A TRIO OF MURDERS

A PERFECT MATCH
REDEMPTION
DEATH OF A DANCER

JILL McGOWN lived in Northamptonshire and
was best known for her mystery series featuring
Chief Inspector Lloyd and Sergeant Judy Hill.
The first novel, *A Perfect Match*, was published
in 1983 and *A Shred of Evidence* was made into a
television drama starring Philip Glenister and
Michelle Collins. Jill McGown died in 2007.

By Jill McGown

Jill McGown

A TRIO OF MURDERS

A PERFECT MATCH
REDEMPTION
DEATH OF A DANCER

PAN BOOKS

A Perfect Match first published 1983 by Macmillan
Redemption first published 1988 by Macmillan
Death of a Dancer first published 1989 by Macmillan

This omnibus edition published 2014 by Pan Books
an imprint of Pan Macmillan, a division of Macmillan Publishers Limited
Pan Macmillan, 20 New Wharf Road, London N1 9RR
Basingstoke and Oxford
Associated companies throughout the world
www.panmacmillan.com

ISBN 978-1-4472-6868-0

1 3 5 7 9 8 6 4 2

A CIP catalogue record for this book is available from the British Library.

Typeset by Ellipsis Digital Ltd, Glasgow
Printed and bound by CPI Group (UK) Ltd, Croydon, CR0 4YY

Contents

A PERFECT MATCH

Chapter One

The September dawn crept over the sky like water on blotting paper, spreading a fine, thin light to supplement the yellow glow of the street lighting. In the town centre shopping precinct, photo cells registered the increase, and the anti-theft store lights clicked softly now and then, obediently switching themselves off. The street lamps, made of sterner stuff, remained on duty – except one, and even that obstinately glowed a dull, dying red. The clock set into Marks and Spencer's wall displayed 6:11 in liquid crystal, and the town slept on, unaware of the coming of the new day, unaware of the milk on the door-steps, unaware that the rain which had lulled it to sleep had moved on, following the thunder northwards.

The town centre was built on the edge of a hill, a hill once part of the forest which still existed in patches of now more manage-able woodland round the new town. Here and there it was allowed to invade the town itself, bringing a little wildness to the unnatural order of a town which had been decided upon, like so many others, in the early fifties. The trees in the heavily wooded parkland at the foot of the hill swayed slightly as the light breeze stirred their branches, and the birds sang, thankful for the storm that had washed away the dust of the long summer. Some had left the trees for the line of semis which stood beside the wood, and the luxury of a bath in the rainwater gathered on the flat roofs of the garages.

The road was busy during the week, busy enough for mini-roundabouts to have broken out like measles all along its length wherever there was a junction; but on a Sunday morning, even when the grey light had become established, the road was empty and quiet. The hum of an engine broke the stillness, and a police car came down the hill from the station, along the line of semis, towards the wood itself, following the curve of the road to the far end, and pulling across to a lay-by. A young policeman, too tall for the compactness of the Panda car, walked on to the soft, heavy ground, crazed and bare in patches, and crossed diagonally to the footpath.

The boatshed-cum-café lay hidden by the trees, and beyond it the artificial lake, spreading back into the wood, the way the car had come. The policeman followed the footpath past the building, across the small parking area, round the water's edge. The ducks swam eagerly towards him as he squelched past, but he had no scraps of food, no time for the ducks. Disappointed, they turned and swam in their own wake, bobbing reluctantly under the surface now and then to make him feel bad.

The creatures who knew the wood at night scattered as he came, darting for safety into the thick undergrowth, making it shiver, releasing drops of rainwater. They knew she was there; they'd known all night.

And now, as he involuntarily closed his eyes, so did the policeman.

Helen Mitchell waved her hand through the steam that rose from the black, traditionally sobering coffee.

'It won't do much good,' Donald said, casting a glance at the sofa. 'It's a bit over-rated, if you want my opinion.'

Donald's opinion wasn't something that Helen wanted too often these days; their twenty-six years of marriage had seen to that. But she was glad he was there, all the same. Chris sat hunched on the sofa, his eyes technically open, his brain almost working.

It had been just before six when Helen had been wakened by the doorbell ringing continuously, like a fire alarm, and gone downstairs to see Donald opening the door to a drunk and dishevelled Chris, shirt-sleeved and shivering.

She'd seen him like that before, his dark hair bedraggled, his chin stubbled with the beard that grew so disreputably fast. At first, Chris Wade had just been a name to Helen; a friend of Donald's, someone he had done some work for, someone who gave him the occasional round of golf. But two years ago, all that had changed, and Chris had become a responsibility.

Now, despite all the water which had flowed under the bridge since, they seemed to be back where they started. Helen helped him hold the mug, when it had cooled enough not to be dangerous, and he drank some of the coffee. His eyes moved with difficulty towards her. He looked even younger like this, and she felt like the mother-substitute she had once been.

'Where's Julia?' she asked him again, for the umpteenth time. 'Is she at your house? Chris?' She shook him gently, but he didn't have to answer. Both she and Donald had rung the number repeatedly in the past hour, and there had been no reply.

'I didn't mean to,' Chris said. 'I didn't mean to.' It was all he had said, virtually. Over and over again.

'Didn't mean to what?' Donald tried. 'What didn't you mean to do?'

'She made me,' he said. 'We went to the café.'

Each time, the conversation had gone the same way. Each time, Helen had looked across at Donald, who was clearly worried; despite the fleshiness with which middle-age disguised his features, he looked almost haggard. Each time, he'd just looked away.

'Is she here?' Chris asked suddenly, trying to struggle up from the sofa, spilling coffee as he did so.

No, she wasn't there. Julia was Donald's sister-in-law, and their weekend guest; Donald had snapped that he wasn't her keeper when it had become apparent that she was spending the night elsewhere. His brother Charles had died only a few weeks ago, but Julia had not allowed her loss to affect her too greatly. It had surprised Helen a little that she wasn't even playing the part of the grieving young widow; she wanted his affairs settled quickly, to get the money for which she had married him, and run. If that had been all there was to it, then only her lack of courtesy should have concerned Donald and Helen when she went off with Chris and failed to return. But of course, that wasn't all there was to it.

It concerned Helen, in a way that she had no intention of explaining to Donald, who thought that extra-marital attachments were his prerogative. It was certainly true to say that Julia's nocturnal activities held no interest for her, as she had indeed said; what she had omitted to say was that Chris Wade's did. And she was certain that it concerned Donald more than he admitted, certain that his relationship with his sister-in-law had ceased to be platonic long before Charles succumbed to his third heart attack. He had been making unfunny jokes in the clipped, off-hand way that he did when he was upset, because Julia had gone off with Chris and had not come back. And Helen had felt like laughing, in spite of it all, at the symmetry of the betrayal.

But now, she had no desire to laugh. Julia wasn't with Chris. Chris was here, saying that he hadn't meant to do it, he hadn't meant to do it.

'Do what?' she asked again, in an urgent whisper, as Donald shrugged and left the room.

Alone with Chris, she squeezed his hand in encouragement. 'It'll be all right,' she said.

'I didn't mean to. I'm sorry,' he said. 'She took me there – I didn't mean . . . I shouldn't just have left her there.'

Donald's normally smooth brow was creased with worry as he sat looking out of the spare bedroom window, through the gloom towards the wood, and the boating lake. Chris had been there – he'd said so, more or less. Why? Why would she take him there? His fingertips massaged his brow, then tapped it rhythmically. What had happened? Why had he come here? He'd got drunk, and then come here. Why? Donald dropped his hand to continue its drumming on the windowsill. As he tried to make some sense of the monosyllabic utterances from Chris, the frown grew deeper, furrowing the skin between his brows. Donald's smoothness of countenance was not the result of a blameless life, free from worry and regret; his was the smoothness of the beach-pebble, that has been buffeted by the wind, moved and turned by the sea, kicked by children, scraped by sand, wearing smoother and smoother, and harder and harder.

Long-sighted, these days, if anything, he focussed on the sweep of road that separated the old wood from the newer pine wood. At the far end sat a car, its rear lights just visible in the increasing daylight, and it was this to which Donald gave his attention as the questions went through his mind. Another car drew up beside it, its unnecessary headlights lending it an air of urgency. There could be no mistaking the activity at the other end of the road, when the two cars were joined by police squad cars with their flashy orange stripes. As he watched, a police mini-bus passed the house and drove along to the knot of cars at the lay-by. Uniformed policemen got out, one after the other, like one of those joke films, disappearing into the trees that sheltered the boating lake.

'What are you looking at?'

He jumped slightly at the sound of Helen's voice, but he couldn't find his own to answer.

'He's sobering up,' she said. 'He hasn't said what happened yet – he said he wanted time to think.'

Donald moved to one side in an invitation to join him at the window. Her eyes met his.

'Oh God,' she said. 'God help him.'

It was a prayer, not a profanity. Donald moved away from the window, and stood helplessly aside.

'A car's coming this way,' Helen said, her voice flat. 'Two cars.' She switched on the bedside light.

Donald rubbed his eyes, hoping he'd wake up, and none of this would be happening. Chris couldn't have killed her. She couldn't be dead. But all those police – he sat on the edge of the bed.

'They're stopping here,' Helen said, coming away from the window. 'He's done something, Donald.' Her grey eyes were tinged with green as she looked at him, as they were when she was tired, or excited, or crying; she had cried too often, he told himself with uncharacteristic honesty. She automatically checked her appearance in the mirror, smoothing down her sleep-tousled hair, still blonde, though here and there streaked with grey. She pulled her housecoat more neatly about her comfortable proportions.

'He's done something,' she said again, to his reflection, as the doorbell rang.

They went downstairs, and Donald opened the door to the police.

'Detective Inspector Lloyd,' the senior man said, nodding to the constable, who walked back to the car. The other car was just parked, with two policemen in it. Donald still couldn't find his voice.

'Stansfield CID,' he continued, with just a trace of a Welsh accent. He had the uncomfortable look of a bearer of bad tidings. 'I believe you may know a young woman – Julia Mitchell? Is she a relative?'

Donald nodded miserably. A time like this, and all he could think was that Inspector Lloyd was small for a policeman.

The coffee had unscrambled part of Chris's brain, allowing him to move more or less as he intended, but his eyes were still reluctant to work properly. There was someone at the door. Wasn't it very early? Maybe not, but it felt early. Too early for visitors. Holding a steadying hand out towards the bookcase, Chris made his way to the door. From the hallway, the voices were muffled and urgent; he shook his head and frowned with the effort of concentration as he gently eased up the lightswitch until it clicked quietly, and the curtained room was dark. Opening the door a crack, he could hear, if not entirely follow, the conversation.

'. . . afraid I have bad news, Mr Mitchell.'

'Where is she? What's happened?' Helen's normally deep voice, higher pitched than usual.

'She had your address in her handbag, you see—'

'What's happened, Inspector?' Helen, impatient.

The inspector lowered his voice, and Chris couldn't hear what was being said, but the reactions were unmistakable. He took a deep breath, and tried to clear his head. She was dead. *Dead*. But that didn't make any sense.

'. . . sorry to have to bring such bad news.' The Inspector cleared his throat. 'Do you know a Christopher Wade, sir?'

'Wade? Yes – I know someone called Wade—'

Donald was playing for time. Giving him a chance. Chris looked round the room, lit by the strand of light from the hallway. What did Donald expect him to do?

'We've reason to believe that Mrs Mitchell was with him at the boating lake, Mr Mitchell. You wouldn't know where he is now, would you?'

Chris held his breath. They'd have to tell him. But he couldn't remember, couldn't get it sorted out in his mind.

'No,' Helen's voice said firmly, and loudly. 'I'm sorry, we don't.'

The silence which followed her statement seemed to last forever as Chris picked his way across the room to the patio window, sliding it back noiselessly on its newly replaced runners. The draught from the window caught the door, opening it slowly, with the full horror-film squeak that it always gave, flooding the room with light.

'Perhaps I could come in for a moment?' the inspector asked.

Chris slipped out into the garden, and slid the window back. The cold morning air that might have cleared his head just made him feel giddy; he made a dive for cover before the already suspicious inspector started looking for him. Crablike, He ran towards the end of the garden, which backed on to the pine wood, and looked back at the curtained house. His foot caught the top bar of the fence as he jumped, and he crashed to the ground, wrenching his ankle. He dragged himself into the wood, crouching below the cluster of new trees. His breath, sharp and cold, was no longer under his control, and he lay on the ground, his eyes closed, gulping air. When at last he could breathe at his own pace, he had time to think. He couldn't stay here. They'd find him, and he still didn't know what to say. He needed time to remember.

He remembered one thing. One place where he could hide, where they might not think of looking. Slowly, painfully, crouching close to the ground, he hobbled away.

Lloyd followed the Mitchells into the sitting room, and noticed the three mugs that sat on the coffee table.

'Is there another person in the house?' he asked.

'No,' Helen Mitchell said quickly. 'They're from last night, I'm afraid – I had a visitor.' She picked up the mugs and took them away.

'May I sit down for a moment?' Lloyd hovered over an easy chair, until Mitchell held out a hand in assent.

Helen Mitchell came back, apologising for keeping him waiting. Both she and her husband looked pale and shocked; both sat quite literally on the edge of the sofa, staring at him anxiously, as he leant back comfortably.

'I realise you've had a shock,' he said, looking from one to the other. 'And I'm very sorry, but I do have to ask some questions.'

'Of course, yes.' Mitchell stood up, his right hand in a fist which he hit gently against his left palm, over and over again. 'You know,' he said, speeding up the little punches and stopping, his hands suddenly helpless, 'it's like a bad dream.'

Lloyd nodded sympathetically. 'What was your relationship to Mrs Mitchell?'

'Brother-in-law,' Mitchell told him, sitting down again, suddenly. 'She was married to my older brother. Charles,' he added, then looked up, almost apologetically. 'He died a few weeks ago,' he said. 'Heart.'

'I'm sorry,' Lloyd said, smoothing down the hair at the back of his neck, feeling the thinning patch, feeling his age, as he always did when he'd got the rotten job. People wanted to be alone with their thoughts, and he was here asking questions. He cleared his throat. 'And did Mrs Mitchell live with you?'

'No,' Helen Mitchell answered. 'She was just here for the weekend. Donald's looking after his brother's estate.' She lit a cigarette. 'He's a solicitor,' she added, as though in explanation.

'Oh?' Lloyd was surprised. 'I thought I knew all the solicitors in Stansfield.'

'You'll know my firm,' Donald said. 'Hutchins and Partners – I don't do criminal law at all. Conveyancing and probate.'

'I see.' You're getting plenty of practice, Lloyd thought.

'I'm actually just the executor of my brother's estate,' Mitchell added. 'My being a solicitor hasn't got anything to do with it.' The last sentence was accompanied by a quick, impatient glance at his wife.

'And Mr Wade is a friend of yours?' Lloyd addressed the question to Mitchell.

'Yes. Yes, he is.'

'Did your sister-in-law know him well?'

'No.' Mitchell shook his head. 'They met by accident, really.'

Lloyd raised his eyebrows enquiringly.

'My brother had a lot of property in this area,' Mitchell said.

'Scattered about – you know.' He was staring at his hands, clasping and unclasping them. 'That's why Julia was here.'

'I know it must be difficult,' Lloyd said. 'There's no hurry – take your time.'

'You probably know that he owned Mitchell Engineering,' Donald continued. 'He sold up some time ago – a good few years ago now – but there are other properties which weren't sold with the main works – they're the ones I mean. A couple of grazing areas, a shop—' he looked up quickly, 'and the boating lake.'

Lloyd was glad to hear a reference to something relevant, and nodded encouragingly.

'It was decided that the simplest course would be to sell these properties off. Julia had no ties in Stansfield – she didn't want to be responsible for property here.'

'Quite,' Lloyd said.

'I put them in the hands of an estate agent,' Mitchell said. 'Chris Wade's brother-in-law, as a matter of fact.' He smiled briefly. 'I know that sounds a bit like jobs for the boys, but he and his wife – Chris's sister – had just moved here, and he'd gone into partnership with a local man. I thought I might as well put some business his way.'

Lloyd didn't know or care about the ethics involved, but he supposed Mitchell would get to the point eventually, and listened politely.

'So last night, I took Julia to see him – to discuss various things.'

'Could I have his name, Mr Mitchell?' Lloyd blinked a little as he reached for his notebook. If he'd known he was going to be dragged from bed at six o'clock in the morning, he'd have gone there before two o'clock.

'Martin Short.'

'Oh yes. I know him slightly.' It was a lie; he didn't know him at all. But sometimes it encouraged them, made them think you were human. You weren't, of course. He certainly wasn't at this time in the morning. He glanced at his watch. It was almost eight o'clock, to his surprise. 'Could I have his address?'

Mitchell gave him the address, and stood up. 'That's where she met Chris,' he said, beginning to pace gently towards the curtained window and back. 'He was at the Shorts, visiting his sister.'

Lloyd frowned a little. 'But she was with you at that point?' he asked.

'Yes – it's a bit complicated.' He stopped pacing and stood with his back to Lloyd, then turned. 'There was a bit of a problem. About the boating lake.' He sat down again, and sighed. 'My brother always intended leaving it to the town,' he said. 'He never got around to putting it in his will, but I knew that he'd meant to. Julia was insisting on selling it to the Council rather than donating it, and I had been trying to make her change her mind.'

Helen Mitchell rose at that point as if to leave the room, but stopped, lit another cigarette, and sat down again.

'You pass the boating lake going from here to the Shorts' house,' Mitchell said, after the slight diversion. 'And Julia said she wanted to check something – I don't know what, now. Probably wanted to count the salt-cellars,' he added.

Lloyd permitted himself a small smile.

'I had one last go at persuading her, and it developed into a row. We went on to the Shorts, but we had had this disagreement, and she wouldn't stay. When Chris realised she intended walking back, he offered her a lift.'

Lloyd put his pen away. 'Well, thank you, Mr Mitchell. You stayed on at the Shorts, did you?'

Mitchell nodded. 'Yes. Not very gentlemanly, but I had had enough of her, to be honest.' He sat back, relaxing a little now. 'That sounds awful,' he said.

'Not at all. Had Mr Wade met Mrs Mitchell before?'

'No. That was the first time they'd met.'

Lloyd frowned. 'So you know of no reason why he'd want to – harm her?'

'Of course not!' Helen Mitchell snapped.

'And you don't know where he is?'

'No,' she said.

'You haven't seen him since he left with Mrs Mitchell?' He addressed the question to Donald Mitchell, who shook his head.

'No,' Helen Mitchell said again, in answer to his enquiring look.

He wondered. He wondered about the three mugs that she was so keen to get rid of. Too late now. 'One more thing,' he said. 'Who is Mrs Mitchell's next of kin? Do you know?'

'It'll be her father,' Donald replied abstractedly. 'But he's on holiday – Spain, I think.'

'Then I'm afraid I'll have to ask you to identify her, Mr Mitchell.'

Mitchell closed his eyes. 'Yes,' he said heavily. 'When will you want me?'

'We'll send a car, Mr Mitchell. Will you be available later this morning?'

'All day.' Mitchell rose wearily and pulled open the curtains, admitting the daylight. 'Helen? Could you put the light off?'

Helen Mitchell switched off the light, and stood by the door. 'Inspector, if you've no objection – I'd rather be dressed if we're to continue talking.'

She was no longer in the first flush of youth, but Lloyd could well believe the rumours that Constable Sandwell had assured him were going round about her and Wade. Wade must be ten, perhaps fifteen years younger than her, but there was a kind of youthful bravado there, defying him to get the better of her, that made her look like a girl – like a little girl, defending what was hers. The mixture of vulnerability and defiance was engaging. Lloyd smiled. 'I beg your pardon, Mrs Mitchell. I'll get out of your way now. I'm afraid I'll be back, though.'

She didn't move as he walked towards the door. 'Do you think Chris Wade killed Julia?' she asked, her voice as calm as if she were asking him if he thought it was going to rain.

'I don't know, Mrs Mitchell,' he said. 'I just know I'd like to talk to him, and he's disappeared.'

She nodded, and moved aside, to let him leave.

Outside in the car, he sat for a moment, looking up at the settled, comfortable house, before nodding to the constable to drive back down the road to the grim scene-of-crime.

At the lake, the breeze was growing stronger, rippling the surface of the water, making him shiver. Everyone had forgotten how to dress for autumn; one or two of the lads had left their jackets in the bus, from force of habit during the heatwave. He raised a hand to acknowledge their presence as he strode towards the beribboned barriers.

Judy was there now, talking to the doctor, having to raise her voice slightly above the snapping of the ribbon. She smiled gravely as he joined them, in the way they all learned to do, her brown eyes troubled.

'Morning, Lloyd,' the doctor said. 'I was just telling your sergeant here – twelve hours at a rough estimate.' He pointed a warning finger at him. 'But it is rough – don't bank on it. Wait for the p.m.'

'We're finished in there,' a middle-aged man called from the building.

'Fine – thanks.' Lloyd turned to Judy. 'Do you want to have a nose around inside? I'll be there in a minute.'

He and the doctor watched as she picked her way across the mud to the pathway.

'Detective sergeants have improved a bit over the years, haven't they?' the doctor said, with a grin. 'Much better legs than they used to have.'

Lloyd laughed. 'Don't let her hear you saying that, for God's sake!'

Judy, new to the area, new to the rank, but a long-time colleague of Lloyd's, heard the laughter, and wondered if it was at her expense. She always did, and always had. It was a form of conceit, her mother had told her when she was small. Assuming that people had nothing better to do than talk about her.

The long, thin rectangle of the boathouse had had a small square partitioned off to produce the café, and it was into this section that Judy walked. Windows had been provided as a concession to the customers, but the high trees blocked out most of the light. Judy picked her way through the forest of chairs upturned on the tables, and stood by the counter. The tables and chairs occupied an L-shaped area, and behind the counter, through a curtain of grimy plastic strips, she could see the tiny kitchen that took up the rest of the square.

Her eye travelled over the flaking paintwork on the door, up to the dingy ceiling. The walls were covered in a plastic material of indeterminate hue to about shoulder height, when they became yellowish-white, with hairline cracks running across them like cobwebs. Through the window, still spattered with the night's rain, she could see the hedged courtyard, where hopeful tables presumably used to be placed on promising summer days. There was a desolate feel to the room, now that its surfaces were smudged and dirty where they had been dusted for fingerprints: the counter, the window ledge, the door. The table and chairs that had been used, presumably by the victim and her attacker, were covered with the unhappy smears, and chalk circles marked the blood-stains, small and almost insignificant, the only sign that anything at all had happened.

The floor was tiled with black and white squares, cracking where the uneven floorboards failed to support them. Judy ran her toe idly round the hole that had appeared in the corner of one tile, and sighed. The gloom of the place was invading her, hurting her. She ran her hand through the newly curly hair that Lloyd said made her look like Kevin Keegan, and wished she worked in Woolworth's.

The door opened suddenly, and Lloyd, a little windswept, strode in, shattering the dark silence, forcing the café back into its original mundane role. His Celtic looks gave him a presence that his inches could not command, issuing an unspoken challenge to everything that moved, especially Judy.

'Well?' he asked. 'Where the hell were you?'

'You know where I was. Running Michael to the airport. I came as soon as I saw the note.'

Lloyd grunted, and joined her at the counter. 'So,' he said. 'How much do you know?'

'Not a lot. I know the girl's name was Julia Mitchell, and that she's the widow of the man who owned Mitchell Engineering originally. Charles Mitchell – was that his name?' She glanced at her notebook. 'And we're looking for someone called Wade, who was seen arriving with her and leaving without her.' She raised her eyebrows in a question.

'It was reported by a boy – he came in this morning. I'll let you have the details later.'

'What's the story, then?'

'She was visiting an estate agent called Short, and Wade was there. He offered her a lift home.' Lloyd spread his hands.

'Do we know anything about Wade?' Judy wandered behind the counter to see what she would see.

'Well – she had no reason to be wary of accepting a lift, if that's what you mean. She was staying with her in-laws, and Wade's a friend of theirs – and the estate agent she was visiting is married to Wade's sister, so he did provide references.'

'Her in-laws – is that who you've just been to see?'

'Yes. Donald and Helen Mitchell.'

'What does he do?'

'He's a solicitor. His brother only died a little while ago, and that's why Julia was here – sorting out his estate. I gather she's been dreaming of this ever since she walked down the aisle.'

'She was a lot younger than him, I take it?'

'Must have been thirty years younger,' Lloyd said. 'He died of a heart attack.' He grinned.

'And Wade's a friend of Donald's,' Judy said, hoping to chase away the grin and failing.

'So he'd like us to think.' The statement was accompanied by his Knowing Look, and Judy felt her irritation with life in general settling firmly on Lloyd in particular.

'Oh? And what do you think?' She brushed through the plastic strips into the kitchen, throwing the question over her shoulder.

'I think he's Helen Mitchell's bit of fluff,' Lloyd said smugly, following her through.

'Helen Mitchell?' Judy asked. 'Donald's wife?'

'The same.'

'On what evidence?' Judy opened the oven door and looked inside, for no good reason.

'Oh – just the way she reacted.' He shook his head. 'Not that it gets us much further forward.'

Judy shut the oven door with a bang. 'What do you want me to do?' she asked.

'You go back to the station – there's a file started. Read it through – see if you can follow anything up today. It would be a Sunday, of course. I'll be back as soon as possible, but I'd better see this estate agent person.'

Judy was about to leave, when she saw the door in the back wall of the kitchen. 'The boathouse?' she asked.

'Yes – it's not locked.'

She pushed it open, and stepped through to find herself in darkness, unable to find the lightswitch. A strip of light showed where the big doors at the end didn't quite fit together, and she could see the shapes of the small boats, as she moved further in. She swore as she banged her hip on the corner of an unsuspected desk. Lloyd followed her in. 'It's smelly,' she said, sniffing. 'Damp.' She ran her hand down one of the boats. 'Oh – they're plastic. I thought they'd be wood.'

'Fibreglass,' Lloyd said. 'They don't need so much maintenance. Which is just as well,' he added. 'As far as I know they don't get any.'

'Does it actually operate?'

'The boating lake bit does, at weekends. The café's been closed for a while now. It was a grand gesture when Mitchell Engineering was on top of the world and everyone wanted British everything. But they couldn't afford it, really. It doesn't even belong to them now – until last night, it was Julia Mitchell's property, I understand. It'll be a good thing if the Council does take it over.'

Judy felt his hand touch hers, where it rested on the side of one of the boats. In the half-light, she couldn't see his face. The contact could have been accidental or deliberate, in fun or in earnest.

'I'll get back then,' she said abruptly, pulling her hand away as she turned.

Light flooded the shed, and Judy could see the offending desk just inside the door, where stood the tall, thin form of Constable Sandwell, his hand on the now obvious lightswitch. He tried hard to show no reaction at all to finding them in the dark, while she chose to stare at the grubby phone on the desk. It would have to be Sandwell, she thought. You-Know-What-I-Heard? Sandwell.

'Excuse me,' she said, brushing past him. Let Lloyd think of a good reason. Let Lloyd pass it off with a smile. She was getting out of it.

Chapter Two

'This is Newsdesk Report with the time at ten a.m.

'Reports are coming in that the body of a young woman has been found in Thorpe Wood near Stansfield town centre. The body has not yet been formally identified, and police are not releasing the name at present. It is understood that they are treating the death as murder, and that a man is being sought. A full-scale search of the woods is under way.'

Donald listened to these words and these only, and they remained in his head long after the radio returned to the inanities of the local DJ. When the music began, he snapped off the radio and lay back on the bed, waiting for Helen to finish in the bathroom. He felt tired, but there was no time to sleep, even if he could, with the horrors of the identification still to come. And more questions – about Chris, and Julia, and last night. And Helen, of course, had lied to the Inspector.

The bedroom door opened, and Helen, smelling of warm terry-towelling and bath-oil, announced that the bathroom was free. Since the Inspector left, the only topic of conversation had been the bathroom. Outside the house, the Panda car still sat with its two occupants, and by tacit agreement not a word was spoken about Julia. Donald presumed that they were there in case Chris turned up, or perhaps they thought he was hiding in the house. Donald half-wished that he was.

The bathroom was still steamy from Helen's bath; condensation beaded the windows and tiles. Donald drew a finger through the moisture on the shower panel, his mind on the wood, and the boating lake, and the mean little café. What could she possibly have said or done to make Chris react like that? He switched on the shower, and tried to drench the thoughts. She must have been so frightened. The warm water sprinkled on to his shoulders, trickling down his back, soothing the tension, calming him. He had to be calm, because worrying wouldn't alter anything. No one would know what had happened until Chris was found – conjecture wouldn't help. He didn't know whether he was glad or sorry that Helen had lied to the police. They'd find out, of course – Helen had only recently taken up deception, and it still had an amateur quality.

He rubbed soap over his body in loops and circles of lather. What did it matter if the police did find out she'd lied? What did any of it matter? The whole thing was a mess, anyway. He knew why she'd lied, of course. He had known for a while, though Chris as suitor – Chris as *rival* – was hardly something that would have occurred to him at first. Helen's inability to prevaricate with any degree of confidence had given the game away a few weeks ago, when he had puzzled over something she had said, and in this very room had cut himself shaving when realisation dawned.

Chris, whom he'd rescued like a drowning puppy in a sack, and truthful, loyal Helen were more than just good friends. How much more, he didn't know; it took him all his time to believe that he was right, though he knew he had to be. The incredulity was no reflection on Helen, and no measure of his egoism. It was merely that he knew her, and knew the sleepless nights that her perfidy must have cost. Sometimes, during the three o'clock in the morning soul-searching in which he had occasionally indulged, he had wondered how he would feel if she were unfaithful to him. Every now and then, having left the warmth of someone else's bed to return, with a glib lie, to his own, he'd wondered how he would react if the tables were turned.

When it finally happened, he was slow to realise, then disbelieving, then fatalistic. And quite proud of the discovery that he did not operate a double standard. If he could do it, so could she, because he didn't really care, and he didn't imagine she did either. Their marriage had been grinding along with a flat tyre for years. Every now and then the sparks flew as the metal touched the ground, but they had carried on, at first for the children, and then for convenience. Now, it was bumping and jolting on the metal all the time, and soon they would have to stop and get out.

And anyway, he liked Chris. He didn't want him to be in this terrible trouble, and he didn't understand why he was. Forget it, forget it, he told himself sternly. One thing at a time. Wait and see. No point in meeting trouble halfway. Having exhausted his supply of wise saws, he lifted his face to the thin jets, screwing up his eyes and letting the water cascade over his face. It streamed down his body, washing away the soap and the fatigue and the worry.

What did it matter? The whole thing was a mess.

'I still can't believe it,' Elaine Short said, handing Lloyd a cup of unannounced coffee, her hand shaking slightly as she did so. She was tall, slender to the point of thinness, and as elegant and graceful as a dancer. She and her husband were both in their for- ties – about his own age, Lloyd judged. Martin Short, looking anxiously at his wife, was about as different from her as he could be. He clearly never skipped lunch; he lumbered amiably about the room in search of things he had mislaid – his cigarettes, his lighter, his glasses, the plans of the café and boathouse. His fair hair never stayed where he meant it to, and he flicked it off his forehead as he spoke.

'You read about this sort of thing,' he said to Lloyd. 'But you never imagine them as real people, do you?' He lit a cigarette, having finally run to earth the necessary equipment to do so. 'I mean, you don't think of them as being ordinary.'

The Shorts had given him the bare bones of what had happened the night before. What time Donald and Julia arrived, that Julia left very shortly afterwards, that Chris offered to run her back to the Mitchells. They had admitted, reluctantly, that she had refused the offer at first; but then, Elaine assured him, people did, didn't they?

He knew now that Wade was a widower, a piece of information defensively given to him by Elaine, as though it might damage his case.

'Your brother's wife,' he asked. 'How long ago did she die?'

'Two years ago,' Martin answered. 'It was a car crash. Chris took it very hard – he was driving.' His eyes flicked over to his wife as he spoke. 'He blamed himself,' he went on. 'But it was no one's fault really – a dog ran out. It was just one of those things.'

'He's all right now, is he?' Lloyd asked.

'Oh yes. It took him a while – he began to drink a fair bit. Don and Helen were very good to him, I believe.' He started looking for an ashtray. 'We weren't here then,' he added. 'We've just moved here.' Finding the ashtray, he sank back into the sofa. 'That's why it's so hard to believe,' he said. 'He wasn't drinking or anything.' Too late, he realised that the statement presupposed his brother-in-law's guilt. 'Not that I think—'

'He didn't kill her!' Elaine Short interrupted him vehemently, bringing down the coffee pot with a thud, and sitting down opposite Lloyd. She didn't share the sofa with her husband as Helen Mitchell had done, and yet Lloyd got a sense of unity from the Shorts that had been singularly lacking from the Mitchells. It was of no importance – he just liked to collect the odd pieces of human behaviour that came his way.

'Nobody knows what happened yet, Mrs Short.' Lloyd sipped his coffee and was pleasantly surprised.

'What happened is that Chris took her home from here, and now she's dead and he's disappeared,' she said, succinctly enough. She jumped up, and walked to the window. 'And you think he killed her,' she added. 'Don't you?'

'I don't know, Mrs Short. Really, I don't. I want to speak to him certainly.' He took another sip of coffee. 'And,' he continued, 'it would be silly of me to pretend that he isn't under suspicion, because he is. But I don't know enough yet to have formed any conclusions.'

'You don't seem to have to know!' she said angrily.

'Oh?' Lloyd finished his coffee and walked over to her. 'What have I done to indicate that?' He stood beside her, looking out at the garden, fresh after the rain, to see yet more rain darken the pathway as he spoke.

'You've got men searching the woods,' she said miserably.

'She was naked, Mrs Short. Her clothes could tell us a lot.' The voice was gentle, though the effect of his words was not meant to be.

Elaine Short was staring at him, and then her husband. Lloyd didn't speak, but nodded as she looked back at him.

'Are you suggesting that Chris—?' she didn't, wouldn't, finish the sentence.

'I'm asking for help, Mrs Short. I want to know as much as you do – as much as everyone who came into contact with Julia Mitchell knows. Then, I can perhaps come to a conclusion. And I don't know until then whether that conclusion will involve your brother or not.'

She walked shakily back to her chair, but Lloyd didn't go with her. 'So,' he said. 'You've told me that Donald Mitchell stayed and your brother ran Julia Mitchell home.' He stayed by the window, and didn't look round at the Shorts. He could feel the eye-signals, and even see a faint reflection in the window as the clouds raced across, darkening the sky.

He turned, quickly, and they tried to look as though no communication had taken place, like schoolchildren caught cheating in an exam.

'Now,' he said. 'I'd like to know what they said, what you said, what you thought, even.' He sat down then, fixing Elaine with his eye. 'And if you don't believe your brother could have killed her,' he said, 'you won't help him by missing anything out.'

'I don't think Elaine had any intention of—' Martin began, protectively, but he was interrupted.

'No, I hadn't,' Elaine said. 'But I would, if I thought it would help. There's nothing to leave out,' she said simply. 'At least, not about Chris.'

Martin shifted uncomfortably as his wife looked over at him. 'It hasn't really got anything to do with us,' he said. 'Or what happened, for that matter.'

'It might, whatever it is,' Lloyd said. 'Tell me. If it's got nothing to do with it, no one will ever know I knew.' He smiled at Martin with the clear-eyed honest look that almost always worked, and wasn't disappointed.

'They had had a row,' Martin said, reluctantly. 'Donald and Julia. They were still going at it hammer and tongs when they got here.'

Elaine rose, and switched on the table lamp. 'She was very angry,' she said. 'She wouldn't stay.'

'Mr Mitchell did mention an argument,' Lloyd said. 'I don't

think you're breaking a confidence.' But there was more, obviously. He smiled at Mrs Short. 'I don't suppose I could beg another cup of that coffee, could I? It just isn't like that when Constable Sandwell makes it.'

'Of course.' She poured another cup for each of them, and came to a visible decision. 'I don't think it really has any bearing on it,' she said. 'But I – that is, we – we think Donald was having an affair with Julia Mitchell.'

Lloyd raised his eyebrows. 'I see,' he said. 'And the row could have been of a more personal nature than I was led to believe?'

'It could have been,' she said, as cautiously as he had.

Lloyd stirred his coffee thoughtfully. 'What makes you think they were having an affair?'

'Not what they were saying,' Martin said. 'That could have been about anything. It didn't make much sense unless you'd heard the rest of the row.'

The coffee was almost gone again. Lloyd tried to make it last, but the cups were very small. 'What were they saying?'

Martin screwed up his face as he tried to remember. 'He said something about her doing something, or not doing something, and she said that she hadn't promised to.'

Setting down his empty cup regretfully, Lloyd asked if either of them could remember the exact words.

'No. I don't think so,' Martin said slowly. 'They were angry – shouting at each other. I don't know exactly what they said.'

'I think I do,' Elaine said. 'As far as I can remember, he said "I wouldn't have believed you'd do this," or something like that.'

'That's right,' said Martin, suddenly coming to life. 'And she said "More fool you" – I remember that. And then that she'd never promised anything. He said it was a row about the boating lake, but—' he shrugged.

'And what makes you so sure it wasn't?'

There was a silence and Martin's skin became slightly pink.

'Tell him, Martin.'

'I don't think it's anyone's business but theirs!'

'Tell him!'

Martin hunched his shoulders like a small boy, then spoke quickly, throwing away the words. 'It's nothing really. I had to be in London for a couple of days a few weeks ago, and I stayed the night rather than do the trip twice.' He began to search for his cigarettes. 'At an hotel.'

'They're on the table,' Lloyd and Elaine said in unison, then smiled with some warmth at one another.

'I was booking out on the Sunday morning, and I saw Donald and Julia coming down the stairs. It was first thing in the morning.'

'Did they see you?'

'No.' Martin looked ashamed. 'I don't think so. I saw them at the top of the stairs, and I went into the phone box as they came round the corner.'

'A bit of a coincidence, that,' Lloyd said. 'Out of all the hotels in London.'

'No – not really. It was Donald who suggested I stay there if ever I was in town.'

'And he still doesn't know you saw him?'

'No.' Martin Short had retreated so far back into the sofa that he was almost invisible.

'Now. Last night. They came in, having a row. How long did Mrs Mitchell stay?'

'Two minutes,' Elaine said. 'Not even that.'

'They stood there,' Martin said, indicating a spot near the door. 'I didn't even have time to offer her a drink.' He pursed his lips. 'Perhaps if she'd stayed—'

'Then he called her a mercenary bitch, and she said she was going,' Elaine said. 'She'd sooner walk home than stay with him – that sort of stuff. And that's when Chris offered her a lift.'

'Right. And when did Mr Mitchell leave?'

'The storm began just after that, and he waited until after eleven – well after – before he left.'

'Thank you.' Lloyd rose. 'You've been very helpful – and the coffee was delicious.' Twelve o'clock, his watch assured him. No wonder he was beginning to feel peckish. 'I've been here a long time,' he said. 'I'm sorry.'

'Never mind about that,' Martin said. 'Just so long as you get to the bottom of it.' He was neatly overtaken by Elaine, who followed Lloyd to the door.

'You still think that Chris did it, don't you?' she asked him, as he stepped out into the gusty wind.

He turned back to face her. 'I don't have any other theory to consider yet,' he said. 'You said it yourself – he took her home, she's dead, and he's disappeared. But they're looking for evidence now – it could change the whole picture.'

'If you want someone else to suspect,' she said, 'you try Helen Mitchell. Ask her where she was when Donald tried to ring her – twice. You ask her that – it's her husband Julia was sleeping with, after all!'

Chris Wade sat in the gloom, his knees drawn up to his chest, his ears straining to hear any sound above the whine of the wind in the trees. There was a window, but years of untroubled grime blocked out most of the watery light. He didn't dare move until it was dark, and he couldn't stand in the confined space. The bench was beginning to assume the comfort rating of a king size double bed, but he must not lie down. He might sleep, and be taken by surprise. He'd made matters worse now, by running away, and the only justification would be if it gave him time. Time to remember, time to make sense of it all, time to go to the police of his own accord.

Helen would be in trouble if they found out he'd been there. He'd tried to tell her; dimly, through the haze of drunken memory, he could remember trying to explain. She had patted him, humoured him, cradled him like a baby. He could feel her arms, soft and welcoming, until he asked her to leave him. And then the police came, and told her Julia was dead. And he, for a single, stricken second, believed he'd killed her. His alcohol-clouded mind told him to run. Donald told him to run, when he took his time answering the police. Helen told him to run, with her direct, atypical lie.

So he had run, and in the safety of his lair, he'd made the mistake of slipping off his shoe to examine his ankle. He couldn't get the shoe on again, which made even giving himself up a difficult obstacle to overcome. But at least his prison was safe – even the vandals had forgotten it existed, and it would be a while before the police remembered. It had seemed so important once – it was an eyesore, a disgrace. But now the tangle of bushes almost hid it, and the good people of Stansfield had forgotten all about it. To Chris it was no eyesore; it was a haven, a safe-house, a resting place where he could have time. Once he'd decided what to say, then he'd go to the police.

It would be nice, though, to lie down. Just for a moment.

One o'clock, and no more news than they had already given. Helen Mitchell switched off the radio, and poured herself a stiff drink. The gin was possibly negating the less fattening qualities of the slimline tonic, but for the moment she didn't care about her thickening waist. She had never been sylph-like; she was the land of woman once called handsome. At fifty she was perhaps more attractive than in her youth – age suited her tall, well-built frame rather better than girlishness had. In her teens, she had felt like an Amazon, in her twenties and thirties, unfashionable. During her forties, her robustness had mellowed into a suggestion of over-weight, and had made her softer, more approachable. Now she kept an eye on the calories as middle-age spread threatened to make her merely fat.

Donald had gone off with the police to make the identification, and Helen had tried hard to feel something, but she couldn't. She was worried sick about Chris, that was all. Julia and Donald and the rest of the world could, and probably would, go to hell. She wanted to know if Chris was all right.

Last night seemed a long time ago. It had all started when Donald had rung looking for Julia, and had suggested that she and Chris might have gone off somewhere together. The irritation she had felt at the suggestion surprised her. Irritation was the name she had given to the sudden sweep of anger, but jealousy would have been nearer the mark. Chris was her business. She had put down the phone with such force that Margaret, who was visiting, had asked her what was wrong, but she had just laughed it off with 'Men!' and there were no more questions, because they had to leave to catch Margaret's train.

At first, she hadn't liked Chris, who had presented himself as a surly, uncommunicative young man, who had usually had too much to drink. She had asked Donald not to bring him to the house, but when he explained about the accident, her sympathy had been roused, and she had taken over the role of keeper, cooking meals for him, listening to him when he was maudlin and berating himself for being the cause of Carrie's death. She had watched the gradual effects of her patient counselling, as he emerged from the self-pity, and his health, both mental and physical, returned. He began to piece together his life and his business, both perilously close to bankruptcy after months of neglect.

Then Charles Mitchell had died, and Donald had to deal with his estate, which meant spending even more time in London, at the Mitchell Development offices. Spending time with Julia. One night, when he rang yet again to say that he was staying over in London, she had told Chris about Julia, and about Donald's other girls. The final, fatal straw had been dropped in place, and the sudden rush of emotion caused their relationship to undergo a sea-change. He was fourteen years her junior, and until a month ago she had been just someone to run to, someone who would put up with him in any mood, in any state. In the last few weeks, everything had changed.

Chris's sister and her husband moved to Stansfield and perhaps it was Elaine who got Chris when he needed cheering up, because it certainly wasn't Helen. She knew he needed her, and now he was saying he wanted her. She had just begun to believe him, begun to accept that his motive was not one of pity, or gratitude, begun to make less of an attempt at concealment of their changed relationship, when this happened.

The clock had turned back two years when he staggered in, breathing whisky fumes all over her. And Helen knew then that she didn't care what happened to her or anyone else. Chris was all she cared about.

'Mrs Marsden?' Judy smiled at the lady who sat in reception, even though she had probably given herself indigestion hurrying up her canteen Sunday lunch in order to see her.

Mrs Marsden was a small woman with a neat figure and greying hair.

'If you'd like to come with me,' she said, and Mrs Marsden stood up.

'I hope it's him you're looking for,' she said in a stage whisper. 'He wouldn't say.' She nodded to Tom Rogers on the desk. 'I'll feel such a fool making all this fuss if it's not.'

'No need, Mrs Marsden,' Judy assured her, pushing open the swing door into the CID room. It was quiet now after the controlled excitement prior to lunch, when everyone had gone around trying to look as though it was all in a day's work. Only Joe Miller held the fort.

'They're all out,' Joe said, with a sigh. 'Or gone back to their own jobs, thank God.'

This was a reference to the Superintendent who was, Judy had already noted with relief, back upstairs where he belonged.

'Through here,' Judy said, as their heels rang through the empty office. She held open the door to the office she shared with Lloyd, and indicated a chair. 'Have a seat,' she said. 'Bring it up to the desk.' She smiled encouragingly. 'Now. You think you've got something that will help us?'

'Only if it's him you're looking for.'

'Who would that be?'

'Mr Wade from the garage on Victoria Street.'

Judy rearranged some files on her desk. 'Is that what you've heard?'

'Everyone says so. You've been at the garage, and it's been closed all day.'

'It's Sunday,' Judy said.

'It normally opens on Sundays,' Mrs Marsden countered.

Judy smiled. 'Do you have some information about him?' She unearthed a piece of paper. 'But before we start – can I have your full name and address?'

'Edna Marsden. 27 Livingstone Drive.' Mrs Marsden waited until she'd written the address. 'I saw him this morning,' she said.

'What?' Judy couldn't remember the last time someone with information really had had information. 'When?' she asked.

'At about quarter past five.'

Judy looked startled. 'You saw him at quarter past five in the morning? Where?'

'At his garage – I deliver his milk.'

'Oh! I see.' Judy laughed, but Mrs Marsden didn't. 'And he was there? At that time in the morning?'

'Yes – he gave me a fright, because I didn't know. You can't see the office light from outside, you see.' Mrs Marsden undid the top button of her coat, getting herself comfortable. She was enjoying herself. She had insisted on seeing Judy as the senior officer – Joe Miller not being good enough. And now she was going to get her money's worth. Still, thought Judy, she really did have information, which was more than she could have expected.

'What happened? Anything?'

'Nothing much – but he was funny. I had just got off the float – I take it right up to the door, you see, and park it behind the pumps. And I was taking the milk out when he spoke, right behind me. He'd got a bottle in his hand, and he was in a state.'

'A bottle? He was drinking?' Judy wrote 'drinking' on her pad.

'Not that kind of a bottle. A milk bottle.'

Judy smiled, crossing the word out again. 'But he was in a state, you said?'

'He was. I think he had been drinking – he was upset.'

Judy drew a neat dotted line under 'drinking', and wrote STET. 'Upset?' she queried. 'How did he show he was upset?'

'He looked upset. As though he'd just had bad news.' Edna stood. 'Do you mind if I take my coat off? It's hot in here – I'm sure your heating's up too high.'

'Probably. Yes – do take your coat off. How do you mean – as if he'd just had bad news?'

'Oh, you know. He looked pale, and his eyes looked red, as though he'd been crying.'

'Where were you at this point?' Judy asked.

Mrs Marsden stared at her. 'At the garage,' she said. 'That's what I'm telling you.'

'Yes, of course. But were you in his office at any time, or on the forecourt – where?'

'Where I said. By the pumps.'

'So the only light would be from the street lamps on the pavement?'

'Yes – but I could see all right.' That Edna resented the implication, Judy could see by the huffy lift of her chin.

'I know you could,' she said quickly. 'I'm just thinking about those lights. They make everyone look a little odd, you know. He probably thought you looked pale with red eyes.' She laughed a little, but Mrs Marsden didn't.

'It wasn't just that! His shirt was unbuttoned, and it was quite cold after the thunder. And when he took the milk, his hands were shaking.'

'Could you describe what he was wearing?'

Lloyd came in as she spoke, and moved noiselessly to his desk. If Mrs Marsden only knew that he was an inspector, Judy's days would be numbered.

'Not very well,' she said. 'The lights make things go funny colours.' It was as though she were making a new point, as though Judy had never mentioned the lights' ability to make things look different. 'Dark clothes,' she said. 'That's all. No jacket.'

'What sort of shirt was Mr Wade wearing? Can you remember? Short sleeved, long sleeved? Tie?' She glanced across at Lloyd, who had begun to listen to the conversation. 'Was it a dark shirt?'

She thought for a moment. 'No – it was light. It could have been red, because his car was there, and it's red. The lights make it go a sort of mustard colour. That's the colour his shirt looked. It had long sleeves – and it was open, so I don't think he had a tie.'

'Good. Anything else you noticed about him?'

'Only that his hands were shaking, like I said. Because I said to put the milk down before he dropped it. And he did,' she added, with a hint of triumph.

'He dropped it?' Lloyd asked, sitting forward.

'He put it down,' she replied, with a withering glance in his direction.

Lloyd laughed, but Mrs Marsden didn't.

At Thorpe Wood, sunlight chased the shadows across the dark surface of the lake as the quickening wind blew the clouds away, and the ducks watched interestedly as the teams of police, who had fanned out from where the body had lain, took a temporary breather. Her clothes had been found, caught up in the tangle of undergrowth. Skirt, blouse and jacket, rolled up together, caught on the thorns of a wild rose-bush. Shoes, some way distant from each other, lying on the ground. No underwear, and no sign of Wade, so they would keep on looking.

The squad cars, Panda cars, private cars, vans and wagons left room for only one lane of traffic. Each car, few and far between, was stopped at the temporary traffic signals, and its passengers questioned. Traffic cones and orange-jacketed police slowed drivers down on every exit road, the men yawning with boredom while they waited for the sparse Sunday traffic. Watchful eyes assessed the handful of people using British Rail's reduced Sunday service; buses were observed, but there was no sign of Wade.

An unmarked car, containing two plainclothes officers, sat quietly in the road that ran down the side of Wade Motors. The building itself had received the attentions of the evidence-gatherers. He wouldn't come back there, but you had to watch, just in case. Another watched his house, another still kept a less obtrusive eye on the Mitchells' house, yet another on the Shorts'. They had just finished in his own house, but they weren't optimistic. There was no reason to believe that he'd been home. Nothing to suggest where he might be now.

By two o'clock, it had settled down to near-routine, but this wasn't routine, certainly not in Stansfield. Drunken stabbings, and domestic rows that got out of hand got headlines in the local papers because they were rare enough.

But this was news, and the ducks were doing well out of the currently access denied reporters and film-crews whose estate cars littered the grass. This was murder, not the unintentional result of a frustrated marriage or a night out with the lads. This was Hunt for Killer of Rich Widow. This was Naked Blonde Death Riddle. This would sell newspapers; this would make good television.

This would feed a lot of ducks.

Chapter Three

Donald thanked the young woman who had driven him home, and stepped thankfully from the car into the invigorating breeze. It had been Julia all right. He had had a dread of not being able to tell whether it was her or not, but he could. When it was over, he had felt light-headed, but relief rather than shock had caused the giddiness. He wondered if that was the usual reason for people fainting – your mind building the thing up to such a pitch that you are prepared for anything. And what you feel is relief that it isn't as bad as you thought.

He was a rich man now that Julia was dead. But that wasn't what was in his mind as he looked at her. Some things were more important than money.

Helen shushed him as he came in the door, and he stood to listen to the news.

'The naked body of thirty-five year old Julia Mitchell, widow of the late Charles Mitchell, was found this morning in the woodland round Stansfield boating lake. The police say that Mrs Mitchell appeared to have been strangled, but that there is no immediate evidence of a sexual assault.

'Her husband, Charles Mitchell, died just seven weeks ago of a heart attack, and Mrs Mitchell was in the area on business connected with her husband's estate. Her body was found less than a mile from her brother-in-law's house, where she had been staying.

'The couple, who lived in London, had strong local connections, Mr Mitchell being the founder of Mitchell Engineering, the largest single employer in Stansfield. When he retired from the engineering world six years ago, Mr Mitchell's keen business *eye enabled him to make a second fortune in London property development . . .'*

The radio went into a rehashed obituary which now included Julia.

'Are you all right?' Helen asked. 'You look pale.'

'Yes, I'm fine. It wasn't too bad, considering.'

Helen held up the whisky decanter. 'Drink?' she asked.

'Please.'

'Are you hungry yet? I've made a salad, and there's cold chicken.'

'Later.' He picked up the paper. 'Oh – that reminds me. The police want a photograph of Julia – to jog people's memory, they said.' He looked at Helen over the top of the newspaper. 'It could have been anyone,' he said. 'It might not have been Chris.'

But Helen shook her head. 'Have you got one?'

'No, not on me. Why would I have a photograph of Julia?' He turned the page, having read nothing. 'That's why I'm telling you. I'll have to go to their place tomorrow and see what I can find. The press are pestering the police for one, anyway. And they want to know where her father's staying in Spain so that he can be told. So I'll have to see if there's a note of that anywhere.' He wondered about her definite shake of the head when he suggested someone other than Chris might be 'being sought' as the radio put it. 'Did Chris say anything to you?' he asked.

'Nothing that made sense.' She poured herself a gin and tonic, and Donald noticed the empty bottle of tonic on the sideboard. He hoped she knew what she was doing.

'Helen?' he said, as people only do when they are about to broach a sensitive subject.

She looked across enquiringly, perhaps a little apprehensively. 'Yes?' she said, trying to sound off-hand.

'Do you know where Chris is?'

She looked faintly surprised. 'No, of course not.' She looked away. 'Why would I know where Chris is?'

The deliberate parody of his reply about Julia's photograph did not serve to make Donald feel any more sanguine. He just hoped Helen wasn't getting herself – and by extension, him – into deep water.

'You could get into real trouble,' he warned her. 'If you're withholding information – it's an offence.' He drank some of his whisky, and waited for it to make him feel just a little bit better, but it didn't.

'You didn't tell them you'd seen him,' she said defensively, spearing the lemon slice with the cocktail stick, and freshening the drink with a new one.

Donald knew this mood. The 'I'm going to get tight so there' mood that happened once in a blue moon. He wondered how many she'd had.

'Only because you lied to the man!' he said snappishly, then wished he hadn't, because that wasn't the only reason. 'And be careful how much you drink, because he'll be back.'

'Oh.' Helen screwed the top on the tonic bottle. 'All right.'

Donald closed his eyes. He could see Maria when he was in London. That would make him feel better.

Lloyd looked up. 'When you saw him,' he said to Mrs Marsden. 'When he spoke and startled you – did you by any chance ask him what he was doing there in the middle of the night?'

'Well, I said "You're an early bird" or something like that. I don't think of it as the middle of the night,' she explained.

'No, quite. Did he say anything?' As witnesses went, Mrs Marsden was pretty good. And patient – he'd been through the whole thing again with her.

'He said he had a big job on,' she said. 'But he was slurring his words, and I didn't see how he could be doing anything.'

Lloyd nodded.

'And he wasn't wearing old clothes,' she volunteered. 'Not the kind of clothes you mend cars in.'

'It might not have been that sort of job, of course,' Lloyd suggested.

'No,' she agreed. 'But if it was paperwork – you'd probably do that at home. I don't think you'd go to work at five in the morning.'

'Possibly not.' His stomach was rumbling, and he coughed to mask the sound, sneaking a look at his watch. Two fifteen – why wasn't he at home having roast beef and two veg like other people? For a moment, he wished the divorce had never happened; that when he did go home it would be to his wife and children. But it was only for a moment.

'Well, thank you Mrs Marsden,' he said, standing up and extending his hand. 'You have been a considerable help.'

Mrs Marsden submitted limply to a handshake. 'People say not to get involved,' she said. 'But I don't think that's any way to be.'

'Quite, quite,' Lloyd agreed heartily. 'I'm afraid we haven't quite stopped imposing on your time – would you just go with the constable, and he'll write out your statement. It won't take long.' All the time, he was ushering her to the door, and now he stood awkwardly, holding it open with one hand and signaling to Sandwell with the other, as Mrs Marsden wrestled with her coat.

'You'll all catch your deaths,' she warned him. 'Having the heating on that high in September.' Lloyd smiled uncertainly. The central heating hadn't been on since sun decided to visit Britain for the fourth time in living memory, and it needed an Act of Parliament ever to get it switched on again. When she was gone, he grinned at Judy.

'So,' he said. Judy was looking in the drawer for something, and Lloyd took the opportunity of perching on the corner of her desk without being glared at. 'What's the story so far?'

She made an exasperated face as she surfaced. 'What's wrong with the chairs?' she asked.

'Have you got it all straight yet?' He ignored her complaint.

'A young man – Paul Sklodowski – I've even learned his name, came in on his way to work this morning to say that he was worried about a girl.' She glanced at the statement, and began to read aloud.

'I saw the car arrive at the boating lake at about half past eight. There were two people in it, a man and a woman. When it left at approximately nine o'clock, only the man was in it. I took the number of the car in case something had happened.' She looked up at Lloyd. 'He didn't have anything to do with it?' she asked.

'Not as far as we can tell – he didn't come last night because he thought we'd laugh at him. But he was worried about it all night, and so he came in first thing this morning.'

'Do you believe him?'

Lloyd made a face. 'I'm not sure. I thought we could go and have a talk with him this afternoon – I haven't seen him myself, anyway. But Tom saw him – he thinks he's telling the truth.' He sighed. 'I'm not so sure – maybe he *and* Wade were up there, and he got cold feet this morning. I've got someone hanging about his house to make sure he doesn't go underground like Wade.'

Judy looked back at her notes. 'Sandwell, acting on Sklodowski's information, went to the boating lake at ten past six, where he found the body of Julia Mitchell.'

'Right. And we now know that she left Donald Mitchell's house at half past seven, went with him to the boating lake, where they had a row, left and went to the Shorts', where they arrived at about twenty past eight.'

'How far is it from the boating lake to the Shorts' house?'

'About five minutes in a car,' Lloyd said.

'What were they doing there all that time? Having this row?'

'Well – the Shorts think there might be rather more to it than that. It seems Donald wasn't obeying all the commandments.' Lloyd took from his pocket the pre-wrapped and sterilised sandwiches that the canteen had sold him, and began unenthusiastically to unwrap them. 'They think it was Julia giving him the brush-off now that she was rich.'

'Lovely – what with that and Wade being Mrs Mitchell's fancy man – still. Go on.'

'She stayed at the Shorts' for less than two minutes, because Mitchell called her names. As she was leaving, Wade offered to drive her back – she wasn't too keen on that, apparently, but he persuaded her.'

'Did she know Wade?'

'No. That was the first time they'd met.'

'Just as well,' said Judy dryly.

Lloyd bit into his plastic sandwich. 'You can only tell by the colour whether it's ham or cheese,' he complained, opening it gingerly to see what colour this one was. It was pink, with a tiny white border. 'Donald Mitchell stayed at the Shorts' until after eleven, because of the storm. Though,' he said, thoughtfully,

'Elaine Short did tell me to ask Helen Mitchell where she was – apparently she couldn't be raised.'

'They've found her clothes, by the way,' Judy said. 'And the preliminary medical report confirms the doctor's theory that there was no sexual assault. It says, in fact, that the clothes were removed with care.'

Lloyd sighed. 'Blows my theory, though,' he said. Wade, turned rapist and killer by the death of his wife in a car crash for which he felt responsible. Nice and neat. Then he brightened. 'No *assault*, but—'

'No sexual activity before or after death,' Judy quoted. 'See for yourself.'

Frowning, Lloyd read the short, much qualified report. If there was no sexual activity, why didn't she have any clothes on?

'It wasn't that hot,' he said. 'Unless—' But he decided to keep it to himself for the moment.

'Unless what?' Judy asked eagerly.

He leant over conspiratorially. 'I'm not sure. I'll tell you later.' He laughed at her aggravated expression. 'A man's got to retain some mystery,' he said, with a toss of the head.

Donald slept in the chair, the Observer having slipped from his grasp to the floor. He hadn't eaten lunch, but he looked better than he had, Helen thought, as his deep regular breathing filled the room. The wind moved into the fresh to strong league, catching the window which wasn't fastened properly, and as she closed it, Donald woke and stretched.

'That's better,' he said, instantly awake, as he always was. He picked up the paper and folded it. 'Has Martin told you about last night?' he asked.

Helen recognised the attempt at a casual question. It was the tone of voice he used when he thought she might have found something out. This would be the explanation, the thing that made it all right.

'I haven't spoken to Martin,' she said. 'I had a word with Elaine, but she didn't say anything.'

'She will.'

Helen sat down. 'Go on,' she said.

'When we left here, we went up to the café – she said she wanted to see it before she decided finally one way or the other.'

Helen nodded. Why the big build-up? She knew that already. 'You told the policeman you'd had an argument with her,' she said.

Donald sighed. 'That was an understatement.'

'Oh?' Helen prepared herself to listen to yet another of Donald's complicated lies. He seemed to think that as long as he included imaginative little details, no one would ever suspect.

'We had a flaming row,' he told her, a little sheepishly. 'It seems ridiculous now.'

'About the boating lake?' Helen tried to keep the skepticism out of her voice, but she could hear it herself.

'Yes!' Donald said, hurt surprise registering automatically. 'About the boating lake – I told you it was ridiculous.' He picked up his almost untouched whisky. 'She was coming into all that money – we haven't even sorted out how much the estate's worth yet – and she was insisting on *selling* that place to the Council.' He downed his drink, and rose to get another. Helen nursed her gin and tonic, mindful of Donald's warning about keeping her wits about her for the police.

'Why didn't Charles put it in his will if he wanted to donate it to the town?'

'Search me. I didn't do his will, if you remember.'

She remembered all right. Charles had found it easier to go to the solicitor who handled the Mitchell Development business in London, and Donald was most put out.

'What made you think you could change her mind?'

'Oh, I don't know. I just thought I'd have one last go at making her see reason.'

'Why did it turn into a row?' Helen normally accepted his stories at face value, said 'yes, dear' and got on with her life. But Julia hadn't seemed in the least interested in the boating lake. The whole thing was just an excuse, and now he was embroidering it.

'It got personal. By the time we got to Martin's, we were calling each other names.'

Helen was sure it had got personal. She raised her eyebrows slightly, but didn't speak.

'She couldn't have cared less about the boating lake,' he said, as though he could read her mind. 'It was just an excuse – something I wanted her to do. Something Charles would have wanted her to do. So she wasn't going to do it.'

Why? Why did he always keep up the pretence? Why did they play this game of lies, excuses, plausible stories? Year after year they had done it. He told them, she listened, and they both knew he was lying. She had come to the conclusion that he had affairs purely for the mental exercise of lying his way out of being caught. The boating lake was just an excuse, all right – an excuse to have Julia there, under his own roof, making the game more challenging than ever.

And now the initial shock had worn off, her death didn't really seem to have touched him at all. It certainly hadn't spoiled the game.

'You want me to come too?' Judy looked at her desk. There was the fire at the school during the holidays – almost certainly arson; there was the purse stealer at Blend-vend, and she was supposed to be preparing a crime prevention leaflet for the Chamber of Commerce, with particular reference to dissuading shoplifters – one point on which was that they mustn't call them shoplifters. Shop thefts, shop thieves. She had to give evidence on Thursday, and there was a lot of paperwork to do on that . . . she stopped thinking about it. 'All right,' she said.

On the way to the Sklodowskis', they tossed theories backwards and forwards like a tennis ball.

'What was Paul Thingy doing in the woods, anyway?' Judy asked.

'Answering the call of nature,' Lloyd said.

'Do you mean having a pee or bird-watching?'

'The former.'

The car picked up speed on the road out to Homewood, where Stansfield's well-heeled residents chose to live. The made-to-measure houses with their swimming pools and tennis courts – much used this summer, for a change – passed in procession.

'Took a hell of a long time over it, didn't he?' Judy remarked, as she turned into Purcell Avenue.

'Couldn't start his motorbike.' Lloyd shrugged. 'I thought he might be a Peeping Tom, but Tom – our Tom,' he said, with a laugh, 'says he'd bet money that he's got nothing to do with it. Says we'll know why when we see him.'

The car drew into the tarmacked driveway of a Spanish hacienda, whitewashed, pink tiled, and shuttered.

'You did say they were Polish?' Judy asked, as they got out of the car, and negotiated the shining new motorbike in the drive.

'Something like that,' Lloyd said, walking back to where PC Alderton waited. 'You can get back to work now,' he said. 'We've arrived with the thumb-screws.'

Mrs Sklodowska was clearing away the remains of Sunday lunch when they went in, having been heartily welcomed by Paul's father, a square, fair man in looks, and almost certainly in temperament, Judy thought. His eyes, even bluer than Lloyd's, looked anxious.

'Alice, this is the police. The other car is not here now.' He turned to Judy. 'You will understand – she not like the car out there so long. I told her – they don't know Paul. He has killed this lady, they think.'

'No, no we don't,' Judy said. 'But we can't take chances.'

'I tell her that.'

Sklodowski's command of the English language was total, but his speech was still peppered with vees, and his syntax was a little eccentric.

'This car is just a car,' he assured his wife, who tucked a strand of greying hair back into her unfashionable bun.

'I'm sorry,' she said. 'But it did bother me a bit. Paul only reported it – I mean, you don't really think he had anything to do with it, do you?'

Lloyd smiled. 'Well, we'd like to talk to him. How old is he, Mrs Sklodowska?'

Judy could feel his smugness in remembering the feminine of the name – especially since Mrs S. was English, and that much more likely to be impressed.

'He's just turned eighteen.' She frowned. 'Do you want to see him alone?'

'Not necessarily,' he said. 'We'll see how it goes.'

A PERFECT MATCH

Paul was called down from his room, and entered shyly, another version of his father. They all got themselves reasonably comfortably seated before Lloyd began.

'Paul – my sergeant tells me that you were on your way to work when you came in this morning. Where do you work?'

'Mitchell's,' he said. 'I was on six to two.'

'Why did you wait until this morning?'

Paul moved uncomfortably. 'I told him. I thought I would be wasting your time. But then it worried me all night, and I decided to come in and tell you.'

Judy looked at him. She could see what Tom meant. He seemed to be a nice-looking, well-built, normal young man. Peeping Toms usually gave off vibrations of failure, and Paul didn't. And yet she didn't think he was telling the truth.

'What else did you think might have happened?' she asked. Paul looked politely puzzled.

'I mean – when you saw the car come back with just the man in it – what reasons did you give yourself? What did you think might be the perfectly simple explanation?'

He looked at Lloyd, then back at her, and mumbled something she couldn't catch.

'Sorry? What did you say?'

'I thought she might have dropped something – she might just have been bending down, and I didn't see her. Or he might just have been dropping her off there – a shortcut or something. But it didn't seem very likely.'

'Anyway,' Lloyd said, smiling benignly at him. 'You took his number, just in case. Do you know whose number it was?'

'No.'

'Are you sure? You didn't recognise the car?'

'No. It was a Cortina, that's all.'

'What colour?' Judy asked, remembering her conversation with Mrs Marsden.

'I can't remember,' he said, his face becoming more miserable by the minute.

'How do you know it was the same car that you saw going up?

He shrugged. 'It looked the same.'

'But it could have been a different car?' Lloyd asked.

Paul shrugged again.

His mother and father did seem a great deal more anxious to help than Paul did. Judy found herself hoping that he would become more forthcoming. She didn't like the idea of taking him in for questioning from under the noses of his parents.

'Got any brothers or sisters, Paul?' Lloyd was asking, as though he were changing the subject.

'Two brothers,' Paul answered.

'Older or younger?' Judy joined in.

'Older.'

Lloyd laughed. 'I'll bet they led you a dog's life, didn't they?'

'No.' Paul looked uncomprehendingly at him.

'Mine did. My big brother – he still bullies me if he gets the chance!' Lloyd laughed. Lloyd hadn't got a big brother.

'My brothers are a lot older than me,' Paul said. 'They were almost grown up when I was born.'

Mrs Sklodowska was nodding vigorously in confirmation.

'So you were spoiled rotten by them, were you?' Judy tried.

Paul smiled shyly. 'I expect so,' he said.

'Let you have everything your own way, did they?' Lloyd was still being jocular.

'I don't know,' Paul said. 'They were always sending me for things – to the shops, or upstairs, or next door.' He laughed a little himself, as he began to relax.

He was a very young eighteen, Judy thought, but that was probably to be expected.

'Helped you with your homework, did they?' Lloyd persisted.

'Sometimes.' Paul looked at his father.

'Were you sometimes a bit jealous of them? They were grown up, weren't they? They could do what they liked, and you had to do what you were told.'

Paul shook his head. 'No, I never minded.'

'Have you ever heard of a man called Christopher Wade?' Judy asked.

'No, I don't think so.' There wasn't a glimmer of recognition as he answered. Not the merest blink. 'Why?' he asked.

'Just wondered,' Judy said, aware of Mrs Sklodowska's eyes

upon her. 'What about friends, Paul? Why weren't you out with your mates on a Saturday night?'

'I don't know.' Paul looked under his fair eyebrows at her.

'Girlfriends?' asked Lloyd.

Paul blushed to the roots of his blond hair.

Judy bit her lip slightly, trying to understand the reaction. Why blush? Boys of eighteen sometimes had wives, never mind girl-friends. Why should the question embarrass him?

'Well?' Lloyd said. 'Don't tell me you've no girlfriends – a good-looking lad like you?'

'There is a girl,' Sklodowski said, interrupting for the first time. 'Why do you not answer? She is a nice girl – we have known her a long time. Why do you blush?' He caught his son's arm. 'Eh? Why don't you answer?'

Paul took a deep breath. 'He's told you,' he said. 'Diane. Why are you asking about her?'

'Just interested,' Judy said. 'Why weren't you out with Diane?'

Paul blushed again, but not so painfully this time. 'Her dad won't let her,' he said.

'What?' Sklodowski stared at him. 'What do you mean? Since when?'

Paul shrugged.

'Don't *do* that!' His father hit him gently on the shoulder. 'Why does he not let her? What have you done?'

'Nothing!' Paul sighed. 'I think it bothers him. Because you got on and he didn't. I don't know why. But he said she's not to see me.'

'What age is Diane?' Lloyd asked.

'Seventeen. It's not long to wait until he can't tell her who to see. We don't mind waiting.' Paul waited patiently for more ques-tions.

'Why were you in the wood for so long?' Judy asked. 'You saw the car arrive, and leave – that was half an hour later, you said.'

Paul nodded dumbly.

'What were you doing?'

'I've said,' Paul muttered. 'I couldn't start my bike.'

'What's wrong with it?' Lloyd asked. 'It's brand new – it was a very warm night – you shouldn't have trouble starting it.'

'I don't know!' Paul shouted.

'Did you go up there? Did you go up to see what was going on?'

'What?' The question came from both Paul and his mother. 'You heard,' Lloyd said, his voice hard. 'Did you want to watch?'

Paul stared at him. 'You're joking,' he finally said.

'Am I? I thought you must be with that story about the bike.'

Paul stood up, and so did Lloyd. Paul was inches taller. 'The bike broke down,' he said. Anger had made him lose his self-consciousness. Suddenly, he didn't seem so young.

'Why didn't you push it? You're a big lad – Wade's garage is just down the road.'

But Paul didn't take the bait that Lloyd was dangling. If he knew that Wade wasn't at the garage, he didn't give himself away.

'Who is this Wade?' he asked. 'Why do you keep dragging him – oh! That's whose car I saw – right? So why should I know him?'

Lloyd walked away from him, over to the window. 'Oh, no,' he said. 'I don't think you know him. At first I did. I thought maybe you knew the car, and didn't want to tell. But now I've got it. You went up to have a look, didn't you? And that's when you saw him. And it frightened you, so you ran away. That's it, isn't it?'

Paul looked at Judy. 'It was nothing like that,' he said mildly.

Judy allowed herself a smile. 'Then tell us what it was like.'

Chris awoke with a start, staring at a damp green wall. For a second, he had no idea where he was, but then the unwelcome memories flooded back. He could see faces – Julia's, pinched and frightened, phone in her hand to call the police. He'd only been trying to apologise, see if she was hurt. She didn't have to do that. He'd tried to explain to Helen – he could see her face, worried and loving. He could vaguely see Donald's. Worried, asking him over and over again what he'd done. She shouldn't have said those things – she shouldn't. He remembered the garage, and the bottle of whisky that he'd found. Whisky to try to blot out the memory, but it hadn't worked. Carrie's familiar face was there. It had all come rushing back to him as he drove away from the wood. Carrie, lying in the street in the rain, covered with someone's plastic mac. The rain teeming down, running off the coat into the road. Police cars, their lights flashing blue through the steady downpour; the ambulance, siren braying, inching its way through the Christmas crowds who couldn't help and wouldn't leave. And he didn't have a scratch. Nothing – nothing wrong with him at all. He had drunk the whisky to make it go away, but it had stayed, and he'd let Helen down.

Now, he felt sick. He had a splitting headache, but he could think more clearly. Julia was dead. He didn't care, that much he did know. But someone else must have come along and killed her, because she was alive and kicking when he left. He tried to think of what they'd done. He'd taken her up there, gone in, tried to talk to her, had a row. He remembered thinking that she must be picking rows with everyone, because she and Donald were having a row when they arrived at Elaine's. She couldn't have died – not from what he did. No one dies, not like that. Not after they've threatened to phone the police and hurled abuse at you. Oh, that was just being stupid. Of course she didn't die from anything he did. Someone went up there and killed her.

God knows, there were probably enough people who wanted to.

The teams of men moved out, widening the area that they were searching. The cameramen were being allowed in now, and they filmed the spot where the girl had been found, and the outside of the building that was still sealed off. Flashes supplemented the daylight, as the press got their photographs of the police searching every inch of the woodland. Reporters hovered, having to make do with press statements until they could find a real live policeman to talk to, because right now they were all too busy.

So they grumbled about the weather, and their accommodation, and the fact that their expenses wouldn't cover their expenditure, what with the hotel costing the bloody earth and it was all right for lorry drivers, they could sleep in the cab. And they sat gloomily in their cars, or on the still damp grass until they discovered that it was still damp, and they watched the people who were working, and wished that they were, or that the pubs were open.

They wouldn't even say who they were looking for, though they obviously all knew. They'd heard the rumours, of course, but you can't print rumours. You can mention the odd disappearance of one Christopher Wade, garage proprietor, which you just happen to have picked up while you were in the area. Is he another victim? But it wasn't as good as coming right out with it. Widow's Death – Local Businessman Sought. Come to that – why hadn't they found him?

Will Lakeside Killer Strike Again?

Chapter Four

Strikes, trouble in the Middle East, trouble in Northern Ireland; they took second place to trouble here in Stansfield, which had caught the attention of the national news, as Helen watched, waiting to hear what was happening. The policeman hadn't come back; not yet, anyway. Donald, less interested, was on the phone to someone, arranging to go to London tomorrow.

The familiar music of the early evening news, opening with the pictures she had already seen in her mind. The police searching the wood; the lake, looking dark and cold as the wind ruffled its surface.

'*The beauty spot where early this morning the body of thirty-five year old Julia Mitchell was found. "We know who we are looking for," says Superintendent James Randall.*

'*Good Evening.*' The newsreader smiled the serious smile that newsreaders keep for these occasions. '*Police have issued a description of the man they wish to interview in connection with the murder of Julia Mitchell, widow of property developer Charles Mitchell. Mrs Mitchell's body was found early this morning, near a boating lake in Stansfield, where she was visiting relatives. Mel Brown has this report.*'

The camera moved round the closed café, showing close-ups of the windows and the door, for no good reason. The reporter walked up to the camera. '*This is the café where it is believed that Julia Mitchell met her death. Mrs Mitchell owned this popular beauty spot, and was in Stansfield to negotiate its sale. She was staying . . .*' Here the camera swivelled round to show the curve of the road, and the houses at the far end. '*. . . just down the road there, with her brother-in-law and his wife, Donald and Helen Mitchell. The Mitchells were not available for comment this* *morning.'* The camera moved back to the café, and the reporter. *'Superintendent James Randall, who is leading the murder hunt, said in a statement this afternoon "We are looking for a particular man whom we know was with Mrs Mitchell yesterday evening, and who may be a vital witness. We are not at present releasing his name." '*

Helen breathed a sigh of relief. Somehow, if his name wasn't mentioned, it didn't seem so bad.

The newsreader appeared again. *'The police have, however, issued a description of the man, who is six feet tall, with dark straight hair and brown eyes. He was last seen wearing brown corduroy trousers, and a light brown shirt. Police appeal to anyone who may have seen him or Mrs Mitchell, who had shoulder-length blonde hair, and was wearing a denim skirt and jacket, to come forward. Thorpe Wood, and the boating lake itself, is a popular spot for courting couples, and the police emphasise that any information will be treated in the strictest confidence.'* Then the film of the police searching the woods again. *'Teams of police are combing the area for clues, and it is thought that her attacker may be hiding out there. Tracker dogs may be used in the search.*

'And now for the rest of today's news . . .'

Helen didn't listen to the rest of today's news.

'The bike wouldn't start.'

Lloyd looked sideways at Judy, and she took over.

'How long did it take to start? I mean – it did start eventually, didn't it?'

He nodded.

'How long?'

The evening sun slanted into the room, landing like a spotlight on Paul. 'I don't know. About ten minutes, I suppose.'

'But you were there for half an hour,' Judy said. 'You should tell your mum to give you All-Bran – half an hour! That's no fun, in amongst the nettles.'

'Could I beg a cup of tea, Mrs Sklodowska?' Lloyd asked. He did want one; the plastic sandwich seemed to be lodged half way down. And he wanted her to go, to see if that made Paul any more co-operative.

Alice Sklodowska went off to comply with his request, and Lloyd caught Paul's father's eye. He looked back steadily, his gentle features placid, secure in the knowledge that his son had done nothing wrong.

'Paul,' Judy said. 'Whatever it is you're not telling us isn't worth it.'

Lloyd rubbed his eyes. They had been here over two hours, and they were no further forward. He decided to go on the attack again.

'All right,' he said. 'You'd better come back with us – the Superintendent will want to see you.'

Paul looked alarmed, as he was meant to. 'What for? I just reported it.'

'No, you didn't. I don't think you're a Peeping Tom – I think you went up there after you saw the car leave. You wondered about the girl, so you went up there, and you found her – on her own. What happened, Paul – did you lose your temper? Don't worry, it'll probably just be manslaughter – particularly if she led you on – did she lead you on?'

Paul stared at him, horrified, as his mother came in with the tea.

'Look – my son, he reported—' Sklodowski began, but he didn't get a chance to finish the sentence.

'Yes!' Lloyd said sharply. 'He reported it. He told us where to go and find a dead body, and we found one. Come on, son – get your coat.'

'But he did not kill this girl – he's just a boy!'

Lloyd looked over at Paul, who still sat, wide-eyed with fear. 'No he's not – look at him. He's a big lad. Strong. She wasn't very strong, was she, Paul? It would be easy to strangle her.'

Paul jumped to his feet. 'I was never anywhere near her! It wasn't me – it was the man in the car! I didn't see anything – I've told you what I saw. Diane can tell you – she was there!'

Lloyd sat back. 'Diane,' he said. 'Is that what this was all about? Diane?' He picked up his tea, and took two deliberate sips before speaking again. 'We,' he said, in his deepest, threatening, but well-modulated tones, 'we have just spent all afternoon here because of Diane? Because Sir Galahad here wanted to protect her reputation?'

'No – it was – yes.' Paul hung his head, and muttered, almost to himself. 'She made me promise,' he said. 'She didn't want me to tell anyone about it at all. Because her dad would find out where she'd been.'

Lloyd contented himself with looking contemptuously at him. 'Right,' he said briskly. 'Her name and address, please.'

'MacPherson,' Sklodowski said quickly. 'Diane MacPherson – she lives on the Queen's Estate, but she's a very nice girl. They lived next door to us when she and Paul were—' he indicated very small children. His fractured English seemed to be mending nicely, Lloyd noticed, and then he realised what name Sklodowski had given.

'MacPherson?' he asked. 'Not Matt MacPherson's girl?'

'Yes – you know Matt?'

'Yes – I worked with him once,' Lloyd said. 'Diane's seventeen, is she? I thought she was about nine.' He laughed.

'It is 39 Victoria Street,' Sklodowski continued, glaring at his son. 'No wonder Matt won't let you see her!' he shouted, aiming an ineffectual blow at Paul, and missing. 'It's flat 5,' he added.

Lloyd and Judy made for the door.

'Don't get her into trouble,' Paul pleaded.

'You're more likely to do that than I am,' Lloyd said. 'We'll need a statement. I'll let you know when.'

Out on the Spanish-style porch, he spoke to Paul's father. 'Don't be too hard on him – we were all young once.'

'Teenagers!' Sklodowski said with as much disgust as he could muster. 'When I was his age we were too busy trying to stay alive to get up to mischief in the woods!'

Despite the talk, Lloyd didn't imagine that Sklodowski had ever been hard on Paul in his life, and he didn't suppose he would start now. Diane MacPherson – well, well. He must be getting old.

It was getting dark, and Chris could venture further afield. He had had one or two furtive excursions outside his shelter when forced to by bodily need, but now it was too dark for them to be searching, and he could find something to eat.

The fresh, pine-scented breeze seemed like heaven after the foul-smelling cell, and he limped away towards the old wood where the wind would have brought down some apples. He tried to work out the last time he had eaten, but he kept forgetting which day was which. It must have been Saturday morning, because he didn't have lunch. Had Elaine given him anything? No, because they'd eaten early. They were expecting Donald and Julia round to discuss the boating lake.

Why hadn't he just dropped her there, like she'd asked? Oh no, he had to take her to the door. She'd left something up there, she said. Just drop her here, she could walk the rest of the way. She'd be all right, you could see the house from here. But she hadn't left anything. She'd tricked him in there with a stupid lie, and he still couldn't see why. God damn it, she hadn't killed herself. Or had she? People did, after all. His mind toyed with that idea for a moment, but it was too fantastic. Why would she want—? For a moment, it did seem to be the answer. She hadn't wanted him to run her back, because she intended doing away with herself. She got rid of him, and did it. Simple. Simple, except that the police were asking about him. Still – it might just be to see if he knew why she'd killed herself. Maybe she drowned herself in the boating lake. Maybe they weren't really looking for him, not like that.

But as he dragged his way back to his hide-out, he knew that he was whistling in the dark. He'd seen all the police cars – even heard a couple of policemen who got too close for comfort. Helen had lied for him. And Julia couldn't have been described as suicidal. When she had admitted that she hadn't left anything at all, said she just wanted to be with him – he had wondered, briefly, what was in store for him. His wildest fantasy would not have included Julia's being dead by morning and his being hunted like a wounded animal.

He crawled back in as darkness began to fall, and released his small load of hard, unappetising apples. He'd give himself up. Even if he couldn't work it out, he'd give himself up soon. Tomorrow. Soon, anyway.

Queen's Estate wasn't far from Homewood, but it could have been a million miles away. The car was parked as inconspicuously as possible by garages, whose defaced and damaged doors no longer closed, and which rarely housed anything as valuable as a car. The six doors presented an opportunity to one paint-spray wielder to inscribe MANUTD upon them in red paint.

'The theory is,' Lloyd said as they walked past, 'that Manchester United has a greater following than any other football club because the fans only need to remember six letters.'

'You know this girl, do you?' Judy asked.

'I thought I did – but she's grown up a bit since I saw her last.'

Judy laughed. 'Peter must be about her age, isn't he?'

'Yes – he'll be eighteen in January. I wonder if he's getting up to mischief in the woods. I suppose he is – I don't see that much of him now.'

'Does Linda still come round?'

'Sometimes. But she's growing up too. I'm glad she doesn't come so often – she must be getting over it.'

They negotiated some broken bricks which lay around for no good reason, and arrived at the surprisingly intact glass door of the flats. On the step, in the same neat, red lettering, was the greeting SHIT.

'My mother was telling me that she came across two schoolgirls the other day – neat white stockings, blue skirts and blazers, satchels, hats – the lot, demurely writing "Mrs Masters is a shit" on the wall with a magic marker,' Judy said, thinking that perhaps it was just that magic markers and paint spray hadn't been invented when she was a demure schoolgirl.

Lloyd shrugged, and they climbed the stairs to the top flat.

'He's always lived here,' he said. 'He thinks there ought to be pockets of resistance.'

'How come it got like this?'

'Nobody really knows. Every now and then they try to brighten its image a bit, but it doesn't really work. Though it isn't as bad as it used to be – there are quite a lot of people who haven't run away. I think it was a sort of vicious circle. One or two bad lots moved in, and we started keeping a special eye on the area. Because we were there, other people wouldn't move in. Still,' he said philosophically, 'you name me a town that hasn't got a seedy quarter. They just happen.'

The door was opened by a pale, thin woman of indeterminate age, with short, mousy hair and a smile of half recognition.

'It's Lloyd, isn't it? It's years since I've seen you! Matt! Matt – look who's here!'

Everyone called him Lloyd. Judy lived in hopes of someone calling him Algernon or Dafydd, or whatever name his parents had landed him with, but no one ever did. And he wouldn't even tell her when she admitted that her middle name was Cornelia.

'Come in, please,' Mrs MacPherson continued. 'The place is a mess – you should have said you were coming.' She stood aside, and Lloyd and Judy stepped in, to be greeted by Matt, whose Scottish accent had not been one whit diminished by living in the east of England for over twenty years.

'How are you doing?' Matt asked, pumping Lloyd's hand, 'And who's this? You've been keeping her a secret.'

Judy felt uncomfortable, because they so obviously thought it was a social visit.

'It's been far too long,' Mrs MacPherson said. She had an accentless voice that could have come from anywhere.

'I'm afraid it's business, Polly. We can't stay. This is Detective Sergeant Hill, Matt – Polly.'

Matt gave Judy an appreciative look. 'There were no detectives like you in my day,' he said. 'All I got were hairy beer drinkers like this one.' He jerked a finger at Lloyd. 'And Welsh, as if it wasn't bad enough!'

'Matt was on the force,' Lloyd explained.

'Aye, but I never had the brains – I couldn't afford it,' Matt said, and laughed.

'Are you working now?' Lloyd asked.

Matt shook his head. 'There's nothing. But there's some sort of an electronics place supposed to be starting up soon – I'll see if they're looking for security men. "Sorry, but we're bringing our staff with us." That's what I'll get.' He had put a high-pitched, mincing accent for the quote, and employed it again. ' "Just leave your name with us, Mr MacPherson – we'll bear you in mind." They're all the same, these places. But I'll take nightwatchman if it's going – I don't want to be idle – see these kids? Half of them are scared to work. But they can get them for nothing.'

By now the group had progressed into the living room, a quietly furnished, airy room, quite unlike its exterior surroundings. 'Mind you, we're all right for now – I've got my redundancy. And if Diane gets that job she's after on the paper—' He broke off. 'Here, where's that beer I brought back?'

'On the sideboard,' Mrs MacPherson's voice came from the kitchen.

'Oh here they are. Will you have a beer?'

'Thanks, I will.' Lloyd said.

'Business, you said?'

'Yes,' Lloyd said, slightly hesitantly. 'Is Diane in?'

'She's in her bedroom reading. She's forever reading, that one – I think she must have read half the library by now.' He paused. 'Why? What's she been up to?'

'Nothing,' Lloyd assured him. 'It's just that we were given her name as being a possible witness.'

'What to?' he asked, suspiciously.

'Nothing, probably. You know what these things are like. It's about this girl – young woman – who was found in Thorpe Wood. Do you know about it?'

Matt looked incredulous. 'Of course I know about it. It's been all over the news – what's she got to do with it?'

'Nothing at all. But we think she might have been around there last night.' Lloyd paused for a moment. 'If we could have a word with her,' he said. 'If she was there, she might have seen something.'

'What would she be doing there?' Matt's dark brows almost met.

'Probably just passing,' Judy said lightly. 'But she might remember something – a car, or whatever.'

'It's just that someone thought they saw her,' Lloyd tried.

'On her own?' Matt opened one of the beer cans with a small explosion of froth.

'Couldn't tell you,' Lloyd lied valiantly.

'She'd better've been.'

'Could I have a word with her?' Judy asked, as though it didn't really matter whether she did or not. She shook her head with a smile at the proffered can of beer.

'Just go through,' Matt said. 'She's used to the law tramping all over the house. That's her door there.' He indicated the door to the right of the kitchen.

'Who was she with? A boy?' Matt asked, as Judy left. 'If she was with that Paul What's-his-name, you'll not be the only one having a word with her. I told her – I'm not having that.'

'I've no idea, Matt. It was just her name we were given,' Lloyd said, getting himself into deeper water than ever.

'Do you know what her mother found in her bedroom?'

Judy by this time had heard 'come in' in a puzzled voice coming from the other side of the bedroom door, and had to guess the answer.

Diane was stretched out on the bed, reading, as her father had predicted, and looked up curiously when Judy walked in. Her mother's face and her father's colouring were an interesting combination; her brown eyes appraised Judy, a slight frown drawing her eyebrows together.

'I'm Judy Hill. I'm sorry to barge in on you, but your dad said it would be all right. I'm a detective sergeant with Stansfield police.'

'Oh. Did you work with my dad?'

'No – but the inspector did. They're having a beer now.' Judy looked round the small, neat room. 'May I sit down?'

Diane slid her legs off the bed to make room, and Judy sat. 'It's about last night,' she said. 'We've spoken to Paul.'

The girl stiffened slightly. 'What about last night?'

'Do you know that someone was found dead in Thorpe Wood last night? A woman?'

The girl clearly did not. 'The woman we saw?' she asked, in a whisper.

'Yes,' said Judy. 'I hope that makes you feel a bit more like telling us what you saw?'

'Of course it does! I wouldn't have – I thought he was making a big thing of it.' She shook her head. 'If I'd thought for a moment that—'

'Let's have your version, then.'

Diane looked up sharply. 'My *version*?' she repeated. 'What do you mean, my version?'

'Your account, then. But it will be a version, whether you like it or not – no two people see exactly the same things, notice exactly the same things. We know what Paul saw, and now I want to hear what you saw.'

Diane pulled her legs up underneath her. 'Does my dad know where I was?' she asked.

Judy sighed. 'Paul said there had been trouble – he very nearly got himself arrested pretending he was there on his own.'

'He would.' She didn't look entirely grateful for Paul's efforts on her behalf. 'What have you told my dad?'

'Just that you were seen in the area. Not where you were, or who you were with.'

'He'll find out though, won't he?' She made a face. 'I'll have to tell him before he reads it in the paper.' She seemed to have resigned herself to that; she faced Judy brightly. 'Go on then – what do you want to know?'

'What you saw.'

'Right. A car drove up the lane – it's a pathway, really, and stopped just opposite us because they had to open the gate. It drove on, and when it came back later, Paul said only the man was in it. There had been a girl in the passenger seat when it went in there.'

'How do you know?'

Diane looked at her more in sorrow than in anger. 'How do you suppose? I saw her, that's how.'

Judy took out her notebook, and made a production out of consulting it. 'What time was this, Diane?'

'Half past eight,' she said immediately. 'When the car came.'

'It was dark then, wasn't it?'

'Yes – I know what you're going to say. But when he got out to open the gate, the car light came oh. And I could see her as well as I can see you now. She was blonde – good-looking, considering.'

'Considering what? Her great age?'

Diane laughed. 'Sorry. She was about your age, I'd think.' She thought for a moment. 'But I didn't just mean that – she looked a bit, well – scared.'

Judy gave Diane the old-fashioned look with which she could infuriate Lloyd on one of his flights of fancy.

'She did! It's not because I know what happened now – I noticed at the time, really, I did!'

Judy made a note to come back to that later. 'Then what?' she asked.

'Two minutes past nine, the car came back down. Paul was over by the bike – his motor bike, and so he was quite close to it. And he came back and told me that the girl wasn't in it. He started to worry about it, and wanted to go up and check, but I stopped him.' She dropped her eyes. 'I didn't know,' she said, 'I'd never have just gone away if I'd thought anything like that had happened. But Paul – he's a big kid, really – you'll know that if you've talked to him – and he likes making mysteries. You know, UFOs and the Bermuda Triangle and all that sort of thing. He'd be just as likely to believe the Martians had got her.'

'You didn't believe him?'

Diane slid off the bed, and tried to put her feelings into words several times before she actually succeeded.

'I believed him,' she said finally, looking out of the window, her back to Judy. 'I believed he hadn't seen her. But I didn't think for a minute that anything had happened to her – I thought she'd just bent down, or it was a short cut to where she lived, and he'd dropped her off there.'

Judy smiled. 'These were your theories, were they?'

'They weren't theories! I just didn't think—' she broke off. 'I was wrong. I'm sorry.' She turned towards Judy, her face worried. 'Was she – I mean, if we'd gone up, would she have been all right?'

'I doubt it very much, but we don't know exactly when she died yet. She was strangled – I expect whoever did it made sure.'

Diane sat down again, her face pale. 'That's all there is,' she said. 'Paul had taken his number. I thought he might ring up, not give his name – but I should have known he couldn't do that.'

'Did you see the driver?'

'Not really. Just a man – I couldn't describe him. I saw her, that's all.'

'What were you and Paul doing when this car arrived, and left?'

Diane raised her eyebrows. 'What do you think?'

'Well,' Judy said. 'That is what I thought. But if you were – let's say otherwise engaged – how come you know exactly when the car came, exactly when it left – what she looked like right down to the expression on her face?'

'It's got nothing to do with you,' Diane said sulkily.

'No, it hasn't, normally.' Judy stood, since standing seemed to carry rather more authority than perching on the edge of Diane's bed. 'And if no one had been found dead, it would have continued to have nothing to do with me. But Mrs Mitchell was strangled. And you and Paul have told me what you saw.' She stepped closer to the bed. 'And what you saw seems to have been a murderer arriving with his victim, and leaving without her. Which is rather important evidence – would you agree?'

Diane didn't answer, or look at her.

'When you are giving evidence in court, the defence will want to know how come you noticed so much, when you could have been forgiven for not noticing anything. And I want to know now.'

'It was awful,' Diane said, addressing her pillow. 'We'd never—' She looked up then, with a quick smile. 'Well, not awful, but not very good. I was frightened someone would see us, and it was too hot, and uncomfortable, and—' She gave a little, nervous laugh. 'When that car came, I nearly died of fright – and then I thought it was coming back again, because it stopped half way along – I heard its brakes. I didn't want to do it then, but I'd said.' She looked back at her pillow then, safe from any reaction. 'So we stayed.' Her face coloured. 'Will I have to tell people this in court?'

'You might have to,' Judy said, coming back and sitting on the bed. 'It depends how much other evidence we get.' She touched the girl's shoulder. 'I'm sorry,' she said. 'But they will want to know how you could be so sure of the times.'

'I'm supposed to be in by half past nine.' She stared hard at the pillow. 'I kept asking Paul the time – I was trying to get out of it,' she said, embarrassed. 'I made him show me his watch when the car came.'

She anticipated Judy's next question.

'It lights up – you know.' She paused. 'And then afterwards I'd got all bits of dead grass on me, and I was trying to get them off. He was over at the bike, and he couldn't get it started, and I didn't dare come home late, not after—' She looked up. 'I asked him what time it was, and he said it was two minutes past nine. And that's when the car came back.'

It had been difficult, and Judy gave her a little pat. 'Did you see the car leave?' she asked.

'Yes, but I was too far away to see who was in it.'

'Thank you. We will want you to make a formal statement, but you won't have to put all that in it.' She smiled. 'Paul seems a nice lad – why doesn't your father want you to see him?'

Diane closed her eyes. 'It's stupid,' she said. 'We've always gone around together. I just thought that if it was getting serious, well, I should – you know. I went on the pill, and my mum found them.' She opened her eyes. 'She told him, and he went mad. I told him nothing had happened, but he didn't believe me.' She shrugged. 'So on Saturday I thought – why not?'

'We won't say any more to your dad than we have to,' Judy said. 'But you'd better tell him something before he finds out some other way.'

'Yes.' Diane wasn't really listening.

'And don't worry,' Judy said, giving a little wink. 'It gets better with practice.'

Diane looked up. 'It couldn't get much worse,' she said, with a wry smile. 'It *was* awful.'

Donald sipped his coffee. 'That was a lovely meal,' he said to Helen, who always found more solace in cooking than in eating, and hadn't really done hers justice. 'It deserves a brandy,' he said. 'Would you like one?'

'Yes please. You don't think that policeman will be back now do you?'

'No.' Donald consulted his watch. 'It's almost ten o'clock. Anyway, a brandy will hardly knock you sideways.' He poured generous brandies and handed one to Helen. 'I don't quite know how to say this,' he said. 'It doesn't seem the right time, but I don't suppose there can be a right time when something like this happens.'

Helen, immediately alarmed, almost choked on her first sip. 'What? Has something else happened?'

'Yes,' Donald said. He really didn't know how to put it. The only way was straight out. 'I don't suppose you knew – I only know because I'm his executor. It's about Charles's will, really. I only thought of it as I came in after seeing Julia. We're rich, Helen. We're very rich.'

Helen took another drink while his words sank in. 'Because Julia's dead?' she asked.

Donald nodded. 'Charles left Julia a great deal of money,' he said, 'which is hers – I mean, it'll go to her father, or whoever has a better claim. But the bulk of the estate was in trust.'

Helen frowned. 'Why?'

'It's not unusual – I'd have advised him the same way. You see, he made the will – what – when did they get married? Five years ago? Six?'

'Five – last March.'

'He made it when they got married, and he expected there to be children. To be honest, I think that's why he married her, despite all the comments.'

'Mostly from you,' Helen reminded him.

'I know, I know. But it did invite comment. I really believe he thought she was expecting his baby. I don't mean he wouldn't have married her otherwise, but she might not have found it too easy.'

'You mean she tricked him?'

'Quite,' Donald said. 'And when he made the will, he assumed children. And so he left her very well off, but he left the rest of the estate to any children of the marriage. He hated all that, you know. It was all I could do to get him to make a will in the first place, and then he had to change it all.' He could see Charles making a nice, general all-purpose will when he got married, so that he wouldn't have to keep coming back to change it.

'If there were no children,' he carried on, 'then the money was to be held in trust for Julia – in other words, she couldn't use it without the say-so of the trustees, and they were his solicitor and the bank. So that she wouldn't do anything silly with it.'

'So what happens now that Julia's dead?' Helen asked. 'How do we end up with it?'

'If Julia died, it was to come to me – just that. Not held in trust – he presumably thought I wouldn't do anything too silly. If I pre-deceased Julia, which at the time would have seemed more than likely, then it had to go to the boys, and so on. Keeping it in the family.'

'So you get it now?'

Donald nodded. 'When I went up to see his solicitor, I read that bit, but I just laughed. It was so like Charles, covering every eventuality he could think of with one great big complicated will. When I remembered, I rang Harper to check. And it's true,' he said. 'We're very rich.' He'd leave the rest until later.

The wind whistled through the trees, moving their branches, filling the air with rustling and sighing. The wood, black and shifting, looked like a wood where someone could die.

The lake, breaking the reflection of the stars into a thousand pieces as the water rippled and turned, looked like a bad place for ducks. But the ducks bobbed and weaved on the water, grimly seeing the night out.

The café stood dark and empty, its door nailed up, its secrets given up.

All, that is, except one.

Chapter Five

Sergeant Jack Woodford knocked and came in. 'Good evening,' he said to Judy, then looked across at Lloyd, who was stifling a yawn.

'I'm on nightshift,' he said. 'What's your excuse?' Lloyd waved a non-committal hand.

'It's quarter to eleven,' Jack persisted. 'How long have you two been working?'

'Don't work it out,' Judy warned. 'It'll only make us feel worse than ever.'

'I,' said Jack, 'have taken pity on the defective branch of the police farce, and any minute now coffee should be appearing—' he twisted round and looked at the door. 'I don't do it often,' he told Judy, his eyes still on the door, 'so grovel if you like.'

'Can I just be pathetically grateful?'

The door swung open, and the young constable whose name Judy could never remember walked in backwards with three steaming mugs on a tray. 'Coffee, sir,' he said awkwardly, having completed a tricky turn to face Lloyd.

'You've got it wrong,' Jack said. 'How many times do I have to tell you? You walk *out* backwards.'

Lloyd smiled tiredly, and reached out a hand for his coffee. Jack was very jovial tonight – he didn't know whether he could take it. He didn't know why he was still there. It would be a damn sight easier if they didn't know who they were looking for; he could be doing something then. Something he could get his teeth into. As it was, no one needed him on a door-to-door. Garages and outhouses could get searched without his experienced hand in the matter. All he could do was speak to the people who might be hiding him, and build up the case for the prosecution. And he could do precious little of that until he got the full post mortem results and the forensic reports. Finding him was the only real obstacle, and that just took manpower.

He drank some coffee, burning his mouth. Since they had left the MacPhersons, he and Judy had sorted out the various accounts of what had happened and the only question remaining was why. Why had Wade suddenly turned on a total stranger and strangled her? Why was she naked? Why had her clothes been rolled up into a bundle? Why were her underclothes missing?

'The reason I came in,' Jack was saying, 'was that we got a telephone call from an anonymous caller saying that Wade had been seen at the Queen's Estate shops. Probably rubbish, but I've sent a car.'

'Marvellous how they all know who we're looking for,' Lloyd said. 'That's the fourth time he's been seen today.'

'Why don't you go home? We'll let you know if anything happens, don't worry. You first, then the Super, so long as you don't tell him.'

'I'll wait and see how the Queen's thing turns out.' He did know why he was staying. He didn't want to go home – he was turning into the kind of policeman who wanted to bring a sleeping bag in and never leave the station. The kind of policeman he swore he'd never be. Or maybe it was because Judy was here – he'd prefer to think that that was why.

'Why are you still here?' he asked Judy. 'You've been up even longer than me.'

Judy used her eyebrows in a sort of facial shrug. 'I thought we'd find him, I suppose,' she said. 'And it could all be wrapped up tonight.'

It didn't sound much more convincing than his reasons. He wondered – hoped, perhaps, that she was staying because he was there.

'We'll see what happens about this so-called sighting,' he said. 'Then go.'

'Do you want a lift?' Judy asked. 'I take it your car's still out of commission?'

'I do, and it is,'

Jack left to see how the lads were getting on in Queen's Estate, and came back to report a false alarm.

'Right,' said Lloyd, putting on his raincoat.

He and Judy walked out of the station into the wind that swirled the rubbish round the car park. Judy's Ford Anglia had seen better days, and Lloyd positively winced at its general condition.

'If you want a lift in a clean car, you'd better ask someone else,' she said. 'It's the dirt that holds this one together.'

He lifted the door slightly before pulling it shut, as he had learned to do now. 'Why don't you buy a new one? A newer one, at any rate?' he asked.

'I like this one – it gets me where I'm going, which is more than you can say for yours at the moment.' She started the engine, a process not to be undertaken lightly, but which with patience usually worked.

'I just wish I knew why,' Lloyd said.

'Why I won't buy a new car?'

He leant back, and rubbed the back of his neck. 'Why someone would want to kill someone else that he'd known for about five minutes. I'd like to know if we're dealing with a nutcase or what. You saw her – there certainly wasn't much of a struggle. So he must have taken her by surprise, and just killed her. No rape – no nothing. Just killed her, as though he'd planned it.'

Judy moved off. 'Maybe he did,' she said. 'Except that he apparently didn't know the girl from Adam – I think we should look more closely there.'

Lloyd nodded. They drove out into the deserted town centre—streets. The pubs were closed, and their customers had dispersed. At eleven o'clock, the town could have been innocent of inhabitants.

'Or he just had a brainstorm,' Judy suggested.

'But what sort? He took her clothes off – or she did. Why? Nothing happened.'

'That might have been the problem. We'll know better when we get the post mortem.' Judy drove past the Mitchell's house, and towards the boating lake, along the tree-lined road to where

Lloyd lived, in a flat that she had so far resisted visiting. Lloyd felt that tonight was not the night to try again.

'Suppose he did know her?' Judy said, pursuing her theory. 'That could be why she didn't want him to give her a lift – why she didn't want to stay in the first place. She did know him, and she wasn't supposed to – two-timing Donald?'

'I've thought of that,' he sighed. 'However unlikely, I've thought of it. But if that was the case, and he just wanted her dead for some reason, why go to the trouble of making it look like some nut had killed her, and then run away? Surely he'd just have gone home, or back to his sister's, said she'd walked, or—' he broke off. 'What am I doing? I don't discuss work when I'm finished for the day. Did Michael get off all right, then?'

'Oh yes,' she said, with an edge to her voice. 'Michael got off all right. Doesn't he always?'

Lloyd wondered, not for the first time, why she had married Michael, whom at best she merely tolerated. He had known Judy a long time, and he knew when she married that it wasn't likely to work. But you didn't say that to people – you just said you hoped they would be very happy. And he had hoped she would – if she had been, he wouldn't be making even the gentle overtures that he was now. Would he? He liked to think that he wouldn't.

Lloyd had started out in Stansfield, and had met Judy when he moved to London. There, they had worked together until she married, and moved with Michael to Nottingham. He didn't know whose idea it was to come to Stansfield, but he was glad they had. His divorce had forced him to acknowledge the fact that he was lonely, and the subsequent gap in his life had been filled by the re-arrival of Judy. At least it gave him something to think about.

Neat houses, arranged in carefully calculated multi-aspect groups flashed past as Judy exceeded the speed limit with a fine disregard for the law she was sworn to enforce. A drunk made his way unsteadily along the pavement; he was doing no one any harm, and they ignored him. The wind hit the car side-on as they turned into Bunyan Road, creating a draught in the old car that ruffled its passengers' hair.

'If you pull up where that van is,' Lloyd said, 'that'll be fine. I I can nip through the alley.' The alley led to the back-door of the flats, running through the garages, which were hidden, from the road by an ornamental wall.

Judy drew the car smoothly to a halt. 'Shall I pick you up in the morning?' she asked.

He opened the door, admitting a blast of air that almost took his breath away. 'Please,' he said, remembering to close the door in the approved fashion, and waving as she drove away.

Inside, he poured himself a large whisky and sat down in the reclining chair which he had bought himself as a divorce present. His book lay on the table beside it; he picked it up, found his place, and tried to read it. It usually worked, this cutting himself off. No matter how long a day he'd put in, how tired he was, a nightcap and a chapter or two made him feel better. But tonight his thoughts kept returning to Wade and Julia Mitchell and what had gone on at the boating lake.

It was no locked-room mystery, he told himself. The body was not lying on the library floor, stabbed with a jewelled paper knife. There was no figure lurking in the gazebo. Wade had taken the girl up there, and for whatever reason, he had strangled her. He had driven away, gone to his garage in the middle of the night, consumed half a bottle of Scotch – the other half was still there. Then he had fled from justice.

Except, of course, that he hadn't taken her up there. She owned the place – she had the key. It was in her handbag, which they'd found in the café. So she had taken him up there.

He opened his book again. Now he knew what had been nagging at him, he began to relax. Tomorrow he could look for the answer. Outside the wind rattled the windows and howled through the alley, but he felt as he had as a child, when he would play in the outhouse, and the concentrated heat would surround his brown summer body like water. If it rained, streaking the dusty window, it was outside. It couldn't get him.

The wind, moaning and sighing, was outside. It couldn't get him.

The wind carried the sound of the church clock chiming midnight into the Mitchells' house. Helen switched off the bathroom light, and went into the bedroom, where Donald was already in bed, leafing through a magazine. As she sat on the bed to remove her slippers, she could feel the waves of potential serious discussion coming from his side.

'Helen?'

'Yes, Donald.' She swung her legs under the bedclothes.

'I've been thinking – about this money.' He half turned to face her. 'Well, most of it won't be money, of course, it'll be shares in the business. But it's the same thing.'

'What about it?' Helen was in no mood for the discussion, but it was impossible to divert Donald once he'd made up his mind.

'You do realise how much we're talking about? Charles was a millionaire – when the radio said he'd made two fortunes, they weren't joking.'

'I know, Donald,' Helen said impatiently. Charles, in the way of most millionaires, had not been all that open-handed when he was alive, but he had left the boys a great deal of money, not to mention Donald. And now that Donald was getting the rest, she knew what sort of money they were talking about. 'Donald – could you get to the point? It's been a very long day.'

And Donald, she knew, had every intention of making it even longer.

'Well,' he said. 'I've been thinking – we're not going to carry on living in a semi-detached in Stansfield, are we?'

'No?' she said, stiffening slightly. This just wasn't the time. Her future was not something which particularly concerned her at the moment.

'Oh, don't misunderstand,' he said. 'I'm not sitting here counting the profits. But there isn't much point in pretending that we've got anything to preserve, is there? And I didn't want you to think that I'd just swan off somewhere once I could.' He paused, apparently waiting for her to say something.

Helen couldn't think of anything much to say.

'I will leave,' he said. 'Whenever we think it's best. But you'll get half of whatever it is I've got by then – I'm not waiting for some judge to sort it out. I just thought you ought to know.'

She nodded. 'Thank you.'

'We could see it coming,' he said. 'It's just that the money made our minds up. There wouldn't be much point in sticking together so we could be miserable in mink, would there?'

'No.' The money had made Donald's mind up. But he was right, of course. 'Was it the money?' she asked. 'Or had you decided anyway?'

There was a heartbeat before Donald answered. 'I'd decided,' he said. 'When I realised what Chris meant to you.'

Helen lay awake in the darkness for a long time, her mind on Chris, as the gales swept in. He must have found somewhere to go, she thought, to comfort herself, but she shivered. So Donald had known all the time – it wasn't too difficult, she supposed. Of all the people in the world, he ought to know the signs.

Judy Hill slept, dreaming that everyone she ever knew was playing tennis in the rain. Her husband wasn't playing; he was standing a little way off, and it wasn't raining where he was. He was complaining, all the same. There was a flapping noise, and a bird swooped down, catching her in its talons. She tried to fight it, but it flapped furiously.

She woke up, her mouth dry, her body tense. The flapping was in the room, and it hurt to move. She lay still, afraid of the noise, until her mind cleared, and she turned to see the curtains billowing out into the room, opened by the wind. The moon was high and small, and silver-edged streams of cloud raced across the sky. Rain, carried on the wind, hit the window as she rose to close it. For some moments she leant on the window sill, looking out at the curve of the road, at the new trees, whose leaves were falling fast. The trees bent in the wind; she wondered if they would survive the wild night.

She lived in the more established part of Stansfield, which meant that the houses were twenty-five years old, and built in terraces, with a single aspect. It also meant that you could find your way from one end of the street to the other. She had gone down in the folklore of Stansfield Constabulary by having to get a member of the public to get her out again when she had entered one of the new pedestrian estates without a compass. The next day, she had found a distress flare on the passenger seat of the car.

She smiled to herself, closed the curtains and went back to bed. She liked Stansfield.

Michael, of course, didn't. But then Michael didn't like anywhere much, and wouldn't, until he could afford to live uptown. Mr Thingy's Spanish hacienda would suit him down to the ground. Living in a council house was something Michael had never got used to, despite having done so from birth. The New York trip meant a lot to him; she wished, a little guiltily, that she had been more enthusiastic for his sake. But then, she argued with herself, everything he does is for his sake, so perhaps he didn't need her blessing. She missed him, in an odd way, when he was off selling computers – this time, he'd only been home two days, and they had been spent sniping at one another, largely because he had failed to sell any computers. And he was worried about New York, because the firm had had to scrape together the money to send him; he desperately wanted to do well.

It was so much easier to be charitable about him when he wasn't there. This morning's row had been the same as all the others – she couldn't remember what had started it, but as always, it ended up being about their standard of living, which suited her and didn't suit Michael. No one in their right minds would live in a place like this, and so on.

And now, of all things, there had been a murder. That was something that Michael would regard as a personal insult if ever there was one. Stansfield had been his idea; she had opened her mouth to tell him that she knew someone there, and had closed it again. Not because it would have put him off, and not because he was likely to read anything into it. Whatever else he was, Michael was not the jealous type. No, she hadn't told him because she knew there was more to it than that. She doubted if she would ever have married Michael if it hadn't been for Lloyd, complete with wife and children.

Perhaps that was what it was with Julia Mitchell. Perhaps they should dig around in her past a little bit, see if Wade figured in it at all. They didn't have to prove motive, but it was so much easier if you knew why someone had done something. She'd look into that tomorrow.

*

At least he'd got out in time. Chris gulped in the cold air, trying to take all his weight on one foot, then washed in the rainwater that had gathered in the dented roof. Once he was certain he wasn't going to be sick again, he went back inside, shivering and exhausted. But the smell of the store of apples hit him, and he had to go back out. He was sweating, and cold. He thought he might die here, and they would find another body in the woods.

He sat on the step, holding his pounding head, trembling in the wind. No, he wasn't going to die. His system had just rebelled against the whisky and the apples and the pain and the fear. With a great effort of will, he held his breath, and moved his provisions out, throwing them as far away as he could.

He'd had more than enough of being a fugitive. He wasn't even sure why he was one, so tomorrow they could have him. He could keep Helen out of it.

Donald was beginning to feel pleasantly drowsy at last. He had almost forgotten what sleep was like, but now he could feel it stealing up to the edges of his mind, gradually blurring the thought processes. Helen slept beside him, breathing deeply; he wished, in a way, that their marriage could continue. Donald wasn't sure what love was – he didn't think he'd ever loved anyone – but Helen had probably produced an emotion more akin to love than anyone else, and he had no desire to hurt her. But he had done, over and over again, and so in the end she had turned to someone else. That was, as he'd told her, when he knew he must call it a day. If Chris could make her happy, then he mustn't hang about to make her feel guilty.

But now, of course, all this had happened, and who knew what was going to happen next? The whole senseless business was threatening everyone's security, not least Helen's.

But he could make her financially secure, which might in some measure make up for the harm he'd done. It was, he concluded sleepily, the best he could do.

As the storm grew outside, Donald turned in the warmth of his bed, and went to sleep.

*

The night winds were sweeping the south-east, lashing the sea into a fury, crashing the waves on to the promenades; further inland, trees fell, blocking roads and railway lines. Hen-houses were left roofless, and cold-frames smashed as slates were dislodged.

In Stansfield, garden gates swung squeakily and Coke tins rattled along the town centre streets. Rubbish swirled into the corners in the back-street delivery areas, whipped up from the communal waste bins.

In Thorpe Woods, the wind moaned through the trees, and the night was alive with the sound of shifting leaves. A hedgehog, seeking shelter, crept under the tangle of nettles and weeds and sniffed curiously at the metal surface. It tempered the wind, and he stayed there.

Inside, Chris Wade tossed and turned on the hard bench, which was not made to accommodate six feet of aching muscle. On the same principle as the hedgehog, he too stayed there.

Chapter Six

Lloyd got into the car beside her, his mood matching the bright Autumn morning. 'The cop-shop, driver,' he said.

Judy didn't reply. Her interrupted night had made her less than sociable, and she could have done without Lloyd's bonhomie.

'Beautiful day,' he said, rolling down the window, and breathing in extravagantly. 'Doesn't that do your soul good?'

'No,' she said.

'Weather forecast said it would rain later – pity.' He grinned. 'It would do your soul good, if you'd got one.'

'I'm sure it would.'

A train rattled past, underneath them, as she drove on to Thorpe Wood Road. The odd one stopped at the station, but most of them roared through, like that one.

'Can you hear the trains at night?' she asked.

'Sometimes, if the wind's in the right direction.' He laughed. 'Last night you could only hear the wind.'

Lloyd lived in old Stansfield, the village that had been there long before the cuckoo in the nest. The flat in which he lived was in one of two blocks, carefully designed to blend in with the atmosphere of the village, as it was still called. The experiment had worked; they were just part of the scenery.

'Oh, look – there's a young tree down,' he said. 'It's hardly a tree at all – only about an inch thick.'

'I thought the one outside our house might fall, but it didn't.'

' "The gale, it plies the sapling double, and thick on Severn snow the leaves",' Lloyd said, winding up the window as the soul-improving freshness proved too much. 'Michael wasn't home very long this time, was he? Had to love you and leave you, did he?'

'In a manner of speaking.' She heard herself give an audible, unintentional, sigh.

'It goes on, you know.'

She frowned. 'What does?'

' "On Wenlock Edge" – you should listen to it. "There, like the wind through woods in riot . . ." '

But she didn't listen. She drove, letting the words wash over her. He didn't need a rapt audience – he just needed someone there so that he wasn't too obviously speaking for his own pleasure. She could imagine him as a fiery Welsh minister, threatening cringing congregations with hellfire, pronounced with about five Ls. Dropping his voice for dramatic effect, raising it at precisely the right moment to make them jump. It was a good voice – an actor's voice. It could be full of reassurance, coaxing a story from a frightened child, or cold and unemotional, if he wanted to alarm. He used speech to make up for the fact that he was the only Welshman in the world who couldn't sing.

The carefully controlled Welsh accent broke through her own private thoughts.

' ". . . Today, the Roman and his trouble are ashes under Uricon." ' He paused. 'What's wrong?'

'You mean apart from the fact that you're reciting poetry at half past eight in the morning?'

'Poets know a thing or two,' he said mildly, 'about feelings. More than computer salesmen.'

'It wouldn't be hard,' she said. 'What's put you in such good humour, anyway? You're not usually this cheerful first thing.'

'I don't really know. Except that it occurred to me last night that if Wade was in the café with her, she must have taken him there, because she had the key.'

Judy thought for a moment. 'Why, do you think?'

'Why did she take him in there? God knows, but at least we can try to find out.'

'No – why did she have the key?'

'It was her café.'

'Yes, but she hardly went around clutching the key to it. She was coming to see it – Donald Mitchell must have had the key in the first place. So why did he give it to her?'

Lloyd shook his head. 'We can ask him today – we're going there. I'm going to take Elaine Short up on her suggestion, and find out what Helen Mitchell was doing.'

Judy aired her own suggestion about taking a look at Julia's history.

'Do you think Wade might have had an old score to settle?' Lloyd asked. 'It's possible, I suppose. But nobody seems to think they recognised one another. Still – that's another thing we can do. See? Things are looking up already.'

They crossed the car park as the sun dipped behind a cloud, and the forecast rain began to fall.

'Sir? I've left the reports on your desk – they're both there.'

Lloyd smiled broadly. 'Today is going to be good,' he said to Judy as they collected good mornings and messages walking through the CID room. He pushed open the door and stood flamboyantly aside to let her through.

Judy watched as he scanned the reports. He threw them across to her. 'All we have to do is find him,' he said.

Judy stooped to retrieve the folder which had, of course, missed her desk and scattered its contents on the floor.

'Sorry,' he said.

Julia Mitchell had died between 7.30 p.m. and 9.00 p.m. 'Death was due to asphyxiation, caused by the restriction of her breathing with tights or a nylon stocking or similar being tightened round her throat. There were minor abrasions, but nothing to suggest that her attacker would be injured in any way. The most noticeable of her injuries was a deep graze below the left eye, in which traces of wood varnish were found. This was thought to have been caused as she lost consciousness and fell, as the small amount of bleeding suggested that it had happened very shortly before death. The blood on the table matched that of the deceased, and the varnish was of a type and age similar to that found in the wound. There was no evidence of sexual activity.

She moved on to the list of stomach contents, listening with half an ear as Lloyd picked up the phone.

'Could you get me Mr Donald Mitchell, please? His number is Stansfield 3074.'

The forensic reports next. They confirmed that she had been in the café; prints matching those found on the steering wheel of Wade's car, on the whisky bottle taken from the garage, and on the shaving mirror taken from Wade's house were found in the café in a number of places, including the door into the boatshed, the counter, and the front door. A jacket which had been identified as Wade's was also found in the café. From the position of the prints on the table, it seemed that he had picked it up and righted it after it had fallen. Another set of prints had yet to be identified; Mr Donald Mitchell would be asked to give a set of prints for elimination purposes. Several prints were found in the boatshed, which had been operational that day, but no clear prints matching any found in the café. Fibres matching those of the deceased's jacket had been found in Wade's car, and a set of unidentified prints on the dashboard. The deceased's prints were not found in the car.

Judy looked up. 'Did you read that bit?' she asked, as Lloyd put the phone down. 'About her prints not being found in Wade's car?'

'Yes – but I don't think it means much, really. If he's a door opener, for instance. Opens the door – all she has to do is get in. Opens the door for her to leave – and she gets out. She wouldn't have to touch anything that would leave any prints.'

Judy pursed her lips. 'What about the other prints, though?'

'We'll have to see what Wade says about them. Might be his sister's, for all we know. We can check that, unless he enlightens us first.'

'You don't think he could have gone up there with someone else altogether?' Judy found herself hoping that he had, and didn't know why.

'I hope not,' Lloyd said, smiling, 'or we'd better start looking for another body – he came back without her, remember.'

'And he's disappeared,' Judy said, resignedly. 'I think he must have gone up there with her.'

'Don't sound so wistful. You haven't even met him and you're beginning to sound like his sister. Chris didn't do it.'

Judy looked at him. 'Tell me honestly,' she said. 'Are you convinced that he did?'

'She was dead by nine o'clock – right? He took her up there at half past eight. Or at the very least, he left the Shorts' house with her at twenty past, and was at the café by half past. What else is there to think?'

'He could have dropped her off there, and gone home.'

'Stopping only to leave his jacket and his prints? And anyway, she was dead by the time he left – these people leave a margin for error – you know that.'

Judy accepted that her theory didn't really hold water.

'I've just asked Mitchell to come in,' he said. 'To establish that the other set of prints in the café are his. If they are—' he shrugged. 'Like I said, all we have to do is find Wade.'

Donald went into the kitchen, where Helen was washing up.

'They want me to go in,' he said. 'To have my fingerprints taken.

Helen turned round. 'Why?'

'Elimination, he says. So that they can sort out what's what at the café.' He poured himself some more tea. 'Do you want another cup? It's still hot.'

'No, thank you. Did he say anything else?'

'Not really. Just that they would be destroyed immediately.' He laughed. 'In case I commit a crime some time in the future. It wouldn't be playing the game, you see, if they already had my fingerprints.' He stirred his tea. 'And they want to clear up a couple of things about Julia, apparently. So I'll pop up there, and then I'll go straight for my train – unless you want me here for any reason?'

'I don't think so.' Helen looked pale and drawn.

'He says someone will be coming here some time this morning to have another word with you – but you won't need me for that, will you?'

Helen agreed that she wouldn't, and Donald went to get ready.

He wondered what they wanted to know about Julia. Probably something he couldn't tell them. They seemed to think he knew her every move. Including, he remembered, her father's hotel in Spain. He had decided to tell them about the will – it wouldn't really do for them to find out from someone else. It might look a bit odd.

'I'm going to tell them about the money,' he said to Helen as she passed him in the hall. He shrugged on his raincoat. 'I think I'd better, don't you?'

'What's it got to do with them?' Helen asked, with an automatic privacy preserving reaction.

'Nothing. But I think I'd better – just so that they know all the facts. You don't mind, do you?'

Helen made a shrugging gesture, and he assumed that she didn't mind.

Chris opened his eyes, which met the rusting walls. He blinked for a moment, then tried to move, but every muscle ached from the exertions of the night. He sat up slowly, light-headed and sore. His ankle throbbed painfully as he tried to stand, and he fell back on to the bench, his back against the moist wall. The swimming sensation left him at last, as he opened his eyes again. At least he didn't feel sick any more. He felt exhausted, and frightened, but he didn't feel sick. He took a deep breath, and launched himself out into the open, stumbling round, searching for something that would serve as a walking stick. Hopping from tree to tree, his hands clutching the wet bark, he scanned the ground until at last he saw a thin branch long enough and strong enough to support him.

The rain was falling in a steady drizzle as he made rather quicker progress through the trees back to his den. He couldn't make it up to the town. He'd wait there until he saw a policeman. He was bound to see one sooner or later.

'Did they come here at all to your knowledge, Mrs Mitchell?'

Helen wasn't sure how good she was going to be at lying to this efficient young woman with the frank brown eyes.

'No – but they could have. I wasn't here all the time.'

'Oh?' Sergeant Hill seemed to be showing nothing more than polite interest.

They were in the sitting room, and the sergeant sat where Chris had. Helen looked out at the garden, which sloped gently towards the pine wood, and she wondered where he was, hiding in its denseness. She wished she was out there, walking through its green solitude, dreaming of life as it should be.

Life as it was sat opposite her, pen in hand, notebook on the coffee table, smart and cool and organised. Her life, Helen felt sure, wouldn't dare to have messy edges.

'Yes. I had to take a friend to the station. She decided to get the earlier train – the 8.50. We left just after Donald phoned for Julia. About half past, I suppose. Perhaps a little later.'

'Do you know why your husband wanted to speak to Julia?'

Helen picked up her cigarettes. 'They'd had an argument – he wanted to apologise, I believe.' She felt guilty even when she was telling the truth. She lit a cigarette, and waited for the next question. The sergeant was writing it all down, and she was talking too much. Don't volunteer information, she told herself. Let her ask.

'Could I have your friend's name and address, please?'

'Is that really necessary? I'd much rather she wasn't dragged into this—'

'I'm afraid so, Mrs Mitchell. We have to check.'

'Why?'

'Because all that we know for a fact is that your sister-in-law is dead, and that Mr Wade is missing. We don't know if he's still alive – so we have to know what everyone was doing at the material time.'

Helen reluctantly agreed that that seemed reasonable. Poor Margaret – she only came for the day, and now she was going to get policemen demanding to know her movements. Margaret was an old school friend, with whom Helen had kept up for the thirty-five years that had passed since their hockey-playing days. She wished she were here now, so down to earth and sensible – she'd know how to deal with this. She wouldn't feel afraid of a young woman with a notebook and pencil.

Helen told the sergeant Margaret's name and address, with a heavy heart. Her opinion of Julia hadn't exactly been glowing, either, she remembered, with a smile. As soon as she had established that Julia and Helen weren't bosom friends, they had had a lovely gossip about her. She stubbed out her cigarette.

'So – you ran your friend to the station, and she caught her train. What time did you get back?'

'About half past nine,' Helen said. 'Maybe twenty-five to ten.'

The sergeant looked up then, with an enquiring look.

Don't volunteer, Helen told herself again. Let her ask. Let her *ask*.

'It was Stansfield station?' she asked, pleasantly enough.

'Yes.'

Was it her imagination, or was Sergeant Hill allowing irritation to cross her composed features?

'And what time did you leave the station?' Still the routine pleasantness. No bare light bulbs, no rubber hoses. Just an attractive young woman, in Helen's own dining room, wearing a cool, pastel-striped shirt that in other circumstances Helen. would have asked her about.

'I'm not sure – I stayed there a few moments. A couple of minutes to nine, I imagine.'

'So you didn't come straight home?'

'Yes.' She had to enlarge on that. 'I did, but the storm broke as I came into Thorpe Wood Road, and I couldn't see a thing. I waited in the lay-by until the rain had eased up.'

'I see.' She smiled at Helen. 'So you were at the lay-by at about – what – five past nine, or so? Possibly earlier?'

'I must have been.'

'Did you see Mr Wade's car – or any car, for that matter?'

Helen's heart was beating so loudly that she was sure it could be heard outside the room. Her throat muscles tightened. How much of the truth?

'No,' she said, trying to sound natural, and failing. She twisted her ring round and round. When was she going to stop asking questions?

'Why didn't you mention this to the inspector yesterday?' she was asking.

'I didn't think. I'm sorry.'

'But we were asking for anyone who was in the area – you did realise that you might be a witness?'

'No – the radio said anyone who had seen them. I didn't see them.'

The sergeant seemed to accept this, and moved on.

'You got back to the house at about half past nine or so – I believe your husband had been trying to contact you?'

How did they know that, for crying out loud? 'Yes,' she said grudgingly.

'Why?'

It's none of your business, Helen thought. Aloud, she said: 'To tell me he was waiting for the storm to ease off, and he'd be later than he thought.'

'Did you discuss Mrs Mitchell?'

'No. Well – yes, he asked if she was there, and I said not yet, or something.'

Sergeant Hill wrote something in her notebook, and Helen stood up, stiff with tension. 'Would you like a cup of tea, Sergeant Hill?'

'No thank you, Mrs Mitchell. I don't want to keep you any longer than necessary.'

Helen cast an almost furtive glance at the clock. Nearly eleven o'clock. She'd been here for three-quarters of an hour.

'Soon be finished,' Sergeant Hill said cheerfully, as though she'd read her mind.

It was almost over then. Helen sat down again quickly, feeling giddy with relief.

'I'd just like you to think back to when you came back from the station,' she said evenly, as though the subject hadn't come up before. 'Did you see any cars on the way back?'

Helen didn't answer, as she tried desperately to think of something to say.

'Mrs Mitchell?' There was a no-nonsense air about her now, like a nanny.

'Of course there were cars,' she said testily. 'Am I supposed to remember them all?'

'What ones do you remember?' She spoke in the same, even tones.

What difference does it make?' Helen jumped up, and took another cigarette out of the packet. 'You've made your mind up, anyway. You've given his description on the radio – you're talking about using dogs!'

The sergeant also stood, and offered her a cigarette lighter.

Helen waved it away, half-turning so that she was not facing her inquisitor.

'We want to talk to him,' she said. 'And either something's happened to him too, or he's hiding from us. Whichever – we do have to look for him.' She sat down again, composed and collected, and looked up at Helen. 'Did you see Mr Wade's car on Saturday night?'

Helen found a box of matches, and shook it, only to find that it was empty. With an exclamation of annoyance, she threw it down on to the table, where it bounced off and fell to the ground.

Coolly, as ever, Sergeant Hill took out the lighter again, suggesting with her eyes that Helen sit down. Despite being irritated almost beyond endurance, Helen complied, and Sergeant Hill flicked the lighter, which lit first time. Helen knew that if the roles had been reversed, her lighter would have clicked impotently and destroyed the whole effect. The flame burned steadily, and her need for a cigarette overcame her desire to leave her sitting there like the Statue of Liberty.

'Did you see Mr Wade's car?'

Helen inhaled deeply, and expelled blue-grey smoke into the fresh, sunlit room. It hung almost motionless in the shaft of light from the window, and it was through the haze of smoke and sun that she looked defiantly at the sergeant, a small muscle working at the side of her face. She had been lulled into a false sense of security, and she resented it.

'There were cars,' she said. 'Other cars.'

'Tell me about them.' She held her pen at the ready over her notebook.

'I don't know – there was a motorbike just beyond the lay-by as I drew in. They were stopped just by the pathway to the boating lake.'

'They?'

'Two people – a boy and a girl.' Helen smoked quickly in between sentences. 'And another car – I don't know what kind. It was open, in all that rain, and the driver was getting soaked.' She was talking quickly now – too quickly, the words tumbling out. 'That was while I had the windscreen wipers going, but then I switched them off and I didn't see anything else. I wasn't taking particular—' she stopped, perilously close to tears. 'Why couldn't it have been one of them? Why does it have to be Chris?' She turned her head away to try to hide the tears.

'It doesn't have to be,' the sergeant said. 'That's why I'm asking you what you saw.'

Liar, thought Helen, looking back at her as a kind of control asserted itself.

'What colour was the car with the open top?'

'Dark – I'm not sure what colour. It was dark.' Smoke came with the words. 'I mean – it was night time, and the car was dark.'

'Did you see Mr Wade's car?' Still exactly the same tone of voice, as though it was the first time she'd asked.

'No.'

'I know Mr Wade is a friend of yours,' she said.

Helen drew herself up. She would have no criticism of their friendship, not from her or anyone else. 'We've made no secret of it,' she said. 'My husband told your Inspector.'

'You might think you're helping him, but you're not – believe me, you're not.'

'I don't know what you mean.' Smoke curled up from the cigarette between her fingers, and twisted into thinning strands.

'We have witnesses, Mrs Mitchell. Witnesses who saw Mr Wade's car leave the boating lake at nine o'clock, and turn right towards the village. Towards his garage, we presume, since he was seen there later. Towards the station, come to that. Did you see his car?'

It was her house. She could just walk out of the room. She could tell Sergeant Hill to leave – she had the right. 'I don't have to answer you,' she said.

'But you do. You know you do. You can't withhold information, Mrs Mitchell. I don't think I have to tell you that.'

Helen made a small, defeated noise. 'All right. Yes, I saw his car. Does that satisfy you?'

'When did you see it?' Her expression hadn't changed. No triumph.

'Just before it rained. He passed me. That doesn't mean he killed her.'

'Did he see you?'

'I don't know. It was at the mini-roundabout where Thorpe

Wood Road and Main Street join – he was waiting for a car. I could see him, but I don't think he saw me.' She thought for a moment, then realised that her statement was misleading. 'I don't mean I could see him – I could see the car. I didn't see who was inside it, so I assumed Julia was with him.' She saw the look on the sergeant's face. 'I'm not just saying that,' she said. 'I just saw the car. It was at the opposite side of the road, on the other side of the roundabout, and there was a car going round between us. When Donald rang, I said Chris must have found no one in and taken her back to his house – I just assumed she was with him.'

The sergeant wrote all this down with what seemed to Helen like exaggerated care.

'I'm sorry,' Helen said. 'I should have told you in the first place. I just didn't know what to do.'

'We do understand, Mrs Mitchell.'

'We!' Helen put as much contempt into the single syllable as she could. 'Why do you people always call yourselves "we"?'

'All right – *I* understand, then.'

Helen shook her head.

'Sir?'

Lloyd looked up, and then up again. 'Yes, Constable Sandwell.'

'I was just thinking – do you remember when they built that road?'

'Which road would that be?' Lloyd stood up to mark off on the map the latest part of the wood to be searched. Turning to face Sandwell, he decided to sit down again, to minimise the inadequacy of his height.

'Thorpe Wood Road. They built it alongside the wood, and then they planted the pine trees. It would be about ten years ago.'

'No. I'd left Stansfield then – I was in the big city. What about it?'

'Well, sir,' Sandwell began. 'I was about nine or ten then.'

Lloyd groaned.

'Sorry, sir.' Sandwell smiled. 'But when they'd finished, there was one of these workmen's huts left on site. And there were arguments about which of the contractors had used it, and which should move it and so on – and me and my mates used to play in it. Nobody would do anything about it – and we used it for ages. When they began planting the new trees – to extend the pine wood, they shifted it back from the road, and eventually you couldn't see it at all. I don't think anyone ever moved it.'

Lloyd smiled broadly at Sandwell. 'When did this thought hit you?' he asked.

'Just now sir. I was saying to Sergeant Watson about how the town had changed, and I just remembered. Do you think he could be there?'

Judy walked in.

'Don't take your coat off, Sergeant, you're not stopping.' Lloyd stood up. 'Come on, Sherlock – get weaving. You can drive us there – if you're right, the arrest's down to you. You'll get your name in the papers.'

Sandwell, delighted, went off to get the car, and Lloyd explained to Judy, who was looking slightly startled at the sudden burst of action.

'So,' Lloyd said. 'Perhaps we can wrap it up now.'

Judy didn't look so sure. 'Perhaps,' she said. 'But I've a feeling we don't know the half of it yet.'

Lloyd hesitated, then laughed at himself. 'He'll just give up,' he said. 'You'll see. He'll tell us the lot.'

The bird that was lying in wait for a rash worm to be drawn to the surface by the intermittent rain flew off as the car drew up. From the safety of a tree, he watched the group of people cross the muddy grass towards the pine wood.

Another figure appeared, bearded and limping, walking towards the group with the aid of a stick. He tried to run, but he couldn't, and he stumbled as he did so. One of the other people helped him, and they took him to the car.

With difficulty, they put him in the back, and then they all got back in again, and drove off. Once they had turned in the road, and were on their way back where they came from, the bird flew down again, and continued his wait for a worm.

If he was very patient, one would turn up sooner or later, like buses.

Like policemen.

Chapter Seven

Judy finished eating, and looked reflectively at Lloyd, then at the room. 'You look after yourself all right, don't you?'

'What did you expect?' He laughed. 'Beer cans on the bare floorboards?'

'No – just less comfort.'

Lloyd looked round at the shabby old furniture, shown up even more by the reclining chair in which Judy was doing just that. 'I got all this lot from a second hand shop,' he said. 'You've got the only comfortable chair there is.'

She smiled. 'But it looks so nice – it reminds me of when I was small. It's the sort of furniture my mum had.'

'It probably is your mum's.'

She laughed, and stretched luxuriously. 'I could fall asleep,' she said. 'You'd better engage me in sparkling conversation.'

'Do you think Helen Mitchell's told you everything now?'

'I don't know,' Judy said drowsily, and sat up. 'I really am falling asleep. She could have, but I feel as though she's still holding something back.' She yawned.

'Why do I feel as though everyone's lying to us?' Lloyd got up to make coffee.

'Automatic reaction,' Judy said, as he went off to the kitchen. 'We're the fuzz.'

'The enemy?' Lloyd said, raising his voice. 'Not usually of sober, white collar, middle-income bracket citizens, we're not. Unless we've got them on a motoring offence.'

He didn't hear what she said, as he ground up the coffee. When the coffee maker was going about its business, he went back in, to find Judy lighting a cigarette.

'I thought you'd given up?'

'I still smoke occasionally,' she said.

'And this is an occasion?' He sat down, then thought he'd better clear away the debris of the Chinese meal that they had eaten picnic style out of the tinfoil containers.

'Well, it's the first time I've seen your flat,' she said, piling things up for him. 'That makes it an occasion.'

It certainly did for him, he thought, as he tipped his load into the swingbin.

'Who else do you think is lying?' she asked, suddenly at his elbow.

'I spoke to Mitchell about the key – he says she asked for it, and he gave it to her. He had no idea why.' He got mugs out of the cupboard. 'I suppose he did. But I got the feeling that the question –' he searched for the word. 'Discommoded him,' he said.

'Do you think they're covering up for Wade – they know something damaging that they're not telling us?'

'Could be.' Lloyd poured the coffee, and handed Judy hers. They would insist on sending Wade to hospital for a check-up. He was beginning to think that the doctor did it on purpose to give the patients time to think up a good story. 'I'll be glad when I can talk to Wade himself.'

They carried their coffee back through to the living room.

'Do you want the comfortable chair?' Judy asked.

'No, no. You're the guest – you have it.' He sat down again on the unyielding sofa. 'You're having a go at Mrs Short after lunch?'

'Yes,' she said. 'When you're becoming a star of the silver screen.'

'It wasn't my idea – it was Randall. "You're better at that sort of thing, Inspector." How does he know? I've never been on television.'

Judy grinned. 'Only because of some grave oversight. Could it be he thinks you like the sound of your own voice? Surely not.'

'Shut up.'

They finished their coffee, and got up to go. Lloyd picked up Judy's coat and held it for her.

'Thank you,' she said, slipping her arm in. 'By the way, I took a phone call for you this morning while you were with Mitchell.'

She turned to face him. 'They wanted to know why you hadn't picked your car up on Friday as arranged.' She smiled sweetly. 'So do I.'

Lloyd thought fast, but no plausible excuse presented itself. The truth, then. 'You know why,' he said.

'So that I'd chauffeur you around.'

'It's not a chauffeur I'm looking for.' He could have phrased it better, but it didn't seem to matter. 'Why didn't you tell me before lunch?'

'Same reason,' she said. 'But I'm not sure it's a very good reason.'

Lloyd took her hands in his. 'You once said you couldn't have anything to do with me because I was married.'

'So I did.' She smiled.

'I'm not married now.'

'I am.' But it was just a statement of fact, not a protest. She took a step towards him, and her lips touched his as the phone rang. She stepped back, leaving the way clear to the phone.

'Thank you very much,' Lloyd said to it, and picked it up.

'Rogers here, sir. They've found her underwear – bra, pants and tights.'

'Great. Where?'

'A long way from either the body or the rest of her clothes, I'm told. The lab's got them now. Can we call off the search?'

'Er – yes. Yes. I think so. But keep the area roped off – and have someone keeping an eye on it. I don't want sightseers.'

'Right, sir.'

Lloyd replaced the receiver and relayed the call to Judy.

'Well,' she said, good humouredly. 'Is that the end of the seduction scene?'

Lloyd laughed, and opened the front door. Lunch, a laugh, and a stillborn kiss. It was better than nothing.

They were in Charles Mitchell's tasteful drawing room, not speaking much. Donald had something to say, but he had not yet fully worked out how he was going to say it.

Maria smiled; he just smiled back, like a stranger, like someone in a waiting room. He touched her to prove that he wasn't.

'It takes a bit of getting used to,' she said. 'That's all.'

'I know,' he said, taking her hand in his. It was cold – he rubbed it gently. 'I can't stay,' he said. 'I've got to get back.'

'You said.' She took her hand away and stood up. 'I'll get your photograph. It's in the bedroom.'

Donald walked round the room, touching the delicate furniture. He ran his hand over the smooth polished wood of the table.

'It's yours now,' she said, reappearing at the door. 'Isn't it?'

'I think so,' he said. 'It's a bit complicated, as I said.' He took the photograph, and glanced at its general amateur fuzziness. 'There aren't any others?' he asked.

'No. Won't that one do?' She came over to him, and looked at it over his shoulder, pushing the fair hair away from her face.

'It'll have to, I suppose.' He gave her a proprietorial peck on the cheek, and put the photograph down. 'Are you going to be all right?'

'Don't worry about me, Donald,' she said, with a touch of sarcasm. 'You've got more than enough on your plate.'

He'd have to tell her. Donald crossed his fingers for luck – not, for once, because he was lying. 'I've told Helen,' he said.

'About me?' she asked sharply.

'No, of course not. I told you – it's a point of honour. But I have told her I'm leaving. I can't just now, not with all this. But I've told her I will be going.'

'Well, well. And I thought now you'd got all this money, you'd just pension me off.' She smiled.

He could have, of course. But Maria had lasted longer than anyone, and he hadn't outgrown her yet. They were holding each other, and the waiting room atmosphere had gone. Maria had been waiting for the blow to fall, and it hadn't. But Donald's fingers were still crossed. 'There is one thing,' he said. 'I've told her she'll have half the money.'

'Half of the money from the will?' She looked horrified.

'Yes. Don't worry – it leaves more than enough for anyone. How much do you suppose this place is worth, for instance?'

'Too much,' she said. 'But even at that. Aren't you being a little over-generous?'

'I don't think so,' he said. 'I'd say it was the least I could do. Helen's had a rough deal.'

'Oh well, you know me. I wouldn't have known what he was worth – too many noughts for me to understand.'

'I could have lied to you,' he said. 'But I'd rather you knew the position.' He put his arms round her. 'It was just that I thought she'd have Chris Wade, but God knows what'll happen now. It was the only thing I thought might make up for everything.'

'Are you sure you *want* to leave her?' It was a serious question, and she was waiting for an answer.

Donald had never had to face the truth so much in his life, and he found it exhausting. 'No, I'm not,' he said with an honesty that took her aback. 'But I do want you, and she doesn't want me any more. All this money,' he said. 'It forces you to look at what's happening, and think about the future. You can't just pocket it and get on with your life.'

'This friend of yours has done everyone a favour, then,' she said.

'I wish to God he hadn't,' Donald said.

'There's nothing you can do, Donald.'

'No.' He looked at his watch. 'I have got to go – I'll try to phone you. I probably won't be able to get back for a little while.' He looked round. 'Where did I put the photograph?'

'On the table. Oh – I got that address. It might not be much good.' Maria took a sheet of paper from a drawer. 'It's the firm's travel agent – her father might have used them. I can't think of anything else.'

'Thanks.' He took out his wallet. 'You're sure there isn't another photograph?' He put it in his wallet as he spoke.

'Quite sure – at least, I can't find any more. She wasn't keen on having her photograph taken, funnily enough.'

'She was probably wanted on three continents,' Donald said, and made her laugh for the first time.

She gave him a kiss. 'Hurry back,' she said.

Donald would be back in about an hour. Helen made herself a cup of tea, and settled down to her hourly ritual of waiting for the news. Now that their marriage was officially over, now that the words had actually been spoken, she could worry as openly as she liked. Donald would be all right; he'd got money enough to satisfy any ambition that had previously been frustrated. She wondered what he would do – go to London, she suspected, to set up in style. He might even live in Charles's house – it was his kind of place. And there would be no shortage in London of a girl or two to keep him company. But, please God, not one like Julia.

If Donald had to stray, why did he have to have such bad taste in women? And why was it so easy for him to have affairs, when she couldn't bring herself to have even one? Chris thought it was because of the age difference, but it wasn't. She was of the old school, and she had promised to keep only unto Donald. Two wrongs didn't make a right. But now that Donald was going, and she might lose Chris, the promise began to seem futile. She regretted and resented her fidelity, if you called it fidelity. Feelings were more important than physical acts, and her feelings were with Chris, and no one else.

The news dealt with what it considered to be the most important matters first, and then the word Stansfield came. '*Stansfield police confirmed this afternoon that the man they wish to interview in connection with the death of thirty-five year old Julia Mitchell on Saturday night has given himself up to the police.*

'*No charges have yet been brought, and it is believed that the man is in hospital recovering from an injury.*'

Relief, despair, fear, worry – Helen didn't know which one to feel first. He was hurt. He was caught, but then he always was going to be. He was safe, and that was the main thing.

Chris had broken a small bone in his foot, he was informed. They would be giving him a crutch, and teaching him how to use it, and then he could be released to the police. In the few moments that he had to wait, he could relax.

The bed was heaven, and he lay back on the pillow, cut off from the rest of the ward by screens, but listening to his fellow patients indulging in verbal slap and tickle with the nurses. At least he was clean and warm and shaved; at least he wasn't hiding any more. Although he was in a ward, he was fully clothed, in the new clothes that Elaine had brought, because the police took away his others. He lay on a bed where they had put him, out of the way. They hadn't let him see Elaine, which was a pity.

But it would be all right. He hadn't killed her, so he had nothing to be afraid of, or so everyone said. He would have liked to have seen Elaine, though, to tell her that he was all right, and that she hadn't got to worry.

They were a long time coming with this crutch. He'd close his eyes. The warmth and comfort claimed him, and he fell sound asleep.

Judy tried to comfort Elaine Short, who paced up and down the room as she spoke.

'He's quite well, Mrs Short.'

She stopped in mid-pace. 'He didn't kill her,' she said. 'He had no reason to!'

'He's not been charged yet. Are you absolutely sure that he didn't know Julia? From some time in the past, perhaps?'

'He didn't know her,' she said helplessly. 'I can't prove it – I can only tell you. Martin knew her, though.'

'Could Chris have met her through your husband?'

'No – Martin had met her at meetings and things, but he didn't know her, not the way you mean. And Chris certainly didn't.'

Judy waited until her pacing brought her level. 'How can you be so sure? Did you know everyone your brother knew? You lived a long way away from him for years.'

The rain coursed down the patio window, obscuring the view, closing everything in. 'He'd have said,' she explained, with exaggerated patience. 'He knew she was coming – he'd have mentioned it.'

'Not if he had some reason not to.'

'You mean if he was going to murder her?' Elaine threw up her hands in a gesture of frustration. 'But you're going round in circles – and he didn't know her.'

'But you will accept that it's a possibility?'

'It's a possibility that he knows Glenda Jackson, but I know he doesn't!'

Judy smiled. 'All right – you're right, we're going round in circles.'

'Why is he in hospital – why is he being kept in, if he's quite all right?'

Judy took a deep breath, this being the third time she had answered that particular question. 'Because he has an ankle injury. They'll be releasing him this afternoon. He is honestly all right. There's nothing to worry about.'

Elaine stopped pacing. 'Oh, no,' she said. 'Nothing at all. You're just going to say that he murdered someone. That's nothing to worry about—' she held the back of her hand to her mouth, and tried to stop the tears.

Great, thought Judy, that's great. Well done, that's the second one you've reduced to tears today. What a lovely job.

'Please, Mrs Short. Don't distress yourself – sit down.'

'I am not distressing myself! This business is distressing me,' she shouted, but she sat down, beside Judy on the sofa.

Judy nodded in what she hoped was an understanding manner. It certainly ought to be, because this business wasn't doing her much good either.

'She came in here,' Elaine said, angrily, 'She came in here, looking for a fight with someone. Maybe she just picked on Chris, and . . .' She shook her head. 'No. No, I don't believe it. He didn't kill her.' She blew her nose.

Judy patted her shoulder. 'I can't pretend that it looks good for your brother,' she said. 'But it could have been something like that – if he was provoked, it's possible that they—'

'I don't think she had the least intention of staying,' Elaine said suddenly, interrupting Judy and saving her from having to finish the sentence. 'She didn't look as though she was staying.' She paused for a moment, and considered carefully before she spoke. 'Have you ever done any acting?' she asked.

'Acting?' Judy said. 'No—'

'Well, I have. You see – I'm sorry, I don't know your name.'

'Judy Hill.'

'Judy. I used to act – nothing spectacular, and not for very long, but I did, before I met Martin. And you know the old cliché situation in plays when someone is walking to the door, and gets called back at the last minute?'

Judy did.

'Well, if you're acting in a play, you've read the script – you know you're going to get called back. And so, unless you're careful, you *look* as though you know. We'd get told to remember that it was up to the other actor to call us back – we had to believe we were going to walk through the door – do you know what I mean?'

'Yes, I know.'

'Julia looked as though she had no intention of staying. She looked as though she was going to leave, long before Donald called her a bitch.' She shrugged, and smiled a quick, apologetic smile. 'I haven't tried to explain that to anyone else.'

Judy said she would bear it in mind. It only strengthened her supposition that Julia knew Chris from somewhere, and had made up her mind to leave the moment she clapped eyes on him, but she didn't voice this opinion to Julia.

'Until we know what your brother has to say, we don't know what's important and what isn't. That's why we're trying to find out exactly what happened – and what you felt happened,' she added.

Elaine smiled. 'Will Chris – I mean, he should have a solicitor, shouldn't he?'

Judy stood up. 'Yes, I rather think he should,' she said. 'He hasn't asked for one yet.'

'Can he ring me? He's allowed to phone someone, isn't he?'

'Yes.' Judy would get him to ring her if it was the last thing he did. 'Don't worry, please. We haven't heard his side of it yet.'

'He couldn't,' Elaine was still assuring her as she made it to the front door. 'He just couldn't.'

She was glad to get away before she found herself agreeing with Mrs Short that her brother couldn't possibly kill a fly.

The fly that had indeed remained unmolested by Chris Wade still buzzed around the workmen's hut, and around the policeman who was checking it. He was waved away, and flew out into the afternoon, where the fitful weather was now shining and summer-like.

He flew across the road, to the building with all the people round it. People meant sandwiches, and mayonnaise jar lids, and sugar.

He settled on a camera lens, and was waved away again, towards the boating lake. Ducks – ducks meant bread. He swooped down on a crust that had missed the water.

This was the life.

Chapter Eight

The nightmare was closing in. Chris had rung Elaine, told her that he didn't want a solicitor. His reasoning was that only guilty people needed solicitors, and he wanted to tell them anything, everything they wanted to know. Elaine had sounded doubtful; he had demanded angrily to know why. Did she believe he'd killed Julia Mitchell? No, of course not, she had said. But perhaps you should get a solicitor.

He sat at a formica covered table, in a smallish room, the walls of which were bare except for the NOTICE TO PERSONS IN POLICE CUSTODY, which he had read and reread until he could recite it. They hadn't charged him yet, which must mean something, pre-sumably. The constable who had remained in the room with him stared straight ahead, not speaking. It was hard to believe he was even thinking, or breathing come to that. He was standing at the moment, at the side of the door, so Chris assumed that he wasn't dead. But then, he thought gloomily, he had assumed Julia wasn't dead.

The inspector had asked him for his version of events, and he'd given it, without interruption. There was a moment while the inspector seemed to be mulling it over, and then he had abruptly left the room, stopping only to advise Chris to think about it.

Think about it. Chris almost laughed. Think about it! He'd thought of nothing else. The steady rain beat down outside, and he tried smiling at the constable, but got no response.

The door opened, and the inspector was back. 'Right,' he said, sitting opposite him. 'Let's hear it again. From the beginning.'

Chris sighed. 'I gave her a lift home from my sister's house.'

'Did you know her? Had you met her before?'

'No.' Chris wondered what he was getting at.

'Why did you give her a lift?'

'Do I have to know someone before I offer them a lift? She was leaving, that's all.'

Lloyd leant back in his chair. 'She'd only just arrived, hadn't she?'

'Yes,' Chris said. 'She didn't want to stay.'

Lloyd nodded, and pushed his chair back so that it squeaked on the tiled floor. He walked to the window. 'Did she want a lift?'

'What?'

'You heard.'

'She said she was going to walk.'

'So? Why were you so keen to give her a lift?' He tutted at the rain, and waited for a reply.

'I wasn't! It was getting dark, and it's a lonely road – there was going to be a storm.'

'A lonely road,' Lloyd repeated. 'It is, isn't it?'

'Yes!'

Lloyd turned quickly. 'Did she want a lift? Did she say yes, thank you?'

'No, she—'

'What?'

'She said she'd walk.' Chris traced a crack in the formica with his fingernail.

'So what did you do?'

'I said she should let me drive her home.'

Lloyd turned back to the window. 'Along the lonely road.' He leant over and looked out, craning his neck as though he were trying to see something, and wasn't really interested in the conversation at all. 'How many times did she refuse?'

Chris stared at the back of his head, and the patch of scalp showing through the dark hair. 'I don't know,' he said, alarmed.

'I do. Four times, according to your brother-in-law. Three or four times, he said.' Lloyd faced him, and smiled. 'But you insisted, didn't you?'

'I suppose so – I just thought . . .' Chris tailed off. He had insisted.

'All right – so she got a lift, whether she wanted one or not. Then what?'

'It wasn't like that – I just—'

'I don't care what it was like! Then what?' Lloyd was leaning over him, hands on the table. Chris shrank back.

'We were going along Thorpe Wood Road, and she asked me to stop the car. I pulled up in the lay-by.'

'Why did she want you stop?'

'She said she thought she'd lost her pen – she looked in her bag for it, and said she must have left it in the café.'

'Her pen. What made her suddenly realise she'd lost her pen? Writing postcards, was she?'

'I don't know. I've told you all this already.'

'And I listened, Mr Wade. But now my critical faculties have been improved by a cup of tea, and now I want to know why.'

'I don't know!' Chris roared, then took a deep breath. 'Sorry.'

'Quite all right, Mr Wade. All right, she'd lost her pen. Then what happened?'

'We've been through all this,' Chris said. 'She looked for it, and decided she must have left it in the café. So I took her up there.'

'Ah yes – you took her up there.' Lloyd sat down again. 'At her request?'

Chris closed his eyes. 'No, not really.'

'You insisted again, did you?'

'She said I had just to go on. She'd walk from there.'

Lloyd tilted his chair back and looked at him for a long time, until he began to feel even more uncomfortable than he had.

'I didn't like the idea of her going in there alone – it's in the middle of the wood, practically. So I said I'd take her up there.'

'But she didn't want you to?' Lloyd let his chair fall forward with a thud.

'No, I suppose she didn't. Look – I thought last night – she might have wanted to—' It sounded crazy now.

'Yes?'

'To – kill herself. And that could be why she didn't want me to come with her. Could she?' They hadn't told him how she'd died. It was still a hope.

Lloyd stared at him. 'I see,' he said in tones of extremely Welsh wonderment. 'If a girl doesn't want your company it must be because she's suicidal? Oh – I've never been that fortunate.

Usually, if a girl doesn't want me it's because she's got something much more interesting to do – that doesn't usually include killing herself.'

'Could she?' Chris persisted.

'Let's say it's unlikely, shall we?' Lloyd smiled.

'How did she die?'

'Now, Mr Wade – you know how she died. But we digress. She got taken up to the café whether she wanted to be taken or not.' He stood up again, and stretched. 'It's been another long day,' he said to Chris. 'So, you take her up there – go on.'

'When we got to the café, she said she'd just run in and see if her pen was there.'

Lloyd leant over the table again. 'Who opened the door?'

Chris didn't know what that had got to do with it, but he'd told them he'd tell them everything. 'She did – she had the key.'

'No – you misunderstand. Who opened the car door?'

'Oh – I see.' He didn't really, but it was easy enough. 'I did. It's very stiff – so I leant over and opened it for her.'

'You leant over and opened it for her – you did open it, did you?'

'Yes. Why—'

'An old trick, but a good one, in my book. Leaning over to open the door – gives you the proximity necessary to make further progress.'

'It was nothing like that! I'd have to lean over to open it for anyone who wasn't used to it.'

'And so she nipped in and got her pen, did she?' Lloyd was walking round now, disconcertingly.

'No.'

'No!' He was overdoing the incredulity a bit, Chris thought, beginning to get his measure.

'No. She came back out and said the light wasn't working and it might take a little while, so I should just go on, and she'd get home herself.'

'And you said rightie-oh, and went on your way?'

'No.'

Lloyd sat down in sheer amazement. 'Fancy that. What did you say?'

'I said I had a torch in the car, and I'd come and help her look for it.' Chris spoke through his teeth. Every word seemed to make matters worse.

'In the café where the light wasn't working? In the lonely café in the middle of the wood? Did she say oh yes please?'

'No.' Chris looked at him. 'No, she didn't. But I went in anyway.'

'Persistent, aren't you, Mr Wade? You must have taken quite a shine to her.'

Chris shook his head.

'Most of us would have been put off by now. She didn't seem to want your company. There must have been a reason for your persistence.'

There was a reason for his persistence. Of course there was.

But it had nothing whatever to do with Julia.

'The boating lake murder – a man is taken in for questioning.'

Thus began the ITV news, and Helen watched it with a gin and tonic and a cigarette for company. Donald had come back, and gone straight out again to the police to see if Chris needed his help.

'The man wanted in connection with the murder of thirty-five year old widow Julia Mitchell gave himself up this afternoon, as the police net was closing in on his hiding-place. He is currently helping the police with their enquiries, and no charges have yet been made.'

Film of Thorpe Wood came up, with policemen searching.

'A large section of the search party returned to normal duty this morning, but police did continue to search for what was described as vital evidence. However, this search was called off at lunchtime. A police presence is being maintained in the area to prevent any possible evidence being tampered with.

'Inspector David Lloyd spoke to Mel Brown this afternoon.'

Inspector Lloyd mouthed silently at the camera for some moments. The film jerked and came to a standstill, and the newscaster appeared, unaware that he was on camera.

He looked up, under his eyebrows, quickly, then down again. Then, with studied confidence, he lifted his head again.

'*I'm sorry, we seem to have some trouble with the sound on that film. We'll come back to it if we can. The police say that they are still anxious to hear from anyone who was in the Thorpe Wood area of Stansfield on Saturday night, and they would like to hear from the driver of a dark, open sports car which was seen at about nine o'clock on the night of the murder.*'

A blown-up fuzzy photograph of Julia smiled out at Helen from the screen.

'*Police have issued this photograph of the murdered woman, which they say was taken some time ago. Mrs Mitchell was wearing a denim skirt and jacket . . .*'

Helen switched off the television. They weren't convinced it was Chris, then. They couldn't be, or they wouldn't be going to all this trouble.

But they didn't seem to be looking for anyone else.

'Ah yes, Inspector. You wanted to know a bit more about the time of death, I believe?' The pathologist's polite Glasgow voice sounded slightly condescending, but pleasant enough.

Lloyd, taking a breather from questioning, had decided to check the details more thoroughly, since Wade's insistence that she was alive when he left was fairly convincing.

'That's right,' he said. 'Is there likely to be any lee-way?' Lloyd had reserved a corner of the blotter for notes on the conversation.

'No, I'm afraid not. I've given you what I consider to be the minimum and maximum. Thought you'd got him, didn't you?'

'Well, we're questioning someone. He's quite ready to admit that he left her after nine o'clock, but he insists that she was in robust health.' Lloyd paused. 'Is it possible for someone to have killed her after nine o'clock?'

'She was dead by nine o'clock, Inspector. Well dead, if you ask me.'

Lloyd looked across at Judy, listening on the extension. 'It's just that I don't want some clever dick turning up at the trial and throwing in a reasonable doubt.' There was no question of that; Wade couldn't prove where he was after nine o'clock either, but it sounded better than admitting that you believed your suspect for no good reason.

'There isn't one, in my opinion. And I think you'd be hard pressed to find anyone to disagree.'

'But pathologists have been known to disagree about time of death,' Lloyd said. 'I don't want that to happen, if possible.'

'Oh, of course they have. It isn't an exact science – far from it. You have to piece together what happened from what you know, what you can deduce – and what you can guess.' He warmed to his task. 'As you no doubt know, you arrive at the time of death using several factors. Body temperature is the most reliable – rigor is the least.'

'And in this case?'

'In this case we had the added advantage of knowing when she last ate. But all these things are variables. Body temperatures for instance. A dead body loses heat, obviously, but in this case it would gain heat after death. Asphyxiation sends the body temperature up, and then it starts to fall. And there was quite an extreme drop in the outside temperature during that night – plus the fact that it was raining very heavily.' He coughed, a deep, bronchial, smoker's cough. 'But you'll know all about that,' he said. 'From other cases.'

'Some of it,' Lloyd said guardedly. 'But it is the first murder-case I've taken charge of where there was any doubt at all. Both the others have pleaded guilty to manslaughter, thank God.'

Girvan laughed. 'Well,' he said, through the hacking cough that the laugh had produced, 'as long as I'm not teaching my grandmother to suck eggs.' He finished coughing, and continued. 'We know certain things. When she last ate, when she was last seen alive – that sort of thing. The stomach is a good guide – but its emptying process can be affected by a number of things, too.'

Lloyd was beginning to wish he'd never asked. 'I'm not over-keen on stomachs,' he said, with a little laugh.

'Don't worry. All I mean is that if we just took that as a guide, it could give us too early a time of death. But the emotions experienced by the deceased come into the reckoning then. Fear slows the whole process down. So, you allow more time from when she ate.'

Lloyd could hear him flicking over pages.

'I believe she'd been having an argument with someone – if she was angry, that would speed the process up – but I think it's fairly safe to assume that there would be a considerable element of fear, from the circumstances.'

'Wouldn't there always be? If someone has been murdered?'

'Yes, I imagine there would. Once they know what's happening. No, I mean over a period of time.'

'She was seen at about half past eight,' Lloyd said. 'We're told she looked scared then – I have to admit we were a bit dubious about that.'

'Ah,' Girvan said. 'That seems quite likely from what we know. And taking everything into consideration, she had been dead for over ten and under twelve hours, which brings you to the times I gave you.'

'But are you saying that it couldn't have happened at five past nine?'

'She was dead by nine o'clock, Inspector – and that's stretching it as far as I can. I'd be happier with 8.45 myself but I allowed a bit more. But not after nine – definitely not.'

He was rather more prepared to commit himself than most, which was something, Lloyd thought.

'Thank you for your time,' he said. 'I just wanted to be sure it couldn't have been later.'

'No. Even if you assume that she was angry, which is the only question mark, that would make it earlier rather than later.' He coughed again, and Lloyd could feel his own chest tightening.

'If your man was with her from – what was it?' He took the opportunity to cough while he obviously flicked the pages back again. 'Half past eight until nine? Then he killed her Inspector or he was there when someone else did.'

Lloyd replaced the receiver, and stood up. 'I'll have another go,' he said to Judy, and walked back down the corridor. He had meant to ask if she'd seen the news, but he might see her later. He pushed open the door of the interview room. 'Tell me again,' he said, removing his jacket, and hanging it over the back of the seat. 'From when you went into the café.'

Christopher James Wade sat at the table, his NHS crutch leaning against it, his plastered foot sticking out uncomfortably, telling the same story every time.

'I went in with her and shone the torch round. A table had been knocked over, I said how did that happen, she said she knocked it over in the dark.' It was said in a sing-song, here-we-go-again fashion. Lloyd was seized with a fortunately controlled desire to kick his bad foot.

'Keep going – I'll stop you when I want more detail.'

Wade glared at him. 'I picked it up. I started looking for her pen, and she said it was all right, she hadn't really left her pen there at all.' He fiddled with the signet ring that he wore on his little finger. I said why were we there, and she said because she didn't want to go back to the Mitchells. I said why, and she said she'd rather be with me.'

Lloyd, tired of the view of the town centre closing down for the night, walked slowly across to Wade. 'And what did you think of that?' he asked wearily.

'I didn't know what to think.'

'Well, then—' Lloyd sat down. 'What did you say?'

'I said she hadn't given me that impression earlier.' Wade tried to arrange his long legs more comfortably. 'And she said that it wasn't a compliment – just that I was the lesser of two evils. I asked her what she meant, and she started going on about Helen. It ended up with a slanging match, and I left.'

For a long time, Lloyd didn't speak, but Wade could play at that game too. 'OK,' he said, running a hand over his face. 'I'm going to have something to eat. And I'll tell the canteen to rustle something up for you to eat. And we are both going to eat whatever it is we get, and then I'll come back, and you can tell me it all again.'

'I am *not* going through all that again!' Wade shouted. 'I've told you twice – that's it. I don't have to speak to you!'

'No, you don't. I told you that, remember? You don't have to say anything, but anything you do say will be written down and may be given in evidence. You say you don't want a solicitor – fine. But you are not telling me the truth, so if you do say anything when I come back it won't just be the same again. You'll be telling me the truth this time.'

'I am telling you the truth!'

'Then why were you hiding out in a workmen's hut running

with damp, used by all the animals in Christendom, making your-self ill? Why? Because you'd had a difference of opinion with someone?'

'Because you were after me for killing her!' Wade hid his face. 'Because I was drunk, and I couldn't be sure.'

'Sure of what?'

'If I'd – I was drunk! I just ran, that's all.'

'From what, Mr Wade?' Lloyd leant forward. 'How did you know there was anything to run from?'

'I—' Wade looked bewildered. 'The radio – they said . . .'

'We were at your garage and your house by half past six in the morning. It wasn't on the radio until much later.'

Wade, tight-lipped, just shook his head.

'I went to see her in-laws,' Lloyd continued conversationally. 'Shortly after she was found. When I arrived, there were three mugs on the coffee table.' He smiled friendly at Wade. 'It was odd, that – struck me at the time. She – Helen Mitchell – said that they were the previous night's. Now me, I'd leave last night's washing up – but her? I couldn't see it myself. But then it got curi-ouser and curiouser. See – she had this friend staying with her. No – I tell a lie – she was visiting, just for the day. But Julia Mitchell was there too. That made four of them. Then her husband and Julia go off – that just leaves two. Then she takes her friend to the station, and she's in on her own. Then her husband comes back – and that makes two again.'

Wade wasn't dreadfully impressed.

'You see? There was no time when there were only three people in the house.'

'There's no law against not having coffee,' Wade said.

'None. Except that we know Julia did – I won't go into that, it's a bit upsetting – and I know her friend did, because I got the local police to ask, despite their thinking I was a bit tapped. And she said "I had a visitor" to explain them – why there were three, and not just two. So that suggested herself, her husband, and – you?'

Wade just sat there.

'That's how you knew, isn't it? Because I was at the door, telling them she was dead and that I was looking for you. Isn't it?'

'No.'

'Then the only other explanation is that you knew she was dead because you killed her. Which do you prefer?'

With that, Lloyd went off in search of food, and found Judy in the canteen, in solitary splendour.

'Are you still here?' he asked, joining her.

'No, I went home half an hour ago. I've had Donald Mitchell touting for business, and three people who were nowhere near the area at the time, and—' she broke off. 'You didn't catch the 5.45 news?'

'No. I was with Wade – how did it go?'

She caught her lip. 'I don't know how to tell you this, really.' She looked suspiciously as though she were going to laugh.

Lloyd narrowed his eyes. 'What?'

'Well—'

He tried not to look too disappointed when she told him. He'd never hear the end of it if he did. It was difficult to know how to look. Laughing it off as though he was on television every night would produce much the same result.

'Not a word?'

She shook her head. 'They didn't fit you in later, I'm afraid.' And with that, the self-control snapped, and she began to laugh. 'I'm sorry,' she said, with difficulty. 'I really am – it was just – of all the things to—'

And her laughter began to make him laugh, until the two of them were giggling like school-girls. It was brought to a sudden and not entirely successful halt by the appearance of more customers, when they tried to behave like dignified officers of the law.

'Do you want to sit in on the rest of this interview?' he asked, when order was restored. 'Someone else there – a different approach. Just ask any questions that occur to you.'

'Yes, I would like to – just kick me if you want me to shut up.'

'I'll remember that,' Lloyd promised.

'Why won't he have a solicitor?' Donald demanded.

Helen carried on laying the table in what seemed to Donald to be a particularly annoying fashion. 'Because he didn't do it,' she said calmly.

'All right! He didn't do it – that's no reason to refuse a solicitor. Solicitors aren't just for defending the guilty, you know! Why in God's name wouldn't he just ask for one?'

'Why are you behaving as though it was my fault?' Helen asked, reasonably enough.

Donald picked up the paper. 'It's so stupid,' he said. 'Of all the people in the world – no one needs a solicitor like Chris Wade does now.'

'Why?' Helen put down the place mats. 'If he's done nothing wrong?'

'For Christ's sake, Helen – you know what he's like. He's never had to stand on his own two feet in his life. First it was his big sister, then it was Carrie, then it was me—' He folded the paper firmly. 'Then it was you – let's not beat about the bush. He's always needed someone to lean on – and now, now of all times, he's got to play the hero.'

'If he's got nothing to hide—'

Donald closed his eyes. Heaven only knew what he was telling them. 'He has got something to hide,' he said. 'He was here – and we lied to the police. You know him as well as I do.' He smiled. 'You know him rather better than I do,' he amended. 'He'll be telling all sorts of stories to cover up for us. And he'll be making matters worse every time he opens his mouth.'

Helen sat down opposite him. 'So it isn't concern for Chris that's got you all hot and bothered?'

'No it isn't. I'm a solicitor! I can't get mixed up in this sort of thing. If he'd just asked for me – anyone – it wouldn't be so bad.'

'But if he didn't do it.'

Donald despaired of her. She really thought that if you didn't do it, there was nothing to worry about.

'Look – he was in there with her. We know that, because he told us. The police know it. He practically forced her to take a lift with him – and then he ran away, and she was found strangled. If he didn't do it, it hardly matters. The police have evidence that says he did. And he needs a solicitor to produce evidence that says he didn't.'

'You could try again.'

'And get touting for business added to my list of offences? No thanks. I went as a friend, to see if I could help, and I was told I couldn't. So that's that.'

He tried reading the paper, but that hardly took his mind off it, since that was the lead story.

Judy looked at the tired, dispirited figure sitting at the table, the remains of his meal pushed away from him.

'The tea's good,' she said. 'Don't let it get cold.'

Wade looked at her, his eyes dull. 'Is this where you're nice to me and he's not?' he asked, nodding in Lloyd's direction. 'I've seen that on the telly.'

'No,' Judy replied. 'Nothing like that. It's where I explain to you that if you didn't kill Mrs Mitchell, then you'd better start telling us the truth, so that we can work out what did happen. If you did kill her, then you'd better explain the circumstances, so that you've got some sort of defence.'

'And you care, do you? Whether I've got a defence?'

'No. But you should – if not for your own sake, then for your friends' – like Helen Mitchell, for instance.'

'What about her?' Wade drank some of his tea. 'You're right,' he said. 'It is good.'

'Hot and strong,' Lloyd said. 'Like love.'

'Speaking about love,' Judy said, as she felt she was being prompted to, 'Mrs Mitchell's very fond of you, isn't she?'

'Is she?' was the only response.

'Fond enough to tell lies for you.' Judy drank some of her own tea. 'She had to tell the truth in the end, though – but she did try.' She glanced at Lloyd, who had got up and was standing by the window. Wade saw the glance.

'You're the one that's telling lies,' he said.

'No, not me,' Judy said. 'She has admitted that she saw you.'

They weren't getting anywhere like this. 'What was your row with Julia about?'

'Helen.'

'She seems to have been in a particularly argumentative mood.

Having rows with everyone – did she say what her row with Donald was about?'

'No.' Wade looked surprised, as though it was the first time he'd thought about it. 'No, she didn't.'

'Why did you go to your garage when you left? Why didn't you go home, or back to your sister's?'

Lloyd had wandered back to the table, and was standing behind Wade, who had twisted round in an effort to see him. 'I was in a bit of a state,' he said.

'Why?' Lloyd asked. 'Because you'd had a row with Julia?'

'Yes.'

'A total stranger? Why should having a row with her bother you?'

Wade turned back to Judy. 'It wasn't the row – not really. It was the accident.'

Lloyd walked slowly round to face him. 'What accident?'

'Oh – it wasn't really an accident – but it reminded me of the accident. That's what made me get drunk.'

'Reminded you?' Lloyd said. 'Of what – your wife's accident?'

He nodded briefly.

'What happened to remind you?' Judy asked, as Lloyd took up his post by the window again.

'Something ran in front of the car as I was going up to the café. I braked, and she fell forward – she didn't hurt herself, but she could have – I swore I'd never do that again.'

'And that upset you?'

'Of course! It was just the same – she could have been hurt. I thought I'd never do that again, and I did. I did exactly the same thing!' He turned his head away.

Lloyd crossed behind him, and went out of the room.

'Your wife died and she didn't – was that what it was?' Judy said carefully. 'You felt angry before you ever went into the café with her?'

'No!'

'But she didn't want you to wait for her – why did you insist on going in with her?'

'I wanted to take her to Helen's – I told you!' He made to jump up, and the constable whose name Judy could never remember leapt to his feet. But Wade winced and sat down again, reaching for his crutch.

'Why? She was a grown woman – she didn't want you.'

Wade shook his head quickly. 'You make it sound as though I forced her – it wasn't like that. She said not to wait for her, and I said of course I would – that was all.' He stood up, this time with the aid of the crutch. 'Do you mind?' he asked. 'I'll get cramp if I have to sit there.'

'Not at all.'

He took a deep breath. 'All right – I wanted to see Helen. Donald was out of the way, and taking her back was a good excuse. If I left her there I didn't have any reason to go to the Mitchells' house. But when I got in there, she said she didn't want to go back. At first she said it was because she'd had a row with Donald and she didn't want to see anyone until she'd calmed down. So I picked up the table and said we should sit down for a moment.'

Lloyd came back in, with more tea. 'Thought we could do with some more,' he said cheerily. 'It looks as though it's going to be a long night.'

'At first?' Judy repeated. 'What did she say after that?'

'Nothing much. She sat down, but she – she looked *scared*. Or cold. But it was so hot, I didn't think she could be cold. Then I thought she might not be feeling well – flu, or something. I took off my jacket, and said if she was cold she should put it on.'

Judy wrote SCARED on her ever-present notebook, and leafed back through the pages to Diane's evidence. *She looked a bit scared*, it read.

'Scared of you?' she asked.

Wade sat down again, easing himself on to the chair, almost falling, as his crutch crashed down to the floor. 'I didn't think so,' he said. 'She had no reason to be.' He retrieved the crutch.

'Scared or cold,' Lloyd said. 'That's what you said, isn't it?'

'Yes.' Wade looked at him sullenly. 'It could have been either.'

'What was she doing that made you think that?'

'She kept her arms folded,' Wade said.

'Her arms folded?' Judy repeated.

'Yes,' Wade said. 'She was standing there with her arms folded. Even when she sat down, she kept them folded.'

'Folded how?' Lloyd sat down beside Judy. 'Show me.'

Wade obliged, folding his arms as they had all been told to at school. 'You know,' he said.

'And she did make you angry?'

'Yes. We sat there for a few moments – then I offered her my jacket, but she didn't want it. I tried to talk to her – just small talk, but she didn't want to know. So I asked if she was feeling all right.'

'And?'

'She said she'd feel better if I would just go. And I said if she didn't feel well, she should let me take her back to Helen's.'

'How long do you think you'd been in there at this point?' Judy asked.

'About ten minutes or so. And she said I should go if that's what I wanted. To Helen's, I mean. She said she knew about us. She said Donald knew.'

Lloyd sat back, tipping the chair dangerously on its back legs, and Judy braced herself for the crash that fortunately didn't come.

'Knew what?' Lloyd asked.

'There's nothing to know,' Wade said. 'That's just it. Helen isn't like her – she doesn't –' he broke off.

Neither Judy nor Lloyd spoke. Wade had at last given up his attempt to say nothing, and they could just sit back and let him go.

'She started going on about her. I said she wouldn't understand about someone like Helen. They'd told me about her – Helen had, and Donald. No wonder someone killed her. She said I only wanted to run her back so that I could—' he stopped, his eyes perplexed. 'She was very crude,' he said to Judy. 'I don't want to repeat what she said.'

'All right,' she said, amiably.

'I told her that it wasn't like that. It's not!' he said, looking from one to the other. 'Helen believes in marriage vows – she won't break them!'

Judy cast a sidelong glance at Lloyd.

'So that just made her worse. She started laughing at me, and telling me to get out and get on with it. She said Helen would be grateful – and in the end she was nearly hysterical – just telling me to get out, so I did.'

Lloyd was drinking his tea unconcernedly when Wade finished his story. He set down the mug, and looked at him. 'That was when you killed her, was it?' he asked quietly.

'I didn't – she was perfectly all right when I left. She was all right – she said she was!'

Judy looked up sharply from her notebook. 'Said she was?'

Wade had gone pale, 'I mean – she was all right.'

'Why did she say she was?'

'I didn't mean that – I meant—' He closed his eyes.

'When did she hit her head on the table?' Lloyd asked.

He opened his eyes again, and frowned. 'She didn't,' he said.

'Well, there was a cut on her face. Her blood was on the table. Varnish from the table was in the cut. What conclusion would you come to?'

'But she didn't hurt herself – she wasn't bleeding.'

Lloyd stood up. 'No, not much. That's because she was dead, Mr Wade. But you seem not to have noticed that.'

'She wasn't! She wasn't dead!'

'Why was she naked?' Judy asked suddenly.

Wade looked slowly from Lloyd to her. 'Naked?' he said. 'She wasn't. She wasn't naked, and she wasn't dead.'

'She was mad at Donald Mitchell with whom she'd been having an affair,' Lloyd said. 'You gave her a lift, and she saw her chance to get her own back on Donald. She took you up there, led you on a bit – why was she naked? I had a theory – you remember?' He turned to Judy, who wasn't sure what her reaction should be. 'I didn't go into it at the time, but it could be right. It was hot – very hot. Right?' he asked Wade.

Wade, bewildered, agreed.

'And there was the boating lake – what was it? Let's have a swim? And you chickened out? Or did you both strip off, and then things developed, and you couldn't cope? You decided to call it a day – and she laughed at you? Was that when she made you angry? Was that when you killed her?'

Wade sat with his head in his hands, saying nothing. When he sat up, it was with a new kind of assurance.

'She was fully clothed, and alive, when I left. She did say she was all right. The reason she said that was that I had *asked* her if she was.'

'In the middle of a row?'

'No. The row ended when I pushed her.'

'Don't tell me we're getting to the truth at last,' Lloyd said. 'You pushed her. When?'

'When she had gone too far. I pushed her away, then I apologised, and asked if she was all right. She shouted yes, and ran into the boatshed. I followed her in there, and I said I was sorry, because I could see I'd frightened her, and I didn't mean to. But she was nearly hysterical. She had the phone in her hand, and she said she would call the police if I didn't leave. So I left.'

'How hard did you hit her?'

'I *didn't* hit her. I pushed her, that's all, and she stumbled and ran away.'

'Was her face cut?' Judy asked.

Wade didn't know. 'It could have been – you could hardly see in there. We only had the torch. I don't think it was.'

'It was,' Lloyd assured him. 'Did she fall against the table? Was that when it got knocked over?'

'No. I've told you about the table.'

Judy decided it was her turn to stretch her legs, and took a slow turn round the room as she formulated her next question. 'You left her there,' she said. 'Alive?'

There was a small exasperated noise from Wade.

'Holding the phone, you said.' Judy looked out through the rain-flecked window to the town and its closed shops. The lit windows of Stansfield's only hotel made her wish she was in there, sipping gin and tonic, relaxing. 'Without leaving her fingerprints?'

Lloyd took over. 'And then you went where?'

'To the garage,' Wade said wearily. 'And I got drunk.' His shoulders sagged. 'That's what I do best,' he muttered.

'And then you went to Helen Mitchell's like you'd wanted to all along?' Judy said.

'Yes.'

'Did you tell her what had happened?'

'I don't know. I don't remember much about it.'

Lloyd stood up, scraping the chair back on the floor. 'I think we should all sleep on it,' he said, and the constable stood up.

Judy watched as Chris limped away, supported by the constable on one side, and his crutch on the other.

'What do you think?' she asked.

Lloyd stretched. 'I think we should go home.' He smiled. 'I didn't have time to collect the car – what with the interview, and this –' he lifted his hands helplessly.

They were both too pre-occupied to chat as they collected their things from the office, and drove home in near silence. Judy tried to cast Wade in the role of murderer, and couldn't. He didn't seem to know how she'd died, or he was very good at keeping his wits about him. She signalled, ready to pull into the garage area behind the flats.

'You don't have to,' Lloyd said, as the car's lights swept over the garage doors. 'I could have—'

'—nipped through the alley,' Judy finished the sentence with him. 'I know.' She switched off the engine, and they were plunged in darkness as she flicked the light switch. 'It might not solve anything,' she said, kissing him lightly on the lips. 'But it would cheer me up no end.'

Lloyd laughed. 'The Superintendent won't like it,' he said, feeding her the line.

'The Superintendent,' Judy said obediently, 'isn't getting it.'

The rabbit saw the headlights, and stopped dead, staring at them. The car drew slowly to a halt, then moved right. The rabbit moved to his left, and the car stopped again.

The rabbit wasn't going to run. He had tried that the other night, and he'd nearly got run over. He was just going to sit there until the car went away.

The car moved back to its left. The rabbit moved to his right, and the car stopped again.

Then the lights weren't there, so the car must have gone. The rabbit raced to the other side of the road, on to the safe grass, away from the cars.

The young policeman put his lights on again, and moved off down the road, where the 'police presence' was being maintained. He didn't know why they were making all this fuss. They'd got him.

He was caught, like the rabbit in the headlights.

Chapter Nine

Could he have killed her? Chris tossed around on the bunk, wishing he could sleep and forget the whole thing for a few hours. The more he tried to tell them his story, the more likely it seemed that he *had* killed her. Could there have been any time he didn't remember? He went through everything again in his head. Driving her home, taking her up there, going in with her, picking up the table, sitting down, talking to her, arguing with her, losing his temper, pushing her, *pushing* her, not hitting her. Could she have hurt herself then? Was it possible for someone to run away, pick up a phone, speak – no, of course it wasn't. But if she did hit her head – but he could swear she didn't hurt herself at all. He left her standing there, holding the phone. He went back to the garage, got drunk – he even had hazy memories of talking to the milk-lady. Staggering off to Helen, and then – then, there was a memory gap. He didn't know how long he was at the garage, how long he was with Helen – he didn't know if he'd gone straight to Helen's.

They said Donald had been having an affair with Julia. Since when? Donald couldn't stand the sight of her as far as Chris knew, and anyway, he boasted about his women. Surely it was whats-her-name – Julia's lady-in-waiting – that he was having the affair with. It had been going on a long time. Helen thought it was Julia – she told him that night, under the impression that Donald's behaviour was news to him. He hadn't corrected her – how could he? Oh, but she wouldn't *kill* Julia, would she? Even if she thought . . . would she?

Judy had thought she might feel guilty, but she didn't. Perhaps that came tomorrow – perhaps it didn't come at all. She felt warm and happy, and glad she'd made her mind up. Lloyd had opened a decadent bottle of wine, and it was just beginning to go to her head as they sat up in bed to finish it off.

'Thank you for having me,' she whispered, then giggled at her own wit.

'I was wrong,' he said, reaching over her for her glass. 'The Superintendent would like it.'

She laughed. 'You forgot to talk like Richard Burton,' she said. 'Did you know? Or is the boy from the valleys just another character part?'

'I don't know.' He poured more wine into her half-full glass. 'It must be – I'm not from the valleys.'

'Oh,' she said sympathetically. 'Do you mean you can't go on about pit disasters and washing your father's back in the bath in front of the kitchen fire?'

He grinned. 'I can go on about anything. It's not very often true.'

'Where are you from?'

'Somewhere even I can't pronounce.' He drank his wine down like water. 'Fishing village – I'd have been a fisherman if we'd stayed.'

'What age were you when you moved to Stansfield?'

'Fourteen.' He sighed. 'Thirty years ago this week, near as makes no difference.'

'What's your first name?'

'Ah, no – you don't get me like that. You'll have to get me drunk – and this stuff won't do it.'

'You told the television people it was David. It's not David. Why would you mind people knowing that?'

She sipped her wine, since it was having rather more effect on her than it was on Lloyd. 'Would you have liked being a fisherman?'

'Not me. I'm too fond of my creature comforts.' His lips touched her hair. 'I'll stick to being a fisher of men.'

'My God, I'll bet that is how you see yourself, isn't it?' Judy shook her head. 'St Peter – that's your name, is it?'

'Different line, different bait – different catch.'

She groaned, and drained her wine glass though she hadn't really meant to.

'Have some more,' he said, the bottle poised over her glass.

She covered it with her hand. 'No thank you – I've got to sober up enough to drive home.'

'You don't have to drive home!' But he put the bottle down, and lay back. 'You want me to throw Wade back, don't you?'

'Hark who never discusses business when he's finished work!' She thought for a moment. 'Is this a private metaphor, or can anyone join?'

'Feel free.' He put his arm round her and pulled her closer. 'Let's have your angle.'

She dug him in the ribs. 'All right. We've got more than one fish in the net. We've only got Helen Mitchell's word for it that she hung about at the station. She could have left sharp, and been at the boating lake before nine o'clock.'

Lloyd shifted round the better to look quizzically at her. 'So what?'

'She could have seen Wade's car go up there. She could have seen it from the house, or on her way to the station. She could have got her friend on to the train and got back there. Gone up to see what was going on – and found that Julia had got her hooks into Chris as well as her husband. She wouldn't be too happy, would she?'

Lloyd made a disbelieving noise, and she sat up, twisting out of his arms. 'Why not?'

'For one thing she was strangled. That takes strength.'

'Helen Mitchell's no weakling – and Julia wasn't what you'd call robust, was she?'

Lloyd frowned. 'But then what? Undressed her?'

'To make it look like a man had done it. Or maybe she didn't have to – maybe she interrupted them at just the wrong moment. Wade runs off – leaving his jacket – and Helen finishes Julia's game for her.'

'But how did she manage all that without leaving one shred of evidence? And why hide her clothes?'

Judy didn't have an answer for that. But it fitted. Wade's shirt was unbuttoned when the milkwoman saw him, which could have meant he'd had to dress hurriedly. His reluctance to bring Helen into it at all – the pathologist's suggestion that he could have seen the murder. She lay back down again.

'Any more theories?' Lloyd asked.

'Mitchell – he came into a lot of money.'

'Mitchell was with Wade's own sister, who would swear black was white if it got her brother off.' He leant over. 'And before you start talking about hit-men and the like, think about it.'

Judy pushed him away. 'I had no intention of talking about hit-men.'

He looked suitably abashed. 'I thought about it. But since only Julia knew she was going up there, she'd have had to cooperate. That seems unlikely. Unless the said hit-man was Wade, of course, in which case he could have forced her up there.'

'And hypnotised her into leaving the Shorts' house early,' Judy said matter-of-factly. That's the answer, of course. How clever of you.'

'That's what I meant. Even I entertained the idea until I realised it was nonsense.'

'Even you! Well, that's all right, then. I'm not such a silly little girl after all.' She helped herself to the rest of the wine. What in the world was she doing? Had she really wished this on herself? 'I must be mad,' she said. 'Even talking to you.'

'I didn't mean it like that – I – oh, to hell. I'm going to get a proper drink!' He put on a dressing-gown that she would have remarked on, if she had been speaking to him.

He was gone a long time; long enough for her to have finished the wine, read an article in Punch, and missed him.

He reappeared, carrying a tray with two steaming mugs. 'Coffee,' he said. 'Black and strong, so that you can sober up as requested.' He handed her a mug, and got into bed.

'Thank you,' she said automatically, absently. She blew at the steam, and tested it carefully. 'It's too hot,' she said, and watched with horror as he took a deep drink. 'Your mouth must be asbestos,' she said, putting her mug down to cool.

His mouth, still hot from the coffee, was on hers. 'You taste nice,' she said. 'Like Gaelic coffee.' She pulled away. 'You haven't put whisky in mine, have you?'

'No.' He held up three fingers. 'Scout's Honour.'

She tested it all the same, but it seemed to be innocent of alcohol.

'It could have been two people,' Lloyd said reflectively. 'The underwear puzzles me. Why would you roll up her clothes and stash them in one place, and bundle up her underwear and hide it yards away in the opposite direction?'

'But even if it was two people – I mean, let's say it was Helen, and Wade saw her and helped her cover it up – why would one person take her outer clothing and the other her underclothing? If they were going to strip her, wouldn't one person do it, and hide it?' Judy picked up her coffee again. 'Why take her clothes off at all?'

'Why do people take their clothes off?' Lloyd asked.

'To have a bath,' Judy said.

'To swim?' Lloyd laughed. 'I think that's a non-starter, really. No one in their right mind would swim in that boating lake.'

'To discuss murder-cases,' Judy suggested with a grin.

They put down the coffee mugs and lay back. Judy pulled pensively at the hairs on his chest until he yelped. 'Sorry,' she said, smoothing them down again. 'Lloyd?'

'Present.'

'Were you ever unfaithful to Barbara?' she asked, not sure of what reaction the question would get.

'Yes,' he said promptly. 'Once. Brief and inglorious.' He laughed. 'She was a rank and file violinist, with the BBC Symphony Orchestra.'

'Are you making that up?'

'No. That's what she was – I always imagine them being drilled. "Shoulder violins! Play, two three four."'

Judy sat up, leaning on her elbow, looking down at him. 'Did you feel guilty?' she demanded.

'A bit. Yes, I did. I think that's why it didn't last very long.' He touched her cheek. 'Why? Do you?'

Judy shook her head, and her hand went to his. 'I should,' she said, smiling suddenly. 'So let's try again and see if it makes me feel guilty this time.'

*

The gales of the night before dominated News at Ten, and Chris was relegated to a mention in the closing stages, before the sport. Donald watched it all without seeing a thing. Another hour passed before he decided not to wait for Helen, who had obviously decided that she was no longer under any obligation to keep him posted about her movements, and had got up and gone out after dinner without a word. She'd be at Elaine's, of course. He knew that without checking up. They could both sit and worry about Chris, as though that did any good. A trouble shared was a trouble exacerbated, in Donald's book.

He switched off the television, and went to bed. Busy day tomorrow – he'd have to start making arrangements to leave. They'd want as much notice as possible, to give them time to find a replacement. And he wanted to start looking through the properties currently on Mitchell Development's books. He was in the market for good premises in a reasonably fashionable area.

'I can't stay,' Judy said, pulling on her tights. 'My car's outside – people have very suspicious minds you know. They might think we were sleeping together.'

Lloyd laughed. 'Who's going to see it?' He sat up and tried to catch her arm, but she pulled it away.

'WPC Alexander, for one,' she said. 'She lives in the flats behind this block.' She zipped up her skirt. 'Where are my shoes?' She looked round the room, and under the bed, and then went out into the living room.

Lloyd put on his dressing-gown, and followed her, shivering slightly as his bare feet hit the tiles in the hallway.

'Mary?' he said. 'She wouldn't say a word. Anyway – you could have been spending the night with her.'

She found her shoes. 'These days that would cause even more talk,' she said, laughing. 'Got them.' She held them up, and saw his dressing-gown.

'You look stunning, my dear,' she said, holding on to him as she put her shoes on. 'Are you wearing that for a bet?'

Lloyd rather liked it, with its gold dragons on a maroon background. 'It was a present,' he lied, because he had bought it himself the year they went to Tenerife.

'Was it? Don't expect one like that from me, will you?'

'I don't expect a thing,' he said, putting his arms round her.

She kissed him, her tongue gently seeking his. 'I've got to go,' she whispered.

'Some more coffee,' he said. 'Make sure you're sober. Maybe you're not – you don't want to be caught drunk in charge, do you?'

He could feel her giving in. 'All right. One cup of coffee.' She took out her cigarettes.

'Oh good,' Lloyd said, 'I was afraid that this wasn't an occasion.'

He made the coffee, humming to himself. She might stay, if he pointed out to her that it was almost midnight and WPC Alexander would have already suspected that she hadn't come for a shilling for the meter. He found some biscuits that he didn't know he had, and piled them on to a plate.

'Coffee and biscuits,' he announced, setting the tray down on the coffee table. 'The biscuits are of a certain age – I don't really advise them.'

'I'm hungry,' she said, biting into one. 'They're all right. A bit soft.'

Lloyd sat beside her on the sofa. 'You know how I never discuss work at home?' he said.

She smiled. 'Go on – you're going to give me my time-table for tomorrow, aren't you?'

'You started it!'

'I did not,' she said. 'You mentioned Wade – I was talking about your childhood.'

'So you were.' He bit into a biscuit, but he couldn't agree with her as to their all rightness. He screwed up his face. 'Don't eat these – I'll make you a sandwich if you're hungry.'

'They're fine. But since you've brought the subject up again, what are you going to do about Helen Mitchell?'

'Randall says I should use my discretion,' he said. 'Assuming Wade's telling the truth, that is. She didn't know he would suddenly disappear as soon as she left him. And then she found herself in a difficult position.' He shook his head. 'One law for the rich.'

'Oh, come on – that's fair enough. It's not as though she knew where he was.'

'Do you think Superintendent Don't-You-Know-Who-I-Am-Randall would have been as sweetly reasonable if it had been some little scrubber and her boyfriend?'

Maybe he would, Judy thought. She had a higher opinion of Randall than Lloyd did, but she didn't say so. 'I think we should talk to her, all the same,' she said. 'About withholding information.'

'And about nipping up and doing in her sister-in-law?' Lloyd asked. 'I could touch on that.'

'We could. I want to see her too. After all, when you think about it, she wasn't so much losing a sister-in-law as gaming access to what Mitchell described as "a considerable estate".'

Judy solemnly finished her revolting biscuit, and washed it down. 'I think he's telling the truth,' she said.

Lloyd raised his eyebrows. 'The whole truth?' he asked.

'If he isn't, he's very good. And the bit about the near miss is probably true – Diane heard his brakes squealing.'

Lloyd knew what she meant, but there was no point in flying in the face of the evidence. 'We'll see what we can get from Mrs Mitchell,' he said. 'Are we missing something? Is it wheelbarrows, do you think?'

'Wheelbarrows?'

'Man wheeling a wheelbarrow covered with a tarpaulin out of a building site. The foreman stops him, looks under the tarpaulin, but it's empty. So he has to let him go. The man does the same thing every day for six weeks, until the job's finished.

'On the last day, the foreman stops him, says he won't shop him, but will he please put him out of his misery, and tell him what he's been stealing, because he knows he's been stealing something. And the man says—'

'Wheelbarrows,' Judy finished, smiling. 'But what could we be missing?'

'Perhaps there's a glaringly obvious reason for taking her clothes off – with care, the report said. Her clothes were removed with care.'

'With care.' Judy thought for a moment. 'So she didn't divest herself in a mad passion.' She leant back, her head on his shoulder, and he smiled to himself.

'Love, oh love, oh careful love,' he said. 'And he didn't tear them off in a frenzy. Someone took them off *with care*, then someone rolled them up and hid them. Why?'

'To delay identification?' Judy suggested.

'It didn't work. Her bag was there, anyway – with letters and credit cards. Not to mention a reminder from her dentist in case we had to identify her by her teeth.' He laughed. 'As cunning ruses go, that one wasn't so good.'

'Even if he was stupid enough to think that we'd fall for rape – he'd surely have just messed her clothes about? Torn them, that sort of thing?' Judy got herself more comfortable. 'And if he was going to hide them, or set fire to them – why roll them all up together like that? Wouldn't you just pick them up?'

'I think they were thrown,' Lloyd said. 'From the car, as it left. They would land about there from the pathway. Then the shoes.' His arm was beginning to go to sleep, and he shifted slightly. 'But why stuff her underwear into the roots of a tree?'

'You didn't tell me that bit,' she said, twisting round.

Lloyd exercised his arm to bring the circulation back. 'Oh, sorry. Yes, stuffed into the roots of a tree.' He rubbed his eyes. 'And I thought we'd have all the answers once we spoke to Wade – if you ask me, he's as much in the dark as we are.'

Judy grinned triumphantly. 'Hah! You don't think he killed her.'

'No, I don't. But Randall says we'll have to charge him tomorrow if we're no further forward, and for once I think he's right. We've got an eye-witness, fingerprints, the time – his own behaviour. We can't ignore all that.'

'Then we'll just have to give Mrs M. a fright,' she said decidedly. 'Let's talk to her on our own ground.'

'Anything you say.' He bent over to kiss her, but she slid deftly away from him.

'I'm going.'

'What's the point? It's well after midnight – your reputation is in shreds, Mrs Hill.'

'I'm still going.' She went to get her raincoat, and Lloyd found himself back in the café, trying to find the wheelbarrows. 'He's lying about one thing,' he said when she came back. 'The phone – her fingerprints would have been on the phone, as you so rightly pointed out.'

'Yes, I don't understand that. Why say it at all?'

'Well, we can see what sort of prints they did get from the phone,' he said, following her to the door. 'It's raining,' he said.

'I'll survive.' They kissed goodnight at the door, like teenagers, and he knew she didn't want to go any more than he wanted her to.

'Julia's prints are elusive,' she whispered, stepping outside.

'The car door's stiff,' he said. 'The passenger can't do it unless they're used to it. I checked – it's true. And his prints bear him out.'

'Everything,' Judy said, kissing him again, 'bears him out.'

Lloyd watched her until she disappeared round the zig-zag of the pathway to the garages.

It was true. Everything did bear Wade's story out. The only conflicting evidence was the phone, which until now hadn't even come into the reckoning. Well, at least he could check that.

He heard Judy's car start up, and wished she had stayed.

Helen Mitchell was driving home late, too. She drove fast along Thorpe Wood Road, feeling better since her visit to Elaine. Insects danced in the lights, and died on her windscreen as she drove, and she could see that the house was in darkness. She hadn't really meant to disappear all evening without telling Donald where she was going, but there was something about his attitude that she found hard to take.

All that seemed to be bothering him was that she had lied to the police, and that Chris might land them in it. Everything else – including Julia's death – he was quite happy to take in his stride. Everything else. And that irked her slightly, she told herself honestly. A little jealousy might have been in order. But he took that in his stride as well, because he'd been going to leave her anyway. As long as it didn't directly affect him, Donald didn't care what happened to anyone. She had tried to tell him about her interview with the sergeant, but he'd been too preoccupied to listen.

Still, Elaine seemed to think that the police weren't entirely hostile. She had even said that Sergeant Hill was nice, an adjective that had not leaped to Helen's mind when describing her. But it had made her feel better, and a little more as though she might come out of this business unscathed.

A cat, blacker than the night, streaked across the road as soon as the car had passed, skittering to a halt at the long grass, overdue for mowing. Above its yellowing fringe danced the daddy-long-legs, bathed in light from the road. The cat dabbed a curious paw at one or two, but she was after bigger game. She moved noiselessly through the grass, into the woods, stopping in the clearing where Paul and Diane had inexpertly consummated their union. She could have told them a thing or two about that, if they'd asked.

She stood motionless, then darted through the trees towards the building. She watched for a moment as the ducks swam away, but they weren't her prey. Into the trees again, and she was there. Invisible against the dark bark, she waited for the mice who would come to nibble the picnic leftovers.

She had to keep her strength up. She had kittens to feed. She washed unnecessarily, her sleek coat shining in the fitful moonlight, and settled down, her eyes closing now and again, but her ears pricked for the tiny sound of an unwitting mouse. She wouldn't miss a thing; she never did.

Oh yes. She could tell them a thing or two, if they asked.

Chapter Ten

Judy woke before the alarm, and lay in a delicious state of semi-consciousness, sleepily aware that she was happy. They had made each other laugh, she and Lloyd, and the knowledge that they could just as easily make each other cry made the laughter all the sweeter. She had laughed at his need for words, but delighted in the sound of his voice, by turns persuasive, funny, soothing, exciting. She had gone home simply because he didn't want her to, and he had laughed at her need for independence, but he hadn't tried too hard to make her stay.

With deliberate perverseness, they had steered the talk round to work; the whispered doorstep conversation had been about Wade, as though they were trying to assure one another that it had all been just for fun. They needed the assurance, because whatever way it had started out, and whatever way it had ended, in between there had been an intensity of feeling that had caught them both unaware.

And she still didn't feel guilty. In fact, she thought drowsily, it was that which was making her happy, because she had never felt like that before. She was glad she was on her own, hugging her thoughts to herself with no temptation to impart them to Lloyd.

The buzzer rudely invaded those private thoughts, and dragged her reluctantly out into the day. The morning paper screamed WOODLAND MURDER – MAN HELD at her. Everyone did it – she did it. You heard that the police had someone helping them with their enquiries, and you thought 'oh good, they've got him'. – it was human nature, though not a particularly praiseworthy aspect of it. She ran her bath, reading the emotional, if not sensational words that accompanied the photograph of Superintendent Randall 'leading the murder hunt'. Murder Weapon Still Missing, read a smaller sub-heading. Woodland Hideout, read another. They knew nothing of Wade – nothing that they could print – and yet without a single libellous word, they managed to produce him to the public, gift-wrapped and guilty.

The morning routine began to take over; it was difficult to remain on a high philosophical plane with the smell of bacon and eggs teasing your nostrils. She ate rather more heartily than might be expected of someone entering a new phase of her life, and drove to work entirely restored to normality.

'Morning Sarge,' Sandwell said as she walked in – an unusually colloquial greeting from him.

'Good morning, Bob – anything I should know about?'

'Forensic's report on the rest of Mrs Mitchell's clothes,' he said. 'It's on Inspector Lloyd's desk, but he's not in yet.'

'My God!' Judy said, startling him a little. Perhaps not entirely restored, she told herself. Freud would have been interested. 'I think he might be expecting me to pick him up,' she said. 'Unless he's gone to fetch his car – I think it's ready now.' She thought for a moment. 'Why don't you give him a ring?' she said. 'And I'll see if that report says anything interesting.'

She left Sandwell to it, fighting the desire to laugh as she walked through the CID room with people in various stages of arriving, bidding them a cheerier good morning than they were used to.

Closing the office door behind her, she waited for the extension to ring, which it duly did.

'Did you do this on purpose?' Lloyd's voice demanded to know.

'No!' She laughed. 'I swear I didn't – I'm sorry.'

There was a small silence. 'But that's *worse*,' he said.

'No, it's not really. Do you want me to come and pick you up now?'

'No thank you,' he said huffily. 'Bob Sandwell's coming for me.'

'I'm sorry,' she said again, there being not a lot else to say. 'I'll see you when you come in.'

'Huh.' And he hung up.

Judy replaced the receiver, and picked up the lab report on the underwear. Like the other clothes, it had merely been removed. Nothing to suggest whether it was before or after death, nothing to suggest forcible or violent removal. The tights had a small run, but that could have happened at any time. They were not the murder weapon.

Not the murder weapon. Everyone had assumed that they must have been, since they weren't found with her other clothes. She wondered if she should see Chief Inspector Royle about releasing men to continue the search, but decided against it. Lloyd might think otherwise, so for the moment she'd leave it. Whatever was used had probably been burned long ago, and it was unlikely to tell them much more than they already knew.

Lloyd came in a few minutes later, and agreed with her that there was little point in searching now, especially since the inch by inch search had yielded nothing.

There was an unspoken agreement that only work would be discussed during working hours. Lloyd stuck to this one, unlike the reverse agreement.

'I think we can take the barriers down,' he said. 'We're not going to learn any more there.' He spoke to Randall, then arranged for the watch to be taken off the boating lake.

'What do you think?' he said. 'Send a car and bring her in for questioning?'

'Yes,' Judy said. 'Let her get the wind up a bit.'

Helen had just put away the breakfast dishes when the knock came to the door. Donald had left early to go to work, because he had missed a day. She had wondered a little about that. She opened the door to an extremely tall, extremely young constable.

'Mrs Helen Mitchell?'

'Yes,' she said. 'Can I help you?'

'It's in connection with your sister-in-law's death,' he said, very formally. 'Inspector Lloyd would like a word with you. At the police station,' he added, slightly hesitantly, very politely.

'Now?'

'Yes, please, Mrs Mitchell.'

'I have already spoken to someone – a lady. A sergeant, I think.' It was supposed to sound casual, unconcerned; it didn't.

'That would be Sergeant Hill,' he said. 'But Inspector Lloyd has a few more questions, if you wouldn't mind.'

And if she did? Helen decided there was little to be gained from finding out, and got her handbag. She glanced up at the sky. She wouldn't need her coat. The sky, a bright jigsaw puzzle blue, held the promise of a warm, late summer day.

As she got into the car, she saw a neighbour's curtain twitch. What did they think of all this, all these polite people who had smiled good morning shyly since it had happened? What did they think of all the police cars, and the reporters still having to be repulsed? The ones she knew merely sympathised; the ones she didn't must wonder.

In no time, they were pulling into the station car-park, and she was being ushered up some steps into the building itself. She had never been inside a police station, a fact that only came home to her as she walked along the corridor. You would think that everyone would have been in one by the time they were fifty, she thought. But she couldn't remember ever having lost her bicycle, like the small boy at the desk. When her purse was stolen, she put it down to experience. That it had happened twice showed that she did not learn by her mistakes.

She followed the young man through a room with three empty desks, to an ante-room in which sat the sergeant who had so easily manipulated her, and Inspector Lloyd, only dimly remembered from the frantic moments of Sunday morning, a hundred years ago.

'Mrs Mitchell. Do have a seat.' It was the cool collected sergeant who spoke, extending her hand towards the empty chair in front of her desk. Helen glanced nervously at the inspector, but he was sorting papers, taking no apparent interest in her presence. She sat down, feeling like a child who has been sent for by the head.

'Thank you for coming in,' the sergeant continued, as though she had had any choice in the matter. Though the constable hadn't said that she must come.

'Mrs Mitchell, I got the impression from you that you want to help Mr Wade in any way you can. Was I right?'

'He is a friend, as you pointed out,' Helen said frostily.

'Quite. That's why it is important that you tell us the truth. I wonder if you are.'

'I am not accustomed to having my word doubted,' Helen said.

It did annoy her, even if there was every reason to doubt it. 'Do you object to my having a cigarette?'

'Not at all.' The sergeant pushed the ashtray towards her with her pen.

Helen smoked nervously, still looking across at Lloyd now and again.

'You did leave one thing out when we spoke before,' the sergeant said. 'And I get the feeling that you have left rather more than that out.'

Helen began to see what Donald meant. She had no idea what Chris had said to them – how much of the truth. She had no idea how much damage the truth would do, or if lying would just hammer the final nail in his coffin. She said nothing, and waited for the next question.

'Where were you at five to nine on Saturday evening?' The question came, disconcertingly, from the inspector.

Helen twisted round. 'I told Sergeant Hill,' she said. 'I was coming back from the station – I had to see someone to a train.'

'Were you?' he said. 'You see – you say you were. But you didn't get home until twenty-five to ten. It's – what? A five minute journey? Seven – eight at the very most. And it was a quiet night – well, it's a quiet road, isn't it? At night.'

'I've already explained –' Helen looked back at Sergeant Hill. '– the storm. I couldn't see where I was going.' She tried to calm herself by drawing deeply on her cigarette.

'Yes,' he said. 'You parked in the lay-by.'

'That's right.

'And did what, Mrs Mitchell?' Sergeant Hill again.

'Nothing.' She looked across at Lloyd. 'Nothing,' she said again, helplessly.

'You didn't go up to the café? Leave your car in the lay-by and go up to the café? Wasn't that where you saw Mr Wade's car? Where you knew you would see it, because you'd seen him – go in there on your way to the station?'

'No!' Helen had never imagined that this was why she had been brought here. 'I told you where I saw his car.'

'After some prompting,' the sergeant said. 'I think you saw his car at the boating take – you went into the café to see what was going on, and you saw Wade kill your sister-in-law. I think you didn't get home until twenty-five to ten because you were helping him. Why did you hide her clothes?'

Helen realised that her mouth was actually open, and hastily closed it. She turned to the inspector. 'Inspector – do I have to sit and listen to this?'

'No,' he said, standing up. He walked over to her, standing close so that she had to hold her head at an uncomfortable angle to look at him. 'No – you can talk; and we'll listen. I don't mind which. But I will tell you this. There seem to be only two people who were in a position to have killed Mrs Mitchell. One of them is Wade, and the other is you.'

'Me!' It had got too ludicrous for her even to be nervous any more.

'What did you think of your sister-in-law?' Sergeant Hill asked, as the inspector melted into the background once more, back to his desk.

'I didn't like her. I never have, and I'm not going to pretend that I did just because she's dead,' Helen said. 'I think you'll find that very few people liked her.' Except Donald, presumably, she thought, then looked at the sergeant. Was that what all this was about? 'Oh,' she said. 'I see. Someone's told you about her and Donald, is that it?'

'You know about that, then?'

'Yes.' Helen stubbed out her cigarette in a shower of angry sparks. 'Why? Were you going to spare my feelings?'

'If possible,' the sergeant said. 'But now that we've got it out of the way – I take it you weren't too happy about the situation?'

Helen lit another cigarette. 'I couldn't have cared less, sergeant,' she said. 'My husband has had other affairs – in which I assume you have less interest – and I do assure you that the ladies are all still alive to tell the tale.' She picked up the ashtray, and held it.

'But this was a little different? She had come into a great deal of money, hadn't she? Enough to tempt your husband away? Whereas, if she were to die . . .' She left the thought dangling in the air.

Donald! He thought he'd better tell them about the money. Now look where it had got her. Helen flicked ash nervously into the ashtray. 'That's ridiculous,' she said, because they seemed to expect her to say something. She looked across at the Inspector, but he had gone. 'I don't care about the money', she said. 'I didn't care about Julia, except that – except that I didn't know why he would prefer her. The others I could understand, but I didn't understand that.'

A policewoman came in, with coffee, followed by Lloyd, who fussed round like a vicar at a tea-party.

'Sugar, Mrs Mitchell? Milk?'

She didn't know what to make of him. One minute he would be like this, and the next he would be calmly suggesting that she killed Julia. On the whole, she preferred the aggressive Sergeant Hill, but that wasn't saying much.

He sat on the sergeant desk. 'Mrs Mitchell,' he said. She looked up at him. 'We have no desire to charge someone for the sake of it. If you know anything about this business that you haven't told us, then please tell us now.'

It was a trick. Frighten her into telling them something that Chris hadn't told them. If she told them what he'd said, it would look as though he'd killed her. And he hadn't. He hadn't. It was a trap, she knew it was. But she couldn't see a way out of it. She shook her head slowly, her eyes tight shut. She had to tell them. Oh, Chris, she had to tell them. Tears oozed from beneath her eyelashes, and she heard the door close. Opening her eyes quickly, she saw a a blurred Sergeant Hill. They were alone.

'I saw his car at the roundabout,' she said, haltingly. 'And I didn't see him again until about six o'clock in the morning. He was drunk,' she said. 'He came to us for help.'

Sergeant Hill nodded. 'It isn't a betrayal,' she said, gently. 'He's told us what he can remember. But there are gaps.'

Helen sniffed back the tears, and saw a warmth in the brown eyes that she hadn't seen before. 'Will it help him?' she asked.

'If he's telling the truth, then you must tell the truth. It can't hurt him,' she said, producing a small cellophane packet of paper hankies from her desk. Helen thought she probably had a tool for taking stones out of horse's hooves and spoke Chinese as well.

'He was drunk,' Helen said again. 'I couldn't make much sense of what he said.'

'It's better not to try,' she said. 'Try just to remember the words. If that's possible.'

Helen nodded. There weren't very many to remember. With what was left of her composure, she gave her account of Chris's visit, tearing the last of her privacy to shreds.

She had told her everything she could remember. When they had been left on their own, and he had begun to sober up, he'd gone quiet, and said nothing more about Julia. The clock behind the sergeant read twenty to ten, and she felt as though she had been here forever.

'Thank you,' the sergeant said. 'There's nothing more?'

'Nothing more about her,' Helen said. 'I don't have to tell you anything apart from that, do I?'

'No.' She stood up.

'Do you believe me? Or do you still think I might have killed her?' Helen had no idea from her demeanour what she believed.

'We have to look at all the possibilities,' she said.

'Oh – wait!' Helen Mitchell's face flushed. 'He asked for her! He asked if she was there – he wanted to speak to her. He did!'

The sergeant sat down again, a dubious look in her eye.

'No – honestly. He did. He said "Where is she? Is she here?" or something like that. He was too drunk to stand up – but he'd hardly be looking for her if he'd killed her, would he?'

The sergeant didn't seem as enthusiastic about it as she was.

'Is it true? Have you got Helen Mitchell here?' Chris jumped to his feet as Lloyd came in to the room, then wished he hadn't, and collapsed on to the bunk again. It didn't hurt unless he forgot. 'Well?' he demanded. 'Have you?'

Inspector Lloyd raised a disapproving eyebrow, and sat down beside him. 'Who I choose to question is my business,' he said.

'Why? Why her?'

'If she's here – why not? You've told me you went there on Sunday morning, and she's told me you didn't.' He sighed. 'It occurred to me that I'd given you an easy way out – I suggested that you'd been there. So now I'm asking her.'

Chris subsided a little. Helen would at least confirm that. Every little helped. Unless, of course, she still thought she ought to keep quiet about it. 'Has she confirmed it?' he asked.

'I don't know. If she does, she's in trouble and if she doesn't, you're in worse trouble. Wouldn't it be easier just to tell the truth?'

Chris massaged his temples, trying hard to keep his temper. 'I am telling you the truth,' he said. 'Whoever killed her is still running about and you won't look for him! You're so sure it's me – how do you know he isn't going to kill someone else?' He lifted his eyes so that they were looking right into Lloyd's. 'I didn't kill her,' he said, as though he were talking to a three year old. 'Do you understand?'

'I understand the words – but the evidence says different.' Lloyd stood up. 'If she provoked you in some way—'

'She provoked me! She seemed to have a talent for doing that – and maybe somebody finally killed her for it, but it wasn't me!' He lifted his leg up on to the bed so that Lloyd couldn't sit there again.

'Did she fall when you hit her?'

'I didn't hit her – no, she didn't fall. She stumbled.' He lay back and closed his eyes.

'What's the difference?'

He knew the difference. 'She didn't fall over. She lost her balance, and recovered it.'

'Did she fall against the table? Cut her face?'

Chris opened his eyes to find Lloyd standing over him. 'No. As far as I know, she didn't hurt herself at all. But if there was a cut on her face, then there was. It didn't happen then.' He swung his leg off the bed again, and reached for his crutch. 'Excuse me,' he said, through his teeth. Jail would be peaceful compared with this.

'She hit her head on the table,' Lloyd said. 'We know she did, so stop telling lies about that, at least.'

Chris stood by the wall, his fist hitting it disconsolately, impotently.

'All right. Who else did you have in your car recently?'

At least it was a different question. 'How recently?' he asked, slightly disoriented by the new subject.

'Well, let's start with the same day. Saturday. We've found a set of fingerprints – they're not yours, and they're not hers. We just wondered whose they were?'

Chris frowned. Saturday? His brow cleared as he remembered. 'It was a girl,' he said. 'She came to the garage looking for petrol, because she'd run out. I ran her back to her car. They must be hers.'

Lloyd was going into his amazed routine. 'I'm lucky to find a petrol station that even employs people any more,' he said. 'And here, you are, running stranded motorists back to their cars! I must remember that – is it a service you offer to everyone?'

Chris leant against the wall. 'It was lunch time,' he said. 'I was closing up anyway. So I ran her back to her car. It's got nothing to do with this.' He had forgotten her; she had been nice.

'Hasn't it? Fond of giving people lifts, are you? Pretty girls, at any rate?'

'I do favours for pretty girls that I might not do for you,' Chris said. 'I think you'll find that's quite normal.'

Lloyd walked to the door. 'If there's anything you know about Saturday night that you haven't told us,' he said, 'you'd better tell me now. I don't think you killed her – at least, not without help. But I'm going to have to charge you, because you're the only one I've got. If you're covering up for someone, believe me the favour won't be returned. You might get your reward in heaven, but here you'll just be sent to prison.'

Chris pushed himself away from the wall, weary of the whole thing. 'You know as much as I do,' he said, and sank down on the bunk. If they thought he'd go to these lengths to cover up for someone, then they must believe the someone to be Helen. They thought she'd helped him – or that she had killed her. 'And leave Helen Mitchell out of it,' he said.

'Jealousy is unpredictable,' Lloyd said. 'Can't leave her out.'

'You're wrong about that, you know. Donald wasn't seeing Julia. It's the girl that worked for her – used to work for her.'

Lloyd looked faintly surprised. 'No matter,' he said, after a moment. 'She *thought* it was Julia.'

*

'I thought you were at work.'

Donald had had more enthusiastic greetings in his time. 'I came home to pick up some of Charles's papers,' he said.

'Would you like to know where I've been?' She threw her handbag down on the sofa. 'While you've been sorting out your nice rosy future?'

Donald was sure he wouldn't like to know, but he was going to be told, anyway.

'I've been to the police station – do you know I've never been in one before? When I do go, I'm on the wrong side of the law!'

'What made you go there?'

'What made me go there?' Helen tore open a new packet of cigarettes. 'What made me go there was a six-foot-four policeman. Because you saw fit to bandy our business about!' She struck a match savagely, knocking its head off, and scrabbled in the box for another. 'I believe I was taken in for questioning. They think I might have killed Julia, so that you could get her money!' She succeeded in lighting the cigarette at last. 'Thank you, Donald. While you're choosing premises in Mayfair or whatever it is you're doing, I'm being accused of murder.'

Donald sat down. They couldn't seriously think – but no, they obviously didn't, or she wouldn't be here.

'Failing that,' she went on, 'Chris killed her, but I helped him cover it up. *I* wasn't very good at it, was I?' She sat down, her hands shaking with anger, and blew her nose noisily.

Donald kept his distance, that seeming to be the safest thing to do. 'They didn't seriously accuse you of all that, did they?'

'As good as.' She relaxed a little. 'Oh, it was just to scare me into telling them that Chris came here.'

'And did you?'

'Yes. Relax, Donald. They've let me off with a smacked hand. And your name didn't even come up – not in that connection, anyway.'

Donald frowned. 'In what connection, then?'

'What do you think? Please stop pretending!'

Donald didn't know what to stop pretending about, and that

worried him. Before he could ask, Helen pushed past him, running out of the room and slamming the front door.

He looked out at the sky, picked up a coat, and followed her.

'Thank you, Mr Muller,' Lloyd said.

Mr Muller was the driver of the brown Triumph Spitfire with the unreliable top. He'd seen the news, and he came as soon as he could get away from work to tell them that it was him. The rain had come on, and he'd stopped to try and get the top over, but it was stuck. So he had driven on with it down, and he had seen a lady in a car in the lay-by, who would, he supposed, be the one who had given his description to the police. It would have been about five past nine, because he was late for an appointment, and he'd looked at his watch when the bloody top stuck. He hadn't seen either the man or the woman, which was why he hadn't come forward before. He hoped he hadn't inconvenienced them.

'Someone helped him out,' Lloyd said. 'There were two people running about with her clothes.'

'But she was in the car,' Judy said. The phone rang, and she picked it up, saying yes and no when appropriate. 'That was the lab,' she said.

'And?'

'The phone has a number of prints on it, naturally. They'd need fingerprints from the normal users to sort them out. Is it worth it?'

Lloyd didn't know. 'Perhaps – can they do anything without that?'

'They're checking the ones that are good enough, but some were obliterated. They say it had been partially cleaned with some sort of disinfectant. Probably one of those telephone wipes.'

'That's all we needed. A hygiene freak for a boatman.'

'That's the funny thing,' Judy said, something obviously sparking off a memory. 'We were in there on Sunday – do you remember? And that phone doesn't get cleaned. Not by any hygiene freak, anyway.'

Clouds had rolled over the blue skies, and rain began to fall, at first in slow, large drops which fell into the pond and caused ripples to roll out, gently rocking the ducks. As it gathered strength, and the spots became small and determined, the odd groups of people who had gathered to look at where she was found began to disperse.

The ducks, fluffing out their feathers, wondered anew who had put out the rumour that they liked rain, and watched the people go. All except one, who sat on the bench in the rain, looking at them, but not seeing them. They swam up to be near her, and caught her attention. Looking round, she picked up a stray crust and threw it, but they could see that she had other things on her mind.

They all grabbed bits of bread.

Chapter Eleven

Helen had so far ignored Donald's entreaties to explain. She stared into the boating lake, its surface spiked with rain, listening to the hiss, smelling the freshness.

'You had to bring her here,' she said. 'Because of some silly game of yours, she's dead, and they think Chris killed her.'

'A silly game?' Donald sounded genuinely puzzled, but she still wouldn't look at him. The grass, greener now that the rain had come, stretched down to the road. And on the opposite side, the tall pine trees which had hidden Chris. During the long summer she and Chris had walked in their cathedral coolness, and they had hidden both of them. Now everyone knew; they constituted nothing more than a woodland hideout, a place where a murderer evaded the police.

'I don't know what you mean,' Donald said. 'It isn't sensible, sitting here in the rain – come home.'

Sensible. What was sensible about any of it? She didn't want to be here. Here, where it all started, where the summer ended.

The rain grew heavier, and Donald took off his coat. 'Here,' he said. 'Put this on at least – you're getting soaked.'

She pushed the coat away. 'Aren't you supposed to be at work?' she asked.

'Yes. What's so terrible about that? Work goes on.'

She shivered. 'I wouldn't have believed you could be that cold-blooded,' she said. 'I know you don't believe in sentiment, but I thought I knew you better.'

'Is this about Chris?' he asked. 'I'm worried about Chris – you know I am! But there's nothing I can do about it – so I have to be practical. I've offered help – he knows he needn't worry about money. But I won't be staying in Stansfield, and the sooner I can sort it out and get out of your hair the better.'

Helen could hardly believe he would take the game to these lengths. She stared at him. 'Not Chris! Nobody would expect you to care about Chris, not now!'

'But I do.'

'You do, don't you?' Helen stood up, and walked to the edge of the pool. Donald was by her side in seconds.

'Helen, I'm trying to understand.' He wiped the rain from his face. 'Can't we discuss this inside?'

'Discuss what?'

'Whatever it is we're discussing!' he shouted, turning away in exasperation. She watched as he squared his shoulders, and turned back. 'I know what I'm like – you owe me nothing. I'm sorry if you want me to be insanely jealous about Chris, because I'm not. I'm glad you found him. I'm desperately sorry that he's in this mess – but I've done all I can!'

'This mess?' Helen shook her head, bewildered. 'This mess? Is that how you see it? You've got money now, so it's an ill wind that blows no one good? I didn't like Julia, but surely she's entitled to more than that from you?'

'You're losing sleep over Julia?' he asked. 'I don't see you in mourning!'

'I wasn't having an affair with her!' Helen cried, as the rain slackened off.

Donald opened his eyes wide. 'And you think I was?' he asked, with total, unmistakable sincerity.

Helen walked slowly back to the wet bench, and sat down, regardless. Donald waited by the water, not looking at her. Her mind was full of all the little proofs of infidelity which had brought her to what had been a jumped-to conclusion. All the visits to London over the last twelve months to see Charles about something, only to find out that Charles was abroad on business on at least two of these occasions. Without Julia, because Julia hated flying. A bitchy little hint from Julia herself, during the duty visit to them last Christmas, when she'd told Maria to remember that Mrs Mitchell was here this time, and that the guest room should be aired. She had allowed the remark to hang in the air, for Helen to draw the inference that Donald on his own didn't need the guest room.

When Helen remembered the pay-off line, she didn't know how she could have missed what Julia was really trying to tell her. She had laughed as though realising what she had said, and added that Donald didn't mind roughing it in the servants' quarters. It would have infuriated Julia to know that her hint was lost on Helen, already firmly convinced that *she* was Donald's away fixture, as he had once himself disparagingly called his infidelities. That was when he was still promising to reform, a long time ago now. It was Maria, then. Attractive, quietly efficient, slightly withdrawn Maria who had taken his fancy, rather than the blonde and beautiful Julia. That must have peeved Julia, even if she had never given Donald a second glance.

'It's Maria, isn't it?' she said, almost apologetically.

'Well it certainly wasn't Julia,' Donald said. 'Give me credit for more taste than that.'

It was hard to know what she felt about Maria – she had never taken much notice of her. She had gone to work for Charles in the hope, Helen had assumed, of catching him herself. But Julia had come along, and tricked poor, gullible bachelor Charles into marriage by pretending she was expecting his child. Charles, who had never wanted a wife, did want children, so that he could pass on all that he had worked for. But Julia wasn't pregnant, and had no intention of ever being, if she could help it. Charles had ended up with a wife and no children.

When Charles died, Maria was out of a job, and a home. It had never occurred to Helen to wonder why Donald, of all people, cared, or why he had told her. But now she knew that it was all part of the game. And she had been too dense to work it out. Not Julia. Maria.

'Maria,' she said aloud.

'I'm going home to change, and then I'm going back to work,' Donald said. 'Are you coming?'

She looked up at him, trying to come to terms with her new knowledge. He was looking holier-than-thou because he'd been wronged; slowly, she rose, and followed him home.

*

'Could someone have received a call at the boathouse?' Lloyd asked, having gone through every wild scenario he could to explain the wiping of the telephone. Even if someone had, it didn't get him anywhere, but it might stop him going round in circles.

'No,' Judy said. 'It's just an extension.'

'Oh.' Lloyd tapped his blotter with the top of his pen. 'So she couldn't have called the police anyway?'

'Yes, she could.' Judy smiled. 'You get an outside line by dialling 9 first – she'd probably not know that, but I don't suppose she cared how it worked, so long as it got rid of Wade.'

'Assuming it ever happened.' Lloyd dropped his pen on to the blotter. 'How come you know all that?'

'How do you think? Bob Sandwell, who knows everything. It used, he tells me, to be an ordinary phone, but whoever happened to be on duty would always find some friend in Australia to ring up. They couldn't leave it without a phone, in case of accidents in the boating lake. So they made it an extension when they got their new system in – now you can still dial out, but it's restricted to local calls.'

'I'd better ring Mitchells – tell them we might need some fingerprints.' He picked up the phone. 'Why do I feel as if Wade's running this enquiry?'

Mitchells' Administration Manager agreed in principle to the fingerprints, but only if the men didn't mind.

'They might not have much choice,' Lloyd said cheerfully. 'But we might not need them, so don't spread any gloom and despondency.'

'Do you think the phone was used when it happened?'

'It could have been, but there's nothing concrete.'

'Because we can help you there,' the voice said. 'The phones are monitored now – we get a print-out with all the calls made.'

Lloyd smiled. That was the first helpful thing anyone had said to him since this whole business started.

'When can I see it?' he asked.

'Let's see – Saturday. Picked up Monday. This is – oh any time now. This afternoon, certainly.'

Lloyd became slightly dispirited again. 'It's possible that the phone was only picked up,' he said. 'It wouldn't show that, would it?'

'No. But if whoever it was started dialling at all, it'll show that. Time, date, the lot.'

'Now, that could be just what we need. It would be at about nine o'clock, we think. You'll let me know when it's ready?'

'Certainly.'

'Oh – by the way. Is it likely that someone would clean that phone at night? Cleaners, caretakers, someone like that?'

'Not very.' He laughed. 'We'll be only too pleased to get rid of the boating lake,' he said. 'As it stands, we man it, but it doesn't actually belong to us. We do the bare minimum – they sweep it out from time to time, but that's all. We did send out little packets of telephone cleaning pads when they all got their shiny new extensions, but in all that time only one extension's asked for a new supply.' He laughed again. 'And that wasn't the boating lake, so I doubt it.'

'Thank you very much – I'll be round to collect your printout as soon as you've got it.'

Lloyd's subsequent enquiries revealed that no packet of telephone cleaning pads had been found.

'So,' Judy said. 'Either someone goes round with them in their pocket, or they used the ones that were there and took them away. Why would you do that?' She thought for a moment. 'If it had never been opened – you'd notice if one had been used. But you might not notice if it was gone altogether.'

Someone picked up the phone, used a pad to wipe the part that they'd held, and removed the packet. Lloyd picked up his pen to help him think. Wade? Why go to all that trouble if your prints were everywhere else? The same went for Julia, even if he could think of a reason for her cleaning her prints off anything.

He drummed his pen on his blotter, then let if roll away. 'If Wade's telling the truth,' he said, 'he'd better pray that Julia starting dialling something.'

In the meantime, he had to tell Donald Mitchell that his sister-in-law's body would be released tomorrow, and he could go ahead with the funeral arrangements. They had traced Julia's father through the travel agent, and he was on his way home. He got a cool, unfriendly Helen Mitchell telling him that her husband was at work; he took the opportunity of telling her that they'd spoken to the driver of her open-topped car.

He got an earful from Mitchell himself, and put down the phone with some force when the call was terminated. They lied to him, and somehow it was his fault. He ought to do them both for attempting to pervert the course of justice. 'This bloody job!' he said. 'I'm going to fetch my car.'

The phone rang again before he had even risen from the seat.

'Lloyd!' he barked into it, unfairly.

'Inspector? Sergeant Hill was asking about the prints on the boatshed phone?'

'Yes, that's right. What have you got?'

'We've got a match – well, it might not be good enough to put into court – but it's good enough for me. A partial print on the phone matches the prints in Wade's car.'

'His prints?'

'No – not his. The other ones. The unidentified ones.'

Lloyd blinked. 'But they're supposed to belong to some – right! Thank you. Mr Wade's got a bit of explaining to do.' He replaced the receiver. 'So much for the lady who ran out of petrol,' he said. 'Someone helped him out, and he's not saying who.'

'He could have known her before,' Judy said. 'She was scared – Diane MacPherson says so, Girvan says so. Even Wade says so, though I can't see how that helps him.'

Lloyd tapped his blotter with his pen. 'Perhaps we should let a doctor see him,' he said. Wade could believe what he's telling us. Believe that he really did leave her alive and kicking. But the fact is that the minute Julia Mitchell saw him, she wanted to leave. And she didn't want him to give her a lift, and she looked scared before anything had happened.'

Judy scratched her head. 'Which do you want?' she asked. 'Does he just go mad and kill someone and then not know he's done it, or did he know Julia and go after her, like she knew he would?'

'If someone helped him, and I'm sure someone did, then I think he just went bananas – that's why he says she looked scared. Because he doesn't know it was him she was scared of.'

'Then how did Julia know to be scared of him in the first place?'

'Stop asking difficult questions. I don't know, but we don't have to prove any motive at all. What we want now is the owner of the fingerprints.' He stopped talking, as yet another scenario presented itself. 'Supposing Helen Mitchell did what you said in the first place? Hurried back from the station, went up to the café on foot – and found that Wade had just killed Julia. Her immediate reaction is to phone the police, but then she thinks better of it – wipes the phone, and they just run out to Wade's car. She ducks down so as no one sees her, then gets out and gets into her own car. That way she would see the kids leave, and Muller would see her. After she's had time to think, she goes back up there and tries to make it look like a sex crime.'

Judy was giving him one of her looks.

'It's not impossible!'

'Why go back up there at all?'

'Because if she could make it look –' he stopped, because he didn't really know what he was going to say. 'Maybe she didn't.' She might have found him there with Julia exactly the way we found her. She got him out of there, then went home. But he turned up again at six in the morning.'

The look was fading slightly. 'It could have been like that,' she conceded. 'Rather than your first version – do you give your imagination full rein in front of anyone, or is it just me?'

Just you, he thought, but he didn't answer her.

'Her fingerprints,' Judy said, 'are on my ashtray.'

Chris lay on his bunk, racking his brains, trying to think of anything that might make the police believe him. Had he been set up? But why? And anyway, he told himself sternly, that was nonsense. She was practically begging him to go away, and he could have, at any time. He needn't even have given her a lift in the first place. She hadn't asked him to. Had he walked into something, then? Someone else's murder? Could she have been meeting someone there, or what?

He sat up. That must be it, had to be it. She was meeting someone there – that's why she didn't want him along in the first place. And all that stuff about Helen – it was to make him angry, so that he would leave. What she didn't know was that whoever she was meeting intended killing her. Or ended up killing her, anyway.

He grabbed his crutch, and swung his way over to the door, using the crutch to hammer on it for attention.

'Hey! Can someone hear me? I want to see the inspector!'

He could hear footsteps, and the door was unlocked by a stout, balding policeman, who stood aside to let the inspector through.

'Your wish is my command, Mr Wade,' he said, smiling. 'Have you decided to tell us at last?'

'No – no, I thought of something.' In the presence of the inspector, waiting sceptically to hear what he'd thought, his solution seemed less and less probable.

'Go on, Mr Wade,' he said pleasantly, and sat on the bunk. 'I'm listening.'

Chris told him what he believed might have happened, as calmly as he could, and the inspector listened gravely.

'Now shall I tell you what we know?' he asked.

Chris looked suspiciously at him. 'Something more?' he asked. 'More than you knew before? I'm not going over the same ground again.'

'Something new,' the inspector assured him. 'We know that whoever picked up the phone left their fingerprints in your car.'

'I didn't touch the phone!'

The inspector was shaking his head. 'No, I don't think you did.'

Chris made an impatient noise. 'Julia. I keep telling you. You know she was in my car.'

'Not Julia. She didn't leave any fingerprints in the car.'

Chris frowned. 'Why not? She was in there.'

The inspector shrugged. 'She probably didn't touch anything. You opened the door for her to get in and out.'

So he had. And she'd sat like a statue, with her bloody arms folded. He half laughed. 'So I could have denied she was ever in the car?'

'Not really, Mr Wade. There are other things. Her jacket, for instance – it was fringed. There were small strands of thread from it – that sort of thing.'

Chris flopped down beside him. 'What's the difference?' he said. 'She *was* in the car.'

'Quite.'

'But no one else was.'

'The prints say otherwise.'

'I've told you about that!' Dear God, did he have to tell them everything eight times? 'I gave a girl a lift!'

'And how do you account for this girl – whose name you don't even know – picking up the phone in the boathouse?'

'I can't.' He hung his head, then lifted it again. 'It doesn't make any sense,' he said. 'Unless she happened to use that phone earlier.'

'It's a private phone – the public don't use it.'

'Then I don't believe you!' Chris said. 'Are you certain they're the same?'

'Yes.' The inspector stood up. 'I thought you might give up this nonsense.'

'If they're the same,' Chris said, 'then they're Julia Mitchell's. What makes you so sure they're not?'

'Oh come on, Mr Wade!' The inspector turned towards the door. 'Even you must know about fingerprints!'

'Then are you sure it's Julia Mitchell you found?'

If his words had an effect, then he wasn't allowed to see it. The inspector left without turning back. The door banged shut, and Chris knew that he would go mad in prison.

It wasn't her. They had to check – they had to realise. She was running about somewhere – maybe she didn't know this was happening. Maybe she killed whoever that was that they found.

And maybe, he thought, as he looked round the cell, maybe he was going mad now. How many days could he stand, cooped up in a place like this? How many years would he be expected to survive?

Donald put the receiver back on the rest, and smiled grimly. Randall might not have said much, but at least he knew how Helen had been treated. Was it his imagination, or had he detected a subtle change in attitude? Was Randall ever-so-slightly deferential, now that circumstances had altered?

Funeral arrangements. He wondered if he ought to be doing something, but decided against it. Her father was on his way back, after all.

He picked up the particulars of a rather nice office suite, and settled down for a good read.

Judy got to her feet as Superintendent Randall came in, and was waved down regally.

'Is the inspector here?'

'Yes, sir – he should be back any minute.' As she spoke, Lloyd came in.

'Good afternoon, sir,' he said, smiling in the brittle way he did with people he didn't like.

'I believe you spoke to Mrs Mitchell this morning,' Randall said.

'That's right.' Judy could hear the danger signals in Lloyd's voice. 'She had been withholding information, as we suspected.'

'But you don't suspect her of any serious involvement in this business, do you, Inspector?' Randall hadn't sat down, and neither had Lloyd.

'It's a possibility, sir.'

Randall cleared his throat. 'Look, I know there's been a bit of talk about her and Wade, but I don't think you should take gossip all that seriously.'

Lloyd sat down. 'We wouldn't get anything done at all if we didn't take gossip seriously,' he said.

Randall looked for just a moment as though he might insist on due deference to his seniority, but if he was going to, he changed, his mind. 'True,' he said. 'But the Mitchells are acquaintances of mine,' he added. 'And I wouldn't like them to be dragged into this any more than necessary. In what way do you think Mrs Mitchell could be involved? Just the fact that she didn't tell us Wade had been there?'

'Perhaps more than that,' Lloyd said. 'She could have helped him escape prosecution – or tried to,' he amended.

Judy liked the 'acquaintances' bit. Just in case they were involved.

'Right. Can you prove it?'

'If she was involved, I should have proof shortly – there was a partial print found at the scene which may be Mrs Mitchell's.'

Lloyd explained how he had come by Mrs Mitchell's prints, to the relief of the Superintendent.

'Let me know what develops,' he said. With that, he was gone.

Lloyd made a face at his retreating back, and made no attempt to find him when something developed immediately. The phone rang, and Lloyd took the message, uttering terse and uninformative comments. He hung up, and looked at Judy with a mixture of disbelief and desperation.

'They're not Helen Mitchell's prints,' he said. 'I was convinced.'

'Why are you looking like that?' Judy asked, though she couldn't have put a name to the look.

'Because Wade could be right.'

'About what?'

'He asked me if I was sure it was Julia we found. Am I? Who identified her? Mitchell. Who comes into a fortune if she's dead? Mitchell.'

'Oh, Lloyd.' Judy shook her head. 'No one would try that. Where's Julia then? And who did we find? It's nonsense – you know it is.'

'I don't know it is. We made him think Julia was dead – I went to his house and *told* him she was dead. He sees visions of the good life, and then when he goes to identify her it isn't her. But he says it is.' He picked up the phone. 'We have to confirm the identification,' he said, defensively. 'It's a reasonable enough doubt.'

But Judy remained unconvinced. It didn't seem reasonable to her. Could they really have been barking up the wrong tree all this time? 'Her father's due back today,' she said. 'He could—'

'No,' Lloyd said. 'We've got the name of her dentist – I assume he doesn't figure in Charles Mitchell's financial provisions.'

But surely, Judy thought, whoever it was would have been missed? You couldn't get away with – she thought hard. 'The photograph,' she said, at last thinking of some concrete rebuttal.

'You look at it,' Lloyd said, 'and tell me that you could swear that that was the girl we found.'

Judy knew she couldn't. Old and blurred, her hair different, her face half turned. You couldn't tell.

'Guess who supplied the photograph?' Lloyd said, as he got through to the pathologist.

Some stopped and stared, pointed out to one another where she had been found, walked up to the barred door of the café, peered in the windows. There was nothing to see, but they did it all the same. They weren't there deliberately – they just happened to be passing, walking in the mid-day sunshine.

But mostly, people just went about their business. It had been news, it would be news again when the trial came up. For the moment it had been pushed to the backs of their minds along with Iran and Poland and the Vietnamese boat-people. They didn't stop and stare, these people with their own problems. They flashed by in cars, or walked past busily, eyes fixed on the pavement ahead.

They didn't turn their heads. They didn't see the ducks, because they weren't looking. If ever they did look, they thought the ducks all looked the same. They didn't, of course.

But they did all answer the same description.

Chapter Twelve

Again and again, Chris retraced in his mind the steps he'd taken on Saturday. He was closing up for lunch when the girl came; she was pretty, and tired, and hot – he could see the perspiration on her blouse, as she waved at him, to stop him from closing. He had sold her the petrol, and chatted to her, the way you do. He had offered her a lift back to her car, and then they had gone their separate ways. He had no way of tracing her, of getting her to prove that she was in his car, and that she hadn't touched anything in the boathouse because she wasn't there. They were wrong about that. He didn't care how reliable fingerprints were. They were wrong about that. He'd driven on then, when he'd got her back to her car – just an ordinary mini, like a million other minis – on, into the countryside. A drive through the villages that clustered round Stansfield, past the meadows and fields that still looked like a Constable landscape; a drive to clear his mind, to think about life in general and Helen in particular.

He'd had no lunch, and spent the afternoon working, like he always did. He was on his own in the garage on Saturdays, a situation he kept meaning to remedy, and never had. Donald usually went to London at the weekend, and he would normally close up and go straight to Helen's. But this Saturday Donald was home, and Chris was at a loose end. So, he'd gone to see Elaine and Martin, arriving just in time to be told that they had already eaten. They were expecting Donald and his sister-in-law round to discuss the boating lake, they said. His ears had pricked up at this – perhaps he could see Helen after all, and tell her what he'd been thinking on his countryside drive.

He'd been thinking that she should stop tearing herself apart, and tell Donald the truth. That there was no point in trying to play his game, and that you could only keep promises if there was a point to them in the first place. Once he'd made up his mind, he had been hardly able to wait for Donald's arrival. He was late – well, later than expected, and Chris had begun to think he might not come at all. But he had, complete with sister-in-law, and in the middle of a blazing row. They hadn't even come in properly, but had stood in the doorway to the sitting room, arguing, with poor Martin trying to sound jovial. Elaine and he had exchanged glances; they could only wait and see who won. Elaine had gone to the door, to try to rescue Martin, and then Chris had joined them.

It was then that she had said she was going, and Chris had realised that his chance might slip away. Donald might take her home, and by the time he could see Helen again, his resolve might have deserted him. And so, he had offered the lift.

She had said she was walking, and he had offered again, until she couldn't refuse. He remembered everything, like a slow motion film; she had tried to shake him off, several times, but he needed the excuse to see Helen. Donald might come home early if there was nothing to discuss; he had to have a reason for being there, for Helen's sake. He hadn't made himself objectionable, he was sure of that. He had simply said he'd help her look for her non-existent pen. Then the row had developed over Helen, and he had pushed her away as she came nearer to him, needling him. She had gone into the boathouse, and she had picked up the phone, screaming at him to go or she would call the police.

And he had given in, and left. He hadn't thought about where he was going; he had just turned away from Helen's, and found himself at the garage.

And there, the memories of the accident had claimed him, and the horror of his inadequacy to deal with anything. He had found the bottle of scotch where he'd stashed it months ago, and he had started drinking. He must have fallen asleep; he heard the milk-float clanking its ghostly way up to the pumps, and it seemed very important that he put out the empty bottle. He had some sort of a conversation with the woman, and then he was on his own again, and he didn't want to be. And he was drunk, and Helen had made him promise that he wouldn't drink, and now he'd let her down. And he had left Julia there, in the boathouse, almost frantic with fear.

So he had gone over on foot to Helen's, grimly determined to get there this time, to apologise to Julia, to tell Helen what he'd been thinking, to tell her he wouldn't let her down again.

He'd got there, eventually, and he may or may not have said any of the things he wanted to, because he had only vague memories of faces, and kindness, until his head had cleared and he was in the room on his own.

If only. If only he hadn't gone to see Elaine in the first place. If only he hadn't been so determined to see Helen. If only he had just dropped her off – if only he hadn't braked for the rabbit – maybe then he wouldn't have got drunk, and made everything so much worse.

He could see it now, darting out in front of him, and feel his foot going down on to the brake again – *again*, as if he hadn't killed Carrie that way. And Julia had gone shooting forward, but he had been going slowly, this time. Slowly enough for her to be able to catch the dashboard and stop herself getting hurt.

Julia, reaching out a hand to save herself. Catching the dashboard. 'No harm done,' she'd said, and she was holding the dashboard. *She was holding the dashboard.*

'She was holding the dashboard!' He leapt from the bed, and in one agonising leap was at the door. 'I want to talk to someone!'

The same stout, balding policeman opened the door wearily.

'Keep your hair on,' was his advice as he went in search of someone that Chris could speak to.

Chris waited impatiently, his hand on the wall to support him as he stood on his good foot, wriggling with impatience, like a child. The girl who had been with Lloyd during one of the interminable interviews came in.

'You wanted to see me?'

'Yes – look, she did touch the car. When I braked – remember? I told you. She touched it then, because she had to stop herself falling forward. She put out her hand and held on to the dashboard.' He stopped, breathless, but there was no reaction from her.

'Don't you see?' he said. 'Don't you understand? Those *are*

Julia's fingerprints in the car. I said so to the inspector – it isn't Julia Mitchell's body!'

'But it is,' she said gently.

'No! Check it, please. Check it again.'

Her face was serious, almost sad. 'We have,' she said, quietly. 'We found a dental card in her bag – everything that's found at the scene goes to forensic. And they're very thorough – they had already confirmed the identification. They told us about five minutes ago that there is no doubt whatsoever. It is Julia Mitchell's body.'

Chris had to be helped to sit down. This time he didn't even hear the bang of the door as it closed behind her.

There was something about the way Judy came back into the office that made Lloyd look up from his desk. She was pale, and upset.

'What's wrong?' He went over to her. 'What's the matter?'

'Nothing,' she said briskly, visibly pulling herself together. 'Nothing, except that I just pulled the lifeline away from a drowning man.' She looked up at him. 'He wanted to tell me that she did touch the car,' she said. 'That when they nearly had the accident, she caught hold of the dashboard.' There was a defiant tilt to her chin. 'And I believe him.'

Lloyd sat on her desk. 'But they're not her prints – and you can't argue with dental identification. We must have been right all along. He knew her from somewhere, or he had a brainstorm.'

Judy had set her chin in its defiant attitude. 'Then whose prints are they?' she asked.

'They probably are this girl's – the one he gave the lift to. The lab said they couldn't swear in court that the ones on the phone were the same.'

'They said they might not be good enough for the court,' Judy said. 'But they were good enough for them – and you know that that means they're the same.' She caught his hand, a thing she would never have done under normal circumstances. The efficient Sergeant Hill was letting her private life spill over into her working life. Lloyd wanted to smile, but he felt that he would get into trouble if he did.

'You were quite willing to believe that there were two people involved a few minutes ago,' she said.

'But he won't say who it is!' Lloyd understood how she felt. Wade was convincing – he seemed to believe that he was telling the truth. But he couldn't be.

'Suppose he is telling the truth?' Judy persisted. 'Lloyd, you've seen enough liars in your time! If you had no evidence but his word – what would you think?'

Lloyd blew out his cheeks. 'I'd think he was telling the truth,' he admitted.

'Then suppose he is.'

Lloyd supposed. If he was telling the truth, then the body was not Julia Mitchell's. But the body *was* Julia Mitchell's, therefore he was not telling the truth. Oh no – that was pathetic fallacy or something. Faulty syllogism. All cows are quadrupeds, therefore all quadrupeds are cows.

'Wade has to be telling the truth,' he said slowly. 'Like a logic problem?'

'Yes,' she said firmly, removing her hand.

Ah well, she'd gone back to being a policeman.

'Wade *is* telling the truth,' he said. 'And the body *is* Julia Mitchell's, therefore the person—' he broke off as WPC Alexander appeared at the door with a youngish man who waved an envelope at him.

'I'm from Mitchell Engineering,' he said. 'I've brought the printout, because I thought you'd be interested – a call *was* made after hours.' He handed the envelope to Lloyd. 'I've done copies,' he said, helpfully, but no one was listening to him. 'I've marked the call with a red cross,' he added.

'The call was made at four minutes to eight,' Lloyd said, and knew that Judy's face mirrored his own in its complete lack of comprehension. He turned to the young man. 'Thank you very much for bringing it,' he said. 'It's even more useful than I thought.' He looked at it again. 'Though I must confess I'm not sure how.'

The young man smiled. 'I can save you some time. The number rung was the Derbyshire Hotel's number. It just happens to be a number I know,' he said shyly, rather as though it was a brothel.

'Lovely. Thanks very much – are you in a car, or can someone give you a lift back?'

'I've got the car, thanks.' He smiled uncertainly, and left.

'Seven fifty-six,' Lloyd said, uncomprehendingly. 'But that's when Mitchell was there.'

Judy nodded slowly. 'She could have phoned someone without Mitchell knowing, I suppose.'

Lloyd wondered. Mitchell had given him the impression that he and Julia were together all the time. But they were having a row, after all; he could have gone out to cool off or something.

'If she did make the phone-call,' he said, 'then she could have been meeting someone, like Wade said. And that's why she wanted to get away from the Shorts, why she didn't want a lift – let's go,' he said, standing up. 'At least we might be able to find out who got the call at the Derbyshire.'

Judy was leafing through her notebook, reluctantly getting to her feet. 'Right,' she said absently. 'I just –' She shook her head. 'I just think he's telling the truth,' she said simply. 'And if he is, then there must be a way that this lot makes sense.'

'Maybe he's just not telling the whole truth,' Lloyd suggested. 'Like who was in the car with him?'

'Maybe.'

The Derbyshire was just a short walk through the town centre.

'Four minutes to eight on Saturday night?' The manager, a small, fussy man summoned by a flustered receptionist, shook his head. 'I'm afraid not.' There was something triumphant about the statement, as though his inability to help were some sort of achievement. He pulled a hard-covered notebook towards him and flicked through the pages. 'We log the calls out, of course. For the bills. But not in.'

Lloyd groaned. 'Were you busy on Saturday night? Full?'

'No, not particularly. About half-full, I'd say.'

'How about people who were just staying over Saturday night?' he asked.

'One moment.' The manager smiled professionally, and opened the register. 'Four,' he announced. 'Four rooms, that is. Five people. One double, three singles.'

'Could I have a note of their names and addresses?'

'Certainly.'

'Did they all pay cash?' Judy asked, as the manager wrote out the names and addresses.

'I'll have to check that,' he said, with just a hint of a sigh. He folded the piece of paper and handed it to Lloyd. 'Excuse me.'

'Any point in checking weekenders, do you think?' Lloyd asked Judy.

She shook her head. 'I doubt it. If someone was involved in this, they'd leave as soon as possible. If we draw a blank we can come back to them, can't we?'

Lloyd nodded, and glanced at the list. The couple that the manager had mentioned, two men and one woman.

'Mr and Mrs Banks paid in cash,' the manager said, returning suddenly and silently. 'And Mrs Williams.'

'Neither of the men?'

'No,' he said, by now clearly irritated. 'Or I would have told you.'

'Cheque – credit card?' Judy asked.

'Guests of local firms – we send accounts. I expect you want to know which firms, don't you?'

Lloyd smiled, and the manager went back into the office.

'You couldn't tell us what any of these people look like, could you?' Judy asked the receptionist.

'No, sorry. I was off sick on Saturday.'

'Could you check the phone list again?' Judy asked. 'See if any of these people made calls out?'

The girl, relieved to have something to do, took the list and busied herself with the log.

'Here you are.' The manager had dropped all professional pretence at bonhomie in favour of a slightly surly approach. 'Mitchell Engineering and Plasticraft.'

Lloyd's eyebrows rose very slightly. 'Thank you. Your receptionist is just checking something for us. By the way – would you be able to give a description of any of these people on the list?'

'No, it was my day off.' He turned to the receptionist. 'You would see them, Maureen – oh, no. You weren't here, were you? Who was?'

'Gina stayed on and did a double shift,' she said.

'Don't tell me,' he said to Lloyd, who had taken a breath. 'You want her address.'

'Please.'

'No phone-calls,' Maureen said, handing the list back to Lloyd. 'Sorry.'

'Just one more thing,' Lloyd said, as he wrote down Gina's address and telephone number. 'Have the rooms been booked out again?'

The manager consulted the register again. 'Two of them have,' he said. 'The double and one of the singles – Mrs Williams'. Why?'

'Could you keep the other two locked? We'll be sending round someone to take fingerprints.'

The manager drew himself up to his full height, which fell short even of Lloyd's. 'We do clean the rooms after they are vacated, Inspector.'

'Well – you never know. Drawers, wardrobe shelves, that sort of thing.'

They passed the lounge on their way out. 'I wish it was opening time,' Lloyd muttered, as they went out into the suddenly brilliant sunshine.

The sun slanted through the tall trees, but the pine wood was cool, as always. The sharp, clean smell that had almost gone during the rainless days was back, and Helen walked slowly, her feet snapping the tiny twigs that carpeted the ground.

Maria. Inside her head, the word was sung, as it was by the latter-day Romeo in West Side Story, and the tune wouldn't let her go. Maria, Maria, Maria.

All her married life, the rules had been simple. Donald told lies, and she pretended to believe them. Anything for a quiet life, for the right to call her soul her own. But she had broken the rules. She had *minded*, and she had refused to accept the lies. And now what? Now that she knew it wasn't Julia after all?

Surely he had been lying. Julia hadn't mentioned the boating lake – Helen couldn't see why it would matter to her what happened to it. Had she really only gone up there to count the salt-cellars? No. No, he was lying, he had to be. But now he was saying that he hadn't had an affair with Julia, and she knew just as surely that that was the truth.

She might have been the only person in the world, as she moved slowly through the pine wood. If she stopped walking, all she could hear was sporadic birdsong, all she could see was dusty sunlight through tall trees. All she could smell was pine.

But in her head, a voice mocked her, as she turned and headed for home. *Maria*, it sang. *Maria, Maria, Maria*.

Donald opened the freezer and looked at the rock-hard chops and steaks, the pizzas and sausage rolls, the labelled and dated pies and stews. Did you have to defrost them? Was that just chicken? The pizza declared itself to be at its very best if cooked from frozen in a preheated oven, and he expected he could manage that.

It hadn't surprised him when he had arrived home to an empty house, though he couldn't remember the last time it had happened. He didn't suppose that Helen would be cooking him too many more meals.

He'd checked the bedroom, to see if she had left him. But there were no clothes missing, no suitcases gone. He was glad. He should be the one to clear out. Helen liked it here, anyway. She liked the town and she liked the house, so obviously she must stay. He'd move out tonight if that made her feel better.

He had just consigned the pizza to the surely-preheated-enough-by-now oven when he heard the front door.

Helen looked pale, but she was calmer than she had been at lunch time, as though she had come to terms with something.

He smiled. 'There'll be some pizza in about half an hour,' he said. 'If you want any.'

But she just shook her head.

'We don't know she rang any of them!' Judy was annoyed at herself, not at Lloyd. She knew she was being negative, but everything about this business *was* negative. The fingerprints in Wade's car were not Julia Mitchell's, the telephone was not used after nine o'clock, there had been no sexual assault, though the body was naked.

'It's a chance,' Lloyd said. 'She's more likely to have rung one of them than anyone else – you said so yourself. And one thing we do know – Wade knows more than he's saying.'

Judy didn't believe that. He wasn't the type – he'd have said something, let slip an unwary word, by now. He just wasn't clever enough, resilient enough, not to.

'He must,' Lloyd said. 'We know that there is another person involved now. Someone who was at the Derbyshire Hotel at four minutes to eight. There's a set of unidentified prints in Wade's car. Are you saying that's a coincidence?'

'No.'

'Then what are you saying?'

'He says they're Julia's prints.'

Lloyd sighed extravagantly, and slumped over his desk in mock exhaustion. 'But we know they're not. Don't we?'

Judy nodded. So he was lying. But why? To protect this person? Something had gone on with all three of them up there, and he wasn't saying what. Her notes now contained the names and addresses of the Saturday night guests at the Derbyshire. The couple had been checked out, and were crossed off. The Plasticraft man was a buyer from Belgium, and he'd been crossed off. That left the Mitchell Engineering man and Mrs Williams from Oxford.

'Why would he want to protect either of them?' she asked Lloyd.

'We won't know that until we know the whole story,' he said. 'But at least we've got the Mitchell connection – that might mean something.'

'That's no connection at all.' She moodily turned the pages of the notebook, not looking for anything in particular. 'The Mitchells haven't had anything to do with Mitchell Engineering for years. He'll be another buyer, like the Belgian.'

'Thank you. You are being a tower of strength.'

Judy smiled her apologies, and turned the pages back again. Statements, opinions, names and addresses, facts. Facts were the only things you could depend on. No suppositions – no presumptions of guilt or innocence. Facts. Like a logic problem. And the facts could not be altered, only seen in a different light.

That light, at last, was dawning. Just a faint glimmer at the very edge of her mind, but it was there, if only she could find it.

The evening shadows lengthened as the sun dipped in the sky, and the woods grew dark. Around the boating lake, the gently rippling water reflected the sun's rays, casting pools of light on to the bark of the trees.

Across the road, the pine wood stood hushed and motionless in the still evening, silhouetted against the reddening sky. A light went on in one of the houses, as the tall trees blocked the setting sun.

The moth saw the light, and made her way towards it, fluttering up and down the glass in an impotent frenzy. There was a smaller window at the top; it was open. Perhaps she would stumble across it in her attempts to beat her way through the glass, and perhaps she wouldn't.

But it was there, if only she could find it.

Chapter Thirteen

'I'll go and see Mitchell,' Lloyd said, looking again at the printout. 'See what he has to say about this phone-call. Could you go and see Gina Whatsit – see if she remembers either of the two we've still got to check – oh, and before you do that, can you—' He could feel his words hit the air and come back to him, like talking in an empty room, and looked up from the print-out to find Judy neatly ticking off notes in her pad.

'Are you listening to me?'

Evidently not. He walked over to her desk. 'Come on – we've got work to do. Leave the bloody notebook!' He caught her arm, but she resisted in an abstracted way.

'It *is* a logic problem,' she said, still not really speaking to him, but to herself.

'Are you back on that?'

'No – this is different.' She looked up, aware of him for the first time in five minutes, he was sure. 'That phone-call was made at four minutes to eight. Right?'

Lloyd nodded.

'So either Julia herself or Donald Mitchell made it?'

'Yes.'

'But neither of their fingerprints is on the phone.'

'No.' Lloyd pulled up the visitor's chair and straddled it, his arms along the back. 'Because it had been wiped.'

'Who by?'

'By whom,' Lloyd said. 'Any of them, I suppose. Julia, Donald Mitchell – this person at the hotel, Wade.' He shrugged.

'But Wade insists that Julia did touch the phone,' she said. 'So he'd hardly remove her prints.' Judy was still turning the pages of the notebook.

Lloyd was puzzled, but interested. 'He'd wipe it soon enough if his accomplice touched it, though,' he said. 'Whoever was in his car touched it, remember.'

Judy nodded, the light of victory in her eye. '*You* remember,' she said. 'And while you're at it, remember that it was Wade who drew our attention to the phone in the first place.'

So it was. 'All right,' Lloyd conceded. 'Not Wade.'

'Next question. *Why* did someone – not Wade – wipe the phone?'

'Please, miss, so that their fingerprints wouldn't be found,' Lloyd said.

'What made them think anyone would be looking?'

'Dead bodies have that effect on people.'

'*Julia's* dead body.' She sat back. 'Which rules out Julia, doesn't it?'

'And leaves Mitchell and the hotel-guest.'

She smiled. 'Mitchell and the hotel-guest – hang on to that, too.' She pursed her lips in a determined effort to concentrate. 'The partial print on the phone matches the ones in Wade's car. So it's reasonable to believe that those were the prints that someone was trying to get rid of. Mitchell had no need to get rid of his – he could have used that phone at any time without suspicion . . . the only reason for the phone being wiped is that it had prints on it that shouldn't be there.'

Lloyd began to see the pieces more clearly. Not quite slotted together yet, but he had a feeling they were going to be.

'Bad acting,' Judy said. 'That's what Elaine Short said it was. Bad acting.' She looked up. 'Have you thought about that dentist's card?'

'Not constantly.'

'What do you do with yours?'

'Dentist's reminders? Burn them,' Lloyd admitted.

'I prop mine up somewhere,' she said. 'To remind me. And then I throw them away when I've been.' She smiled, to prove how successful this method was. 'I'm not saying she wouldn't keep hers in her bag – but wasn't it lucky? You find a naked body that could be anyone, and umpteen proofs of identity in her handbag, including the name of her dentist.'

Lloyd thought about it. 'Because it was important that she should be identified? However long it took to find her?'

'And think about what Girvan said about the time of death. The earlier the better – as early as the circumstances allow.' She moved her pencil down the neat lines of writing. 'Yes – here it is. We knew when she had last eaten, and he said that if you worked it out from that, it could give too early a time of death. He assumed fear – and we had reason to think he was right to – which slows the digestive processes down. So he ended up with a later time of death than he'd thought at first.' She looked up, her face eager. 'But supposing she wasn't afraid? Before people kept telling us she was, we thought she'd been taken by surprise, without a struggle, even. Which gave her no *time* to be afraid, and that brings you back to the early end of the range. Nearer eight o'clock? About five to eight?'

Lloyd sat up slowly. 'Mitchell killed her? Then made the call to the hotel?' He got up, picking up the chair and putting it back against the wall.

'Mitchell. Who needed her to be identified. And who had to remove her clothes with care because someone else was going to wear them. Pretend to be Julia.' She suddenly deflated, like a pricked balloon. 'Except that Short already knew her,' she said. 'I should have known it was too good to be true.'

'Did he?' Lloyd said, reaching for her phone, sitting on her desk.

'Yes. He even saw them on a dirty weekend at that hotel in London.'

'Did he? Why? Why go to an hotel? Who'd go to a crummy hotel when they'd got the run of what I gather is virtually a mansion?' He asked for a number. 'I don't need notes,' he said. 'I remember things.'

'Greenwood and Short,' said a pert voice.

'Mr Short, please.'

Martin Short came to the phone. 'Can I help you?'

'I think you can, Mr Short. Lloyd, Stansfield CID.'

'Good afternoon, Inspector.' Short was his usual affable self. 'How can I help you?'

'You mentioned something to me, Mr Short. A chance meeting that you had with Mr Mitchell in an hotel?'

There was a slightly embarrassed silence. 'Not a meeting, thank God,' he said. 'I mean – he didn't see me.'

'When was this, Mr Short?'

'Oh – about three weeks ago, I think. Just a second, my diary's here somewhere.'

It took a lot longer than a second, but Short came back to the phone eventually. 'Yes,' he said triumphantly. 'Three weeks ago on Saturday.' He flicked the page. 'It was the Sunday morning that I saw them, when I was checking out.'

'Thank you Mr Short,' Lloyd said. 'Two more things. One – how many times did you actually meet Mrs Mitchell?'

'Three – if you count that time. Once, at her house in London, not long after her husband died, to discuss the various properties they wanted me to handle. The hotel – and then at our house on Saturday.'

'And two – could you let me have the name of the hotel that you were staying at, please?'

Short obliged, in a puzzled tone, but Lloyd merely thanked him, with no explanation.

'I think the much maligned Mr Wade has been proved right again,' Lloyd said, as he put down the phone.

'Right about what this time?'

'He says that it wasn't Julia Mitchell that Donald was seeing – it was her housekeeper. And the London hotel seems to bear him out – again. Why would Julia have to go to an hotel with him?'

Judy practically bundled him out of the door and into her car. Her haste was justified; Gina remembered Mrs Williams well. She invited Lloyd and Judy into the flat that she shared with two other girls, both obviously pleased to have become involved in the murder enquiry, however vaguely.

'I checked her in,' Gina said. 'I remember her because you don't often get women on their own. She was blonde – quite attractive.'

'Did she go out at all?'

'Yes – she went out at about eight o'clock – just after I'd put a call through to her, so I thought she must have a date. But she was back just after nine, so I don't suppose it was.'

'And, to coin a phrase,' Lloyd said, 'would you know her if you saw her again?'

'Oh, yes. I think so.'

'We'll be in touch,' Judy said. 'You might be asked to pick her out of a line – do you think you'd be able to do that?'

Gina thought she would and it came as no surprise to them, when they got back to the station, to be told that Thames Valley couldn't trace a Mrs Williams at the address given. Were Stansfield sure that the address was Oxford itself, or could it be one of the villages near Oxford?

They went into the office, and as the light flashed and flickered into reluctant life, Lloyd sat down with a sigh, feeling as though he had just got his mythical brother off a murder charge. He rang the number of the Mitchell house in London, and hung up when the phone was answered.

'I thought she'd move back in,' he said. 'Why not? Donald Mitchell owns the place now.' He picked up the phone again, and rang for a car.

And so it was that just two hours later, they were standing on the doorstep of the Mitchell residence, which was indeed practically a mansion, inviting Maria Fraser to accompany them to the local police station. Maria was surprised to see them. She was attractive, as Gina and Diane had both said. Her hair was up, whereas Julia's had been down – fairer than Julia's, but who'd notice degrees of fairness? Make-up and clothes would turn her into an identical police description. Blonde, early thirties, denim skirt and jacket.

She complained, as they escorted her from the house, that she didn't know what was going on. Lloyd smiled when Judy assured her that she would pick it up as she went along.

He had never seen such a perfect match. She had caught the dashboard with the four fingers of her right hand, and she couldn't have done it better if she'd been trying to leave a set of fingerprints. Which, of course, she had been trying very hard not to do. She had done the only thing she could think of to stop herself touching anything. She had folded her arms.

No wonder, thought Lloyd, that she was none too keen to accept a lift from Wade. No wonder she looked scared, as he insisted on coming into the café with her. No wonder she was almost hysterical when he wouldn't leave.

She wasn't hysterical now. She sat between Judy and Lloyd on their way back to Stansfield, staring straight ahead, saying nothing, apparently calm.

'We'll be asking you to take part in an identification parade, of course,' Lloyd said, conversationally.

'Of course,' she said.

The car doors slammed, and Helen watched as the police drove off with Donald, under arrest. It hadn't really come as a shock – more, perhaps, as a relief, because the responsibility had been shifted from her shoulders. She had seen Donald's hand in it from the moment she realised that it was Maria with whom he'd been having an affair. It had all worked out too well.

Donald wasn't a lucky man – he made his own luck. Julia's death meant that he could have money, and Maria, and a clear conscience, because Helen would be provided for.

She had known him too long. He was worried about Chris – far too worried, because nothing really worried Donald that didn't affect him personally. Chris worried him, because Chris had blundered in where he wasn't wanted. And then there were the lies. The lies about Julia's obsession with the boating lake. Helen knew when he was lying; she always had. Walking on her own in the pine wood, trying to sort it out, she had realised that if the lies were not to cover up an affair, then they must be for some other reason. And the reason had to be the murder.

And now, she didn't have to choose. She stood in the sitting room where a moment ago the police had arrested Donald for murder, and she thanked God for saving Chris.

And yet she couldn't hate Donald, though she knew that he would have let Chris go to prison. She walked slowly out to the car, and prepared to enter a police station for the second time in her life.

Chris had thought he was going to be charged. He had prepared himself for that; he had decided to get a solicitor, to see what someone else could do, but in a way he had resigned himself to the fact that he had lost.

So that was what he had expected to hear, when the duty sergeant came to see him. Not that he was free to go. At first, the words didn't mean anything, and he felt like an actor who had been given the wrong cue. The sergeant went on to tell him that he might be required to give evidence, and still it didn't mean much. He was being shepherded out of the cell, up to the main desk. He was being thanked for his co-operation, he was being apologised to, he was being given back his money and his belt.

He asked if he could telephone his sister, and they said of course he could.

Donald saw Maria arrive, flanked by the inspector and his rather fetching sergeant, out of the corner of his eye, as he was taken into a small room and invited to stay there until the Inspector could see him. A burly young man stood in front of the door in case he should wish to leave.

After some minutes, both the inspector and his sergeant came, and he stood up to greet them.

'Sit down,' Lloyd said.

'Don't worry, Inspector,' said Donald. 'We agreed – once Wade had got himself mixed up in this – that if you got to Maria, the game, as they say, would be up. We can't even try to fight. You have a number of people who can identify her, I'm sure.'

'Five or six at the last count,' Lloyd said.

'It could have worked,' Donald said, almost dreamily. 'If young Mr Wade hadn't been so keen to give her a lift home. None of these people would have been likely ever to see her again – and if they did the passage of time would have made all the difference.'

'You have been cautioned, Mr Mitchell,' the sergeant said.

'I have indeed,' he said. 'But it was a gamble, and we lost.'

'Whose idea was it?' Lloyd asked.

Donald thought, and discovered that he really didn't know. He said as much to the inspector. 'It was a joint enterprise,' he said. 'We both like the finer things in life, and neither of us counted Julia as one of these.'

'You were very convincing,' Lloyd said. 'When I came to break the news.'

'Oh, that.' Donald shook his head, remembering the mind-numbing emptiness of that moment, when fact seemed to have overtaken the fiction that he had created. 'That wasn't acting, Inspector. When I saw the state that Wade was in, and all the police arriving – I really thought that it was Maria you had found.' He leant forward. 'She is very important to me,' he said. 'More important than the money, I discovered.'

'Julia Mitchell left your house at 7.50 p.m. on Saturday,' the Inspector said. 'Perhaps you'll take it from there?'

'Certainly,' Donald said, and sighed. 'I left with Julia, and told her I wanted her to see something at the boating lake. It was quite dark in the café – the trees block the light, you know – and besides, I had taken the precaution of removing the light bulb. It was really quite easy – much easier than I'd imagined.' He looked from inspector to sergeant and back again. 'I strangled her,' he said.

The sergeant was looking back at him, her brown eyes widening just a little. 'What with?' she asked.

'Tights,' he said helpfully. 'I've burned them, I'm afraid.'

'And then you rang Miss Fraser at the hotel?'

'Yes.' How did they know that? It wasn't supposed to end like this, but that's what gambling was all about. Tearing up your betting slip. 'While she was on her way from the Derbyshire, I removed Julia's clothes – and Julia, I hasten to add.'

The inspector opened his mouth, then seemed to change his mind.

Donald waited politely, then carried on when it seemed that the inspector was not after all going to speak.

'Maria and I went on to the Shorts – the idea was that she would leave almost immediately, in a huff. Start walking home, and disappear.'

'While you were safely visiting the Shorts,' the sergeant said.

'Quite. She would have gone back to the café, left Julia's handbag, changed back into her own clothes, and got rid of Julia's. Gone back to the Derbyshire, and left Stansfield on the Sunday morning.'

Once again the inspector opened his mouth, a little hesitantly, but this time he proceeded with the question. 'Why did you remove her underclothes?' he asked.

Donald looked and sounded like a professor answering a bright student. I thought it looked better – you might have wondered, if they had been intact. Wondered why, I mean. So I took them off and hid them under a tree on the way back to the café. Maria was there by then, and we just went on our way.'

'When did you plan all this?' the sergeant asked.

'The moment Julia gave Maria notice, I suppose,' Donald answered. 'Just after Charles died. It started as a sort of joke, really. Then Maria had to move into digs.' The awful digs that she had hated, where the thought that Julia was worth shoving under a bus had become less of a joke, and more of a discussion. 'We realised that it might not be all that difficult. We saw snags, but not too many.' He smiled. 'And not the right ones, it would appear.'

His audience did not respond, and he went on. 'I arranged for Martin Short to meet Maria at Julia's – we had a key, of course. It was easy – we just had to wait until Julia went away for a while.'

The sergeant was writing everything down, her pen making little swishing noises as she wrote.

'The meeting lasted quite a long time,' he said. 'But Maria was only there for a few moments. Just long enough for him to get a general impression of her. So that he would be a good witness when the time came.' He smiled, a touch ruefully. 'But when the time came, Wade happened,' he said. 'I imagine you'll be asking Maria about what happened then.'

'We will,' the inspector said. 'But go on.'

'He offered her a lift – she did her best to refuse, but he wouldn't take no for an answer. She couldn't go on refusing – the Shorts would have got too good a look at her. So she tried to get rid of him, but he stuck like a leech.' He shook his head. 'He even picked up that table and sat down for a nice chat. But you'll know that.'

'Yes, we know that.'

'In the end, she was frantic – she'd tried everything else so she grabbed the phone and threatened him with the police. It worked.'

He sat back. 'She tried to get rid of her fingerprints – was that the mistake?'

'One of them,' the sergeant said.

'Well – she felt she couldn't just leave them. And she thought if she wiped the phone clean, you might wonder about that – so she tried to wipe the parts she'd held. We didn't think it would matter too much – her fingerprints shouldn't mean anything to you.' If they did, he wasn't going to be told, he realised. 'Anyway, she changed back into her own clothes which were in one of the boats, and walked back to the hotel. She rolled up Julia's clothes and threw them as far as she could into the wood.'

'Then *you* kindly provided us with a fuzzy photograph of Julia.'

'Yes – a bit too recognisable for my liking, but there weren't any others, except the wedding photographs, and we got rid of them. But there you are – that wasn't what let us down. Even after you'd got Wade, I thought we had a chance. He'd obviously seen nothing – he didn't know it wasn't Julia he was with. Maria even thought he'd done us a favour – taking the suspicion away from me, but I wasn't so sure. I'd have preferred it to have been an unknown assailant.'

'The best laid schemes,' the inspector said, a trifle unoriginally, in Donald's opinion.

'As you say, Inspector. But I still don't understand why you were so reluctant to charge him.'

The inspector looked steadily at him. 'You should have left the underwear,' he said, shaking his head. 'Two different people got rid of her clothes. That's what puzzled us, Mr Mitchell.'

Oh, dear. Helen was always telling him about that. He always thought that if he added artistic little touches, he could get away with murder.

Judy pushed the typewriter away, and held her hands to the small of her back. 'Done it,' she said, but Lloyd had long since fallen asleep, his head resting on his hand. She looked at him for a moment, trying not to think of her marriage, or of what sort of future she might have, because it was too soon, and too difficult.

Last night hadn't been a beginning; they had known for years that it would happen one day. But it wasn't an ending – it wasn't an itch that they'd scratched and now it was gone. It was just another stage in their curious detached relationship.

Lloyd opened his eyes, as he realised that the typing had stopped. 'What did you want to do that tonight for, anyway?' he asked.

'It's tidier,' she said. 'And I don't have to come in to it in the morning.'

'It is the morning,' he grumbled. 'Can we go now?'

'I've never been in court with you,' she said, switching off the light as they left.

'No?'

'No. But I'll be there this time. I can't think why I didn't do it years ago.'

Lloyd looked sleepily uninterested.

'You can't tell a court of law that your first name's David,' she said, pushing open the door to the car park.

'Oh yes I can.' Lloyd turned his collar up against the soft rain.

'But that's not your name.' Judy got into the car, and pushed open the passenger door.

'It is now,' Lloyd said, getting in beside her. 'Officially, at least.' He lifted the door, and closed it quietly. 'I just kept the initial.'

That ruled out Shirley or Marion, Judy thought. She grinned. 'It's that bad? You actually changed it?'

'As soon as I was old enough. And I'm not going to tell you, so you might as well give up.'

Judy began the process of starting the engine. 'But other people know – people you grew up with. Went to school with – they know.'

'Some,' he said. 'Which is how come everyone calls me Lloyd.' The car coughed its way into a semblance of life. 'Because they know,' he continued, his voice flat, 'that regardless of age, infirmity or sex, I will flatten them if they use it.'

Judy put the car in gear and splashed it through the puddle that had formed at the entrance. 'I'll find out,' she promised him. 'Somehow.' She glanced across at him.

He closed his eyes. 'No doubt,' he murmured, sleepily. 'But you're not exempt.'

*

Stansfield was a carpet of orange lights in the darkness, as the owl flew silently over, on his way to a wood he knew where an owl could get a decent meal.

An old, dirty Ford Anglia made its way through the village, turning into the garages behind some flats. It disappeared as its lights went out. The owl flew on, towards the dark blot in the orange lights, towards his late-night snack.

He glided down, ghostly pale against the dark sky, and sat on the roof, motionless and ready. It was quiet tonight; the lake was dark and still. The gentle rain had barely dampened his feathers before it had stopped, and the night skies were clearing. It was pleasant, and cool, and not like the other night, when he'd perched here. When the storm was coming, and it had been so hot and heavy. That had been unpleasant. Yes, he thought, as movement caught his eye, and he swooped down upon his supper, that *had* been unpleasant.

In fact, that had been murder.

REDEMPTION

Hail, O ever-blessèd morn!
hail, redemption's happy dawn!
sing through all Jerusalem:
'Christ is born in Bethlehem!'

Chapter One

Lloyd finished the last chapter of his library book, and closed it with relief, wishing that it was in his power to abandon books half-way through. But no matter how obvious the plot, how stilted the dialogue, he was obliged by some natural law to finish them. The worse they were, the more likely he was to devour them, reading into the small hours to get them out of the way. Good books relaxed him, and he would fall asleep with them in his hand, but no such luck with the lousy ones.

He balanced the book on top of the others on his bedside table, and ran his hand over his hair to smooth it down. It was habit – he couldn't get used to his hair being so short now. He had decided that people who were rapidly losing their hair should not draw attention to the fact by keeping the remaining hair long. He still thought it looked odd; Judy said she liked it. He had wondered about growing a moustache, to make up for the shortfall on his head – he craned his neck to see himself in the dressing-table mirror, and pulled a face. His unshaven face held the ghost of what a moustache might look like, and he didn't think it would do. Tall, military types could carry off moustaches, but he had come in at the low end of the regulation height. Too small and dark, he decided. He'd look like a bookie's runner.

He lay back, wide awake, aware that the pile of work which awaited him was being added to as he lay doing nothing. Added to by pre-Christmas burglars who helped themselves to the presents under someone else's tree – added to by the ones who stole the trees, come to that; the chain-saws got stolen around August, the trees in December. Added to by the drunks, added to by the jolly Christmas spirit that brought out the pickpockets and the handbag snatchers, the credit-card frauds and the conmen in the market square.

One small, striped package and the odd Christmas card were the only hint of Christmas in Acting Chief Inspector Lloyd's flat. Not that he had any objection to glitter and tinsel – in fact, if he were truthful with himself, which he quite often was, he was a bit of a sucker for jingle bells. But there was another natural law which decreed that no man be alone at Christmas, and he would once again be made welcome by Jack Woodford and his nice, comfortable wife in their nice, comfortable house. Lloyd didn't really know if they actively desired his presence at their festivities, but they knew that they had to ask him, and he knew that he had to accept. And he would give their grandchildren presents that their parents would insist were too expensive, as he had done for the past three Christmasses, and the collective Woodfords would give him a bottle of malt whisky.

He liked buying presents for the children; his own were grown up now, and just got presents like everyone else's. He had missed his annual excursion into the magic world of children's toys. His Christmas visit to his own offspring consisted of an hour or two on Boxing Day, with Barbara making polite conversation as though they hadn't been married for over eighteen years before it all came to pieces in their hands. So he was glad of the Woodfords' goodwill, and he enjoyed the cheerful, noisy family Christmas. Especially this year, now that his father was beginning to get used to the idea of being a widower, and had decided to go back to Wales to live, which he'd wanted to do ever since he'd left. What with that, and Judy about to have her in-laws staying with her, Lloyd would have been very much alone.

Judy was the detective sergeant with whom he'd worked, off and on, for seven of the fifteen years since he'd met her. He had been married then, and the twenty-year-old Judy had rejected his advances, her eyes sad. Eventually, she herself had married, and moved away. Because Barbara had wanted it, and because it might have saved his marriage, Lloyd had requested a return to Stansfield, but the divorce had happened anyway. Then, eighteen months ago, Judy had arrived back in his life, a brand new detective sergeant. Since then they had, with a sense of inevitability, become lovers. Occasional lovers, he thought, with an audible sigh. Very occasional.

When Michael was at home, he and Judy weren't lovers. And Michael's promotion had ensured that he was home for considerably longer periods than before. Michael, a computer salesman turned sales director; Michael, to whom Judy professed an unexplained wish to remain married.

The covert nature of their relationship was beginning to irk Lloyd, though Judy seemed happy enough with things as they were. He wished she was with him now, in his three o'clock in the morning wakefulness, though even that pleasure would have been qualified by her ability, figuratively at least, to keep him at arm's length. He looked at the little gift-wrapped parcel on the dressing table. It ought to be tied with ribbon, he decided. And under a tree. He'd get one tomorrow. And some lights. Tomorrow was Christmas Eve; today, he corrected himself. Judy was on leave to play hostess to Michael's parents. He probably wouldn't even see her until after the holiday, but her present would be under a bloody tree if he had to keep it there until March.

He switched off the light, and closed his eyes. He wondered if it was still snowing, as it had been when he'd retired with his dreadful book. A white Christmas – it looked pretty, but the roads hadn't been gritted, and the traffic lads would be busy. His thoughts dwelt on work until at last his mind began to shunt itself into a siding for what was left of the night. Filtered through the fog of sleep, the sighing of the wind reached his ears, and his last conscious thought was for the traffic division, if the snow drifted.

George Wheeler rubbed his eyes as the early morning sun glinted on the snow. Not so early morning, he realised. It was ten o'clock, and he still hadn't written a word.

'I'm sure *you* understand, Vicar, being a Christian.'

Perhaps it was when those words were addressed to him by someone whose motives he had no desire to understand, and with whose values he had no desire to be aligned, that George Wheeler had stopped believing. Not in God, for he knew that he had never honestly believed in God as a being, an entity. As a force for good, perhaps – something inherent in man – but not as some sort of super-caretaker.

Stopped believing in himself? No, that wasn't right either. George believed in himself, for there he was, flesh, blood and bodily functions. And bodily desires – was it perversion to find himself appreciatively eyeing the young mothers at the church play group, or mere perversity? Was it middle-aged conceit that made him imagine that young Mrs Langton was seeing past his clerical collar to the man, or a sign that soon he would be roaming the streets of Soho, a *News of the World* headline *manqué*?

He put down his pen, and sat back in his chair, the better to contemplate the prospect. He had played a bit of soccer in his youth, and he still did some refereeing when he got the time. He'd kept in shape, more or less. Good enough shape for the lovely Mrs Langton to fancy him? He smiled to himself. Chance would be a fine thing. Though he still had all his hair – its sand colour was diluted here and there by silver, but that was distinguished, according to his wife. George believed in himself enough to be vain about his appearance, so that wasn't it.

No, he had stopped believing that he believed. It wasn't something that it had ever crossed his mind to wonder before. His family went into the Church. His grandfather had made it to Bishop, and there had even been rumours that he was on course to make it all the way to Canterbury, but George rather thought that his grandfather had started those himself. At any rate, he didn't. It was taken for granted – by George as much as anyone else – that he would go into the Church. It was a career decision, if decision it could be called, not a spiritual one. There was the Church, the armed services, the Civil Service. George had chosen the Church.

He addressed himself once more to the pale lines of the A4 pad in front of him, but inspiration, divine or otherwise, eluded him. George had been expected to do well, to rise through the ranks as had his grandfather before him, and as his nephew was doing even now. But George wasn't a company man. He was well enough connected to have secured a living in one of the prettiest villages in England, complete with a vicarage about which anyone might be moved to write poetry. Verdant lawns, bushes, shrubs, climbers; light-filled rooms with elegant lines, and old, good furniture. Wonderful views from its hilltop site, across three counties which today all lay under a shifting blanket of snow. And just twenty-five minutes from Stansfield, with its new-town bustle, its supermarkets and cinema, trains, and buses. The best of both worlds, and for twenty-nine years George had clung tenaciously to his well-behaved flock and his uncomplicated life. Lack of ambition, said his superiors. Pure selfishness, George knew now.

It would take rather longer than usual to get into Stansfield today, George thought, glancing out of the window as the wind whipped up the fallen snow. It was drifting badly on the road, and the cars were already having trouble on the hill.

It was no crisis of faith, for there never had been faith, but it was a crisis of the heart, and the words for the midnight service simply wouldn't come. He put down his pen, and stood up, holding out his hands to the one-bar electric fire. Central heating would make the vicarage truly a poem. As it was, there was still a sliver of ice on the inside of the study window. The parish couldn't afford central heating, and neither could he. Until now, he had accepted that as his lot, just as he had accepted everything else.

He had accepted God, to the extent of praying to him in church, and sometimes out of it. Praying for the rescue of people in peril: physical, in intensive care, or spiritual, in the back of a Vauxhall Chevette. Prayer perhaps helped those who prayed, but that was all. And then there was worship. George had never worshipped God. He had taken part in acts of worship – if saying a few words about the sanctity of life and tossing off a couple of hymns to the less than talented Jeremy Bulstrode's organ accompaniment counted as worship. But it didn't. Not in George's book.

Worship was naked, open adulation, to the point of total self-lessness. George had never lost his sense of self, not even on a morning like this, when the elements combined to put man firmly in his place. Not even when he had fallen hopelessly in love, at thirteen, with his cousin from Canada, five years his senior and only in the country for a fortnight. Not in the throes of more mature passion, or grief, or anger. And not, certainly not, in the pulpit of St Augustus.

And yet he knew how it felt, this loss of self, this giving over. Once, long ago, he had felt it. He walked to the window, and ran his finger down the sliver of ice, which melted to his touch. It wasn't a woman, he thought, with a smile at himself. A few courteous and cautious walkings-out before Marian, and marriage. A happy, fulfilled marriage, but not worship. Joanna? No, not even her. He loved his daughter with all his heart, but it was still *his* heart. It was long ago, before any of that, before adulthood.

The dog. Of course, of course. His grandfather's dog, whom he had had the privilege to know all his life until the old soldier died, when George was eleven. Perhaps only a child could truly worship, for he would have died instead, if he could have. So, he thought, as the sun shone blindingly on the white carpet below him, he had broken the first commandment.

Come to that, he had spent all summer spraying greenfly in a deliberate act of destruction. Did greenfly count? Birds did.

His father had shot birds; George had joined him once or twice on shoots, but he was a miserably bad shot, and had barely inconvenienced the game.

He had loved his father and mother, but that was no big deal. It wasn't hard to love people who loved you, and it certainly wasn't an honour to be thus loved. If honouring them meant putting flowers on their grave on the infrequent trips to his remaining relatives, then it was Marian who did the honouring. If it meant being straight with them, then he had dishonoured them by joining the Church.

And *by* joining the Church, he broke one commandment regularly, every Sunday. The Bible might not count taking Sunday services as work, but he certainly did. Standing in the pulpit, in the ever-present draught that gave him a stiff neck, seeing the same old faces staring back at him, not expecting anything from him. They were there, like him, from habit and custom; presumably they did find something that they needed in the chill air and the stained-glass light, but he never had. Whatever kind of fulfilment he sought, it was not to be found in St Augustus on a Sunday morning.

Could Mrs Langton provide it, he wondered? VICAR IN PLAY GROUP LOVE TANGLE. Except that she probably hadn't given him the eye; it had probably never occurred to her that his mind ever dwelt on such things. But it had. Not *News of the World* stuff, then. A question on a game show, perhaps.

'*We asked one hundred vicars: Do you ever have sexual fantasies about the mothers in your church play group? How many vicars said yes, they did have sexual fantasies about . . .*'

'I've brought you some coffee. You must be frozen.'

He jumped at the sound of Marian's voice, and turned from the window.

'Sorry,' she said. 'Were you working or day-dreaming?'

He smiled. 'Oh, day-dreaming,' he said, walking back to the electric warmth.

'I've got the fire going in Joanna's room,' Marian said, handing him the mug. 'It took about six fire-lighters, but it's caught now. And George,' she said, in her scolding voice, 'must you leave your overalls in a heap on the hall floor?'

'Sorry. I was looking at the car.'

'What's wrong with it?' Marian asked.

'Nothing. I was just—' But she had never understood his love for things mechanical, so he didn't try to explain. He put both hands round the mug of coffee, and stared at the empty pad on the desk.

'Are you having trouble?' she asked.

'You could say that.'

Marian wasn't what he thought of as a vicar's wife. Even he saw the situation comedy notion of Vicar's Wife, when he thought of the actual words. Vicars' wives were either dowdy, shy and full of good works, or blue-rinsed, tweedy and full of good sense. Marian had short, curly, dark blonde hair, and mischievous eyes. Her fiftieth birthday had just passed, and those eyes had tiny wrinkles that he supposed had once not been there, but which were a part of her that he felt he had always known. She had the suggestion of freckles on her nose, and a wide, generous smile. She wasn't tall, and seemed even less so once Joanna had grown up to become three full inches taller than her. He smiled. His adulterous thoughts had made him feel quite frisky, and vicars weren't supposed to feel frisky at ten-thirty on a Wednesday morning, especially not on Christmas Eve.

'Which one?' Marian asked.

'Sorry?'

'Tonight's or this afternoon's?'

He stared blankly at her. 'Sorry?' he said again.

'Which sermon are you having trouble with?'

'Oh. Tonight's. This afternoon's for the children really. It's easy to talk to children.'

'Well, I hate to break it to you, but Jeremy Bulstrode's on his way over, in a state about something. He can't play this afternoon.'

'He can't play, period.'

'Something to do with his wife's brother,' she went on. 'He's on his way over for high-level discussions. What will you do?'

'See him,' George said, with a sigh. Ah well, it was highly unlikely that the vicar's wife would want to know at ten-thirty on Christmas Eve morning anyway. And it just wouldn't do for Jeremy Bulstrode to come in and find the vicar and his wife *in flagrante delicto* on the study floor. Would that interest the *News of the World*, he wondered? Or would it have to be the vicar's wife who found him and Jeremy Bulstrode?

'I mean about this afternoon. Shall I fix up the record player?'

'Oh – no, that might not be necessary. Mrs . . .' He hesitated over the surname, not in deliberate deception, but none the less deceptively. 'Mrs Langton plays,' he said. 'I believe.'

'Oh, good,' said Marian.

Mrs Langton was a newcomer to Byford; eight weeks ago she had moved into the cottage at Byford Castle, with her two-year-old daughter.

'I'll pop round and ask her,' George said.

'But Jeremy's coming.'

'After Jeremy,' he said.

'I can go, if you're busy.'

'No,' he said. 'I'll go. It'll be a good excuse to get rid of Jeremy.'

He pushed away his pad. 'Maybe visiting someone will give me an idea for this,' he said.

'What about tomorrow? Have you still got to write tomorrow's as well?'

'No. I say the same things every Christmas Day.'

'Do you?' She frowned. 'I hadn't noticed.'

'More or less,' he said. 'It's the midnight service I like to get my teeth into. But the one I'd written won't do.'

'Why not?'

He looked at her. He couldn't tell her she was married to a fraud. He couldn't tell his congregation that they had been listening to a fraud all these years. He didn't know what to say to her, or them. Perhaps seeing Eleanor Langton would help. He found it easy to talk to her, to be himself with her, and not the character actor that he had become, even with Marian.

Eleanor had told him a little of herself – she had been a research assistant, and was now employed by Byford Castle to work during the winter on preparing their archives for publication, and to oversee the guided tours in the summer. She was a widow, and she was lonely. She had told him that because he was a vicar, he assured himself; that's what vicars were for. But he felt as though it was vaguely guilty knowledge, because he *hadn't* imagined her interest in him, and she had seen and recognised his in her. Unspoken, unacknowledged, but it was there, and it had been for weeks.

'George? Are you feeling all right?'

He smiled, almost laughed, at himself. 'Just considering my suitability for getting into the *News of the World*,' he said.

'Do you *want* to get into the *News of the World*?'

'Other vicars do,' he replied.

She smiled. 'You haven't developed a passion for choir boys, have you?'

'Good Lord, no. Nasty little brutes. Can't think what all those unfrocked vicars see in them.' He moved reluctantly from the arc of warmth, back to his desk. 'And that's another commandment gone,' he said, sitting down.

Marian bent down and sniffed. 'You've not been drinking,' she said.

'No. But I took the Lord's name in vain. I do it quite a lot.'

'Yes,' said Marian.

'I suppose,' he mused, 'if I worked my way through all ten commandments – that might qualify me for inclusion.'

'Well,' Marian said, picking up his empty mug. 'I don't care how much you covet it, you're not bringing that ox in here.'

Judy Hill switched on full headlights as the drifting snow swirled round the car, reducing visibility to what seemed like three feet. Mrs Hill senior sat beside her in the car, and Mr Hill sat in the back, tutting at the weather. Judy felt as though she was somehow being blamed.

'Idiot,' she said, as a car swept past her through a gust of snow-filled wind.

'I'm looking forward to seeing the new house,' Mrs Hill volunteered, after a moment.

'We haven't finished decorating yet,' Judy said. 'But it's looking pretty good.'

'Michael says he's thinking about converting the loft,' said Mr Hill from behind her.

Judy slowed down still more as she felt her tyres become unsure of their grip on the deepening snow. 'Yes,' she said absently, peering through the flakes which were falling yet again. The windscreen wipers worked hard, piling snow into the corner of the windscreen, but the weather was beating them. 'I'm not sure why,' she went on. 'There's more than enough room for us as it is.'

'Maybe he's thinking of the future,' Mrs Hill said.

Judy hooted angrily as a car cut in ahead of her. The future? My God, it wasn't a granny flat she had in mind, was it?

'Adds to the value,' came the voice from the rear. 'When you sell.'

Oh yes. Nobody actually bought houses to live in, not in Michael's world. You bought them as a rung on some socioeconomic ladder.

'It would make a nice nursery,' said Mrs Hill.

'Not too far now,' Judy said, hearing a note of desperation creeping into her voice already, and they weren't even installed

yet. Michael didn't even *want* his parents' company over
Christmas; he just wanted to show off his enhanced lifestyle. She
signalled left with a mental sigh of relief. Almost there.

The little road was almost clear of snow, and her heart sank
as she saw why. The driveway was inches deep, with snow piled
up against the garage door. She pulled into the pavement, and
stopped the engine.

'Oh dear,' said Mrs Hill. 'Someone will have to get busy with
a shovel.'

You? Judy thought sourly. 'Yes,' she said, brightly. 'Let's get
you settled in first.'

Mrs Hill got out, and fiddled unsuccessfully with the front
seat.

'I'll do it.' Judy tried hard to keep the edge out of her voice as
she tipped the seat forward to allow Mr Hill to clamber out.

'There's a present here, ducks,' he said, handing it to her.

Damn, damn, damn. She had meant to go via the police station, and drop it in to Lloyd. The weather had driven all thoughts
out of her head, save picking up the Hills and getting them home
in one piece. 'Thank you,' she said, putting it in the glove compartment. 'It's for someone at work.'

She led the way up the path, and kicked away the snow from
the front door. 'Go on in,' she said, realizing that she had left her
car lights on. 'I won't be a moment.'

Back at the car, she switched off the lights and opened the
glove compartment, as if staring at his present would somehow
magic it to Lloyd. She couldn't just leave the Hills there, even if
the thought of just driving away again did have a certain mali-
cious charm. With a sigh, she closed the car up.

'It's a lovely big room,' Mrs Hill was saying, as Judy went in,
shaking the snow from her dark hair.

'It's a bit of a change from the last one,' Judy said. 'We swing
a cat every now and then to celebrate.'

'Pardon?'

'Nothing,' Judy said, taking out her cigarettes.

'Oh, now – I thought you'd given that up,' said Mr Hill. 'You
should read what it says on the side of the packet before you
light that.'

Judy lit it without improving her mind. 'I only have one very occasionally,' she said truthfully. When she felt she needed one. Like now. 'I expect you'd like a cup of tea. Or something stronger?' she added, hopefully.

'Tea,' Mrs Hill said firmly, as Mr Hill opened his mouth. 'Thank you.'

Michael came in while Judy was in the kitchen, and she could hear his mother fussing over him. He wasn't, apparently, wearing warm enough clothes.

'The driveway's blocked,' he said, when he joined her.

'I know. What are you doing home?'

'Office party,' he said. 'It started at about half past eleven.' He leant on the fridge.

Judy pushed him to one side as she got out the milk. 'Aren't you supposed to stay?' she asked. 'To mingle with the common folk?'

'I pleaded bad weather,' Michael said. 'I can think of better things to do than trying to get my hand up some typist's skirt, even if Ronnie can't.'

Judy laughed. 'Ronnie doesn't turn into an office Romeo at Christmas, does he?'

'Does he not.' Michael looked through his double-glazed window at the weather. 'I'd better start digging,' he said. 'I can't leave the car out in that.'

'The car' was his car. His company car.

'You won't be able to get it out again if you put it away,' Judy pointed out.

'What you've just said would have had Ronnie in stitches,' Michael said, with a smile. 'Do you blame me for running away?'

Judy smiled too, shaking her head.

Michael stood, still looking out, momentarily lost in thoughts which Judy knew she didn't share, his thin face slightly, pink from the cold air. They were doing well, so far. A good five minutes without a cross word. She set mugs on a tray, and Michael, back in the real world, looked pained.

'What's the matter?' she asked.

'We do have cups and saucers,' he said.

And still, teeth gritted, Judy didn't allow the very cross words she was thinking to pass her hps. They would have shocked Michael even more than the mugs had.

'George – come in.' Eleanor Langton had decided to stop calling him Mr Wheeler the last time they had spoken, but she hadn't had the nerve. She waited apprehensively for his reaction, as though he might tell her off.

'Thank you,' he said, brushing snow from his coat as he came in.

'I'd take my coat off, if I were you,' she said. 'It's a bit warm in here.'

'Thank you,' he said again.

'Is this a social visit?' she asked, as he slipped off his coat. 'You're in civvies.'

He smiled. He really did have a lovely smile, she thought. It made him look about six years old.

'I've come to beg a favour,' he said.

'Anything. I must owe you several favours.'

'What for?' he asked.

Eleanor indicated a chair. 'Listening to my moans,' she said.

'You don't moan. And if you did, it's a vicar's job to listen.'

Eleanor brushed her blonde hair back from her face. 'What favour?' she asked.

'My organist has let me down, or turned up trumps, depending on your ear for music,' he said. 'In any event, he can't play, and I've got a children's carol service this afternoon. Nothing tricky,' he added. 'Just the usual carols to the usual tunes.' He paused. 'Will you play for us?' he asked.

'Oh,' she said. 'I only play an electric organ.'

'It is electric,' George said. 'It used to be a harmonium, but I didn't see why the church shouldn't move with the times.' He smiled again. 'No pumps, no bellows,' he said.

'I'd love to,' said Eleanor. 'I was taking Tessa anyway.'

'Wonderful.' He sat back. 'Where is she?'

'At the film-show. Mrs Brewster took her, bless her.'

'Oh, yes. In the church hall. I'd forgotten about that.' He sat forward a little. 'Eleanor,' he began, slightly hesitant. 'You – you're not going to be alone tomorrow, are you?'

'No. Richard's mother's coming – well, she was. If this goes on much longer . . .' She shrugged, glancing out of the window at the snowflakes dancing through the air.

'Well, the vicarage is at your disposal,' he said. 'Marian always buys an enormous turkey – it lasts until about April.'

Eleanor laughed. 'That's very kind of you,' she said. 'Will you have a Christmas drink with me? It's almost lunch time.'

'I'd love to. I feel as if I'm playing truant,' he said.

'Why?' Eleanor stood up. 'What should you be doing?'

'Writing tonight's sermon.'

'Oh dear. You're cutting it a bit fine. I can only offer you whisky or sherry, I'm afraid.'

'I'd better have sherry,' he said.

'Is the sermon proving difficult?' She handed him his sherry, and sat on the sofa.

'Yes,' he said, getting to his feet. 'Do you mind if I take my jacket off? It's a little—'

'It's very,' Eleanor said. 'The boiler has two modes – off or equatorial.'

He took off his jacket, but he didn't sit down again. He walked over to the sideboard and picked up the photograph of Richard. 'Your husband?' he asked, turning.

Eleanor nodded.

'Is this your first Christmas without him?'

'Not really.' She could talk about it now. There had been a long time when it was impossible, when the tears that were denied her at the time would suddenly surface. But she was over that now. 'Richard was in a coma for a very long time,' she explained.

George carefully replaced the photo. 'I'm sorry,' he said.

'Tessa never knew him, not really. I took her to the hospital when she was born, but—'

George looked horrified. 'Oh, forgive me,' he said. 'I didn't know the circumstances—'

'It's all right,' Eleanor assured him. She took a breath. 'It was a motorbike accident. Head injuries.'

Driving without due care. That was all the driver had been charged with. Her life was shattered because someone drove without due care. It was anger that she felt now, more than grief. More than anything. But that would pass too.

'He only died in October,' she said. 'But – well, this is the third Christmas without him.'

George sat down beside her. 'How dreadful for you,' he said.

'It was,' said Eleanor. 'To start with. They said I should talk to him – you know? At first, you feel self-conscious, but in the end, it became—' She paused. 'A habit, I suppose,' she said, looking away from the hazel eyes that she was saddening. She hadn't meant to talk about Richard. 'After he died,' she heard herself saying, try as she might, 'I kept a diary. Telling it the things I would have told Richard.' She looked up. 'But I haven't had to do that since I started working here.'

George stroked his upper lip for a moment before he spoke. 'Did you have your family to help you?' he asked.

'Richard's mother. I'm not from Stansfield. My brother came down as often as he could—' She broke off. 'I'm sorry,' she said. 'I really didn't mean to bend your ear with all this.'

'I told you,' he said gently. 'That's what vicars are for.'

'I don't think that's why I'm telling you,' she said quietly, and there was a silence.

The man wasn't just married, he was a vicar. A *vicar*. The first man in whom she had had a flicker of interest, and he was a married vicar. 'I'm supposed to be listening to your problems,' she said, her voice sounding false, even to her.

'My problems?' He loosened his tie slightly.

'With your sermon.'

'Oh, that.' He sighed. 'That's easy. I don't think I have the right to preach to people.'

'Then don't,' she said. 'Just tell them what's on your mind,'

He looked at her, into her eyes, and smiled, 'I don't think that would be a very good idea,' he said.

Eleanor closed her eyes for a second; George loosened his tie some more. Another silence. She had to say something, do something. 'I'm sorry it's so hot,' she said.

'Have you had anyone to look at it?' he asked.

'The castle said they'd get someone, but they haven't yet.'

A TRIO OF MURDERS

'I could look at it for you.' He smiled. 'I'm quite good at that sort of thing.'

'Would you?'

He put down his drink. 'Lead the way,' he said, getting up.

'Oh – but you're too busy just now.'

'It might just be that the thermostat's set too high,' he said, following her into the little outhouse which had been tacked on to the cottage. The cottage itself had been built on just after the Civil War, to accommodate the family while they repaired the ravages of Roundhead occupation.

George caught his breath as he walked through the wall of heat to which Eleanor had become acclimatised. 'You could grow tropical fruit in here,' he said.

Eleanor watched as he pored over the yellowing manual, and she fetched screwdrivers and pliers when requested, like a nurse assisting a surgeon.

He mopped his own brow, however, and stood up, 'Why they want to put the damn thing in the most inaccessible—' he said, and bent to his task again, his tie trailing in the dust at the back. He stood up again. 'Would you undo my tie?' he asked. 'It's getting in the way, and I can't let this go.'

He kissed her as she undid his tie, as she had known he would. Just a gentle kiss.

She slowly pulled his tie from his collar.

'A dog-collar wouldn't have afforded me the opportunity,' he said, with a little laugh. 'Maybe that's why I came in mufti,'

Eleanor didn't speak, because she couldn't.

'Are you angry with me?' he asked, after a moment.

She shook her head. There were so many things she wanted to say. About the months and months of willing someone to live, but waiting for him to die. About the relief when the end finally came, and the resultant guilt at that relief. About being locked into a kind of limbo, neither married nor widowed, with a baby to bring up. A limbo where you shrivel up inside. About how it simply wouldn't do for the person who broke through that terrible barrier to be him, of all the men it might have been. Her tongue couldn't find the words. Any words. But she reached for him, and

194

it found a different kind of eloquence until the doorbell made them spring apart.

'Tessa,' Eleanor said.

He nodded. 'I think I have mended your boiler,' he said. 'It wasn't just a ploy.'

Eleanor stepped back to let him pass. 'We're not going any further with this, are we?' she asked.

George shook his head. 'I don't think we're cut out for it,' he said, as they went along the corridor to the sitting room. He put on his jacket. 'I love my wife,' he said, but it merely undermined the effect of his previous statement.

She handed him his coat.

'But I don't want to pretend that it never happened,' he said quickly. 'I'm not sure what I want.'

'You mean we should keep it in reserve?' Eleanor asked, smiling.

'Perhaps I do.'

Eleanor went to the door. 'What time's the carol service?' she asked, as Mrs Brewster came in with Tessa, who immediately turned shy.

'Here we are,' said Mrs Brewster.

'Three,' George said.

'Did you have a lovely time?' Eleanor asked Tessa. 'Stay and have a cup of tea, won't you, Mrs Brewster?' She turned back to George. 'Three?' she said. 'I'll get there for about half past two, then. All right?'

'Lovely.' He ruffled Tessa's hair, and passed the time of day with Mrs Brewster. 'Thank you again, Mrs Langton,' he said, as he left.

And beyond the door, where the others couldn't see him, he smiled at her again. And *winked*.

Eleanor turned back to Mrs Brewster. 'You couldn't possibly keep your eye on Tessa for another ten minutes, could you?' she asked. 'I have to make a phone-call.'

Marian stared coldly at the young man on her doorstep.

'I just want to talk to her,' he said. 'She is my wife.'

'I'm aware of that.'

'We can't go on like this for ever,' he said.

'She isn't here, Graham. Not at the moment.'

Graham Elstow looked every inch the successful young accountant that he was. He dropped his eyes. 'I've got to see her,' he mumbled.

There were steps up to the vicarage door; Graham had retreated after ringing the bell, and for once Marian had the luxury of looking down at someone. The parting in his well-cut fair hair was neat and straight, like a schoolboy's. Behind him, beyond the porch, the weather grew wilder, and Marian began to be a little worried about Joanna, who had gone into Stansfield to do her Christmas shopping at the last minute, as usual.

'When will she be back?' Graham was asking.

'I've no idea.' Marian scanned the whiteness, hoping that she wouldn't see Joanna's car, hoping that she would. It was a perilous world.

'Can I come in and wait?'

'No, Graham,' she said. 'You can't.'

He looked surprised. He actually looked surprised.

'I've got to talk to her,' he said again.

'Then I suggest you come back when she's here.'

'But—' He turned and waved a helpless hand at the blizzard.

'I can't help that. I don't want you here. I'm sorry.'

He dropped his eyes again. 'I can understand that,' he said.

Then go away, Marian thought. Go away and leave Joanna alone.

'I'll never forgive myself.'

Marian didn't speak. All she could do was pray that Joanna wouldn't forgive him. Not this time. Surely not this time.

'Is it all right if I come back after lunch?' he asked, half turning to go. 'If I get something at the pub, and come back? Will she be back then?'

Marian wouldn't answer, and he walked through the snow back to his car. She watched until it had driven away before she closed the door, her legs weak, her hands shaking. For a moment, she stood with her hand on the door-handle, gathering herself together.

It was about half an hour later that Joanna appeared, pink-cheeked and bright-eyed. 'It took me over an hour just to drive from Stansfield,' she said, depositing bags round the kitchen, where warmth could be ensured in the draughty old house. She unwound her scarf, pulling a face at the wet folds of wool. 'I'd better hang this up,' she said. 'It'll drip everywhere – that was just coming from the *car*.'

'Graham was here,' Marian said baldly. There wasn't any way to dress it up.

Joanna's smile vanished. 'When?'

'A little while ago. He says he's coming back.' She watched as Joanna sat down at the table, her fair hair bedraggled, her hands tight around the scarf. 'He says he wants to talk,' she carried on, sitting beside her. 'You don't have to see him, Jo.'

'I do,' she said.

'Not yet. Not today.' Marian took the wet scarf from her, and hung it over a chair. 'You can see him when *you're* ready.' She held Joanna's hand in hers.

'Now's as good a time as any,' Joanna said, as the front door banged. Her grey eyes looked apprehensively into Marian's.

'We're going to get snowed in,' George said, as he came in, rubbing his hands and walking to the fire. He stood with his back to it, and looked at them, frowning slightly. 'What's up?' he said.

Joanna let go of Marian's hand, and left the room.

'What's wrong?' George said again.

Marian told him. He exploded, as she had expected.

'Coming back, is he?' he said, angrily rebuttoning his coat. 'That's what he thinks. The pub, you said?'

'George,' Marian said wearily. 'Joanna wouldn't thank you.'

'I'm not looking for thanks! I won't have that little rat in my house – not today, not ever.'

'He's her husband.'

'Marian – he'll talk her round again. She'll go back with him.'

Marian rubbed her eyes. 'She's got more sense,' she said.

'She didn't have more sense the other times!'

'She hadn't left him.'

'She forgave him, though.'

'But she hadn't left him,' Marian repeated. 'It's been two months. She won't go back to him. She hasn't even said she'll see him.' She stood up. 'Now,' she said briskly. 'Lunch is ready. Give Jo a call.'

George stared at her. 'How can you behave as though it wasn't happening?'

Because it was the only way she could deal with it. George could fly into rages, could go marching off to the pub, and make a scene. But Marian had to think about problems, and work out a strategy for dealing with them.

'You still have to eat,' she said stubbornly. 'He isn't here now, so there's nothing we can do.'

'There's something I can do!'

'But you're not going to,' Marian said, deliberately barring his way. 'Take off your coat, and tell Joanna her lunch is ready.' She looked up at him, aware suddenly of their relative strength; aware that the only reason she could actually stop him leaving was because George, like most men, operated a voluntary hand-icapping system.

He reluctantly unbuttoned his coat again, and threw it over the chair with Joanna's scarf.

They ate lunch in near silence, until George gave up his brief attempt at minding his own business. Minding other people's was his job when all was said and done, Marian supposed.

'Well?' he said belligerently, looking up at Joanna.

'I've got to talk to him,' she answered.

George stabbed a piece of potato, 'I don't want him here,' he said.

Joanna laid down her knife and fork. 'There's nowhere else,' she said, reasonably enough, in Marian's opinion.

'You don't have to see him at all.'

'I do, Daddy! He's right. We have to talk. If it can't be here, then I'll have to go there.'

Marian, her head turning from one to the other, saw the angry colour rise in George's face.

'Well then,' Joanna said, putting away her volley. Advantage.

'If you're seeing him, I'm going to be here.'

'No,' said Joanna. 'Anyway – you've got the carol service.'

'That can be cancelled.'

'No, it can't,' said Joanna. 'And how do you expect me to talk to him with you and Mummy outside the door, listening for—' She broke off. 'Just go to your service. And you go and do your Santa Claus bit,' she said to Marian. 'I'd much rather be alone when he comes back. He finds it difficult here anyway.'

'He finds it—' George began, his face purple.

'It's my problem, Daddy. I'll deal with it.' Game. Joanna pushed her plate away. 'Thank you,' she said, getting up. The handshake at the net. 'I know you want to help. But I'm just going to talk to him, that's all.' And she left.

George looked at Marian. 'Are you still going out?' he asked.

'I have to, George. And I think I should. I don't want her to feel she's got an audience – it would only make it more difficult for her.'

George sighed, and finished his lunch. Marian was sure he had no idea what he was eating. 'I'd better get changed,' he said.

'Where's your tie?' asked Marian, suddenly realising that it was his open-necked casualness that was making George look different.

His hand went to his collar. 'Oh – I took it off,' he said, 'I must have put it down somewhere.' He stood up. 'Maybe I'll have a more Christian attitude to that little toad when I'm dressed for it.'

Marian began to clear away.

'What if she goes back to him?' George asked.

'She won't,' Marian said resolutely, squirting washing-up liquid into the bowl. 'Not this time.'

But she looked anxiously back over her shoulder when she and George left the house, an hour later. Perhaps he won't turn up, she told herself.

And she kept looking at the phone while she was talking to the matron of the children's home, barely following what the woman was saying.

It's none of your business, Marian Wheeler, she told herself severely, as the matron repeated what she had just said, and Marian still wasn't listening. You *can't* phone her. Wait until you get home. She won't go back with him. She *won't*. She's got more sense.

*

'You're just not listening to me, are you, Graham?'

Graham picked up her father's decanter, and waved it at her.

'No. And I don't think you should have any more,' she said.

'Mustn't drink all Daddy's whisky? I'll replace it.'

'You've had enough, Graham. You'd had more than enough when you got here, and that's your third!'

He saluted her with his glass. 'One of the perks of bachelordom,' he said. 'You can get pissed without being nagged.' He dropped his hand, and sat down, his head bowed. 'I'm sorry,' he said. 'I'm sorry. I just wish you'd come home and we could sort it out on our own.' He looked up. 'I can't – I can't get *through* to you here. It's too—' He shrugged. 'Too nice, too Enid Blyton. I'll bet you're back in your old room, as if I'd never happened.'

'Why have you had so much to drink?' she asked. Drinking, despite what he'd just said, was not one of Graham's faults. 'Why?' she asked again.

'No reason,' he muttered.

'Because you were coming here?'

'No!' he shouted. 'Forget it. Look – Jo. Just come back. Don't stay here. Shouldn't your father be telling you that? I mean – isn't he supposed to believe all that about those whom God hath joined together?'

Joanna's eyes widened. 'Graham – you're talking as if I had left you on a whim.'

'I know,' he said, shaking his head. 'I know what I've done. It won't happen again.'

'It will.' She got up and went to the window, watching the snow fall from a darkening sky as the silence enveloped them. It was cold in the sitting room; she had chosen it as the site for negotiations rather than the cosy, homely kitchen, where she might be lulled into a false sense of security.

'Joanna, I swear. I'll never, never do it again.'

His voice was suddenly close to her, and she turned to find him behind her.

'Don't look like that,' he said. 'Please. Please don't be frightened of me.'

'I am frightened of you.' She turned away again.

'But it isn't me,' he said. 'You're not frightened of me.' He put his hand lightly on her shoulder, and she faced him again. 'Something gets into me. Something just snaps.'

'Then you should see someone. Talk to someone.'

'No. I can work it out for myself.'

'Not with me.' She pushed past him, and put as much distance between them as the room would allow.

'It has to be you. You're my wife.'

'And you think that gives you the right?'

'No!' He drained his glass. 'But—' He sighed. 'All right,' he said, 'I will see someone. I promise.' He waited for her response, which was not forthcoming. 'I *promise*!' he shouted.

Promises. As though they had never had this conversation before.

'What do you *want* me to do?' he asked, striding across the room.

Joanna moved away again, as he picked up the decanter.

She closed the curtains on her reflection. 'Why *are* you drinking so much?' she asked again. 'What's wrong?'

'Nothing. No reason.'

'Is it because of me?'

'Nothing to do with you. I met—' He paused. 'I met someone. Nothing – no one. Forget it.'

He wasn't making sense. 'Don't drink any more,' she said.

'Why not? What do you expect? You walk out on me—'

'I didn't exactly *walk* out,' she said sharply.

'Oh God, Jo,' he whispered. 'I'm sorry. I'm so sorry. Tell me what you want me to do, and I'll do it.'

'See someone,' Joanna said. 'Tell them what happens to you.'

He put down the decanter, his face growing a painful red. 'I couldn't,' he said.

'Because you don't want to admit it?' She took a deep breath. 'Well, that's what you're going to have to do,' she said. 'If you do that – if you prove to me that you're trying to get help . . .'

'You'll come back?' he said eagerly.

'You have to do it *first*,' she said.

'I will, I will.' He came towards her. 'Don't walk away from me, Jo,' he said. 'Help me. I'm not sure how—' He waved a hand. 'You know. How to go about—'

'I'll do that. I'll find out who you should see. And I'll go with you. To the doctor, or whatever. We'll get advice.'

'Yes. Good.' He put down his empty glass. 'Thank God,' he said.

Joanna looked at him for a long time. 'It's your last chance, Graham,' she said.

'I know. I know.' He took her hands, 'I know,' he said again, kissing them. He smiled, and kissed her on the cheek. 'Let's go,' he said.

'No, Graham. You've got to make the first move.'

'But you said we'd do it together.'

'We will. But you've promised before, Graham. I'm not going back until I know you're doing something about it. I will help you. I will. But I'm living at home until I'm sure.'

The clock whirred quietly, preparing to chime, as Graham dropped her hands. She knew the faintly puzzled look.

'What did you say?' he asked, and she knew the tone of voice. She knew what came next.

Chapter Two

Eleanor had played at the carol service, catching his eye only to indicate in mime, her back to the congregation, that he had left his tie there.

He had told the children about all the people in the world who didn't have turkey and Christmas pudding, and had smiled gravely at the earnest, concerned faces which had looked back at him. If only that concern could last, he thought, into Cabinet Ministerhood. But it couldn't. By then, delicate international situations would seem much more important than feeding hungry mouths.

He locked away the collection money – he must have convinced some of the adults too, because there was even a fiver in there. He picked up the cash-box, then paused, and opened it again. Another fiver joined the first, and he locked the box again. He'd make sure it went to Save the Children or someone. The church roof could wait. Church roofs didn't cry.

He walked out into the already black night, and looked up at the starless, snow-laden sky. He'd have to get the tie back some time. He wondered about Eleanor's reasons for not bringing it with her. In case someone saw her give it back? Or because she wanted him to have to go back for it? Either way, it was a complication that he could have done without.

He should have worn boots, for the snow was covering his shoes, and he looked round for clear ground, but there was none. Sighing, he turned up his coat collar as a flurry of snow went down the back of his neck. He needn't worry about his sermon for tonight, he thought. He'd be the only one there.

As he rounded the church, the wind hit him. Head bowed, he set off to where the road could still just vaguely be seen, a faint fold in the white blanket. He heard the car as he walked along what he thought was the verge; he moved to the side, but it hooted. He lifted his head to see Marian.

'Lift?' she said, reaching over and opening the passenger door.

George got into the car, and pulled the door shut. 'Oh boy,' he said.

'The Stansfield road's blocked,' said Marian.

'Great.'

Marian drove a little more quickly than he would have done under these circumstances. As the car shimmied round into the vicarage driveway, she slowed down. 'His car's still here,' she said, pulling up outside the house. She looked at him. 'She won't go back to him,' she said. 'She's got more sense.'

'Not where he's concerned.' George got out and ran up the porch steps. As he opened the front door, he heard the bedroom door close upstairs. 'Jo?' he called.

He and Marian exchanged glances.

'They just want some privacy,' Marian said.

'They could be private downstairs,' George said darkly.

Marian stood for a moment, looking anxiously upstairs. Then her eyes went slowly to George's. 'She won't go back to him,' she said defiantly.

George felt that a closing bedroom door was hardly a sign of irretrievable breakdown. But she couldn't, she *mustn't* let herself be persuaded to go back. He felt helpless; all his working life he had helped people in trouble, and all he could do was fight with Joanna, as though it were her fault.

'What can we do?' he asked.

'Not much,' Marian said, with another glance upstairs. 'I think we should carry on as normal.'

'Go out, you mean?' He and Marian always spent a couple of hours in the village pub on Christmas Eve. It had been Marian's idea – she said you were more likely to get people into church if you were manifestly seen to be a person. 'What if he wants to come with us?'

'We'll cross that bridge when we come to it.'

'Will we?' he said dubiously.

'Yes,' she said. 'Let's go and get changed.'

'Upstairs?' The thought embarrassed him. Joanna's bedroom was at the other end of the landing from theirs, but he still felt as if he would be intruding.

'Well, that's where our clothes are,' said Marian. 'George, I am not going to let him spoil things. It's my house, and I'll go wherever I like.'

He changed, keeping his fingers crossed that the tie wouldn't come into the reckoning, and it didn't. She just told him to take what she called his work shirt down with him when he went, because she would be washing.

'On Christmas Eve?' he asked.

'Why not?' she demanded, a little on the defensive.

Marian always found something useful to do when life got complicated. He held up his hands in surrender. 'Just asking,' he said.

'What do you think?' she asked, holding up a dress he hadn't seen before.

'When did you get that?' he asked.

'It's your Christmas present to me.'

'I've got very good taste,' he said. 'It's lovely.'

'Joanna found it. She said you'd approve.'

George sat down to put on his shoes. 'Why should you need my approval?' he asked.

'What?' Marian came over to him. 'You're still in a funny mood, aren't you?' she said, her arm round his shoulders. 'What is it?' she asked, kissing the top of his head. 'Joanna?'

He patted the hand that rested on his shoulder. 'Partly.'

'And partly what else?'

He looked up at her. She believed in him. She believed he was what he said he was. And she didn't think for a moment that he visited Eleanor Langton because she had good legs and long blonde hair.

'Male menopause,' he said, as she sat beside him, her head touching his. He put his arm round her. 'I wanted to make love to you this morning,' he said.

'Why didn't you wake me?'

'You were awake,' he said. 'But I thought it might embarrass Jeremy.'

She laughed.

'Is this place important to you?' he asked.

Marian frowned slightly. 'The house?' she said. 'Or the village?'

'Either. Both.'

'On a scale of one to ten,' she said, 'I'd give it seven, I think.' She looked concerned. 'Are they trying to make you move to Brixton?' she asked.

He laughed. 'No. Nothing like that.'

Living here was important to her, he thought, tying his laces. Which just made things more difficult. Marian, you're married to a fraud, but I'm an honourable fraud, so I have to resign. He picked up his shirt, and they went downstairs.

'Someone's left the light on in the sitting room,' he said.

'I think it was Easter when we used it last,' said Marian. 'Let's hope it hasn't been on ever since.'

George saw Joanna when he opened the door. She looked up, her face streaked with tears, her eyes already bruising, her mouth swollen.

'My God,' he said.

'George?' Marian came in behind him, and ran to Joanna.

George watched, his brain numb. Joanna burst into tears again, and Marian took her into the kitchen, where she bathed the bruises, her face pale and set. Joanna was mumbling something, rendered incoherent by the sobs. And he just watched, feeling a creeping coldness in his limbs. Then he remembered the closing bedroom door.

'He's upstairs,' he said, making for the door.

'No!' Joanna shouted suddenly. 'Leave him, please. Leave him. He's drunk. He'll be sleeping it off—'

George was out of the kitchen before she'd finished the sentence, but Marian was behind him, her hand on his arm, as he reached the bottom of the stairs.

'George, do as she says.'

'I told him what would happen if he laid a finger on her again,' he said, starting up the stairs, but with a strength that he hadn't suspected, Marian hung on to him.

'It wouldn't do any good,' she said.

'It would do *me* some good!'

'It would get you into trouble! You'd upset Joanna – and what for? It wouldn't undo anything, would it?' Her face, still grimly sensible, looked up into his. 'Come back, George,' she said. 'Let him sleep it off.'

'In my house? He's leaving. Now.'

'He can't,' Joanna said, appearing in the hall.

George looked at her, bruised and battered, and felt tears of rage prick his eyes. She'd even got dressed up for him.

'He can't drive anywhere,' Joanna said. 'He took your whisky up with him. He's had far too much to drink.'

'I'll put him in a taxi when I've finished with him,' George roared, but he still couldn't make any progress on the stair, with Marian clinging to his arm.

'The road's blocked,' Marian reminded him. 'He can't get back to Stansfield anyway.'

'I don't care where he goes, as long as he leaves my house!' George shook Marian off at last.

'Please *leave* him!' Joanna cried, and there was real fear in her voice.

He stopped, and turned, but Joanna had gone back into the kitchen. He sat down heavily on the stairs.

'What's the point in causing more trouble?' Marian asked, joining him. 'If you hit him, that's all you'll be doing.'

'Here,' he said, pushing his laundry into her hands. 'You wear it.'

'George—'

'I mean it. I'm not fit for it. Not if you're meant to turn the other cheek. Not if you're meant to love someone like him.'

'I'm not being particularly Christian,' Marian said. 'Just sensible. Joanna's had enough – she doesn't need you and Graham brawling into the bargain. She needs us to be with her.' She stood up, and held out her hand.

George looked up at her, and took her hand, heaving himself off the step. 'He's loving all this, isn't he?' he said, with a malevolent look at the closed bedroom door.

'Talk to him when you've calmed down and he's sobered up,' Marian said, leading him downstairs. She stopped at the bottom. 'I'd better make up the bed in the back bedroom,' she said. 'For Joanna.'

'Of all the—' George spluttered. 'If anyone had told me that I'd be offering hospitality to—'

'And I think you should take Joanna out,' she said firmly.

'What?'

'If he gets up, I don't want Joanna here. Or you, come to that,' she added.

'She won't come,' he said.

'Yes, she will – you can persuade her. You know you can.' She patted him. 'Go on. Go and talk to her.'

George sighed, and went into the kitchen, where Joanna was sitting by the fire, ineffectually raking the coals.

'Your mother thinks you should come out for a drink with me,' he said.

She shook her head. 'Like this?' she said.

'Well, that's what I thought.' He pulled a chair from the table and sat down beside her. 'But unless you're thinking of keeping yourself prisoner, you'll have to go out sooner or later.'

'Later,' she said.

'And then they'll see you in ones and twos,' he said. 'Why not come out with me and let them all see you at once?'

She smiled, still tearfully.

'I'll go along with whatever you want to tell them,' he said. 'Will you come?'

She didn't reply.

'It'll look worse tomorrow,' he said, in a matter-of-fact way that was entirely manufactured. He wanted to break down and cry. He wanted to go and ram Elstow's own medicine down his throat. He wanted to run naked through the snow and get into the *News of the World*.

'Is this so as you can talk to me?' she asked.

'I rather hoped you might talk to me,' he said. 'But I don't care if you talk or not.'

'Do you really want me to come?'

He nodded.

'All right,' she said. 'I might be telling a lot of lies,' she warned him.

'Fine,' he said. 'I've been telling a lot of lies for years.'

'What do you mean?'

'Oh – I'll tell you some time.' He smiled. 'When you're older.'

Marian watched Joanna's car move off slowly down the driveway. Perhaps spending the evening together would bring them closer; they had grown apart recently.

She glanced at the bedroom door as she got the bedding for Joanna, then walked quickly downstairs to the back bedroom, frowning in concentration. Had they had this chimney swept? They had had discussions about whether or not to include it, since the room wasn't really used now. Yes, she remembered. She had sensibly decided to get it done, just in case.

Just in case they had to accommodate her daughter's vicious husband.

Eighteen months, Marian thought, as she quickly and efficiently spread the sheets on the bed. Married eighteen months, and already an old hand at being knocked about. It wasn't too bad this time, she had said. Not compared to last time. Marian shook her head, and smoothed out the blanket. Perhaps you got grateful when he only blacked your eyes.

She sat on the bed, remembering the first eighteen months of her own marriage. Discovering George, realising that she wasn't obliged to be his right arm, and finding that she wanted to be, anyway. They hadn't had many rows – they'd been lucky. She'd become aware of his temper, of course, but it was usually aroused by something beyond their domestic boundaries.

The first time he'd actually been angry with her was when they'd been married about six months. She remembered the occasion; where they were when the row blew up. They were in the garden shed, of all the unlikely places for her to find herself. It was something to do with the garden – she had interfered with one of his precious plants, or something. He told her she'd killed it. He was furious. She tried to imagine how she would have felt if he'd attacked her physically, but she couldn't. She couldn't begin to imagine being frightened of George.

She finished making the bed, and set about the fire-building process with rather less efficiency. Twenty-six years of coping with the vicarage fires had done nothing to make her any more expert, but she thought that if it was lit now, it would be just right when she got back.

As Marian scrubbed the coal-dust from her hands, she could hear again what Joanna had said while she was bathing her eyes. Quietly; so quietly that George, still shocked, hadn't even heard her.

But Marian had.

Joanna was getting used to the stares; she had told those who'd asked that she had been to the dentist. She had once seen someone come back from the dentist with black eyes. The swollen mouth added to the effect, but even so, there were one or two polite but old-fashioned looks.

They were in a corner, where they could speak without being overheard. She looked at her father, whose face was still dark with brooding anger.

'He needs help,' she said.

He sipped his beer. 'He needs something.'

'He's going to see someone.'

'Not before time.'

'I'm going back with him,' she said carefully. She paused. 'We're going to get help.'

Her father stared at her, slowly putting down his mug. 'You're not serious,' he said.

She knew what she was doing to him, but she had to go through with it. 'It isn't his fault,' she said.

'I don't *care* whose fault it is,' he whispered fiercely. 'I don't care, Joanna. It's you I care about!'

'He doesn't—' She stopped as the barmaid came along, picking up empty glasses.

'You've been in the wars,' said the barmaid cheerfully.

Joanna smiled weakly.

'Dentist, Bill said. Eye-tooth, was it? I know they can do that to you.' She laughed. 'Your husband must be getting some funny looks,' she said, and went off to pass a few cheery words with someone else.

'He doesn't know what he's doing,' Joanna carried on.

'He knows well enough to stop doing it when he hears someone coming,' her father said. He leant closer. 'What would have happened if we hadn't come back, Jo? It would have been like last time, wouldn't it? Maybe even worse.'

Joanna stared into her barely touched cider.

'He's *dangerous*, Jo. You must see that. You can't go back to him! It's—'

'He doesn't understand you,' she said, interrupting him.

George drank some beer. 'I should hate to think that he did,' he said coldly.

'He doesn't understand why you're so against us trying to work it out,' she said. She was hurting her father more than she'd ever hurt anyone, and she loved him. 'He thinks you should be stronger on letting no man put asunder,' she said.

'I think he should be stronger on cherishing,' said her father.

'But you're supposed to believe in all that,' she persisted. 'If I was a stranger, you'd be helping me. You'd be helping Graham.'

He looked shocked; she wished she hadn't said it. But it was true.

'Do you love him?' he asked suddenly.

Joanna looked away. 'He isn't like that all the time,' she said.

'Do you love him?' he repeated.

'I did! When I married him.'

'And do you still?'

Joanna looked round the little pub, full of people in various stages of Christmas cheer. 'I don't know,' she said. 'It's hard to separate one thing from the other. It's not his fault. Yes. Yes, I do.'

'But you didn't make any attempt to get in touch with him, did you? Why not?'

Joanna's eyes were throbbing. She sipped her cider.

'Why not, Joanna?' he asked again.

'I was afraid,' she said. 'I shouldn't have left. It's only made things worse.'

'How can you love someone you're afraid of?' he asked.

Joanna looked over her glass. 'You should know,' she said. 'Aren't you supposed to fear God and love him at the same time?'

Her father sat back. 'I can't help you, Jo,' he said. 'I don't know how, because I don't understand. All I can do is tell you how to fight back. Don't drop your guard – learn how to punch. Learn how to put your weight behind a blow, how to duck and weave—'

'Stop it.' She had never heard him so bitter about anything. 'We're just making one another unhappy,' she said. 'This wasn't a good idea.'

'No,' he said. 'Perhaps it wasn't.' He finished his half pint. 'How can you talk about going back to him when he's just done that to you?' he asked.

'I've got reasons,' Joanna said. One reason. One that she wasn't going to share with anyone.

Eleanor was attempting to assemble the first toy. Didn't people used to buy toys already made? She stared at the instructions for the pedal car. What on earth was a . . . ? She screwed her eyes up to read the small, smudged print, but she still didn't know what it was, never mind which one of the parts at her disposal it was likely to be.

She had finally located the thread of a plastic bolt when the doorbell rang, and the nut slipped backwards and off. Eleanor glared at the door. Trust someone to come just when it seemed she had got the hang of something. She flicked the curtain back, and smiled. George's car – he must have come for his tie. He'd know how to get the car together.

What was it he wanted from her, she wondered. Was this the harmless flirtation that one read about in problem pages? She picked up the tie and, on an impulse, draped it round her neck. Maybe she could get her own back.

She opened the door, and froze.

'Good evening,' said Marian Wheeler.

She couldn't take it off; she'd notice. 'Oh, hello,' she replied, certain that her face had betrayed her if the tie hadn't.

'I'm calling to confirm George's invitation,' she said. 'You'd be very welcome.'

'Thank you,' Eleanor said, still transfixed.

'Please don't hesitate to come over,' Marian went on. 'Any time. Don't worry if there's no one in when you get there – the door won't be locked. Just make yourself at home.'

'Thank you,' Eleanor said again, as her wits slowly returned.

Ask her to come in, she told herself. You'll have to – she's just invited you for Christmas. 'Would you like to come in?' she asked, but it really didn't sound convincing.

'No, thank you – I've got some other calls to make.'

'Well – thank you for coming.'

'Not at all. Oh – and if you did want to contact anyone tonight . . .' She paused, just for an instant. 'Your mother-in-law, is it, that you're expecting? I'll be pleased to pass on a message – I know you can't leave your little girl.'

Had she seen the tie? Was that why she stopped speaking for a moment? Oh, God, had she? 'It's very kind of you,' Eleanor said. 'But I – no. No, thank you.'

'You're welcome. And do bring Tessa over to see us some time over Christmas anyway. It's a long time since there was a little girl at the vicarage.' She turned to go. 'A long time,' she said again.

Lloyd drained his glass and set it down on the bar.

'Another?'

'No, thanks, Jack.' He looked at his watch. 'I think I'll get off now,' he said. 'Get an early night.'

'It's only ten o'clock,' Jack said. 'I thought you never went to bed the same day you got up?'

Lloyd slid off the stool.

'Got a date, have you?' said Jack.

Lloyd looked at him quickly. Jack had his Dutch uncle voice on. 'I just don't want to miss Santa,' he assured him.

'Judy rang in,' Jack went on. 'She said to say she's sorry she missed you, and happy Christmas.'

That was something, Lloyd supposed. 'I hope she's having fun with her in-laws,' he said.

'In-laws are obligatory at Christmas,' Jack said, and finished his pint. 'You're right,' he said. 'Shouldn't stay out too long on Christmas Eve. I'll go home and surprise the wife. Any chance of a lift?'

'Sure.' Lloyd smiled. Jack Woodford was the most complete family man he had ever met, but he liked to give the impression that he wasn't. Lloyd had been a family man too, once. Before the rows, which weren't so bad because you could always kiss and make up. Before the long silences, which were awful, because the air never cleared, and it got hard to breathe. Before the complaints about the hours he worked, and the accusations of neglect. Now, Barbara seemed almost like a stranger. Perhaps she always had been.

'Trouble with this job,' Lloyd said, holding the door open, 'is that you know your colleagues better than your family sometimes.'

'Or they know you better,' Jack said, as they went out into the dark, slushy car park. 'I mean, there's things you can't talk about to your family – not even your wife. Things they wouldn't thank you for talking about.'

'Things they wouldn't understand if you did,' Lloyd said, unlocking the passenger door. Little things. Minor irritations, minor triumphs, shared with people to whom they did not have to be explained.

'Yeah,' said Jack, mind-reading, as he often did. 'Like that bloody book.'

Lloyd laughed. The Super's ideas of efficiency weren't meeting with general approval. The book was instituted so that the desk sergeant could see at a glance . . . Lloyd couldn't quite remember what. 'Like that bloody book,' he agreed.

'Still,' Jack said, arranging his legs more comfortably. 'You've got all that sorted out, haven't you?'

'The book?' asked Lloyd, puzzled.

'The problem.'

Oh. Lloyd didn't answer, as he negotiated the slippery carpark entrance. Snow began to fall again, and he sighed.

'You and Judy Hill,' Jack said, not one to beat about the bush for ever, if the birds didn't rise. Stick the gun in and shoot them there.

'I thought I was overdue for a lecture,' said Lloyd.

'I'm not lecturing you – just pointing out that it's not very clever.'

'Yes, thank you, Sergeant.' He leant slightly on the rank.

'Don't try that with me,' Jack warned. 'There are promotions in the wind – Barton's getting a shake-up in the new year.'

Jack was ten years older than Lloyd, but he behaved as if he were old enough to be his father. It was Jack, a sergeant at twenty-seven, who had interested Lloyd in making the police his career. Jack himself had never tried to get further than sergeant, having found his niche.

Lloyd switched on the windscreen wipers. 'I'm not all that ambitious, Jack,' he said.

'And Judy? Is she not ambitious either?'

Lloyd had never really thought about it.

'Look, Lloyd. I don't know how serious it is – I'm just saying watch your step, that's all. You've all but got your promotion – they'll come down on her harder than they will on you.'

'It's not against the bloody law!' It wasn't even happening at the moment. He'd barely even seen Judy out of working hours since Michael became desk-bound.

'If her husband took it into his head to complain . . .' Jack said, leaving the sentence unfinished.

'So what?' said Lloyd. 'What do you think they'd do, Jack? Break her on the wheel? She'd get shifted to another station, that's all.'

'As sergeant. No promotion – and it's hard enough for women to make inspector without having the reputation of—'

The car swerved slightly as Lloyd took his eyes off the road. 'She has *not* got a reputation!' he shouted.

'Sorry, sorry. I didn't mean it like that. It would be a black mark, that's all. One that a woman can't afford in this job.'

'When did you get Women's Lib?' Lloyd muttered, running the window down to check for traffic.

'She's a nice girl – and she's good. I'd like to see her get on.'

Lloyd pulled up outside Jack's house, and Jack undid his seat-belt, but he didn't get out. He turned to Lloyd. 'If it's just a fling, she's risking more than you. That's all I'm saying.'

Lloyd sighed. 'It's not really like that,' he said. 'Judy and I go way back. To before she was married.'

Jack raised his eyebrows, 'I didn't know that,' he said.

'No. You don't know everything, O Wise Grey-haired One.'

'Sorry. None of my business,' he said, as he got out.

'No. But I'll pass your message on.'

'Right.' Jack leant back into the car. 'Come whenever you like tomorrow,' he said. 'Lunch will be at about two-thirty.'

'Smashing. Thanks, Jack – oh, and . . .' He smiled. 'Thanks for the warning.'

It was after eleven by the time he got to the flat, and well past midnight by the time he had the little tree under control. He picked the pine-needles from his sweater, and strung the lights through the branches. Then he solemnly brought the little present from the bedroom, and took out the white nylon ribbon. With considerable lack of skill, he finally persuaded it into a bow, and snipped the ends until it looked more or less even. He swept the pieces of ribbon into the big empty ashtray that only Judy ever used, and switched on the tree lights.

Standing back to admire his handiwork, he wondered if Judy wanted to be a DI in Barton.

Michael's mouth brushed her neck, beginning its comfortably predictable quest, and Judy turned towards him, responding to the familiar overtures almost without conscious thought. She frowned, puzzled, as he drew away from her.

'What's the point?' he said.

'Michael?'

'It's no good.'

'How do you know? We haven't done anything yet.'

He swung his legs out of bed, and sat with his back to her. 'Would you have noticed if we had?' he asked.

'Michael! That's not fair.'

'No?' His shoulders hunched slightly. 'It's all so—' he began, and abandoned it. 'You were on automatic bloody pilot,' he said.

The protest died on her lips as she acknowledged the truth of his complaint. 'Sorry,' she said, touching his shoulder. He didn't respond, and she took her hand away. 'Come on, Michael,' she said. 'What do you expect? We've been married too long for—'

'For what? A simulation of some interest in the proceedings?'

'I wish you'd get back into bed,' Judy complained. 'It's freezing.'

'I don't expect passion,' he went on.

'We were hardly at the passionate stage, were we?' Judy said.

'We never have been,' he said, turning to look at her. 'But there used to be some enthusiasm. Not now.' He looked at her for a moment. 'Now, it's a way of passing the time. Like doing a crossword, but without the emotional involvement.'

'Are you saying that's just me?' she asked hotly.

'Keep your voice down,' he said urgently. 'They're just across the landing!'

'I will not keep my voice down! Our marriage may not be anything to write home about – but lack of emotional involvement is your speciality, not mine!'

He looked away again. 'I'm sorry if I bore you,' he said.

Judy frowned. 'You don't bore me,' she said. 'Are you bored? Is that what it is?' She sat up, and smiled. 'Is it unnatural practices time?' she asked.

'Don't be silly.'

She lay back on the pillow. 'What's all this leading up to, Michael?' she asked.

Did he know about her and Lloyd? She was surprised to find a cold pool of dread beginning to form. Not guilt, she noted dispassionately. Just panic at being found out before she was ready. But it couldn't be that. Michael must have decided long ago to push any suspicions about her and Lloyd to the back of his mind, and leave them there. So why would it bother him now, when she wasn't even seeing Lloyd?

'*Do* you want to do something?' she asked. 'Tell me. The worst I can do is say no.'

'There is something I'd like us to do,' he muttered, only just loudly enough for her to hear. He looked over his shoulder at her.

Judy waited, ready for anything.

'I'd like us to have a baby.'

Almost anything. She felt as though the world had stopped, as she stared back at him, at the eyes no longer bleak now that he had unburdened himself.

'It's not such an unnatural practice,' he said.

A baby had no place in Judy's scheme of things, if she had a scheme of things. Life was complicated enough without that. 'Why?' was all she could ask, when she found her voice.

'Why not?'

Why not? My God, she could give him a dozen reasons.

'You like babies, don't you?' he asked, the words incongruous coming from him, from Michael, from room-at-the-top Michael.

'I have a marginally higher opinion of them than Herod,' she said.

'Oh, for—' He flopped on to his back. 'You agreed we'd talk about it one day,' he said.

'Did I?' She couldn't imagine under what circumstances. 'So, we're talking about it.' Now, she really was on automatic pilot. Suitable words were filling up the spaces, while her mind raced through the impossibility of it all.

'I'm talking about it,' Michael said. 'You're doing one-liners.'

'When did I?' she asked, suddenly galvanised into life. 'You've never shown the slightest interest in starting a family.' Her eyes widened as she realised. 'It's your mother, isn't it?' she said angrily. 'It's your mother who wants us to have a baby!'

'Not so loud,' he said again. 'Yes, all right, she's mentioned it. She wants a grandchild – that's not unnatural either.'

'Well, tell her I'm sorry, but it just isn't convenient.'

'We can't wait for ever.'

'What's this *wait*? I'm not waiting for anything.'

Michael sat up. 'But this is when we should start a family,' he said. 'I'm not flying half-way round the world any more. We've got this house. It's time we put down roots.'

Judy's mouth fell open. 'You and me?' she said. '*Roots?*'

'Why not you and me?'

'Because we live separate lives,' she said.

'But we've been apart,' Michael argued. 'We're not apart now.' He lay back. 'People expect someone in my position to be a family man,' he said.

'I thought I'd heard it all, Michael,' Judy said wearily.

'Will you think about it?'

She shook her head.

'But that's what marriage is for,' he protested.

'Not our marriage.'

'What's *wrong* with our marriage? We've stayed together ten years,' Michael persisted.

Judy sat back. 'We've stayed together,' she said, 'because it's convenient. You married me because I had a career of my own, and I wouldn't be hanging on to your coat-tails. Because I wouldn't complain about your being away half the year, and I wouldn't ask too many questions when you got back. Because being married was a desirable plus on your CV – like children, presumably. That's why you married me.'

He didn't deny it. 'Why did you marry me, Judy?' he asked.

Because she couldn't have Lloyd. 'For all the wrong reasons,' she said.

The bedside phone rang, making them both jump.

'Half past one,' Michael said. 'I expect it's for you.'

Judy picked it up.

'Judy?' Lloyd said. 'Sorry, but you're needed; we've got a murder.'

Chapter Three

Lloyd waved back as Judy appeared at the window. A few moments later she came down the path, stopping at her own car and taking something out. Then she joined him, bringing with her a blast of freezing air.

'Happy Christmas,' he said.

'Very funny.'

'I wasn't being funny.'

She looked apologetic. 'Happy Christmas,' she responded belatedly, handing him a heavy, rectangular parcel. 'I was going to come in this morning,' she said. 'But I couldn't.'

He smiled, and put it on the back seat. 'Yours is at home,' he said, as the car bumped oversnow already freezing now that the wind had dropped.

'Where are we going?' Judy asked, her voice flat and uninterested.

'Byford village.'

'I thought the road was still blocked,' she said.

He smiled. 'We've got our own personal snow-plough.' Judy didn't seem as impressed as he had been.

'Are we going to be first there?' she asked, with a sigh in her voice.

'No,' he said. 'There's a village bobby these days. I expect he's coping.' He glanced at her, but it was too dark to see. 'What's up?' he asked.

'What sort of murder is it?' she asked, ignoring him.

'Domestic.'

She groaned.

'They have their advantages,' he pointed out. 'No incident rooms, no house-to-house – no breaking it to the relatives since they were probably all there at the time.' Still no reaction. 'That's why I had to get you,' he said wickedly. 'Domestics need a woman's touch.'

But not even that elicited a response from Judy. There was something wrong. But then, he thought, she had been dragged out at two o'clock on Christmas morning. 'Sorry,' he said.

She hadn't even asked for details, and he had been looking forward to imparting them.

'One man dead,' he said. 'That's all I know. But you'll never guess where it happened.'

No response. Not even irritation. He soldiered on. 'The vicarage, would you believe? Our very own *Murder at the Vicarage*.'

'Sorry?'

'*Murder at the Vic*—' He sighed. 'Of course, you're not an Agatha Christie fan, are you?'

'No.'

'Vicarages, snow-bound villages,' he said, with a grin. 'With any luck we'll find a retired Indian Army colonel, a gigolo, a faintly sinister Austrian professor, and an old lady who'll sort it all out for us.'

'Mm.'

'Are you listening to anything I'm saying?'

'I didn't think you were saying anything important,' she said, then immediately repented. 'I'm sorry,' she said. 'Don't take any notice of me.'

Ahead, Lloyd could see the yellow flashes from the snow-plough. 'We'd better let him get further away,' he said, pulling the car up. He waited to see if she would talk to him, but she didn't.

'Someone is head-hunting you, if my little bird's got it right,' he said.

She turned to look at him, at least. 'What do you mean?'

'Moves afoot in Barton. Coming up in the new year, I'm told. But – there's a but.'

'But what?'

'But your relationship with me could rock the boat.'

'Why?' she asked. 'What's it got to do with anyone else? We wouldn't even be working together any more.'

'It shouldn't matter,' he said. 'Unless Michael complains about me.' Despite his dismissal of the consequences, Lloyd knew that Jack was right.

'Michael doesn't know,' she said.

'Can you be sure?' Lloyd asked.

'Yes,' she said. 'If he did, he'd have packed his bags by now.' She gave a sigh. 'Or mine,' she added.

'Suppose he finds out?'

'Michael won't complain,' she said. 'That would be regarded as making an exhibition of himself. Michael doesn't do that.'

'So you'll go after it?'

'Let's wait until it's officially there to be gone after, shall we?' she said.

The yellow light had slowly moved over Lloyd's horizon, and he set off again, through the moonscape. Following yonder star. He smiled, remembering how he used to long for it to snow at Christmas, and it never did. Christmas used to be fun. '*I can never remember,*' he quoted, '*if it snowed for six days and six nights when I was twelve, or twelve days and twelve nights when I was six.*'

'Dylan Thomas,' she said.

'See?' he said. 'I've taught you something.' Judy's lack of soul was something about which he complained, but which pleased him, really. It gave him something to work on. 'Unless it was a guess,' he added.

'*A Child's Christmas in Wales,*' she said, and he could tell that she was smiling at last.

He wound down the window as they approached the all-conquering snow-plough.

'All clear ahead,' a voice shouted. 'For now. You might not get out again, though.'

'And a merry Christmas to you,' Lloyd shouted back, and his voice sounded dead, in all that high-piled insulation.

A chorus of unsuspected voices called season's greetings. Judy behaved as though they weren't there. Lloyd frowned. No point in asking what was wrong, not while she was in this mood.

A lone police car sat outside the vicarage, and a young constable approached as they got out of the car.

'Chief Inspector Lloyd?'

'Yes – this is Sergeant Hill,' he said, waving a hand at Judy.

The constable nodded. 'Parks, sir,' he said. He stamped his feet.

Lloyd smiled. 'Parky by name . . .?' he said.

The constable smiled, and Lloyd was truly grateful to him, after the hard time Judy was giving him. 'So,' he said. 'What's gone on here, then?'

Constable Parks led them up on to the porch steps, where he seemed to regard it as warmer. 'The dead man's called Graham Elstow,' he said. 'He's been battered to death with a poker.'

Lloyd groaned, and exchanged glances with Judy, who looked a little apprehensive.

'It's not too bad,' said Parks, sympathetically. 'There are three other people in the house. George Wheeler – he's the vicar, sir. His wife Marian, and daughter Joanna – that's Elstow's wife. She identified the body, sir.' He rubbed cold hands together. 'They reckon it happened while they were out, and Elstow was in the house on his own.'

'But you don't?' Lloyd asked, hearing the disparagement.

'The daughter's been beaten quite badly, sir. By her husband, I believe.'

'Wonderful,' said Judy.

'It's not my fault, Sergeant.' His breath streamed out as he turned to her, the vapour caught in the light from the door.

'Right, thanks. Let's go and have a look,' Lloyd said. 'Do you know the family?'

'I've passed the time of day with Mr Wheeler,' he said. 'And I know Mrs Wheeler and the daughter by sight – but I've not been here long.' He pulled the door to, in case he was over-heard. 'The daughter's been staying with them since October,' he said. 'I didn't know she was married until tonight.'

Lloyd nodded, and pushed open the door again.

They trooped into a long, wide, Christmas-decorated hallway, where there was a tree surrounded by presents.

'The body's upstairs in one of the bedrooms,' the constable said. 'The family are in the kitchen, and no one's been in the other rooms since I arrived. They say it must have been an intruder, so I thought you would probably want to check the rest of the house, just in case.'

'Quite right,' Lloyd said. 'Good lad.' As he spoke, another car appeared in the driveway. 'Freddie,' said Lloyd to Judy. 'It's the doctor, constable – show him upstairs, and ID the body. OK?'

'Sir.'

Lloyd briefly introduced himself and Judy to the family, who sat round the kitchen table, rather as though they were at a board meeting. A big, well-built man who looked slightly out of place in a clerical collar. A pretty wife – wearing a trouser suit, which rather surprised Lloyd. He still expected the wives of clergy to wear twinsets and pearls, but it had been about thirty years since he'd had anything to do with that sort of thing. A daughter who was probably pretty when she hadn't been beaten up. No tears, no hysterics. Mr Wheeler stood up to shake hands.

The courtesies completed, Lloyd apologised. 'I'm afraid the snow's caught us all on the hop,' he said. 'We're a bit short-handed here. We'll be back in a few moments, if you'd excuse us.'

'You'd better go and say hello to Freddie,' he said to Judy, once they were out in the hallway. 'Send Parks down, will you?'

So it wasn't straightforward, and he would have to bring forensic in. Lloyd glanced up as Parks came downstairs. 'What's it like up there?' he asked.

'Well,' said the constable, 'I wouldn't want my mum to see it.'

Poor Judy. Lloyd left Parks phoning for back-up, and went back in to the silent group in the kitchen.

'Are you all right, Mrs Elstow?' he asked. 'Do you want a doctor?'

'No,' she said. 'I'm all right, thank you.'

Her face, pale beneath the discoloured skin, belied the polite answer.

'Well,' he said gently. 'Let's start with what happened to you.'

She glanced quickly at her mother, who took a preparatory breath.

'I'd rather hear it from Mrs Elstow herself,' said Lloyd quickly.

'I – that is . . .' the girl began, then stopped. 'Graham – that's my husband – he . . .'

Lloyd sat down at the table. 'You'd left him,' he said, hoping his guess was right.

She nodded.

'And why was he here?' asked Lloyd.

'He came to ask me to go back with him,' she said, dully. 'I wouldn't.'

Lloyd put his chin on his hands and looked at her. 'And that was how he hoped to persuade you?' he said.

Her eyes met his defiantly. 'He got angry,' she said, and it was said in her husband's defence.

Lloyd sat back, and nodded slowly. 'And when was this, Mrs Elstow?'

Again, a glance at her mother, who looked down at her hands.

'This afternoon. Evening. I don't know.' Then she added, in a low voice, 'About five.'

'Mr – Lloyd, is it?' said Wheeler, 'I don't quite see what this has to do with what happened.'

Lloyd raised his eyebrows at him.

'We were all out,' he said. 'Someone must have—'

'So when was he found?' asked Lloyd, talking through him.

'Just before one o'clock,' said Mrs Wheeler. 'I found him. We'd been to the midnight service.'

'Thank you,' said Lloyd. 'Which of you saw him last?'

They all looked at one another; no one looked at him.

'I did,' said Joanna Elstow. 'At five.'

Slowly, painfully, the story emerged. Lloyd didn't ask for detail, or for clarification. He made a mental note of the points that puzzled him, but he didn't ask about them. He just listened. George Wheeler and his daughter had left the house at seven. Mrs Wheeler had gone out at about ten to eight. Wheeler and his daughter had returned first, to find themselves locked out. Mrs Wheeler had let them in when she got home, and they had all left again at eleven for the midnight service.

Lloyd had heard the others arrive during his patient questioning of the family. When Marian Wheeler completed the story with her account of finding Elstow, he thanked them, giving every indication that he accepted their story as gospel. Which was appropriate, he thought, as he stood up. 'Excuse me again, please,' he said, and went upstairs, where Judy was directing the activities of the photographer. The fingerprint lad was whistling quietly, as he carefully stepped over the body; the photographer impassively snapped away, the doctor was making interested noises, and Judy looked green.

'What do you think?' Lloyd said.

'I think I want to go home and let Miss Marple get on with it,' she said.

So she had been listening to his one-sided conversation in the car, he thought. She was just being bloody-minded, which at least was in character. 'You go down and see what you can get,' he said, having given her the bare bones.

Judy escaped, and Lloyd looked round the room. The poker lay on the floor by the body; he peered at it before it was bagged up, then squatted down beside the doctor. 'Well?' he said. 'How long?'

'Under twelve hours. Anything between five and eleven hours. That's very rough – I'll be able to narrow it down.'

Lloyd checked the time. 'Between four-thirty and ten-thirty p.m.?'

'Well – my *guess* is eight to ten hours. The PM will probably confirm that.'

'Could a woman have done it?' Lloyd asked.

'Oh, yes. They're heavy blows, but a woman with a good double-handed backhand could have done it.' He grinned, altering his thin, serious face. 'Judging from that,' he said, nodding at the decanter which was being dusted for prints, 'and the smell, I'd say he made it easy for whoever did it. I'll confirm that at the lab.'

'His wife says he'd had a lot to drink before he got here.'

Freddie nodded. 'I expect so,' he said. 'And he'd been hitting someone.' He smiled broadly again. 'If that's any help.'

'His wife,' said Lloyd.

'Ah. The Case of the Turning Worm?' asked Freddie.

'They were all out when it happened,' said Lloyd, his eyes wide, his hands held out in helpless innocence.

'Of course they were,' said Freddie. 'Can you give me a photograph from this angle, please?' he asked the photographer, indicating what he meant. 'Looks like a woman's prints on the poker.'

The flash made Lloyd blink. 'How long between the attack and death?' he asked.

'Not long. Look.'

Lloyd didn't really. He'd developed a trick of making his eyes blur.

'Not all that much blood.'

'What?' Lloyd looked at the bed.

'Oh, there's a lot splashed about,' Freddie said. 'But he didn't lie bleeding on the floor for long. I'll know better when I've had the chance to make a proper examination. I can do it today, if you want to arrange for someone to be present,' he said. 'Spoil someone's Christmas dinner.'

'It had better be mine,' said Lloyd.

'Pity,' said the doctor. 'I thought I might get a couple of hours in Sergeant Hill's company.'

Lloyd smiled. 'I'm not that cruel,' he said.

'Is it the blood, or me?' asked Freddie.

'Sir!'

Lloyd went to the fireplace, where it was just possible to see the charred remains of clothing.

Freddie bent down to take a closer look. 'Oh, yes,' he said. 'Enough left to identify it, I'm sure.' He straightened up. 'You're home and dry this time, Lloyd.'

Joanna sat at the table, her mother on one side, and Sergeant Hill on the other. Her father was over by the fire.

Sergeant Hill was very attractive, Joanna thought absently. Good clothes.

'Can you tell me why he hit you?' she was asking.

'He came to see if I would go back with him, and I wouldn't,' Joanna said, her voice light. She wasn't going to cry.

'I'm sorry,' the sergeant said. 'I know this must be very difficult for you, and I won't keep you long, I promise. But I do have to know what went on in here tonight.'

'That wasn't tonight,' her father said. 'It was this afternoon. It had nothing to do with what happened tonight.'

The sergeant looked over her shoulder. 'Were you here, Mr Wheeler?' she asked. She was simply requesting information, but Joanna saw her father's colour rise a little.

'No, I was not!'

'George,' said her mother, 'the sergeant has to ask questions.'

'Sorry.'

'Don't worry about me, Mr Wheeler,' Sergeant Hill said. She turned back to Joanna. 'When did it happen?' she asked.

'I told the inspector,' Joanna said. 'Five o'clock.' She could still hear the clock chiming as Graham advanced on her. Her head ached, and she wanted to close the eyes that it was so painful to keep open. She wanted to be alone, to assess her position, to work out what it all meant, how she felt. Graham was gone. And with his going, the ever-present fear had slipped away from her. But that wasn't all she was going to feel. She needed the chance to find out.

'He only stopped because he heard us coming home,' her father said.

'You and Mrs Wheeler?'

'Yes.'

'What time was that?' asked the sergeant.

'Let's see,' said her father, 'I stayed at the church for a while. I must have left at about quarter-past five, I think. Is it important?'

Sergeant Hill smiled apologetically. 'You never really know at this stage in an investigation,' she said.

'There were other people there until just before I left,' he said. 'You could check with them.'

'I picked you up at about twenty past,' said her mother. She turned to Sergeant Hill. 'We came straight here,' she said.

'And is that right, Joanna?' the sergeant asked. 'He stopped because he heard your parents coming in?'

'When he heard their car,' Joanna said miserably. 'He went upstairs.'

The inspector came back in then, and apologised for all the disruption, as if it was his fault.

'I'm afraid we'll be here for some time,' he said. 'There's a great deal of difficulty getting vehicles here. And there's—' He waved a hand. 'A lot to see to,' he said.

He meant that they couldn't get Graham out yet, Joanna thought grimly.

'Especially,' he went on, 'since you say it happened while you were out.'

'Say?'

Joanna flinched, hearing the danger signals in her father's voice.

Inspector Lloyd came over to the table, and leant both hands on it, bending down almost conspiratorially. 'We've had to get the lab boys in,' he said, and Joanna noticed his Welsh accent for the first time. 'To tell us what went on in there.' There was a pause. 'And they can,' he said, straightening up. 'Make no mistake. Everything in that room's got a story to tell.' He looked directly at Joanna when he spoke again. 'So if any of you could save us some time and trouble . . .' He waited.

Joanna looked steadily back at him. He had blue eyes.

'Mrs Elstow?' he said.

'I've told you all I know.'

He stepped back from the table, and went over to stand by the door, as though she might make a break for it.

'Joanna,' Sergeant Hill said. 'You said just now that Graham ran upstairs? Where did you have the fight with him?'

'It wasn't a fight,' Joanna said helplessly. Then again, almost to herself, 'It wasn't a fight.'

'I'm sorry. Where were you when he hit you?'

'The sitting room.'

'Where's that, love?' the inspector asked.

'The last door on the left,' she said.

He opened the kitchen door, and looked down the hall. 'You weren't upstairs with him at any point?' he asked.

'No.'

The sergeant glanced at him, and Joanna saw him give a tiny nod.

'Are you sure, Joanna?' the sergeant asked.

'Of course I'm sure.'

'Did you try to defend yourself?'

Defend herself. Joanna shook her head. 'I just tried to get away,' she said.

'How?'

'I ran to the door, but he slammed it.'

The inspector got up and went out; for some reason that she couldn't fathom, Joanna felt safer with him there.

'Didn't you try to fight back?'

Joanna looked at her, at the clear brown eyes that watched her so closely. 'You *can't* fight back,' she explained, to this woman who had never been in that position. For all Joanna knew, Sergeant Hill regularly waded into pub brawls and mad axe-men. But she had never been knocked off her feet by her own husband.

'You must have been angry, Joanna.'

'Angry?' Joanna repeated, genuinely puzzled.

The sergeant frowned. 'Weren't you?' she asked.

'No. I was frightened,' she said. 'Frightened.'

The sergeant wrote that down. She wrote everything down. It was beginning to irritate Joanna.

'What did you do after he'd gone upstairs?' she asked.

'Nothing.'

'But your parents had come home,' she said. 'Didn't you see them?'

'No. I didn't leave the sitting room. I heard them come in, and then they went upstairs.'

'And you stayed where you were?'

'Yes.'

'For how long?'

Joanna shook her head. 'I don't know,' she said.

'It would be about a quarter of an hour, twenty minutes,' her father supplied. 'We didn't know any of this had happened, and we just went up to change. We thought—' He broke off. 'We thought Joanna was in her room,' he said. 'We didn't want to disturb her.'

The sergeant looked back at Joanna. 'But you were downstairs all the time?' she asked.

'Yes. Until Daddy came in and found me.'

'Why, Joanna?'

'Look – is this really necessary?' her father demanded.

'Why?' asked Sergeant Hill again.

Joanna swallowed.

'Why didn't you come out when your parents came home? Why didn't you tell them what had happened?'

'Because—' Joanna could feel her skin redden, as she tried to explain. 'Because you feel ashamed,' she said.

*

Eleanor quietly placed the pedal-car at the foot of the bed. The pale moonlight lit the room, with assistance from the snow, and for a second, she recalled exactly the moment of waking to find her stocking bulging and lumpy with presents.

Tessa would be awake in a couple of hours, she told herself. It wasn't sensible to stay up half the night worrying about something she couldn't alter.

She cried, as she watched Tessa sleep. If only Tessa had known him; if only he could have seen her. But the tears weren't for Richard. He was beyond tears, and had been from the moment the car hit him. For a while, during the long evening, she had thought that she had been released from the crushing loneliness. George had needed her, and it had been so long since anyone at all had needed her.

Tessa needed her, she reminded herself, as she watched her turn, and sigh contentedly. But that was dependence, and that wasn't the same. A two-year-old takes love where she finds it; she was as happy with her grandmother as she was with Eleanor. But George had needed *her*. Not someone who would feed him and clothe him, and keep him safe. He could do that for himself. He had needed her, and she had helped him. She hadn't been able to help Richard, and that had been the worst part. It had been a long time since she had been able to offer rather than ask for help. It had been a step towards the open door, the light from which now paled the edges of her darkness.

Today had been a turning point. But she shouldn't have done what she did; she knew that even at the time, though she couldn't have stopped herself. She had waited so long. So perhaps the tears were remorse. A brief moment of satisfaction, followed by the reckoning. The tears were for herself.

She tucked the quilt round Tessa's sleeping figure. Perhaps it hadn't been the release she had longed for, but it had been a moment's respite; she deserved that.

And the tears were drying.

They were taking the tumble-dried clothes out of the washing-machine. They had asked politely enough, and George had given his permission with a co-operative readiness that he did not feel.

George watched the two constables who were carefully listing the clothes, then dragged his attention back to the inspector.

'When did you and your daughter get back from the pub?' he asked.

'Just before ten,' said George quickly, not looking at Joanna. 'Joanna was tired, so we left a little earlier than usual.'

'And you came straight home?'

'Yes,' said George. 'But as Joanna said, we were locked out. Surely that's important?' he asked. The inspector hadn't seemed terribly interested. 'It wasn't accidental,' he said. 'We never lock the doors.'

'Never?' the sergeant asked.

'No,' he said. 'There's still no need to lock doors in Byford. Not the vicarage doors, at any rate. We've nothing here worth stealing.'

'But you still think someone came in to steal tonight?' the inspector asked.

'I think we had an intruder,' George said carefully. 'When whoever it was went into Joanna's room, Elstow presumably startled him. And for some reason, he must have locked the doors when he left.'

Joanna buried her face in her hands, and Marian put her arm round her shoulders.

'Whoever it was would have needed a key for the back door,' said the inspector.

'The key's kept in the door,' said George.

'I thought Graham had done it,' Joanna said, not taking her hands from her face, 'I thought he was just—'

'And the front door's a Yale lock,' said the inspector, almost to himself. 'But why would anyone want to lock the doors?'

George wasn't sure if a reply was needed. He shook his head.

'Well,' said Lloyd. 'We'll see what prints we can get. Lucky you had a key, Mrs Wheeler.'

'There's one on the ring with the car-keys,' she said.

'Before you left for the pub,' asked Sergeant Hill, 'did anyone check on Mr Elstow?'

'No,' George said heavily. 'Marian asked me to let him sober up first.'

'After you came back?'

'We thought he'd locked us out. We left him to stew.'

'So from five o'clock, nobody saw Mr Elstow at all?'

'No.'

'Mrs Elstow?' asked Lloyd.

Joanna, her face still buried in her hands, shook her head.

'The front door,' Marian said, 'I pushed the catch up again as we left for the midnight service. I've probably spoiled any fingerprints.'

'What about the back door?' asked the sergeant.

'I unlocked it,' said George. 'It annoyed me – I thought Elstow . . .' He ran his hands over his face. 'It has to have been a burglar,' he said.

'But nothing was taken,' Sergeant Hill said quietly. 'You've got presents under the tree in the hall – why would he go upstairs?'

'I've no idea. Evidently he did.'

'Why would he come in and go straight to the one room that had someone in it?' she asked.

He looked from her to the inspector. 'I don't know,' he said. 'But that's what must have happened.'

'That's it,' said the policewoman who was making out the laundry list. 'Would you sign it, please, Mrs Wheeler?'

Marian signed it, and was given a copy.

'We'll try not to hang on to them too long,' said the inspector. 'But what with Christmas and everything, I can't promise. We really do appreciate your co-operation.'

'We understand,' George said. 'You're welcome to take anything you think will help.'

'I suppose you've got your job to do,' Marian said, and the inspector looked a little uncomfortable.

'Well,' he said. 'It's just that whoever did do it must have changed his clothes. We have to eliminate possibilities as well as investigate them.'

Marian stood up. 'If there's nothing else you want Joanna for,' she said, 'I think it's time she got some sleep.'

'Of course,' said Lloyd.

'I know you're taking these clothes away because you think I did it,' Joanna said.

'We're trying to establish what happened,' Lloyd said. 'That's all.'

George almost believed him. He kissed Joanna, and Marian took her off. He turned back to face Lloyd, his shoulders sagging. 'You do think Joanna killed him,' he said.

'It's a possibility,' said Lloyd. 'Isn't it?'

George got up and filled the kettle. 'I think I'd like a cup of tea,' he said. 'Good old English stand-by. Will you join me? I'm very aware that we are ruining your Christmas.'

The sergeant frowned a little. 'I don't suppose,' she said slowly, 'that your own Christmas has been improved.'

He filled the kettle, and switched it on. 'Sergeant Hill,' he said, turning to face her, 'my Christmas was ruined when that young man came here this afternoon. The fact that he will hopefully soon be leaving my house, albeit feet first, is a source of considerable satisfaction to me.'

Sergeant Hill's eyes widened.

'You think a man of the cloth should be showing more compassion,' he said.

'Or more discretion,' she said, with a smile.

He laughed. Really laughed. He liked this lady with the shrewd brown eyes and quick tongue.

'All I know is that Joanna won't suffer at his hands any more,' he said. 'And quite frankly, 'I don't *care* who killed him. But it wasn't Joanna.'

'You seem very protective of your daughter, Mr Wheeler,' Lloyd said.

'Do I?' he asked. 'No more than any other parent.'

The sergeant wandered over to the window wall, where Marian had begun pinning up the photographs of Joanna when she was three weeks old. George watched her as she perused them.

'My wife had two miscarriages before Joanna was born,' he said. 'We were told she shouldn't have any more children after Joanna.'

'She's very pretty,' said Sergeant Hill.

'But you have to find that out from a photograph,' George said. 'She isn't very pretty tonight.' He stood up, and walked over to where the sergeant stood. 'She's twenty-one years old,' he said, and tapped the wall. 'That's all twenty-one years of her.' He looked at the photographs. 'Two months ago, I had to bring her home from hospital, Sergeant.'

'Hospital?'

'Oh, yes,' said George. 'Cracked ribs. A broken collar-bone. Battered – that's the word, isn't it?'

'Did she bring charges against him?' she asked.

George shook his head. 'I thought you'd understand about battered wives, Sergeant,' he said. 'They're too ashamed – too scared. Too—' He shrugged, and walked away. 'I don't know,' he said. 'Do you have children, Sergeant?'

'No.'

'Inspector?'

'Two,' Lloyd said. 'A boy and a girl.'

'How would *you* feel?' George asked. 'How would you feel, if you found your daughter in the state that mine is in tonight?'

Lloyd's blue eyes looked at him steadily. 'Angry,' he said.

George nodded. 'That's how I feel,' he said.

'And,' Lloyd carried on, 'I'd think he'd deserved all he'd got.'

George sat down heavily.

'And if I came in,' said Lloyd in measured tones, 'and found her laying into him with a poker, I might feel inclined to . . . fix it?' he suggested. 'Fix it so that she didn't get the blame.'

'So might I,' said George. 'So might I. But, fortunately, it wasn't necessary.'

Lloyd didn't believe him, he could see that.

Marian sat with Joanna until she fell asleep, her poor battered face almost peaceful. Upstairs, people still moved about, rattling up and down the stairs, going in and out of the door. Using the telephone. Talking in low voices. Across the hall, they were even in the sitting room. She bent down and kissed Joanna as she had when she was a child, and said a prayer for her. Then she straightened up, and went back to the kitchen.

'Mrs Wheeler,' Inspector Lloyd said, getting to his feet. 'I think I'm in your seat.'

'Oh, no. Please. Sit down again. I'll sit here.' She sat at the table with the sergeant.

'We'll be out of your hair soon, Mrs Wheeler,' she said.

Marian looked across at George, who smiled quietly at her. 'What time is it?' she asked him.

He looked at his watch. 'Twenty-five to five,' he said.

Marian had thought it must be much later. 'Why are they in the sitting room?' she asked the inspector.

He cleared his throat before he spoke. 'Your daughter says that she and her husband were in there when he lost his temper,' he said. 'She was pretty badly knocked about, Mrs Wheeler. The room isn't.'

'I tidied it,' Marian said. 'Before all this. After we found her in there.'

She watched realisation dawn in the inspector's eyes. 'Of course,' he said. 'I didn't think – I must be tired.'

Marian was surprised that she wasn't. She ought to be. But somehow it just felt as if this was happening to someone else. 'Are you accusing Joanna of killing him?' she asked.

'We're not accusing anyone,' said the inspector. 'Not yet.'

'Mrs Wheeler?' the sergeant said. 'No one at all saw Mr Elstow between five o'clock, when he left your daughter, and just before one, when you found him. That's right?'

'Yes,' said Marian, a little worried.

'No one went to check on him, or try to talk to him?'

'No.'

'So what made you go up when you did, Mrs Wheeler?'

She looked at George. It must be agony for him, sitting there, putting up with all these questions, hardly answering back at all. He'd called it pretending to be a vicar, earlier on. He'd been in such a funny mood all day. And that sermon was odd, too. As she watched, George pulled out his handkerchief and mopped his brow. And there, hanging out of his pocket, was his tie.

Marian stared at it, transfixed by it for the second time. Oh, my God. My *God*. He'd said he'd been with Joanna all evening. Oh, my God.

'Mrs Wheeler?'

She blinked at the sergeant. 'Sorry?' she said.

'What made you go up to him when you did?'

'Joanna,' Marian said, trying to drag her thoughts away from the tie. 'She said she wanted to see if he was all right. It was Christmas Day, that sort of thing.'

'Joanna felt sorry for him!' George said angrily, interrupting her. 'So I told her that if anyone was going to see him, it would be me, and that I would talk to him in language that he understood.' He turned to the sergeant. 'I'm sorry, Sergeant Hill, if I'm failing to live up to your expectations of the clergy. Clearly, I disappoint my daughter – even my son-in-law, I was told tonight. But that's how I felt.'

'He'd got Joanna and George at each other's throats,' Marian said. 'So I went up. Just to let him know what he was doing to us. And I found him,' she finished.

'Did you touch anything, Mrs Wheeler?' Inspector Lloyd asked.

She shook her head. 'I just called George,' she said, still barely aware of what she was saying. George had been with Eleanor Langton.

'Then I phoned the police,' George said.

'Just one more thing,' said the inspector. 'Where did you go when you went out, Mrs Wheeler?'

'I checked up on the older people in the village. Because the weather was so bad. To make sure they were all right.'

'Could I possibly have a list of the people you saw?' he asked. 'Not now, of course. Perhaps tomorrow?'

'Yes. Yes, of course.'

Marian acknowledged their leave-taking with half of her brain. She wasn't sure she could cope with this.

George came back in. 'You could go to Diana's,' he said. 'You don't have to stay here.'

Marian shook her head, getting up slowly from the table. She looked across at her husband, her face sad.

'How many commandments have you broken today, George?' she asked.

'Well, Watson?' said Lloyd, starting the engine. 'What do you think?'

Judy leant back and closed her eyes. 'I think it's all very depressing,' she said. 'And he's a very odd sort of vicar.'

'Is he? I don't know much about vicars,' Lloyd said.

'He's not like any one I've ever known,' Judy said, and yawned. 'But then, I haven't known very many.'

'Someone tried to burn some clothing,' Lloyd said. 'Can't tell what yet. But we'll find out, as I told Mrs Elstow.'

Judy frowned. 'Why the business with the washing-machine?' she asked. 'If you'd already found the clothes?'

Lloyd smiled. 'Confuse the enemy,' he said. 'And never take anything at its face value. What's your verdict?'

'That Joanna got hit once too often, and got her own back when he fell asleep,' Judy said. 'And they're covering up for her.'

'Then what about the doors?' Lloyd said. 'Why mention that at all? It just buggers up their own intruder theory.'

Judy was too tired, too confused, to listen to one of Lloyd's flights of fancy. 'You don't seriously think it was an intruder, do you?' she said sharply.

'No.'

'Then can we leave it until we know what we're talking about?'

'Yes, miss.'

She rubbed her forehead, where an incipient headache was forming.

'Do you fancy taking on young Mrs Elstow in single combat?' he asked.

'Poor kid. Yes, I think that might work.' She yawned again. 'When?'

'Tomorrow afternoon, I suppose,' he said.

'By tomorrow, I take it you mean today?'

'I'm afraid so.' He smiled. 'You should worry. I've got the post mortem.'

Judy closed her eyes again. 'Michael will go through the roof,' she said. 'He already thinks it's the height of bad manners to get yourself murdered at Christmas time.'

'Just go to Byford when you're ready,' Lloyd said, obviously none too interested in Michael's problems. 'No need to let them know you're coming.'

The car bumped over the snow, as a new fall came floating down.

'I should be back at the station at about four,' Lloyd said. 'You can let me know how you've got on.'

'Eleven hours from now,' Judy said gloomily, her eyelids heavy.

'Let Michael cook the dinner,' Lloyd said.

'Looks like I'll have to,' said Judy.

Lloyd lapsed into an unnatural silence then. Lloyd loved speaking. Judy sometimes loved to listen. But this time she was grateful for the silence, as he concentrated on his driving, through conditions which had worsened still further.

'At least the road's not blocked,' she murmured, closing her eyes again. Just for a moment.

'We're here,' Lloyd said, and she was startled to find herself in the police station car park. 'Oh, Lloyd, I'm sorry,' she said.

The heating had, of course, broken down, and Judy began writing up her notebook until her hands became too numb. Lloyd left instructions for the day-shift, and at last decreed that they could leave.

She flopped into the car. 'Home, driver,' she said.

'Come to the flat first.'

Judy turned to him. 'Lloyd, I've got Michael and his parents expecting a jolly Christmas Day, and it's almost six in the morning!'

'That's why you need to unwind. Come to the flat.'

Unwinding would be nice, she thought.

'Just for a cup of coffee,' he persisted.

Lloyd's quiet, restful flat, or Mrs Hill banging on about Christmas being for the kiddies, really. 'All right,' she said. Though even Mrs Hill would not be banging on about Christmas at six o'clock in the morning, she reflected, as Lloyd drove off. She curled into a cold, uncomfortable heap, until at last she was in Lloyd's flat, in the exquisite, centrally-heated warmth. She took off her coat for the first time since she'd left home.

'I'll get the coffee on,' he said, stopping at the kitchen door. 'You go through.'

She opened the door to find the living room in darkness, except for a tiny tree, its coloured lights filling the room with exotic shadows. She smiled. 'It's lovely,' she said, going in.

Lloyd came in after her, and her present to him joined the one under the tree. 'I thought it was pretty good,' he said, catching her hands. 'Happy Christmas, Sergeant Hill.'

He was kissing her, holding her close, and it was so peaceful, so good to have him to herself. Too good. 'Put the light on,' she said.

'Why?'

'Because you said just a cup of coffee, not kisses by coloured lights.'

He smiled, and reached over to a table lamp, which filled the room with a soft glow.

'That isn't much better,' Judy complained, her hands still clasped behind his neck.

'What do you expect in a bachelor flat?' he said. 'I've only got seduction lighting.'

Judy laughed. 'It would take more than lighting,' she said. 'A few pep-pills and some rhinoceros horn, maybe.' She kissed him. 'When did you get the new lamp?' she asked.

'About six weeks ago,' he said.

Now Judy felt guilty. 'It's ages since I've been here,' she said.

He nodded. 'I'll go and really put the coffee on.'

Judy loved Lloyd's flat, which bit by bit was being made the way he wanted it. It was quiet, and tranquil, and not at all like him.

He came back in. 'Five minutes,' he said. 'And Santa's been.'

He sat on the sofa; she sat on the floor, and opened her present to find the little ebony cat that she'd seen months ago, and told Lloyd about. 'Lloyd,' she said, 'I didn't mean you to *buy* it.'

'I know you can't take it home,' he said. 'Before you tell me. But you can keep it here, can't you? Or at work, I suppose.'

She smiled. 'Where do I need the most luck?' she asked.

He didn't reply, but picked up his present.

'It isn't as romantic as yours,' she warned him.

'I'd be disappointed if it was,' he said. 'One romantic is enough in any relationship.'

She watched anxiously as he opened it, and his smile seemed genuine. 'The new one,' he said. 'I've been waiting for this.' He opened it. 'It's *signed!* How did you manage that?'

'I queued for two hours,' she said.

'That's romantic,' he pointed out. 'What was he like?'

'Like someone who'd been signing books for two hours.'

She joined him on the sofa for the rest of the five minutes, which stretched to ten. 'Coffee,' she said, pushing him away.

'Coffee.'

He came back with a tray on which were set two mugs, the coffee jug, cream, and a bottle of brandy. 'Right out of pep-pills and rhinoceros horn,' he said.

They drank the coffee with liberal helpings of brandy, which seemed to have the opposite effect to pep-pills, and this rather counteracted any similarities it may have had to rhinoceros horn. They sat on the sofa, arms round one another, eyes half-closed. Judy squinted at her watch. 'It's after seven,' she said, 'I have to go.' But she didn't move.

'What's wrong, Judy?' Lloyd asked.

'Oh, nothing. Everything. I don't know.'

'Michael's parents getting you down?'

'Yes. And Michael's getting me down. And the weather. It took almost an hour just to get here from Byford.'

'I know,' he said. 'I was driving.'

'Sorry I fell asleep on you.'

'Well,' he said, squeezing her. 'It was better than being ignored.' He looked at her. 'Have you had a row with Michael?' he asked.

'Yes.'

'What about?'

'Nothing.'

'Tell me.'

'No – it doesn't matter.'

'Come on,' he said. 'It might help if you get it off your chest.'

She sighed. 'He said he wanted us to have a baby,' she said, her eyes closed. She felt Lloyd pull away from her.

'What did you say to him?' he demanded.

'Oh, Lloyd! What do you think I said?'

He sat for a long time without speaking. Just looking at her.

'Lloyd – I've got no intention—'

'Judy,' he said, talking through her. 'Judy, I don't think I can go on sharing you.'

Oh, God. She felt like one of those rubber dolls that bounced back to get knocked over again. 'Not now, Lloyd,' she said. 'Please, not now.'

'It's how I feel now,' he said.

'I've already had one row with Michael,' she said, running a hand through her hair. 'I've been up all night, I've had to look at a man with his brains bashed in. I've got my in-laws expecting Christmas dinner – I don't *need* this, Lloyd!'

'No,' he said, getting to his feet. 'And it's what you need that matters, isn't it? Always.'

'I don't want a row,' she said, wearily.

'It's not a row. It's just the truth. I can't bear thinking of you and him—'

'Then *don't* think about it!' she shouted.

'I can't ignore it any longer – don't you see? That's the whole problem!'

She stared at him. 'I've been straight with you from the start,' she said, almost in tears. 'I've never pretended it would be any other way.'

Lloyd poured brandy into his empty cup. 'Things change,' he said. 'I don't want it to be like that. Not now.'

'If you're driving me home, you can leave that until you come back,' she said hotly.

He put the cup down. 'You're afraid to leave him,' he said. 'Because he asks nothing of you, and I would.'

Judy's head was spinning. 'This isn't fair,' she said. 'It isn't how this is meant to be.'

'No. You were meant to carry on with your nice safe marriage, and I was meant to sit around like a bottle of bloody aspirin, waiting for you to have a headache.'

Judy didn't know if this was an unprovoked attack, or simple home-truths. She'd have to sort it out later, when she'd had some sleep. It seemed like an unprovoked attack.

'I don't want that any more,' Lloyd said.

'Will you take me home, please?'

He drove her home in silence, and this time she didn't enjoy it. She had always been aware that she was walking a tightrope between triumph and disaster. And now she had fallen off.

'You'd better stop here,' she said, as she saw the side road, worse than it had been when they left. She got out of the car, and took a deep breath of sharp, cold air before looking back in. 'Is it all over?' she asked.

Lloyd reached over to the open door. 'No, you silly bitch! I want to marry you!' And he slammed the door and drove off, his back wheel spinning in the deep snow at the edge of the road.

She'd fallen off the tightrope all right. But she was damned if she knew which way.

Chapter Four

Eleanor opened the door, and let out a sigh. 'Thank God,' she said. 'The radio just said—' She stepped out into the frosty courtyard.

'You've heard, then,' said George.

'My mother-in-law did. I didn't know what to do – thank God you're all right.'

'It's Elstow,' George said. 'Elstow's dead.'

She nodded. 'How? What on earth happened?'

George licked dry lips. 'Someone battered him to death,' he said.

'Someone?' The wind that had once again begun to bluster across the fields suddenly swirled round the courtyard, lifting a stinging flurry of hard snow. Eleanor stood like a statue, just staring at him, blinking as her hair blew across her eyes.

'Eleanor?' Her mother-in-law, George presumed, appeared at the door, an Instamatic in her hand. 'Is it all right if I take photographs? The castle looks lovely with the snow.' Mrs Langton senior smiled at George expectantly, but Eleanor was too preoccupied to satisfy the curiosity that had prompted the photographic urge.

'Yes,' she said. 'Help yourself.'

'Oh, my goodness.' Mrs Langton shivered. 'Don't stay out here too long, will you? You'll catch your death.' Then, perhaps just a little reluctant to begin her quest, she set off with her camera.

Eleanor waited until she had disappeared round the thick castle wall. 'Come in,' she said.

He followed her into the living room, and saw Tessa, engrossed in a cartoon.

'Is it good?' he asked, crouching down beside her.

She nodded, laughing delightedly as Bugs Bunny emerged unscathed from a crippling fall.

George smiled, 'At least that's all she's got to worry about,' he said.

'Look!' Tessa demanded. 'Look, Mummy, look!'

'I can see,' Eleanor said.

George stood up straight. 'I thought you ought to know,' he said, plunging in at the deep end. 'I've told the police that I was with Joanna all evening.'

Eleanor, still obediently watching Bugs Bunny, looked slowly away from the screen, towards him. 'Was that wise?' she asked.

'I don't know,' he said wearily. 'Wisdom didn't seem to come into it.' He looked away from her. 'It's entirely up to you what you do about it,' he said.

'*Watch*, look! He's *flat*!'

'Do about it?' Eleanor asked. 'Why should I do anything about it?'

George sat down. 'We think it was an intruder,' he said. 'But the police aren't inclined to believe us.'

Eleanor sank down on to the sofa, her worried eyes not leaving his. 'What are they doing?' she asked. 'The police?'

'The usual things,' he said. 'They're asking questions. All over the place – checking up on where we were, what we were doing. Even what we were wearing.'

Tessa's laughter made George look at the screen. It was easy there. If you got bent out of shape you just shook yourself, and everything was all right again.

'They'll find out,' Eleanor said. 'If they're asking questions they'll find out that you—' She glanced at Tessa, obviously trying to think of words that would mean nothing to her, but she clearly wasn't listening anyway. 'That you weren't entirely straight with them,' she said.

'Perhaps not,' George said. 'The pub was very busy – they wouldn't necessarily know how long we were there. But yes,' he sighed. 'They'll probably find out.'

'More?' Tessa enquired as the credits came up.

'I don't know, Tess,' said Eleanor. 'Wait and see.'

There was more, and Tessa turned her attention once more to the television.

'What do you want me to do?' Eleanor asked.

'Whatever you think is right,' he said. 'I had no right to lie. So if you want to tell them the truth, then you must.'

Eleanor shook her head. 'I won't go to them,' she said. 'But if they ask – I don't know, George. Why did you lie?'

'Are they going to ask you?' he said. He hadn't answered her question, and she didn't answer his.

There were good reasons for his lie, but he didn't offer them to Eleanor.

'George,' she said quietly, 'do you know what really happened?'

Judy was having Christmas dinner with the Hills. That's what it felt like – not like her own house at all. She hadn't even produced the meal.

She had arrived home, tip-toeing upstairs to find Michael getting dressed.

'I couldn't sleep,' he had said.

Judy, cross and confused, had tried hard not to take it out on Michael, whose fault it certainly wasn't. The realisation that the whole mess was entirely her own fault had made her slightly less confused, but even more cross. So when Michael had touched on the subject of Christmas dinner, she had bitten his head off.

'Oh, for God's sake, Michael! Everything's *done* – you've only got to put it *on*. I'm sure your mother wouldn't mind doing it anyway.'

He had listened, maddeningly patient, until she'd finished.

'I just meant should we leave it until evening so that you can get some sleep?' Mild, solicitous, and calculated to make her feel guilty for jumping down his throat.

'Sorry,' she had said. 'No – no, I'll just need a couple of hours. I'm sorry, Michael,' she had said again, but there had still been an edge of irritation in her voice. Unwarranted. Unfair. Unkind. 'I've had a bad night,' she had said. 'I'm sorry. I really am.'

Michael had looked a little puzzled at her reaction to what had been an entirely routine skirmish. 'Was it a nasty one?' he asked.

A brief nod of confirmation, and he hadn't asked any more questions. 'And I have to go out again this afternoon,' she had warned him.

'Oh.' He had turned to leave, then turned back. 'I take it that it is really necessary?' he had said.

'Yes.'

'Well. You'd better get some sleep, then.'

'I want a bath. You haven't used all the hot water, have you?'

A cool bath, and an uneasy sleep punctuated by the sounds of the neighbours' children having a snowball fight, doubtless having abandoned all the batteries-not-included goodies laid before them in favour of playing with the weather, were to be her lot. And it seemed she had barely closed her eyes when it was time to get up again, time to drink a sherry and open presents with the Hills. Time to eat with the Hills.

She tried to enjoy the meal, which was, of course, delicious. Mrs Hill never forgot to warm the plates, or allowed the vegetables to overcook. Her turkey was never too dry. Michael must have sorely missed his mother's cooking, but he had never said so. Lloyd would have done, she thought. But then Lloyd didn't automatically assume that women did the cooking.

There was no point in weighing up advantages and disadvantages; there was no comparison between Lloyd and Michael.

Mr and Mrs Hill and their son Michael spoke a language that Judy didn't understand. They spoke about things in which she had no interest. She watched Michael, so engrossed in his conversation with his father that he was quite unaware of her scrutiny.

The sound of their voices faded and merged, just a confused background jumble, as she studied Michael as though he were a close-up on a cinema screen. His thin face was animated, even when he was listening rather than talking. His eyes went from his father to his mother when she spoke. He drank some wine, and poured more for everyone, including Judy. But he was in a world where she didn't really exist; a world of property chains and loft conversions, of the mileage you could get from Austin Princesses compared to Rovers, neither of which any of them owned. A world of small investments, of tax concessions and pension funds.

She had seen a man who had been battered to death.

What sort of masochism was it that she was so intent on practising? Why cling to something alien, instead of to someone who understood? Someone she could understand? What was it that

Michael got from this fake marriage that he was prepared to introduce a baby to it? She knew the answer. Independence. The mere fact that they *were* married to one another meant that no one else could own them. It was why they had thought it would work. It hadn't, but they wouldn't let go.

She got through the rest of the meal, as she always had before, on these rare family occasions. Michael must feel like this when they visited her family. Making no contribution, not expecting to be included.

After lunch, she went to see Joanna again.

Joanna didn't want to speak to Sergeant Hill, but she didn't seem to have much option. They were in the back bedroom, with the fire burning brightly, reminding Joanna of childhood ailments, when the bed in here would be made up so that her mother didn't have to run up and down stairs all day. No matter how itchy the spots, how sore the throat, being ill had been almost fun, in this cosy little room, with the fire going. It made her feel secure, and she wasn't at all sure that she should, with Sergeant Hill's watchful brown eyes on her. She had been aware of the danger with Graham, when she had relegated her interview with him to the sitting room. She must still be aware of it now, she reminded herself, as the sergeant waited for an answer with infinite, unbearable patience.

'I tried to *protect* myself,' Joanna said, when she couldn't stand it any longer, and looked away. 'Not defend myself.'

'All right,' said Sergeant Hill. 'I'll ask you something else.'

Joanna's eyes slid unwillingly back.

'You said that the row with your husband—'

'It *wasn't* a row,' Joanna said stubbornly. A row. That was twice she'd called it that. She had simply no idea. No idea at all.

'You said that your husband became violent at about five o'clock,' she said.

Joanna nodded, hearing the chimes, seeing Graham's face.

'And that he stopped when he heard your parents' car,' said the sergeant.

Joanna stiffened. She'd thought that this bit was over. 'You've asked me all this,' she said. 'It's in your notebook.'

Sergeant Hill nodded, and pointed to the notebook. 'It says that your parents came home at half-past five,' she said.

'Yes.'

Sergeant Hill looked at her for a moment without speaking, then carefully turned to a clean page in her notebook.

'That wasn't going on for half an hour,' she said, pointing to the bruises. 'Or you'd have been in hospital again.'

Joanna blushed. She didn't know they knew about that.

'So let's start again,' said Sergeant Hill.

'I don't see what it's got to do with it,' Joanna said. 'It's private.'

'He stopped long before your parents got here,' she said, as if Joanna hadn't spoken. 'Why?'

Joanna didn't answer.

'Were you upstairs with him, Joanna?'

'No.'

The sergeant looked thoughtful. 'Something stopped him hitting you,' she said. 'And it wasn't your parents' car driving up, was it?'

Joanna didn't speak, didn't look at her. It was no one else's business. No one's.

'People will understand,' Sergeant Hill was saying. 'If you picked up something to defend yourself.'

'I didn't. I've *told* you what happened.'

'But you haven't told me the truth.' She reached over and touched her hand. 'You said yesterday that it made you feel ashamed when he hit you,' she said.

Joanna looked down.

'I know you think I don't understand any of this,' she went on. 'But I can understand that.' She sat back again. 'Now, something made him stop hitting you,' she said. 'At the moment, it looks as though you fought back.'

'I didn't.'

'I don't think you did,' said the sergeant. 'So what did happen? You've nothing to be ashamed *of*, Joanna.'

'Ashamed?' Joanna repeated, puzzled. 'Oh,' she said. 'Sex? Is that what you're talking about?'

'It's not an unusual pattern,' said the sergeant. 'Some men get—'

'Get turned on by it? Perhaps they do, but that isn't how it was.'

'I'm sorry if I've offended you.'

'It would help if you called a spade a spade!' Joanna said angrily.

Sergeant Hill smiled. 'I expect it would,' she said. 'All right. Something stopped him, Joanna. And if it wasn't being battered to death, then what was it?'

Joanna's eyes filled with tears. 'The baby,' she said, in a low voice. 'I'm going to have a baby. I thought Graham had hurt it, and that's why he stopped.'

'Did he know you were pregnant?'

Joanna shook her head. 'Not until then,' she said. 'I was so frightened – I screamed at him, and he stopped.'

'Why in God's name didn't you tell me that in the first place?' the sergeant shouted, angry with her.

'Because I didn't want anyone to—' But she had suddenly and uncontrollably burst into tears. 'I didn't want to tell them,' she sobbed, as Sergeant Hill put her arms round her. 'That's why I stayed in the sitting room. I didn't want to see them.' But the words were incoherent. She couldn't speak, couldn't even breathe, for the convulsive sobs. She tried desperately to control them.

'It's just reaction,' said the sergeant. 'You cry.'

But it wasn't reaction. Joanna knew what it was, and it would be so easy to tell her, just tell her and get it over with. But she couldn't. She gulped in air with the sobs, her face buried in the sergeant's shoulder, until the shuddering stopped.

And then she tried to explain. She wanted Sergeant Hill to understand. But the words she could find didn't really describe her near-hysteria, and Graham's remorse; the tears, the gentleness, the closeness. The common fear that the baby had been hurt in a battle that Joanna was only just beginning to understand.

She looked up, expecting scepticism, but not finding it. 'I wanted to go home,' she said. 'I wanted to go home, and start again. With Graham and the baby. I wanted to do it *right*. But we heard the car, and I made him go upstairs and stay there, or my father would have killed him.'

Sergeant Hill's arms were still round her; Joanna felt the slight reaction to her words, and pulled away. 'It's an expression,' she said. 'It's just an expression.' But oh God, why had she used it?

'I know,' said the sergeant.

'I was so scared,' Joanna said again. 'I was scared about the baby.' Tears ran down her face again. 'I knew I'd tell them if I saw them,' she said. 'I didn't want to tell them.'

The sergeant took some tissues from her bag, and handed them to her. 'Do they still not know?' she asked.

'No.' Joanna took a deep, difficult breath. 'It's not their baby,' she said. 'And it's not going to be.'

A nod; understanding, perhaps, a little. 'Have you seen a doctor?' she asked.

'Yes. She's made an appointment for me to have tests. But she says there's nothing to worry about.'

'Good.'

'Sergeant Hill? You won't tell them, will you?'

She shook her head. 'But they'll have to know sooner or later,' she said.

'I know. It's silly, I know, but just not yet.'

'That I *can* understand,' said the sergeant, with a little laugh. 'Believe me.'

Everyone had their problems. Joanna wondered what Sergeant Hill's were.

'How long were you married?' she asked.

'Eighteen months,' said Joanna. Eighteen months, she thought. A June bride.

'Was he always violent?'

'Not really. Not to start with. He'd get angry with me— He didn't like . . .' She looked away. 'He didn't like my parents very much,' she said. 'And it just somehow started.'

'You said he'd been drinking – was he often drunk?'

'No – he didn't really drink. He said he'd met someone. I suppose they just—' She shrugged. 'It's Christmas,' she said. 'People drink too much.'

She looked round the safe, secure, comfortable room. 'He hated this place,' she said. 'He said I'd never come out of the womb.'

It was when Freddie was cheerfully removing bits of Graham Elstow that he dropped his unintentional bombshell.

'Between seven o'clock and nine o'clock,' he said. 'That's right, isn't it, Kathy?' The question was thrown over his shoulder at his assistant, who seemed equally happy in her work as she industriously checked samples.

Lloyd's face fell. 'What?' he said. 'What about five?'

'Five? No. Definitely still alive and digesting at five. He ate at two o'clock, according to the barmaid.'

The barmaid had had good reason to remember Elstow, who had refused to leave at closing time. In the end, she had brought in reinforcements, and Elstow had left, protesting that no, he hadn't got a home to go to, no one could call that a home . . .

'Still alive at five,' Freddie went on. 'And at six – almost certainly still at seven.' He flashed a wide smile at Lloyd. 'And definitely dead by nine,' he said.

'Don't *do* this to me, Freddie! We've got a theory.'

Freddie sucked in his breath. 'Tricky things, theories,' he said.

'Our theory,' Lloyd went on, 'says that Elstow arrived in the afternoon to make things up with his wife. He's successful, and they go up to her room. But Elstow has to knock her about to get in the mood – and when he's sleeping it off, she gets her own back with the poker.' He raised his hands. 'Simple,' he said.

'Simple is the word,' said Freddie. 'Simple, neat, tidy – what a pity it doesn't fit the facts.'

He didn't sound too cut up about it, Lloyd thought sourly.

'He didn't die until Mrs Elstow was safely in the pub,' he went on, then picked up some papers. 'Preliminary report from forensic,' he said. 'Have you got yours?'

'No.' Lloyd glared at him.

'It's probably on your desk now. They don't have much to go on yet – they're working with a skeleton staff, and half of them couldn't get in. But it does say that Elstow's full handprint was on the inside of the sitting room door – as it would be, if he'd slammed it shut, like Mrs Elstow said. And there were scuff marks on the polished floorboards, consistent with two people struggling.'

'All right, all right,' Lloyd said. 'Stop being so smug.'

Freddie laughed. 'He was lying on the bed when he was attacked,' he said. 'Probably asleep.' He looked up. 'That fits in with your theory,' he said. 'If only he'd died a couple of hours earlier.'

Joanna had been a fairly conspicuous visitor to the pub, with her black eyes. They had all seen her arrive with her father, at about ten past seven. Still, Lloyd thought, Freddie said he could have died *at* seven.

'Could she have killed him before the pub?' he asked.

'And ten minutes later she's sipping cider?' Freddie said. 'No, Lloyd. I think he was alive at seven, anyway.'

'But it's possible? In theory?'

'Theoretically, he could have died at seven. But for Wheeler and his daughter to be in the pub by ten past – which several witnesses say they *were* – they have to have left the house by seven. The weather precluded speeding – if we assume they travelled at a reasonable speed, it would certainly take ten minutes from the vicarage to the pub.'

'Are you saying he couldn't have died even a few minutes before seven?' asked Lloyd.

'I am. Seven and nine are the absolute outside times, Lloyd. Between seven-thirty and eight-thirty would be my guess.'

'So I have no leeway?'

'No,' said Freddie. 'Not on the time. But there are two other interesting points,' he said, brightening up.

Lloyd shook his head. 'Other people would object to their Christmas Day being broken into in this fashion, Freddie. Why don't you?'

'I'm happy in my work,' he said, with a shrug.

Lloyd looked at Freddie's work, and shook his head again.

'This has *made* my day,' he went on enthusiastically. 'It's a puzzle, Lloyd. If you look at the—'

'I'll take your word for it, Freddie, whatever it is.'

'Right. Two of the blows occurred after death. They're not particularly heavy – nothing like as heavy as the others.'

'Whoever did it expended a lot of energy,' said Lloyd.

'Sure, sure. The last blows wouldn't be as strong,' Freddie said. 'But if you were that tired – why hit him again?'

'She just kept going until she was certain,' said Lloyd. He couldn't see what there was to get excited about.

And he didn't miss Freddie's raised eyebrows at his use of

gender, but it was Freddie who had said that he thought the prints on the poker were a woman's.

And Lloyd thought they were Joanna Elstow's, and would continue to do so until he was proved wrong. But God knew when that would be. It was Christmas Day, and it was snowing; that apparently meant that the system ground to a halt.

'Elstow died almost immediately,' said Freddie. 'But he got hit again, twice, some considerable time after he had died.'

Lloyd frowned. 'Why would anyone want to do that?'

'You're the detective,' said Freddie. He grinned.

Lloyd regarded him sourly. 'When you haven't got your hands in a corpse, you're nice and miserable like the rest of us,' he said. 'You're only really happy round death. That's weird, Freddie.'

'So I've been told. I like dead bodies.' He smiled. 'I like some live bodies, too. Has Sergeant Hill recovered?'

'Yes, thank you,' said Lloyd. 'You said two points. What's the other?'

'The prints on the poker – oh, I forgot. You haven't seen the report yet.'

'What about them?'

'They agree with me that they're probably a woman's,' said Freddie. 'Of course, since we haven't got the comparison with the family's prints yet ...'

'The Wheelers' prints were taken as soon as possible,' Lloyd said with exaggerated patience. 'Don't blame me because they've got stuck in some bureaucratic snowdrift.'

Freddie laughed. 'It's lonely at the top, Acting Chief Inspector.'

'Is that it?' Lloyd said. 'That they're a woman's prints?'

'*Could* be a woman's prints. And yes, in a way, that is it, because the poker was held with one hand. Now, it's not impossible, but I'd have said that to inflict blows like that, the average woman would have needed both hands.'

Lloyd nodded. 'A good double-handed backhand, you said this morning.'

'That's still what I think,' said Freddie. 'So there you are. You go away and puzzle that lot out, and I'll get busy on the details. If and when we can get any,' he added.

Lloyd groaned. 'It only happened today,' he said. 'And it's Christmas Day, Freddie – a day we simple folk celebrate.'

'Until we've got them, you don't know if you're looking for an intruder or not,' Freddie said.

'Intruder!' Lloyd snorted. 'It's a domestic, Freddie. Pure and simple.'

'Like your theory?'

Lloyd sighed. 'Don't remind me,' he said. 'I've just sent Sergeant Hill to lean on someone that you tell me was in a pub with a hundred witnesses when the deceased met his maker.'

Freddie bristled slightly. 'Let's hope she left her rubber truncheon at home then,' he said. 'Look – you shouldn't have gone on my estimate at the scene. I told you it was rough – I even told you it could be down to eight hours.'

Lloyd held up a conciliatory hand. 'I know,' he said. 'I know. But young Mrs Elstow is not telling the truth about what went on, wherever she was when he was killed,' he added.

'When did he stop beating his wife?' Freddie said.

'Quite.' Lloyd shook his head. 'How you can make jokes in a morgue is beyond me,' he said, looking at his watch. Four forty-three. Surely Judy would have been and gone by the time he got to the station. 'I'm off,' he said. 'Enjoy yourself with the rest of Mr Elstow.'

'I shall,' said Freddie cheerfully. 'I shall.'

'It's Graham's father,' said Marian to Joanna. 'On the phone. I didn't say you were here.'

She had almost gone in when she'd heard Joanna crying. She *had* gone in as soon as Sergeant Hill had left. But Joanna had said that everything was fine. It had just caught up with her, she had said. Sergeant Hill had comforted her, she'd said. She hadn't made her cry. So all that worrying had been in vain.

'I'll talk to him,' said Joanna. 'I think it'll be about the funeral arrangements. I called him, but he wasn't there.'

The funeral. Marian hadn't given it a thought. It was as if once they had removed his body from the house, that was that. But it wasn't, of course. It was very far from being that.

'No one can do anything until the police say so, anyway,' said Joanna. 'I ought to go and see him, really.'

'Yes,' said Marian absently. 'Perhaps you ought.'

She could hear the rise and fall of Joanna's voice on the phone. It would be over, she told herself. One day, it would all be over, and they could get back to normal.

'The vicar,' Eleanor said, in answer to the inevitable question that had been an unnaturally long time coming.

Penny's smile faded. 'The *vicar*?' she repeated. 'You didn't tell me you *knew* them.'

'I don't really.' Eleanor was very fond of her mother-in-law, who had been everything to her for the last two years: her mother, her friend, her adviser, a shoulder to cry on, a baby-sitter. But she was incurably interested in other people's business.

'Why was he here?'

Eleanor pushed her chair away from the table, and eyed the remains of the Christmas dinner. Tessa's plate, abandoned in favour of Dumbo in the other room, was particularly uninviting. Two-year-olds had no preconceived notions about what you could eat with what.

'We'll get this done in no time,' Penny said reassuringly, standing up. She hesitated. 'You're not—' she began, then obviously decided that even she couldn't continue that particular line of enquiry. 'Why *was* he here?' she asked, taking the direct approach.

'They'd invited us over,' Eleanor said. 'He came to explain what had happened.'

'Oh.' Penny began to pile up plates. 'Are you going to finish your pudding?' she asked.

Eleanor shook her head.

'I thought you were worried this morning. Why didn't you tell me you knew them?' She made a hideous pile of left-overs.

'I didn't want to worry you,' Eleanor said. 'One of us worrying was enough.'

'Who was killed?' Penny asked, her voice low.

'I'm not sure,' said Eleanor, departing from the truth. 'He didn't go into details. Someone who was visiting them.'

Penny tutted. 'How did it happen?' she asked.

'They think it was a burglar.'

'You mean someone just got in and *killed* someone?' Penny pushed open the kitchen door. 'Haven't they caught anyone?' she asked, alarmed.

'No, I don't think so.' Eleanor picked up the cream jug and the barely-touched pudding. She didn't know how much of this third-degree she could take.

'I don't like the idea of your being here alone,' Penny said. 'Why don't you and Tessa come back with me? Spend the rest of the holiday in Stansfield?'

Eleanor managed a smile. 'I'm not really on holiday except for today and tomorrow,' she said.

'It seems so lonely here,' Penny persisted. 'Tessa's all on her own.'

'Not usually. There's the play-group – there are lots of children in the village.'

'But for Christmas, I mean. The people next door to me have got a little boy a few months older than Tessa – that would be company for her, wouldn't it?'

'We're perfectly all right here, Penny. We won't be murdered in our beds, I promise.'

Penny sighed, and went into the kitchen. For a moment, all that could be heard was water running into the dish basin. Then it was turned off, and there was a little silence.

'Someone was,' she called through. 'Don't forget that.'

Chapter Five

'Something odd,' Jack Woodford said, as his head appeared round Lloyd's door. 'Got a minute?'

'All the time you want,' Lloyd said. 'Something odd means we're getting there.'

Jack looked less certain of that than Lloyd, as he came in, a sheet of paper in his hand.

Judy arrived before Jack had closed the door. 'I thought I'd better report in,' she said.

Lloyd had indeed successfully avoided her the day before, after his visit to the morgue; he had rather hoped that she wouldn't come in today.

'You thought you'd get away from your in-laws,' said Jack.

'That too,' she confessed with a smile, taking off the new leather coat that she was wearing.

'Jack's about to give us something to go on,' said Lloyd, glad that Jack was there. Their row had been yesterday; it seemed like a year ago. But it was still only Boxing Day, and this interminable festive season ground on around them, with no shops open and no proper programmes on the telly, even if he'd had the energy to watch.

Jack laid the sheet of paper on Lloyd's desk. 'My lads have been checking up on the people Mrs Wheeler visited,' he said. 'On Christmas Eve.'

Lloyd glanced down at the list. Beside the names, Jack had jotted down times.

'They're only approximate,' Jack said, as Lloyd opened his mouth to ask. 'People didn't think to look at their watches in case the vicar's wife needed an alibi for murder.'

'No,' said Lloyd.

'But she says she left the vicarage at about ten to eight – right?' He didn't wait for the unnecessary confirmation. 'And the earliest visit we can find is . . .' He leant over, reading the sheet upside down. 'Mrs Anthony,' he said, running his finger down the list of names. 'And that was at eight twenty-five. The thing is – Mrs Anthony's house is in a row of cottages right beside the drive up to the vicarage.'

Lloyd remembered passing them just after they had spoken to the snow-plough crew.

'If Mrs W. had gone on her hands and knees into a force eight,' Jack went on, 'she'd have taken no more than five minutes getting there. Which seems to my untrained eye to leave half an hour unaccounted for.'

'Well, well, well,' said Lloyd briskly, looking over at Judy. 'I think we'd better go and talk to this Mrs Anthony – don't you?'

On the way, Judy expanded a little on the notes she'd left him on her interview with Joanna. She had obviously believed her; Lloyd trusted Judy's instincts, but he had a question.

'If she'd made it up with him,' he asked, 'why didn't she go up to see him?' He slowed down to let Judy read the numbers on the cottages.

'Eleven, thirteen – seventeen must be that one with the yellow door,' she said. 'I don't know. That is a bit odd.'

'It's not like you to miss a trick,' he said.

She got out of the car without replying. He'd said it to annoy her. She had said nothing at all about their row, or about his parting shot. In fact, she was behaving as though nothing had happened, obeying Lloyd's own rule that their private relationship mustn't affect their work. But she was much more of a professional than he would ever be, and the ease with which she donned her policeman's helmet irritated him. Irrationally, he conceded. But it did.

Mrs Anthony took some time to come to the door; when it opened, they saw a frail old lady backing her wheelchair away. Lloyd introduced himself and Judy, and they were shown into a small, neat living room.

'Do you remember Mrs Wheeler coming to see you on Christmas Eve?' Judy asked, raising her voice slightly, enunciating clearly.

Lloyd suppressed a smile as Mrs Anthony regarded Judy with a bleak eye. 'I am almost eighty years old,' she said. 'I sometimes have to use this wheelchair. I would prefer to be thirty-five and walking about, like you, but I do assure you that neither of these disadvantages affects my hearing, my acumen, or my memory.'

Judy's face grew pink. 'Oh – I do apologise if I gave the impression—'

'You did,' said Mrs Anthony sharply.

It gave Lloyd just a little perverse pleasure to see the efficient Sergeant Hill so firmly on the carpet.

'I'm sorry,' Judy said.

'And now that we have established that I can remember all the way back to the day before yesterday, what did you want to know?'

'We'd like to know what time she got here,' Lloyd asked.

'Eight twenty-five. Between then and half past, that is,' said Mrs Anthony, without hesitation.

'Can you be sure about that?' Judy asked.

'What was the point of asking me if you don't think I can tell the time?' demanded Mrs Anthony.

Judy looked uncomfortable. 'I just wondered how you could be so precise,' she said.

'Because the programme I was watching had just got to the end of part one,' said Mrs Anthony, relenting slightly. 'The advertisements were on when the doorbell rang, and I hoped that whoever it was wouldn't stay. She did, though,' she added.

'How did she seem?' Lloyd asked.

'Not her usual self,' said Mrs Anthony.

'You know her quite well?' asked Judy.

'If I didn't I wouldn't know what her usual self was, would I?' snapped the old lady. 'I've known her all her life.'

Lloyd decided that he didn't really like witnessing Judy being eaten for breakfast after all. 'And what was her usual self?' he asked.

The world-weary eyes regarded him. 'She was always a very determined girl,' she said, thoughtfully.

'Oh?' Lloyd, who had been standing by the radiator, came over and sat near to Mrs Anthony. 'What makes you say that?' he asked.

'Poor George Wheeler,' she said, smiling softly, as though at some memory, 'I don't imagine he'd still be a vicar if he hadn't married Marian.'

A silence fell, and Judy jotted something down. She looked up, frowning slightly. 'What do you mean, Mrs Anthony?' she asked. 'Why wouldn't he still be a vicar?'

Mrs Anthony smiled her soft smile again, but the eyes remained lack-lustre. 'Lack of faith,' she said. 'But Marian thought it was right to encourage George's scepticism; she thought it made him more accessible. One of the boys. And Marian always thinks she's right,' she added.

'And you don't think she was right?'

Mrs Anthony raised her eyebrows, 'I think a leaning toward religion is preferable in a vicar,' she said, 'I think if George had married someone else, he would have realised that a lot sooner than he has.'

'You think he has realised now?' asked Lloyd.

'Oh yes,' she said. 'His sermon at the midnight service made that obvious. To me, at any rate.'

'And what was his sermon?'

'Being true to yourself,' she said.

Judy and Lloyd exchanged glances as Mrs Anthony wheeled herself closer to the radiator. 'Marian just wants people to be true to her,' she said. 'That's all she asks. But she couldn't protect George from his own thoughts,' she said, turning up the temperature control. 'She had a damn good try, though. I'll give her that.'

Judy, perhaps a little apprehensively, looked up. 'Do you think this has got something to do with what happened at the vicarage?' she asked.

'Let's just say it doesn't surprise me that you're asking about Marian Wheeler,' she said. 'It doesn't surprise me in the least.'

She wheeled herself back to where Lloyd and Judy sat. 'And I'll tell you how she seemed,' she said to Lloyd. 'She seemed upset. Nervous.'

Judy's face assumed an expression Lloyd knew well. 'How did this manifest itself?' she asked, her tone matching the disbelieving look.

'For one thing,' said Mrs Anthony, her eyes suddenly alive,

'her hands were shaking so much that she spilled coffee on her dress.'

And Judy, overmatched, took refuge in her note-taking.

'Fortunately,' continued Mrs Anthony, 'most of it went in the saucer.'

'Did she say what was upsetting her?' asked Lloyd.

'She'd hardly do that, would she, Mr Lloyd?'

It wasn't a crime to be upset, as Lloyd pointed out to Judy on their way up to the vicarage.

Marian Wheeler opened the door, and gave a short sigh when she saw them.

'Joanna's resting,' she said. 'Unless it's really important, I'd rather you didn't talk to her just now.'

Lloyd smiled. 'I quite understand,' he said. 'But it's you we've really come to see, Mrs Wheeler.'

'Oh.' There was a strange mixture of apprehension and relief on her face. 'You'd better come in.'

They followed her through to the kitchen, where George Wheeler was drying dishes.

'It's the police,' said Mrs Wheeler.

'Any further forward?' asked Wheeler, turning round.

'Things are moving,' said Lloyd smoothly. 'Slowly, I'm afraid. But they are moving.'

'Good.'

'Why we're here, Mrs Wheeler, is to clear up a small . . . inconsistency, I suppose.'

He explained the nature of the small inconsistency, while Wheeler dried the cup that he held in his hand until he had almost worn it away.

'Are you certain that you left the house at ten to eight?' Lloyd concluded.

Marian Wheeler frowned. 'Yes,' she said. 'I must have missed someone off the list.'

Judy handed her a copy of the list, and Mrs Wheeler took glasses from her handbag. 'I can't think who,' she said as she looked at it. 'But I was a bit shaken up when I wrote it out. I can't honestly remember.'

'Perhaps you wouldn't mind thinking about it?' asked Lloyd.
'Let me know if you remember.'

'Certainly I will.' She handed the list back.

'Mrs Anthony said you seemed upset,' said Judy.

'Did she?' Marian Wheeler took off her glasses. 'Yes – yes, I
suppose I was. Of course I was, after what had happened to
Joanna.'

Wheeler at last put down the cup. 'What are you suggesting?'
he asked quietly.

'Nothing at all,' said Lloyd. 'But we have to try to account for
half an hour that has somehow got itself lost.' He turned to
Marian Wheeler. 'I'm sure it'll come back to you,' he said. 'You've
got the number to reach me, haven't you?'

'Yes, thank you.'

'Well – thank you for your time. Don't worry – we'll see ourselves out.'

They didn't stay long at the station, and Judy left before Lloyd
did. He decided that now was as good a time as any to make his
duty visit to Barbara and the kids.

Two hours later, he went back to his flat, none the better for
seeing his family, who had merely added to his worries and irritations. He consoled himself with a large glass of the Woodfords'
present, and a few chapters of Judy's.

And by the next morning, the things that had been moving
slowly started moving fast, now that the world had got itself over
the twin difficulties of snow and holidays. Late Saturday afternoon found him reading the first detailed forensic report.

The fingerprints on the poker were Marian Wheeler's; another
set of her prints had been found beside an attempt to clean a
blood-stain off the landing floor. One of her shoes bore traces of
blood. Lloyd looked up thoughtfully from the report.

He wondered about Freddie's belief that a woman would have
had to hold the poker in both hands. Any woman, according to
him. So – what would he think of Marian Wheeler, small and slim,
wielding the poker one-handed? Not a lot. Much more likely that
she had interfered with the scene once she'd found Elstow. She
had run into the room, picked up the poker – got blood on her

shoe. Then what? Why not just say that that was what she had done?

And yet, Lloyd knew, people reacted oddly under stress. TV and books had done a wonderful job in instilling into the public the vital importance of leaving murder scenes untouched; if only they could direct this talent to pointing out the beneficial effects of not murdering anyone in the first place, he thought irrelevantly.

But it was possible that she thought she shouldn't have touched anything, and so denied going into the room at all. But she'd hardly have given Elstow a couple of thumps with the poker, he thought, and shrugged, giving his attention once more to the report.

No traces of an intruder, inside or out. No fingerprints other than those of the deceased, Mrs Elstow, and Mr and Mrs Wheeler. Nothing disturbed, nothing taken, nothing vandalised. Just one dead body.

The clothing. Forensic said it was a woman's dress, probably size 12, in a pink or peach-coloured unpatterned material, judging by the reinforced collar and cuffs which had failed to burn up as well as the rest of it had. There were traces of blood on one cuff. Type B, similar to the deceased's.

Size 12. Judy was a 14; so was Barbara, and so, if he was any judge, was young Mrs Elstow. Mrs Wheeler would be a 12. Things did not look good for Marian Wheeler.

He felt that there was probably something a little suspect about a man who could sum up a woman's dress size at a glance, but there it was. Gigolos and detectives were supposed to notice things like that.

Marian Wheeler would have to be brought in.

He dialled Judy's number, which barely rang out at all before she picked it up.

'We've got work to do,' he said.

'Thank God for that.'

He smiled at the dialling tone, and replaced the receiver.

'A man-made material,' the inspector said. 'Plain – probably pink or peach-coloured.' He looked from Joanna to Marian. 'Do either of you own such a dress?'

Marian saw George's head turn involuntarily towards her as the inspector spoke. She heard Joanna try to smother the confirmation that had escaped, despite her efforts.

Christmas was over; the waiting was over. The police, suspicious from the start, had taken away clothes and shoes, had come every day, politely and courteously making them tell their stories over and over again. They had been all over the village, asking questions.

'If it was an intruder' – slight accent on the 'was' – 'then someone must have seen him. He would be badly blood-stained.'

That had been the explanation offered for their checking-up on the comings and goings from the vicarage, when Marian had demanded one. It had been given to her by the crisp, concise Sergeant Hill.

Now she was here again, with the inspector. They looked a little stern, a little sad. And they were looking at her.

'Was it your dress, Mrs Wheeler?' The sergeant.

They had taken away the ashes from the fires in Joanna's bedroom and the kitchen, and Marian had endured Christmas somehow. Though it wasn't really Christmas, not with all that had happened. The house always seemed to have some figure of authority in it. If it wasn't police, it was clergy. There had been a lot of work to take her mind off it.

'Mrs Wheeler?' The sergeant again, not impatiently.

She took almost as much on herself as Chief Inspector Lloyd. Marian found herself inconsequentially wondering if that annoyed him. She decided it couldn't, or presumably he would have stopped her doing it. Whereas often he would almost melt into the background while she did the asking.

The sergeant came over to her. 'Mrs Wheeler,' she said. 'Was it your, dress?'

'Yes.'

Inspector Lloyd cleared his throat. 'Mrs Wheeler, I'd be grateful if you could come with us to the police station,' he said. 'There are questions we would like to put to you concerning the murder of Graham Elstow.'

'This is outrageous!' George roared.

'George,' said Marian. 'It's their job – they're only doing their job.'

George gaped at her, then shook his head.

'Mrs Wheeler,' said the sergeant briskly, 'if you could get your coat—'

'No!' Joanna shouted. 'I don't understand – what are you doing?'

Inspector Lloyd looked far from happy. 'Mrs Wheeler has simply agreed to help us with our—'

'Agreed?' George said. 'I didn't hear her agree.'

Lloyd glanced at Marian. 'Mrs Wheeler?' he said.

'George is right,' she said. 'I haven't actually agreed to come.'

'Are you going to force me to arrest you?' asked Lloyd.

'Yes!' shouted George. 'If you want my wife to go with you, you're going to have to arrest her.' He took a step towards the inspector. 'So you had better be very sure of your ground, Chief Inspector Lloyd,' he said.

Marian saw the inspector shrug slightly at the sergeant, and she was being arrested.

They were telling her she didn't have to say anything. She knew that. She knew the wording of the caution. She wondered when the British police would feel obliged to alter their simple, direct sentence into whole paragraphs of statutory advice, like the Americans. Or was that just New York? America was funny, with all the states having different laws.

They were taking her out to their car. George was white, and Joanna walked with her arm round his waist, holding on to him like a child. George was saying something about a solicitor. The sergeant got into the back of the car with her, the leather coat she wore creaking slightly, smelling new. There was a constable at the wheel of the car, and he closed the passenger door as George kept the inspector talking.

Joanna had gone back into the house, obviously on George's instructions, and re-emerged, carrying coats. She got into her car as George at last walked away from the inspector, turning twice on his way to call something angrily over his shoulder.

The inspector got in then, slamming the door. Marian could see the tension in the back of his neck, as the car moved off through the new fall of snow. Five days of it, Marian thought, and it still hadn't given up. Not constant, or the vicarage would have disappeared under it. But snow, every day, and the driveway was deep again now. The incessant cars had churned it up into slush, and it might freeze. Someone could break their neck. They said you were responsible, if someone did. If they were there for a reasonable purpose. Postmen, newspaper boys. Policemen.

The sergeant was speaking to her, but she hadn't been listening. 'Mrs Wheeler?'

Marian turned to face her. She had a nice face, Marian realised. Not just nice-looking – which she was – but something more. People could have beautiful faces that weren't attractive. Sergeant Hill wasn't beautiful; she had a good face, the kind photographers like. Warm brown eyes, and an open friendliness that was there even when she was briskly arresting you.

'Are you all right, Mrs Wheeler?'

'Oh – yes. Thank you.'

On, through white-banked roads, into Stansfield, with no one speaking at all. Skirting round the now pedestrianised centre of the town to the police station at the other side. Marian had sat on the Young Offenders Committee in there, in her time. It had folded, not through any lack of young offenders, but because it hadn't really helped.

The sergeant was opening the door as the driver pulled round to park. She was out of the car as it stopped moving, her hand held out to assist Marian, who was then taken – no doubt about it – *taken*, the sergeant's hand lightly holding her elbow, into the building. She was taken to the desk, where another sergeant began filling in forms. He repeated that she didn't have to say anything, but if she did . . . She signed a form. Then she was taken into a room with a formica table and chairs, like the one the YO committee had used. A woman police officer came in, and the sergeant told Marian to sit down. Told her.

It was odd, for someone who was used to being shown and asked, to be taken and told.

'Just leave it here,' said George, as Joanna pulled up at the police station.

'I can't,' she said. 'It's double yellow lines.'

Double yellow lines. Marian had just been arrested, and she was worrying about double yellow lines. But that was just like Marian would have been, George thought, if the positions had been reversed.

'You go in. I'll take it round to the car park,' she said.

George strode into the station, and saw Inspector Lloyd talking to Sergeant Hill. Ignoring the desk sergeant, he walked purposefully up to them. 'Where's my wife?' he demanded.

Lloyd broke off his conversation and turned. 'Mr Wheeler, you can't see your wife at the moment. I'm sorry.'

'She has the right to have a solicitor present,' George said.

'Of course she has,' said Lloyd.

'But how do I get hold of one?' George found himself asking. Pleading. 'It's Saturday afternoon!'

Lloyd pointed back down towards the entrance. 'Go to the desk sergeant,' he said. 'He'll help you.'

'Will he?' George felt bewildered. In the last few days, the police had altered their image for George. They had gone from being symbols of security and order to being invaders of privacy. Now, they just seemed like the enemy. Why would they help?

But help they did, and the solicitor said he would come right away. George looked round helplessly as he finished his call, but he couldn't see the inspector. He went out the front door, and walked round to the back, where he found the car park, and Joanna's car.

'Why would she burn her *dress*?' Joanna asked, as he got in.

'I don't know.'

'But why?' she said again. 'What possible reason could she have for doing something like that?'

'I don't *know*!' George shouted, but he wasn't angry with Joanna. 'No,' he said. 'Perhaps I do.'

'What?'

Eleanor. It had to be Eleanor. 'Perhaps,' he said, hitting the flat of his hand against the dashboard as he spoke. 'Perhaps I do. She could have burned it because she was angry with me.'

Joanna turned, her eyes wide. 'What have you done that would have made her angry enough to burn your Christmas present?' she asked.

George closed his eyes. 'It doesn't matter,' he said. 'A misunderstanding. It's possible, that's all.'

Joanna frowned, but she didn't ask again.

They waited in the police station car park, not knowing what to say or do. The solicitor was taking his time, thought George. He'd said he'd come right away.

There had to be a simple explanation. There *had* to be. But she hadn't given them one. And he had thought that they were just trying to alarm her into producing an explanation, when they'd asked her to go with them. That was why he'd said they would have to arrest her. Because he thought they couldn't, not just on that. But they *had* arrested her, as though confirmation about the dress had been all that they had needed. What else could they possibly have found to link Marian to it? And so what if she *had* burned the dress? It was her dress. She could do what she liked with it.

At the back of his mind, a doubt was creeping in. He'd told her she was wrong about Eleanor. Surely, *surely*, she would have told him about having burned the dress then? Or was she ashamed of having done it? He'd asked her why she wasn't wearing it, once he'd noticed. She had said it wasn't a good fit. Why hadn't she just told him the truth? Or had she just hoped that he would forget about it? Hadn't she realised the consequences of failing to mention it to the police? Hadn't it occurred to her what the police would think when they discovered it? Or did she think that the fire would have destroyed it completely?

Anyway, his mind asked him, despite his conscious effort to make it stop, *when* did she burn it? Elstow was in the room all the time . . .

George's eyes were tight shut. 'I need some air,' he said, scrambling out of the car. He ran to the bushy hedge that ran along one side of the car park, and was violently sick.

Joanna watched impassively as her father bent over in the bushes, his shoulders heaving. She couldn't help him.

Whatever nonsensical idea the police had got would be

disproved; if her mother had burned the dress in a fit of pique – though that was hardly like her, but if she *had* – then she would tell them, and they would let her go. But she obviously hadn't told them, doubtless in a misguided attempt to shield her father from embarrassment. And if that was the case, then he should go in now, and tell them why he thought she'd burned the dress.

It was ridiculous, her mother being in there, under arrest. Almost laughable. She supposed her father thought that eventually they would realise what a ludicrous mistake they were making, without his intervention. And they would, of course, in time.

Joanna was rather looking forward to the moment when the sharp-eyed, sharp-tongued Sergeant Hill would have to climb down and apologise. Because she would have to; there was no possibility of their continuing to imagine her mother guilty. None. It was a combination of circumstances, that was all. It would get sorted out. It probably took them hours to unarrest someone. It *would* get sorted out. It had to. Tears rolled down her face, unchecked. But crying wouldn't help. Throwing up in the bushes wouldn't help.

She dried her eyes, and got out of the car. Up some steps to a door, slightly ajar. Joanna took a deep breath, and went in.

She was in a corridor, with doors off it, all closed. There must be someone somewhere, she thought, as she walked along. She heard footsteps behind her, and turned to see a young constable.

'Can I help you?'

'I want to see Sergeant Hill,' she said.

'If you'll come with me,' he said, 'I'll see if we can find her for you.'

She followed him round into the main entrance, where he asked her to wait.

A few minutes later, he came back, and she followed him once again, through a room full of people, into an ante-room. Sergeant Hill stood up when she came in.

'Joanna,' she said, her face concerned. 'Have a seat.'

'No, thank you.' Joanna didn't know what to say now that she was here. Screaming abuse at her would hardly help, but that was all she really wanted to do.

'We were given no option but to do what we did,' Sergeant Hill said.

'No option?' Joanna shouted. 'You can't seriously believe my mother killed Graham!'

'We just wanted to ask her some questions, Joanna. It needn't have been like that.'

Somewhere, at the back of her mind, behind her desire to call her names, Joanna knew that she was right. Her father had forced them into a corner.

'But why?' she demanded. 'Why did you want to question her? Because of the dress? My father thinks she did it because she was angry with him – it was his Christmas present to her.'

'Oh?' said Sergeant Hill. 'Why was she angry with him?'

'I don't know! You'll have to ask him that.'

'Where is he?' she asked.

'Being sick!'

'I'm sorry,' she said. 'Please sit down, Joanna.'

Joanna felt some of the anger drain away, to be replaced by hopelessness. She sat down. 'Why have you arrested my mother?' she said again.

'I can't discuss it with you,' Sergeant Hill said. 'But in view of what you've said about the dress, I would like to talk to your father.'

Joanna went to find her father; he was angry with her for telling the sergeant.

'If you think she had a good reason for burning the dress, you have to tell them!' Joanna said.

'I didn't say she had a—' He sighed. 'Sorry,' he said. 'It's not your fault.'

Joanna waited for him by the desk. It would get sorted out.

'Yes,' Eleanor said, as brightly as she could, 'I will think about it. I promise.' And she waved as her visitor drove out of the court-yard, then closed the door with a sigh.

'You should go,' said Penny, as she went back in.

'I can't see myself at a New Year party,' said Eleanor.

Penny shook her head. 'You've got to start some time,' she said.

'And the sooner the better. You don't have to stay long. But you should start going out.'

Eleanor knew all that. But how could she start going out now, for God's sake? Penny didn't understand. And she wouldn't, for as long as Eleanor could keep it that way.

'I'd look after Tessa,' Penny went on. 'You know that.'

Eleanor smiled, 'I know,' she said. 'You're right. But I just don't think I could face it.'

'At least do what you said you'd do,' Penny said. 'Think about it.'

'I will.'

'I was wondering,' said Penny, 'I know you won't come – but would you mind if I took Tessa back with me when I go tomorrow night? There's nothing much for her to do here, is there – and you'll be working. It would be more fun for her. There's a little boy next door that she could play with.'

'You told me,' said Eleanor, with a smile.

'Well? It would be a few days rest for you, and I'd love to have her.'

'Yes, of course,' said Eleanor.

'If she wants to come, that is,' said Penny.

Tessa would want to go. There was only one thing she liked better than visiting anyone, and that was visiting her grandmother. They couldn't ask her then and there because she was off visiting the Brewsters, who had three of the children that Penny kept insisting were non-existent in Byford.

'Thank you,' Eleanor said. 'It would be nice to have a break.'

George Wheeler hadn't been very forthcoming as to why his wife should have been angry with him. He had just sat there, looking like death, saying that it was a misunderstanding, until Judy had told him he could go.

Lloyd raised his eyebrows when she told him. 'Sounds a bit desperate to me,' he said. 'The best excuse he could come up with.'

'I know.'

'All the same,' said Lloyd. 'I don't think Freddie's going to go much for Mrs Wheeler as a likely candidate.'

'Has she said anything yet?'

'No,' said Lloyd. 'Do you want to come and have a go?'

Judy got up. 'Is her solicitor here?'

'No. I suppose Wheeler did ring one,' he said. 'Every time I see him, he's rushing into the loo.'

Judy went to the door. 'Are you coming?' she asked.

'Yes,' he said wearily. 'Why not?'

Marian Wheeler sat at the table in the interview room, looking entirely unperturbed.

Judy sat down. 'Have you remembered where you were on Christmas Eve?' she asked.

'No.'

'Can you give us an explanation for your fingerprints being on the poker?'

'No.'

Judy clasped her hands, and thought for a moment. 'Did you go into the room when you found Elstow's body?'

'No.'

'Were you in that room at all on Christmas Eve?'

'I was in and out during the day,' she said. 'The last time would have been at about two, I think. Just before I went out in the afternoon. I made up the fire.'

'You're sure that was the last time you were in there?'

'Yes.'

'Oh, come on, Mrs Wheeler!' Lloyd suddenly spun round to face her from having his back to her.

His voice startled Judy, but Mrs Wheeler looked as calm as ever.

'Your fingerprints were on the poker. There had been an attempt to burn a dress – *your* dress, which had blood on it. Type B, Mrs Wheeler. Elstow's type.'

Marian Wheeler didn't speak.

'You must give us some explanation for these facts, Mrs Wheeler,' Judy said, her voice as calm as Mrs Wheeler's.

'I understood I didn't have to speak to you at all.'

Judy sighed. 'You'll have to give an explanation to someone, some time,' she said. 'You will have to defend the charges, won't you?'

'You haven't charged me, have you?' Mrs Wheeler looked eager; interested. Not as though it was happening to her at all.

'No,' said Judy. 'We haven't. But we will, Mrs Wheeler, unless you have an explanation. Do you?'

'No,' said Mrs Wheeler.

'No?' Lloyd said. 'You mean you don't *know* how the blood got on your dress? You don't know how your fingerprints got on the poker?'

He leant over the table, and Mrs Wheeler pulled back a little.

'You say you were never in the room, Mrs Wheeler. So how come blood got walked out of that room on to the landing on the sole of *your* shoe?'

'I don't know. I'm sorry.'

'You don't know,' he said, his voice menacingly low and Welsh. 'Someone tried to clean up the blood on the landing – did you know that? Someone who left their fingerprints by the stain.' His own hand, fingers spread, thumped down on the table. '*Your* fingerprints, Mrs Wheeler. You don't know how that happened?'

She was getting to Lloyd. Judy could tell when simulated anger was turning to real frustration. 'I've just been talking to Joanna,' she said, conversationally.

Mrs Wheeler stiffened.

'She suggests that you burned the dress because you were angry with her father.'

'Does she?' A frown crossed the serene face.

'Were you angry with him?'

'No.'

'So that isn't why you burned the dress?'

'No, of course it isn't.'

A silence fell, and Lloyd sat down, leaning back, relaxed.

'But you did burn it, didn't you, Mrs Wheeler?' Judy asked quietly.

Mrs Wheeler nodded, and Judy felt her heart skip a little.

'I wanted him to leave,' Marian Wheeler said. 'I wanted him out of the house just as much as George did. I just wanted to ask him to leave. To go away, and stop hurting Joanna. So I went up. But – but when I spoke to him, he just . . . *came* at me. He was drunk, I suppose. I told him to stop, but he was threatening me. I picked up the poker. I told him to stop. I *told* him I'd hit him.'

Judy glanced at Lloyd, whose eyebrows twitched a little.

'Are you saying it was self-defence?' she asked Mrs Wheeler.

'Yes,' she replied, 'I was frightened. I warned him. But he kept coming. Then he lunged at me, and I hit him. He fell,' she said. 'I realised he was dead.'

'We don't think it was self-defence,' Judy said carefully. 'Our evidence suggests that he was lying on the bed when he was attacked.'

Marian Wheeler's eyes widened and for a moment she said nothing. Then she shook her head.

'He wasn't lying on the bed?'

'No. He was coming at me.'

'Where was he when you hit him?' Lloyd asked.

'Near the fireplace,' said Mrs Wheeler. 'That's why I could pick up the poker.'

'And that's where you're saying you struck the first blow?'

'Yes,' she said.

Lloyd looked at her for a long time, without speaking. Mrs Wheeler looked back, wide-eyed. Judy stayed out of it. After a while, Lloyd sighed heavily, and rubbed his face. 'I told you that everything in that room had a story to tell, Mrs Wheeler.'

Mrs Wheeler looked away from both of them, as though something had caught her attention.

'Blood stains,' Lloyd went on. 'They talk, Mrs Wheeler. Elstow was nowhere near the fireplace.'

She looked back then, her eyes defiant. 'Yes,' she said. 'He was.'

'Then what?' said Lloyd, abandoning the topic.

'There was blood on my dress. I took it off, and put it on the fire. It wouldn't burn properly, because the fire was almost out. So I used matches, and firelighters. Then when I left, I could see I'd made marks on the landing. I cleaned my shoe, and then I cleaned up the stain.'

She paused. 'I washed, and went into my own room. I put on different clothes, and different shoes, and then I went out to check up on the old people, since that was what I had been going to do in the first place. And I *did* lock the doors,' she said. 'So that no one would find him.'

Judy noted the emphasis – 'I *did* lock the doors' – but its significance escaped her.

Mrs Wheeler's statement was being typed when her solicitor arrived, full of apologies to his client for the long delay, occasioned by his car breaking down in the middle of nowhere. He couldn't even find a phone; he had had to walk to a garage through the snow. He advised her against signing the statement, but she did anyway. Lloyd still didn't charge her; her solicitor wasn't happy about that either, but Judy understood his reluctance.

Back in the office, Judy tidied up her desk. They had informed Mr Wheeler of the course of events, and he'd gone rushing outside. Joanna Elstow had stared uncomprehendingly at them, then followed him. The solicitor had sighed, and gone after both of them.

'Let's go and talk to Freddie,' said Lloyd.

Judy looked at her watch. 'At the hospital?' she said. 'Will he be there this late on a Saturday?'

'Of course he will. He practically lives there.'

Judy drove them in her car; Lloyd's had been left at home in favour of the front-wheel drive of official vehicles. Her car might not be in the first flush of youth, she pointed out, but it didn't get the vapours at a little snow and ice.

Freddie was, as predicted, at the path lab, as joyful as ever with his choice of profession. 'Confessed?' he beamed. 'Well, there you are. You do win some.'

'Do we?' Lloyd said. 'By the time it gets to court, she may well have changed her mind.'

Judy hated the smell of the place. She didn't want to be there, and she wasn't sure why she was. But Freddie was always pleased to see her, so that cheered her slightly.

Lloyd continued. 'She's either going to plead self-defence or not guilty,' he said. 'How good a case have I got?'

'She won't plead self-defence,' Freddie said decidedly. 'If she brings in her own pathologist, he can't not agree with me. The man was lying on the bed when the first blow was struck.'

'She says he was by the fireplace,' said Lloyd.

'Well, you know he wasn't.'

'Could he have fallen on to the bed? From being hit?'

Freddie shook his head. 'He was on the bed,' he said. 'There's no argument – look at the bedclothes, man!'

'I'd rather not,' said Lloyd.

'All right,' sighed Freddie. 'Let's suppose we get given an argument. Wherever he was, he wasn't standing up. Or if he was, then his attacker was standing on a step-ladder. There is no way a blow of that force could have been delivered except from someone with a considerable height advantage – so if you've got someone nine feet tall on your list, that's your man.'

Lloyd smiled. 'So what will the defence do with a not guilty plea?' he asked. 'Apart from produce a nine-foot tall suspect?'

'Well,' said Freddie, 'if I was defending, I *would* go on build. I wouldn't produce the giant theory, but I would point out how small and slim Mrs Wheeler is.'

'You said a woman could have done it,' Lloyd said in injured tones.

'Certainly. But Mrs Wheeler's height and weight would suggest that she'd need two hands to produce blows that strong.' He warmed to his task. 'She only used one hand on the poker. So if I can produce a good reason for her prints being there, and ram home her diminutive stature . . .' He left the rest of the sentence eloquently unfinished.

'Are you saying she'll get off?'

'No,' he said. 'Because she *could* have done it. If she was frightened enough. Or angry enough.'

'So what *are* you saying?' Lloyd asked testily.

Freddie smiled. 'If she sticks to self-defence, she's got no chance,' he said. 'If she simply says she didn't do it, well – you've got her confession, her prints, and the burnt dress on your side. She's got the fact that she's small, pretty, female and a vicar's wife on hers.'

'And the fact that she was alone with him in the house at the material time,' Lloyd said. 'I've got that on my side, too.' He thought for a moment. 'Suppose she *did* hit him by the fireplace?' he said. 'Ineffectually. Making him dizzy – he grabs hold of her as he falls. So she's only got one hand free, and she's terrified. What then?'

'Is that what she says?' asked Freddie.

'No,' Lloyd said. 'But could that produce what you've found?'

'If he happened to fall on to the bed,' said Freddie. 'Which I suppose he could have done. It's highly unlikely.'

'But self-defence might work?'

Freddie shook his head slowly. 'No,' he said. 'That could just conceivably have been what happened. But he must have let go. And she didn't stop hitting him. Two blows were after he was dead, remember.'

'Yes, I know,' said Lloyd. 'That's what puzzles me.' He got up. 'Thanks, Freddie,' he said. 'See you in court.'

'Are you going to charge her?' Judy asked, as they got back to the car.

'Not tonight,' he said. 'I'm not happy with any of this. Why would she hit him twice after he was dead? And why wouldn't she tell us that she had?'

'Do you still think she just tried to tidy up after someone else?'

Lloyd looked tired, as he shook his head. 'I can't see *when*,' he said.

Judy frowned. 'So what do you think?' she asked, puzzled.

Lloyd smiled. 'You'll give me one of your looks if I tell you,' he said.

'Try me.'

'Well,' he began a little sheepishly. 'I'm beginning to think she wasn't there at all.'

Judy stared at him, giving him one of her looks. 'Someone else burned her dress?' she said incredulously. 'Someone *else* put blood on her shoe?'

He nodded.

'And she's *letting* them?' Judy shook her head. 'What about the prints on the poker?' she said.

'Ah, yes. There are those.'

Judy smiled, and started the car, and there was silence then, as though leaving the lab was a signal that the working day had ended, and now she and Lloyd were back to being just two people who didn't know what to say to one another.

The headlights lit the snow-covered verges as the car sped along a country road now dry and cold, and it was the first time they had been alone together, out of working hours, since Christmas morning. It seemed to Judy that Lloyd had engineered their lack of privacy; perhaps it was because she hadn't responded to what she assumed had been a proposal of marriage, or perhaps because he was regretting it already, and wanted to avoid any discussion on the matter.

Judy thought of several things she should be saying, but she didn't voice them. A minute and painful examination of her position had forced her to see things from Lloyd's point of view. She did want everything her own way. She did want to run back to the safety of her marriage, and it wasn't a marriage, not really. It never had been. But where she and Michael bickered and complained at one another, she and Lloyd had rows. Real rows, where feelings were involved. Lloyd, with his quick Celtic temper, could forget them five minutes later. Judy couldn't. It was all too raw and emotional for her, and the rows would haunt her for days. But this one, despite having ended in the odd way that it had, seemed to have left its mark on Lloyd too, and she knew why.

'I didn't know I was hurting you,' she said.

'You're not,' Lloyd said, his voice surprised. But Lloyd could do that. Surprise, sorrow, anger. Whatever was needed.

'You said you felt like a bottle of aspirin,' she said.

'That's irritating,' he said, as she slowed the car down, and signalled left. 'It doesn't hurt.'

'Then why have you been avoiding me?'

He didn't answer for a moment, and Judy affected deep concentration on her negotiation of the turn into the old village, where Lloyd had his flat. Stansfield, town of supermarkets and light industrial estates, of civic theatres and car showrooms like the one she was passing, had once just been a farming village, like Byford.

She could abandon the decision she had come to in the path lab; she could drop Lloyd off by the alleyway. But she drove on, turning through the entrance to the garages, parking beside Lloyd's car.

'I had no right to say these things,' Lloyd almost muttered.

'But they're true,' Judy said gloomily, stopping the engine. She looked out at the blackness of the garage area, only marginally relieved by stray beams from a failing street-lamp, and not at all in the shadow of the ornamental wall. She was surprised as always that the place wasn't littered with the unconscious bodies of muggees. But throwing empty bottles at the garage doors seemed to be the most popular pastime in this particular back alley.

'No,' Lloyd protested, 'I knew the position all along. You were right.'

This wasn't helping, thought Judy. Trust Lloyd, who could always be relied upon to defend himself, to turn sweetly reasonable on her.

'I am being selfish,' she said, 'I know I am. But—' She stopped. How could she explain it to Lloyd? She and Michael didn't need one another; they needed the marriage. That was why Michael had thought up his ridiculous notion of starting a family – it was one way to keep the marriage going. A marriage they both needed because it was safe, and predictable, and pleasantly boring, like a cricket match which will inevitably end in a draw.

'So what if you are?' said Lloyd. He gave a short, unamused laugh. 'If you'd given in to my lustful advances in the first place, you'd have the bachelor flat, and I'd be the one hanging on to my marriage.'

It was a joke, of sorts. But it wasn't true.

'No,' she said. 'You're braver than me.'

'Why won't you tell him about us, Judy?' he asked.

She didn't reply.

'I can't believe he hasn't guessed,' Lloyd went on.

He may have guessed, thought Judy. But she didn't think so. And guessing wasn't the same as finding out for certain. And it certainly wasn't the same as being *told*.

'Why?' he asked again.

Judy tried to explain. 'There's only ever been Michael and you,' she said. 'And you could come from different planets.'

'The trouble is,' said Lloyd, 'we're on the same planet.'

'Yes,' she said. Worse; they were in the same town. But she had to run some risks for Lloyd, or it was all too selfish for words. 'I'm here now,' she said. 'But I can't stay long – you do understand that.'

It had been a hard decision to make; she hadn't reckoned on Lloyd's reaction.

'What?' he said, taking his arm away.

'What's wrong?' she asked. It was an innocent question.

'What's wrong? What's wrong?' His voice grew louder. 'You can't see, can you? You still don't understand!'

He was shouting so loudly that Judy glanced fearfully up at the flats in case someone might hear.

'I told you what was wrong on Christmas morning,' he said. 'I don't want to share you any more, Judy. Do you understand? I don't want to share you *any more*!' And he got out and slammed the door so hard that the car rocked.

Chapter Six

Marian Wheeler had been awake when they brought her breakfast. The girl, an uncompromising young woman with sensible legs – though, Marian supposed, you didn't have much option but to have sensible legs in uniform – seemed almost apologetic. But there was nothing wrong with the food. She had sampled the canteen cooking in her YOC days; she had never imagined she would be eating it in a cell. She was by herself, because the others being detained were men. It gave her time to think.

By the time lunch had arrived, she had worked out what she was going to do. The solicitor had come, but she had refused to see him. Once she knew he was gone, she told the policewoman that she wanted to change her statement.

And now a sergeant was here; not the desk sergeant from last night, but it wouldn't be. He'd be on a different shift. This one had grey hair, and a kind, bored expression. Last night's had been a little surly, she thought. This one said his name was Woodford. Did she want someone to take down her new statement?

'No,' she said. 'I'll write it myself, if that's all right.'

'Yes,' he said. 'That's fine.'

The girl gave her a form, and the sergeant told her what to write at the beginning.

> *I make this statement of my own free will. I have been told that I need not say anything unless I wish to do so and that whatever I say may be given in evidence.*

She signed that, and the sergeant left, leaving the girl with her. That inhibited her a little, like the invigilator in an exam, when he walks between the desks. But in the end, it was finished.

'Read it through,' said the girl. 'Make sure it says what you want it to say. Then sign it.'

Marian read it through.

> *In my statement dated 27th December, I said that I had killed my son-in-law Graham Elstow in self-defence. This was untrue. I was about to leave the house at about ten minutes to eight, but I did not want to leave him alone in the house, and I decided to try making him leave. I only intended speaking to him, but when I went up and told him to leave, he wouldn't answer, and he wouldn't turn round. He pretended to be asleep, and that made me angry. I suppose I just wanted to hurt him because he had hurt Joanna. I picked up the poker, and hit him. He sort of sat up, and fell off the bed. I kept on hitting him. I knew I had killed him. I had blood on my dress, and I burned it. I left the house at approximately eight twenty-five.*

Marian signed it.

'I thought you didn't believe in it?'

Eleanor's voice, quiet, as befitted someone speaking in church, made George start.

'I'm used to doing my thinking in here,' he said.

He had behaved like someone about to steal the poor-box when he had arrived to do his thinking, making sure that his emergency stand-in had gone.

'What did Marian say?' she asked.

'What?'

'About your decision?'

She didn't know. Of course she didn't. How could she? It had only happened yesterday evening, and Eleanor, up in the castle, wasn't on the village grapevine. He tried to tell her. It was simple. The words were simple. *They've arrested Marian.* But he couldn't say them. He stuck on 'they' as if he had a stammer.

'They what? What's wrong?' She made an impatient noise at her own lack of tact. 'Sorry. But you know what I mean – has something else happened?'

George stood up, and walked into the aisle, where the stained-glass sunlight cast colours on to the floor. 'When I got engaged to Marian,' he said, 'Rosalind Anthony – do you know her?' He carried on as Eleanor shook her head. 'Rosalind Anthony told me that since she didn't know who gave vicars good advice when they were about to marry, she'd do it. She'd been married three times,' he told Eleanor. 'She'd be about . . . about Marian's age then, I suppose. She'd divorced two and buried one.'

Eleanor looked puzzled, and sat down.

'She was quite a girl in her youth, I believe,' he said. He paced along a few feet, turned and paced back, as he spoke. 'She said Marian would never let me down, and that I might find that hard to take.'

He looked across at Eleanor, who sat still, her hair touched by the soft colours from the window. She frowned slightly, not understanding.

'And I said something pompous about that being what marriage was about,' he went on. 'But she said that I might not want to be protected and shielded all my life.' He sank down on to a pew. 'She was right,' he said. 'She was right.'

'Has something happened with you and Marian?' Eleanor asked. 'Was it when you told her?'

'Told her?' He blinked. 'Oh – no.' He ran his hand over his face. He hadn't shaved. He hadn't slept. He must look awful. 'Rosalind said that if I married Marian, I'd have to go on pretending to be a vicar. She was right about that, too.'

Eleanor made sense of one thing. 'You *haven't* told Marian you're leaving the Church, have you?' she said.

'No.'

'Who have you told?'

'Only you.'

'And now you're not going to do it?'

George shook his head. 'I can't,' he said. 'I can't leave.' How could he leave? He was in prison. A prison that Marian had knitted for him. He dropped his eyes from Eleanor's. 'And now—'

'Now?' she asked, when he didn't continue.

'She's told the police that she killed Elstow,' he said, and he

could practically hear the snowflakes fall outside. He looked up.
'She *didn't*!' he shouted. 'She didn't – don't you see?'

Eleanor shook her head, as if to rid it of confusion. 'But you
said everyone was out all evening,' she said.

'We were. But – but Marian . . .' He sighed, and tried to tell her
rationally. 'At first, she said she left the house at ten to eight, but
now she says she didn't. And then, well – there was the dress, and
I don't know – there must have been more. But she's *confessed* –
don't you see?' He buried his head in his hands.

'Dress?' said Eleanor, uncomprehendingly. 'What dress? What
has a—?' She broke off. 'George?' she said. 'What did you say?
What time did Marian say she'd left the house?'

He lifted his hands away, and held them up helplessly. 'She says
she didn't leave until later,' he said. 'I don't know. What difference
does it make?'

'It's important, George.' She sounded impatient, almost angry.
'She's made up some story to protect you, hasn't she?'

George looked up slowly. 'Me?' he said.

'I thought that's what you meant. When you told me about this
Rosalind person. That Marian thought *you'd* done it.'

'What?' he said. Did she? No. Perhaps. He didn't know.

'Whatever her reason,' Eleanor said. 'Did you say eight?'

He frowned. 'Ten to,' he said. 'She said she left at ten to eight.
They say she couldn't have, and it's got something to do with Ros
Anthony. *That's* why I was telling you. She's always had a down
on Marian – I wouldn't put it past her—'

'George.' Eleanor broke into his illogical accusations. 'George.
We have to go to the police,' she said.

'You shouldn't have *let* her make statements!' Joanna said firmly.

Mr Barrington, a young, dark man with a worried expression,
pulled papers from his briefcase, and laid them out on the kitchen
table. 'I've made some notes,' he said. 'Some odds and ends that
might help us.'

'Why didn't you stop her?'

'I can't tell your mother what to do, Mrs Elstow,' he said. 'I can
only give advice.'

'Once you get there!'

'I have apologised for that – I couldn't get to a phone. And I did advise Mrs Wheeler not to sign the first statement, but she did. She wouldn't see me either of the times I called there today. And I wasn't there when she made the second statement.'

Joanna was making coffee for her visitor; it was like saying thank you to an automatic door, or apologising for bumping into a lamp-post. Making coffee for vicarage visitors was second nature, even if they'd come to tell you that your mother had confessed to the deliberate murder of your husband.

'But she *can't* have said she did it deliberately!' Joanna filled the coffee pot with water, and banged the kettle down.

'I'm afraid she has,' said Mr Barrington. 'And it ties in with the medical evidence.'

'I don't *care*!' Joanna tried to calm down. Deep breaths. 'Of course it does,' she said. 'Maybe they dictated it for all I know – maybe they made her sign it!'

Mr Barrington coughed. 'I doubt that very much, Mrs Elstow,' he said.

'Oh – I suppose you think the police are whiter than white?'

'No,' he said, his reasonable tones beginning to strain just a little. 'I'm sure some police officers are not above bullying known criminals, or convincing teenage boys that it'll be better if they confess. But I don't think they'd be likely to do it to someone like your mother.'

'It would be easier with her,' Joanna said, noisily removing mugs from the cupboard. 'She's not used to being arrested – being questioned.'

'She could certainly have been confused,' said Mr Barrington, clearing away some papers for her to put the coffee things down. 'That is one of the points I've made.' He pointed to his hand-written notes. 'She must have been alarmed, and tired – and perhaps she just told them what they wanted to hear. It does happen. But I know the inspector, and I'm sure that he would do nothing . . . nothing *underhand*.'

'You're chums with the inspector. Great.'

'I didn't *say* that, Mrs Elstow. I—'

But Joanna felt the tears coming again.

'Oh – Mrs Elstow. Er – please. Look – have some coffee, a glass of water?' He searched his pockets fruitlessly, and then pulled some kitchen paper from the roll. 'Mrs Elstow?' he said, pushing the wad of paper into her hands. 'I'm sorry. But I—'

This time, at least, she was under control. She blew her nose. 'Graham's *dead*,' she said. 'And they're accusing my mother, and I don't know what to *do*.'

'There isn't a great deal you can do at the moment, Mrs Elstow,' he said. 'But there are things I can do – look. I've made notes on them. I really came to talk to your father – I should have waited for him. I shouldn't have bothered you.'

Her father. Whose answer to the situation last night had been to disappear into his study until it was time to go to bed. Who had spent most of the night in the loo, and stayed in his room all morning. Who had eaten lunch in silence, and left without a word.

'No,' she said. 'He's not very well. I'm all right now,' she assured him, sitting up straight. 'What happens next?'

'Well,' he said helplessly, 'I take it you mean what happens to your mother?'

'Yes.'

'She'll be charged, and go before the magistrates. That doesn't take more than a few minutes. I can't promise anything, but there's a possibility that she'll be released on bail.'

'And if she isn't?' Joanna couldn't take it all in.

'Once she's been committed for trial,' Mr Barrington went on briskly, as though she hadn't spoken, 'I'll be able to brief counsel.'

Joanna pulled at the screwed-up paper towel in her hands. 'And he'll have all the answers?' she asked bleakly.

'She,' Mr Barrington said. 'She may have some. It's what she's paid for. It does rather depend on your mother.'

'My mother didn't kill Graham.' There was no response to her words, and she looked up to find Mr Barrington watching her closely.

'Then someone else did,' he said. 'So she must be protecting someone.'

Of course she was, thought Joanna, as she shredded the paper towel. 'It was someone who came in,' she said obstinately. 'A burglar.'

'There's no evidence of a burglar,' he said gently. 'And your mother – if she *is* protecting someone – doesn't believe it was a burglar.' He looked away from her. 'Mrs Elstow,' he said. 'It is a very serious situation.'

Joanna frowned. 'Do you think I don't know that?' she asked, and then her brow cleared. 'You think she's protecting me, don't you?'

'Is she?'

'Probably,' said Joanna. 'But she's wrong.'

He wasn't convinced. Or perhaps he just believed her mother's confession. Joanna didn't know, but she wished her father had found someone older, more experienced.

'Mrs Elstow – is there anyone else who might have felt that violently about your husband?'

Joanna didn't answer.

'I mean someone he might have admitted to the house.'

Joanna shook her head. 'I don't think so,' she said.

'You see—' He cleared his throat, a little embarrassed. 'It's possible that – in view of the fact that you had left him – your husband took up with someone else. It's just possible, since there is no evidence of an actual intruder, that someone was invited into the house, and subsequently—' He opened and shut his mouth a few times.

'Up to my bedroom?' Joanna supplied.

'That's where it happened,' he said, almost defensively. 'Whoever did it was in the bedroom with him.'

Joanna wiped the tears away. 'You think Graham could have had another woman? But why should she be here?'

Mr Barrington sighed. 'It isn't at all likely,' he said. 'But I understand that he may have met someone here – at the pub, I think your father said.'

'Yes,' said Joanna doubtfully.

'It's worth investigation,' he said. 'If there was someone else, she may be the person he met in the pub. It's a very long shot,' he stressed. 'But I'll put an enquiry agent on to it, if you think it's worth it. In my experience, men who show violence towards their wives do so towards other women with whom they have relationships. If someone else was here, it could have turned violent.'

'But he didn't have anyone else here, did he?' said Joanna. 'The police didn't find any other fingerprints, or anything. And Graham wouldn't have done that anyway,' she added.

'It's ... well, I won't pretend I'm not clutching at straws, because unless your mother co-operates, that's all I can do, other than to set out the mitigating circumstances. And I gather your father doesn't want that. Not yet.' He began to put away the papers that Joanna hadn't even looked at. 'I could wait, and talk to him,' he said. 'When will he be back?'

'I don't know.'

'Well, then – I'll ring later. Do you think he'll agree to an enquiry agent?'

'Yes.'

'Good.'

Eleanor finished her story, and glanced at George, who sat tight-lipped, not looking at her. She looked back at the inspector.

He ran his hand over his hair, and drew in a slow breath. 'Well, well, well,' he said. 'An alibi.'

Eleanor frowned.

'Well, I mean,' he said, and he sounded much more Welsh than he had to start with. 'Convenient, isn't it?'

'Do you think I'm making it up?' she asked, startled.

He picked up the file that he had brought in with him, stood up and walked to the window.

Eleanor exchanged glances with George, but all George's bluster seemed to have gone. He looked almost furtively away again.

'Langton, Langton,' the inspector said, consulting the file, murmuring her name. 'No,' he said. 'No Langton on Mrs Wheeler's list of visits.' He looked out of the window, his back to her.

'Mrs Wheeler was at my house at five past eight on Christmas Eve,' Eleanor repeated, her voice firm.

'Was anyone else there?' He didn't turn round.

'Only my daughter. She's two and a half years old, and she was sound asleep.'

'Not much good, then,' he said.

He still hadn't turned round, which was beginning to irritate Eleanor.

'Friend of the family, are you?' he asked.

She said no, just as George said yes.

Then Lloyd turned. Of course he turned. 'Shall I go out?' he asked. 'Give you a bit more rehearsal time?'

'I help out with the church play-group,' Eleanor said, aware that she was going pink, as she did with unsophisticated ease. 'I know Mr Wheeler. I've only met Mrs Wheeler a couple of times.'

'One of those times being five past eight on Christmas Eve?'

'Yes.'

The door opened and Eleanor turned to see a young woman come in, glancing over at George, who just looked through her.

'Well, then, let's see,' said the inspector. 'If you saw her, perhaps you can give me some sort of proof. What was she wearing, for instance?'

'I never notice what people are wearing.'

Eleanor had only been aware of what she herself had been wearing. George's tie.

Inspector Lloyd sat down again. 'Definitely under-rehearsed,' he said.

Eleanor refused to take the bait. 'Someone like him could have had enemies,' she tried. 'Why don't you look for them?'

'Someone like what?'

'Like Graham Elstow. Someone who beats up women, for a start.'

'Wouldn't that make his wife's mother an enemy?'

'She was with *me*.'

He leant forward. 'And why do you suppose Mrs Wheeler didn't tell us that?' he asked.

'I don't know,' Eleanor said.

'Perhaps,' said Lloyd, 'it's because she doesn't know that that's suddenly where she was. She was out making certain that old people were keeping warm enough, according to her original story. Where do you fit in?'

'That isn't why she came to see me,' Eleanor said. 'She wanted to confirm Mr Wheeler's invitation for Christmas lunch. And I'm not on the phone,' she added. 'So she had to call personally.'

'Why?' asked Lloyd. 'It was hardly necessary.'

Eleanor frowned. She had never thought about it.

'Going out on a night like that just to repeat an invitation?' He shook his head. 'That sounds very weak, Mrs Langton.' He leaned forward. 'Even weaker, if I may say so, with Mrs Wheeler's husband sitting beside you,' he added.

He thought they'd made it up. Or he wanted them to think that was what he thought.

'That's why she came,' she repeated stubbornly.

'How long would it take her to get from the vicarage to the castle?' Lloyd asked.

'About fifteen minutes,' Eleanor said. 'By road.'

'By road?'

'There's a shortcut,' she said. 'Across the fields. But Mrs Wheeler was in the car.'

'Quarter of an hour,' Lloyd said, and sat back tipping his chair up. 'Imagine you are Mrs Wheeler,' he said, then flicked his eyes at George and back to her. He raised an eyebrow.

Eleanor wished that George would at least *react*.

'And you are going to call on about half a dozen people in the village,' Lloyd went on. 'Would you start with someone who lived . . . what? Three miles away? Then go on to someone who lived at the bottom of the drive? Then off somewhere else altogether?' He opened the file again. 'No,' he said. 'You'd start or finish with the person closest, wouldn't you? Which is what Mrs Wheeler did, Mrs Langton.' He tapped the list of names. 'She started with Mrs Anthony. And she didn't call on you.'

'Why would I make it up?' she asked.

'Oh, I don't know,' Lloyd said. 'Misguided loyalty.' He looked at George again. 'Or perhaps it's just women sticking together. Women against this, that and the other. Especially the other. Wife-batterers deserve all they get.'

Eleanor refused to let him get to her. She stood up. 'Look, Inspector. I don't know what she was wearing, and I don't know why she didn't tell you, but Mrs Wheeler was at my house at five past eight. I put Tessa to bed at seven. I decided to wait an hour before doing her stocking. I checked on her at eight, and I started to assemble the pedal car. About five minutes after that, Mrs Wheeler arrived. I want to make a formal statement to that effect.'

He sighed.

'If George—' She stopped, then decided that to amend it to Mr Wheeler would make things worse. 'If George and I had cooked it up, would we have come here together?'

'You'd have been better going to Mrs Wheeler's solicitor,' Lloyd said. 'But you can make a statement if you want.' He stood up. 'I notice George hasn't had much to say for himself,' he said.

George had gone pale, and Eleanor could see beads of sweat on his forehead. Lloyd had been deliberately trying to provoke him, all the time, and he still didn't say anything.

'And I must warn you,' Lloyd went on, 'that if you make a statement you can be prosecuted if you say anything knowing it to be false.' He opened his office door. 'Still want to make it?' he asked.

'Yes.'

He brought in a young man who took it down and read it back. Eleanor signed it with an angry flourish and handed it to Lloyd.

'Thank you for coming in,' he said.

She left, with George following behind her like a large dog. Outside, he sat down on the wall.

'You only said one word, and that made me look a liar,' Eleanor said angrily, then saw how he looked. 'Are you all right?' she asked.

'I will be,' he muttered. 'Once Marian's out of there.'

Eleanor sat down with him. 'Why didn't you ask to see her?' she said.

He shook his head, and they walked round to her car.

'He didn't believe a word,' George said. 'Not a word.'

'Oh – that was just theatre,' Eleanor said. 'I told him she had the car – someone's bound to have seen it.'

'Let's hope so.'

She looked at the pale, defeated face. 'Look, George, she *was* there! They can't make out in court that I've got some daft female solidarity reason for saying so.'

'What if she doesn't want you to give evidence?' he asked.

Eleanor's hand stopped in the act of unlocking the car door. 'Don't be silly,' she said, after a moment. 'She's bound to. You saw what he was like – no wonder she confessed. He was making me feel as if I was lying, and I'm not being accused of anything.'

They got into the car. 'Let's go and see the solicitor,' said Eleanor. 'He'll know what to do. Where does he live?'

George took a card from his wallet, and handed it to her in silence. She had to stop twice on the way to let him out to be sick.

'It'll be all right,' she said, arriving at the house. She squeezed his hand. 'You'll see. It'll be all right.'

'Do you really think she's making it up?' Judy asked, picking up Eleanor Langton's statement.

Lloyd shrugged. 'I don't know what to make of it,' he said. 'It sounds a bit unlikely. And George Wheeler didn't seem too keen on it himself.'

'No,' said Judy. George hadn't acknowledged her presence at all; she could have understood if he'd been resentful, like Joanna, and simply hadn't spoken to her. But it hadn't been like that. It was as though she hadn't been there. No, she amended. It was as if *he* hadn't been there.

'And there's this,' said Lloyd, putting a handwritten statement on her desk.

Judy read Marian Wheeler's new statement and looked up at Lloyd. So that was why he'd called her in.

'Now it makes a bit more sense,' she said.

But something didn't; she knew that even as she said it. She frowned at the statement. It seemed all right – it confirmed Freddie's findings.

'More sense,' Lloyd agreed. 'But we told her he was on the bed, didn't we? And she knows he ended up on the floor.'

Judy nodded. 'What does Freddie think?'

'Would you believe I haven't been able to get hold of him? He must take the last Sunday in the year off.'

'*I kept on hitting him,*' Judy quoted. 'Could that account for the blows after he was dead?'

Lloyd shrugged. 'Probably,' he said. 'That's what I wanted to ask Freddie. That, and—' He smiled. 'No,' he said. 'Forget it.'

Judy flicked through her already thick notes. It all seemed to fit, but there was something that wasn't right.

'What's up?' asked Lloyd.

'I'm not sure. Something doesn't fit.'

Lloyd came over, picking up the statement, and sitting on the corner of her desk. It usually irritated her, but this time she was glad.

'About this?' he asked, reading it through.

'No. I don't think so. It makes sense. It fits in with the forensic evidence – it maybe even explains the two extra whacks.'

'*Lizzie Borden took an axe, and gave her . . .*' mused Lloyd. 'But you don't believe it,' he said.

'I might,' said Judy. 'If I could find what I'm looking for.' She looked up at him. 'Because if you've got a piece left over after you've finished the jigsaw, it must belong to another puzzle – right?'

'There are quite a lot of puzzles,' Lloyd said. 'Little puzzles. What was Mrs Anthony hinting about George Wheeler, for instance?'

'What was Marian Wheeler angry with George about?' asked Judy.

'If she was,' said Lloyd. 'I'm inclined to think he made that up, like today's little pantomime.'

But Lloyd wasn't really dismissing Mrs Langton's statement just like that, Judy thought. It had set him thinking; he was going to ask Freddie something, and he wouldn't say what. So he had to be back on his frame-up theory. No point in asking; he'd tell her when he felt like it.

'And why *didn't* Joanna go up to talk to Graham in all that time, if she'd made it up with him?' she asked. 'Eight hours, Lloyd.'

'Well,' he said. 'If this statement's true, none of that is any of our business.'

There was a knock, and Jack Woodford came in. 'Just going to the machine,' he said. 'Anyone want anything?'

'Coffee,' Lloyd said, digging in his pocket for a coin. He threw it. 'Thanks, Jack,' he said, as his phone rang, and he slid off Judy's desk. 'We'd better talk to Mrs W. again,' he said, as he picked up the phone. 'Lloyd.'

He listened.

'Right. Thanks. Tell them to wait – I want a word with them before they go.'

He hung up and turned to Judy a little sheepishly. 'Just something I have to talk to Bob Sandwell about,' he said.

Judy gave him one of her looks for good measure, for whatever he was up to, he clearly deserved one. She watched the door close behind him, and uncharacteristically put down her notes, thinking about Lloyd, and Michael, and the dreadful mess her life was in.

Next door, two typewriters clattered, one expertly, one inexpertly. There were voices, laughter, as someone was being teased. Outside, a bus churned through the slush to the bus-station. Someone walking past was whistling *Plaisir d'Amour*. She wished she could be in Lloyd's flat, quiet and peaceful. Their few snatched moments on Christmas morning had been shattered, and she was afraid that her life might be going the same way.

The last time she'd been there – really been there – had been how long ago? She looked at the calendar on the wall. Almost three months ago. My God, was it that long? No wonder Lloyd had had enough. She had known then about Michael's promotion, and she had wondered, as she and Lloyd had made love, what she was going to do. She had pushed the thought away, told herself that it would all resolve itself somehow. But it wouldn't. It couldn't. *She* had to resolve it.

The door opened suddenly, jerking Judy back to her surroundings with a heart-stopping jump.

'Lloyd's coffee,' Jack said. 'He's gone off somewhere – he said just to give it to you.'

'Thanks,' said Judy, taking the paper cup. Her hand trembled slightly from the start she had been given, making coffee spill over on to her desk.

'Don't worry – I've got it,' said Jack, mopping it up with blotting paper.

Judy stared as the brown stain spread over the paper.

'All right?' Jack asked.

'Yes,' she said absently. 'Yes. Thanks, Jack.'

He went out, and she picked up her notebook, leafing through to find the right page.

Her hand shook. Spilled coffee on dress.

Well, fancy that, Judy thought. She sat back, looking at the sentence for a moment. Then she put on her coat, scribbled a note to Lloyd, and left.

The phone was picked up this time.

'Freddie? Where the hell have you been?'

'Out,' said Freddie. 'Playing Trivial Pursuit, if you must know.'

'I didn't know dead bodies could play Trivial Pursuit,' said Lloyd.

'Neither did I, until my wife took it up.'

Lloyd smiled. 'How does your wife put up with you?' he asked.

'She's a saint, Lloyd, a veritable saint. What can I do for you?'

Lloyd read him Marian Wheeler's second statement.

'Mm.'

'Mm?'

'It fits.'

'But?'

There was a pause. 'Same buts as before, really. Still, she's admitted it, so that's that. Though—'

'Though – what?' Lloyd said eagerly.

'Two confessions seems like one too many to me,' he said. 'It's a funny one, Lloyd.'

'I know,' said Lloyd. 'And what I wanted to know was – does her second statement account for the two post-mortem thumps?' he asked.

'Not really. I don't know what to make of them.'

'Freddie?' Lloyd said, preparing him for the silly question. 'Is there any doubt about the murder weapon?'

He heard Freddie draw in a slow breath. 'No,' he said. 'But if you were to bring me something else that general size and shape, I'd certainly consider it.'

'Like another poker?' Lloyd said. 'The one from the kitchen?' He held his breath.

'The one we've got gives every indication of having been used,' said Freddie.

'Could it have been used just for the two extra blows?'

There was a long silence. 'It's improbable, but just possible,' Freddie said at last. 'You bring me the other poker, and the chances are I'll know if it was used.'

'Good,' said Lloyd. 'Because it's on its way here now, with any luck.' He had dispatched Bob Sandwell and one of the uniformed lads to the vicarage an hour ago.

Freddie laughed. 'What's your theory this time, Lloyd?' he asked.

Lloyd didn't know what sort of reception it would get. 'Marian Wheeler had been using the poker in Elstow's room,' he said. 'When she made up the fire earlier that day. Someone could have killed him with one poker, cleaned it, put it back – then bopped him a couple of times with the one that already had Marian Wheeler's fingerprints on it.'

'What about the fingerprints on the landing?' Freddie said.

'Coincidence. It's a polished floor. Chances are, her prints are all over it. From polishing.'

'Maybe,' said Freddie, unconvinced. 'I'd have thought that polishing was supposed to have the opposite effect. And are you saying she's just going along with all of this?'

He sounded just like Judy. Lloyd didn't answer, because he hadn't worked out that part of his theory.

'And what about the dress?'

'Someone else could have bumed the dress, too,' Lloyd said, beginning to feel cornered.

'She was *wearing* it, Lloyd,' he said. 'But it's an interesting point about the poker. Send it to me anyway.'

'Don't worry,' said Lloyd, irritated. 'I will.'

He put down the phone, and there was a knock at the door.

'Sir?' Bob Sandwell came in. 'We've brought them both,' he said, handing him two pokers, in separate bags. 'Mrs Elstow told us about this one.' He held it up. 'It's from the back bedroom,' he said. 'She says her mother got a fire going in there on Christmas Eve, so her prints might still be on it. I checked the other rooms, but they've all got gas or electric fires. No other pokers, sir.'

'Thank you,' said Lloyd. 'Give them to Sergeant Woodford, will you? Tell him I want them taken to the lab first thing in the morning.'

Sandwell departed, ducking under the door, though he wasn't quite that tall. Lloyd sat forward. He was still lost in thought when Judy came in.

'I've tried my theory out on Freddie,' he said.

'Your frame-up theory?' she asked.

'Yes. Plus my poker theory.' He gave her a brief résumé. 'And all that Freddie could find to fault it was that she was wearing the dress,' he said. 'But she may not have been wearing it. She changed into it when she thought she was going to the pub – but she ended up doing a whole load of housework instead, didn't she? She did a washing, and made a bed up for Joanna – she even got a fire going in the back bedroom. Heaving coal about? In a brand new dress that she wanted to wear to the midnight service?' He sat back. 'Perhaps she wasn't wearing the dress at all,' he said. 'Perhaps she laid it on the bed, ready to change into when she got back from visiting.'

'Except that she *was* wearing it,' Judy said again. 'When she went visiting.'

Lloyd smiled. 'All right,' he said, 'I suppose you can prove it.'

'Yes,' said Judy.

'Oh, well,' Lloyd said resignedly. 'Another theory gone west.'

Judy shook her head. 'No it hasn't,' she said.

Lloyd smiled. He loved it when Judy got on to something. She looked just like a gun-dog.

'The dress,' she said. 'When we saw Marian Wheeler on Christmas morning, she was wearing a trouser-suit. There wasn't a dress in the washing, and there wasn't one with coffee stains on it anywhere else; But according to Mrs Anthony, she spilled some coffee on *her dress*. I've been back to Mrs Anthony,' she said, 'I got a good description. Peach, full skirt . . .'

Lloyd frowned, as he realised what that meant. 'But if she was wearing it at half past eight,' he said, 'she couldn't very well have thrown it on the fire some time previously.'

'No,' said Judy. 'She couldn't.'

'She spilled coffee,' said Lloyd slowly. 'And went home to change yet again. Are you saying that someone burned the dress after that?'

'Not after,' said Judy, sitting forward. 'Lloyd – if someone frames you for murder, I imagine you don't usually just go along with it, do you?'

'Well, I normally protest my innocence, I must agree,' said Lloyd.

'Make fun of my grammar if you like,' she said. 'But there is one circumstance in which you *wouldn't* protest your innocence.'

'Is there?' Lloyd thought hard. 'You mean I'd want to be framed?' he asked. 'I'd have to have framed myself.' He hit his head when he finally saw the point. 'Let's talk to the lady,' he said. His eye caught Mrs Langton's statement as he stood up. 'You'd better take that,' he said to Judy.

Judy picked up Mrs Wheeler's statements too, and read all three while they waited in the interview room.

When she was brought in, Marian Wheeler looked as calm and composed as she had when they had arrested her, but the slightly far-away look had been replaced by watchfulness.

'Some more questions, Mrs Wheeler,' said Judy. 'You understand that you don't have to answer them, and you can have your solicitor present if you choose?'

'I understand.'

Judy laid Mrs Wheeler's two statements down in front of her. 'Do you want to make a third?' she asked.

'No,' she said. 'I've told you everything.'

'Except the truth.'

Mrs Wheeler didn't speak.

'Right,' said Judy. 'Where were you at five past eight on Christmas Eve?'

'I've told you in my statement,' she said.

'Where were you at five past eight on Christmas Eve?' Judy asked.

Lloyd watched Marian Wheeler. He'd never been able to perfect Judy's trick of asking the same question over again, just as though it was the first time. It was dreadfully irritating, and almost always produced a response.

'I've just told you.'

'You were in your daughter's bedroom?'

'Yes.'

'Laying into her husband with a poker?'

Marian Wheeler raised her eyebrows. 'Yes,' she said. 'If you want to put it like that, I suppose that is what I was doing.'

'And then you burned the dress, and went to see Mrs Anthony?'

Mrs Wheeler didn't reply, but the watchfulness became wariness, and she sat a little further back in her chair.

'Where were you at five past eight on Christmas Eve?' asked Judy, pleasantly.

'I – I was at home.'

'Battering your son-in-law to death?' enquired Judy.

Marian Wheeler looked shocked. 'Sergeant, I don't think there's any need to—'

'There isn't a gentle way to say it,' said Judy. 'Someone battered him to death.'

'I did,' said Mrs Wheeler. 'I've told you.' She picked up the statement.

'And then you burned your dress?'

'Yes.'

'No,' said Judy. 'You were wearing the dress when you saw Mrs Anthony.'

'No! No – Mrs Anthony's a very old lady—'

'We made that mistake,' Lloyd said, chiming in. 'She's old, but she's *sharp*. Right, Sergeant?'

'She's described it to me, Mrs Wheeler,' said Judy. 'Peach, full skirt, deep cuffs . . .' She paused. 'You spilled coffee on it. You went home to change.'

'Yes,' said Mrs Wheeler. '*That's* when I did it – I got confused, that's all.'

'You didn't leave Mrs Anthony's house until ten past nine. Graham Elstow was already dead.'

Mrs Wheeler's eyes had lost their wariness, their defiance, and Lloyd knew that Judy had won.

'Where were you at five past eight on Christmas Eve, Mrs Wheeler?' asked Judy, in the same interested, polite tones.

'At the castle,' she said, her voice flat. 'I went to see a girl called Eleanor Langton. She's working there. A sort of archivist or something.'

Lloyd sat down. 'And *then* you went to see Mrs Anthony.'

She nodded. 'But while I was there I spilled some coffee on my dress. Well,' she said, 'she told you that, didn't she? I was still shaking. What if we hadn't come back, Mr Lloyd? What would have happened to Joanna if he hadn't stopped?'

'And yet despite how you felt – and despite the weather – you went all the way to the castle first?' said Lloyd. 'To confirm an invitation? I almost didn't believe Mrs Langton when she told me.'

'I wish you hadn't,' she sighed. 'Yes – that's what I told her. But I just wanted to . . .' She gave a short laugh. 'See what I was up against,' she said. 'She's been taking up rather a lot of my husband's time lately.'

'I see,' said Lloyd.

'I wonder if you do,' said Mrs Wheeler. 'Anyway, I *did* want to confirm the invitation. I wanted to be sure she knew that it was from both of us, if you see what I mean. I went there first to get it over with.'

'And then you went to Mrs Anthony's, and from there you went home to change,' said Lloyd. 'Go on.'

'I went upstairs,' she said. 'And I looked along the landing. Joanna's bedroom door was open. I thought Graham had left. I went in, and . . . and found him,' she said. 'He was dead. I didn't know what to do. I thought—'

Lloyd stood up, and walked slowly round the room. 'You thought your daughter had killed him,' he said.

'Yes,' she said. 'He deserved it!' she shouted. 'He deserved it – he put her in hospital – did you know that?'

'Yes,' said Lloyd. 'So what did you do then, Mrs Wheeler?'

'I didn't know what to do,' she said. 'I knew Joanna must have done it. That was why she wouldn't let her father go up to him.'

She looked up at Lloyd. 'I wasn't going to let her suffer for him any more,' she said. 'So I . . . I made it look as if I'd done it.'

Lloyd sat down, feeling tired and old. 'What did you do?' he asked.

'I cleaned the handle of the poker,' she said. 'And I held it. But then I thought – they can tell, can't they? They can tell *how* you've held something. I've read it in books. So I hit him, to make sure I was holding it right. I hit him twice.'

Someone walked along the corridor outside. Lloyd leant on the table, his chin resting on his clasped hands. She hadn't switched pokers, he thought. Other than that, his theory was pretty good. 'And the dress?' he said.

'I burned it,' she said. 'I got blood on the sleeve, and I realised that if I burned it, you'd find it.' She looked at Lloyd. 'What difference does it make?' she said. 'You've got *me* – why don't you charge me? I'd have done it – if I'd seen him hitting Jo, I'd have done it!'

Lloyd was beginning to lose what little patience he'd had left. He counted off on his fingers. 'One, you have wasted police time. Two, you have tampered with evidence. Three, you have made false statements. And if I can think of any more, I will, Mrs Wheeler. You can be prosecuted for these offences – perhaps that will feed your desire for martyrdom.'

She looked at him with vague surprise. 'I wasn't being a martyr, Mr Lloyd. I was just—' She obviously decided that he would never understand, and gave up with a shrug.

Then, Lloyd realised what she had done. What she had really done, and he was assailed by something worse, much worse, than mere irritation. 'When you left the house in the first place,' Lloyd said, 'you left it unlocked, as usual?'

Marian Wheeler looked haunted for a second. 'Yes,' she said.

Lloyd closed his eyes. Between ten to eight and ten past nine, the doors were unlocked. And someone went in. How the hell were they supposed to find out who? Marian Wheeler was out visiting, Wheeler and his daughter were at the pub . . . Well, they could make more vigorous enquiries about all of that. But the other possibility loomed before him.

'Someone could have got in,' he said slowly, angrily. 'Just like you said.'

Marian Wheeler's mouth opened, but she closed it again.

'And you destroyed any evidence that there might have been,' he went on. 'You misdirected us, you obliterated possible fingerprints, you tampered with the scene of the crime. You have given him time to get away, to destroy his clothing – in short, Mrs Wheeler, you have made our job practically impossible.'

He walked out of the room, resisting the temptation to slam the door. Bloody woman. Bloody stupid interfering woman. Who the hell could have got in and murdered the man? Why? Someone he knew? It had to be. Someone he didn't know? Lloyd's heart sank. Someone who might do it again. There had to be a coat, something, that the murderer had jettisoned. He'd get men looking tomorrow. Thank God they had taken the intruder suggestion seriously enough to issue a warning. But now an intruder wasn't just a desperate explanation thought up by the Wheelers. It was a real possibility. And they would have to start looking into Elstow's background.

He met someone in the pub. He'd ignored that. Now, he'd have to talk to the villagers, find out if they had seen a stranger hanging round. Oh, God, this should have been done days ago!

But some of it had, he reminded himself. Elstow had been alone in the pub, according to the barmaid. He had come in alone, and remained alone. And they only had his wife's word for it that he had ever mentioned meeting anyone. He calmed himself down, and walked back to the office. Joanna Elstow still seemed the likeliest candidate, even to her mother. Lloyd sighed. He'd taken her word for it that her row with her husband started at five. He was going to have to rub out anything that that damn family had told him, and start again.

Judy came in. 'I'm driving Mrs Wheeler home,' she said, then closed the door. 'Should I come back?' she asked him.

'No,' he said. 'There isn't much we can do tonight.' He looked up from the desk. 'Is there?' he asked, and he sounded bitter.

'I thought perhaps there might be,' she said quietly.

'No.'

Her direct brown gaze held his for a moment. 'Don't do this to me,' she said, almost under her breath.

'I'm not the one who's doing it,' he replied.

He watched as she slipped on the dark grey leather coat that Michael had given her for Christmas. He'd like to have given her something like that. As it was, they had to be content with the sort of thing that wouldn't be remarked on. Suddenly, he understood why long-standing mistresses would deliberately get pregnant. It wasn't vindictiveness. It was desperation of a sort.

He watched out of the window as she drove off with the would-be martyr, and darkly formulated the charges against Mrs

Wheeler. Because he *would* prosecute, and Judy would tell him he was being uncharitable.

But maybe not, he thought, sitting down again. Not if she was busy being a DI in Barton, and he'd made it clear that she wasn't welcome. Damn it, she was more than welcome, she was *necessary*. He needed her, and his bloody pride would have to take a back seat. Sharing her might not be ideal, but it was better than feeling like this. He just hoped he hadn't blown his last chance.

He picked up Eleanor Langton's statement. He'd better apologise – be really had been a bit high-handed with her. Perhaps he should go now, he thought, glancing at his watch. Why not? It would keep him out of the flat for another hour or two. And apologising to her might rid him of this nagging notion that he ought to be apologising to *someone*.

He was getting heartily sick of the journey into Byford, rendered utterly monotonous by the snow. In spring, the fields would shade from pale yellow to dark green, relieved here and there by the dark brown of a ploughed acre. Crows would rise noisily from the treetops, flapping across the road, and rabbits would dart from the fields, bobbing along the verges, occasionally coming to grief. But the snow deadened everything; no colour, no sound.

Up Castle Road, reluctantly past the pub, and on to the top, where he turned into the castle gates, the car bumping over the cattle grids. In the unlit castle grounds, he drove cautiously, only knowing he was on a road by the regular 5 m.p.h. speed-limit signs. On his left, suddenly looming into the night sky, was the castle, a dark, forbidding fortress. A reminder that there had once been worse things to worry about than muggers and vandals. Or even the odd murderer. He'd brought the kids here once or twice, when they were younger.

It had never made him shiver before.

Through the huge gatehouse, into the protected heart of the castle, lit by the odd wall-light where there once had been flaming torches. Turn left as you come out of the gatehouse, and left again at the end of the gatehouse walls, he'd been told.

He turned left, into a large, moonlit courtyard. Stables, whatever their function now, ran along the whole of one side, and Lloyd could practically hear the horses' hooves on the frosted cobbles, now broken up here and there by flower-beds. He pulled up beside two other cars and got out, walking past the shop which sold books and bric-à-brac, looking for Eleanor Langton's door. Beside the souvenir shop, the ever-knowledgeable Constable Sandwell had told him, and beside the souvenir shop it was.

A black door, with a brass knocker shaped like a lion's head. Through the window at the side, a light showed faintly from the rear. He knocked.

Mrs Langton let him in with a courtesy that he felt he didn't deserve. He followed her down the hallway to find an older woman sitting at the table in the small dining room.

'Oh, I'm sorry,' he said. 'I'm interrupting—'

'We've finished,' Mrs Langton said, and the other woman smiled. 'This is Chief Inspector Lloyd, Penny,' she went on.

'Acting,' said Lloyd, conscientiously.

'Some might say over-acting,' said Eleanor Langton in a quiet aside, as she began clearing away.

Lloyd was surprised, and smiled, pleased to discover that at least he'd been picking on someone his own size.

'This is my mother-in-law, Inspector. Penny Langton.'

'How do you do, Mrs Langton,' he said, shaking hands. 'It's a bit confusing,' he added. 'Two Mrs Langtons.'

'Then you'd better stick to Eleanor and Penny,' said Eleanor.

'Right.' He felt a little awkward now that he was on Eleanor Langton's home ground. She was in command here. She was enjoying herself.

'I'll be back in a moment,' she said, and Lloyd leapt to open the door to the kitchen as she made for it with both hands full. 'Thank you,' she said, and he was relieved to be left alone with her mother-in-law.

'You'll be here about the business at the vicarage?' said Penny, her eyes worried.

'Connected with it,' Lloyd said. 'Mrs . . . er . . . Eleanor has been very helpful.'

'Have I?'

He hadn't heard her come back, and he turned to see her in the doorway, flicking her long blonde hair back from her face. She was very good-looking, in a Scandinavian way. But there was something about her that reminded Lloyd of the snow-scene outside.

'Yes,' he said. 'I'm here to thank you for coming in, and to confirm that I have no reason to doubt the accuracy of your statement.' He paused. 'And to apologise if I . . .' He searched for the appropriate words. 'If I offended you in any way,' he said.

Her eyes held his, and there was a hint of amusement in them that he didn't like.

'Why the change of mind?' she asked.

Lloyd thought for a moment. 'Further evidence has come to light that . . . casts a new light on the incident,' he said, annoyed with himself as soon as the words were spoken, because they had been clumsy. She unnerved him.

'Thank you for the apology,' she said. 'Will you join us for coffee?'

He hesitated, because he wished he'd never come at all. But it was a tedious drive back, and if she was prepared to offer him coffee, the least he could do was to accept it. 'Thank you,' he said.

Over the coffee, Mrs Langton senior did most of the talking. Lloyd learned that her son had died in a motor accident, that Eleanor had coped wonderfully, and that Tessa was the most delightful grandchild anyone could ever want.

'I'll just look in on her,' said Eleanor. 'Help yourselves to more coffee.'

Penny Langton waited until she closed the door. 'It's very difficult for her,' she said. 'Bringing up Tessa on her own.'

'It must be,' said Lloyd.

'It's not money – she got some compensation after the accident. She doesn't *need* to work here, if you know what I mean. It's more for something to do – but I wish she'd move back to Stansfield. It's lonely here, don't you think?'

Lloyd couldn't but agree.

'But she says she really likes the job, and of course, another kind of job might be difficult, with Tessa, but . . .'

Lloyd waited.

'But the thing is, I'm worried about her being here,' she said. 'Is she safe?'

'Sorry?' said Lloyd.

'I mean – is she in danger, Mr Lloyd? If she's got some sort of evidence . . . if she's mixed up in it somehow.'

'Oh,' said Lloyd. 'No – she isn't involved in it. She's in no danger. Eleanor just cleared up a small mystery for us.'

She looked slightly less anxious. 'I was so worried, you see. Because Eleanor rang on Christmas Eve to say that the snow would probably block the road into the village, and I'd better listen for the road reports before I set out. So I put on Radio Barton in the morning, and the first thing I heard was that someone had been murdered in the village. I just got into my car, and thank God, the road had been cleared.' She paused for breath.

Lloyd nodded. He wasn't sure what he was supposed to be saying.

'What's happening about it, Mr Lloyd? The radio didn't even say who was killed. A man, that's all.'

'I'm sure Inspector Lloyd has better things to do than gossip,' Eleanor said.

Lloyd wished the damn woman wouldn't creep about. 'We have advised people in the area to keep their doors and windows locked, of course,' he said, thankful that that was the truth. 'And not to open the door to anyone they're not sure about—'

'Did someone get in?' asked Penny Langton. 'I haven't even seen an evening paper since I've been here.' She looked accusingly at Eleanor.

'I've *told* you, Penny. I'm not in any more danger than anyone else. I just told the police something I thought they ought to know.'

'But you won't talk about it.' She turned to Lloyd. 'Have you caught anyone?' she asked.

Lloyd took a breath. 'Our enquiries are proceeding,' he said. 'And I'm sure there's no cause for general alarm.' He was sure, he told himself. He was *sure*.

He suddenly felt sorry for Penny, stuck in the middle of nowhere with her enigmatic daughter-in-law, frightened to leave her alone. 'The facts are that the vicar's son-in-law was the victim, and that we are following a number of lines of enquiry, including the possibility of a break-in of some sort. And that's about as much as it said in the paper.' He smiled. 'We have no reason to think that the incident was anything other than a one-off,' he said.

'Do you mean it was someone in the *vicarage*?' she asked.

Lloyd refrained from glancing over at Eleanor. She had obviously told her mother-in-law nothing at all.

'Our enquiries are proceeding,' he said again, and rose.

Eleanor came out with him, almost closing the door, so that the only light was from the ghostly moon, full and low in the misty sky. 'Have you let Mrs Wheeler go?' she asked.

'Yes,' he said. He pulled on his gloves. 'You haven't told your mother-in-law about it?'

'No. I've tried to play it down,' she explained. 'Penny gets very nervous.' She shivered slightly in the cold air.

'I'd have thought that a village this size would know every detail,' said Lloyd. 'She'd hardly need the evening paper.'

'It's a very large village,' Eleanor said, proprietorially.

'By area,' Lloyd agreed. 'But most of that's farmland. There aren't so many people, are there? It can't be easy to keep a secret.'

'Probably not,' said Eleanor.

And you probably have one to keep, thought Lloyd, thinking about George.

'But we're sort of cut off from the rest of the village here.' Eleanor smiled. 'And I'm a newcomer.'

Lloyd glanced round at the stone walls of the castle. 'Is the family here?' he asked.

'No. They winter somewhere exotic.'

He frowned. 'Are you alone?' he asked.

'For the moment,' she said. 'They do have a couple of staff who live in, but they're on holiday too, just now.' She smiled her cold smile. 'The place is riddled with burglar alarms connected to the police station,' she said. 'I'm perfectly safe. I just wish they'd hurry up with the phone.'

'Aren't there any pay-phones?'

'One, would you believe? In the café, which is closed until Easter.'

'Well,' said Lloyd, slightly diffidently. 'I know the telephone manager – do you want me to put in a word?'

'It's not British Telecom who are dragging their feet,' she said, and smiled suddenly. A real smile. 'You don't have to worry about me,' she said. 'This place has survived Cromwell, hasn't it? I'm as safe here as I could be.'

Lloyd said goodnight, and got back to the car. He glared back at the snow when he turned on his headlights, and regretted bringing his own car back into service as he steered it gently over the icy ground back to the untreated estate road. He wondered, as he slowly made his way out, why Eleanor Langton was so unwilling to share her knowledge with her mother-in-law. Because of George? But it was idle curiosity, more than anything else. It was none of his business.

And apologising hadn't made him feel better in the slightest degree.

Chapter Seven

'Did you manage to see the kids?' Judy asked.

They were in the lounge bar of the Duke's Arms in Castle Road, where the Reverend Mr Wheeler and his daughter had spent some time on Christmas Eve. That much had been established; what they wanted now was a clearer indication of when they left the pub, but so far all they had done was wait. Voices floated in from the public bar, but she and Lloyd were alone in the lounge, except for the landlady, who couldn't help. Some of the regulars might, she had said. But they wouldn't be in until lunch time, and what with people taking the whole week between Christmas and New Year, there might not be many of them.

Lloyd laughed. 'Kids?' he repeated. 'Yes, I managed to get over for a little while on Boxing Day.'

'How is everyone?'

'Fine,' he said. 'Except – Linda's got some ridiculous idea about going to London. She's far too young.'

Judy smiled. 'I hope you didn't tell her that,' she said.

'No. In fact, I wondered . . .'

Judy raised an eyebrow, recognising the wheedling tone.

'You were a single girl in London,' he said. 'You know how difficult it is – accommodation, that sort of thing. I thought you might talk to her.'

'There wouldn't be much point,' said Judy.

'Why not?'

'For one thing, I lived with my parents, which is hardly the same thing: I don't know any more than she does about flat-hunting and finding a job – probably a lot less.'

Lloyd looked glum.

'And for another – Linda can barely bring herself to speak to me.'

'Oh, no,' Lloyd assured her. 'She's over all that, I'm sure.'

'Is she?' said Judy, disbelievingly. 'All right – she says hello if we meet, but she still doesn't think much of the idea of you and me.' She sipped her drink. 'It must run in the family,' she said.

'Judy,' Lloyd began. 'I don't—'

'I know, I know. I'm breaking the rules. But since you won't see me in anything *other* than working hours, I—'

The door banged open, and a middle-aged woman breezed in.

'You got back then,' said the landlady, unnecessarily. 'Did you have a nice time?'

'Oh, you know,' said the other woman. 'So so. It's nice to be back in my own house.' She hung things up on various pegs. 'But anyway—' she began, excitedly.

'You didn't have too much trouble getting there?' interrupted the landlady.

'What? Oh – it was past midnight before I arrived. You wouldn't *believe* the number of cars out at that time on Christmas Eve. But never mind that,' she said. 'I can't turn my back for five minutes, can I?'

Judy could see the landlady in the mirrored wall, as she mouthed 'police', nodding over to their table.

The barmaid, for such she proved to be, looked over at Judy. 'We can't go to jail for talking about it, can we?' she asked, with a laugh.

Judy smiled.

'I couldn't believe it,' she said, and turned back to the landlady. 'I felt awful when I heard,' she said. 'I mean, I'd made a joke about it – you know the way you do.'

'A joke?' queried Lloyd, twisting round.

'About her black eyes. She said she'd been to the dentist, and I said something about her husband getting funny looks. I never dreamed it *was* her husband. And now . . .'

Villages. Judy didn't know how people could bear to live in them, with everyone knowing everyone else's business. When she had been Joanna's age, she would have died if she had thought her private life was common knowledge.

And when she *had* been Joanna's age, she reflected, her private life had been Lloyd, just as it was now. A secret, guilt-ridden, unconsummated love affair. She glanced at Lloyd, who was joining in the gossip. What was it now, now that it had been consummated? There was no guilt; Barbara was no longer part of Lloyd's life, and Judy owed Michael nothing. But there was still secrecy, because once Michael found out, champion of Victorian values that he was, her bridges would be burned, and she wasn't sure she could face that. And because of that, she was right back where she had been, when she had been Joanna's age. Sitting opposite Lloyd in a pub, staring unhappily into a half pint of lager, trying to disguise her cowardice as principle, and failing.

'They say he put her in hospital,' finished the barmaid.

'I'd heard that that was why she'd left him,' said the landlady. 'I didn't believe it myself. A vicar's daughter.'

'You never told me!'

'No. Well. You shouldn't repeat gossip.'

'See what I have to put up with?' the barmaid demanded.

Judy laughed; Lloyd picked up his drink. 'So you were here on Christmas Eve, then?' he said. 'And you spoke to Mrs Elstow?'

'Who? Oh – is that her name? Only for a minute. She was with her father – they were talking about something. In fact,' she said, 'he was angry with her, I'm sure. I remember thinking that the poor little girl could do with some sympathy, not being glared at.'

'Did you notice when Mrs Elstow left?' Lloyd asked.

'No,' she said slowly. 'No, sorry. We were packed – well, you know what it's like on Christmas Eve.' She thought hard. 'No, I just don't remember,' she said. 'I know when he left, though. The vicar.'

Lloyd turned back, glancing at Judy. 'They didn't leave together?' he asked carelessly, finishing his beer. He stood up. 'I'll have another one in there, love,' he said.

She pulled another pint, and handed it to him. 'He left on his own,' she said. 'About half past eight. There's always carols on Christmas Eve, and the pianist came in just as Mr Wheeler was leaving. I thought it was funny, because he and his wife normally stay for that. I wondered if she wasn't well, because she's usually with him. I don't think that girl was well enough to be out, quite honestly . . .'

She chattered on, and Lloyd looked as though he wasn't really listening, as he sat at the bar, reflectively sipping the beer Judy knew he didn't want. But he was paying much more careful attention than the barmaid suspected, for through her he was learning the habits of the Wheelers on Christmas Eve.

Habits which had, for one reason or another, been broken.

'Why did you do it?' Joanna was asking, her face sad and cross at the same time. It was the first time she had mentioned it; Marian had thought that she had escaped interrogation.

'The inspector thinks I wanted to be a martyr,' she said. 'But that wasn't it.'

'You can't really blame him,' said Joanna.

Marian considered her motives, now that she had been asked. 'I just think,' she said, after a few moments, 'that if you love someone, you should be prepared to help them.'

Joanna's eyes widened. 'But it was crazy!' she said. 'And unnecessary. You didn't *have* to do something like that.'

'People don't think it odd if someone dies saving their child from a fire,' Marian said. 'They don't call them martyrs.'

'But I didn't *do* it!' Joanna shouted suddenly. 'Everyone thinks I did – but I didn't, I swear I didn't.'

The front door banged, and George came back from wherever he had been. Marian could hazard a guess.

'It's very slippery at the top here,' he said. 'I almost broke my neck.'

'I'll put some ash down, shall I?' Joanna said, getting up.

Marian didn't think that was at all a good idea. 'No, dear,' she said. 'I don't think you—' She stopped. 'It's a very dirty job,' she said.

'I'll wear the overalls,' said Joanna.

'I'll do it,' said George.

'But you're not well,' protested Joanna.

George sighed. 'I'm all right,' he said. 'Doing something physical might help.'

Marian rather thought that was just what he had been doing. It didn't seem to help at all.

'It's just all this business,' he said.

Marian saw Joanna's eyes flash. Joanna was sometimes so like George.

'You're sick because you think I killed Graham,' she shouted. 'That's why you told the police you were with me all evening!'

Well, thought Marian. It was the reason advanced, at any rate. But unlike Joanna, she knew the real reason for the lie.

'I *don't* think you did it. I just thought it would clear you of any suspicion. It was stupid, I know. But it's done now.'

'You lied to them. Either you think I did it, or—'

'You think I killed him? I wish I had, Joanna. Believe me, I wish I had.'

Marian didn't want to hear this. She didn't want to know.

'Yes! Because then you could take the blame. You think I did it – you both do! The police do – and now they'll be convinced,' she added, with a flash of something less than gratitude at Marian. 'You don't have to *lie* for me, do you understand? I can take care of myself.'

'Oh, can you? Then perhaps you'll enlighten us—'

'That's enough!' Marian's voice, rarely raised, brought the shouting to a halt. Normality. Ever since Graham Elstow had turned up, she had got by on normality, and so would they.

'Sorry,' muttered George. 'We're all a bit on edge.'

'Me too,' said Joanna, sitting down.

Marian relaxed. That was better.

Joanna frowned slightly. 'Where are the overalls?' she asked.

'*I'm* doing the path,' said George firmly.

'No – I mean where *are* they?'

Lloyd relieved himself of some of his liquid intake, and sighed. So, he thought, George and Marian always stayed for the carol-singing, which went on until ten-thirty. But this year, everything was different. It probably meant nothing, he told himself. But George must have gone somewhere.

He came out of the gents, and stopped at the door of the lounge bar, as he saw Judy. She looked a little sad, sitting there on her own, he thought, and he wished that things were different.

It still looked odd to him, a woman alone in a pub, but he was doubtless a male chauvinist. He breezed in. 'Right?' he said.

'Right.' She finished her drink and stood up.

'I've a good mind to charge the lot of them,' he said, as they left.

'You don't have enough evidence.'

'We know they've all lied to us.' He unlocked the car angrily, dropping the keys in the snow. He swore, and picked them up. 'We know Marian Wheeler interfered with the scene of the crime.'

'All that proves is that they've protected Joanna from the cradle,' said Judy briskly.

He opened her door, and she got in beside him. 'I think that's why Elstow got so violent,' she added.

Lloyd grunted.

'Did you look at those photographs of Joanna on the kitchen wall?' she asked. 'Joanna crawling, Joanna walking, Joanna's first tooth, first day at school – no wedding photographs. No photograph of Graham Elstow at all.'

'Are you surprised?' asked Lloyd.

Judy nodded. 'Yes,' she said.

'Well,' said Lloyd, reversing gingerly on to Castle Road. 'They'd hardly have Joanna's first black eye, would they?'

'But there's never *been* any,' Judy persisted. 'They're all written up – there haven't been any removed. They're in date order,' she said. 'And her wedding's been ignored.'

Lloyd got the car pointing the right way, and stopped.

'And George Wheeler was angry with her,' Judy went on. 'About Elstow. He wasn't frightened for her, like her mother. Joanna makes him *angry*.'

'What does that prove? She makes me angry too. Why the hell did she put up with it?'

Judy sighed, 'I think,' she said slowly, 'because she knew, really, *why* Elstow behaved like that. Imagine it, Lloyd. Coming up against all that jealousy. It was as if he didn't exist.' She turned to him. 'Elstow was frustrated,' she said. 'And no wonder. How would you feel?'

He smiled at the worried brown eyes that looked into his. 'Well, I wouldn't start knocking you about,' he said. 'I'd probably buy a twelve-year-old malt, sit down, and have a long heart to heart with your father.'

'Not everyone has your way with words, Inspector Lloyd,' Judy said, smiling. 'And not everyone is a push-over for expensive whisky.'

'Your father is,' said Lloyd.

Her face grew serious again. 'My father isn't in love with me.'

Lloyd started the engine again. 'Wheeler and his daughter?' he said. 'Is that what you think?'

'It's a possibility,' said Judy.

Lloyd pulled out on to the main road, and headed for the vicarage. 'Spiritual or physical?' he asked.

'Who knows? Behind closed doors, and all that.'

Lloyd settled in behind a lorry. 'Reciprocated?' He glanced at her.

'Oh, I don't know,' she said. 'I'm not even sure I really believe that. But why *didn't* she go up to Graham?'

'I asked you that,' said Lloyd.

'I'm not sure she knew what she wanted,' Judy said.

'I think she did,' said Lloyd grimly. 'She wanted rid of Elstow.'

'I don't think she had anything to do with killing him,' Judy said. 'It's Wheeler who left the pub, remember.'

So Wheeler killed him? It was possible, Lloyd thought, in theory. But there was a practical side to murder, particularly this murder, where the Wheeler solution just didn't fit. Clothes. They'd found nothing. No clothing of any sort. And Wheeler was wearing the clothes he'd worn in the pub when he and Judy arrived at the vicarage on Christmas morning. He smiled at his next thought. Surely the congregation would have noticed if his clerical robes had been covered in blood? His smile vanished. Had anyone checked the vestry?

'We are dealing with a family of pathological liars,' he reminded her.

'I think Joanna's telling the truth,' she said.

'The whole truth?' he asked, and she didn't answer.

He did trust Judy's instincts. But perhaps Elstow had trusted his, and look how he ended up.

For the next few minutes, he formulated several ways of telling Judy that he was quite prepared to share her with Michael. He didn't utter any of them, partly because they were in working hours, and he ought to obey his own rule, partly because it wasn't really true, and partly because she might tell him the offer was closed.

The castle's pale stone walls were just visible through the naked trees as they drove up to the Wheelers' drive. It was no more than a ten-minute walk over the fields, sharing the hilltop with the vicarage. Lloyd could even see the stables, but only because they had cleared the land for fanning. In the Civil War, the castle had been totally camouflaged; it had commanded views of all comers from all sides, and couldn't be seen itself. It had succumbed to the Roundheads' gunpowder in the end, but as Eleanor had pointed out, it had survived. In daylight, it looked settled, peaceful. Pretty, even, in the winter light. But at night. . . He shivered again.

George Wheeler was waving a dustbin about. Lloyd frowned, but as they got closer, he could see what he was doing. They got out of the car.

'Good morning,' Lloyd said.

Wheeler scattered more ash. 'Doesn't look very pretty,' he said. 'But it works. This is something you can't do in centrally heated houses, now I come to think of it. Perhaps we're not so badly off, after all.'

'I'd like a word, Mr Wheeler.'

'Oh?' he said, shaking out dark gritty ash as he walked along. 'What about? Have you come to arrest my wife for cleaning her own landing? She tells me you intend to prosecute. Don't you think you'd be better employed looking for who really did it?'

Lloyd, who had never had the least desire to use his fists, knew how Elstow must have felt. But he recognised bravado when he heard it. This was George fighting his desire to throw up. This was George thinking that attack was the best method of defence.

Wheeler had stopped blustering, and stood waiting for a reply. So Lloyd didn't speak at all. And he could stand there in silence all day, if he had to. Judy affected a deep interest in her notebook. For a long time, all three of them stood, saying nothing at all.

The disintegration of George, thought Lloyd, as he watched Wheeler's eyes begin to move furtively from him to Judy, and back. He wiped his upper lip. 'Well?' he said.

'Well what, Mr Wheeler?' asked Lloyd, politely.

Wheeler didn't speak, and Lloyd looked down at the grey ash on the white snow, a fair approximation of Wheeler's complexion.

'Look,' said Wheeler. 'Marian went out, someone came in – and you haven't lifted a finger to find out who, or why. You're tearing this family apart, do you know that?'

Lloyd looked up from his contemplation of the black-speckled ash at his feet, stung into a reaction.

'We have carried out extensive enquiries in the village,' he said. 'We have been searching for days for any trace at all of someone gaining entry to your house. We're looking in six-foot high snow-drifts for abandoned clothing.' His feet crunched on the ash as he moved toward Wheeler, having to look up at the taller man. 'Your wife destroyed evidence, and misled us quite deliberately,' he said. 'So don't blame me for what's happening to your family, Mr Wheeler!'

George Wheeler looked down for a moment, then picked up the dustbin again.

'If you really want to help,' Judy said, stepping out of the way of a cloud of dust, 'you'll tell us where you were on Christmas Eve.'

'I was at the pub with my daughter,' he said. 'I've told you a dozen times.' He tapped the last of the gritty ash from the bin, and put it down.

'Let's go somewhere we can talk,' said Lloyd quietly.

Wheeler hesitated. 'My study,' he said, in the end, and led the way to the house, where Marian Wheeler and Joanna met them in the hallway.

'Joanna,' said Judy. 'Could we have a word, do you think?'

The girl looked apprehensively at her mother.

'You can come into the kitchen,' said Mrs Wheeler.

'Oh, I don't want to put you out of your own kitchen, Mrs Wheeler,' said Judy.

Marian Wheeler, tight-lipped at being thus dismissed, turned and went back into the kitchen by herself.

'We can use the back bedroom,' Joanna volunteered.

'What's going on. Inspector?' asked Wheeler.

Lloyd held out a hand, ushering Wheeler into his own study. 'I'll tell you, Mr Wheeler,' he said, looking at Joanna as he spoke. 'We don't like being lied to. That's what's going on.'

Joanna closed the bedroom door. 'What does he mean?' she asked.

Sergeant Hill raised her eyebrows. 'I think you know what he means,' she replied, turning to look out of the window.

'No,' Joanna said warily, sitting down on the bed.

The sergeant turned, sunlight suddenly breaking through the grey clouds, lighting her as though she were on stage. Dramatic light and shade; Joanna felt as if she were an actor in a drama. Guiltily, she was finding that she rather enjoyed it. Like long ago, when the room they were in had been the sick-bay. She had been the centre of attention then, too.

'I thought we had a bit more trust going for us than this,' the sergeant said.

'Trust?' repeated Joanna. 'You arrested my *mother*, and you expect me to trust you?'

Sergeant Hill gave a short sigh, and looked at her reflectively. After a moment, she turned away, looking out into the strong sunlight. 'People pay taxes,' she said slowly. 'Good money. For a police force. Who are supposed to prevent crime, and investigate the ones they've failed to prevent.'

You never knew where you *were* with her, Joanna thought worriedly. Now, she was to be given a lecture on police-work? She sat back, her elbow on the pillow, in a studied attitude of detached interest.

'The thing is,' the sergeant said, turning back again. 'The bobby on the beat might prevent ten shops being broken into, but nobody knows that. All they know about is the eleventh shop, which does get broken into. And they want results.'

Joanna looked back at her. 'So?' she said.

'So that's where I come in,' she said. 'I have to find out who broke in to the shop – and prove it.' She came over to the foot of the bed, and sat down. 'And the only way I can do that is if people trust me enough to tell me the truth.'

'Why should they?' Joanna sat up. 'You hear all the time about policemen on the take, planting evidence—'

She nodded. 'Just like you hear about the eleventh shop,' she said. 'But the rest of us are just doing our jobs. And the whole system depends on people telling the truth. On both sides.'

Joanna looked away from her.

'Where were you on Christmas Eve?' she asked.

'At the pub,' Joanna said. 'With my father.'

'And did you stay there after he'd left?' she asked.

Joanna froze. 'What?' she said, when she could say anything at all. But the sergeant didn't speak, and Joanna turned her head slowly to look at her.

'Your father left the pub alone at eight-thirty,' she said. 'And I want to know what you did. Did you stay there? What did you do, Joanna?'

'You think I killed Graham,' she said, almost inaudibly.

'I don't.'

Joanna's eyes widened with surprise.

'But your lies make it hard for me to justify my position,' she went on. 'What did you do after your father left the pub?'

Joanna's mind raced. 'I went to see Dr Lomax,' she said truthfully.

The sergeant opened her inevitable notebook.

'She's our doctor,' Joanna said. 'A friend of the family.'

Our doctor, she thought. Her doctor, her parents' doctor. Poor Graham.

'Were you seeing her as a friend or a patient?'

'I was worried about the baby. I told you I'd seen a doctor. I stayed there for a while. We talked about Graham – she told me where he could get help. And then I came home, but I couldn't get in because the house was locked up.' The words were coming fast now. 'I knocked and knocked, and I thought Graham was just being stupid.'

'What time was this?'

'I got here at about half past nine, I suppose. I sat in the car to keep warm. And then my father came home.'

'When?'

'Half an hour after that,' she said.

'Did he have his car?'

'No. Mummy had it. He was on foot – he came over the field.'

'The field?' queried the sergeant.

'It's a short cut to Castle Road,' said Joanna, and with the words, she realised where her father had been. 'He waited with me until my mother came home. She was only a few minutes after that.'

'Why did you lie to us, Joanna?'

'I *didn't*,' she said indignantly, before she could stop herself.

The sergeant slowly turned back the pages. 'No,' she said quietly, looking up. 'I'm sorry. You just went along with a lie.'

And if she hadn't initiated the lie, then her father had, and the implication was obvious. Joanna could have bitten her tongue off.

'Joanna,' said the sergeant, apparently unconcerned about that. 'You told me you'd made it up with Graham – you'd decided to go home with him.'

'I had,' she said, puzzled.

'Didn't you want to talk to him?'

This was getting worse and worse. Joanna shook her head.

'All that time,' said Sergeant Hill. 'From five o'clock. Didn't you want to see him?'

'Yes! Yes, of course I did,' Joanna said. 'But it would have caused trouble, and that would have upset my mother.'

The sergeant nodded, looking a little baffled.

'When I did say I was going up to see him, it caused a row,' she said. 'Just before Mummy found him.' The tears threatened again.

Sergeant Hill closed her notebook. 'Thank you,' she said.

'The solicitor that my father got for my mother,' Joanna said. 'He said that Graham might have been seeing someone else – she might have come here that night.'

Her heart sank when she saw the look in Sergeant Hill's eye. But she had to try. Try to get them to look somewhere else for the murderer.

'Please,' she said. 'He was going to check up – get a private detective. But he won't now, and I can't afford to – *please*.'

'We already are looking into it,' said the sergeant. 'Graham said he'd met someone at the pub, didn't he? We're trying to find out about that.' She stood up. 'You didn't go to the house when our people checked it, did you?'

Joanna shook her head.

'You should,' she said. 'You're more likely to spot any indication of another woman than we are.'

Joanna hadn't thought of that.

'But Joanna,' she said, in the warning voice that Joanna had come to recognise. 'We have found nothing to suggest another woman, and there is simply no evidence at all that anyone else was in here that night. You do understand that, don't you?'

Yes, Joanna understood.

'And I hope you do think you can trust me,' she said. 'Because you can, you know.'

As she made to leave, Joanna made up her mind. Because she did trust her. 'Sergeant Hill,' she said. 'There's – there's something else. Something you ought to know.'

George had reiterated that he'd been in the pub with Joanna all evening, and said that the barmaid must have been mistaken. Then the inspector had chosen to take him through the whole evening again, and George was beginning to feel sick.

'Look, I've told you this three times! Why aren't you out looking for whoever came in here? I'll tell you why! Because you're convinced that my daughter killed him, that's why!'

Lloyd looked faintly surprised at the sudden outburst. 'We're not convinced,' he said. 'I don't know so much about you.'

'You have already suggested that I am somehow covering up for my daughter, Inspector.'

'Her mother did,' Lloyd said imperturbably.

'I am not her mother! What her mother did was—'

'Extremely foolish,' said Lloyd. 'If there ever was an intruder, she carefully wiped away any traces of the fact.' He stood up, and toured the room. 'But she wouldn't have been that thorough,' he said. 'There would have been something. Fingerprints we couldn't identify. He came in from all that snow – there would have been footprints. Someone would have seen *something*. How could he have left here in that state without someone noticing him?'

George clamped his teeth together. He had to see this through; he couldn't let his stomach be the boss. 'I don't know,' he said, releasing his breath, and turning to look out of the study window at the frozen, still landscape. There was ice on the inside again. 'You know what I keep thinking?' he said.

'What's that, Mr Wheeler?'

'That if we'd had central heating, it would never have happened,' George said slowly, touching the ice, watching it melt and dribble down the glass. 'Silly, isn't it?'

'Not really,' Lloyd said. 'You get more shotgun murders in farmhouses than you do in penthouse flats, for instance. You can't pick something up if it isn't there to *be* picked up. And not too many people get bludgeoned to death with thermostats.'

A shotgun, George thought. He had a shotgun. His father's shotgun. He put the back of his hand to his mouth. The fields. Look at the fields. White, clean, fresh. Cold. Sweat trickled down the back of his neck. He turned, his stomach lurching. 'If that's all you wanted, Inspector,' he said, as civilly as he could, 'I do have some things to be getting on with.'

'No, it isn't all,' said Lloyd. 'I want the truth.'

George fought the nausea. His legs were shaking. He sat down, and tried desperately to get control. They *knew* he'd left the pub. He'd have to say something. 'I was at Eleanor Langton's,' he said, not looking at him.

'Eleanor Langton's,' repeated Lloyd.

George looked up, not sure what reaction to expect. Shock? Disapproval? Or a boys-will-be-boys wink? He got none of those things.

'Times?' Lloyd said.

'I went straight there from the pub,' said George.

'When did you leave?'

'Not until I had to,' he replied bleakly.

'When was that?'

George stared out of the window. 'A little before ten,' he said. 'The snow had drifted off the field, so I went that way. It only took a few minutes to get home.'

Oh, Eleanor, why aren't you on the *phone*? He looked at the ash on the snow. Ashes to ashes, dust to dust. Heaven and hell, life or death. To be or not to be, that was the question.

The inspector was leaving. 'Thank you, Mr Wheeler,' he said, opening the door to find Sergeant Hill waiting in the hall. 'Right, Sergeant,' he said, his voice unnecessarily loud. 'I think we've finished here.' He glanced back in. 'For the moment,' he said, closing the door.

When he heard the front door shut, George went to the window, and watched as they went down the porch steps. As they crossed the driveway, the inspector glanced back, and George automatically stepped back from the window. They got into their car, and drove away.

To Eleanor's, no doubt. George fled upstairs to the bathroom.

Eleanor lay on the sofa, pampering herself with a dry sherry and a box of chocolate mints. Tessa had gone off with her grandmother as arranged, ostensibly to give Eleanor a rest; but Eleanor knew what was really on Penny's mind. If a blood-crazed murderer was going to break in here one dark night, he wasn't going to get Penny's grandchild. Eleanor smiled, as she had at Penny's efforts to get her to go back to Stansfield with them. But it did give her a rest, so she would enjoy it. And of course, there was a knock on the door.

Eleanor's heart sank when she saw the inspector, with the policewoman who had come in during her interview.

'This is Sergeant Hill,' he said. 'May we come in?'

'Yes. Please do.'

They walked ahead of her into the sitting room. Eleanor took a deep breath of cold air before she closed the door.

'I was just having a sherry,' she said, as she joined them. 'Would you like one?'

'No, thank you, Mrs Langton,' Lloyd said.

She smiled. 'I thought we'd agreed on Eleanor.'

She was interested to see the sergeant's immediate and hastily cancelled reaction.

'Mrs Langton,' the inspector said. 'Did you see Mr Wheeler on Christmas Eve at any time?'

Eleanor indicated the armchairs, and sat down on the sofa

again. 'Yes,' she said carefully. 'He came here in the morning to ask if I would play the organ that afternoon.'

'Did you see him again?' asked the sergeant.

'At the church,' said Eleanor, noticing that the sergeant wore a wedding ring. Interesting. She wondered about that fleeting look of concern, and thought that she might play up to it. It would be quite fun to land Inspector Lloyd right in it. 'I didn't get the chance to speak to him,' she added.

'And these are the only times you saw him?' asked Lloyd.

'*It's up to you what you do about it.*' George's words. This was her chance *to* do something about it. She forgot about making a fool of Lloyd, as she tried to decide what to do.

'Mrs Langton? Could you answer the question?' said the sergeant.

'Yes,' she said firmly. 'I'll answer it. I saw him later. He came here about half an hour after Marian did. I know he's told you he was with his daughter, but if you ask me it's time she was responsible for her own actions.'

She didn't even try to gauge what sort of effect her words were having on her audience. She had started now.

'If she finally had the guts to take a poker to her husband, then she should have the guts to admit it,' she said.

'And that's what happened, is it?' asked Lloyd.

'I don't *know* what happened! All I know is what it's doing to George – it's making him ill. It's what he thinks happened – that's why he said he was with her! It's why her mother did what she did. Joanna must be protected at all costs – well, I think it's costing too much. Whatever he's told you, George was here. Until about quarter to ten.'

She looked at them then, for their reaction. They didn't seem very impressed.

'Half an hour after Marian left,' said Lloyd. 'That would be what – half past eight?'

'Something like that,' said Eleanor. 'Maybe a few minutes later. And whatever George has told you, *I'm* telling you the truth.'

'That is what he told us,' the sergeant said. 'Thank you, Mrs Langton.'

They had left before the full impact of what the sergeant had said hit Eleanor.

George. They'd been checking up on *George*.

Chapter Eight

Eleanor took the mini, though the pub was so close, preferring to brave the elements on four wheels. The car park was filling up now that it was lunch time, but she found a space; she hadn't been able to find one on Christmas Eve, or she might never have seen him.

Her foot slipped on the icy ground as she got out, and she walked carefully towards the back entrance. On Christmas Eve, she had had to park in Castle Road; she had used the main entrance. And so had Graham Elstow, coming in as she was going out, the mere sight of him tearing at emotions already exposed by George's visit.

She pushed open the door, and found herself glancing along the corridor to the bar, checking who was there. But Graham Elstow was one person she was never going to bump into again. The phone was being used; Eleanor waited, her face hot with the memory of that day, her heart beating too fast. But the man hung up, and said 'All yours, darling', as though she wasn't in an advanced state of panic. She thanked him, and dialled the number, clutching the coin hard, so that her hand didn't shake too much.

'Byford 2212.'

'Is Mr Wheeler there, please?' Eleanor was surprised at how ordinary her voice sounded.

'I think so,' said the voice. Marian's? Joanna's? Eleanor didn't know Marian well enough to tell, and she didn't know Joanna at all. 'Who's calling, please?'

Oh God, she hadn't thought of that. But come on, Eleanor. Pull yourself together. You've called him before – you have business with him. And what's changed, what's really changed?

'Eleanor Langton.'

There was the tiniest of pauses. 'Just a moment, please.'

She could hear footsteps in the hallway, then muffled voices.

'Hello – Eleanor?' He sounded ordinary too. Not like the tortured man he was.

'George.' She glanced along the corridor. No one around. And the people in the bar too far away to hear. 'I've had the police,' she said.

There was a silence. Then, 'Yes?'

'Yes!' she said impatiently, 'I told them you were with me,' she said.

'Yes,' he said again, 'I thought you probably would.'

He sounded so unconcerned. So matter-of-fact. What if she'd told them that she hadn't seen him? Wasn't that what he'd asked her to do, in his oblique way? Was he relieved or angry that she'd told them?

'But George—' She turned her back on the people in the bar.

'Well,' he said. 'Thanks for ringing.'

Eleanor realised. 'Oh, hell, there's someone with you.'

'That's right.'

'I've got to *talk* to you.'

Another silence. 'Yes – perhaps tomorrow?' The casual tone was beginning to sound a little desperate.

'Tomorrow?' Eleanor echoed. 'Can't you come before that?'

'No,' he said, and she could hear paper rustling. 'No, sorry.'

'All right,' she said weakly.

'Fine. Tomorrow, then. First thing.'

Eleanor hung up, and let out a sigh.

'Stood you up, has he, love?'

She whirled round, her face burning, to see the man who had been using the phone before her.

He looked a little alarmed. 'Nothing personal,' he said. 'Just a joke.' He picked up the receiver. 'At least you got through,' he said. 'That's more than I did.'

Eleanor stared at him. What had he heard? Had she said anything? She'd called him George. Oh, George was a common name – she could have been ringing anyone called George. And why would he care, anyway?

She turned and almost ran from the pub.

*

'Joanna,' said her father, as he slowly replaced the receiver. 'Did you want something?'

She had stayed in his study after she had told him about the call. If she hadn't, she would have listened in on the hall phone, and conspicuous eavesdropping seemed preferable, morally.

'What did she want?' she asked baldly.

'Just play-group business,' he said.

'Play-group business?' Joanna said angrily. 'Come off it! All that diary consulting – was that for my benefit? You're not *doing* anything just now!'

He slammed his diary shut. 'I will not be cross-examined about my private phone-calls!' he shouted.

That was just the problem, thought Joanna. He probably would be. She sat down. 'That's where you were on Christmas Eve,' she said. 'Isn't it? You were with her. You told me you'd stayed at the pub.'

'Yes.' He sighed. 'It's called bearing false witness, in the trade,' he said.

'And what you were doing with her?' Joanna asked sharply. 'What's that called?'

His eyes widened. 'It's called minding my own business,' he said. 'Just like you were minding yours. You weren't exactly forth-coming about where you'd been.'

But she hadn't lied to him. And she hadn't been . . . She closed her eyes. 'Is that why Mummy was angry with you?' she asked.

'She wasn't angry with me,' he said, and he sounded almost wistful.

'Was that another lie?'

'No!' He stood up. 'It was a possible explanation for her burning the dress, that's all.'

'Does she know about you and her?'

'Now, look!' He banged his fists down on the desk. 'Whoever this concerns, Joanna, it does not concern you.'

'Doesn't it?' Joanna asked bitterly. 'Then why *did* I find myself lying to the police?'

His body sagged a little, and he sat down heavily. 'I'm sorry about that,' he said.

'Why?' she asked again. 'So that you didn't have to admit that you were with her?'

'I just didn't want Eleanor's name brought into it,' he said, swivelling the chair round, and looking out of the window.

'I'll bet you didn't.'

'Have you told them where you were?' he asked.

'Yes,' she said, but that wasn't entirely true.

'But you still won't tell me? Or your mother?'

'No.' No, no, *no*. She didn't want them to know about the baby. Not now. Not ever, but she had very little option about that. Not until they had to, at any rate.

'Then we'll just have to respect one another's privacy, and hope that the police do the same,' he said.

He was still staring out of the window when Joanna left.

They had spent the afternoon fruitlessly going through the mounds of paperwork that had developed on the Elstow business. Next door, people collated and cross-referenced, and tried to produce some kind of coherent sequence of events from the observations of those not involved, and therefore not likely to be lying. But they were likely to be exaggerating, or imagining things, or simply mistaken. Marian's movements were checkable, and had been checked. She had called on half a dozen people, staying just a couple of minutes at each place, and would have arrived home at about ten, just as they all said she had. Wheeler had been seen walking up Castle Road; Joanna hadn't been seen at all. Someone knew that it was the gypsies. If there had *been* any gypsies, Judy thought, she would have gladly gone and interviewed every one of them. Joanna's information about the overalls had gone down the pipeline, so now people knew that that might be what they were looking for; at least that was something.

Outside, the afternoon had grown dark, and evening had descended. Another day almost over, and they were no further forward.

'The overalls are our best lead so far,' she said, looking up at Lloyd.

'To what?' Lloyd got up and stretched, then sat on her desk. 'To some intruder who went in, saw them, and popped them on just in case he came across someone he wanted very messily to murder?'

Judy shook her head. Lloyd was edgy, ready to dismiss anything she said. He'd been like that since they'd seen Eleanor Langton. 'Are you still convinced it was one of the family?' she asked.

Lloyd looked away in disgust. 'Of course it was,' he said. 'I'm still convinced it was Joanna Elstow, if you want to know.'

'But the doctor confirmed her story,' said Judy.

Joanna had arrived, a little upset, according to Dr Lomax, some time after half past eight. About quarter to nine, she thought. She had stayed for thirty, forty minutes. Something like that.

'The friend of the family,' corrected Lloyd, 'confirmed her story.'

'Oh, Lloyd! Do you think the whole village is party to a conspiracy?'

'I wouldn't be a bit surprised,' he said sourly. 'A domestic. A domestic – you're supposed to get there and find someone in tears saying that she was cutting some bread when the knife slipped. And that's that.'

Judy smiled. 'I don't believe she killed her husband,' she said. 'For one thing, she wasn't there – and for another, I don't believe she wanted to.' She paused. 'I think we should take a closer look at Elstow. He was sober when he arrived at the vicarage in the first place,' she said. 'What made him get drunk?'

Lloyd sighed. 'Becoming involved with that bloody family, that's what,' he said. 'It would drive anyone to the bottle.' He ran a tired hand down his face.

'But he didn't drink,' Judy said. 'Not as a rule. And why would he choose to just then? He was trying to get Joanna back, not put her off.'

'And yet he succeeded, according to her,' said Lloyd, tapping Judy's notebook. 'Does that seem likely to you? He arrives drunk, gets drunker, beats her up, and it all ends happily ever after? Or would have done, if the invisible man hadn't popped in and murdered him?'

Put like that, it seemed highly unlikely, but it had seemed true enough when Joanna had told her about it. If Lloyd had been in a more receptive mood, Judy might have tried to explain that.

'I think our first theory was right,' Lloyd said. 'I think Marian Wheeler was right. Joanna went for him with the poker.'

'But the time of death is wrong,' Judy pointed out reasonably.

'I'm going to get Freddie to have another look at that,' he muttered.

The overalls. White nylon overalls, which George Wheeler had left in the hall, and which had now disappeared. They were important, thought Judy. If they found the overalls, they might get some answers.

Left in the hall. A thought occurred to her. 'Wheeler,' she said. 'He'd know—'

'Wheeler doesn't know if he's coming or going!' snapped Lloyd. 'If you ask me, he doesn't know what day of the week it is, never mind anything else.'

'If your theory's right about Joanna, he'd have to know more than he's telling us,' said Judy, stubbornly.

'Not necessarily. He says he heard the bedroom door close as he went in. That could have been Joanna. Shutting herself in the bedroom with her husband, after she had killed him. Wheeler and his wife go upstairs to change, Joanna creeps down, and into the sitting room, where the original fight took place, and where they found her.'

Judy looked up at him.

'Don't look like that! It fits all the forensic evidence. It explains why she didn't come straight out and tell her parents what had happened. And it means that George Wheeler's telling the truth, and doesn't know what the hell's going on.'

'Except,' said Judy patiently, 'that Freddie says Elstow didn't die until two hours after that, when Joanna was sitting in the pub.'

Lloyd grinned suddenly. 'That's its only drawback,' he said.

'So you're going to ask Freddie if by any chance he's made a two-hour error on the time of death?'

'You never know,' Lloyd said. 'I'm going to ask him to assume that nothing that we have been told is accurate.'

'But we know it's accurate! We know what time they arrived home, we know what time Elstow ate—'

'We only know because people have told us,' said Lloyd.

'The barmaid,' said Judy. 'The people at the afternoon service – why would they lie, Lloyd?'

'People can make mistakes. This is a domestic murder, Judy, whatever way you look at it. The intruder theory is laughable.'

'Maybe,' said Judy. 'But he did meet someone at the pub.'

'According to Joanna,' said Lloyd.

'Isn't there anyone else who might have had it in for him?' she asked hopefully. She had believed Joanna; she wasn't going to admit defeat yet.

'No,' said Lloyd. 'You know there isn't. He didn't gamble, he didn't owe money except in the usual way. We can't find anything on other women – his own wife admits he didn't even drink to excess. The one offensive thing he did was to beat his wife.' He smiled. 'The house *looks* as if a bomb's hit it, but that seems to have been Elstow himself rather than the Battered Wives' Liberation Army.'

'Do you think it's funny?' Judy asked sharply.

Lloyd sighed. 'No,' he said. 'You know I don't. But if you don't laugh at this job . . .' He shrugged.

You cry, thought Judy.

'Sorry,' he said. 'But what have we got here? We've got a cave-man. Dressed up like an accountant, but a cave-man, all the same. Frustrated and inarticulate – you said that yourself. A man who beats his wife, Judy – you find him with his head bashed in, who do you look for?'

Judy nodded sadly, and Lloyd looked at her, his face serious.

'You've got too involved,' he said. 'You like her. You want to believe her. You don't blame her, do you?'

'No,' Judy admitted. 'Not after what he did to her.'

'See?' said Lloyd. 'What are you defending, Judy? Her innocence? Or her actions?'

She'd walked right into the trap. But there was no triumph in his voice.

'Joanna was home before anyone else,' Lloyd went on. 'Saying she had been locked out.'

'She had been,' Judy said. 'Marian had locked the doors.'

'Why?' asked Lloyd.

'Because she'd found Elstow's body,' said Judy.

'Why lock the doors?' Lloyd repeated.

Judy had just accepted it, until now. Marian had locked up the house in order that no one would find Elstow's body. But why shouldn't it have been found? What difference did it make?

'I don't know,' she said slowly.

'She didn't,' Lloyd said. 'She didn't lock the doors at all. There was no reason to, whether or not there was a body in the bedroom. But there wasn't, because Elstow was in the bedroom, alive. And whoever murdered him locked the doors.' He sat back. 'And then claimed that she had been locked out all along,' he added.

'The time of death is *still* wrong,' said Judy. 'Elstow had been dead half an hour before Joanna got back from Dr Lomax.'

Lloyd made an impatient noise. 'No one was synchronising their watches, Judy! It's all arounds and abouts. Joanna says she got back at around nine-thirty – Freddie says Elstow died at about nine o'clock. Easy enough to lose half an hour that way.'

'*Before* nine o'clock,' Judy reminded him, then realised that she had been steered completely off course. 'And anyway,' she said. 'There's the overalls.'

'What about them?'

'You've seen the house,' she said. 'Whatever else Mrs Wheeler may be, she's a very conscientious housewife.' Lloyd had entertained her to a number of things which, in his opinion, Mrs Wheeler was. 'And it seems that he left these overalls in the hall,' Judy said. 'Mrs W. was doing a washing, wasn't she? I don't think she'd leave a pair of dirty overalls in the hall for long – especially not when it was all decked out for Christmas. I think,' she said simply, 'that she would have washed them.'

Lloyd got off her desk and walked around, which meant that he was actually thinking about what she had said. 'And if she *did* wash them,' he said slowly, 'then the intruder would have had to know that he was going to *need* overalls. And that he could find a nice pair all washed and tumble-dried in the machine.'

Judy nodded. 'And when we took the washing away, Marian Wheeler knew the overalls should have been there,' she said. 'But they weren't.'

Lloyd stared at her. 'Of course,' he said. 'Of course. That's when she bundled Joanna off to bed.' He sat on her desk again. 'Did you notice what she was like when she came back?' he asked.

Judy had. Marian Wheeler had been distracted, unsettled. Her mind seemed to be somewhere else altogether. 'She kept looking at George,' Judy said. 'And he's the one who threatened Elstow in the first place. He's the one who lied about where he was.' At last, Lloyd was really listening. 'Marian Wheeler wasn't protecting Joanna at all,' said Judy. 'She was protecting *George*. Because if Elstow *had* died at five, we would hardly have been asking her where she was two hours later, would we? She knew that. Perhaps it was never Joanna she suspected in the first place.'

Lloyd tore a piece off her blotter, and rolled it into a ball as he thought. 'But when did he do it?' he asked, flicking the pellet at the wastepaper bin, and missing.

'Would Mrs Langton give him an alibi, do you think?' Judy asked.

Another pellet pinged against the metal bin, and landed on the floor. 'She seemed to think she was spoiling one,' said Lloyd.

'Not his,' argued Judy. 'Joanna's. She was very keen to put suspicion on Joanna – and take it right off George.'

Lloyd flicked another pellet, which landed satisfactorily in the bin. 'Arrest the whole lot of them,' he said, getting to his feet. 'That's the answer.'

'Including Eleanor?' Judy asked wickedly. 'You mustn't get too involved, Inspector Lloyd.'

'With her?' said Lloyd, with genuine horror. 'Don't worry.'

They laughed, and the moment could have been seized, but Judy let it go. Two rejections were enough for anyone.

'Elstow met someone at the pub,' mused Lloyd, trying one more attempt at the waste-bin. He missed. 'There are too many little puzzles,' he said, picking the coats off the pegs, and – throwing Judy's to her. 'Let's call it a day.'

And they called it a day, going to their separate cars. Judy drove towards home, considering giving her car star markings to indicate its freezing capacity, as her feet and hands began to lose their feeling. Other people looked forward to going home, she thought.

But she was going home to the Hills, and earnest discussions about whether gas or electric central heating was better, about whether their furniture had really been a sensible buy, about how the future really mattered, because it was what you gave your children. 'When they come along,' Mrs Hill had said, with a twinkle, as though she and Michael were newly-weds. And Judy didn't believe that Mrs Hill had missed a word of the Christmas morning discussion between her and Michael.

The Hills might have been sitting with her in the car, pointing out how hard Michael had worked to get their beautiful house, which would be even more beautiful once it had all the necessary things done to it. Pointing out that Judy didn't really *need* to work now, because Michael was doing so well. Pointing out that time was going on – it was hard to believe that it was ten years . . .

She was almost home. Just next left, and then a right, and her twenty-minute journey would be over; she would be safe in the bosom of Michael's family. She pulled the car into the kerb, and sat for some minutes, the engine running. Then she started the car, passed the left turn, stopped, and reversed into it. She stopped again, for a long time, until her breath began to mist the cold windscreen; she wiped it with a tissue, and started the car, indicating right. Back along the road she had just travelled. Twenty minutes later, she passed the police station. Left at the big roundabout at the bottom of the hill. Left, to the old village.

She parked her car beside Lloyd's, remembering the last time. The jolt to her ego of his rejection had been considerable, and she walked almost on tiptoe.

He might have heard the car, and simply not answer the door, she thought, as she pushed open the glass door to the flats.

He might be out. You couldn't tell with the thick curtains and that silly lamp. He'd strain his eyes if he read by it.

He would just tell her to go away again, she decided miserably, as she climbed the stair.

When she got to his door, she was out of breath; she had been holding it all the way up. All the way *there*. She gave herself a moment before ringing the bell, then heard the inside door open, saw the light going on. She could see him through the fluted glass. The door opened, and she was inside, in his arms. He was apologising. Why was *he* apologising?

'You're frozen,' he said, letting her go, ushering her into the warmth of the sitting room. He helped her with her coat, and put a finger to her lips as she tried to speak. 'Later,' he said. 'We can discuss things later. Let's get you thawed out first.'

She sat down, while he went to the kitchen, coming back some minutes later with a steaming jug of coffee and the brandy.

'Just coffee,' she said.

'Fine.'

The coffee warmed her, but the silence unnerved her. It must have unnerved Lloyd too, because he began making conversation in the way that he'd told her he did with Barbara. Carefully avoiding any mention of work; even more carefully avoiding any mention of their situation. She took as much of – it as she could stand, then waited for a lull.

'I thought you would be—' she began.

'I'm just glad you're here,' he said, interrupting her. He smiled. 'Do you want to eat?'

She shook her head.

'More coffee? Or would you like a brandy now?'

'No,' she said.

He switched off the lamp. 'Kisses by coloured lights?' he said, with a little laugh, and this time he met with success.

They went into the bedroom, arms round one another. The room was chilly; Judy shivered a little as she pulled off her sweater. Lloyd's lips caressed hers as he began to unbutton her blouse.

'It'll be a lot quicker if I do it myself,' she said.

Lloyd smacked her hand away. 'And a lot less fun,' he said. 'You have no soul. *Andante*, Sergeant Hill. *Andante*.'

But Lloyd didn't realise just how many layers of clothes she wore in weather like this. He soon found out, laughing with delight as he discovered what he insisted on calling a vest.

'It is *not* a vest,' said Judy. 'It's a T-shirt.'

'It's a vest. And you thought you could whip it off while I wasn't looking.'

'Shut up,' she said. 'You get yourself undressed.'

'Oh, no,' he said, grabbing her. 'I don't want to miss anything. What have you got on under the trousers?' He took a peek. 'Long johns,' he said.

'They're *tights*,' she squeaked indignantly. 'It's all right for you – your car's got a heater that works. They keep me warm.'

'They don't,' he pointed out.

'Look,' she said. 'They've got feet. They're tights.'

But Lloyd had discovered skin, and was tickling her. They collapsed in a heap on the bed, and the more they laughed, the more *andante* it became, and the more they enjoyed it.

Judy had thought about this moment on the way to the flat. She had thought it would be awkward and intense if it happened at all; at best, she had imagined it would be a kind of self-conscious re-establishment of the status quo. But instead, it was like this, and she lost herself completely in the laughter and the love.

Which was why, when her senses returned, she got up, taking Lloyd's dressing-gown from the door as she went into the sitting room, pulling the belt tight around her. She stood for a moment in the near darkness; she wanted a cigarette, a B-movie cigarette, and she felt in her handbag for the packet, not wanting even Lloyd's seduction lighting. Her hand trembled as she struck the match.

She heard Lloyd arrive in the room; she didn't turn round.

'And I thought it was the faithful come to Bethlehem,' he said, after a moment.

She didn't need him talking in riddles. She inhaled deeply, and expelled the smoke. 'What?' she said, still not looking.

'Joyful and triumphant.'

She smiled, despite herself. 'It was.'

'Then what's wrong?'

The smoke was drawn through the coloured lights, curling round the tree. 'I'm frightened,' she said.

'Of me?'

She didn't dignify that with an answer.

'Of us,' he amended, and this time she didn't have to answer.

He came up to her. 'Because you forgot to keep back a little piece of yourself?' he asked.

She put her cigarette in the ashtray, and turned to look at him. Acting came to Lloyd as naturally as breathing. His voice, his expression, his mood. But he dropped the act with her. He pretended that what was underneath was just another act, but it wasn't; it never had been.

'But it makes you so vulnerable,' she said.

'Yes.'

She hugged him close to her. 'I love you,' she said.

He reached past her, and switched on the lamp, which seemed suddenly brilliant.

'What did you do that for?' she asked.

'Say it again. When I can see your lips move.'

She hadn't meant to say it in the first place. She had spent fifteen years not saying it.

'Where did you get that?' Judy touched the sleeve of the new dressing-gown that Lloyd was wearing.

'Don't change the subject.'

'It's nice,' she said, and glanced down at the one she had wrapped round herself like some sort of fig-leaf; it had afforded her about the same protection.

'The kids gave me it for Christmas.'

'They've got better taste than you,' she said.

'Say it again.'

'They've got better—' She smiled. 'I love you.'

'You've never said that before.'

'I've said it now.' She smiled again. 'Twice. So that should keep you going for another fifteen years.'

'But what does loving me mean?'

'I'm not sure,' she said. 'It means I'm here, when I should be at home with Michael. *And* his parents. God knows what I'll tell them. I'm a rotten liar.'

'So tell them the truth.'

Mrs Hill probably wouldn't believe her if she did, thought Judy.

'Sorry,' he said. 'Forget it. Do you want something to eat?'

'Poor Lloyd,' she said smiling. 'You're hungry.'

'Starving,' he said. 'What would you like?'

'Nothing,' she said quickly. 'I've got to go, Lloyd.'

He let his arms drop away from her, and walked off into the kitchen, slamming the door.

It was bitterly cold, and the wind had come back, moaning through the trees. But George stood in the garden in his shirt sleeves, looking across at the castle, its battlements visible in the clear, starlit night. He was trembling, already. Because it was cold. Too cold to stand out here. The frozen snow glistened as the temperature dipped even further.

The coldest Christmas period since eighteen seventy-something, the radio said. Hypothermia was a killer, they said. Make sure old people wear lots of layers of clothing. Tell them to heat one room only if they're worried about bills. Make sure they have hot meals.

He had ten years to go before he collected his pension, before he was consigned to that section of humanity assumed to be incapable of making sure for itself that it wore warmer clothes in winter – who couldn't even listen to advice on the radio. Ten years to go before other people had to listen to the radio for him, and tell him what it had said. Ten years. He wasn't old. And yet he felt old. Too old to start again.

He could go across the fields, to the castle. To Eleanor. She wanted him there. She needed him. But he wouldn't go. He would stay at home with Marian.

'George?' Marian's voice. 'George, are you all right?'

'Just getting some fresh air,' he said.

He could hear her footsteps crunching on the snow, as she walked over. She came up to him, putting her arm round him. 'A bit too fresh,' she said. 'Come back in. You'll catch cold out here.'

'I always understood that you could only catch colds from other people,' he said.

'And you're testing the theory?' Her arm tightened round him. 'We've just got to carry on,' she said, in a quiet voice.

He looked at her, and smiled. 'You're better at that than I am,' he said.

She kissed him, her face warm against his. 'Don't make yourself ill,' she whispered. 'It's happened. We'll survive it. We've survived other things.'

Lost babies, lost parents, lost dogs. And it was always Marian who kept herself and everyone else together. He kissed her, suddenly and fiercely. But she couldn't help him through this.

'Dinner's ready,' she said.

He gave a short laugh. 'Not much point in my eating it,' he said, patting his stomach.

'Is it just as bad?'

George looked at the castle. 'It won't get any better until this business is over and done with,' he said, and he followed her into the house.

For a few moments, out there in the cold, it had gone. Out in the sharp, breathless cold, there had been no desperation in the pit of his stomach, making him ill.

But now it was back.

Lloyd turned down the gas under his rice, and surveyed the multi-coloured piles of matchstick vegetables, ready for stir-frying. Slicing them up had been good therapy. Removing a table mat and fork from the drawer, he went into the sitting room. She wasn't there.

He picked up the ashtray, in which Judy's cigarette had burned away, leaving ash and melted blobs of nylon ribbon. They were lucky she hadn't set the place on fire. As he put it down, it reminded him of something, and he frowned, looking at it again.

He set his solitary place, and went into the bedroom, where Judy sat, dressed and ready to leave. But she hadn't.

'I thought you were in a hurry,' he said.

She looked up at him. 'I didn't want to leave while you weren't speaking to me,' she said.

Lloyd sat beside her, and took her hand in his. 'I want to explain how I feel,' he said.

She looked away. 'This must be later,' she said.

'Yes.' Her hand still rested in his; his thumb moved back and forth across it as he tried to phrase his statement. 'Judy,' he said at last. 'Going to bed with you is lovely. It's great. Tonight, it was better than ever.' He paused. 'Look at me,' he said.

She turned, her face a little apprehensive.

'But it's not why I want you here,' he said. 'It's not what this is about. And your being here just long enough for us to hop in and out of bed seems . . . sordid, somehow.'

'Sordid!' She turned away again.

'Yes, damn it! Sordid. It's not all I want out of this,' he said. 'But I'm – well, I'm afraid that maybe it is all you want.'

She looked back, her face angry. 'That would be funny,' she

said. 'If it wasn't so—' She pressed her lips together, and took a moment before speaking again. 'Listen to me,' she said. 'I've been married to Michael for ten years. Ten *years*, Lloyd.'

Lloyd was listening. But she was saying nothing new. 'So he's got the prior claim, is that it?' he asked.

'No,' she said, her voice exasperated. 'He has, I suppose, but that's not it. Because I don't think it would break his heart.'

Lloyd was lost again.

'Until this year, he spent half his time abroad,' she said. 'He did what he pleased when he was away, and I could have done the same, I suppose. But I didn't.'

'Until I came along?'

'Not even then,' she said. 'Because this *isn't* the same, is it?'

Every time Lloyd thought he'd got hold of something, she seemed to change tack. 'I don't understand,' he said. 'What are you saying? That you were faithful to Michael until I came along and seduced you, or what?'

She closed her eyes. 'No,' she said, opening them again. 'You,' she said. 'If I was faithful to anyone, then it was to you. Because I've never wanted anyone else.' The tears weren't far away when she spoke again. 'So, no – I'm not just after your body,' she said, her voice bitter.

She had been hurt by that; Lloyd put his arms round her.

'I'm sorry,' he said. 'Truly, I am. Take no notice of me.' He held her close. 'But I don't understand why you won't just *leave* him,' he said.

'Because I'm a coward,' she answered, her voice muffled. 'You said I was frightened to leave him, and you're right. I'm scared to change my whole way of life just like that.'

'But you wouldn't be on your own!'

'I know,' she said, standing up. 'And I do have to go,' she said.

'It's this or nothing? Is that what you're saying?'

She nodded. 'Unless it's too sordid for you.'

He looked up at her. 'My tongue gets carried away sometimes,' he said. 'It's Welsh. You have to make allowances.'

She didn't reply. After a moment, he heard the outside door close.

He'd done it again. It was some time before he could make himself move, go into the kitchen, and carry on. And he ate his stir-fry, but his appetite had gone, and he didn't enjoy it. He tried to watch television; some of the proper programmes were back, but they were all, to his jaundiced eye, unwatchable. After the news, which he would have been better advised not to have watched, he went to bed, at an unreasonably early hour for him. He was tired, but he took his book, as he always did.

He opened his eyes when it landed on the floor. Blinking, he picked it up again, and carried on reading, as though to fool it into believing that he'd never been asleep. The words were easy enough, but he didn't know what they meant. Then the print moved and swam before his eyes, and the book slid away again. This time he caught it, admitted defeat, and closed it. But the action involved had made him properly awake, now, and he might as well carry on reading.

He opened the book, almost against his will, at the inscriptions. A hastily written 'Best wishes from' followed by the indecipherable signature of the author. Underneath, in her neat, clear, writing, 'and from me.'

But he didn't want to think about Judy, or the arrangement that he no longer wished to live with, or without. He closed the book again, and switched off the light.

He was drifting off to sleep again, when an image came into his mind. George Wheeler. George Wheeler, emptying ash from a dustbin on to the vicarage driveway. Grey ash, black speckled.

Just like the melted nylon ribbon in his ashtray.

Marian Wheeler watched her husband as he got ready for bed. At first, he wasn't aware of it; she watched him become aware, try to ignore it. She watched him become awkward, as if she were a stranger.

He buttoned his pyjama top. 'What?' he said. 'Why are you staring at me?'

Marian took a deep breath. 'What's making you sick, George?' she asked.

'I told you,' he said lightly. 'This business. You know what I'm like – I used to be sick for a week before exams. I was sick in the vestry before I gave my first sermon.'

'Is it because you're being unfaithful to me?' she asked, when he'd finished.

George closed his eyes briefly, and sat on the edge of the bed. 'No,' he said. 'Nothing happened on Christmas Eve, Marian. I went there to get my tie. That was all.' He sighed. 'But I realised that I could stay there or come back here and spend the evening with my son-in-law. So I stayed.'

Marian didn't speak.

'Nothing happened then, and nothing's happened since. I'm not being unfaithful to you.'

'Because you haven't actually slept with her?'

George looked away.

'Why don't you, George?' she said. 'Perhaps it would settle your stomach.'

'Marian—'

'I mean it,' she said. 'If you want to break commandments, go ahead and break them. Don't agonise over it.'

George didn't say anything at all. He turned the bedclothes back slowly, and got into bed.

Marian put out the light, and lay back. She had known about Eleanor Langton's effect on George long before he had noticed it himself; she had prepared herself for the reckoning, unlike him.

Poor George, making a fool of himself over a girl not much older than Joanna; becoming, Marian was sure, the subject of behind-the-hand murmurings amongst the other play-group mothers. Making himself sick with worry and guilt, and for what? A fantasy. Well, Marian would back herself against a fantasy any day.

And yet, she was grateful to Eleanor Langton, in a way; at least she *had* been with George on Christmas Eve, and that proved that he couldn't have killed Graham.

If only she could be that sure of Joanna's whereabouts. But nothing she could say would make Joanna tell her where she'd gone that night. Marian toyed with the idea of a similar assignation to George's; she even considered the possibility of Joanna's being pregnant by another man. Perhaps that was why she hadn't told them about the baby.

Perhaps it was this man that Graham met in the pub; why he

got drunk, why he became violent. It would explain why Joanna had just stayed in the sitting room after she and George had come home, because she wouldn't want to answer questions until she was ready. It would explain why she hadn't taken them into her confidence about where she had been that night. For it would be natural, wouldn't it, to go to him, to tell him what Graham had done.

It explained everything, but Marian knew that it was nonsense. Joanna had been too hung up on her odious husband to have been looking elsewhere.

Chapter Nine

It was nice, not being stared awake by Tessa. Nice, but odd. Eleanor switched on the light, and looked at the clock, to discover that habit and worry had overcome freedom. Six o'clock. That was even earlier than Tessa's start, but she was awake now, and she could never go back to sleep. She lay back, and considered the situation, which didn't seem so bad, after a night's sleep. She felt calmer now that she'd spoken to George, even if it had been an unsatisfactory communication. He couldn't have told the police, or surely the inspector would have asked questions? Or would he? He was fond of drama. The anxiety returned, as she slowly got out of bed.

Not even daylight, she thought, as she ran the bath that at least she could have all by herself, without Tessa's ministrations. She could soak for hours, if she wanted.

The knock on the door made her jump. My God, who came at this time in the morning? Police. It had to be the police. Shouting that she'd just be a moment, she hastily grabbed her clothes, hopping about on one foot as her jeans refused to co-operate. She pulled on a sweater, and opened the door to George. Her mouth opened and closed again.

'When you say first thing, you really mean it,' she said; when she had got her breath back.

'I had a bad night. I could see your light, so I came over.' He went into the sitting room.

Eleanor followed him in. 'You told them you were here,' she said.

'Yes.' He was by the window, looking out at the courtyard. He didn't look at her.

'So did I,' she said.

'Yes.' He turned from the window. 'Just as well we told them the same thing,' he said. 'Or it might have looked rather odd.'

'It might.' Her eyes searched his, trying to make contact with him through the barrier of his blank, bland stare. 'Why were they checking up on you?' she asked him.

He shrugged. 'They have to suspect someone.'

'I didn't tell them anything else,' she said, bracing herself for his reply.

The smile that had attracted her to him slowly appeared, for the first time in days. 'Neither did I,' he said, and Eleanor felt the anxiety slip away.

His eyes, alive again, took her in from head to toe, and back again. 'Eleanor—' he said, then suddenly, almost audibly, the barrier came back down. 'I have to go,' he said, walking to the door.

Eleanor tried not to think of the man she had met two months ago; the man who had called on Christmas Eve. The man who had fleetingly reappeared with the smile.

'George?' she said. 'When did you start feeling ill?'

He turned, frowning. 'When they arrested Marian,' he said. 'She has to be the mother-hen. Protecting her egg from predators. Offering herself up.'

Eleanor turned away from him. 'Eggs are supposed to hatch out,' she said.

She heard his footsteps coming towards her, felt his tentative hand touch her neck. As she turned, he walked away again, the front door closed, and she was on her own.

Joanna drove out of the vicarage, taking Judy Hill's advice to check the house. There wasn't much conviction about the action, but it was something to do, something that might, just might, make the police start looking elsewhere. There was still an hour till sunrise, so with any luck she should avoid the stares of the neighbours.

Her father's car emerged from Castle Road. She doubted if he'd seen her, other than as another road-user. He had withdrawn into a world where other people didn't exist. Except Eleanor Langton. Joanna had heard him leave even earlier than she had; what was so urgent that he had to visit her practically in the middle of the night? Eleanor Langton was doing her father no good, that much she did know: she had heard him during the night, walking up and down. The last time he'd had as bad an attack as this had been when he brought her home from hospital.

She drove into Stansfield, and took the right turn into the private housing estate where she and Graham had lived, remembering the first time they ever saw it. Before they were married, they had come here, looking for a house. What were now neat if yet to be established gardens had been a sea of mud and builders' rubble, the houses approachable only by planks laid precariously on bricks.

The show house had been one of the expensive ones, beyond their range. So she and Graham had gone to look round one of the others, and she had got whistles from the workmen as she had picked her way up to the front door, still without the steps it needed. Graham had lifted her up, like a child. He had been excited about the house; it was just an ordinary house – one of the bedrooms was barely larger than the larder at the vicarage. '*But it'll be ours*,' he'd said.

They had got into trouble from the site foreman, who had shouted at them about its being private property, and his responsibility if they got hurt. If they wanted somewhere to do their courting, they could find somewhere a lot bloody safer than a building site.

They had bought the house a couple of doors away from that one. Joanna pulled up outside, her heart beating fast. It was almost as though he would be there when she went in, in a mood, as he always was when she'd been home.

Home. That was what had caused one of Graham's rages; when she had called the vicarage home. Was that this time? She couldn't remember clearly. Only the chimes, and Graham's face. What had triggered the violence was lost.

But he wasn't here, not now, not any more. There was no need for apprehension. It was an empty house, that was all.

She walked into the house, through the sitting room to the kitchen, feeling like a visitor, like someone who had come to feed the cat. It was unbelievably untidy, with every surface covered in either dust or whatever Graham happened to have put down and never picked up again. The ironing board was up, with the iron still on it. At least it was unplugged. Graham had been used to having someone who washed dishes and dusted and hoovered carpets for him, especially since the firm she had worked for had done a moonlight, leaving the gates locked and thousands of pounds of bad debts. She hadn't been there long enough to get any recompense, and Graham hadn't wanted her to apply for unemployment benefit. So she'd had no money, and the mortgage meant that there wasn't much left over from Graham's salary. Her mother had given her a fiver now and then, but after the first time, Joanna had made sure that Graham didn't find out.

The kitchen was worse than the sitting room. There were dirty dishes in the sink, and she wished she hadn't come. There were too many memories, too much grease clinging to the cooker, too many coffee mug rings on the formica, too much pain.

Through the archway, over which hung the painting that Graham had bought from a street-artist in Paris on the first day of their honeymoon weekend, to the stairs – and they hadn't seen a brush for weeks. He had been brought up to think that men didn't do that sort of thing, even if they had no alternative. The alternative was to carry on exactly as though someone was going to come along behind and make it all neat and clean again.

The bed was made – even Graham knew how to pull a duvet straight. He had changed the bedding at least once, she thought. It was the blue set, and it had been the pale yellow ones. She remembered everything about their last night in this house, except what had caused it all, just like at the vicarage. It was easier to remember the externals; the chiming clock, the yellow duvet.

She remembered the ambulance men; she remembered Graham saying that she'd fallen downstairs. She had gone along with it, though it was clear that no one at the hospital believed it. Her father thought it was because she was afraid to do anything else, but it wasn't.

She sat on the bed, and looked round the room. Her slippers, which Graham had failed to pack in his remorseful co-operation with her mother, still lay where she had kicked them off that morning.

No, she had gone along with Graham's story for a dozen

different reasons. It was easier than admitting to strangers what had really happened. It was unthinkable to go to the police, to go through a court case. And besides, it hadn't all been like that. They'd had *fun*. Often. They'd had fun buying the house, doing it up, furnishing it. The mortgage payments had got difficult once she had lost her job, but they'd managed. The garden had been hard work, because neither of them knew the first thing about it, and she had been wise enough by then not to seek advice from her father. But even it had been fun, and they'd done it in the end. They had a lawn, and flowers. Graham even had vegetables at the back. She stood and looked out of the window, but the snow covered everything.

Beneath the surface, there had been tension. She'd put it down to having to get used to one another. They were from different backgrounds; they had different opinions about how things should be. But everyone had to compromise, she had told herself, when they had had the odd argument, the occasional two-day huff. That had resolved nothing; she could see that now. And so the tension had gone on building, until at last it erupted into violence, and tears, and vows never to do it again. And forgiveness. But he had done it again, and again, until her parents couldn't fail to notice. Their consequent concern had made matters worse; her mother had taken to calling unannounced, and Joanna had started going to see her more and more often to render such spot-checks unnecessary. It was as though everything had been planned, arranged, leading up to that night.

The externals. Like a silent movie. Pulling up outside, like today, after a visit to her mother. Graham, cold-shouldering her when she went in, picking up his evening paper and going upstairs with it. Following him up after a while, to see if she could get him out of his mood. She couldn't remember what she had said, but she remembered that Graham hadn't been listening, and that had upset her.

She frowned. A flash of memory, like a dream. She could see Graham, handing the paper to her, asking if she'd read something.

'Yes,' she had said, annoyed by the interruption. '*I saw the paper at home.*'

The little silence. She had dropped the paper on to the bed.

She remembered trying to get to her feet, grabbing at the bed, but all she had got hold of was the yellow duvet which slid down, taking the paper with it. She could see the paper, as it was kicked under the bed in the struggle. Slow motion action replay.

Then her mind went blank, shutting out the memory, until the moment that she had realised it had stopped, and she could get away from him. She had made it downstairs, then had collapsed at the foot, unwittingly offering Graham his explanation of her injuries. She remembered hearing his voice on the phone. Then the ambulance men, and the hospital. Her mother and father. No Graham. She had asked the doctor to check, just in case. Being told that the baby was all right was the confirmation of what had merely been a possibility, unsought and unmentioned.

The bedroom was covered in Graham's cast off clothes. The laundry basket was full, as though he'd thought she might come along and do his washing. He'd piled more things on top of it. His wardrobe only had some empty hangers in it; his drawer was stuffed full of unironed shirts. Two dry-cleaning bags lay on the floor, and underneath one she could see the corner of the paper, still under the bed.

She reached down and pulled it out, still open at the page he had wanted her to read. One side was advertisements for used cars, but that wasn't likely, because they had just bought hers when Graham got a backdated increase. News items on the other side. She glanced at them. It was probably just something that had caught his eye. A funny misprint, or a bit of local bureaucracy gone mad.

She read the headings, COUNCIL VETOES SUNDAY OPENING; ASBESTOS SCARE – NO RISK, SAYS FIRM; NEW MOVES IN BUS DISPUTE; PENSIONER ROBBED.

Then, along the bottom, the one that made her eyes grow wide, and her face grow hot. It had to be it. It *had* to be. It couldn't be a coincidence.

Morning. Judy's eyes half-opened, then closed again, despite the angry buzzing by her left ear. After a moment, she sat up, and cancelled the alarm. At first, she wasn't really aware of Michael's non-presence; she had spent half of her married life waking up alone. Then she realised, and remembered. Michael had gone to Edinburgh.

He'd be there by now, she thought sleepily, looking at the clock. And his parents, thank the Lord, would be sleeping soundly in Nottingham.

She had arrived home to find Michael packing; for a moment, she had thought it was instant retribution. And when she had been told that Ian had come down with flu, and that Michael was going to have to go to Edinburgh in his place, her mistaken impression had struck her as irresistibly funny. She had had to feign a sudden need to race upstairs to the bathroom, where she had pulled the chain and turned on the bath taps, muffling the laughter, nervous, painful laughter, in a bath towel.

Mrs Hill had been discreetly anxious to know if everything was all right; she was doubtless irritated that another month of the limited time at Judy's disposal had apparently slipped away. And she informed Judy that Michael's train stopped at Nottingham, so she and Mr Hill had decided to go up with him, instead of waiting the extra day, since Judy was so busy. He would be glad of the company.

She had driven them all to the station, Michael being unhappy about leaving his car there at this time of the year. They had all remarked on the lack of heat in the car; they hadn't been driving all over Stansfield in it half the night.

Michael had told her that he would be returning on the overnight train arriving in Stansfield at seven thirty-two on Wednesday morning. Judy had said she would meet it, and had queried the wisdom of travelling overnight to a meeting and overnight back again without a break. He had said that nothing would induce him to be in Scotland once Hogmanay had started. Somehow, she thought, that summed up the differences between them.

And the difference between him and Lloyd, she thought, her heart heavy. Once again, what should have been good had turned sour; once again, it had been her fault. She sighed, and was preparing herself to crawl out from under the warm duvet to begin another day, when the phone rang.

Lloyd? She picked it up almost timidly.

'Sergeant Hill?'

Not Lloyd. Constable Sandwell's voice.

'Yes,' she said. 'Good morning, Bob.'

'Morning, Sergeant. I'm sorry to ring so early, but I've got Mrs Elstow here, very anxious to see you. I said you weren't due in until nine, but she said she'd wait.'

Judy took that in. 'And you think I should come in now?' she asked.

'Well. It's just that she seems to think that she's found something that will help you with the case, and I thought she might change her mind if she had to wait. You know what they're like.'

'They' covered anyone who wasn't a police officer, in Sandwell's book. He had been seconded to CID, and was proving useful.

'She won't tell me,' he said. 'Or anyone else.'

'Right,' said Judy. 'I'm on my way.'

In under fifteen minutes, surpassing even her Christmas morning sprint, Judy was out in the bitter weather, persuading her car to start. Once it obliged, she got out, and cursed the ice as she scraped it off the windows, realising as she took this exercise that she hadn't eaten since lunch time the previous day, and that she was ravenous.

Back into the ice-box, in which she seemed to be spending her entire life, and off on the twenty-minute journey, which she had made, one way or the other, six times in the last twelve hours.

Something kept teasing her mind; something she couldn't catch hold of; at first, she dismissed it, thinking that it must be a fragment of a dream. But it wasn't. It had something to do with the murder. Something Lloyd had said, but she was certain that she hadn't written it down, which was odd, because she wrote up her notebook every night, and she wrote *everything* down. People laughed at her notes, but Lloyd knew why she took them. She had a dreadful memory. It probably wasn't important. And if it had been something about the murder, she'd have jotted it down somewhere. Maybe just a word, or a question mark against a previous note. She would look through her notes as soon as she got time.

Joanna Elstow jumped up as she walked in, and Judy smiled at her, grateful to her for delaying the moment when she would see Lloyd.

'Good morning, Joanna,' she said, sounding a little like a head-mistress greeting a pupil. 'Is there an interview room free?' she asked Sandwell.

'You can take your pick, Sergeant,' he said.

'Good.' She led the way, and went into the first one, closing the door. 'Take a seat,' she said. 'What can I do for you?'

'I've been to the house,' Joanna said.

'Oh?' Judy reached into her bag for her notebook. 'Were there signs of someone else having been there?'

'No,' said Joanna, with a reluctant little smile. 'Or if there was, she must have been as untidy as Graham. And if she was as untidy as Graham, there would have been signs.'

Judy smiled at the logic. 'Well,' she said. 'It was always unlikely.'

Joanna nodded, and pushed a newspaper across the table to her. 'But I found this,' she said. 'Graham asked me to read it.'

Judy frowned. 'When?' she asked, thinking for a moment that Joanna had been communing with the spirit world.

'The day . . .' Joanna faltered a little. 'The last day I was there,' she said. 'The day I went to hospital.' She leant over. 'Look,' she said, pointing to a news report.

COMA MAN DIES, read the headline, and Judy's eyes widened as she read the report.

'He must have known him,' Joanna said.

Judy agreed that it was unlikely to be a coincidence. 'Though they do happen,' she warned Joanna.

Joanna smiled. 'I know,' she said.

Judy felt foolish then. She always found herself speaking to Joanna as if she were a child instead of a married woman. A widow, she reminded herself. About to become a mother. But a child. A child of the Byford vicarage; a protected, cushioned child who had become the victim of savagery.

Along the corridor, into reception, through the CID room. Keep walking. Don't stop to talk. Get it over with.

'Hello,' said Lloyd.

'I've got Joanna Elstow here,' she said.

Even if they hadn't been at work, with the possibility of

someone barging in, there was very little she could say. Perhaps they had said it all last night.

George didn't like guns. He fumbled with the cartridges; it was cold in the study, but he hadn't put on the electric fire.

He thought of Eleanor, and closed his eyes. Standing there in front of him, hands in pockets, barefooted in her jeans and sweater, her hair swept up in a careless knot on top of her head. Young, and beautiful, and free. Free as a bird.

He was awkward with the shotgun; it had been a long time since he'd shot anything. Marian did clay pigeon shooting at the castle, when they held competitions, in the summer. She'd once won a bottle of whisky.

His fingers were stiff; he flexed his hand, and laid the gun down on the desk as he stood up. Marian's prize had reminded him that there was some brandy somewhere. A drink might relax him. Give him Dutch courage, at any rate. He pulled open the cupboard door, and revealed the bottle, with a tot left in it. No glass. He didn't want to go out to the kitchen; he swigged the brandy from the bottle, surprised by the amount, by the suddenness of it on his throat. Pushing the stopper back, he stood for a moment with the empty bottle, remembering its origins.

Joanna and Graham had brought it with them when they'd come over for the silver wedding celebrations. Fourteen months ago. It was just after that evening that Joanna had sported a bruise for the first time, and told them some story to account for it. George threw the bottle into the empty grate behind the electric fire, but it didn't break, didn't even make much of a noise.

'*When did you start feeling ill?*' Eleanor's question echoed in his mind. When they arrested Marian. Because Marian was offering herself up; guarding, protecting, defending her nest. It couldn't go on. It mustn't go on. He stared at the gun, then hoisted it to his shoulder, as if following a bird in flight.

He pulled stuff out of the cupboard until he could lay the gun down inside, and covered it with the papers and bits and pieces until it couldn't be seen. He closed and locked the door, then went back to his desk, looked at what he had written, and tore it into tiny pieces, letting them fall from his hands into the waste-paper basket.

Eleanor, turning away from him. 'Eggs are supposed to hatch out,' she had said. She must have had to dress quickly, after he had knocked at the door; the sweater label stuck up at the nape of her neck. And he had gone back to her, and tucked the label in.

'*Eggs are supposed to hatch out.*' Yes. Yes, they were.

If the little bird inside couldn't break the shell, then it died in there.

And here was Eleanor Langton again, Lloyd thought, popping up for the third time in this investigation. He scanned the page. Could Graham Elstow have been going to show his wife something else altogether? It was possible. Anything was possible. But it surely had to be something important, something that over-rode the fact that he wasn't on the best of terms with his wife at that particular moment? Lloyd thought back to the huffy silences which had descended on him and Barbara. You didn't break them for a discussion on the dangers of asbestos, or the desirability of Sunday trading.

He read the Sunday trading piece, in case Wheeler's views had been sought, and Graham had been looking for an argument about Joanna's father. But no, there was nothing there.

Joanna seemed as mystified as they were. The unnamed motor-cyclist on whose bike Langton had been riding pillion was reported as having been 'saddened' by Langton's death. But he wasn't Elstow, because he was also reported as having just returned from working in West Germany for eighteen months.

'We'll check it out,' he said.

Joanna nodded.

They were all in the office now. Joanna sat at Judy's desk, and Lloyd at his own; that way he had the width of the room between them. He could get up, walk round. Affect deep interest in wall charts and floor tiles. It all helped to confuse the enemy.

Judy was talking to Joanna, jotting down the odd thing now and then. She gave him a cool glance as he toured the office with no apparent aim; he wished things could be different, as he had at the pub. But the regret was pushed to one side by the thought that then occurred to him, and he went back to his desk, opening his diary to give himself something to do while he thought it through.

'But you don't recall him ever mentioning Richard Langton?' said Judy.

His ever mentioning, thought Lloyd, automatically.

'No, never.'

Lloyd looked up, and smiled at Joanna. 'Forgive me,' he said, 'but something is bothering me a little, Mrs Elstow.'

She looked across at him, her eyebrows raised in enquiry.

'Sergeant Hill tells me that you and your husband had reached some sort of understanding after . . .' He finished the sentence with a wave of his hand in the general direction of Joanna's bruises.

'Some sort,' she said dully. 'I think I really only began to understand this morning.'

'Oh?'

'What I was doing to him,' she said. 'What I was letting her do to him.'

'Your mother?' Lloyd stood up, and leant on the edge of the desk.

She nodded again.

'And yet – you didn't make any attempt to communicate with him afterwards,' he said. 'In case it upset your mother.'

Joanna looked at Judy, not at him. 'I didn't want to cause any more trouble,' she said.

'So you left him upstairs,' Lloyd said, his voice slightly raised. 'Not knowing whether he should come down and face the music, or start knotting sheets together.' He shook his head. 'I don't believe that, Mrs Elstow.'

Joanna shot Judy a desperate look, but she was involved with her notebook.

'I – I didn't get the chance,' said Joanna. 'My father took me to the pub.'

'Ah, yes,' said Lloyd. 'The pub.' He pushed himself away from the desk. 'It was your father's idea, wasn't it?'

'No,' she said. 'Not really. It was my mother who suggested it.'

'But it was your father who persuaded you to go?' Lloyd sat down again. 'Yes?' he said.

'Yes.'

'I don't imagine that you wanted to,' he said. 'Not after what had happened. You must have felt a bit rough. And – forgive me again – you must have looked a bit rough.'

'He said it would just look worse later,' said Joanna. 'He was right.'

'So he persuaded you to go with him.'

'Yes.' Joanna sounded wary.

'And having persuaded you, he just got up and left you there, on your own?'

Joanna's mouth opened slightly, but no words came out. Again, she looked at Judy for help.

'Did he, Joanna?' Judy asked.

Joanna's shoulders sagged. 'No,' she said.

'No,' said Lloyd. 'Your father left the pub alone, but he left after you, not before you. Right?'

'Yes.'

'When did you leave?'

'About eight,' she said, and there was no expression in her voice. 'I knew my mother was going out, so I gave her time to be well away.' Her hand absently touched the bruise under her eye. 'I wanted to get Graham to come with me to Dr Lomax,' she said. 'But I couldn't get him to open the door. I thought *he'd* locked it,' she said. 'I thought he'd got in a mood again, and—'

Judy looked up from her notes. 'But your mother didn't lock the house up until after nine,' she said.

'My mother didn't lock up the house at all! Don't you see? She thinks *I* killed Graham. She thinks *I* locked the doors. But it wasn't me! Graham let someone in, and they locked the doors so that they wouldn't be *disturbed*. Don't you see?'

'Someone?' said Lloyd.

'Whoever he met at the pub,' said Joanna.

'We can't find any trace of his meeting anyone at the pub,' said Lloyd. 'He came in alone, drank alone, ate alone, and was ejected. Alone.'

'He said he met someone,' Joanna repeated mutinously.

Lloyd stroked his chin. 'Perhaps you'll tell us why you didn't volunteer this information?'

'I couldn't,' she said. 'Not after my father said he'd been with me all evening.'

Lloyd picked up a pen, balancing it on his finger as he spoke. 'And why did he say that, do you suppose?' he asked.

'Because he thinks I did it! They both do!' Her eyes filled with tears. 'So do you,' she said. 'But I didn't. I *didn't*.' She got up, and came over to him, jabbing a finger down on the newspaper. 'What about this?' she said.

Lloyd picked up the paper. 'You think your husband knew Richard Langton,' he said. 'And by extension, Eleanor Langton.'

'Yes, of course I do.'

'Perhaps,' said Lloyd. 'But knowing him hardly constitutes motive for murder.' He looked at Joanna's bruises as he spoke. On the other hand, he thought, perhaps it did. 'And Mrs Langton was at home,' he said. 'All evening. According to both of your parents.'

Joanna stood up, very erect. 'Are you going to check this?' she asked.

'Oh, yes,' Lloyd said. 'We'll check it. Thank you for coming in, Mrs Elstow.'

The door closed behind her, and Lloyd picked up the phone. 'Bob? Come in a moment, please.'

'Let's see what Eleanor Langton has to say,' Judy suggested.

'No,' Lloyd said quickly. 'Not yet.'

'Why not?' asked Judy.

Lloyd was loath to explain why not. Because she made him feel uncomfortable. Because she didn't look at people, she *watched* them. Because if he were to engage in a battle of wits with Eleanor Langton, he wasn't at all sure that he would win.

'Because,' he said, as Sandwell knocked and came in. 'When we go to see Mrs Langton, I don't want to ask her if she knew Elstow, I want to *tell* her she knew him.' He looked up, and handed Sandwell the paper, with the report ringed in red. 'Details,' he said. 'As quickly as that dreadful machine can produce them.'

'There's sometimes a bit of a delay, sir. It depends on whether—'

'No lectures about ROM and RAM and downtime,' groaned Lloyd.

'No, nothing like that, sir.' He opened his mouth, then wilted under Lloyd's stare. 'Sir,' he said, taking the paper and leaving.

Lloyd sat down as Judy began flicking through the pages of her notebook. He smiled as he watched her. No one took notes like Judy did. Perhaps she was going to write a book one day.

'Besides,' he said. 'We've only got Joanna Elstow's word for how she came by it.'

Judy closed the notebook. 'The paper is dated the day she went into hospital,' she said. 'And if we're embarking on a course of taking no one's word for anything, we'll never do anything at all. How can you take Sandwell's word for it that the computer gives him whatever answer it does? Perhaps he'll make it all up.'

'Sandwell has not proved time and time again to be telling lies,' Lloyd pointed out. 'She has. And her parents.'

'You don't like it because it's putting a dent in your domestic theory,' she said.

'No, that's not why,' said Lloyd, thoughtfully and truthfully. 'Why I don't like it is that it's yet another puzzle. We've got more little puzzles than enough.'

Judy opened her notebook again. 'I think I'll write them down,' she said.

Lloyd laughed. 'Writing them down does not solve them,' he said.

'Who says? We think they're connected to the case, don't we? So if they're all written down together. It might . . .' Her voice tailed off, as a good reason failed to present itself. 'Help,' she finished lamely.

Lloyd was having nothing to do with it. He needed answers to questions, not parlour games.

His shoes had deposited enough of George's ash on the floor of his car to constitute a sample, and it had gone to the lab. At least that was an answer to one question.

He watched as Judy worked her way through her copious notes, in which every little puzzle had of course been entered, and he found himself thinking how soft and shining her hair looked, how pleasing the line of her jaw.

Unprofessional. He had never admired Sandwell's hair, or Jack Woodford's jaw-line, fine specimens though they doubtless were.

She worked carefully, checking every page so as not to miss anything, making a neat list on a sheet of paper. Anything less sordid than Judy was impossible to imagine. And he had probably ruined everything, throwing words about in the way other people might throw crockery. Crockery was less dangerous. Perhaps even someone like Elstow was less dangerous. He had hurt Judy just as surely as if he had punched her.

She sat back and looked at the list, the tip of her tongue brushing her upper lip as she thought hard about something. Unfair, thought Lloyd. She turned to look at him, and neither of them said anything, until they both spoke at once.

'Judy, look, I've—'

'Lloyd – listen to this.'

He held out a hand. 'You first,' he said, because what he had been going to say had had very little to do with the murder of Graham Elstow.

'The things that puzzled us,' she said. 'We know the answers to some of them.'

'Good.'

'We wondered what Mrs Anthony was hinting about George,' she said, and then looked at him enquiringly.

'Presumably she'd noticed that he was taking too healthy an interest in the beautiful Mrs Langton,' said Lloyd.

'Yes. And why Marian Wheeler was still so upset when she was at Mrs Anthony's. She'd just been to see . . .' She held out a hand, waiting for him to supply the answer.

'Eleanor Langton.'

'And we wondered what Wheeler thought could have made his wife so angry that she would destroy his Christmas present.'

'Eleanor Langton,' said Lloyd, slowly, tipping his chair back as he thought about the little puzzles, and the ubiquitous Mrs Langton at the bottom of every one of them, including today's. Everywhere he looked, there she was, with her long blonde hair and her fine features, and her watchful eyes. Who had provided Marian with her alibi? Who had provided George with his? And who was careful to unprovide Joanna with hers?

'You'll fall one day,' said Judy.

'That's the beauty of it,' said Lloyd, righting the chair, and the allusion was not lost on Judy. 'Any more puzzles?' he asked.

'Who Elstow met at the pub, and why he got drunk,' said Judy.

Eleanor Langton? But they mustn't jump to conclusions. And Sandwell's computer wasn't going to come across for a while yet. Its coaxial cable must have got caught in its zip.

He stood up, and felt a little like an adolescent seeking his first date. 'I . . . er . . . I'd like to go somewhere nice for lunch,' he said. 'And I'd like it much better if you came with me.'

She looked as if she might be going to find some words of her own to throw at him, but then her eyes softened a little. 'Good idea,' she said.

It was a long way to the pub he had in mind, especially when it was necessary to negotiate ungritted country roads and the impacted snow of the by-passed village in which it lived. But it would be worth it for the food, and the atmosphere. They could talk there, perhaps. At least they could relax there.

It had changed hands.

'Not one of my better ideas,' Lloyd said, as they were leaving, encouraged to do so by the simple expedient of the staff suddenly appearing in outdoor clothing, and putting out as many lights as they could.

Judy, who had chosen the less than inspired Chef's Special, laughed, and got into the car, shivering.

It had even been cold. There was a notice apologising, but that hadn't made it any warmer. They had had to stay, since they were miles from anywhere else that sold food at all.

'I'm sorry,' he said.

'You couldn't help it,' she answered.

'That's not what I'm sorry about.'

They were alone in the car park, the staff having beaten them to the exit, and he kissed her, as he'd wanted to do all day. Her response was less than passionate.

'Are you still angry with me?' he asked.

She frowned. 'Angry?'

'About what I said.' He looked down. 'My tongue runs away with me,' he said. 'It always has. You should hear some of the things I say to my sisters – even my mum, once.'

'Your *mother*?'

He smiled at Judy's horrified expression. 'My dad clouted me for that,' he said. 'And he'd have clouted me again if he'd heard what I said last night.' He took her hand. 'He thinks you're the greatest thing since rugby union,' he said, kissing it.

'But you must think it's sordid,' she said. 'Or you wouldn't have said it.'

Lloyd sighed. 'That's the whole point,' he said. 'I don't think. At all. I've never thought anything of the sort.' He let go her hand. 'Am I forgiven?' he asked.

'I suppose so.'

It was as much as he could hope for. He drove back to Stansfield, only to discover that he could no longer delay his visit to the dreaded Mrs Langton. For a visit, if you could believe Sandwell's computer, was undoubtedly called for.

Graham Elstow had been the driver of the car which had hit Eleanor Langton's husband. Elstow had lived with his parents, next door to the Langtons, and had been coming out of the road just as the motorbike had turned in.

'He clipped its rear wheel when he tried to avoid it,' Judy said.

She was reading the print-out while Lloyd drove towards Byford. He was beginning to hate the place, which was a pity.

'The pillion passenger fell off, and went under Elstow's car.' Judy folded the sheets. 'Richard Langton,' she said. 'But the motor-cyclist hadn't passed a test, and shouldn't have had a passenger anyway – and Richard Langton wasn't wearing a helmet, or it might not have been so serious.'

'And the upshot was that Elstow was charged with driving without due care,' Lloyd said thoughtfully.

Judy put the print-out into the glove compartment. 'A bit hard to take,' she said.

'Quite,' said Lloyd. 'She might well be prepared to give Wheeler an alibi, given her relationship with him, *and* this.' He turned almost reluctantly into the castle grounds, 'I rather think that's what Joanna is afraid happened,' he said, slowing to a snail's pace along the narrow road. His car's heater had trumped Judy's car's road-holding qualities.

Eleanor Langton admitted them, a resigned look on her face. 'I'm working,' she said. 'Will it take long?'

'I couldn't honestly say, Mrs Langton,' replied Lloyd.

'Well,' she said, leading the way into the sitting room. 'I don't suppose you'd be here if it wasn't important.'

Other people might have meant that he wouldn't waste valuable time on trifles. But Lloyd was uncomfortably certain that Eleanor Langton knew that she intimidated him.

She stood by the window. 'Please sit down,' she said.

'I'll stand, thank you,' said Lloyd.

Judy sat down, producing the notebook.

'Mrs Langton,' said Lloyd. 'Did you know Graham Elstow?'

'Yes,' she said, without hesitation.

'You didn't tell us.'

'You didn't ask.' She sat down on the low seat by the window. 'Richard and I lived next door to him and his parents,' she said.

'There's a bit more to it than that,' said Lloyd.

Her face hardly registered any emotion. But something changed about it. 'He was responsible for my husband's accident,' she said, her voice clear but quiet.

'And you didn't tell us that because we didn't ask,' said Lloyd.

'No,' she said, looking away from him, out of the window behind her. 'I didn't tell you because I wasn't very proud of what I'd done.'

Lloyd glanced at Judy.

'I met him,' she said. 'That lunch time. At the Duke's Arms.' She turned back. 'I'd gone to phone my mother-in-law,' she said. 'And I met Graham Elstow as I was coming out.' Her fair skin began to grow a painful red. 'I'd had a difficult morning. I'd been talking about Richard, and seeing Graham was the last straw.' She turned her head again. 'I asked him how he'd been for the last three years,' she said. 'I told him how I'd been. Every detail. I told him what it had been like, what Richard had been like. I told him about Tessa, being born to someone who just lay there and did nothing, and said nothing, and never would again.'

Her voice was coming from behind the long blonde hair that covered her face, and Lloyd sat down as she spoke.

'I could see I was upsetting him. Terribly. He'd been a friend of

Richard's. I was making him go through it all again. And I couldn't stop. Eventually, he just walked away from me. Into the pub.'

Lloyd sat back.

'And I felt *good*,' she said fiercely, then moved her head, to look at him again. 'But it didn't last.'

Lloyd didn't speak.

'It helped, a little,' she said. 'Saying unkind things. I think perhaps you can understand that, Inspector.'

She'd be reading his palm next.

'Then when George came that evening, he told me what his son-in-law had done to Joanna, and eventually he called him by name. And I realised that I was probably responsible for the whole thing. I felt terrible. Then the next thing I knew, Graham Elstow was dead. And I didn't tell you because I hoped I wouldn't have to go through all this.' There were tears in her eyes.

'And that was the only time you saw Elstow that day?'

'Yes, of course.' The answer was ready enough, but her eyes were wary. 'Why do you ask?'

'Someone murdered him.'

Judy had relegated herself to note-taker general, he noticed. Perhaps Eleanor Langton unnerved her too.

'I saw him once,' said Eleanor. 'At lunch time. I had no *idea* he was Joanna's husband! I'd never met her, and I didn't know her surname. People in the village call her Joanna Wheeler. I didn't even know she was married.'

Neither had Constable Parks, thought Lloyd. And the barmaid at the Duke's Arms hadn't recognised her surname. Graham Elstow was a non-person as far as the Wheelers were concerned, so there was no reason to disbelieve her on that score.

'Mrs Langton,' said Judy. 'When Mrs Wheeler left here on Christmas Eve, she was upset. Can you tell us why?'

She nodded, and again a blush suffused her face. 'Something happened,' she said. 'Something very trivial and silly, but . . . yes. She could have been upset by it.'

'Thank you,' said Judy, and she didn't press for details.

'I'm sorry I didn't tell you all this before,' said Eleanor. 'But it really doesn't help you, does it?'

Lloyd stood up. 'Oh, I think it does, Mrs Langton,' he said. 'There were a number of things puzzling us. Small things. But they do have to be investigated.'

She nodded. 'In that case, I do apologise,' she said. 'I didn't realise that I would be hindering your enquiry. But I didn't want to have to discuss my involvement. Especially not with Richard's mother here.'

'You couldn't keep it from her for ever,' said Lloyd.

'No.' She stood up, and went towards the door. 'But she was worried enough without my telling her it was Graham Elstow who'd been murdered.' She opened the door, and Lloyd felt as though he was being dismissed. He *was* being dismissed.

'I upset Graham, and he got drunk and took it out on his wife. So she took a poker to him. And it was all my fault,' she said.

Lloyd looked over at Judy, then back at Eleanor Langton. 'Mrs Langton,' he said. 'That's the second time you've accused Mrs Elstow of killing her husband.'

'Well, didn't she?' said Eleanor bitterly. 'Isn't that what Marian Wheeler's charade was about? And isn't that why George is making himself ill?'

'Mrs Langton,' he said. 'Has anyone indicated to you that that is what happened?'

'Of course not,' she said. 'George likes to believe it was this fictitious intruder.'

Lloyd drove back to Stansfield, beginning to feel that he was getting somewhere at last. He wondered what Eleanor Langton had been like before the accident, before she'd had to spend years waiting for someone to die so that she could get on with her life. But, she'd told him what he wanted to know. She was the answer to the remaining two puzzles. And since all the little puzzles could be accounted for by her presence in the Wheelers' midst, it was easy enough to put her to one side, and look at what he had left. A domestic. Wife kills brutal husband.

He said as much on the way back, and Judy didn't argue. But that, he told himself, was possibly because she wasn't speaking at all. So he turned his attention to other matters; he asked her again to talk to Linda, and she agreed, absently. She was preoccupied, barely listening.

'What's wrong?' he asked.

'Nothing,' she said, frowning. 'When I was at school,' she went on, 'I sometimes even forgot my satchel.'

Lloyd laughed.

'It was one of those satchels that you carried on your back,' she said. 'For cycling.'

Lloyd liked the idea of Judy cycling to school.

'And I'd eventually be aware that I was too light,' she said. 'That's how I feel now. Too light. Because I'm *missing* something.'

He drove into the police station car park, but Judy didn't get out of the car. 'Why not Wheeler?' she said.

Lloyd sighed. He'd never known her to get this personally involved before. 'Wheeler was with Eleanor,' he said.

'Before we got there, you thought she might have been prepared to give him an alibi,' said Judy hotly. 'What does she do to you, Lloyd? You didn't even *ask* her!'

'She would just have said the same thing,' Lloyd said. 'There was no point in asking her.'

'So you'll take what she says as gospel, but not what Joanna says?'

'You said that if you had pieces over when you'd completed the jigsaw, then they must belong to a different puzzle,' Lloyd reminded her. 'Eleanor Langton belongs to a different puzzle.'

For a moment, Judy subsided, considering her own words. Then she came back into the fray. 'You can't say that,' she said. 'Not when you didn't even ask her about it.'

'Neither did you.'

'I was taking my cue from you.'

'I'd sooner tackle George about it,' said Lloyd. 'Eleanor Langton hasn't got a weak stomach.'

'Huh.'

All right, so the woman had an effect on him. He hadn't asked her, because he knew that she would answer him clearly and concisely, and tell him exactly what she wanted him to know, and no more. He hadn't asked her, because she'd been *expecting* him to ask her, and just for once he wanted to get the better of her.

'She's a witch,' he said, 'I kept expecting to see her familiar curled up on a broomstick.'

Judy laughed.

'It's not funny,' he grumbled. 'Look what she said about saying unkind things.' He looked at her shamefacedly. 'How did she know about that?' he asked, only half in fun.

Judy smiled. 'Because you did much the same to her,' she said.

He got out of the car, feeling slightly better. But there was no doubt that Eleanor Langton made every Welsh superstition in his body rise to the surface and leer at him.

'You fancy her,' Judy said.

Fancy her! Not a chance. Wheeler fancied her, though. No wonder he was a nervous wreck, if he was bedding Mrs Langton. No, Lloyd didn't fancy her. But that just would be Judy's explanation, he thought. She had no soul for Mrs Langton to probe.

'And Wheeler might never have been near the place on Christmas Eve,' she added.

'All right,' he said, as they walked up the steps. 'What's the alternative?' He opened the door. 'That Wheeler went straight home when he left the Duke's Arms, right?'

'Right.'

'So how did he get there? He was on foot, and the main road would have taken him the best part of an hour, remember. And no one, but no one saw him cross the field. They *did* see him walking up Castle Road.' Of course they did. The vicar and Mrs Langton were the object of considerable interest in the village.

They walked through the CID room, and Lloyd stopped to pick up another sheaf of papers. Information gleaned from the full-scale house to house that had now been completed, and none of it, he knew without looking, any damn good. 'Practically the whole village goes to the pub on Christmas Eve,' he said, as they walked into the office. 'It's a tradition. And a lot of them use the shortcut from that side of the village. But no one saw George.'

Judy took off her coat, and sat down.

'Besides which,' he said. 'If your little girl's telling the truth, the house was locked up before George ever left the pub.'

'The barmaid could have mistaken the time,' said Judy.

'What? I thought we had to believe what we were *told*.'

'If my little girl's telling the truth,' Judy said, 'she didn't murder her husband.'

Lloyd sat down, his face serious. 'George was in the pub, then went straight to Eleanor Langton's. Eleanor was at home. Marian was out visiting. We've got witnesses to all of that, Judy. And Joanna was at the vicarage, and keeping very quiet about it.'

Judy sighed, at last admitting defeat.

Lloyd nodded. 'If you ask me, Joanna left the pub, and went home. She could and did get in. She put on the overalls, went upstairs and killed her husband. She burned the overalls in the back bedroom, because the fire in her room would practically be out by then. And she knew that she'd be the first person we'd suspect, so she locked up the house, went to Dr Lomax, then came home and waited, saying that she had been locked out. But she wasn't to know that her father had his own reasons for keeping quiet about where he'd been, and before she knew it, he was giving her a different alibi. One that hopefully covered him too, as far as his wife was concerned.'

He tipped his chair back, as the scenario presented itself. 'I don't believe Marian Wheeler did go home to change her dress,' he said suddenly. 'That's why she doesn't know *when* the doors were locked. Why would she go home? She was wearing a coat, and she wasn't going to stay anywhere else long enough to take it off. She finished her rounds of the old folk, and *then* came home. That's when she went up to change her dress – *that's* when she found Elstow.' Oh yes, he thought, it was all coming clear now. 'She thought Joanna had killed him that afternoon. That's when she burned the dress and put her own prints on the poker.'

He let the chair fall forward. 'I think that when we got there, she was as mystified about the doors as anyone. She denied locking them, remember. But then she finds out that Joanna and George weren't at the pub all the time, and she begins to put two and two together. She realises what must have happened, and why the place was locked up. And that's why she was so keen to point out that she *had* locked the doors – check your notebook,' he said, 'if you don't remember. I saw you underline it.'

'I remember,' Judy said dispiritedly. But she still didn't quite give in. 'Why did Joanna tell us about the overalls, in that case?' she asked.

'Someone would, eventually. She thought it might be better if it came from her. So that you would say just what you are saying.'

'Forensic can't tell us very much,' said Judy.

'No,' agreed Lloyd. 'But if we can tell the Wheelers something they don't think we know, that might just do the trick.'

'That they burned the overalls,' said Judy. 'Does that mean you still think the whole family's involved?'

'I think Wheeler's stomach is very involved,' said Lloyd. 'He knew when Joanna left the pub, at least.' He got up. 'Home time,' he said. 'Hours past home time.' He smiled. 'At least you won't get into trouble with your mother-in-law tonight.'

'No, thank God,' said Judy.

'Tell you what. Why don't you come back to the flat for something to eat?' Lloyd asked. 'Make up for lunch time.'

She hesitated, but she accepted. He was winning.

Seven o'clock. Where on earth had Joanna got to? Marian laid the table, still determined that she would go on as normal. At least she could dig George out of the study, to which he had retreated immediately after lunch. He seemed to spend all his time in there. All the time that he wasn't spending in the bathroom, she thought worriedly. It was going on too long. She walked into the study, and stopped dead.

'What are you doing with that?' she asked.

George sighed. 'It was my father's,' he said, a faraway look in his eye. The gun rested on his arm, pointing towards her.

'I know that,' said Marian. 'George – please put it down,' she added nervously, as his inexpert finger strayed towards the trigger.

'What?' he said vaguely. 'Oh.' He laid it on the desk. 'It's not loaded,' he said.

'Good,' she said, walking slowly over to the desk. 'Why have you got it?'

'He killed things with it,' George said.

Marian sat down. 'What were you going to do with it?' she asked gently.

George's shoulders hunched a little, like a child's. He reminded Marian of Joanna when she didn't want to go to bed. 'I was just . . . looking at it,' he said.

Marian looked at it. Oh God, what was happening? 'Why, George?' she asked.

He didn't answer; didn't even seem to hear her, or see her. She glanced round the room, and saw the open cupboard, a pile of things on the floor beside it. 'Did you find it in there?' she asked, startled.

He still didn't answer, and she got up to look in the cupboard, as though it could give her some answers. She always kept the gun in the sitting room, locked up. 'George? Where did you get it?'

His eyes seemed to focus slowly as he looked at her. 'The usual place,' he said.

'And you brought it in here?' She looked again at George's cupboard. Normality. Pretend that this is all normal. 'Were you thinking of keeping it in there?' she said, striving to make her voice sound unconcerned. 'Because I don't think it's a very good idea,' she said. 'That lock's very flimsy.'

He'd picked the damn thing up again. Marian carried on gamely. 'After all,' she said, 'if someone broke in, they could get hold of it. We have to keep it secure.'

'It was my father's,' he said.

Was that it? It was his father's, so he wanted it? Anything was worth a try. 'Would you rather I didn't use it?' she asked.

'What?' George looked puzzled. 'Good Lord, no. You use it whenever you like.' He put it down again.

Marian sat opposite him. 'George – don't you think you should see a doctor?' she asked gently.

He looked faintly surprised. 'The stomach?' he said. 'No. It'll pass.'

Marian dragged her eyes away from the gun to look at George himself, 'I think . . .' she said hesitantly, afraid that the wrong word would spark the quick temper that seemed to have died. Marian wanted to see it back, see George back to his old self. But not while he was like this. 'I think you're a bit run down,' she said. 'Depressed.'

'A nervous breakdown?' he asked. 'Is that what you think it is?'

'It could be,' said Marian carefully.

'*I* think it is,' George said, disconcertingly.

Marian's mouth was dry. This frightened her; George had

always just been George. But now, his eyes held an almost accusing look, and she didn't know why. 'What *is* wrong?' she asked.

Suddenly, he came to life. 'You ask me that? Joanna's husband is murdered in this very house, and you ask me what's *wrong*?'

At least bluster was something she understood. 'This started long before Graham Elstow turned up here,' she said. 'You've been . . .' She plunged in. 'You've been acting very oddly for a long time,' she said. 'Since before that.'

'Before that I had to bring my daughter home from hospital. That's when I was sick before,' he said.

'It's not just being sick,' said Marian. She wouldn't be swayed. 'All that stuff about breaking commandments,' she said. 'What was all that about?'

He didn't answer.

'It started when Eleanor Langton came here, didn't it?' she said.

'Ah.' George sat back. 'My mid-life fantasy,' he said.

'Well isn't she?' Marian asked.

'Probably,' said George, his voice tired.

'Don't let her make you ill,' she said. 'Whatever you've done – whatever you do, I'll be here.'

'I know,' said George, and his eyes went to the gun.

Marian stiffened. 'George,' she said, alarmed that she had said the wrong thing. 'Are you in love with her? Or do you just want to kick over the traces?' She paused. 'Break a commandment?'

He gave her a half smile. 'I've broken lots of commandments, Marian,' he said.

Marian stared at him, perplexed. 'Diana Lomax,' she said, bringing common sense to the rescue. 'Go and see her, please, George.'

'She'll cheer me up, will she?'

'She'll recommend someone who can help,' said Marian. 'It *would* help, you know. If you could talk to someone.'

'It does,' said George. 'It helps when I talk to Eleanor.'

'What about?' asked Marian.

'Anything,' George said. 'She's spent a long time just watching people, you know. Listening to them. Not joining in, so she had time to take stock of them, to assess them. She understands people.' He smiled, the strange, faraway smile that he'd had when he was holding the gun. 'A lot of the other play-group mothers don't like her. That's because she understands them, sees through them. It makes them feel uncomfortable.'

'But she helps you?' Marian asked, frowning.

'Yes. She understands.'

'Don't I?'

He shook his head. 'On Christmas Eve,' he said, 'she helped me write my sermon. She suggested it.'

Marian felt a little numb. 'It was her idea, was it?' she asked. 'Shakespeare?'

'Yes. Not the Bible. *To thine own self be true*. I'm not true to myself.'

'Aren't you?'

'No!' he said, with disgust. 'I'm not a vicar, Marian. I'm pretending to be one. I don't believe in any of this. You do,' he said.

'That's why you're breaking commandments?'

He smiled, and Marian didn't recognise this man. 'It's a start,' he said.

Marian shook her head, the sturdy common sense rising again. 'Don't you see?' she said. 'All this is because of how you feel about her. You want to go to bed with her, it's as simple as that. And you think you've got to throw everything up because of it.'

'The Church wouldn't take too kindly to it,' George said.

'The Church wouldn't know,' said Marian. 'Unless she told them. Is that what's worrying you?'

George didn't speak for a long time. Then he sat back, and looked at her. 'I have never heard of any other man sitting down and discussing his potential adultery with his wife,' he said.

'She's making you *ill*, George. And if I thought telling you to forget her would work, that's what I'd be saying.'

'But you think that indulging my fantasy will do the trick?'

'What?' said Marian, guardedly.

'You think if you give me permission, you'll put me off the whole idea,' he said.

Marian didn't answer. Yes, that was the hope at the back of her mind. It had certainly been her hope when she had suggested it before. But now . . . now she didn't care what George did as long as it helped. And there was no way that Eleanor Langton could live up to George's fantasy. He'd find out what a ridiculous waste of energy it had been. She didn't even blame him. Eleanor Langton was blonde, and beautiful, and young. She was lonely and vulnerable, and she had sought reassurance from George. He was flattered, of course he was. But she wasn't worth all this soul-searching, and he'd find that out if he turned his fantasy into reality.

'I just don't want you to feel like this,' Marian said.

George sighed. 'That's not why I'm sick,' he said.

'Of course it is,' said Marian. 'You've been sick ever since you started spending half your time over there. Is that where you were this morning?'

He nodded.

'Why? What do you find to say to her?'

'We've a lot in common,' he replied. 'Graham Elstow, for one thing.'

Marian stared at him, speechless.

'Elstow was responsible for her husband's death.'

She couldn't have heard him. 'What do you mean?'

'He was driving the car that hit her husband,' George said. 'He was in a coma for almost three years.' He shivered. 'Three years,' he repeated.

'Have you told the police?'

'No, of course not.'

'What do you mean, of course not? They should know.' Marian's head was spinning. Eleanor Langton?

'It's up to Eleanor whether she tells them or not,' said George. 'For all you know she has.'

That's what was making him sick. Marian couldn't take it in. George thought that Eleanor Langton had killed Graham Elstow, and he was keeping information from the police. Her mind wouldn't cope with the rest. Faint, vague feelings of betrayal; none that she could put into words. He'd watched her being arrested – practically *forced* them to arrest her . . . She looked at the gun, at George, his face ashen.

'She didn't do it, Marian,' he said. 'She wouldn't. She *wouldn't*.'

'What difference does it make?' asked Marian, her voice weak.

'None.' He clasped his hands, laying his forehead on them, and he looked as if he was praying. Marian hoped that he was.

She stood up slowly. 'Will you let me have the gun back?' she asked.

'Take it,' he said. 'I don't want it. Throw it away.'

Marian took it, and left the study. She was on her way to the sitting room, when she realised that she couldn't keep it in the house. She didn't know this George. She didn't know what he'd do. She walked out to the car, and opened the boot, automatically checking the gun before putting it in.

The cartridges stared back at her, two eyes gleaming in the light from the door.

Chapter Ten

Joanna glanced at her watch as she got out of the car. Almost nine o'clock. She crunched over the ashes to the front door, gloomily aware that her mother wouldn't be pleased. She hadn't even told her where she was. She had been at the house all day; cleaning, dusting, tidying, until it looked like her house again. She felt better, now. But it would be difficult, telling them she was going back there to live. Still, she would do it. Tonight.

The vicarage seemed strange; normally, she could hear her parents talking, or movement, at least. Had the car been there? She opened the door again. No. That was odd; her parents were creatures of habit. Her mother, at any rate. Her father's behaviour over the last few days was far from normal. She went into the kitchen, and stood for a moment at the doorway, a frown forming. This wasn't right. The table was set, but no one had eaten; she could smell the food. She opened the oven door to find a dried up casserole, and she switched it off, beginning to feel panicky. Had there been an accident? She should have rung them, told them where she was. She ran out of the kitchen, and through to her father's study.

He sat at his desk, staring at a lined pad, his pen in his hand. He had written nothing. He didn't look up, or speak. Joanna swallowed, and went over to him, almost afraid to make a noise.

'Daddy?'

He looked up, his eyes not really taking her in. 'Yes?' he said.

'Where's Mummy?'

'Isn't she here?' he said, but there was no interest in the question. Just an automatic response.

Joanna shivered. 'Did she say she was going out? Did you forget to eat?'

He shook his head.

'What's going on?' Joanna cried. 'What's happened?'

'Nothing,' he said mildly.

'It's freezing in here,' Joanna said. 'Come into the kitchen. I'll make you something to eat.'

He stood up, and followed her.

'She must have told you to get your own dinner,' Joanna said. 'You must have forgotten.'

'No,' he said.

'Where's she *gone*?' Joanna asked again. 'What's wrong? What's the matter with you?'

He looked at her then, for the first time. 'Your mother thinks it's a nervous breakdown,' he said.

Joanna stared at him. 'Has she gone for Diana?' she asked.

Her father smiled. 'They can't listen to your chest for a nervous breakdown,' he said.

'*Are* you ill?' Joanna asked, bewildered, slightly suspicious.

'Your mother thought I wanted to kill myself,' he said, and his voice was calm now. Rational; conversational, almost.

'Why?' demanded Joanna. 'Why did she think that?'

'Because of the gun,' he said.

'Gun?' The word chilled her. 'What gun?'

'My father's shotgun.'

'*Were* you going to kill yourself?' Joanna still wasn't sure that she was dealing with a breakdown.

'I'm not sure,' he said.

'Where *is* she?' Joanna looked round helplessly, as though her mother might materialise.

'She might have gone to Diana's,' he said, as though she had never mentioned it.

'Did she say that was where she was going?'

He frowned slightly. 'Where have you been?' he asked mildly. 'It's late, isn't it?'

Oh, God. He couldn't stay on one subject for two seconds; it was hopeless. 'Have you taken something?' she asked, alarmed by the thought.

'A couple of pills.'

'What pills? How many?'

'The ones you got after you came home from hospital. Just a couple. I thought they might help.'

Joanna ran to the medicine chest, and the bottle was there, still with a good supply of pills. She let out her breath, and took the bottle out, putting it in her pocket.

'Where've you been?' he asked again.

'At home,' she said with a sigh.

'Were you?' He sounded puzzled. 'Were you in your room? I thought you were out.'

Joanna closed the medicine chest, and turned to look at him. '*My* home,' she said.

He stared at her uncertainly, then mumbled something, and fled.

She listened to the now familiar sound of her father's feet pounding upstairs, and sank down at the table. The table set for dinner. The dinner which was dried up and ruined in the oven. Something had happened. Something terrible. Slowly, she rose and went into the hall, but she arrested her hand as it reached for the phone.

She was being silly. Her mother wasn't here, that was all. She had told her father to serve himself, but he had forgotten, mixed up by the pills. It wasn't late, not yet. Not really. She had just heard the clock chime the half hour. Half past nine wasn't late. She mustn't let her father's nervous state get to her. She heard him walking about upstairs; he wasn't well. Her mother had probably gone to get Diana. But she would have *phoned* Diana, said a voice in her head.

She looked at her watch. Quarter to ten. That wasn't late, no matter how you looked at it. So what *was* late? Eleven, she decided. She would give her mother until eleven. Then she would start ringing round. There was no need to panic. She must be somewhere. Joanna glanced anxiously upstairs. She must be *somewhere*, she told herself sternly.

She must be somewhere.

Eleanor Langton got out of the bath, and towelled herself dry, pulling on her bathrobe, and rolling up its sleeves. She had, after a great deal of thought, decided against going to the party.

Instead of a quick bath and an evening out, she had had the long luxurious bath she had promised herself, and was washing her hair.

She had been getting ready to go out, having decided that perhaps she could face it, after all; she was coming out of her prison, making a new start, and a New Year party seemed appropriate, even if it was two days shy of the end of the year.

But then she had looked at the ticket. They seemed to think you'd bring a partner, and she had thought that she might feel conspicuous without one. The others had said that lots of people were going alone, what with husbands on shift-work, or husbands who wouldn't go to a disco if you paid them, but they might have just been saying that to make her feel better about not having a partner. Everyone else, she had thought, might turn up complete with a man, and she'd be left alone at the table while they all danced.

Someone might *ask* her to dance. Eleanor had wondered, then, if she could handle that. But what was there to disco-dancing? You hardly knew who you were dancing with. She had never actually danced at a disco, because Richard had run one for years in his spare time and she had helped. She had even played keyboard in a short-lived group that Richard had got together, before they were married.

Another Eleanor, another life. Now she played the organ for the carol service.

She had looked at herself in the mirror, and hadn't been sure about the dress. Perhaps it should be separates; jeans, even. And reflected in the mirror, she had seen the bedroom, so obviously solo. Going to a party might help, she had thought; she might meet someone.

But she *had* met someone; slowly, Eleanor had unzipped the dress, and stepped out of it.

She had just put on the second lot of lather when the knock came to the door. George. She lifted her hair up and looked at her watch on the windowsill. It was after ten. Surely it was George. She squeezed some of the water out of her hair, and opened the bathroom door, dripping shampoo on to the floor. 'I won't be a minute!' she shouted anxiously. 'Don't go away!'

George picked wonderful moments to call, she thought, as she rinsed the shampoo out of her hair. She was pleased that he'd come, that he still needed her. This morning he had been so distant, and odd. And yet, for a moment, she had thought that at last they would make love, and keep the promise that they had been holding in reserve since Christmas Eve. But it had only been for a moment.

'Coming,' she called again, as she wrapped her hair in a towel, and ran along the corridor, throwing open the door.

Again.

'I'm sorry,' said Marian Wheeler. 'I know it's a bit late. But I've got to talk to you.'

Eleanor felt a surge of panic. This wasn't *fair*. 'Yes, of course,' she heard herself saying. 'Come in.'

In the sitting room, she waved a hand vaguely at the chairs, and Marian took off her coat, and sat down.

'I'd better come straight to the point,' she said. 'George isn't at all well, Mrs Langton. But I expect you know that.'

Eleanor nodded. 'He told me it was a nervous reaction,' she said. 'That he always got like that if there was an upheaval of some sort.'

'Yes,' Marian said. 'That's true. But I think this time it's worse than that.'

'Do you think he's really ill?' Eleanor asked, alarmed.

'I think he's having some sort of nervous breakdown,' said Marian. 'I'm here because – well, I'm here for several reasons, to be quite honest.' She took a breath. 'Tonight, I found him with his father's shotgun. He said it wasn't loaded, but it was.'

The words hung in the air, while Eleanor stared at Marian, open-mouthed. George? George, who joked about keeping their tentative affair in reserve? George, who winked at her behind Mrs Brewster's back? But no, not that George. George, who could barely think straight any more. George, who had called at six o'clock in the morning, then had hardly even spoken to her. *That* George.

'Why?' she whispered, '*Why?*'

'I've brought the gun with me,' Marian said, hesitantly. 'It's in the car. I wondered if you could possibly put it in the gun room here – I daren't leave it in the house.'

Eleanor agreed, automatically, with a distracted nod of her head. 'Thank God you found him,' she said.

'He may have been waiting for me to find him,' said Marian.

It seemed odd to Eleanor that Marian was here. If George was that bad, shouldn't she be there?

'Shouldn't someone be with him?' she asked.

'Joanna will be back by now,' said Marian. 'I just wanted to get that gun out of the house.'

'Yes, of course,' said Eleanor.

'I think George needs help,' Marian said firmly.

'Yes.' The word came out with a shudder, like a sigh. 'I had no idea he was that bad.' Her mouth felt dry. 'Look – can I get you something? A drink, perhaps?'

'Coffee would be lovely,' said Marian.

'Coffee. I'll . . . er . . .' She pointed vaguely in the direction of the kitchen. 'I shan't be a moment.'

She almost ran along the corridor again, and stood for a moment in the kitchen, taking deep breaths. What was coming next? A third-degree on her and George? Eleanor made coffee, the situation beyond her. And surely not of her making? But that was what Marian thought, or she wouldn't be here.

'Can I help?' Marian appeared in the kitchen.

'You could help yourself to milk and sugar,' Eleanor said.

'Thank you.' Marian took her time, obviously working on her next reason for being there.

'You see,' Marian went on, 'I've spent all evening just sitting in the car, trying to work out what's happened to George.' She looked up, and gave a little shrug. 'You happened to him,' she said.

'We're not lovers,' said Eleanor. 'If that's what you think.'

'Oh, but you are,' said Marian. 'In the old-fashioned sense.' She stirred her coffee. 'It might be better,' she said, 'if it was in the physical sense.' She sat down. 'You see,' she said, 'I think you're the only one who can help him.'

Eleanor's head shook slightly. This wasn't happening. Marian

Wheeler wasn't here, practically inviting her to have an affair with George. This wasn't happening.

'Shall we have the coffee in here?' Marian asked, for all the world as though they were swapping recipes.

Eleanor sat down too, still bemused.

'At least get him to see a doctor,' said Marian. 'He will, if you tell him. I know he will.'

George didn't need a doctor. No one thing had happened to George. It was a mixture of *all* the things that were happening to George. Meeting her; his crisis of faith; Joanna, Graham Elstow – Marian's love, smothering him. And was Marian here, now, out of that love? Was she seeking help for George, no matter what she had to do to get it? Protecting him, forgiving him. And not even his attempted romp through the ten commandments could put her off.

'He needs your help, Eleanor.'

Eleanor didn't speak. There were things she could say: Mrs Wheeler, my relationship with your husband consists of a few frantic moments in the out-house, and hours of listening to him tell me that you love him, and that he loves you. That doesn't make me responsible for his welfare. That doesn't mean that you can lay the blame for this at my door. She didn't voice her thoughts; what did it matter who or what had driven George to this point?

But it did matter, of course, and as George would doubtless have said, it was up to her what she did about it.

'He seems to value your opinion very highly,' said Marian, and there was no trace of sarcasm.

Eleanor lifted her eyes slowly to Marian's. 'But it isn't my opinion that he should see a doctor,' she said. 'It's yours.'

Marian tutted impatiently. 'He must see a doctor,' she said. 'And he won't listen to me. You're the one who has done this to him, Eleanor. You're the only one he'll listen to.'

'No,' said Eleanor quietly. 'I haven't done this to him. It was already done before I met him. George wants—' She broke off, then decided to go through with it. 'He wants freedom,' she said.

Marian's head went back slightly. 'So that he can do the decent thing by you?' she asked archly. 'Are you holding out for marriage? Is that what it is?'

'No, no, no!' Eleanor shouted. 'Not that sort of freedom,' she said, her voice quieter. She thought for a moment. 'You called us lovers,' she said. 'But we're not, you know. Not in any sense of the word. If George wanted me, he could have me, and he knows that.' She paused. 'But he doesn't,' she said. 'He thinks he does, but he doesn't.'

What *was* she to George, she wondered for the first time. A fellow prisoner? Or just a stick to shake at Marian? The one thing that he hoped would make her angry? And when that didn't work ... was that what the shotgun was about? Marian had said that perhaps he was waiting for her to find him. Yes, Eleanor could see George doing that, trying to baffle Marian into something other than patient understanding.

Failed again, George, she thought. Failed again.

'I'm just a ... a sort of focus,' she said.

'A focus?' Marian repeated.

Eleanor couldn't tell Marian what she meant. She and George had both been in prison; but she was on the other side of the bars now, free, while George was still painfully tunnelling out. Hers was the freedom of the newly released long-term prisoner; the world was a frightening, alien place. She and George needed one another, that was all.

'A focus for his dreams?' said Marian.

'If you like,' said Eleanor.

'A damsel in distress, that he had to come and rescue?' asked Marian. 'A sleeping beauty that he had to awaken with a kiss?'

Eleanor felt her face grow hot, and Marian nodded. 'He told me about Graham Elstow,' she said, after a moment. 'About his having caused your husband's accident.' She leant forward. 'He was with you on Christmas Eve,' she said. 'What time did he get here, Mrs Langton?'

Eleanor frowned. 'What?' she said.

'It's a simple question,' said Marian. 'What time did he get here?'

'What are you suggesting?' asked Eleanor, her voice horrified. 'That George killed Graham Elstow? On *my* behalf?' She jumped to her feet. 'Why? Why would you think that? George didn't . . .? No,' she said. 'He didn't tell you that. Why then? Just because you think he was going to kill himself? Is that why?'

Marian looked up at her. 'I don't think I said anything about George killing *himself*,' she said, barely stressing the final word.

'My God,' said Eleanor. 'If you can't sacrifice yourself for your daughter, you'll sacrifice George. You're trying to blame George.'

'*Blame* him?' Marian repeated, with an uncomprehending movement of her head.

Eleanor sat down again. No. Marian had never blamed George for anything. 'But you can't *really* think it was George,' she said. 'Marian – he was in the pub, and ten minutes later he was with me.'

Marian nodded again. 'And you had thirty minutes,' she said. 'Thirty minutes between my visit and George's arrival.'

Eleanor's eyes widened slightly.

'*That's* what is making George ill, Mrs Langton,' said Marian. 'That thirty minutes.'

George Wheeler splashed water on his face, and looked at himself in the bathroom mirror. If he saw that man walking down the road, he wouldn't recognise him.

Had he been going to kill himself? People asked him questions, all the time. And he didn't have the answers. *To thine own self be true.* Had he been going to kill himself? Marian had gone to the police; she must have done. And wasn't that why he had told her? So that she would protect him from that, too? She would go to the police, not him.

He'd gone to see Eleanor this morning. Why? Because she'd called him yesterday, said she had to see him. He hadn't slept, and then he'd been pacing the floor, deciding to die. Yes, then he *had* been going to kill himself. He'd seen Eleanor's light, and gone to her. Just once, he had thought. He wanted her just once before . . .

Before he killed himself? But his courage had already waned, even then. He couldn't have Eleanor; he couldn't even die.

Had he been going to kill himself?

Eleanor. When had he realised? Not when Marian found

Elstow's body, not even when they arrested her. It was later, after that, that it had begun to dawn on him. It was the day after that, in the church, with the sunlight streaming through the stained glass. Eleanor, coming in. Talking quietly. Almost angry when he had told her about Marian; just at that moment he could have sworn that Eleanor had thought *he'd* done it. But then, as she rushed him off to the police station, he had realised. Eleanor had been angry because someone else had been implicated, and she hadn't meant that to happen; she had urged him into the police station, desperate to clear Marian's name.

But she hadn't told them about Elstow's involvement in her husband's accident, and neither had he, even though Marian was under arrest. Marian thought that it was his betrayal of her that was making him ill, and so had he, until now. But it wasn't.

'*When did you start to feel ill?*' When they arrested Marian, he had said. But it was Marian, of course, who knew when he had really started to feel ill. '*It started when Eleanor Langton came here, didn't it?*'

Had he been going to kill Marian? Marian, who sat there calmly discussing the pros and cons of his adultery, Marian who had confessed to the police because she thought *he'd* done it? Not Joanna, for Marian knew Joanna too well to think that she was capable of it. Joanna had loved Graham Elstow; she had been frightened of him, but she hadn't hated him. No, Marian had been protecting *him*. Her other egg. Or so she believed. But all the time, she had been protecting an intruder, defending a cuckoo's egg.

'*Eggs are supposed to hatch out.*' Eleanor understood. He was trying at last to break out of the shell, and that was what was making him ill. Yes, he had wanted to blast his way out with his father's shotgun, and he could never be sure which way he would have pointed it, if he'd had the nerve to pull the trigger.

Lloyd carried the empty plates into the kitchen.

'It was lovely,' Judy called through. 'Well worth the wait.'

'Good things take a little time,' Lloyd called back, smiling. 'I've told you before. *Andante.*' He piled the plates in the sink, and took mugs out of the cupboard.

'I could have made something in ten minutes,' she said.

'I'm sure you could, but I wanted one decent meal today,' he said, hunching up his shoulders as he waited for her reaction.

She arrived in the kitchen. 'I can show you a school report,' she said. 'It says, "Judith shows an interest in and aptitude for domestic science." So there.'

'What happened?' Lloyd put the sugar bowl on a tray with the mugs. 'Black or white?' he asked.

'White.'

'Take that through, will you?' he said, indicating the coffee jug.

'Do you trust me to?' She took it.

He poured milk into a cream jug, then remembered that he had cream. 'Cream or milk?' he called.

'Milk.'

He shrugged. No soul. It was good to see her back to her old self again, but it did make him feel more than ever like a bottle of aspirin. He carried the tray through, to find Judy looking at his Christmas cards. 'You won't find it there,' he said. 'If anyone had the nerve to put it on a card, it would go in the bin.'

She turned, smiling, 'I don't have to,' she said.

'You're bluffing.'

'Am I? All right,' she said, sitting on the sofa. 'Call my bluff.'

'How?' He picked up as many things as he could carry from the table, and went through to the kitchen. Judy was under strict orders to do nothing. This was an occasion. He came back through. 'How can I call your bluff?' he asked.

'If I'm bluffing, give me permission to tell Jack Woodford,' she said.

Her eyes glowed with mischief. But she *was* a rotten liar, as she had pointed out last night, and she didn't look as though she was bluffing. She must be, though. How could she have found out?

'Well?' she said. 'Can I tell him?'

'No.' He picked up the salt and pepper and table mats, and turned to see her grinning at him. 'If you know,' he said, 'you must have gone to Somerset House.'

She shook her head. 'It isn't Somerset House any more,' she said. 'And that would have been cheating.'

'Certainly would.'

Back in the kitchen, he illogically put away the table mats and the salt and pepper, and left, closing the door on the piles of dishes. 'So you are bluffing,' he said, as he came back in. 'I'm not calling it,' he added quickly.

'Am I allowed to pour the coffee?'

'No! You're to be waited on hand and foot.'

'So how come I had to carry the coffee in?'

'It's good luck,' he said solemnly, pouring the coffee. His first name had haunted him all his life. She didn't know it. 'How could you have found out?' he asked.

'You took me to visit your father before he went back to Wales,' she said.

Lloyd joined her on the sofa, relaxed, now. 'Then you're definitely bluffing,' he said, drinking some coffee just to see Judy wince. He liked it when it almost burned his mouth. 'If it's possible,' he said, 'my father is more ashamed of it than I am.' Even his father just called him Lloyd. And his mother had settled for a shortened version, which could have been the diminutive of something less awful.

'What did he call you when you were a baby?' she asked. 'He didn't call you Lloyd then, surely?'

'I don't know,' Lloyd said. 'The baby, I suppose. That was his problem.'

Judy's dark eyes regarded him as she gently blew at the steam from her coffee. 'No,' she said. 'He didn't tell me.'

Lloyd laughed. 'You gave in too soon,' he said.

'I've not given in.'

He frowned. 'What's my father got to do with it, then?' he asked.

'You and your father went off to look at some furniture,' she said. 'To see if you wanted an old dresser, or something.'

An old dresser or something. A genuine . . . He began to feel uncomfortable again. Because that bit was true. 'So?'

'So I was left alone,' she said. She left a pause. 'With the family Bible.'

The family *Bible*? They didn't have one. Did they? Oh, God, yes. He could remember it. A huge black one that he'd grown up with and seen every day, and to which he had never paid the least attention. But even so, they didn't write *names* in it.

Judy sipped her coffee.

'I'd know,' he said. 'If they'd written babies' names in it.'

'How? Your sisters are older than you. There weren't any babies after you.'

Lloyd finished his coffee, and his mug still steamed. 'What are *their* names?' he demanded.

'Megan and Amelia.'

He poured himself more coffee. 'I've told you that,' he said. 'I must have.' Megan and Melly. That's what he called them. He never thought of Melly as Amelia. But then his father sometimes called her Amelia. That's where she got that from. But he couldn't be sure.

'All right,' he said. 'If you know, tell me.'

She looked horrified. 'You said you'd flatten me if I ever used it,' she protested.

'You *are* bluffing.' He pointed at her. 'But just in case you're not,' he said. 'Don't you ever utter it. Ever. Not even when you're *alone*. Or I'll—'

'Flatten me,' she said.

'Worse. I'll put a notice up in the CID room that you wear a vest. That'll put a dent in your image, Sergeant Hill.' He smiled. 'I'm very glad you're here,' he said, giving her a squeeze.

'I'm glad I'm here.' She lay back, her head on his shoulder. 'Talk to me,' she said.

'What about?'

'Anything. It doesn't matter. I don't listen anyway.' She closed her eyes. 'Anything except double-glazing and cavity wall insulation,' she said.

Lloyd smiled. 'Well, that leaves the field fairly open,' he said. 'What would you like? The influence of Roman culture on ancient Britons?' He kissed her, and her response was rather more to his liking than it had been in the car park of that dismal pub. 'An analysis and comparison of the French and Russian revolutions,' he said, as she began to loosen his tie. 'Flora and fauna of the Florida everglades . . .' Her mouth touched his as he spoke. 'The pre-Raphaelite Brotherhood,' he said.

'Eleanor Langton,' she said.

'The habitat of the natterjack toad,' he carried on, and kissed her as she laughed.

'You said she was in all evening,' said Judy.

'The decline of Twelfth Night as a popular festival.' She wasn't wearing a vest tonight. 'The effect of television on the British film industry,' he murmured in her ear, as he undid her bra.

'But she might not have been.'

'Can't you think of anything else? Pick a subject.'

She smiled. 'The pre-Raphaelite Brotherhood,' she said. 'Marian saw her at five past eight, for about five . . .'

Lloyd drew her into a long kiss, but it had to end.

'. . . minutes, and George got there at about twenty to nine.'

'In the middle of the last century,' Lloyd began, his lips on her shoulder, 'three artists – Rossetti, Holman—'

'And it only takes a few minutes across the fields,' she said.

'Holman Hunt, and Millais,' he went on, his lips travelling with the words, 'decided that they didn't think much . . . she'd get there at twenty past,' he said, tackling her zip. 'At the earliest.' Or long johns. She'd catch her death.

'Plenty of time to do it,' said Judy.

'I know,' said Lloyd. 'But I'm in the mood *now*.'

'Eleanor had plenty of time to kill Elstow.'

Lloyd sat back. 'Except that if your little girl's telling the truth, then she would have been there by the time Eleanor Langton arrived,' he said.

'Joanna could have been and gone by twenty past.'

'In which case, she wouldn't have found the door locked, would she?'

'Are you saying that Joanna is telling the truth?'

'No,' he said, with great patience. 'I'm saying that if it was Eleanor, then there's no reason to disbelieve Joanna. And if there's no reason to disbelieve Joanna, then it wasn't Eleanor. You like logic problems – sort that one out.'

Judy took his hands. 'Sorry,' she said.

'I'll forgive you,' he said. 'But only because I'm damned if that family's going to spoil this evening.'

Judy smiled, and lay back, taking him with her. 'What family?' she said.

'Will you stay the night?' he asked.

'Oh, Lloyd, I can't,' she said.

'You've never spent the night with me.'

'I *can't*,' she said. 'Please, Lloyd, I don't want another row.'

'Why can't you?' he asked. He didn't want another row. He wanted her to stay.

'I have to meet Michael's train at half past seven in the morning,' she said.

'There is a half past seven in the morning here,' Lloyd said.

She kissed him. 'I'm sorry,' she said. 'It would be too obvious that I hadn't been home. There would be too many questions.'

Don't go on at her, he told himself. Don't spoil it again. He smiled. 'And you can't tell lies,' he said.

She shook her head.

'What you need,' he said seriously, putting his hands on her shoulders, 'is a piece of magic chalk.'

'All right,' she said. 'I'll buy it. What's magic chalk?'

'Well,' he said. 'Dai's going home from work, and calls in for a quick drink. And there at the bar is the most beautiful blonde he's ever seen. He can't believe his luck when she buys him a drink. So he sits down, and chats her up a bit, and then she says would he like to come home with her and make love to her.'

Judy smiled.

'Would he not?' Lloyd went on. 'So Dai throws caution to the wind, goes home with her, and makes love to her for hours. But all good things must come to an end, and Dai's getting dressed to go home when he sees the time. "My God," he says. "Look at the time. What am I going to tell the wife?" '

'Are you making this up as you go along?'

Lloyd grinned. ' "Don't worry, Dai," she says. "I've got some magic chalk here, see?" And she gives him a piece of chalk. Well, it just looks like ordinary chalk to Dai, but she swears it's magic. "Just put it behind your ear," she says, "and tell your wife the truth." '

Judy moved closer to him as he spoke. 'You *are* making it up,' she said.

'Dai doesn't fancy that at all,' said Lloyd. 'But the blonde just smiles again. "Trust me," she says. "It's magic." So Dai goes home, taking the chalk with him.'

'Does this go on all night?' Judy asked. 'So I'll have to stay – like Whatshername telling stories?'

'Scheherazade,' said Lloyd. 'Now, he doesn't have much faith in this chalk, but he's got no chance otherwise. When he gets home, he puts it behind his ear, and goes in. "Where have you been, then?" says his wife. And Dai takes a deep breath. "I've been making love to a beautiful blonde all night," he says. "Don't give me that, Dai Griffith," says his wife. "You've been down the Legion playing darts – you've still got the chalk behind your ear!" '

Judy laughed, but then her eyes widened, and the smile faded. She twisted away from him, reaching for her handbag.

'Leave it!' he ordered. 'Don't dare bring out that notebook!' Gun-dogs were supposed to *obey*.

She leafed through the pages, and looked up. 'It's all here, Lloyd,' she said. 'We had all the pieces. You were asking the right questions, all along.'

Lloyd looked over her shoulder at her notes, but he couldn't decipher the mixture of Judy's own form of speedwriting, the odd clear word and dozens of question-marks and asterisks. 'I hope your official notebook doesn't look like that,' he said.

'Why did Marian Wheeler go all the way to Eleanor Langton's, and then all the way back to Mrs Anthony's?' Judy said, her eyes bright with triumph. 'Why go to Eleanor Langton's at all?'

He had indeed asked those questions. It seemed to him that they had been answered, but obviously not.

'Why did Marian Wheeler deny locking the doors, and then insist that she had? Why lock them in the first place?'

He thought that they had established that Marian Wheeler *hadn't* locked the doors, whether or not Judy's little girl was telling the truth. Which, judging from Judy's almost indecent excitement, she was.

'Why bother going home to change her dress?' asked Judy.

'You wrote that *down*?'

'Yes,' she said, surprised. 'What I *didn't* write down was when you told me just to tell the Hills the truth.'

Lloyd was relieved to hear it.

'And I thought how they wouldn't believe me if I did,' said Judy.

Lloyd sat back, and looked at her. Feed in a few wild scenarios, and Judy would sift through them, rejecting everything but the facts, because she had no imagination to get in the way of the truth. She gathered facts. Some were tiny and vital; some were pages long, and useless. But they were all in there, like that dreadful computer of Sandwell's. Much more fun, though. It wouldn't be sitting there, beaming from ear to ear.

'Go on,' he said.

'Marian was alone in the house with him,' Judy said. 'So she had to have an alibi.'

He nodded slowly.

'And that's why she went to see Eleanor Langton. It *was* a trumped-up excuse. It had to be Eleanor, because she had no obvious friendship with Marian – in fact, gossip would say just the opposite. But Eleanor would be certain to know all the details – know that the time of Marian's visit *mattered*. George would tell her everything, and Marian Wheeler knew that.'

Lloyd sighed. 'And then Mrs Anthony,' he said, feeling weary. 'Whom Marian has known from childhood. She *knows* the old lady's as sharp as a tack. If anyone was going to notice her new dress, it would be Mrs Anthony.'

'That's why she stayed there long enough to take off her coat,' said Judy. 'Unlike anywhere else. Then she spilt some coffee, to give herself an excuse to go home.'

'Where she burned the dress,' said Lloyd. 'For us to find, along with all the other evidence.' Of course, of course. If she had simply denied murdering the man, the chances were that they would find some evidence anyway. So she just gave them a bit more. 'And she did her trick with the poker,' he said. 'To make it look like faked evidence.'

'And if she had trotted out her alibi,' Judy said, picking up her notebook, 'we would have been a lot less inclined to believe it. But as it was,' she said, 'she let us discover her alibi for her. And congratulate ourselves on how clever we'd been. *Don't give us that, Mrs Wheeler,*' she said, in a very fair imitation of Mrs Dai

REDEMPTION

Griffith's accent. '*You've been down the Legion, playing darts.*'

Lloyd stood up, and began to pace round the little room. 'She had to lock up the house,' he said. 'She couldn't risk Elstow being found before she'd finished leaving evidence for us.'

'And she had to keep it locked,' said Judy. 'Because she still didn't want him found too early. Or we might have got too accurate a time of death.'

Lloyd nodded. The trouble with alibis was that you couldn't really be in two places at once.

'She had to lose half an hour,' said Judy.

He nodded, his back to her. Easy enough to lose half an hour, he'd said. And when she confessed to killing Elstow, she simply made it half an hour later than it actually was. Half an hour which she had spent beetling back and forth across the village.

He ran a hand over his face, and stood staring at the Christmas tree. 'And she burned the overalls in the back bedroom,' he said, turning to face Judy. 'Knowing that when we found burnt clothing upstairs, we wouldn't *look* for any other fires.'

'I wonder how she felt when she saw George spreading them all over the driveway,' said Judy.

Lloyd shook his head.

She closed the notebook, looking sad, and still a little confused. 'She must have known we would suspect Joanna,' she said. 'She even told us she thought Joanna had killed him. How could she *do* that to her, Lloyd?'

'She didn't.' Lloyd sat down heavily. 'The locked doors,' he said. 'The Mystery of the Locked Bloody Doors. That was the one piece of evidence that we *weren't* supposed to know about.'

Judy frowned.

'Marian and George always went to the pub on Christmas Eve,' Lloyd said. 'Every year. And every year, they stayed until ten-thirty, singing carols. So she packed George and Joanna off in the belief that they'd do the same, and would therefore have cast-iron alibis. She would be home first, and no one would ever know the house had been locked up at all.'

'But they didn't stay,' said Judy.

'No. They didn't. And Joanna arrives home at ten past eight to find herself inexplicably locked out.' He looked across at Judy.

393

'She thinks it's her husband being bloody-minded, and goes off to see the doctor. She doesn't tell her parents that, because she doesn't want them to know about the baby. When she gets home again, she waits for them to come home. They get in, and now *she's* the one who feels bloody-minded. So she does what her mother asks, and doesn't go up to see her husband. Off they all go out again, and when they come back and find Elstow . . .' He bowed his apologies to Judy. 'In all innocence, she tells us that they were locked out. Which puts Marian in a fix, because she didn't want us to know.'

'And then, she realises that they *weren't* together all evening,' said Judy. 'You said that too.'

'So she has to tell us that she *did* lock the doors. To prove that it couldn't have been Joanna, because she couldn't have got in. Only she didn't know about Joanna's earlier trip home, did she? She thought she had covered her when she said she'd locked the doors at nine. Those doors,' he said. 'They were bothering me all along.'

The phone rang, and there was a moment before Lloyd snapped back, and picked it up. 'Lloyd,' he said.

'Sorry to bother you so late, sir, but I thought I'd better ring you. We've had Mrs Elstow on the phone, saying that her mother's gone missing.'

'Missing?' said Lloyd. 'Has she now?'

'Young lady sounded pretty desperate,' he said. 'I've sent WPC Alexander – didn't think I should send Parks. Not on his own, anyway.'

'Right,' said Lloyd. 'Thank you. Let Parks get his beauty sleep. I'm on my way.' He almost hung up, then put the receiver back to his ear. 'I'll pick up Sergeant Hill on the way,' he said, with a wink in her direction.

'But I think,' he said to her as he replaced the receiver, 'that you should probably do up at least some of your clothes.'

She had been gloriously unaware of her *déshabillée* through-out both his bringing it about, and her triumphant unearthing of the truth. Lloyd straightened his tie, and grinned.

'Ready?' he said.

*

Marian had wanted to kill Graham Elstow when she had stood by Joanna's hospital bed. She had wanted to, but the thought of actually doing it hadn't occurred to her. Not then. And she had wanted to kill him when she had gone to the house for Joanna's clothes, with him in attendance, mumbling apologies at her as she packed. But she hadn't thought of actually doing it, because Joanna wasn't going back. So he didn't matter any more, and Graham Elstow hadn't so much as entered Marian's mind from the moment she had left that house with Joanna's suitcase, until Christmas Eve, when he turned up at the vicarage.

And she hadn't thought about killing Eleanor Langton at all, until now.

She had come looking for help, that was all. George needed help. He was ill because he was so convinced of Eleanor's guilt that he was displaying the symptoms; Marian had enjoyed the effect that her words had had on Eleanor, who sat at the kitchen table, her head on her hand, her coffee cold beside her.

Marian had thought that George's infatuation with her was a passing phase, something that at worst a few illicit afternoons would have cured. The towel round Eleanor's head accentuated the fine bone structure, the youthful, unlined face. She wouldn't have blamed George if he had given in to a physical attraction.

Eleanor slowly unwound the towel, and her hair fell down in damp golden strands. The movement caused the bathrobe to fall open slightly, revealing long, shapely legs. Marian compared herself with the girl who sat opposite. Twenty-six, seven? Slim. Elegant. Wearing only a bathrobe, and she had thought that it was George at the door, just like last time.

And yes, Marian would back herself against a fantasy any day. But Eleanor Langton was no fantasy. Whatever George wanted, one thing was clear. One thing was certain. And it was more potent than all of Eleanor's physical attraction. Eleanor Langton wanted George.

Eleanor absently rubbed her hair with the towel as she looked at Marian. 'You're wrong,' she said.

'Wrong?'

'Perhaps George does think I killed Graham Elstow,' she said.

'But that isn't what's making him ill.' She sat forward slightly. 'He needs the freedom to be himself, Marian,' she said.

'Freedom,' repeated Marian thoughtfully. 'Yes, perhaps you're right.'

And she thought again of those cartridges, in the gun that George had pointed at her. She stood up.

'Perhaps you're right,' she said again. 'But at least we can make sure that he doesn't get it at the point of a gun. I'll go and get it.' She turned on her way to the door. 'If that's still all right with you,' she said.

'Of course,' Eleanor said tiredly. 'It should be out of harm's way, whatever he was going to do with it.'

'Quite,' said Marian.

She walked along the corridor to the front door, leaving it open as she stepped out into the icy night. There was a thick layer of frost on the car already, and for a moment, she thought that the boot lock had frozen. But it gave at last, and she took out the gun, leaving the boot open. Slipping her hand into the pocket of her jacket, she felt for the cartridges. Light streamed across the courtyard from the open door, and eventually Eleanor would come out, to see what was wrong. And she would come up to the car. Closer. Closer.

It was a dreadful accident. Dreadful. I couldn't leave the gun in the house, not with George behaving like he was. So I thought the best place would be the gun room at the cattle. I only ever use it there anyway, and the castle could always use an extra gun. I was so stupid, not checking it. But George had thought it wasn't loaded – that's what you told me, wasn't it, George? It was dreadful. Eleanor came with me to get it; I took it out of the boot, and it just . . .

Marian would never forgive herself for not checking the gun. But she would forgive George his lie. She would be patient, and sympathetic, and understanding.

And he would come back to her, just like Joanna.

They left George and Joanna with WPC Alexander. They didn't know where Marian was, they said; they had rung everyone they could think of. And Judy had seen Joanna's face when Lloyd had said that there were some more questions he wanted to put to her mother, if she contacted her or her father. Joanna had not been surprised.

They were on their way to the castle for inscrutable reasons of Lloyd's. 'What if she's in bed?' Judy asked, as Lloyd carefully drove at five miles an hour through the castle grounds.

'Then we'll go away again,' he said. 'But you heard George – he thought that Eleanor had killed Graham Elstow, and Marian knows it.' He glanced at her. 'And I think Marian would be very keen to drop that snippet of information into Eleanor's lap,' he said.

'But do you think she's still here?' asked Judy. 'It's late,' she pointed out. 'By most people's standards.'

'No,' said Lloyd. 'But Mrs Langton just might know where she's gone. Or make a good guess,' he added, with a laugh. His tiredness was evident in the Welshness of his accent, usually carefully controlled and measured. 'Besides,' he said. 'Eleanor Langton's been the answer to all the other puzzles, hasn't she? Let's see what she can do with this one.'

The castle appeared on their left, huge and black. 'I don't think you should drive right in,' said Judy. 'It really is very late, Lloyd. We might frighten her.'

Lloyd pulled up at the gatehouse, and they walked over the frozen, snow-covered gravel, through the massive entrance, into the castle proper, their footsteps deadened by the snow and the fourteen feet thickness of the walls.

They heard Eleanor Langton's voice softly calling Marian's name.

Marian Wheeler said something that they couldn't catch, as she and Lloyd arrived at the turn into the courtyard. Lloyd, a yard or so to her right, couldn't see what Judy could see.

It happened so quickly; it happened so slowly. She had seen it in films, when they slowed the action down. She had thought it was just for effect, but that was how it was.

Eleanor Langton, walking towards the Wheelers' car. Marian Wheeler, hidden by the open boot, gun raised, pointed at Eleanor, her finger on the trigger.

'*Mrs Langton!*' Judy's own voice, echoing round the ancient buildings. '*Stay where you are!*'

Marian Wheeler turning. Turning instantly, turning in slow motion. Turning, her finger pulling the trigger.

Seeing the ground rushing towards her, as the shot shattered the still night. Hearing glass break, feeling pain tearing at her leg. Running feet; Lloyd calling out. Hands touching her. 'Get inside!' Lloyd's voice. Lloyd's hands. Blackness.

Opening her eyes. Lloyd was kneeling beside her. 'I'm all right,' she said. 'I'm all right.'

'Thank God.' He pressed his forehead to hers.

She tried to get up, but she felt dizzy, and leant back against the wall.

'Wait,' said Lloyd. 'Take it easy. You were out for a couple of minutes.'

'Was I?' She frowned. 'My leg,' she said. 'It hurts.'

Lloyd looked down. 'It's cut,' he said. 'Quite badly. You must have caught it on one of those spikes when you went down.'

Judy looked at the wrought iron, foot-high spikes which carried an ornamental chain round a flower bed.

'Is she all right?' Marian Wheeler's voice, afraid; it came out of the darkness. She was close, but Judy couldn't see her.

'I'm all right, Mrs Wheeler,' she said, grunting with the effort of getting to her feet. She leant on Lloyd. 'I think you got one of the castle windows,' she said, trying to sound positively jolly.

'I didn't mean to shoot at you,' said Mrs Wheeler. 'It was *her*. It was *her*.'

Lloyd put his arm round Judy's waist. 'Come on,' he said. 'Sit down in the car.' He led her to the Wheelers' car, and opened the door for her. From there, Judy could see Eleanor, inside the house, framed in the light from the doorway.

'She was going to take George away from me,' Marian said. 'I couldn't let her do that. I let Graham Elstow take Joanna, and look what happened.'

Judy looked at Lloyd, who shrugged. 'Let her go on talking, I suppose,' he said quietly, in answer to her unvoiced question. 'Can you see her?'

Judy peered into the deep shadow of the castle, and shook her head.

'It should be all right as long as Eleanor stays in the house,' Lloyd said, crouching down. He gently lifted the torn cloth away from Judy's leg. 'I think I should rip it some more,' he said. 'Keep it away from the wound.'

Judy nodded, and closed her eyes while he dealt with it.

'Are you OK?' he asked doubtfully.

'Yes.' She glanced down unwillingly, and looked away again. 'I don't think it's as bad as it looks,' she said. 'It hurts like hell – isn't that a good sign?'

He smiled, and stood up. 'Mrs Wheeler?' he said. 'The sergeant's hurt. I think she should go to hospital.'

'Then take her. I didn't mean to hurt her.'

Lloyd sighed quietly. 'I know that,' he said. 'But I don't think we can leave without you.'

There was silence.

'We know what happened, Mrs Wheeler,' he said.

'But I had to kill him,' she said. 'We'd never have got rid of him. I had to. I had two hours to work out what to do. It was quite clever, don't you think?'

Judy shivered.

'Yes,' said Lloyd. 'It was quite clever.'

'Joanna's having Graham Elstow's baby,' Marian said. 'She thinks I don't know. But I was washing her poor face, and I heard her. I heard her. *Let the baby be all right.* I *heard* her. A baby. A baby! He'd have rights. Even if she left him, he'd have rights. Over *my* grandchild. We'd never have got rid of him. I had to kill him.'

Judy closed her eyes, as the pain throbbed through her leg.

'Mrs Wheeler,' Lloyd said, his voice soothing. 'Why don't you come out where I can see you? And you don't need the gun, do you?'

'Oh, yes,' she said, sounding surprised. 'It's all over. Don't you see? It's over. I just wanted to explain.'

The throbbing increased with Judy's heartbeat, as she looked at Lloyd. She put her hand on his, where it rested on the car door.

'No, Mrs Wheeler,' he said. 'It's not all over. People will listen. They'll help you.'

'They'll send me to prison.'

Practical, sensible, thought Judy. But then Marian Wheeler was a realist.

'Yes,' said Lloyd. 'They might. But even if they do, they'll still help. You know that.' He paused. 'You've helped people, Mrs Wheeler. So now they'll help you.'

She moved then, and they could just see her shape standing out from the shadow of the castle walls. Judy patted Lloyd's hand.

'Mrs Wheeler,' he said. 'I really think that Sergeant Hill should go to hospital. Will you come with us?'

The sirens were faint at first; they grew louder, until the sound filled the air, punctuated by a shotgun blast.

Post-Mortem

Exhaust fumes hung in the cold, still air; sirens whined down as the cars' engines were switched off. Lights flashed, and the winking colour on the pale, ancient stone seemed almost festive. Judy stood watching, supported by the car door, unable to help.

Lloyd, grim-faced, walked through the chaos towards her, shaking his head.

'All right, what's going on here?' A torch played on their faces. 'Inspector Lloyd?' said the voice, disbelievingly.

'A woman's just shot herself here,' Lloyd said angrily. 'She's dead, I'm sure, but I want the doctor here. Now.'

The sergeant ran back to his car, and reached in for his radio. After a few minutes, he came back, still looking confused. 'I've to tell you that Freddie's at the station, and he's on his way,' he said.

'Good,' barked Lloyd. 'Now you can tell me what this circus is *doing* here!'

The sergeant looked offended. 'The burglar alarm went off in the station,' he said. 'We were using it as an exercise.'

'The *burglar* alarm?' Lloyd repeated, then sighed. 'The window,' he said to Judy. 'She broke a window.' He took a short, calming breath, and explained in more detail to the bemused sergeant.

He turned back to Judy. 'Do you think you can walk to the house?' he asked.

'I'm sure I can.' She limped to the doorway, her arm round Lloyd. Eleanor Langton stood just inside, shivering.

'Do you mind if we . . .?' Lloyd began.

'Of course not,' she said.

'Mrs Langton,' he said gently. 'You'll get pneumonia if you don't get dressed.'

She looked down at herself almost in surprise. 'Yes,' she said. 'Yes, I will. Then I'll make you a hot drink, Sergeant Hill. I don't think you should have anything stronger – they say it isn't . . .' She foundered. 'There's a first aid kit in the kitchen,' she said. 'I'll bring it.'

Judy smiled. 'Don't bother,' she said. 'You get dressed.'

Lloyd helped her to the sofa. 'I think your leg should be up,' he said, easing off her shoe, and pulling the coffee table towards her.

'I'm not dripping blood all over the carpet, am I?' she asked. She wouldn't look.

He smiled, shaking his head, then sat down beside her. 'Some coward you turned out to be,' he said.

'She was going to *shoot* her, Lloyd!' Judy said, springing to her own defence.

'And you thought it would be a much better idea if she shot you,' said Lloyd.

'I didn't think anything! I just warned her.'

'I don't understand,' Lloyd said. 'You're frightened to change the way you live, but you're quite happy to get in the way of a deranged woman with a double-barrelled shotgun.' He stood up. 'I have to get over to the vicarage,' he said, with a sigh. 'Break the news.'

Judy nodded. Poor George, she thought. Poor Joanna. 'Lloyd? Tell Joanna I'm sorry I couldn't come myself.'

'Sure.' He looked at her for a moment. 'I thought you were dead,' he said.

She caught his hand, and squeezed it. 'So did I,' she replied.

Joanna gave her father a little encouraging smile as he went off with the inspector. She had wanted to say she was sorry, but she couldn't, because her father must never know the terrible thing she had thought, when she had finally rung the police.

Her poor, gentle father.

The inescapable truth, which should have been shattering, had come almost as a relief. Almost as though she had known all along. Perhaps she had. And perhaps so had her father, who may have convinced himself that Eleanor Langton had killed Graham, but had failed to convince his stomach. And now, her mother was dead. But she couldn't take that in. Not yet.

She waited until the sound of the police car's powerful engine had dwindled to nothing before she closed the door.

'I've made a big pot of tea,' said the policewoman. 'You come and have a cup of tea with me, love.'

Joanna allowed herself to be steered into the kitchen, where the fire burned brightly and WPC Alexander bustled plumply round her. She had offered to go with her father to the castle, but he had said she should stay. Two hours ago, he couldn't have summoned up the will to make such a decision, but he could now.

Because with the inspector's terrible news had come a reawakening of her father's spirit.

At least she hadn't lost him.

Eleanor found as many containers as she could for coffee, which she was providing on a conveyor-belt system for the people who were working out in the bitter cold. It seemed ridiculous that just across the courtyard there were dozens of cups and saucers in the café, and she couldn't get into it. She found herself thinking that she would have to speak to her employers about that, as though this happened every week; she almost made herself laugh.

Thank God Tessa wasn't here, though in truth, the events of the night had barely affected Eleanor herself. A shout, a shot. Another shot.

Now that they had told her what had happened, she knew how close she had come. But at the time, it had just been a confused sequence of sights and sounds, like a scene from a badly directed play.

She handed the tray to a grateful policeman, and picked up the first aid kit. Sergeant Hill had refused several offers of medical assistance, but Eleanor thought she really ought to do something.

'Ah, just the job!' A tall, thin man with an unexpected smile appeared in her kitchen and took the box from her. 'Doctor,' he explained.

'Oh, good,' she said. 'I'm sure I wouldn't be very good at it.'

'Neither will I,' he said. 'But you have to give the public what they want.'

*

George had nodded his confirmation that it was Marian, then had walked away, feeling detached from it all. Perhaps it was the pills. For a long time, he stood unnoticed in the shadow, watching as the numbers dwindled, and only Chief Inspector Lloyd and the officer who had driven him remained. When the ambulance came, bumping over the frozen ground to Marian, he slipped into the courtyard.

The door was open; he walked in, and could see Eleanor at the end of the corridor, sitting in the dining room. She stood up as he went in, her face pale.

'The police are waiting for me,' he said. 'I just wanted to be sure you were all right.'

She nodded, but her eyes were worried. 'George?' she said. 'Did I cause all this?'

'You?' He took her hand. 'Oh, Eleanor. No.' He shook his head. 'No.' he said again.

They were putting Marian in the ambulance; they asked if he wanted to wait until it left, but he shook his head. It was odd, he thought, as he was driven back home. Now that everyone else was feeling sick, he didn't.

Not any more.

Lloyd watched as the ambulance drove away with Marian Wheeler's body, and rubbed his eyes. Would she have come with them if the damn squad cars hadn't arrived? He passed the shattered window that had brought them, and shrugged. He'd never know now. All he knew was that his immediate future would be filled with enquiries and questions and statements, and the depressing likelihood that the file would quietly be closed on Graham Elstow's murder.

He shivered, and arrived at the cottage as Freddie was leaving.

'Bloody cold out here,' said Freddie, his breath streaming out as he spoke. He smiled. 'I never thought I'd get that close to Sergeant Hill's legs,' he said.

Lloyd rubbed cold hands together. 'Isn't there something about medical ethics?' he said.

'I have to take my pleasures where I find them,' said Freddie.

'Most of my patients are past their best.' He opened the car door and threw in his bag. 'Like Mrs Wheeler,' he said.

'Must you be so cheerful?' Lloyd said. 'The woman has just blown her brains out.'

Freddie grinned. 'I'd sooner look at Mrs Wheeler's brains and Judy Hill's legs than the other way round,' he said.

Lloyd smiled reluctantly.

'The leg's not bad,' said Freddie. 'The wound, I mean. I've bandaged it up – but she should get an anti-tetanus injection.'

'Now?' asked Lloyd.

'Now would be best.' He got into the car. 'And she should take it easy for a few days,' he added. 'But they'll tell her all that at the hospital.'

Lloyd lifted a tired hand as Freddie reversed out of the court-yard, and roared off into the night. He knocked quietly at the door.

Eleanor Langton gave him a little smile as she opened it. A real smile. 'Come in,' she said. 'I'll make you a cup of coffee – you look frozen.'

'Great,' said Lloyd. 'Thank you. Are you all right?'

'Yes,' she said. 'I didn't really know what was happening until it was all over.' She walked down the corridor a little way, then turned back. 'Your sergeant saved my life,' she said.

Lloyd nodded briefly, and walked into the sitting room, where Judy sat, her now bandaged leg still resting on the coffee table. 'Right,' he said. 'A quick cup of coffee and then we have to get you to hospital.'

'Hospital?' she said.

'Freddie's orders. Besides, I want a real doctor to look at it.'

She laughed. 'Freddie is a real doctor,' she said.

Lloyd raised his eyebrows. 'Laugh-a-minute Freddie?' he said.

'That's just how he copes,' said Judy. She patted the sofa. 'Come here,' she said.

Lloyd sat beside her on the sofa, as she gingerly removed her foot from the coffee table, and moved closer to him.

'We have to sort ourselves out,' she said.

'Yes,' Lloyd agreed. 'But I don't really think this is the ideal place,' he added, with an uncomfortable glance at the door. 'She'll be back any minute.'

'Oh, but it is the ideal place,' said Judy. She looked down for a moment, then her head came up resolutely. 'I'm not very proud of what I've been doing,' she said. 'To you or Michael.'

Lloyd took her hand.

'I should have left him when it started,' she went on, then shook her head. 'I should never have married him in the first place.' She looked away again. 'For a moment tonight,' she said, 'I honestly thought I was dead. And I've wasted too much of everyone's time. Michael deserves more than this, and so do you.' She smiled sadly. 'So I'm leaving him,' she said.

'Are you sure?' Lloyd gently touched her bandaged leg. 'You'll never have a better piece of magic chalk.'

'I'm sure.'

Her lips touched his, gently at first, then with an urgency that took him by surprise. They broke away as the normally silent Eleanor positively banged her way down the corridor, rattling cups.

Lloyd frowned. 'You set this *up*,' he said, incredulously.

Judy grinned. 'They don't call you a detective for nothing,' she said.

'You *told* her? About us?'

'She told me,' said Judy.

'I told you she was a witch,' said Lloyd, as Eleanor just happened inadvertently to bump into the door with her noisy cargo.

'Sorry I was so long,' she said. 'I made a couple of sandwiches.'

A sandwich and a cup of coffee later, Lloyd went to bring his car round from the gatehouse. He stood for a moment looking down at the moonlit village. It was exactly like the Christmas card he'd got from the Woodfords.

And this place had made him shiver, he thought, touching the rough surface of the wall. Perhaps his Welsh superstition had been right.

Mrs Anthony could have told them. She hadn't been hinting about George at all. She had been telling them, in words of one syllable, about Marian. And hadn't he said that they would find an old lady who would solve it all for them? Pity they hadn't been listening.

Murder at the Vicarage, he thought, as he got into the car. He must read it again some time.

DEATH OF A DANCER

Chapter One

NO ROAD TRAFFIC BEYOND THIS POINT –
ALL VEHICLES TO CAR PARK

Philip Newby turned in the direction of the arrow, along a road which ran between two buildings. Behind the larger of the two, he could see the car park, and pulled in, thankful to find a space close to the road. He emerged from the car with difficulty, shivering as he stepped out into the bitter January wind. This winter was never going to end. There were always going to be heaps of snow along the pavements, making them narrower than they were to start with. The frost that lay along every branch of every tree, every television aerial, every telegraph wire, was there forever, frozen and permanent.

Reaching back into the car, he took out the walking-stick, and made his way back along the side road. It seemed like a long way to the school itself, which was on the other side of the grounds, its roof visible above the other buildings. Between him and the grey, dignified building was a curving tarmac roadway slippery with slush; it might just as well have been a minefield. But the school had been there for a hundred and fifty years, and he didn't suppose it was going to come to him. He clamped his teeth together as he walked up the slight incline that he once wouldn't have recognised as one.

He walked quickly; too quickly, the doctor had said. Certainly too quickly for the conditions. But he *walked*, and there had been a long time when it was thought that he might not, because of the back injury. It had healed more quickly than his leg, as it had turned out. It ached, from time to time. He couldn't turn quickly. But he did exercises, and through the pain he could feel it strengthening. With the leg exercises, all he could feel was the pain. His long stint in a wheelchair had, however, made his arms stronger than they'd ever been; an ironic twist.

He made the final assault with a burst of speed that took him up the stone steps at the front of the building in seconds; the best way to deal with steps, he'd found. He winced each time his weight came on to his right foot, as it had to, but the pain afforded him some pleasure; it was proof that his leg was still there, and still functioning.

Heat wrapped round him like a blanket as he went into the building, and he stood for a moment, savouring it. In the large entrance-hall, an old-fashioned finger-post pointed the way to the office, where he joined a queue, a mixture of boys and staff, who looked at him curiously or incuriously, depending on their nature. Staff didn't get preferential treatment, he noticed. First come, first served. He approved of that.

Another finger-post greeted him: CLASSROOMS 1–14, STAFF ROOM, LADIES' REST ROOM, STOREROOM, BOILER ROOM. It pointed in all directions, including up. CLASSROOMS 15–21, that one read. HEADMASTER'S STUDY, PHYSICS LAB, LAVATORIES. He looked at the wide, curved staircase, counting the steps he could see, in case LAVATORIES indicated the only facilities available. Like an old man. An old man with a stick, afraid of a flight of stairs. He'd bought the stick specially; the hospital had said that theirs was very carefully designed to give the best support, and hadn't been too keen on the idea, but if he had to walk with a stick it would be a stick to be proud of. It was a silver-topped walking-stick, slim and elegant. All right, the surgeon had said grudgingly. But keep the other one in case that one snaps. The balance was all wrong, with that heavy knob; these sticks weren't for *walking* with, they were for show. So Philip was showing it. The other one was with his luggage, in the car.

First day of term; that was the reason for the queue. There were questions to be answered, children to be checked and registered and comforted, staff to be given timetables and instructions and notes about epileptics and Muslims. He joined the end, and shuffled up with the others. He'd been told not to, in a letter. The headmaster would meet him, show him round, it said. But none of the people he had seen had been the headmaster. His memory was a bit faulty, but not that bad. Treadwell had come to see him just before Christmas, to check that everything was all right, and that he could start in the new year.

He had seemed very solicitous. Too solicitous. Philip must tell him, he had said, if there were any obstacles that could perhaps be overcome or made less troublesome. There would be no obstacles, Philip thought darkly. He was thirty-seven, God damn it. He was in the prime of a life that he enjoyed, an uncomplicated life, doing more or less what he pleased. He was . . . he was just temporarily inconvenienced. He wasn't disabled, and he never would be. He just used a walking-stick, that was all.

An all-male queue; but in the office two women came into view as Philip at last achieved the window position, with only a man and a small boy ahead of him. The blonde receptionist was dealing with the queries; she caught his eye, as she would, for Philip was taller than the rest of the queue, and she smiled. Philip smiled back automatically, but he was looking past her to where another woman sat perched on the desk, talking on the phone. She was a little younger than he was, at a guess. Dark eyes, clear skin, dark hair drawn away from her face. Delicately coloured eyelids, and lips that matched the pale, polished nails. A wedding ring encircled one slim finger. No other jewellery. He felt as though he knew her, but he didn't.

'Are you sure you don't mind?' she was saying. 'It's just that it's only on that one night. But I did say I'd—?' She paused. 'Thank you,' she said. 'I'm really grateful, Diana.' She twisted the telephone cord lightly in her fingers as she spoke.

Lifting her hand to his mouth, kissing the long, slim fingers . . .

'You'll have to hire one,' the receptionist was saying to the man. He was about fifty, stockily built, slightly overweight, wearing jeans and a sweatshirt.

'Hire one?' the man repeated, in a London accent which, if it ever had been polished up, had returned to its native roughness. 'Do you know how much the bloody things *cost* to hire?'

His lips touching her eyes, her cheekbones . . .

'Fucking dinner-jacket,' the man said, walking down the corridor.

There were embarrassed giggles from the boys, but neither of the ladies seemed shocked, or even surprised.

'You'll have to excuse Sam,' the dark one said, her hand over the mouthpiece as she addressed him over the head of the small boy in front. 'He's a law unto himself.' She turned back to the phone. 'Just apologising for Sam,' she explained to the caller. 'He's trying to shock people, as usual.'

'They'll all be taller than me,' the boy now at the head of the queue complained, and Philip could see that this would indeed be the case, whatever the child was talking about.

Like the previous customer, the child left disgruntled, but refrained from swearing, at least in anyone's hearing.

His mouth seeking hers . . .

'Can I help you?'

Unwillingly, Philip's eyes turned to the young receptionist. 'Newby,' he said. 'I believe you're expecting me.'

'Mrs Knight,' the girl said, over her shoulder, 'Mr Newby's here, but Mr Treadwell isn't in his office.'

She was Andrew Knight's widow.

'Oh – thank you, Kitty,' she said, and hurriedly finished her call. She stood up and went out of sight for a moment, then came out of a corridor door. She was taller than he'd thought. Longer legs.

'I'm Caroline,' she said. 'Mr Treadwell must have got held up – you know how it is on the first day. Everything that can go wrong does.' She smiled.

'Philip.' He shook the hand she extended, and frowned slightly. Her greeting had reminded him of something. It was always happening – things people said, did – sometimes just the tone of voice or a gesture, and he would be groping around in the void of his memory-gap. Bits were coming back, slowly. Nothing came back this time.

She smiled. 'I heard a lot about you from Andrew,' she said.

He had probably heard a lot about her. But he couldn't remember anything about that day. Or the days that followed it.

'I expect you'd like to go straight to the flat,' she said.

The staff block turned out to be the smaller of the two buildings by the car park. That side of the grounds could be reached through a sort of alleyway that he hadn't noticed. It made the walk shorter, but he embarked with dread on the cobblestoned surface, and tried to look as though he was strolling, rather than picking his way. It was a difficult effect to achieve in the biting wind that whistled through the alley.

'Is your stuff in your car?' she asked, with a glance down the side road towards the car park. 'We'll collar a child to bring it in.'

They were at what had once upon a time been a single house, which had been split into two flats. Caroline opened the door, and let him in to the ground-floor rooms; large, cold, sparsely furnished, but adequate.

'You'll be sharing,' she warned him. 'Did someone tell you?'

He nodded.

'Well,' she said. 'At least you're here at last.'

Philip should have started at the school almost eighteen months before. He had come for the interview, had been offered and had accepted the job. He was to have started that September. Andrew Knight had been running him back to London when the accident had happened. He had known Andrew since their school days; they would surely have done a lot of catching-up, but he couldn't remember. He couldn't even remember whether or not he had met Caroline; from what she had said, he assumed that he hadn't.

Smiling, mouths meeting, the tip of his tongue moving over perfect teeth . . .

She shivered. 'Sam should have put the fire on,' she said, going over to the gas fire, and kneeling in front of it. She looked up. 'That's who you're sharing with,' she said, her voice slightly apologetic. 'Do you have matches?'

The driver of an oncoming car had seen fit to overtake the vehicle in front, on a road too narrow for such a manoeuvre, and hadn't survived the experience; neither had Andrew Knight. Philip had, but he had no recollection of it.

Trying not to lean too heavily on the stick, he knelt beside her. Kneeling was one of the few physical feats he could achieve without too much difficulty. He produced matches, and the jets lit with a quiet little explosion.

'This is terrible,' she said, holding her hands out to the warmth. 'We can't even offer you hot food today, I'm afraid – some crisis in the kitchen. But there's a pub just down the road that does lunches.'

'It's better than last time,' he said.

'It must have been dreadful for you,' she said. 'All that time in hospital.'

'I survived.' There *was* something familiar about her, he thought, and he coloured slightly, not wanting to admit any non-visible defects. 'This is the first time we've met, isn't it?' he asked.

'Not quite,' she said. 'I came to see you in hospital.'

'Things from before and after the accident are sometimes a bit hazy,' he said.

'It doesn't matter,' she said. 'I didn't expect you to remember me. You were in a bad way.'

Her lips parting to admit his questing tongue . . .

He must have seen the car coming, he supposed; he must have closed his eyes and waited for the impact, but he could remember nothing. He couldn't even remember arriving at the school, or anything about the interview, except tiny, fragmentary, frustrating snatches. The last thing he really remembered was getting on the train to come here.

'It seems amnesia's not uncommon,' he said. 'Something to do with the pain. Your memory blanks it out.'

'I wish mine could,' she said.

'It was good of the school to keep the job open all this time,' he said.

Unbuttoning her top button, slipping a hand inside her blouse . . .

'The least they could do,' she said.

'It wasn't the school's fault.'

Cupping her warm, silk-encased breast in the palm of his hand . . .

'Perhaps not,' she said, handing him back the matches, and standing up. 'Well – I expect you'd like to rest before you start looking round.' And she left, closing the door behind her.

Philip closed his eyes, hearing the quiet roar of the gas fire. He leaned on the stick, and slowly, painfully, got to his feet, standing motionless for a moment. Then his hand gripped the wooden shaft of his stick, and he raised it above his head, bringing it down

DEATH OF A DANCER

on the table with all the strength he possessed. Pain shot through his body as the stick shuddered in his hand, and he let it go, watching it roll along the floor.

Now he would have to pick the damn thing up again.

Barry Treadwell watched Diana Hamlyn from the window as she crossed the courtyard, towards the playing-field, on her way to the junior dormitory. He sighed, sliding open his desk drawer, and feeling at the back for the bottle. He drank from it twice before replacing the cork, and putting it back. The phone rang as he did so; he answered it to Kitty, the receptionist.

'Mr Treadwell – Mrs Knight said to tell you that she's looking after Mr Newby.'

Damn. He'd forgotten all about him. 'Good,' he said. 'Thank you, Kitty.'

'And . . .'

He knew he didn't want her to go on.

'. . . there's been another theft,' she said. 'A ring.'

Treadwell took the receiver from his ear, and sat with it in his hand for a moment; when he put it back, she was still on the other end of the line. 'Where from?' he asked wearily.

'The ladies' loo,' said Kitty. 'Miss Castle says she took it off to wash her hands, and remembered about it as soon as she got back to the staff room. She went back, but it had gone.'

'Is she sure?' he implored. Treadwell was fifty-six, but on the first day of term he always felt twenty years older. Now this.

'She's quite sure. She's here. Do you want her to come up?'

No, he didn't want her to come up. A boys' school shouldn't *have* ladies' loos, was his first reactionary thought. Then it wouldn't have ladies taking their rings off in them. So no one could steal them. He had been at the school for two and a half years. The previous head had agreed with the governors' odd notions when it came to staff; employing women was just one of them. If he had had anything to do with it, he would have fought the idea, just as he was fighting the suggestion that they admit girls. But he had already lost that, and the first of the female pupils would be starting next year whether he liked it or not.

The first woman had been Caroline Knight, who had come four years ago as some sort of package deal with her husband, Andrew. Two vacancies had been advertised, the newly married Knights had applied, and the idea had appealed apparently. It would not have appealed to Treadwell, but it had been an established fact when he arrived, and it seemed to have worked, for as long as it had lasted.

His heart felt heavy as he thought of Andrew Knight; deputy head, a good teacher, a good man. For poor Andrew had been wiped out in a car crash less than a year after Treadwell started, and Treadwell didn't want to think about that.

Anyway, Caroline had been the first, and save for the months immediately following Andrew's death she was level-headed and logical and even quite good company. But she had opened the door for the others, and now one of the damn women was saying her ring had been stolen.

'Send her up,' he said.

He listened to her story, and had to admit that unless (as he tended to suspect) the woman had no brain at all, then she had taken her ring off in the ladies', walked along ten feet of corridor into the staff room, remembered, walked back, and it had gone. Yes, she said coyly when he asked her, there had been someone else in there, but she didn't want to accuse anyone.

But Treadwell knew, without her assistance, who it must have been. Perhaps if he called in the police it might bring her to her senses; he needn't voice his suspicions.

'We'll have to get the police this time,' he said to her and, sighing, he picked up the phone.

'Oh,' she said. 'It wasn't my engagement ring.' She waved her left hand at him to indicate its continuing presence on her finger. 'I mean, it isn't valuable or anything.'

No, he hadn't supposed it would be. The things that went missing never were.

He asked for the chief superintendent, and saw Miss Castle raise her eyebrows just a little. Why shouldn't he? The man was a friend of his. He wanted to be sure it was all handled properly, he thought, running a hand through springy grey hair. Nothing irritated the middle classes so much as having their sons suspected of theft.

He just wished it was one of their sons he suspected.

The canteen was virtually empty, much to Sam's delight. There were many things about teaching art in a small, fifth-rate private school that he didn't like; eating with blazered youths was just one of them.

'Salads?' he said incredulously. 'What do you mean, there's only salads?'

'The electricity went off to the cookers,' the girl explained patiently. 'It's only just been fixed, because we couldn't get an electrician any sooner.'

'You can't call salad *food*, woman! How do you expect me to exist on—?'

'Hello, Sam. Still complaining?'

Sam turned to see one of the few things he did like about the place.

She rubbed her cold hands together. 'Oh, it's cold out there,' she said, shivering.

'Good afternoon, Caroline,' he said. 'Don't expect any rib-sticking stew to take the cold out of your bones, whatever you do. We're being fed like sodding rabbits today.'

'I know,' she said. 'So would you if you ever read any notices.'

'This place has got more signs and notices than a bloody—' He broke off, being unable to think than what. 'Besides, I'm an artist – I don't have to be able to read.'

They picked up their salads, and went to a table beside one of the old-fashioned radiators. Sam sat down and looked reflectively at Caroline. 'I take it that was Philip Newby at the office this morning?' he asked.

'Yes,' she said.

'Are you all right?'

She frowned. 'Why shouldn't I be?' she asked.

'Well – it's a reminder, and all that.'

Her eyes grew hard. 'I hadn't forgotten,' she said.

'No, well,' said Sam, 'you know what I mean. Anyway – what's he like?'

'He's all right, I suppose.'

'Oh, come on! I've got to live with the guy – I want to know what he's like. For all I know he's queer.'

'I don't think you need worry on that score.'

'Oh – what's up? Did he make a pass at you?'

'Of course not!'

'Well – what didn't you like about him?'

'Nothing,' she said, decidedly on the defensive. 'He's all right, that's all. He didn't say much.'

'There's something about him you didn't like,' Sam persisted.

'Oh, for God's sake! I exchanged about three sentences with the man. He'd had a long drive, his leg was probably hurting him, you were the first member of staff that he clapped eyes on, and then he found out he was sharing a flat with you! No wonder he seemed a bit odd.'

'He has to be odd,' Sam said, 'or he wouldn't be eligible to work here.' He looked up as some more members of staff wandered in. 'Look at them,' he said. 'Flotsam and jetsam – we take what other schools throw out. How this place has staggered on for a hundred and fifty years is beyond me.'

She looked up. 'I wasn't thrown out by another school,' she said.

No. But she had come as one of an inseparable pair; Sam knew for a fact that they had tried several schools before this one. Positively unnatural, in Sam's view, being so wrapped up in one another. Especially at their age. And she was an odd one herself. Blew hot and cold.

Maybe she fancied this Newby; he'd heard it took some people like that. Though it was hard to imagine Caroline fancying anyone. He'd taken her out once or twice since she had begun to get over Andrew's death, and the relationship had moved from entirely platonic through sub-teenage to long discussions about how she didn't feel ready. Sam didn't really mind. He liked her company, and if it developed beyond that – fine. But in between the outings and the discussions he seemed to be the last person on earth that she wanted to spend time with. Perhaps he embarrassed her. He hoped he did. At any rate, she had never given the least hint that she was remotely interested in him other than as an occasionally necessary social accessory.

'How long was he in hospital?' he asked.

A little frown creased her forehead. 'Who?' she asked.

'Newby.' She knew damn well who.

'He was in and out for about a year, I believe. He's had dozens of operations.' She gave a short sigh. 'He's been at some sort of recuperation place for six months.'

'It was hard luck,' Sam said.

'Hard luck? Is that all you think it was?'

Sam shrugged. 'What else? Some nutter comes out of a line of cars, Andrew gets killed, Newby gets crippled – bad luck. Fate, if you'd rather.'

She just looked at him, not speaking, not arguing.

'Well,' he said, 'what would you call it?'

She sighed. 'Forget it,' she said.

'What's he doing for lunch?' Sam asked.

'I don't know. I told him he could get something hot at the pub.'

Sam frowned. 'Does he know where it is?' he asked.

'I don't know!'

'You mean you just left him to fend for himself?'

'Can we drop the subject of Philip Newby?' Oh, well. Presumably his presence had upset her. But someone had better see that the man got fed.

'Are you going to this party tonight?' Caroline asked.

'If you are,' he said. 'Does cocktails with the Hamlyns turn you on?'

'Not really,' she said. 'But I suppose it would be a bit off not to celebrate his promotion.'

'Robert Hamlyn – deputy head,' said Sam, in tones of wonderment. 'Who would credit it?'

'Robert's all right,' said Caroline, determined to disagree with him about everything, obviously.

'*He's* all right,' Sam agreed. 'But I don't think the deputy headmaster's wife should be the good time that was had by all, do you?'

She shook her head. 'Probably not,' she said.

'No other school would employ him, never mind make him the deputy head.'

The deputy between Andrew and Robert Hamlyn had

abandoned ship during the summer break, having realised all too quickly what he had got himself into. Sam had his own ideas as to why Hamlyn had been thus exalted.

'What's wrong?' asked Caroline. 'Do you think it should have been you?'

'Oh, very funny. No, but there are one or two people I think it could have been. You, for instance.'

She looked at him strangely, again, then smiled, shaking her head.

'The boys would have been queuing up to have you discipline them,' he said, pushing away his barely touched salad, and standing up. 'I think I'll see if Newby wants to come to the pub,' he said.

Caroline was no fun when she was in one of her moods, and it was with something like relief that Sam stepped out into the sleet which was now slicing its way through the air, and walked down to the staff block, letting himself in to find Newby sitting by the fire.

'Waters,' he said. 'Sam. I teach art because no one buys my paintings.' He held out his hand.

Newby looked a little startled, then smiled. 'Newby,' he said. 'Philip. I teach English because I like it.'

'They're feeding us on grass at the canteen,' said Sam. 'I wondered if you fancied something at the pub.'

'I've heard of you,' Newby said slowly. 'You had an exhibition at the Tate – it was quite successful, wasn't it?'

'It was five years ago,' Sam said, surprised as he always was when anyone had heard of him. 'Are you interested in art?'

'Yes,' said Newby. 'I went to the Tate a lot when I was in London – I like the things the tabloids make fun of.'

'So do I,' said Sam thoughtfully. 'Yes – the exhibition was quite successful. But you have to die in my business before you earn enough to live on.'

Newby smiled. 'I don't suppose you're too pleased about having a room-mate,' he said.

'Oh, I don't know,' said Sam truthfully. 'I'll be glad of the company.'

'I'll be looking for somewhere of my own,' Newby said.

'Good luck. The nearest town is Stansfield, and that's twenty miles away,' said Sam. 'And if you get anywhere in one of the villages you'll have even less privacy than you get here.'

There was a knock at the door, and Sam watched as Newby went to answer it, moving in the oddly quick way he had, almost as though the stick wasn't there at all. He could have gone, but he had a feeling in his bones that that wouldn't have been a wise move.

'Philip,' Barry Treadwell's voice boomed. 'So sorry I couldn't meet you myself this morning, but there were a million things to do.' He walked in, nodded to Sam, then turned back to Newby. 'Still,' he said, 'I'm sure you'd rather have Caroline showing you round than me!'

Newby didn't react with the expected polite smile. If Sam were to be asked, he would say that he saw a faint flush on Newby's face.

'Now – are you settling in all right? Got someone lined up to bring in your stuff?'

'Not yet,' said Newby.

'Soon remedy that.' He went back to the door, and bellowed at the youth who was passing to get someone else and start unpacking Newby's car. 'Keys?' he said, turning back.

'It's open,' said the still bemused Newby. 'The back door doesn't lock.'

Treadwell relayed this information to the young man who had answered his summons; Matthew Cawston, head boy and smooth bastard. Sam didn't care for him.

'Good,' Treadwell said. 'That's got that organised. You didn't see much of the place when you came for the interview, did you? And it was a long time ago, now. So have a good look round, and anything you think you need – come to me. Anything we can do to make things easier . . . just pop into my office – any time. Sorry I can't stay and chat.'

Sam looked at Philip Newby when Barry had gone. 'So,' he said. 'You've met the lovely Caroline?'

Newby nodded.

'Forget it,' Sam said. 'I've got my name down.'

'I'm sorry?' Newby said.

There was another knock on the door, which opened to reveal Cawston and a bearer. The smaller boy staggered in, loaded down with suitcases.

'Where would you like your things, sir?' asked Cawston.

'Oh – just dump them in my room,' said Newby, going to open the door for the panting child. 'Anywhere,' he said.

Sam watched as Cawston supervised. 'Cawston,' he said. 'Try going back to the car and picking up a few things yourself. You never know, it might just work.'

Cawston's back stiffened for a moment. 'Yes, sir,' he said.

'And don't call me fucking sir!' roared Sam, as Cawston left. 'Lazy young sod,' he said to Newby, as the other one emerged from the bedroom and scampered out before he got sworn at, too.

Newby was trying not to look startled, and manfully got back to the matter in hand. 'Er ... you and ... Mrs Knight,' he said. 'Are you ...?' He finished with a movement of his head.

'Well,' said Sam. 'Let's put it this way. There are four hundred males and twenty-three females in this place.'

Cawston and his labourer returned with various items of Newby's luggage.

'Eight of them are under ten – I don't know if you're into paedophilia, but I'm not,' Sam continued, enjoying Newby's consternation at his discussing such things within the boys' earshot. 'Twelve of them are married, and one, as we all know only too well, is engaged to be married. If they stray, they don't do it here.'

'Is there more in the boot, sir?' asked Cawston.

'Except for one, of course,' said Sam. 'But she's a nympho.'

'No,' Newby said, with a quick, disapproving glance at Sam. 'It was frozen up this morning – I couldn't use it.' He dug in his pocket for change.

'And you can get too much of a good thing,' Sam went on, ignoring Newby's embarrassment.

Newby hurriedly tipped the boys, thanking them, shepherding them to the door.

'One is Matron,' continued Sam, 'who is twice my size and coming up for sixty-five. And the other one is Caroline.'

Newby closed the door with a sigh of relief, and took cigarettes from his jacket pocket. He lit one as he considered Sam's words. 'Which one's the nympho?' he asked.

Sam had been expecting a reproof. He grinned. 'You'll find out,' he said. 'Are you coming to the pub?'

'Mrs Knight! Mrs Knight!'

Caroline turned in the direction of the peremptory treble.

'Mrs Knight – Mrs Hamlyn says could you possibly pop up to see her if you have a moment?'

The faithful reproduction of Diana Hamlyn's request made Caroline smile, and she followed the child back to the junior dormitory, and popped up to see Diana, who sat amid trunks and suitcases and sundry grey-blazered small boys, a blonde, vivacious splash of colour.

'. . . and this has no name-tag.' She looked at the child over her reading-glasses, which were perched on the end of her nose. 'You can write your name, can you, young man?'

The child smiled shyly at her mock sternness, and Diana went on. 'Two white shirts, two—' She looked up and smiled. 'Oh, super, Caroline. Are you on your way back to the staff block by any chance? The thing is that I only found out about this new chap this morning – I mean, he hasn't had an invitation for drinks. I'm stuck here with these horrors, and I'm hours behind – could you be an angel and pop in to tell him he's more than welcome?'

I'll bet he is, thought Caroline, as she tried to think of a way of refusing. Diana always welcomed a new man. She was an odd mixture of sense and sensibility.

'Can you?' Diana asked. 'Or are you fearfully busy?'

No, Caroline wasn't fearfully busy. But she hadn't been able to get away from Philip Newby fast enough, and she had no desire to go back. She still tried to think of a plausible excuse, but none presented itself. She supposed she was being silly; it wasn't as if he *had* actually made a pass at her or anything. And, if the worst came to the worst, she could certainly run faster than him.

Diana smiled her thanks. 'Two vests,' she said, carrying on with her inventory. 'I'm assuming you have one on.'

He smiled again, pinkly confirming her supposition. Diana was in her element with the little ones, thought Caroline, and not for the first time wondered why she had none of her own.

And she delivered Philip's message from Diana. At first he was diffident, almost shy; she wondered if she had imagined the whole thing until after a few moments she became aware of his intense interest once more.

It surprised her a little that she thought of him as Philip. Not as Philip Newby, or Mr Newby, or just Newby, as Sam called him. There was something about Philip that she recognised, and understood. The shared experience of the accident, perhaps; she didn't know.

'Is it the sort of thing I ought to go to?' he asked her calves.

'Well, he's just been appointed deputy head,' she said. 'That's what they're celebrating. I don't know how strong you are on keeping in with the bosses. But it's a good way to meet the rest of the staff.'

His eyes travelled up, lingering now and then, before meeting hers. 'I suppose I should go,' he said.

She resisted the temptation to pull the collar of her blouse together as his eyes rested on the little line of cleavage of which she was now as intensely aware as he was. She stood up. 'They live at the top of the junior dormitory,' she said. 'That's the building just across the side-road.'

'The one that backs on to the car park?'

'That's right,' she said, going to the door, wondering if he was actually listening to anything she said.

'What about the Grand Tour?' he asked, getting to his feet.

Damn. She'd forgotten about that. He did listen, apparently. 'Of course,' she said, her heart sinking at the thought.

He wanted to see everything, but she could see that trying to keep his feet on the slippery cobbles of the little lane through the buildings was painfully difficult. She was uncharitably grateful to the road surface for taking his mind off her anatomy.

Over the years, buildings had been added to the grounds until it looked like a small village; a tour merely confused new people. But, she assured Philip as they went into the main building, he would find his way about eventually.

She showed him the staff room, and one of the classrooms, then popped her head round Barry Treadwell's door.

'Oh, I beg your pardon,' she said, when she saw that he had someone with him. 'I was just showing Philip round.'

'Come in, come in,' Treadwell said. 'Philip may as well find out that it's not all roses.' He gestured towards the dark-haired woman with him. 'This is Detective Sergeant Hill,' he said.

Sergeant Hill was about her own age, well dressed, and attractive. Caroline nodded to her, puzzled by her presence, and delighted that she was female, which would not please Barry at all.

'Something's gone missing,' Barry said by way of explanation. 'Already.'

'We've got a thief,' she said to Philip. 'Watch your valuables.' She turned back to Treadwell. 'I'll leave you to it,' she said.

They left the headmaster's study, and went back downstairs, where she ticked off doors as they passed. 'Storeroom, boiler room – and this,' she said, opening the insignificant door at the end of the corridor, 'will surprise you.'

She liked introducing people to the Great Hall by its internal door, watching their faces as they found themselves in its baronial splendour.

Philip looked up at the exposed beams arching across the high ceiling, and walked slowly towards one of the carved pillars, his face breaking into a slow smile at the sheer chaotic bad taste of it all.

'It's called the Great Hall,' she said, as they crossed over, towards the double doors by which people more usually entered. 'The original school had it built on, for reasons best-known to the founder. It's used for assembly, prize-giving, lectures – that sort of thing. This is where we'll be holding the Sesquicentennial Ball.'

'Lovely word,' he said. 'You'd have to celebrate it just so you could use it. It's next month, isn't it?' he asked.

'Yes. Friday the fourteenth. St Valentine's Day.'

His face broke into a sudden and engaging smile. '*That's* what Sam needs the adjectival dinner-jacket for!' he said.

'Correct,' she said, laughing, as she pushed open the double doors to the entrance-hall.

'Loos, cloakroom, telephone,' she said, tackling the huge, arched outside door which weighed about a ton, and stepped out into the courtyard.

Philip followed her, his step becoming unsure once more as he made his way across the cobbles.

'What are all these buildings?' he asked, stopping by one, trying not to look as though he was recovering from his short journey across the courtyard.

Caroline pointed to the one behind the Hall. 'That's the Dining Hall,' she said. 'Most people just call it the canteen. And the new one behind that is the gymnasium.'

Philip nodded. 'What's in here?' he asked, trying the handle of the door he was pretending not to lean on. 'Oh,' he said, as visitors always did, when he found himself looking directly at the snow-covered playing-field through the open wall at the other side.

'The Barn,' said Caroline. 'At least that's what it used to be. It's even got a hay-loft.' She led the way in.

'So it has,' said Philip. 'Do you have some use for hay?'

Caroline stiffened slightly. 'Not to feed animals,' she said. Diana sometimes had a use for hay, she thought, but she didn't burden Philip with explanations. He looked a little puzzled at her cryptic answer, and she smiled briefly. 'Anyway – that lot's well past its sell-by date,' she said. 'We tend to use this place like other people use attics.'

'So I see,' said Philip.

Boxes, old books, builders' left-overs lined the floor along the walls. But you could still have held a dance in what was left. They almost had, but the effort of getting it cleared out had proved too much for Barry.

'Couldn't it be put to some better use?' asked Philip. 'All this space?'

'Ah – you and Sam had better get together,' Caroline said. 'He wants it to be turned into a new art room. The big doors face north, apparently. He wants glass put in their place, and all sorts of things.' She smiled. 'But that costs money, and this school doesn't have a lot of that.'

They wandered out, and Caroline slid the barn doors shut.

'They're supposed to be kept closed,' she said. 'But the kids play in here.' She turned. 'That's the junior dormitory,' she said, pointing across the playing-field. 'The Hamlyns' flat is at the top.' She smiled at his confused expression. 'You'll get your bearings,' she said.

'Don't you have a garden, or something?' Philip asked.

'No,' she said. 'There's no room. We've got buildings everywhere there was once a space.'

He frowned a little. 'I thought I remembered a garden,' he said.

As they moved off again, his stick skidded on the frozen cobbles, shooting out of his hand; Caroline retrieved it, examining it for damage.

'There's a little crack just about halfway down,' she said concernedly.

He almost snatched it from her. 'I know,' he said.

They carried on, more slowly now that he was taking care with the stick, and on their way back to the staff block Caroline explained the buildings that huddled round the lane. There had been a time when the enrolment had increased rather than decreased every year, and the result was a wonderful mixture of periods and mock-periods. The whole place was an architect's nightmare, and Caroline liked it.

Philip suddenly stopped, as they emerged from the lane. 'There's no need to see me home,' he snapped.

Caroline raised an eyebrow. 'I live here, too,' she pointed out.

His unexpected smile appeared again. 'Sorry,' he said.

Caroline smiled back. When he wasn't ogling her, or biting her head off, he wasn't all that bad. In fact, he reminded her of Andrew; she wasn't surprised that they had been friends.

Outside the light faded, and Judy Hill tried to sound interested in Mr Treadwell's problems.

'And it began about eighteen months ago?' she asked, taking out her notebook.

'Yes, just about. A year ago last September – at the beginning of the autumn term. At first, we didn't even realise we had a thief – the odd thing went missing now and then, but it wasn't constant. There would be months when nothing went missing. But eventually we knew it couldn't be coincidence.'

'Do you have a list of the stolen items?'

'Not as such,' he said. 'I've noted them down here and there, but I haven't done an actual list. I can let you have one, if you like.'

'Yes, please,' she said, trying not to yawn. 'Have you done anything yourself about the thefts?'

'I made an announcement at assembly. Told everyone to keep a careful eye on anything that might be stolen, and to report anything that was. I advised the thief to stop, because if he was caught he would be expelled.'

Dynamic leadership, Judy thought, and her brown eyes widened a little as she wrote. 'You're certain it is one of the boys?' she asked.

'Well,' he said, 'yes. Yes, I imagine it is.' He got up and looked out at the darkening sky. 'I think we must be seen to be doing something about it.'

'What's gone missing today?'

'A ring – not worth much but, then, none of it is. It belongs to one of the teachers. She'd left it on the . . .'

Judy wrote down what he was saying. There wasn't much you could do about this sort of stealing, with upwards of four hundred suspects. On the first day of term, everyone was all over the place. There were no classes; there was nothing to pin anyone down to a particular place at a particular time. Whoever it was, he bided his time, and took great care not to get caught. It was obviously purely to irritate.

Trust Lloyd to land her with this on her first day back. 'As a favour to Chief Superintendent Allison,' he had said, blue eyes shining with suspect honesty. 'The headmaster doesn't want uniforms all over the show.'

'What's wrong with Sandwell?' she had asked.

'Mr Allison thinks a woman would be less threatening to the lads.' He had grinned mischievously. 'And I thought it would be a nice way to ease you back into harness.'

This, of course, was Lloyd's way of getting at her, Judy thought darkly, as she glanced at her notes, at the list she had made of where the thefts had occurred.

'Would I be right in thinking that these are mainly staff areas?' She glanced down the list. 'Staff room, sports pavilion, secretary's office, kitchen, storeroom . . .' she read.

'Yes,' he said testily, then apologised. 'It is popularly believed to be a member of staff,' he admitted. 'But that's out of the question.'

'Well,' said Judy, 'I'd better start with the boys, if you think it's one of them.'

'How?' asked Treadwell, alarmed.

'Do you have a head boy?' Judy asked.

'Oh, yes.'

'Perhaps if I speak to him. If it is one of the boys, he quite probably has an idea who.'

'He'd never tell you if he did. That would be sneaking.'

'I know. But he might warn off whoever it is. Or just knowing that the police have been called in might put the thief off. And, if it is a member of staff, they might get an attack of conscience if the boys seem to be being suspected.'

That was what Treadwell was hoping.

She closed her notebook. 'It isn't very satisfactory, but . . .'

'Yes, yes.' Treadwell stood up. 'I'll send Matthew in,' he said. 'In the meantime, I'm sure you could do with a cup of tea.'

Judy smiled, and Treadwell left. Again, she found her thoughts turning to Lloyd, and was irritated with herself for being unable to divorce her personal life from her professional life. She had always been able to before.

The tea came, brought in by a youth who looked to Judy far older than most of the constables with whom she worked. She stood up and relieved him of the cup and saucer. He was slightly taller than she was, and somehow contrived to make his uniform look like what the fashionable man-about-town was wearing, with exactly the correct amount of cuff showing, and an air of elegance that Lloyd would have envied. Lloyd somehow never looked like that. Someone she knew did, though; he reminded her of someone. Not his features. His manner, his personality.

'Matthew Cawston,' he said smoothly. 'Mr Treadwell said that you wanted to speak to me.'

Judy turned her mind once more to work, until at last she was leaving the school, and on her way home.

Two weeks since her promise. Two weeks of steeling herself, lecturing herself, loathing herself for being such a coward, had crystallised into two words. Tell him. Tell him at breakfast, before he goes to work. Tell him when he comes home from work. Tell him in the evening, when he's settling down to watch television. Tell him before you go to bed, tell him at breakfast. It wasn't as if it would come as all that much of a surprise to him; Michael had probably already guessed about her and Lloyd. But somehow none of that made it any easier. And it had only been a fortnight ago that she had made her mind up to leave him; she had to pick the right moment.

She drove home with the words beating in her mind like a pulse. It was a half-hour drive from the school, which contrived almost literally to be in the middle of nowhere, but which somehow came under the purview of Stansfield Constabulary. At last she saw the orange lights flanking the snow-lined dual carriageway into the new town, and now-familiar landmarks came into view. The industrial estate with its neat factory units looking like terraced houses, and the superstore looking like an enormous Swiss chalet, with its seemingly permanent covering of snow. The DIY store with swings and see-saws and slides; the adventure playground, with tyres and planks.

A left turn, and she would be in the village that had been there since Elizabethan times. The old Stansfield, where Lloyd lived.

Tell Lloyd that you still haven't told Michael. I dare you.

She took the right turn.

Michael smiled when she came in. Don't *smile*, why would you smile? Criticise me for something, God knows that's what you usually do. Say that it's high time we moved out of this town. Go on about how much we'd get for the house if we put it on the market. Tell me that you've got filing clerks earning more than I do, so it's not as though my job's that important, and you could get a job anywhere. Prove you don't understand, don't want to understand – *don't smile.*

'How did it go?' he asked.

'What?'

'Your first day back.'

'Oh. Fine.'

'Are they going to give you a medal or something?'

'Good God, I hope not.' She took off her coat and went out into the hallway to hang it up.

'Why not?' he called through. 'You were hurt in the line of duty – you could have got killed.'

She went back. 'Well, I wasn't,' she said.

'No, thank God.'

Tell him. 'Michael, I want to tell you—'

'Shall I tell you something funny?' he said, interrupting her.

She sat down with a sigh.

'When I came home, and the house was in darkness – I forgot you were back at work. I was expecting you to be here.'

Oh, here we go, she thought. How nice it was to have her at home. So why didn't she just give up her job and go with him to a nice middle-class town and have a baby before it was too late?

'And for a moment ...' He laughed a little shyly. 'For a moment, I thought you'd left me.'

She looked up at him. 'Left you?' she repeated dully.

'It wasn't such a strange thing to think,' he said. 'Was it? I mean – we're not even ... Well, I just thought you had. And then I realised you were just at work,' he said. 'But I thought ... other men don't think their wives have left them just because the light's out. And I know things haven't been too good since I got the promotion – but that's just because we're not used to being together all the time. We've drifted apart, that's all.'

Judy couldn't speak.

'But we've stayed together ten years, and I don't want to lose you, Judy.' His eyes dropped away from hers. 'I really thought you'd gone,' he said. 'And I felt exactly like I did when I was three years old and lost my mother in Woolworth's. Total panic.'

Judy listened to the little speech with a dismay which she felt must show on her face, but he didn't seem to notice.

He metaphorically picked himself up and dusted himself off. 'Well, now I've said it. What were you going to tell me?'

'Oh,' she said, looking away from him as she told a rare lie. 'Nothing. I don't remember.'

'Can't have been anything important, then,' he said, with a smile. 'Would you like a drink?'

*

Matthew Cawston looked up at the windows of Palmerston House, checking that all the lights were out. His fellow-prefects would go from room to room, opening the doors; Matthew thought that a waste of energy. Tonight, something was going on in the junior dorm which interested him. And they hadn't all arrived yet.

He stepped out of the shadow of the building, and walked to the end of the lane, where he lit an illicit cigarette. He shook the match out and buttoned his jacket against the chill. He was glad to be back at school, and away from all the rowing at home. He had caused it, of course, by refusing to be put into some sort of pigeon-hole by his father. His mother had taken his side, as she always did, so before long it was his mother and father who were shouting at one another.

School was infinitely preferable to that. Here, they only wanted him to shine for them, and he could do that without trying. He drew deeply on the cigarette, watching stars begin to appear as the clouds drifted off, and the temperature fell once more.

'What are you intending doing with your life?' his father had demanded to know during one of the interminable sessions.

Matthew didn't know, but he couldn't explain that to his father. He was sixteen. Why should he start mapping his life out? He didn't know if what interested him now would still interest him at twenty-six, or forty-six. He wasn't sure what did interest him now, anyway. He was good at most things; studying came easily to him, and passing exams was taken for granted. His father expected him to go on and get a double first at Oxford, but that didn't interest Matthew. There was no challenge in that.

The only subject in which he had any real interest was English. English wasn't like other subjects, where everything was cut and dried, right or wrong. He enjoyed the books that the others moaned about having to read; he liked discussing them, dissecting them, criticising them. He'd seen the new English teacher limping about with Mrs Knight, and wondered what he'd be like. He must be good, for them to have kept his job open for such a long time.

The tip of the cigarette glowed red in the darkness, and Matthew moved back into the lane, in case some over-zealous fellow-prefect spotted it. The housemaster was at the Hamlyns' do, so no fear of his creeping up behind him. All in all, it wasn't a bad school. It had rules and regulations, like all schools, and Matthew enjoyed that; it gave him the chance to break them without getting caught. His expertise was evidenced by the fact of his having been made head boy, an honour which Treadwell had solemnly conferred upon him while Matthew kept a straight face.

Footsteps came along the road from the staff block; Matthew dropped the cigarette and stood on it, strolling out into the light again.

'Good evening, Mrs Knight,' he said.

'Hello, Matthew. Is there something wrong?'

'No, not at all. I just felt like a breath of air.'

'How did you get on with the policewoman?' she asked.

'Very well, thank you. She said that it was really crime prevention at this stage – a case of advising everyone to lock desks and rooms, and so on. She said we should report to Mr Treadwell if we saw anyone hanging round the lockers or anything like that.'

She nodded. 'I don't suppose there's much the police can do about it, really,' she said.

'No.' Matthew let her get a couple of steps away. 'Oh – Mrs Knight. I was pleased to hear about Mr Hamlyn.'

'I'll tell him,' she said, smiling.

Matthew watched her go. He *had* been pleased to hear about Hamlyn's promotion; he liked him, liked his absent-minded professor air, which was entirely genuine. Hamlyn knew what he wanted to do with his life, and he was doing it, to the exclusion of all else. He wanted to immerse himself in maths and logic and solve complicated puzzles. It wouldn't do for Matthew, but he admired Hamlyn's single-mindedness, his courage. Because it took courage to do what you wanted to do, and to hell with what people thought. And that even included his choice of wife. Matthew smiled as he thought of Mrs Hamlyn, as unlike her husband as it was possible to get, and still be of the same species.

He gave Mrs Knight time to get upstairs to the Hamlyns' living-quarters, then walked quickly across the road, down the side-road to the car park, and along to the junior dorm's fire-escape. The light went on in the Hamlyns' bedroom as it had with each new arrival, and went off again after a moment.

Mrs Knight's late arrival had made it more of a challenge than it might have been; people might even be thinking of leaving soon. But, then, again, people were innately polite, and wouldn't go as soon as someone had arrived. He would give himself three minutes, he thought, glancing at his watch in the dim, almost non-existent car park lighting.

A glance over his shoulder, before he ascended the metal steps; there was no one else about on this cold night.

On the balcony, it was simplicity itself. Interior décor was not something for which the school was renowned, and the curtains, made for a quite different window, left a gap down the side through which he could see the darkened room. It was easy to step from the balcony to the window-ledge, after he had knocked away the frozen snow. The window didn't close properly; Matthew had already established that. It pivoted open, and he put his arm through, pushing down the handle of the balcony door.

Slowly, carefully, he opened it; to his surprise and horror, it made a deafening squeak, but it couldn't have been that loud inside the house. He waited a second or two before going in, and noiselessly crossed to the light-switch. He smiled at the heap of coats on the bed, and began going through the pockets. He didn't care what he found; if he found nothing, he would take the travelling alarm-clock that sat on the bedside table. But he would prefer it to be something out of a coat, or a jacket.

It had been accidental, to start with. The very first thing he had taken had made them all decide it had to have been Mrs Knight; now, he shadowed her, taking things when the opportunity presented itself. It was fun. And this morning he had struck gold in the ladies' loo, waiting until she had left it empty, then slipping in unseen. He could hardly believe his luck when he saw the ring.

He moved to the side of the bed, standing still as the door blew shut again, with another loud squeak. Then he picked up the sheepskin jacket affected by Newby, the English teacher, and his hand closed over a packet of cigarettes, followed by a box of matches. They went into his pocket, joining his own; a further search of the coats produced a lady's comb and a pound coin.

At first, he didn't recognise the sound; by the time he realised that it was the tap of Newby's stick on the corridor, it was too late. He thought he would have time to make it back out before Newby got to the room, but Newby moved faster than he'd suspected; desperate, Matthew slipped behind the curtains, drawing his feet up on to the window-sill as the door opened. He couldn't get out without pushing open the balcony door, and he couldn't do that without attracting attention. So he just had to stay there.

Through the gap in the curtains, Matthew watched as Newby pulled coats aside to reach his jacket. He was feeling in the pockets, frowning, when Mrs Hamlyn appeared, standing in the doorway.

'Not leaving us, are you, Philip?'

'Just came to get my cigarettes,' Newby said. 'But I must have left them at the flat.'

'Is that why you left?' she asked. 'Or is it because Caroline's arrived?'

Newby looked down at his feet for a moment. 'I don't know what you mean,' he said.

'Yes, you do. But she's much too complicated for you, Philip. Take my advice – don't get involved.'

'I don't even know her, Mrs Hamlyn. I only met her this morning.'

'I'm very uncomplicated,' she went on. 'You'd be much better off with me.'

Matthew held his breath.

'Mrs Hamlyn, I—'

'She's never got over Andrew,' Mrs Hamlyn went on.

'That's hardly any of my business,' said Newby.

'It's everyone's business,' said Mrs Hamlyn. 'She's making it everyone's business – if your cigarettes have gone, that's probably because Caroline's just been up here.'

'What?' said Newby.

Mrs Hamlyn gave a slight shrug.

'You're not suggesting that Caroline—?'

Matthew so far forgot his unenviable position to permit himself a smile.

'She can't help it,' said Mrs Hamlyn. 'I'm just warning you.'

'I've probably left my cigarettes in the flat,' Newby said again, his tone growing angry. 'And I hardly think they merit warnings being issued.'

Mrs Hamlyn smiled. 'I'm not warning you to keep an eye on your cigarettes,' she said. 'I'm warning you not to get involved with Caroline. She's supposed to be seeing a psychiatrist or something, but she doesn't.'

'I can't imagine what you mean, "get involved".'

'Oh, come on, Philip. I saw the way you looked at her.'

There was an uncomfortable silence, during which Matthew didn't dare breathe, and Newby grew red and sullen, like one of the first-years caught reading a girlie magazine.

Mrs Hamlyn glanced down at Newby's leg. 'Does it give you much trouble?' she asked, nodding at it as she spoke.

'Not really,' said Newby, recovering some composure now that the subject had been changed.

'I mean – it would be a frightful bore if it interfered with your normal activities.' She lifted her eyes to his again. 'I do hope it doesn't,' she said.

It sounded like an innocent remark, but its implication was not lost on Matthew, or Newby.

'Hardly at all,' he said. 'I'd better be getting back.' Newby went towards the door in the sudden way he had of moving. He didn't look awkward with the stick; it was as if it was just a part of him. 'If you'll excuse me, Mrs Hamlyn,' he said.

She didn't move.

'Could you excuse me?' he asked again.

'I'm sure you could squeeze past,' she said, not moving.

Matthew's eyes widened. He'd heard the stories about Diana Hamlyn, but he had always assumed they were exaggerated.

'Mrs Hamlyn, I—'

'How formal. Do call me Diana.'

'Mrs Hamlyn,' he said firmly. 'I think I should get back.'

She smiled. 'I'd be more fun than a cigarette,' she said. 'And much better for you.'

Newby gave a brief smile. 'If you could just move, please,' he said.

She came in, then, closing the door, and leaning on it. 'I've moved,' she said.

A mixture of fear and fascination warred within Matthew as, open-mouthed, he watched her turn the key and remove it from the lock. Fascination won; he forgot his own predicament as he watched Newby deal with his.

'I presume this is your idea of a joke,' Newby said.

'It is quite amusing.' She came up close to Newby, and smiled.

'We met exactly an hour ago, Mrs Hamlyn,' said Newby. 'I hardly know you.'

'We could remedy that,' she said, lightly touching his chest.

Newby moved away from her, and sat down, his hands crossed over the top of his walking-stick. 'If the positions were reversed,' he said, 'you could slap my face – even shout for help. As it is, I'll just have to wait for you to get bored.'

'You were a friend of Andrew Knight's, weren't you?' she asked.

'Yes.' Newby sounded guarded.

'Oh, don't worry,' she said. 'I wasn't. Not like that, anyway. He had no time for me – he was too much in love with Caroline.' She sighed. 'I've a dreadful suspicion that so are you,' she said, and smiled, throwing him the key.

He didn't try to catch it; it clattered to the ground, perilously close to the window, and Matthew closed his eyes. He opened them as Newby addressed himself to the problem; he saw the pain on his face as he leaned as much of his weight as he could on the stick, and scooped up the key. For a moment, as Newby straightened up, it was as if he were looking directly at Matthew, but he wasn't. He was waiting for the pain to go before he turned to face Mrs Hamlyn.

'Thank you,' he said, going to the door, unlocking it.

'Making sheep's eyes at Caroline won't get you anywhere,' Mrs Hamlyn said. 'Sam's been trying for months.'

Newby coloured a little. His stick tapped quickly down the corridor, and Mrs Hamlyn smiled to herself, putting out the light as she left.

Matthew let out a long sigh of relief, and waited until it was safe before pushing open the treacherous balcony-door and making his exit. Outside, he repeated the exercise in reverse; his arm through the window, he pulled the door shut. He closed the window as much as it ever closed, checked that he still had everything he had taken, and almost strolled back down the fire-escape steps, back to Palmerston House.

Detective Chief Inspector Lloyd poured himself a beer, picked up his plate of sandwiches, and went through to the living-room, kicking the door shut behind him.

He put the sandwiches on the table, the beer on the floor, and eased off his shoes, sitting down in the reclining chair that had been his first major purchase after his divorce. He picked up the television remote control, and the television flashed into silent life as he muted the sound. He'd waited years for this film to be shown again. He'd had hair the last time it had been on. Well, rather more than he'd got now, anyway.

There was something to be said for living alone, he thought, as he reached for the video remote. You could watch films that went on until one fifteen in the morning, *and* record them, without being nagged to death.

Judy would think he was quite mad, of course.

'Why watch it in the middle of the night when you're recording it anyway? Why record it when you've seen it three times already? Why even watch it twice?'

'Oh, for God's sake, I just want to watch the film. Go to bed if you don't like it.'

'I'll hear it through the wall – how can I sleep?'

'Then, watch it with me.'

'I don't want to watch it.'

He smiled. It would be better, he conceded, if she was actually there, saying all that, instead of just in his head. As it was, she had never stayed all night with him, and all their rows were about their situation, not about normal domestic differences.

'As for people fantasising rows . . .'

Judy would have him certified if she knew everything that went on in his head.

He wondered what she was doing now, then wished he hadn't. Her assurances that the marriage was all over bar the shouting didn't help, though he knew it was the truth. She still spent her nights with Michael instead of with him, and what was or wasn't happening was of secondary importance.

She had promised to tell Michael, and she would. But she hadn't promised when, and Judy had a positive phobia about commitment.

But perhaps, he thought, with a total lack of conviction, perhaps she was telling him even now. Perhaps she would turn up at his door in half an hour, saying that she had finally left him. He smiled to himself. If she did, she would spoil the film, and wouldn't that be just like her?

The credits rolled on the news programme, to which he had not been listening, and he turned up the sound. He checked the video. Right channel. As a slide of tomorrow's early programmes went up, he started the tape, and paused it, ready to roll on cue.

'*And now*,' said the announcer smoothly, '*in a change to our advertised programme* . . .'

Lloyd stared at the screen, at the 'tribute' to the actor whose death had presumably been reported in the previous programme. One of his old films. How dragging a few reels of film out could possibly be regarded as a tribute was beyond him. Anyone who wanted to see the damn thing wouldn't know it was on.

He was still watching, still recording, as though it would somehow transform itself into *his* old film, but it wouldn't. With a deep sigh, he switched off the television, and stopped the tape.

He bit disconsolately into a sandwich. No chance of her turning up now.

Chapter Two

The Sesquicentennial Ball had finally arrived; Caroline had other plans, which included Sam. 'Are we still on for tonight?' he asked, sitting opposite her.

She barely looked up from her newspaper. 'Yes,' she said.

It was hardly enthusiastic, but it was in the affirmative. Sam picked up his knife and fork, as she turned her attention once more to what seemed to be the racing pages. He prodded the potatoes. 'What did you have?' he asked.

'The quiche.'

'I think so should I have done.' But despite his misgivings he began to eat; he was ravenous. He glanced up now and then at Caroline's absorbed face. 'Are you fond of a flutter?' he asked.

'No.'

God. Was she going to be like this tonight? Sam didn't care for hard work, and that's just what Caroline was. He was beginning to see Matron's attractions. She presumably had the appropriate anatomy, which was the only qualification required.

But Caroline had got hold of tickets for a midnight showing of some foreign film of which he'd never heard, but which, it appeared, anyone worth his artistic salt would kill to see. And since it was at midnight she obviously didn't want to go alone. So, call for Sam, who she knew would welcome any excuse to leave the festivities. He was under no illusion about why he had been thus honoured, but he had no pride.

He was to leave the ball at eleven, and pick Caroline up from the junior dorm. The film, he understood, concerned itself high-mindedly with erotica; perhaps she had picked him because she imagined that artists, like doctors, viewed these things with a detached professionalism.

They didn't. At any rate, *he* didn't. He couldn't wait any longer for Caroline.

'I trust Diana's suitably grateful for your offer to babysit,' he said. 'Imagine – the Great Hall full of men, and she might have been stuck with a load of eleven-year-olds.'

'Diana isn't obliged to look after them,' she said, not lifting her head from the paper.

'Then, I trust the school is suitably grateful,' he persisted. At least he'd got a whole sentence out of her.

'Look – I didn't mind organising it, but I certainly didn't want to go to this thing. Both Robert and Diana have to be there at least until the speeches are over. Someone has to supervise the kids, so I volunteered – is that all right with you?'

Sam decided that saying nothing was the wisest course.

'And she is leaving early so that you and I can go to this film,' Caroline added.

'She's probably, got some man lined up,' said Sam.

'My God – they say women are bitchy.'

'You're a woman,' said Sam. 'You don't know what she's like. Ask Newby, if you don't believe me. She's been trying to seduce him for weeks.' He sat back a little. 'But he's only got eyes for you,' he said.

'Have you got your dinner-jacket?' she asked, transparently changing the subject.

'Not yet.'

'Oh, Sam!' She got up.

Sam shrugged. 'I'm picking it up this afternoon,' he said. 'Don't you worry.'

'I'm not worried,' she said. 'But you can only get away with being just so eccentric, you know. Even famous artists have to conform sometimes – or they might lose their cushy jobs.'

She walked off, and Sam watched her go out of the corner of his eye. Cushy job, he thought sourly, returning to his stew and potatoes. Trying to teach the rudiments of art to a lot of talent-less youths who wouldn't know a Picasso from a pikestaff. That wasn't cushy; it was soul-destroying.

And now they wanted him to sing for his supper; stand up and make speeches to blue-rinsed women and paunchy men about how they should keep the school going for another hundred and fifty years by sponsoring scholarships which would be named after them; sales-talking local yuppies into sending their sons there. And, come to that, their daughters – next year, they were accepting girls – how positively modern could you get? And who better than 'one of our foremost modern artists' to give them the sales pitch?

He supposed, to be fair, that anyone would be better than Barry Treadwell, who thought women were of no practical use whatsoever – and who could blame him, with Marcia for a wife? And who was to say that he was wrong, come to that?

He couldn't think why he was so hungry; he persuaded the girl to give him a second helping, and sat down. He hadn't felt as hungry as this since he was doing stuff for the exhibition. In the golden days, when inspiration never seemed to dry up; when the desire to work was so strong that it sharpened his senses and his appetites, and he would eat and drink and . . .

It had been so long that he had failed to recognise the symptoms. He looked round. Yes. Yes, there were things here, even here, that could inspire. Look at *that*, he thought, as the girl splashed tea into a mug from a push-button urn. Machines. He loved machines. He didn't know what he would paint yet. That still had to come. But he would paint something, soon. And in the meantime the hunger would burn, and would have to be staved off in other ways. Food. Women. Only when he started painting, could it truly be satisfied. It was difficult, this period of increased awareness; difficult to live through, difficult to control. But it meant that he was working again. He might look as though he was sitting here eating stew, but he was working. And this school could stuff its contract. And its dinner dance. He smiled. But no, it would be a shame to waste the opportunity.

He pushed his plate away. He'd go, complete with dinner-jacket. And he'd make them sit up.

As the speeches droned on, Matthew glanced round the Hall at the talent, as his father called females. Earlier in the day, they had been the subject of brisk trade-offs.

'*And* your pen-knife.'

'It's a Swiss army knife! She's not worth that.'

'Then, you can't have her.'

'You hang on to your knife, Simmons – women aren't worth it.'

'You'd know, and I don't think.'

The reason for the black-marketeering was the First Dance, which was how it had been described in the handout from the office, and the only way in which Matthew could think of it, with capital letters.

The senior boys had each been allocated a partner for the First Dance; they were to politely request (sic) the First Dance, dance with the lady, and return her to her table. This was in honour of St Valentine, apparently, in view of the 'happy coincidence' of the dates.

The ladies were a mixture of staff, governors, various wives, and sundry local schoolgirls, and it was this last which had brought out the entrepreneurial skills of those who had drawn them.

After the First Dance, the boys could dance or not, as they wished. The desirability of getting the right partner first time round was obvious. They were in school uniform, which hadn't pleased anyone, and therefore the chance to impress was more necessary than ever. Not necessary enough, however, to part with a Swiss army knife. In the end, the lady went, for a give-away solar-powered calculator, to another bidder altogether.

Matthew had drawn the headmaster's wife, but he hadn't joined in the bidding for a more suitable partner, because she would give him access to the top table, and that had given Matthew an idea.

He was working on something very special for tonight, and Marcia Treadwell was going to help him, albeit unwittingly, to achieve it. Trust Treadwell, he thought, to have married someone like that. A woman for whom the word vacant might have been coined; a downtrodden doormat of a woman who was about as exciting as a piece of boiled cod, and who went pink if she thought she had done or said anything of which others might disapprove.

Matthew's eyes were fixed firmly on the top table, as he waited for his moment to arrive. Anything would do; he didn't mind what it was, just as long as it was on the top table.

Sam Waters finished his speech; what little Matthew had noticed of it had seemed very ordinary. People were clapping with some enthusiasm, which was a disappointment. Matthew had rather hoped that Sam at least could be relied upon to say something deeply offensive. He had imagined that their illustrious and foul-mouthed art teacher might sit down to boos, but no such luck. His jacket took a bit of getting used to, though, he had to give him that.

The applause had barely died away when Waters just walked out. Matthew smiled, as Treadwell, already on his feet, watched him leave. Good old Sam, he thought, frowning a little as he tried to make out the object on the table where Sam had been sitting.

When he realised what it was, he smiled broadly, and clapped vigorously as Treadwell cleared his throat to indicate the start of his speech.

It was his chance.

The knock at the door made Caroline jump; she wasn't expecting anyone. Please God, don't let it be one of the boys, she thought. No temperatures, no spots, no sore throats, not tonight. She opened the door to Sam, and stared at him without speaking, not sure whether it was his presence or his attire that had actually struck her dumb.

'What on earth are you doing here?' she said at last.

'The speeches are over.' He smiled. 'Mine is, at any rate, and who wants to hear any other bugger's? I thought I'd come and keep you company.' He looked at her expectantly. 'Well,' he said. 'Do I get to come in?'

'Did you really wear that to the dinner?' she asked, as he walked in past her.

'I did. And very splendid everyone agreed it was.'

'Where in God's name did you get it?'

He grinned. 'Theatrical costumier,' he said. 'A friend of mine. I asked him for something which would be worn by an MC at a strip show, and this is what he came up with.' He strolled up and down, modelling it. 'Good, isn't it?'

Caroline didn't smile. 'You enjoyed showing Barry up, did you?'

'Yes,' he said. 'Yes, I think I did.'

'We can't go yet,' she said. 'Diana isn't due for at least an hour.'

'I know,' he replied conspiratorially. 'How about a cup of coffee, then?'

And she found herself in the kitchen, making coffee, wishing Sam was anywhere but there, wishing that the Hamlyns had a more plebeian taste in coffee. It seemed to be taking for ever.

'What kind of music do the Hamlyns run to?' Sam called through.

'I don't know. Don't put it on too loud.'

'Boys that age can sleep through anything,' Sam said. 'Besides, they're downstairs. Oh – *Hits of the Fifties* – that sounds like my scene. Who'd have thought Hamlyn was a rock fan? You're a bit young, I suppose. Still – we'll give your ears a treat, shall we?'

When she took the coffee through, the record was being played at what even she had to agree was a modest level. He had removed the jacket to reveal an even more hideous shirt; he sat in one armchair, and the jacket lay over the other. She handed him his coffee, and sat on the sofa.

'I'm not going anywhere with you dressed like that,' she said.

'I thought it was a dressing-up do,' he said.

'It is. It isn't a fancy-dress do.'

He grinned. 'Don't worry. I'll change into a respectable suit before we go.' He got up, and joined her on the sofa. 'But I had to let you see it, didn't I?'

His arm was round her shoulders, and his lips planted a chaste kiss on her cheek. 'Fifties music, fifties ploy,' he said.

'What?'

'Sit in one chair, throw jacket over the other. The girl feels obliged to sit on the sofa, where, in due course, you join her.'

His lips were on hers, and she turned her head away. 'Don't, Sam, please.'

He sat back with a sigh. 'Christ, you're hard work,' he said. 'It's St Valentine's night – relax, for God's sake.'

'Don't be silly, Sam,' she said, pushing him off. 'I think you should go and get changed.'

'I'm willing to get out of these clothes any time you say.' His lips were at her temple.

'Stop it, Sam,' she said. 'Please. We've been through all this.'

'Don't I know it? You're not ready. Great. Well, I am, and we're not kids any more.'

Go away, she thought. Just go away.

'We've been going out for months – it's time to get grown-up, Caroline. We're much too old for goodnight kisses on the door-step.'

'We haven't been anywhere,' she reminded him.

'I could have waited until I brought you home,' he said, the wheedling tone back since masterful dominance wasn't working. 'But you'd have thought it was the film that had given me ideas.'

'So what has given you ideas?'

'You,' he said. 'I don't need erotic movies. I find you sexy even when I've been listening to Robert Hamlyn make a speech.'

She laughed at the little joke, and instantly his mouth was on hers in a prolonged, passionless, tongue-thrusting kiss. Her lack of response didn't put him off; it was probable, indeed, that he hadn't even noticed.

He began to unbutton her shirt, his hands everywhere; grappling with her bra, groping her with bruising thoroughness. She passively endured the invasion, because maybe he was right; maybe it was all she needed to put her grief behind her.

Forcing her bra up, out of his way, he grasped her exposed breast, squeezing it hard, muttering some form of encouragement before his mouth turned its attention to it, and his hands were free to continue undressing her. And still she didn't stop him, because he might be right.

He was already fumbling under the navy satin cummerbund for his zip, and she didn't even like him. It wasn't necessary to like him, she told herself. Sex never used to be that important to her, in her single days. It had always just been a bit of fun, no big deal, before she met Andrew. Perhaps it should be again. Sam might be right. It might be all she needed.

It might be. But it wasn't going to be here, and it wasn't going to be now, and it wasn't going to be Sam.

The speeches were no more or less boring than speeches usually were; Robert's, indeed, had really been quite amusing, which had surprised Philip. Sam Waters's had been entirely conventional, unlike his dinner-jacket. Philip smiled again as he thought of it.

It was a quite wonderful dinner-jacket; midnight-blue velvet with pale-blue shot-silk lapels and pocket flaps, it set off the ice-blue dress-shirt with navy ruffle and solitaire-studded bow-tie to perfection.

Sam had left as soon as he'd finished speaking, and just as Treadwell had stood up to speak, in what seemed to have been a calculated insult. He'd get away with it, of course, thought Philip. He always did.

Philip's eyes had searched the Hall in vain for Caroline, and it was with a mixture of relief and disappointment that he had learned of her babysitting activities. He had tried to talk to her, even rehearsed asking her out for a drink, but he couldn't. All he could do was so pathetically sick that it destroyed him, but he couldn't stop it. St Valentine's Day, he thought sourly. Once, it would have been easy.

Barry was using index cards for his speech; it was impossible to tell whether he was in the middle of it or nearly at the end; one could only hope it was the latter, as he had been speaking for over twenty minutes. He got a murmured laugh, and seemed to be winding up; Philip shifted slightly in his seat as his leg began to complain, and joined in the applause.

Philip drank to the next hundred and fifty years, feeling a bit as though he had been there for the first hundred and fifty. He had drunk to everything; indeed, the speeches had been made easier on the ear by virtue of finishing off each glass of wine while the next one droned on. The young woman who kept refilling his glass was by now wearing a permanently worried expression. Philip smiled at her.

The music struck up; a plague of grey blazers suddenly rose from the tables, and descended on the ladies, who tried to look surprised as they took to the floor.

Philip watched as they danced; people who could move, some more elegantly than others, exactly as they chose, and he hated them all. He sighed, wishing Caroline was there, and turned to the other two men who remained at the table as they included him in the inconsequential conversation, but he was having some difficulty following what they were saying.

The dance was over; the boys began to see their ladies back. Returned to the top table, Diana Hamlyn didn't even sit down, but instead came back across the room towards him, almost, it seemed, pushing people out of her way in order to get there. The music began again, and his companions rose to dance with their returned ladies.

He was alone at the table when Diana arrived.

'Is this a frightful bore for you, Philip?' She leaned over as she spoke, her face close to his.

He didn't answer.

'How's the leg holding up?' she asked, as her hand rested lightly on his good leg.

The girl he had been seeing before the accident had come to the hospital when he lay paralysed, with no one able to say if the immobility was permanent or not. It had been the most casual of relationships; she had not unnaturally taken fright at the possibility of being cast in the rôle of paraplegic's loyal girlfriend, and he hadn't seen her again.

But he hadn't had fantasies about her, to whom he really had made love. And he didn't have fantasies about Diana Hamlyn, whose hand really was pressing his thigh.

She straightened up, slowly slipping her hand away. 'Sorry I can't stay,' she said. 'Duty calls.'

And she made her way to the exit, just as Sam had done; Philip watched her go, swearing under his breath. Damn the woman. Damn her. She'd been using him as some sort of decoy. But he couldn't even ask her to dance, never mind anything else, so what good would he be to her? He didn't want her anyway.

He wanted Caroline.

'Isn't Mr Waters coming back?' asked the wife of the chairman of governors, whose name Treadwell was constitutionally incapable of remembering.

'Er . . . no,' he said, his eyes still on Diana as she left the Hall. 'He did say that he wouldn't be able to stay long,' he said. 'He had a previous appointment.'

'What a pity,' she said. 'I had hoped to get the chance to talk to him.'

Thank God you didn't, Treadwell thought. He had scarcely been able to conceal his relief when Waters told him he wouldn't be staying. When he had seen the jacket, the relief had been doubled; if that was the Statement, then the speech would probably be free of four-letter words and innuendo, which had proved to be the case.

'But he and Caroline aren't leaving until eleven,' said Marcia, with the wide-eyed innocence that Treadwell, despite having been married to her for over thirty years, still wondered about. 'Are they?'

'Eleven?' repeated Hamlyn, in a startled voice. 'Then, why did he leave at half past nine?'

'Just a misunderstanding, I expect,' Treadwell said. He glared at his wife, who looked flustered.

'Diana seems to have misunderstood, too,' said Hamlyn. 'She also left as soon as she had discharged her duties.'

Treadwell smiled weakly. 'I'm sure there's an explanation,' he said.

'I think we all know the explanation,' said Hamlyn.

Treadwell wanted to die; he signalled frantically to the girl to bring more wine. Hemlock, for preference.

'It's an odd time to have an appointment,' laughed the bloody woman who wouldn't let the subject of Sam Waters go. 'Whenever it's for. Still, artists are supposed to be unconventional.'

'Mr Waters is certainly that,' said Hamlyn. 'Wouldn't you say, Barry?'

The new bottle arrived. 'More wine?' Treadwell asked, his voice a shade desperate. But any hopes he had of the subject having been dropped were dashed.

'You'd think the man would have more of an idea of dress sense, if he's meant to be an artist,' said the bloody woman's husband.

'I think,' said Robert Hamlyn quietly, 'that that was Sam's idea of a joke, rather than his idea of dress sense.'

'A joke?'

Treadwell smiled broadly. 'As your wife says,' he laughed,

'artists are supposed to be unconventional.' He poured more wine for himself.

'I don't really see the point, if it was a joke.'

'We're the point,' said Hamlyn.

'Sorry?'

'We never see ourselves, do we?' He smiled. 'As others see us,' he added.

Treadwell watched with dismay as his guests' faces grew slightly pink.

'Here we are,' Hamlyn went on, in the quiet voice that carried as far as it had to, after years of lectures and talks. 'Here we are, sitting up straight in our best bibs and tuckers, and there's Sam, doing exactly what he pleases.' He paused, and looked straight at Treadwell. 'With my wife,' he added.

Treadwell's glass froze at his lips. He had expected trouble from Waters; he had anticipated it, told him in no uncertain manner that his fixed-term contract had not been agreed by him, and did not have to be renewed. It would never have occurred to him that Hamlyn, who lived for the most part in a world composed entirely of logic and mathematics, would be the nigger in the wood-pile. Almost automatically, he told himself that he mustn't use that expression any more. The fly in the ointment, then. Presumably there were no pressure groups for fly rights yet. Why now, for God's sake? Why now? Why here?

'You're worrying these good people,' he said, trying to laugh, sounding hysterical, he knew he sounded hysterical. 'They'll think you mean it.'

'You mean I'm worrying you,' said Hamlyn, still smiling.

Treadwell shot a look at Marcia, who looked like she always did. Polite, a little apprehensive, not understanding what was going on, and quite unaware that she had caused it all.

It was just then that he saw Philip Newby get up and move quickly through the dancers to the doors.

'Do you want coffee?' Lloyd asked, his voice as surly as he could make it, given the deliberately non-contentious nature of the question.

They were in Lloyd's flat, surfacing from yet another row; Judy shook her head, not turning to look at him, and opened the window a little to watch the rain pouring down, leaving a slippery film on everything, as it battered away at the piles of snow. It had come suddenly, unpredicted by the weathermen. Hopefully, it was at least signalling the end of winter.

She had looked at her watch, apparently. Not, she would have thought, the most inflammatory of gestures, but it had sparked off the quick temper to which she doubted if she would ever become accustomed. Michael was at a colleague's stag party, and wasn't going to be home until the early hours. But it was well after midnight, and, bearing in mind her Cinderella status, she had looked at her watch.

And she was getting no better at holding her own during such hostilities; the cutting remarks and wild accusations perhaps stung a little less than they used to, but not much.

The question had broken the ten minutes of silence which had followed the angry words; it was, Judy knew from experience, the prelude to a more reasoned statement of grievances, to which she was supposed to reply in equally reasonable tones, until Lloyd made some feeble joke that they would both pretend was funny.

She let the cold air cool the cheeks that had grown hot with indignation as the hurtful words had been hurled at her; she had no weapon to match Lloyd's tongue, and he knew it. Afterwards – after the silence and the peaceful negotiations, which Judy hated even more than the row, after the pipe of peace had been smoked – he would blame his Welshness, and try to make her laugh at the English reserve which stopped her giving as good as she got.

She closed the window and braced herself for the unnecessary but obligatory discussion of their situation; when Lloyd didn't speak, she turned to look at him. He stood up, and held out his arms.

'This is crazy,' he said, hugging her. 'I want you to live with me, and all I can do is fight with you.'

It was far from all he could do. The rows blew over, and he had every right to feel frustrated and angry as the weeks went by. But she couldn't explain to Lloyd why she hadn't made the break. Michael's dependence on her, unsuspected and unsought, was a factor that Lloyd didn't know came into it, and to tell him would seem more like a betrayal of Michael than her infidelity ever had.

'Are you having second thoughts about leaving him?' he asked.

'No!' She pulled back to look at him. 'He just won't accept that it's all over. We've got separate rooms, Lloyd, I told you.'

It was an unnecessary denial of one of his angry suggestions, and he pulled her close to him again. 'I didn't mean any of that,' he said. 'But you can't leave him in stages, Judy.' His lips touched her cheek. 'Hoping he won't notice.'

She closed her eyes. 'Do you ever take time off?' she asked.

He gave a little laugh. 'Sixteen years ago it was Barbara you didn't want to hurt,' he said. 'But someone is going to get hurt.'

She had known Lloyd since she was twenty years old; she had loved him since she was twenty years old. But he had been married to Barbara then, with two young children. So – as a direct result – she had married Michael, with whom she had had an easy relationship for years. Marriage had put an end to that. Her path had crossed Lloyd's again two years ago, when she and Michael had come to live in Stansfield.

Thus began what was supposed to have been a no-strings-attached relationship with Lloyd, except that there were strings attached, and always had been. They had just pretended that they couldn't see them, until they pulled so tightly that it hurt, and even she had to admit to their presence.

With that admission, and the spoken acknowledgement of it, had come a flood of relief, and love, and guilt, laced with a generous measure of panic. But the panic was over; now she truly didn't want to hurt Michael. So she was hurting Lloyd instead.

'You,' she said miserably. 'I know I'm hurting you. Because you'll put up with it.'

He smiled. 'You'd better go,' he said, kissing her gently.

Judy looked at her watch again, but this time she took it from her wrist, and slipped it into Lloyd's pocket.

'Sure?' he asked. 'It's even later now.'

'I'm not going anywhere,' she said, as the phone rang.

Lloyd picked it up with a shrug of apology to her, then listened, his face growing grave. He sighed. 'Yes,' he said. 'I'm on my way.'

She was going somewhere now, she thought, as they went out to their cars. Hers coughed and spluttered like a sixty-a-day

smoker, and she had to abandon it and go in Lloyd's. They were
going, as fast as they could in the non-stop rain, to what Lloyd
had described as 'that school of yours'. He seemed to hold her personally responsible for the rape and murder which had apparently
taken place there.

They arrived to find what seemed like half of the county constabulary there already; squad cars, doors open, radios crackling
messages, were parked in the wonderfully eccentric fashion
known only to squad-car drivers. Lloyd pulled up beside the
pitch-dark playing-field, where the knot of onlookers suggested
that they would find the body.

'Get rid of them,' Lloyd muttered, as he got out of the car.

Judy sometimes wished he wouldn't make allowances, but on
the whole she was glad that he did. It helped a little if she could
get into her stride before she had to look at the victim.

She got out, and prepared to go into the routine of telling them
that there was nothing to see; this time it was entirely true.
Portable lighting equipment was on its way, but for the moment
there was only the light from the building, and it lit the onlookers,
not the scene of the incident. But the crowd, mostly boys, wasn't
sightseeing. It was quiet, and still, shocked by the news. The boys
spoke to her of someone they had liked, someone who had meant
a great deal to each of them. She caught a glimpse of the one she
had spoken to about the thefts, but she couldn't remember his
name. Coatless, he stood shivering in the rain, and in the aftermath of tragedy he looked like the schoolboy he was. Not the
elegant man-about-town; an awkward schoolboy, all wrists and
ankles. Another blinked furiously as he told her that he would
have run away when he was eleven if it hadn't been for her. None
of them could help with what had happened; they only knew
what they had been told, and what they had overheard. She
moved them away, and watched them go, moving off slowly,
looking back over their shoulders at the dismal, rainsoaked scene.
They were still boys, still children. They were sad, not angry.

She was angry.

Her husband had found her, almost falling over her in the darkness as he had crossed the playing-field from the Great Hall to the

junior dormitory. The ambulancemen who had been called had treated him for shock; there was nothing they or anyone else could do for his wife.

The ambulance had had to leave almost as soon as it had arrived, to pick up the injured from a crash on the treacherous road. It had happened close enough to the school for the mournful sound of a jammed car horn to reach them, and Lloyd had sent someone to investigate. Now half the men were out at the accident, coping with something which had taken and continued to take more lives than all the murderers there had ever been.

But deliberate destruction was still much harder to take. Lloyd watched as at last they set up the lights, which had taken an hour to arrive because of the road diversion, and another hour to fix up. By torchlight, they had cordoned off the playing-field. Now, in the steady rain, they ran ribbon along either side of the tarmac path, and round the area where the attack had taken place. No murder weapon was immediately to hand; they would have to start searching at first light. So much time was wasted in winter, waiting for the sun to come up. The cold, relentless rain was washing away evidence, and the killer was getting further and further from their reach.

The lights went on, illuminating the little patch of playing-field like day; Freddie looked round the small lit area for anything that might give them a clue to her attacker, but there was nothing. He shook his head, and crouched down beside the young woman's body, under the canvas that sheltered it from the rain; it seemed an uncomfortable position for his tall frame, but he wouldn't move until he'd finished, for fear of disturbing some minute piece of evidence. He had done what he could when he arrived, two hours ago. Now he could really begin his work. His thin face looked pinched and cold as he drew a quick sketch of the area, and dictated initial thoughts and findings to his assistant, a slight frown furrowing his brow. The girl wrote with blue hands, stopping now and then to rub them together.

Even with the lights, they could see nothing in the immediate area that could have inflicted the injuries. Slowly, Lloyd moved back towards the body, under the makeshift shelter. It had been bad enough by torchlight.

'Several blows to the head,' Freddie was saying, as the girl wrote. 'Non-manual. Our old friend the blunt instrument.' He peered closely at the body. 'An attempt, possibly successful, at strangulation,' he said. 'Bare legs and feet, no shoes. No underpants. No coat. One, two – two buttons missing from dress at front. Brassiere torn. Injuries to—'

'Sex murders,' Lloyd said bitterly, like the obscenity they were.

'Don't knock them, Lloyd,' said Freddie cheerfully. 'Chances are I can learn a lot more from a sex murder than from any other kind.'

'Well, that's all right, then,' said Lloyd. 'I'm sure Mrs Hamlyn was pleased about that, if nothing else.'

Freddie looked the part, all right. All tall thin seriousness, until you became aware that his looks disguised a genuine, even engaging enjoyment of his work. But Lloyd couldn't share his appreciation of rape as an aid to detection.

The photographer arrived, and began setting up, as Lloyd heard another car arrive; its headlamps lit up the gentle slope from the gates as it joined the other cars. He looked out from the bright light into the wet, cold darkness, taking a moment to make out the chief superintendent's figure.

'Morning, Lloyd.'

'Sir.'

Chief Superintendent Allison was twelve years younger than Lloyd, which had illogically irked Lloyd when he first arrived. His grudging admission that at least Allison was better than his predecessor had given way in the end to a slightly less grudging respect for the man's ability. And he wasn't all that much taller than Lloyd, which gave him several merit points.

Together, they sorted out what was being done, what could and would be done. There was someone on the gates, checking cars in and out; that would continue until the living-in member of staff who was missing had either come back, been accounted for or placed firmly on the suspect-list. Judy had spoken to the gathering in the Great Hall, and was currently taking statements from anyone with anything to say.

Allison would be addressing the school at assembly next day. There were other women at the school, small children and young boys; neither the police nor the school could take chances with their safety. The evening assemblies would be suspended until further notice to avoid the necessity of the younger boys walking round after dark.

Theoretically, anyone could have come into the school grounds and attacked Mrs Hamlyn as she walked across to the junior dormitory. Realistically, it was unlikely that a total stranger would chance on a night when everyone was safely in one place, rather than coming or going. Everyone except the victim, that was. She was using the short cut from the Hall to the dormitory, alone and in the darkness. Anyone in the school, however, could have known that; it had hardly been a secret. Any of the guests could have followed her.

And statistically it was more likely to be someone she knew. Lloyd sighed. It was the same problem as Judy had with the thefts. Too many suspects.

Allison glanced round the dark playing-field. 'How wide a search are you doing?' he asked.

'Ten feet either side of the footpath,' Lloyd said. 'To start with.' Daylight was still hours away. He sighed again.

'Do you want any more photographs?' asked the thin man with the beard. 'The doctor's got all he wants for tonight. I'll be back in daylight.'

'Fine.' Allison sighed, too.

It was the universal reaction to something that could never be righted. Insurance replaced burgled goods; shop windows could be renewed; supermarkets could mark up their prices to take account of shoplifting. But, no matter what anyone did, the young woman on the ground was no more. Lloyd's anger might help him get to the bottom of it, but it wouldn't bring her back.

'Bob Sandwell's been talking to the catering staff, I understand,' the chief superintendent said, as the photographer thankfully packed away his camera.

Detective Constable Sandwell seemed to discover things by osmosis. Already, he was the one everyone asked if they wanted to know which building was which; he doubtless knew all the catering staff by their first names. Lloyd waited to hear what he had discovered from the ladies.

'And it seems that Mrs Hamlyn had something of a reputation,' said Allison. 'To put it mildly.'

'Does that matter?' said Judy's voice, from behind them, startling them. 'Sir,' she added, with a delayed, acid politeness that bordered on insubordination.

'All right, Sergeant,' he said good-humouredly. 'I'm not suggesting it was her own fault.' He looked down at Diana Hamlyn's corpse.

Carefully, Freddie turned the body, and continued his patient eyes-only examination before taking samples. He finished with a minute description of the still-frozen ground below the body, and a final taking of the temperature.

'We'll be in a better position once we've had the postmortem results,' said Allison, for want of something to say, in Lloyd's opinion.

'. . . as at two fifty-five hours,' Freddie said, dictating the body temperature to his assistant, whose own didn't look much higher. He gave her the ground temperature, and looked up at them.

'That's about it until I can examine her properly,' he said, packing away swabs and tapes. 'She can go to the mortuary now.' He stood up, flexing his back. 'Is there somewhere Kathy can go and thaw out?' he asked, taking the notebook from her.

'Yes,' said Sandwell eagerly, appearing from nowhere. 'I'll show you,' he said to Kathy, who gratefully followed his tall figure out of the light, towards warmth.

'How long?' asked Judy.

'I'd say between two and five hours,' Freddie said with suspicious promptness. He was normally very loath to give estimates at any time, and never liked to be asked before the post-mortem.

Lloyd looked at his watch. Between ten and one. But they already knew that, of course. She'd been seen in the Hall at ten, and the treble nine call had been made at ten past one. 'Thank you,' he said to the smiling Freddie.

'What do you expect? There's dozens of factors to be taken into consideration.' He stepped carefully back, out of the shelter.

'Is there a chance of narrowing it down?' Lloyd asked into the darkness.

'For once there might be,' Freddie's disembodied voice said.

'She'd just had dinner for a start.' He came back into the light. 'And the temperature readings are interesting – I think I'll be able to narrow it down a little. She was nice and fresh.'

He couldn't disguise his enthusiasm, and never tried to. Freddie liked dead bodies.

'Sir?' A young uniformed constable looked uncertainly from the chief superintendent to Lloyd. 'Mr Waters has just come in. He's the art teacher – the one that was missing. We've asked him to wait in the Hall.'

'All yours,' said Allison. 'I'll have another word with the head.' He turned back. 'He seems to have been a bit liberal with the medicinal brandy,' he said. 'I don't think you'll get much out of him until the morning. Shall I tell him to expect you then?'

Allison left as Sandwell delivered Freddie's assistant back to him, and they roared off in Freddie's powerful car, with little regard for the younger residents, who until then had slept on, unaware of the drama going on.

Lloyd and Judy walked into the building, through a cloakroom in which only Mrs Hamlyn's coat remained.

'She didn't mean to be out in the rain for long,' Judy said.

The catering staff moved round the Great Hall in a silent pall of disbelief, having been told that they could at last clear away. The party's abrupt and shocking end was evidenced by the balloons still trapped in the netting slung from the rafters.

They found Mr Waters sitting at a cluttered table, wearing jeans, a thick sweater, and a surly expression.

Lloyd introduced himself and Judy, and asked Mr Waters where he had been, immediately eliciting hostility.

'Why should that concern you? What's going on?'

'A crime's been committed here,' Lloyd said.

Waters raised his eyebrows. 'So? I wasn't here, was I?'

'What time did you leave here, Mr Waters?' Judy asked, her notebook at the ready.

'How the hell should I know?'

'Were you at the dinner here tonight?'

'Yes. I left early.'

'Would you mind telling us why?'

'Yes.'

Lloyd sat down beside Judy, opposite Waters. 'Someone was murdered here tonight,' he said, his voice almost conversational. 'Would you know anything about that?'

Waters's eyes widened. 'Murdered?' he repeated. 'Who?'

'A Mrs Diana Hamlyn,' said Lloyd, watching carefully for Waters's reaction. It wasn't any of the things he had expected.

'Diana?' he said. 'Murdered?' He looked almost amused. 'Are you telling me that Hamlyn finally cracked?'

Lloyd sat back in his chair and regarded Waters for some moments; until Waters began to look uncomfortable. 'Do you have some reason to think that Mr Hamlyn murdered his wife?' he asked at last.

'I'd have murdered her,' he replied.

Lloyd smiled coldly. 'But you didn't,' he said.

Waters shook his head. 'She wasn't my wife,' he said.

'And had she been your wife? What would have been your motive for murder?' asked Lloyd.

'Only that she was screwing half the men in this school,' Waters replied.

'Does that include you?' Judy asked, with polite interest, not looking up from her notebook.

Judy waited for a reply, as Lloyd watched Waters argue with himself.

She looked up. 'Does that include you?' she asked again, as though he might not have heard.

'Yes, all right. It did, at one time.'

'Mrs Hamlyn was raped,' said Lloyd.

A broad smile spread over Waters's features. 'Raped?' he repeated incredulously. 'Diana Hamlyn, *raped*? You have to be joking.'

'I wish I were. But it would be a joke in very bad taste.'

'Who the hell would need to rape Diana?' he said.

'Why did you leave the dinner?' Judy asked.

Waters didn't reply.

'Where did you go?'

Waters just looked at her without speaking.

'What were you doing?' she tried.

'Minding my own fucking business,' said Waters.

'That'll do, Mr Waters,' said Lloyd.

Waters clapped his hand to his mouth. 'Oh, am I offending the lady?' he asked.

'I wouldn't know,' said Lloyd. 'You're offending me.' He got up, and walked round the table to Waters, bending down to talk to him. 'The English language is a very flexible instrument, Mr Waters. The use of entirely inapposite adjectives offends me very deeply.'

It was a lie, of course. Lloyd could throw in as many inapposite adjectives as the next man. But Judy would never forgive him if he admitted that it was using them in her presence that he found offensive. He stood up, and looked again at Sam Waters. 'I take it you didn't attend the dinner dressed like that?' he asked.

Waters raised his eyebrows. 'No,' he said. 'Is my dress something else that offends you?'

'Not in the least,' said Lloyd smoothly. 'But you've changed your clothes, Mr Waters. And I'd rather like to see the ones you were wearing earlier.'

'What?' Waters stared at him. 'You think I did it?'

'You won't tell us what you *were* doing,' said Lloyd.

'It's none of your bloody business, if you'll forgive another inapposite adjective.'

'Oh, but this time the adjective is right, and you're wrong. It is a bloody business – but it *is* mine. And I'd like to see the clothes you were wearing this evening.'

'Don't you need some sort of warrant?' Waters said, and got up. 'Oh, what the f—' He put a finger to his lips. 'Oops,' he said. 'Hell. Is that all right?'

Lloyd ignored him.

'They're in my flat. And since I've had a bloody awful evening which culminated in being sent five miles out of my way by a road diversion, only to be accused of murder when I finally get here, that is where I'm going.'

Lloyd smiled again, with no more warmth than before. 'Then, we had better come with you,' he said.

'Suit yourself,' he said, striding away.

Lloyd had rarely disliked anyone as much in so short a time.

But, he reminded himself as he and Judy followed Waters out of the Hall, that didn't make him a murderer.

It just made him an inapposite adjective good candidate.

Chapter Three

Philip Newby lay awake in the darkness. It was cold in the little unheated bedroom, but there were beads of perspiration on his temple as he lay still clothed on top of the bed, afraid to move. He would have to move, sooner or later. It would be daylight in a few hours, and he could hardly walk around like this. Thank God it was Saturday.

He swallowed, his mouth dry, and forced himself to sit up, closing his eyes as the pain gripped his lower back. Perhaps he wouldn't be walking around at all by the morning. But he *could* sit up; he could ease himself off the bed. He stood one-legged, and moved round the room, supporting his weight on the chair-back, the dressing-table, the end of the bed, until he reached the light-switch.

He could see himself in the dressing-table mirror. Bent over like an old man, his blood-stained shirt hanging out, his jacket and trousers smeared with mud. He had to straighten up. He had to. The image went as he screwed his eyes up against the pain, and lifted his head, wanting to howl like the wounded animal he was. Little dots of light swam in front of his eyes when he opened them, but when they cleared he could see himself again. Erect. And that was a joke, he thought.

Now, no joke – he had to get the clothes off. It was difficult enough at the best of times. He weighed up the pros and cons, and decided to start with the trousers. It was a slow, agonising operation.

He had got the trousers and the jacket off, and was standing in his shirt and underpants when he heard Sam's key turn in the door. One hand on the desk, he allowed as little of his weight as possible to fall on his bad leg as his good one kicked the clothes out of sight under the bed. Just in case he was too stiff to get rid of them in the morning.

He could hear voices; a woman's, and at least one other man's. He could hear the rise and fall of a voice that wasn't Sam's.

The wardrobe was just within his reach, and he pulled open the door, fumbling amongst the clothes for the stick. It was the middle of the night, and the voices sounded urgent, official. He had no desire to be discovered in this condition.

His hand grasped the metal, and he pulled the stick out. At last he could move more freely. He got into his dressing-gown, pulling the belt tight, covering his shirt. Perhaps the pain was lessening, he told himself, as he opened the door.

'What's going on?' he asked, his voice failing as the agony seized him again.

He could hardly think, as the man introduced himself. Chief Inspector Lloyd, he heard, and those three words were all that went through his head, like a mantra, as he tried to cope with the pain. Other words fought their way through. This is Sergeant Hill. Sorry to have disturbed you at this time of night. Serious incident.

'Would you be better sitting down, Mr Newby?'

He didn't know if he could sit down. Or get up again if he did. He shook his head.

'Are you all right?' Sam asked, the first time he had spoken.

Philip nodded, teeth clenched together.

'What happened to you?' the sergeant asked.

'Car crash,' he said.

'When did it happen?'

'Eighteen months ago. It's not usually as bad as this.'

'Well, Mr Waters?' asked Chief Inspector Lloyd.

'It's over there,' Sam said, jerking his head towards a large box in the corner of the room. 'Help yourself.'

The chief inspector went over, and took out the suit, his eyes widening when he saw it. Philip frowned as he watched him examine it.

'It's damp,' said the chief inspector.

Sam shrugged.

'Is it hired?'

'Borrowed,' said Sam. 'Do you want to take it away? Examine it for blonde hairs?'

'Yes, thank you. Since you have been kind enough to offer. Do you want to tell us where you were tonight between ten and midnight, Mr Waters? It would save a great deal of time.'

Sam told the chief inspector that he had no intention of divulging this information, but he took only two words to do it.

Philip stared at him, at the chief inspector, at the sergeant.

'Very well, Mr Waters,' said Lloyd. 'We'll be back, I've no doubt.'

Philip marshalled his wits, and looked again at Sam. 'What's this *about*?' he asked.

Sam smiled. 'Someone raped Diana,' he said.

'*Raped* her?' said Philip. 'What do you mean, raped her?'

Matthew had hidden the evidence somewhere which was itself a challenge; he'd have to get rid of it all now, but for the moment he was safe. He had got back to the Hall, and had asked Mrs Treadwell to dance; as far as he could tell, he hadn't even been missed, but it didn't really matter if he had.

The ball had been almost over when Hamlyn had come stumbling in like a drunk; Matthew had been contemplating whether it would be going over the top to invite Mrs Treadwell up for the last waltz. It was, after all, conceivable that Mr Treadwell would feel obliged to take his wife on to the floor, but he hadn't danced with her all night, and Matthew had thought she might appreciate the gesture. But the moment never came; Hamlyn had run blindly up to the top table, Treadwell had stared at him for a moment, then had moved uncertainly towards the dais, and the music had petered out. Then he had said that there had been a serious incident, and that the police would have to be called, and asked everyone to stay until they got there.

Matthew was awake, working out what to do next, how much – if anything – he should tell the police. The others hadn't talked much about what had happened; they had silently got into bed, and eventually had gone to sleep.

But Matthew watched. From the window, he could see the line of police cars at the far side of the playing-fields. He was stiff and cold, after hours of watching. Two of the cars still sat there, but the one the sergeant had come in had moved, and just five minutes ago he had watched it sweep round the road to where it now stood outside the junior dormitory. Sergeant Hill and the man had got out of it, and had gone into the building, presumably up to the Hamlyns' flat, where the light had burned all night.

Matthew didn't like it when he didn't know exactly what was happening. He even contemplated the fire-escape again, to eavesdrop, if he could. He abandoned that idea, but he was going to carry on watching.

All night, if he had to.

'Raped?' Caroline Knight stared at Chief Inspector Lloyd.

'Yes, Mrs Knight,' he said, with just a trace of a Welsh accent. 'I'm afraid so.'

She had been told, when someone had finally got round to telling her, that Diana was dead. That her body had been found on the playing-field. No more.

'Does that surprise you, Mrs Knight?' The cool question came from the sergeant. Caroline remembered her from last month, when she had come about the thefts.

'Well . . .' Caroline felt a little uncomfortable under the sergeant's steady brown gaze. 'No one's really told me what's going on. I knew someone had . . .' She broke off, not wanting to say the word. 'But I had no idea that she had been raped.' She sat down. 'That's dreadful,' she said.

Sergeant Hill wrote something in her notebook, and Chief Inspector Lloyd took over.

'Forgive me, Mrs Knight,' he said. 'But you did seem a little more surprised than shocked.'

'Yes,' she admitted. 'It was silly of me.'

Robert Hamlyn was being attended to by Matron, and Caroline had found herself in sole charge of the junior dormitory by default. The police had asked if they could speak to her, but had said that it could wait until the next day. Caroline had said they could come in; she couldn't sleep anyway. But she hadn't been prepared for the almost hostile sergeant.

'Shall I tell you some of the other reactions we've had?'

Sergeant Hill was saying, as she made a business of turning back the pages of her notebook. 'We've had "Who the hell would need to rape Diana Hamlyn?", and "What do you mean, raped?" Now you say you're surprised. Why?'

Caroline Knight looked at her thoughtfully. 'If you've been asking questions, then I expect you already know the answer,' she said. 'Diana had . . . well, a problem.'

'A problem?' queried Lloyd.

'With men. I mean – I'm no psychiatrist, but she seemed to me to be a . . .' She paused, not wishing to sound melodramatic. But it was the truth, after all. 'A nymphomaniac, I suppose,' she said. 'She was promiscuous, at any rate.'

'Oh?' said Sergeant Hill. 'Does that mean she can't have been raped?'

'No, of course not.' Caroline didn't want to think about it; she really ought to tell them, but perhaps she'd imagined it. She wasn't sure. And, if she said anything, the crazy thought that went through her head at the time might get spoken, and she really couldn't do that to Sam. She'd been jumpy, that was all. Better not to say anything at all, unless she had to.

'Well,' said Chief Inspector Lloyd, 'let's get away from that. I understand, Mrs Knight, that you intended supervising the children until about eleven, when Mrs Hamlyn was due to relieve you. Is that right?'

'Quite right.' She pushed her long hair away from her face. 'I rang the Hall at about quarter to, and was told that she had left about half an hour before that.'

'Were you worried?'

'I thought it was odd, but I wasn't exactly worried.'

'You must forgive me again,' Lloyd said. 'But I'm not all that sure how the school runs. Am I right in thinking that Mrs Hamlyn was not actually employed by the school in any capacity?'

She nodded. 'But housemasters' wives do find themselves in this position,' she said. 'And she had said she'd be pleased to let me go at eleven – I was going out, you see.' She glanced down at herself, all dressed up. 'So it did seem odd that she hadn't turned up, but – well, I never dreamed anything had *happened* to her. Not until Mr Dearden came and—' She broke off.

Lloyd nodded. 'And Mr Hamlyn?' he asked. 'Was he worried? I take it that's who you spoke to at the Hall?'

'No,' she said slowly. 'Robert didn't come to the phone. Barry did. He said he'd have a look round for her, but he didn't ring back or anything. So I just stayed. I . . . we . . . well, Barry and I both thought she might have gone off with someone.'

'You didn't ring Mr Treadwell back?' asked Lloyd.

'No – because my plans had fallen through anyway. The next thing I heard was when Mr Dearden came and told me she was dead. That someone had killed her. I couldn't believe it.'

'Did he leave you here on your own?' asked the sergeant.

'Well – you . . . the police were all over the place. I told him I'd be all right.'

'Now,' said Chief Inspector Lloyd, 'you didn't hear from Mrs Hamlyn at all?'

Caroline shook her head.

'The path across the playing-field,' he said. 'It's a short cut, I take it. How many people would be likely to be using it?'

'No one,' said Caroline. Sam. Sam must have used it.

'No one?' Lloyd frowned a little. 'Why is there a path, then?'

'The younger boys have always used the playing-field to get from the school and the Hall to here. For years. Eventually, they wore a path, so in the end they tarmacked it. Mr and Mrs Hamlyn use it, of course. But everyone else uses the lane.'

'What lane?' Sergeant Hill and the chief inspector chorused.

'There's an old lane from the main buildings,' Caroline explained. 'The senior boys are in houses – the lane runs past them.'

'How come we didn't see that?' asked Lloyd.

'It goes through the buildings,' she explained. 'You wouldn't know it was there unless you were looking for it. That's why we can't allow cars to come right in – it would be too dangerous, with boys shooting out of there.'

'And everyone else uses that rather than the footpath?'

'Well – anyone going to the boys' houses, of course, or any of the other buildings off the lane. Or anyone going to the staff block or the headmaster's house. The field's only a short cut to this building. The lane's the quickest route to everywhere else.'

'Thank you, Mrs Knight,' Lloyd said, standing up. 'I suggest you try to get some sleep now. There will be officers patrolling, so you don't have to worry.'

'I still don't think I'll sleep,' she said.

Lloyd and Judy left the junior dormitory and crossed over to the other side of the road. The lane snaked and zig-zagged along, shadowed by the darkened buildings that flanked it; the boys' houses, the sick-bay, and others that only Bob Sandwell could have sorted out.

Lloyd glanced at Judy. 'I want this place searched,' he said. It seemed to him a much more likely trysting-place than the middle of the playing-field. It was dark, private. Perhaps she had come along here with someone, on their way to the staff block; he tried not to see it as Sam Waters, but without success. Perhaps she had been killed here, and dumped on the playing-field. Freddie might be able to tell them that. It looked like a good place to hide the weapon. Plenty of nooks and crannies.

The doctor who had been called to Mr Hamlyn had said that he mustn't be disturbed until the next day, so there was no more to be done until then. The living-in staff were all accounted for now; a couple of other members of staff and the odd guest had gone AWOL from the ball, and that all still had to be sorted out. Lloyd wrapped it up for the night, and four-thirty found them on their way back to Stansfield.

'Do you want to try your car again?' he asked.

'No,' she said. 'There's no point until it dries out a bit.'

Lloyd smiled. 'That might not be until August.' He took her watch from his jacket pocket and handed it to her with a shrug. 'I'll take you home,' he said.

The road had been cleared, but they could see the debris of the accident.

Lloyd shivered a little. 'Any thoughts?' he asked her.

'Well,' she said, 'I think it's a bit of a coincidence that both Sam Waters and Caroline Knight seem to have had appointments that late at night. If they were going somewhere with each other – I think I'd like to know why the plans fell through.'

'And why Waters was so reluctant to tell us what his plans had been,' said Lloyd. He sighed as he thought of Waters.

'Aren't you always trying to convince me that artists are sensitive?' said Judy, her voice mischievous.

Lloyd spent a great deal of time trying to educate Judy in the fine arts; it was probably a lost cause, but he tried anyway. 'Sometimes,' he said, 'I feel I should apologise for the male of the species. This is one of the times.'

And Waters may have thought he had got off lightly, but he hadn't. He had left the Hall about three-quarters of an hour before Mrs Hamlyn, which hardly suggested a tryst, but he wasn't prepared to tell them what he had been doing. He would get another visit from Lloyd before he was much older.

'None of them seemed to care all that much,' he said. 'At least Waters was truthful about it, I suppose.'

'Caroline Knight was upset about the rape,' Judy said encouragingly.

'Yes,' Lloyd said. 'Though I would have thought that being dead was the more pressing of Mrs Hamlyn's problems.' He yawned wearily.

'Do you want me to talk to Treadwell tomorrow?' she asked, after a moment. 'I have met him before,' she added.

He grinned. She was never going to forgive him for that. 'Yes,' he said. 'My first appointment's going to be with the chief super,' he said. 'I'll meet you at the school after I've been to the postmortem. I don't suppose you want to join me?'

He didn't want her to join him. Freddie's black humour usually went down better with Judy than it did with him, but he had a feeling that he might find himself being the referee if she went this time. It wasn't difficult to dissuade Judy from attending a postmortem, and she didn't even bother to confirm his supposition.

The rain stopped suddenly as they came into Stansfield. You could almost hear the sigh of relief.

'It could just have been someone who got in, and was wandering about the grounds,' Judy said. 'Is Allison setting up an incident room?'

'They're sorting out an office for us,' said Lloyd. He glanced at her. 'But you know as well as I do that it was probably someone she knew.'

'Why does that sound as though it was all her own fault?' Judy asked, as the car made its way through Stansfield.

Lloyd didn't answer as his tyres threw up spray from the side of the road where the rain had at least made some impression on the heaps of snow. He moved out a little. The car's tyres hissed through slushy puddles which reflected the orange street-lamps, and Lloyd knew how people felt when Judy was questioning them. She was waiting for him to answer, and the question would hang in the air until he did.

'Because women *do* sometimes play with fire,' he said carefully. 'Sex *is* an aggressive act. From the male point of view.'

She snorted.

'All right, assertive, then. If the assertiveness wasn't there, it couldn't happen at all. And it doesn't take much to turn it to aggression – there is sometimes a very thin line between sex and violence. It's not always nonsense when the man says he was led on.'

'And being led on gives him the right to rape her?'

'No,' he said vehemently, shaking his head. 'It doesn't excuse it. But it gives him a reason.'

'Oh,' she said. 'So it's *reasonable* for him to rape her?'

Lloyd sighed. 'Yes, in a manner of speaking,' he said. 'It implies that he had not lost his reason. That he knew what he was doing.'

'Is that better or worse than if he *had* lost his reason?' she asked.

Lloyd shook his head. 'I don't know,' he said tiredly. 'But it's more likely to be someone she was with – someone she felt safe with. Safe enough to cross a pitch-dark field with.'

'You ended at least two sentences with prepositions there,' she said wickedly, as she got out of the car. 'I'll report you.' She leaned back in. 'I'm telling Michael today,' she said, kissing him on the cheek. 'I'll have left by tonight, I promise.' She smiled, and closed the door.

He was startled, as she had intended; he smiled broadly as she walked up her front path, her shoulders set in the way he recognised when nothing and no one was going to stop her doing what she intended to do. He had almost given up hope of seeing that resolve being used out of working hours. But this time she meant it, and he watched until she went into the house. She waved, and he drove off.

He knew that the suggestion that the victim might have played a part upset Judy, but it was something which had to be considered. Because if it wasn't someone Diana Hamlyn was with, then they could soon be playing a repeat performance of tonight, and that sort of show could run and run.

That was why the victim's own contribution was important; if she had made one, it made investigation easier, and a solution more likely. It reduced the likelihood of further crimes, and the proportions of the one being investigated to ones that he could understand. That a lot of men could understand, including judges. And that was what angered a lot of women, including Judy.

Back in his flat, he poured himself a large whisky, and put on an episode of an old, entirely escapist, quite ridiculous television series, the entire rerun of which he had taped. He went to bed at half-past six, allowing himself two hours' sleep.

Judy would think he was quite, quite mad.

Judy's alarm brought her to consciousness, and she opened her eyes to Saturday morning proper with some reluctance. The injury received in the line of duty had caused her to see what a mess she was making of everyone's life; she had made her original promise to Lloyd, and had used the excuse of a painful leg to move into the spare room. She had never moved out again. She pulled on her dressing-gown, and went downstairs, to find Michael in uncharacteristic pose, at the cooker.

'Good morning,' she said.

'Morning. I didn't think you'd be getting up yet,' he said, serving himself his large English breakfast as he spoke. 'I heard about the murder on Radio Barton.'

Judy raised her eyebrows. 'Do you actually *listen* to local radio?' she asked. 'I mean, when there are no extremes of weather?'

'No,' he said. 'I do when my wife's out all night, and I want to know why. You didn't leave a note.'

'Sorry,' she said. 'I didn't know it would take so long. There was a bad accident as well – it held everything up for hours.'

'Where's your car?' he asked, as he picked up his knife and fork.

'It wouldn't start,' she said. 'I had to leave it.' It was so easy, telling selective truths. So easy and, now, completely automatic. But it had to stop.

'Oh, of course,' he said, and carried on eating, unfolding the morning paper. 'The rain.'

'Michael,' she said.

There was a silence after she had spoken his name, during which he pretended to read. Then he shut his eyes briefly, and looked up at her.

'The car's at Lloyd's,' she said. 'I was with him when we got called out. That's why I didn't leave a note. Because I wasn't here.'

'I see,' he said, arranging a look of slight puzzlement on his face, then turned back to the paper.

'Don't pretend you don't know what I mean!'

His eyes didn't leave the newspaper. 'You were in bed with Lloyd,' he said. 'Is that what you mean?'

'No, as it happens,' said Judy. 'But I have been, and I would have been if we hadn't got called out. And I'd have stayed the night, and I would have told you when you asked where I'd been.'

He nodded slowly at the newspaper. 'And despite fate's intervention you're telling me anyway?' he said.

'I've been trying to tell you for weeks.'

'I know. I didn't want you to tell me.' He looked up, and it was her turn to look away.

'I'm sorry,' she said.

'Are you?'

'I'm sorry about the whole thing! I should have told you a long time ago. I shouldn't have married you, come to that.' She met his eyes.

'Was it going on when we got married?' he asked.

Judy had met Lloyd in London, when she was a WPC and he was a detective sergeant. Almost sixteen years ago. What a waste of time. 'Yes,' she said. 'I wasn't sleeping with him, but . . . yes.'

'Why *did* you marry me?' He sat down, and looked at her, his thin face showing no emotion as he asked the question.

She took out cigarettes and lit one before answering. 'Because I liked you,' she said. 'Because we got on well together, and because you were going back to live in Nottingham, which was a long way away from Lloyd and Barbara and the children.'

'How very strong-minded of you.'

'I didn't see myself as a home-wrecker,' she said wearily.

'But you don't mind wrecking this one?'

'This isn't a home! We share a house – it's all we've ever done. And it's my fault, I'm not pretending it isn't.'

'How long has it been going on?' he asked. 'If you'll forgive the cliché – one can hardly avoid them.'

'Does it matter?'

'Yes.' He picked up his plate and tipped its contents into the swing-bin. 'Did you know he was in Stansfield? When I applied for this job?'

She nodded. 'And I knew he'd been divorced,' she said. Lloyd's marriage had ended the year before Judy arrived in Stansfield.

'You kept in touch with him? All that time?'

She nodded again.

'So when did it start? As soon as you got here?'

She shook her head. 'It wasn't quite the way it sounds,' she said, and gave a short sigh. 'It was about six months after we came here.'

'And I didn't know,' said Michael. 'Not for certain. I've no doubt everyone else did – all your friends at the police station, for instance – but I didn't.' He smiled coldly. 'Until you moved out of my bed, I was sharing you with Mr Lloyd. And I didn't know.'

Lloyd had envied Michael that; he had hated knowing. And poor Michael was under a handicap just discussing it. Lloyd's first name was so awful that even she didn't know it, and he was universally referred to by his surname. Michael had to put in the 'Mr' to indicate his hostility.

'You've had other women,' she said. 'Don't pretend you haven't.'

'I'm not. But a one-night stand in Brussels isn't quite the same thing, is it? I think I could have lived with it if you'd been filling in time between planes, as it were. But that's not how it is.'

'No, it isn't,' she agreed hotly.

'For God's sake, Judy, you knew about all that! They didn't mean anything – they were casual girlfriends, that's all!'

'A girl in every port?' said Judy. 'I know, Michael. I was one of them. And it should have stayed like that. But you decided it was time you were married. Now you've decided it's time you had a family. But the fact is that it's time we were divorced.'

He shook his head.

'I don't care, Michael,' Judy said. 'Don't you see? I don't care, I've never cared about other women. This has never been a marriage – we've never been a unit. You should have someone else,' she said. 'Someone who loves you. Someone who wants children – someone *you* love. You don't love me.'

'Don't I?'

'Do you?' she asked, getting up.

'It rather depends on what we mean by it. If it means not being able to live without you, then – no, I don't love you. I don't claim the grand passion that you and Mr Lloyd have apparently found.' He looked away. 'I don't know, Judy,' he said. 'I know how I felt when you got hurt. You can't live with someone for ten years and feel nothing for them!' He looked up at her. 'Or can you?'

'No,' she said, sinking tiredly down again. 'But it's over, Michael. Whatever it was, whatever it is. It's over, and I'm leaving.'

'And moving in with Mr Lloyd?'

'Eventually,' she said. 'When I get my transfer.'

'Because the powers that be wouldn't like it while you're both still at Stansfield?'

'Quite.'

'So where will you go in the meantime?'

'I'll get somewhere,' she said. 'I can share with someone. It's only until June.'

'Stay here,' he said.

Judy's eyes widened. 'What?' she asked disbelievingly.

'Stay here. Why not? We've got separate rooms – if you're going to share with someone, share with me.'

'I can't do that!' she said.

He nodded. 'Of course. Mr Lloyd wouldn't like it. Well,' he

said, with a grim little smile, 'I know where I come in the pecking order, don't I? I come a poor third to your bosses and your boyfriend.'

Judy shook her head. 'Why on earth do you *want* me to stay?' she asked.

He dropped his eyes away from hers. 'I can't cope with this,' he said. 'I can't cope on my own.'

'Michael, you're a grown man!'

He put his head in his hands. 'Maybe that's just what I'm not,' he said.

A little boy in Woolworth's. Judy got up, and put her arm round his shoulders. 'You can't hold on to this,' she said. 'Not just because of—'

'I know,' he said, interrupting her. He took his hands away, and looked up. 'Just stay,' he said. 'Until your transfer. Give me time to get used to the idea. Don't walk out on me now. Please. Give me time to find somewhere. I can't rattle about this place on my own.'

Judy frowned slightly as she looked at him. 'I never knew you felt like that,' she said.

'Well, I never knew about Lloyd. That makes us quits,' he said.

Her arm was still round his shoulders. She gave him a squeeze. 'No,' she said. 'It doesn't.' She straightened up. She would have to break her promise. 'I'll stay until the transfer,' she said. Her heart sank at the thought of telling Lloyd, but she managed a smile. 'And this does make us quits,' she said. 'OK?'

He smiled. 'OK,' he said.

The rain had offered false hope; it was falling again, but this time as sleet, as snow, adding to the problem that they already had. It was difficult just to keep upright on the slippery pavement. Judy took a taxi to Lloyd's flat. The obliging driver took her into the garage area, and waited until her own car was coaxed into starting, driving off with two cheerful blasts of the horn when the exhaust fumes belched out, indicating success.

She was looking forward to living here, in an apprehensive sort of way. In the relentlessly modern Stansfield, the old village was reassuring, with listed buildings and family shops and people who had lived there all their lives. But it was enough like part of a much larger town to be reasonably anonymous. Her comings and goings from Lloyd's flat doubtless amused his neighbours, but it remained none of their business. And Lloyd's flat itself was a kind of haven; a little bit of the initial magic was always there.

Judy got ready to go and interview Treadwell, trying to bring her mind back to work, and away from how she was going to tell Lloyd what she had agreed with Michael.

Sam prepared a canvas; he would be painting soon. The image danced just beyond his vision, but it was there. Outside, teams of police combed the playing-field, and nosed up and down the lane; they didn't know what they were looking for, either.

He looked up as the knock came to the door, and Caroline walked in.

'Philip said I'd find you here,' she said, wrinkling her nose a little at the smell.

'Philip was right.' He went back to his canvas. Fifties song, fifties ploy, fifties frustration. He hadn't ached like that since he was fifteen. The brief moments of gratification that he had finally achieved hadn't been worth it. Women never were.

'I owe you an apology,' she said.

'Yes,' he said, still not looking at her.

'I'm just not ready,' she said.

'You seemed ready enough to me.' He looked up. 'Are you ready to come to the pictures?'

'What?'

'Well, we missed out last night,' he said, wiping his hands on a rag. 'So let's go this afternoon. To a real cinema. Saturday afternoon flicks. It won't be very artistic, but what the hell? I don't know what's on, but that doesn't matter.'

She looked shocked. 'We can't do that,' she said.

'Why not? It's Saturday, isn't it?'

'That's got nothing to do with it!'

'Oh,' Sam said. 'Because Diana Hamlyn's dead? Not coming to the pictures with me isn't going to change that.'

'I can't! What would people think?'

'I don't give a f—' He gave a mock bow. 'A fig what people think. And Diana Hamlyn's demise is another thing I don't give a fig about.' He gave a broad smile. 'It looks like she had one fig too many,' he said. 'Doesn't it?'

Caroline just looked at him.

'So,' he said. 'The afternoon showing's at about three, I think. I'll pick you up in the car park at quarter past two – all right?'

'I'm not coming to the pictures with you,' she said carefully, as though he were a bit slow. 'Do you understand?'

'Of course you will. You want to.' Why was he being so persistent, for God's sake? They were all the same in the dark. But he wanted *her*, for the same reasons, he supposed, that a fisherman might struggle for hours to land an inedible fish.

'Is Philip all right?' she asked, ignoring him.

'I think so,' said Sam. He didn't, but he wasn't about to discuss Newby with Caroline.

'He seemed to be in a lot of pain when I saw him,' she said.

Sam grinned again. 'He always looks like that when you're around,' he said. 'Hadn't you noticed? Everyone else has.'

This time he achieved a real blush. You would think it would make her angry, the way Newby looked at her sometimes. But it didn't. At least it embarrassed her.

She turned away and walked to the door.

'Two-fifteen,' he said. 'I'll be waiting with bated breath for your arrival.'

He went to the window then, as there was a flurry of activity in the lane outside. They seemed to have found something.

'I wouldn't, if I were you,' she said. 'Because I won't come.'

Sam grinned. 'I wouldn't really expect you to,' he said. 'Not in the back row of the cinema.'

'Is that it?' asked Treadwell, pointing to the ring.

'Yes,' said Miss Castle, and reached out a hand to take it.

'I'm sorry,' said Sergeant Hill. 'But we'll have to hang on to it for the moment.'

'Oh, of course,' she said.

Treadwell indicated that she could leave, and Miss Castle reluctantly took the hint.

'Where did you say they were found?' he asked.

'In the loft above one of the houses,' she said, tagging the ring.

'Which one?'

'The one at the far end of the lane,' she said, consulting her notebook. 'Palmerston.'

'Worrying about theft seems a bit ridiculous after what's happened,' he said gloomily, then brightened. 'Still, it does seem to have been one of the boys after all,' he said.

There was a little group of items which remained untagged; they were all things that people might never even have missed. Loose change, cigarettes, a pocket handkerchief. Except that there was a pen there – it looked expensive.

'It's odd that the pen wasn't reported,' he said, picking up the plastic bag. It was old; well used. The pattern along the side had almost worn away.

'Yes,' agreed the sergeant. 'I'll see if anyone recognises it. But to get back to why I'm really here,' she said briskly. 'Was there much coming and going from the Hall last night?'

Treadwell thought for a moment. 'No, I don't think so. Waters left at about half past nine, and Mrs Hamlyn went just after quarter past ten. And Newby went early . . . . I left briefly, when I went to look for Mrs Hamlyn. And Robert went back to the flat at about one o'clock – that's when he found her, of course.'

'Mr Newby left early?'

'Yes. He said his leg was bothering him, I'm told.'

She jotted something down. 'He seemed to be in quite a lot of pain when we saw him,' she said, responding to the note of disbelief.

Treadwell shrugged. 'He moved fast enough when he left,' he said.

'When was that?'

'Just minutes after Mrs Hamlyn left. Five at the most.'

He sat down, motioning to the sergeant to do the same. His office felt cold this morning.

'Did Mr Waters mention to you where he was going last night?'

'Is he being difficult?' he asked, but she didn't answer.

'He was supposed to be going out with Caroline Knight,' he said.

'Mrs Knight didn't attend the dinner,' said the sergeant. 'Why was that?'

'She didn't want to, and I didn't press her. She was in a very bad way after Andrew's death.' He sighed. 'I asked her to organise the dinner. I thought having something specific to do might help. And it did seem to – she's quite like her old self. But she wouldn't attend. Not without Andrew, she said – so . . .' He shrugged. 'Perhaps I'm not such a good doctor,' he said, with a smile.

'But she was going out with Mr Waters?'

'Well,' said Treadwell. 'She said she was. Some film, I believe.'

She frowned. 'At that time of night?'

'It was a special showing for St Valentine's Day. Midnight.' He smiled again. 'It doesn't sound like Waters's cup of tea to me. I think it was an excuse they cooked up to get him out of having to stay at the ball.'

She wrote what seemed to be all of that down. 'Is that obligatory?' he asked, pointing to the thick pad.

She smiled. 'It is if you've got a memory like mine,' she said. 'Do you mean you don't think that he was really going out with her? You don't believe the film existed?'

He held up his hands. 'Who knows? Sam – well, you've met him. Enough said, I imagine. But Caroline is quite friendly with him, for some reason. She might have let herself be used as an excuse.'

'Mrs Knight telephoned to speak to Mrs Hamlyn at . . .' She consulted her notebook. 'Ten forty-five. Why was it you rather than Mr Hamlyn who spoke to her?'

Treadwell wasn't sure how to handle this. The woman must have heard about Diana by this time, but . . . well, she *was* a woman. It was all a little indelicate. 'Hamlyn thought she'd gone somewhere with Sam Waters,' he said. 'He refused to take the call.'

She gave a little nod. 'You were gone from the table for about quarter of an hour?'

'Yes,' he said. 'Yes, I must have been.'

A little frown appeared between the sergeant's eyebrows. 'I got the impression from Mrs Knight that the call was quite brief,' she said.

'It was. But she wanted to speak to Diana, and I said I'd look for her.'

'Where did you look?'

'Does it really matter?' Treadwell snapped. He hadn't expected a *woman*. Simon Allison had said the chief inspector would see him. Not a woman.

'Well, one of the people at your table told me that when you returned you were ...' Again, she leafed through the notebook. '... "soaked to the skin",' she said. She looked up at him. 'Were you?' she asked.

'Hardly,' said Treadwell. 'But I did get wet. It was raining very hard.'

'Where did you look?' she asked again.

Treadwell could feel perspiration on the back of his neck. He wished the woman would just go away, but she was waiting patiently for an answer.

'Various places. Places she might have gone with ... with ... well, you know.'

'Mr Treadwell – do I understand that as soon as you were told that Mrs Hamlyn wasn't where she was expected you assumed that she was with a man somewhere?'

'Yes, I'm afraid so.'

'Wasn't she a bit of a liability?'

'In some respects.' He resisted the temptation to run his finger round his shirt collar. 'But she was a very good housemother. She understood children – the youngsters are devastated.'

'Did you ever try to do anything about her behaviour?'

'Like what? It's Hamlyn that we employ, not his wife. What she did was her business.'

'And yet you went looking for her?'

'Mrs Knight wanted to speak to her.'

'Where did you look?' she asked.

Treadwell thought he'd got her off that. 'I went across to the Barn,' he said. 'I just thought she might be there.'

'The Barn?'

'The building behind this one.' He waved a hand behind his shoulder, indicating the Barn through the window.

She got up to look out. 'Why?' she asked.

He closed his eyes briefly. 'I once had occasion to go into the

Barn for something,' he said, his voice flat. 'She was in there with someone.'

'Who?'

'Does it matter? He's no longer employed by the school.'

'Yes, it matters,' she said, in a voice as crisp as the white blouse she wore.

Treadwell sighed. 'It was a young man who was employed as a sort of handyman,' he said. 'I dismissed him on the spot.'

'So he might well feel very resentful towards Mrs Hamlyn?'

'I don't see why. Anyway, it was eighteen months ago – it was a year ago last July.'

'She got him into trouble – she lost him his job.'

'Hardly,' said Treadwell. 'It is the man who takes the lead in these matters.'

He could only be thankful that Marcia had never looked at anyone like Sergeant Hill was looking at him.

Chapter Four

'. . . internal bruising, together with injuries—' Freddie broke off as he realised that Lloyd had come in. He smiled. 'Good morning, Chief Inspector,' he said. 'You almost missed it all.' He smiled broadly.

'Pity I didn't,' Lloyd said sourly, as Freddie finished off the note he'd been making.

'– to neck, breasts, and thighs, consistent with sexual assault.' He looked up. 'Swabs are positive,' said Freddie. 'If it was someone at the school, we might clear this up quite quickly. But it's an interesting one, Lloyd.'

Lloyd groaned. Freddie's 'interesting' was everyone else's headache. He looked at Kathy, which was a more pleasant activity than looking at what Freddie was doing. She smiled at him, as she wrote down Freddie's findings. How could a nice girl like her possibly want to do this for a living? Sandwell was smitten; Lloyd didn't blame him. But he wasn't sure that he could fall for a pathologist's assistant.

'She died of asphyxiation,' Freddie said, peering at something.

Lloyd frowned. 'What about the head injuries?' he asked.

'They didn't kill her,' he said. 'They would have done. He hit her often enough to drop an ox.'

Lloyd nodded, and was left in limbo while Freddie worked, whistling quietly to himself, stopping to get Kathy to make notes, then picking up the tune where he left off. At last, he looked up.

'But all her attacker knew was that she wasn't dead. He thought he wasn't making much of a job of it like that, so he restricted her air supply instead.'

'What with?'

'Ah – well, that's one of the more interesting aspects,' Freddie said eagerly. 'Something rigid – quite thin, probably quite long. Made of wood. And it broke, eventually. We're working on the splinters – should know the sort of wood quite soon, I imagine.'

'Can you give me some sort of description?'

Freddie nodded. 'The blows were made with something blunt, about five, six inches long, with rounded edges. Probably metal, but not particularly heavy – that's why it didn't do the job very efficiently. Unless he went with a positive armoury of weapons, I'd say he adapted whatever he'd been using; just pressed it down on her throat instead of hitting her with it.'

'Can you hazard a guess as to what he used?'

'Taken in conjunction with the neck injury, I'd say you were looking for something with a long, stiff wooden shaft, and a pro-tuberance at one end. Like a golf-club,' he said, and smiled. 'Can't get much closer,' he said. 'I'm not sure what I'd take – a sand iron, do you think?'

'I wish you sometimes had a hangover,' Lloyd said. 'Maybe you wouldn't be so cheerful.'

'Anyway,' Freddie said, 'he underclubbed, whatever he took.'

'Is the golfing analogy going to be a feature of this investigation?' Lloyd asked.

'Just trying to bring a little sunshine into your life,' Freddie said. 'Speaking of which – why do you keep Sergeant Hill away from me?'

'Freddie, believe me. In this case, I'm doing you a favour. She wouldn't take too kindly to your remarks – it's quite difficult to say anything, never mind make jokes.'

'Why?'

'Sex murders don't exactly give her a warm, secure feeling.'

'No, I don't suppose they do. This is a funny one, though.'

'Freddie,' Lloyd sighed. 'Don't make difficulties.'

'I'm not,' said Freddie, sounding a little hurt. 'But it's possible that we're not dealing with rape and murder.'

'Freddie,' said Lloyd, with exaggerated patience. 'She was found in the middle of a field, in the middle of February, in the middle of a downpour, in the middle of the night. Her clothes were torn. She wasn't wearing any underwear. She had been beaten and strangled.'

'I know it wasn't her *day*,' said Freddie. 'I'm just saying she might not have been raped.'

'Oh, come off it!' said Lloyd.

'She was very sexually experienced,' Freddie persisted.

Lloyd raised his eyebrows. 'There would be a lot more blood and guts in here if Judy heard you say that,' he said. 'What's her sexual history got to do with it?'

'It makes rape easier to achieve, and harder to detect, for one thing,' said Freddie. 'And with rape and murder you usually find—'

'Usually!' snorted Lloyd. 'Rape murders aren't usual.'

'They're getting that way,' said Kathy.

They both turned, to look at her, rather as if the corpse had spoken, and Kathy looked faintly guilty for having an opinion at all, but she carried on, glaring at Lloyd.

'It used to be something people did if they went crazy,' she said. 'Now it's something they do if there's nothing good on the telly.'

'– that the rape itself is extremely violent,' Freddie said, determinedly finishing his sentence.

'It sounded violent enough to me,' Lloyd said, waving a hand at Kathy's notes.

'And me,' said Kathy, obviously emboldened by the discovery that she did not get struck by lightning for speaking her mind.

'There was a not inconsiderable degree of sexual violence,' agreed Freddie. 'It was crude, and very forceful. But, if that had been that, it's quite probable that she wouldn't even have sought medical assistance. Her injuries would have mended themselves. And they were occasioned before the head injuries,' he added. 'But she didn't fight back.' He indicated her fingernails. 'These could do a lot of damage,' he said. 'She didn't use them.'

'Perhaps she couldn't get her hands free,' said Lloyd.

Freddie admitted the possibility with a slight nod of his head. 'Perhaps,' he said. 'If the attack had taken place in a confined area, where she couldn't move freely. But, as you so Welshly point out, it took place in the middle of a field, et cetera. And there is no indication that she was restrained in any way.' He smiled suddenly. 'In any sense of the word,' he added.

Lloyd glanced at Kathy, but she was letting that pass. Judy wouldn't have.

'The ground was rock hard, and uneven,' Freddie went on. 'She wasn't forcibly pinned to it, or there would be indications.' He paused. 'The sexual violence was' – Freddie thought for a moment – 'cynical, if you like. The sexual equivalent of a professional foul. He wasn't out of control. He knew what he was doing.'

Lloyd listened thoughtfully as Freddie almost echoed his words to Judy.

'I don't think you're looking for someone who frenziedly raped and murdered her as she was crossing the field,' said Freddie.

'What *are* we looking for?' Lloyd asked.

'Whoever killed her was certainly very frightened – or very angry. The murder *was* particularly violent. And in that context the sex wasn't. She could have put that down to experience. Quite probably a not entirely new experience – possibly not even an unwelcome experience.'

Lloyd's eyes narrowed a little as he tried to work out what Freddie really thought. Freddie's opinions were rarely offered; it didn't do to dismiss them. Or very angry, he had said. 'Do you think she was killed because she had been discovered with someone?' he asked.

Freddie raised reproving eyebrows. 'That's a theory, Lloyd,' he said. 'I don't have theories. Facts, the odd opinion if I feel strongly enough . . .'

'The very odd opinion,' grumbled Lloyd. 'Are you seriously saying that she *consented* to sex in the middle of a field, et cetera? I don't care how many men she had before breakfast – she wasn't about to do that.'

'No,' conceded Freddie. 'But she could have been chased on to the field from somewhere else. We've found nothing yet to confirm that anything other than the murder took place on the field – we're still looking, of course, but the intercourse could well have happened somewhere else.'

'Why do you have to take a perfectly obvious rape murder and complicate it?'

But he was giving Freddie's opinion his consideration all the same. Hamlyn? Did he find her with someone, and kill her in a terrible rage? That seemed to be what Freddie was unofficially suggesting. Freddie who never had theories, because they always came to grief.

'Where would he get hold of a golf-club?' Lloyd asked. 'If it was some sort of row that blew up after the sex?'

Freddie smiled. 'Not my job,' he said. 'The facts are that it certainly looks like rape, and that the rape' – he glanced at Kathy, and smiled seriously – 'though fairly violent, wasn't as violent as the murder. We won't have the results of the tests for a while – before that, anything is guesswork. So, as far as my preliminary report is concerned, Mrs Hamlyn was raped and murdered.'

'Good,' said Lloyd.

'She died between ten-fifteen and eleven-fifteen,' Freddie said. 'I could stretch that to eleven-thirty, but no more. She had been dead at least two hours when I first saw her, and she was last seen alive at ten-fifteen.'

Lloyd nodded. At last, something was going his way. Most murders weren't discovered soon enough to have that good an estimate of the time. But it meant that his theory about Hamlyn had come to grief already.

Waters had a little bit of talking to do, though, and he wasn't going to find Lloyd such an uncritical listener this time.

'Did you think Mrs Hamlyn was with Sam Waters?'

Treadwell rubbed his hands over his face. He had a hangover, and this woman was going to be here for the rest of his life, asking him questions, the same questions, over and over again. 'She did have a bit of a . . . a thing with him, once. But that was well over a year ago. It wasn't still going on.'

'But her husband thought she was with him?'

'Well, as I said, she left forty-five minutes after he did,' said Treadwell. 'That doesn't sound like even circumstantial evidence to me. But Robert made a bit of an exhibition of himself about it.'

'Are you surprised?' she asked.

'Well, I don't think—' He stopped. He'd already been made to discuss things that he would never normally discuss with a woman. Not even Marcia. He had never spoken to her about Mrs

Hamlyn's behaviour with that young man in the Barn; he had not wanted to speak to Sergeant Hill about it.

'You didn't think she was with Mr Waters,' she said, her pen moving over the pages.

Perhaps he could try to make it clear without having to go into any sort of detail. 'The boys danced the first dance with the ladies – just a silly sort of token thing for Valentine's Day,' he said. 'As soon as Diana had finished dancing, she made a bee-line for Philip Newby. I'm not exaggerating – she practically fell over young Matthew Cawston in her hurry to get to him. She talked to him for a few moments, and then she left.'

She waited patiently while he worked out how to phrase the next part.

'He watched her leave,' he said. 'And I understand that he said his leg was bad. But he moved out of there fast enough, believe me.'

She wrote it all down, but her question wasn't about Newby, and she couldn't have made it much plainer.

'Do you know if Mr Waters did go straight to see Mrs Knight?' she asked.

'How would I know?' he said, almost shouting at the stupid woman who couldn't see what was staring her in the face.

'Was he with her when she was told about Mrs Hamlyn?'

'No,' said Treadwell. This seemed to have nothing to do with anything, but at least he could talk about it. 'Dearden said she was on her own – he was a bit worried, because he already thought she seemed jumpy, even before he told her about Diana. But that was half past two in the morning, so I'd hardly expect Sam to have been with her.'

'Everyone left her on her own?' Sergeant Hill asked. 'After what had happened to Mrs Hamlyn?'

Oh, God. 'Yes,' said Treadwell. 'I know it must seem a bit—'

'No one even went to check up on her until half past two?' she asked incredulously.

'No.'

'You didn't ring Mrs Knight back,' the sergeant carried on remorselessly.

'Sorry?' said Treadwell, desperately hanging on to the ropes.

'When you failed to find Mrs Hamlyn – you didn't ring Mrs Knight. Why was that?'

'I had left my guests for rather too long as it was,' said Treadwell. 'Caroline would have gathered that I hadn't found her.'

She didn't believe him, but if she had been going to question him further, he was saved by the door opening, and two of the boys tumbling in excitedly, without even knocking.

'Sir! We've found these!'

'I'm glad I caught you,' Sergeant Hill said. 'I'd like to have another word with you, if it's convenient.'

Caroline invited her in. 'Take a seat,' she said.

Sergeant Hill sat down, and took her notebook from her handbag.

Caroline sat down, too, a little warily. 'I don't think I can tell you any more than I did last night,' she said.

The sergeant smiled. 'I think perhaps you can,' she said pleasantly. 'There are a few things – things that might not have seemed relevant last night.'

Caroline sat back a little, trying to look relaxed, like she did at the dentist. But the efficient, smartly dressed, quick-witted Sergeant Hill made her feel even more uncomfortable than the dentist's chair ever had.

'Did Mr Waters stand you up last night?' she asked suddenly.

Caroline was taken by surprise, as she was meant to be, and she had no time to think. 'No,' she said. 'No, he didn't.' What if he had? Caroline didn't know why she was being asked.

'But your plans – to go to the cinema, was it? – fell through.'

Caroline shrugged slightly. 'It's a film club,' she said. 'Not really a cinema. Of course they fell through. Diana didn't turn up,' she said sarcastically.

A tiny frown appeared on Sergeant Hill's brow. 'I don't think,' she said, consulting her notebook, 'that that was what you said yesterday, was it?'

Caroline didn't know what she'd said yesterday. She wasn't sure what she was saying now.

'Here it is,' said Sergeant Hill. '*My plans had fallen through anyway.*' She looked up. '*Anyway,*' she repeated. 'Whether or not Mr Treadwell had been able to locate Mrs Hamlyn?'

Caroline felt cornered. 'Yes,' she said. 'It was going to be too late for us to go by then.'

'At quarter to eleven? Surely it didn't start until midnight?'

Caroline assumed the question was rhetorical. 'Was Mr Waters with you when you rang the Hall?'

'No,' said Caroline.

Sergeant Hill looked puzzled. 'But he had been with you?'

'Yes.'

'So when did he leave?'

Caroline didn't answer, as she tried to gather her thoughts. She didn't know why they were so interested in Sam. But all his remarks and comments about Diana were echoing in her head, and if he'd said that sort of thing to the police . . .

'About what time did Mr Waters arrive?'

'Half past nine or so.'

'And leave?'

'He left at about ten past ten, I think,' Caroline said, still not sure what relevance Sam's movements had.

'Oh? Did you have some sort of argument?'

'He went to change his clothes,' said Caroline, feigning puzzlement. 'He was wearing a ridiculous dinner-jacket – I wasn't going out with him in that.'

'But when Mr Waters did go out he wore jeans and a sweater. You were all dressed up, Mrs Knight.'

'I don't understand!' Caroline shouted. 'Why are you asking me all these questions?'

'On television they ask if the deceased had any enemies,' said Sergeant Hill. 'I'm afraid we're more likely to ask if she had any friends.'

'But why pick on Sam?'

'We're not picking on him,' the sergeant said calmly. 'But Mr Waters has refused to tell us anything, including where he was. So I have to find out from other people. It's my job, Mrs Knight.'

'To suspect everyone who isn't prepared to tell you all his private business?'

'I'm afraid privacy is at something of a premium in the wake of a murder,' she said.

Caroline made an exasperated noise. 'Sam's just being pig-headed!'

'Perhaps he is,' she said. 'Had you had an argument? Or were you never really going out with him at all? Was that an excuse so that Mr Waters could leave the ball early?'

Caroline frowned. What was that supposed to mean? It was none of her business anyway.

'If he was here, he left early. Did you have a row?'

Oh, God. Caroline could see his baffled face again, and her own face grew hot. 'What makes you think that?' she asked, trying to give herself time to think.

'I think perhaps you rang to tell Mrs Hamlyn that she needn't come at all.'

'So?'

'You were meant to be going out together, but Mr Waters left after half an hour.' She raised her eyebrows. 'In my experience, that equals a row.'

'Yes, all right! We had a ... disagreement – what of it?' Caroline didn't know how to cope with this. Everything she said seemed to get her in deeper.

'What was it about?'

'It's got nothing to do with you!'

'Someone raped and killed Mrs Hamlyn,' she said, her voice still maddeningly calm, like someone manning a Samaritan line. 'That's got something to do with me.'

My God, she thought it was Sam.

'Sam didn't rape her!' she shouted, more to convince herself than Sergeant Hill. 'I know what he's like – I know the sort of things he says and does. But he wouldn't *rape* someone! My God, if he'd been going to rape anyone, it would have been me!' She could hear her own voice echoing in the air for what seemed like hours after she had spoken.

'It would have been you?' repeated Sergeant Hill quietly.

Now what had she done? Caroline couldn't believe she'd said it. How had she made her say it? She dropped her head in her hands.

'Mrs Knight,' she heard the sergeant say. 'You are going to have to explain that.'

Caroline wouldn't look at her. Her hands still covered her face.

'Mrs Knight?' she said again, after a moment. Still calm, still patient.

Caroline looked at her.

'Are you saying that Mr Waters tried to assault you?'

'No!' said Caroline, horrified. She took a moment, then tried to explain. 'I know Sam swears and says outrageous things,' she said. 'He tries to shock people all the time. I don't even like him all that much. And last night was a mistake – things just got out of hand. It wasn't his fault,' she said quickly. She pushed back a straying strand of hair. 'I didn't mean to, but . . . I – I suppose I gave him the wrong idea.' Her nerve deserted her a little under the sergeant's unwavering gaze, and she stopped speaking.

'Go on,' said Sergeant Hill.

'I stopped him,' she said. 'He wasn't very happy about it – that's why he left. He didn't do anything.'

Sergeant Hill showed no reaction.

'I don't know why he didn't just say he was with me, except that it did end like that, and – well, that might just be Sam's version of chivalry.'

The truth. It was a relief, in a way. But now what would she think about Sam? And what if he *had* . . .

'I was going to tell Diana not to bother coming back early,' she said, in a low voice. 'But when I couldn't speak to her I decided to go anyway. By myself.' She sighed. 'I don't suppose I would have had the nerve.'

She was going, thank God. But she stopped at the door. 'Did Mr Waters frighten you?' she asked.

Caroline shook her head.

'Did something frighten you? Mr Dearden seemed to think you were already a little nervous before you knew about Mrs Hamlyn.'

Caroline sighed. 'I think there was some sort of prowler here last night,' she said.

'Oh?' She came back in, and sat down again.

'I . . . I think someone was watching me,' she said. 'When I was changing.'

'Where did you change?' she asked.

'In the Hamlyns' bedroom. I felt as if someone was watching – but I ignored it. And then – well, the curtains don't close properly, and . . .' She shivered again, as she thought of it. 'I'm sure I saw someone,' she said.

'Did you look out?'

'No!' No, she had run into the living-room, too scared to look.

'When was this?'

'Just after eleven,' she said.

'Were you going to keep that to yourself?' Sergeant Hill asked, her tone still polite, interested, like a television interviewer.

'I – I thought perhaps it was . . .' No. No, she couldn't say she thought it was Sam, trying to upset her. 'My imagination,' she finished.

The sergeant wrote that down. 'Thank you,' she said, standing up again.

Caroline showed her downstairs, and out of the building, more to assure herself that the woman had actually gone than out of courtesy. She began to climb the stairs again, then stopped, and looked reflectively at the door of the downstairs flat. Then she turned, came back down, and knocked.

After a moment, Philip opened it, and smiled, but she could see the pain he was in.

'Wasn't he in the art room?' he asked. 'He's not back yet, I'm afraid.'

'Oh – yes, he was,' she said. 'I just came to see if you were all right.'

'Of course I am,' he said, affecting surprise.

She shook her head. 'You can hardly walk,' she said.

'I was in a road accident,' he said, his voice bitter. 'Didn't I tell you?'

'You know what I mean! You can't even stand up straight. Should you see your doctor?'

'No!' he said firmly. But he stood aside. 'Are you coming in?' he asked.

She hesitated, then went in. 'Does it often get as bad as this?' she asked, sitting down.

He moved slowly to the sofa, and lowered himself down, leaning on his stick. There was something different about him, apart from the obvious difficulty he was having in moving. Caroline couldn't quite work out what it was.

'Now and then,' he said. 'It's probably the weather.'

She nodded. 'Have the police been to see you?' she asked.

'Why should they see me?'

'No reason. They seem to have spoken to everyone else, that's all.'

He shook his head. 'I saw them,' he said. 'In the middle of the night – but it was Sam they were interested in. They didn't ask me anything.'

In the middle of the night? What on earth had Sam done that had got them so suspicious?

'Why were they interested in Sam?' she asked.

'I think it was just because he wasn't around when they arrived,' he said. 'And he'd changed.'

Caroline swallowed. 'He wasn't here? Do you know where he was?'

'He wouldn't tell me.' He shrugged. 'And of course he wouldn't tell them.' He smiled again. 'Can't you get done for using abusive language to a police officer?'

Caroline began to understand that the police weren't really picking on Sam. He was picking on them, enjoying being under suspicion, wanting to make them look foolish, if he could.

Philip was looking at her again, his eyes hungry. She tried to ignore it; it wasn't easy, but she was used to it by now.

'Is Sam working on a painting?' she asked, breaking the silence.

'No idea.'

'Do you get on all right with him?'

'Yes,' he said. 'He's not too bad.'

Caroline wasn't at all sure she agreed, but she smiled. 'What did you think of his dinner-jacket?' she asked.

Philip's face broke into his sudden smile, despite the pain, despite whatever his imagination was up to. 'It was fantastic, wasn't it?' he said, turning back into the person she liked. 'Can I get you a cup of coffee or something?'

'I'll get it,' she said.

'No.' He got to his feet, his face growing pale with the effort.

'Philip – are you sure you shouldn't go to the doctor?'

'I'm all right!' He limped over to the kettle, and shook it before plugging it in. 'When did you see his jacket?' he asked.

'He came to see me at the Hamlyns',' she said.

Philip smiled a little shyly. 'Are you and Sam . . . well, a couple?'

'No!' she said vehemently. 'We've been out a few times. That's all.'

'Oh – none of my business. I just . . .'

'What's he been saying?'

'Nothing,' Philip said, spooning coffee into two mugs. 'Well – you know Sam.'

Yes, she knew Sam.

Philip poured the water on to the coffee, then picked up one mug, and reached over to her, the knuckles of his other hand white as they gripped the stick.

The stick. That was what it was. He was using an NHS one.

'Where's your proper stick?' she asked.

'This one's better when it's bad,' he said.

Caroline drank her coffee, but he was at it again before she'd finished; she hurried it, and left.

Matthew watched with dismay the comings and goings of the police, of lab technicians, photographers. They were everywhere. They'd found his hiding-place.

Could they prove anything? If they could, it would be better if he told them himself. Admitted the thefts, saved them the time and trouble of finding him. Let them get on with the serious business. Almost heroic, he told himself.

No – not heroic. Frightened. That would be better. He'd get sympathy then. He could tell them he had been too scared to come forward. Too scared, by what he knew. The sergeant would go for that, he decided, as he watched her talking to one of the teachers. She had a kind face. He would make a full confession. But not now. Not here. After a struggle with his conscience; after he had convinced himself that the police wouldn't let any harm come to him.

Yes, he thought, as he left the house and walked along the lane to the school, that would be best.

He was going to offer Mrs Knight some help in setting up some project that she was doing for Monday. He'd heard her mention it to Treadwell; she had said she would need the key for the store-room. Before, that would have presented a glorious opportunity to take something, and make it look like she had done it. He walked quickly through the drizzle to the main building, and along past the office to the storeroom, where the door was open, and he could see Mrs Knight reaching up to the top shelf for some old books.

'I'll do that,' he said.

She turned quickly, her hand at her mouth, her eyes wide with alarm. 'Oh, Matthew,' she said, breathless. 'I thought there was no one else in the building. You gave me a fright.'

'I'm sorry,' he said. 'I didn't think.'

'Not your fault,' she said. 'Are you taller than me?'

He came in and stood beside her, but there was no difference in their heights. 'I'm afraid not,' he said, looking round.

There was a pile of out-of-date encyclopaedias, and he began piling up the enormous old books.

'No,' she said. 'What if you fell?'

'I won't fall.' He really did seem to have frightened her; he sup-posed, now he came to think of it, that it wasn't surprising. He constructed a platform of books, and tested it with one foot. It seemed quite stable.

'Well,' she said. 'All right. You hand them down to me.'

They got them all down, and began transporting them to the classroom. He met her on the stair as he went back down after dumping his first load; she seemed calmer. But she had been nervy since her husband's accident; Mrs Hamlyn's being murdered wouldn't have done her much good.

'In the Barn,' said Judy. 'Some of the boys found them. Shoes, bag, tights, the lot. One of the shoes was squashed. And the underwear and tights were in the bag.'

'Why didn't anyone check the Barn last night?' Lloyd demanded.

They had obediently parked in the car park, and were walking through the lane, making for the main building. Lloyd held the door open for her with a flourish. 'Ladies first,' he said, with a grin.

'Because no one knew the Barn had anything to do with it,' said Judy. Including Lloyd, but she thought it wiser not to point that out.

It was like any other school building on a Saturday; somewhere, they could hear the caretaker, raking out the boiler, doing whatever uncanny things caretakers did to heating systems to ensure that they belted out heat all weekend and broke down at precisely six o'clock on Monday morning. Judy was instantly transported to her grandmother's warm kitchen; would that she could be, she thought, as her heels rang out on the uncarpeted corridor, making the place seem chillier than ever.

'I suppose every kid in the school got his fingerprints all over them,' said Lloyd gloomily, as he pushed open the office door.

They had temporarily taken over Treadwell's office; Judy once again looked out at the Barn, and was furious with herself for not having got it checked as soon as Treadwell mentioned it. 'Of course they did,' she said, turning from the window. 'I suppose everyone makes mistakes,' she added, almost to herself.

Lloyd laughed. 'Yes,' he said. 'Even me.'

'But Treadwell said he'd looked there,' she said, turning back.

'I don't know who you're arguing with. No one's blaming you. As you said – no one knew it had anything to do with it.' He joined her at the window as one of the scene-of-crime officers emerged from the Barn and lit a cigarette.

'So what do you make of it?' he asked.

'She was raped in the Barn, ran away, and he caught up with her on the playing-field,' she said.

'You know Freddie's theory.'

Judy knew Freddie's theory, and she didn't think much of it. And the Barn seemed no more likely a place for consenting sex than the field, not in the middle of winter.

'Her pants and tights were in her bag,' Lloyd said, correctly interpreting her silence. 'Isn't that more likely to be something she would do?'

'You're asking that as though I were some sort of expert on the protocol,' she said.

'Oh, come on!' he laughed. 'It's not always been in bed, has it?'

She didn't reply.

'It has,' he said gleefully. 'We'll have to remedy that.'

'Don't you have some sort of rule about not mixing our private lives and our professional lives?' she reminded him sharply.

'I didn't mean right *now*,' he said.

He was in one of his skittish moods, when she would wonder what she ever saw in him in the first place. Sometimes if she so much as said his name in the wrong tone of voice he'd be reminding her about his rule.

'Let's hope Freddie can tell us a bit more tonight,' he said.

'Tonight?' Judy repeated.

'We're all going for a drink,' he said.

'You and me and Freddie?' she said. 'Tonight?'

'You and I and Freddie,' he corrected.

'Why?'

'We've got something to celebrate,' he said.

Her heart plunged, but she didn't let it sway her from her investigation. 'You invited Freddie for a drink because we've got something to celebrate?' she asked.

'Well, no. Freddie invited me. Yesterday. But since we've got something to celebrate, I'm inviting you.'

'Oh.'

'It'll just be for an hour or so,' he said. 'Before he goes home to the long-suffering Mrs Freddie. But he might be able to tell us something in advance of the report. You don't mind, do you?'

She shook her head, smiling. She liked Freddie. And she liked the fact that he constantly chatted her up, and that this irritated Lloyd, which served him right for being at times so excessively irritating himself.

She gave him the gist of her interview with Caroline Knight.

'Do you think Sam's our man?' he asked.

Judy shrugged. 'We only know as much as she's prepared to say. Women do sometimes protect men in these circumstances.'

'You concede that, do you?' said Lloyd.

'And she was careful to say that she wasn't all that keen on him,' Judy said, ignoring him.

'We'll talk to Waters. Tell him we know what sort of mood he was in when he left Mrs Knight. That might rattle him a bit.'

'Any chance of eating first?' Judy asked, alarmed that he might abandon lunch in favour of talking to Waters. She had to get the chance to tell him, or she would have to go round with this lead weight inside her all day, and she didn't think she could stand that.

'You bet,' he said. 'I'm told there's a pub round here does a very good lunch. We'll tackle Mr Waters after some food.'

She wished he wasn't in such a good mood, as they went back along the lane to the car park through a cold snow-filled rain that saturated everything.

'It's all right,' he said, as they drove out of the gates. 'We won't get lost – I got directions from Bob Sandwell.'

They didn't get lost, and already she could see the pub sign. Lloyd would soon be off-duty and available to be Spoken To. He pulled into the car park, which was up a three-in-one gradient, and parked the car in an impossible space, with an ease that Judy always envied.

Judy's stomach churned. Music played at a pleasant level, and they were in a private, intimate booth for two in the dining-room. The place was full; people must come for miles, Judy thought, so the food must be good. She wouldn't know, as she pushed it about her plate, but he was enjoying it, and she had no desire to ruin his lunch into the bargain. She would have to wait until he had finished.

As the coffee arrived, Lloyd beamed at her. 'I was talking to the chief super this morning,' he said.

Please, please, don't let it be a long story, she thought. He was deliberately not asking her about Michael. Saving it up, in the same way as he opened all his bills and junk mail before he opened real letters.

'Lloyd, I—'

'And he said to me, "Lloyd," he said, "is Sergeant Hill really a left-wing feminist lesbian from Islington, or is someone having me on?" And I said, "Someone is having you on, sir. She's a left-wing feminist lesbian from Southwark." '

Judy managed a smile. She wasn't going to be able to stop him, so she might as well let him tell his story. 'I take it that the bit about talking to the chief super is true,' she said. 'Let's go from there.'

'He asked if last night was just a gut reaction on your part, or were you a bit political about it.'

'He actually said "gut reaction"?' she asked.

Lloyd smiled. 'He did. Don't blame me. So I said that you held very firm views on the treatment of rape. And he said that he might give you an argument on some of the finer points, but that he just wanted to be sure it wasn't a feminist stand.'

Judy frowned a little.

'And then he said that they were thinking of transferring you to Malworth, instead of to Barton.'

Her face fell. 'Barton would be more exciting,' she said. 'I thought they needed a DI.'

'They do. But they can have any old DI. At Malworth, you would be heading up a small CID section, and second-in-command of the station. Congratulations.' He smiled. 'He said some stuff about ability and leadership and courage – but you don't want to hear all that.'

'Well,' she said.

'That's it? Well?' He called the waiter, and gave him his credit card. 'They're trying you out, Judy. Seeing how you handle command. Before I know where I am you'll be back here as my superintendent.'

'That'll be the day,' she said, and took a breath. 'Well, maybe I should give you my news now.' And she told him, watching him go from delighted to disbelieving.

'Judy – leaving him means that you move *out*!'

The waiter came back, and Lloyd signed the chit angrily. She had known it would be like this. She waited for the waiter to go away again. 'Lloyd, Michael and I have been married for over ten years, and this is the first favour he's asked.'

'So of course you have to grant it.'

'Yes!' she said hotly.

'Why, for God's sake? He's going to try to hang on to you! You know that as well as I do! What sort of basis will it be on? A sort of *ménage à trois*? "I'm off now, dear, just popping over to Lloyd's. I'll be back in time to make your hot chocolate." I know you! You'll still be looking at your bloody watch!'

His voice was growing louder; Judy could see people look round the corners of the other booths.

'He's given you a safety-net. You're not going to leave him.'

'Of course I am,' she said.

'He knows you'll never go if he can stop you now.'

'It's not like that,' she protested in an agonised whisper. She should have known not to embark on this in a public place. 'It's – it's difficult,' she said. 'I can't just walk out like I was going to.' And now she would have to betray Michael, too. She had to explain. 'I didn't realise how much he needs me.'

'And I don't?'

'You've got me.'

Lloyd got up and left.

Judy looked under her eyelashes at the people who tried not to look as though they were looking at her. The waiter brought back the credit card, and left it on the table.

With slow determination, Judy finished her coffee, picked up his credit card, left a tip, thanked the staff, and walked out into the car park. He was still there.

Judy got in, and neither of them spoke until she finally broke the deadlock.

'I owe him this much,' she said stubbornly. 'It's only until June.'

He didn't even look at her, as he started the car, and lunchtime was over.

They drove in silence back to the school; this time, Lloyd swept angrily past the NO ROAD TRAFFIC BEYOND THIS POINT notice, and parked right in front of the building.

Back up in Treadwell's office, Lloyd made phone calls while Judy went over her notes. That pen was odd, she thought. Why wasn't it reported? Maybe she should show it to a few people. She took it out again, and looked at it more closely.

'Waters,' Lloyd said, as he hung up the phone. 'Let's talk to him.'

'Just what I was going to say,' she said, and followed Lloyd out into the corridor.

They frowned at one another as the noises reached them from one of the classrooms, the door of which stood ajar; a strange scraping sound, and a woman's voice uttering mild, slightly breathless oaths. Lloyd went first, pushing open the door, and they watched Caroline Knight continue her argument with the easel she was setting up until it was finally upright; she straightened up, and saw them.

'You win on points,' said Lloyd.

'Were you looking for someone?' she asked, smiling.

'No,' said Lloyd. 'We've commandeered the headmaster's office.'

'That's the lot, Mrs Knight.'

Judy turned to see the head boy again. She still couldn't remember his name.

'Hello, Sergeant Hill,' he said politely.

'Hello,' she said. 'It's . . .'

'Matthew,' he said, with a smile.

'Of course. I'm sorry.'

He put down the briefcase he carried, and shrugged on the expensively casual leather jacket that lay over one of the chairs, his elegance fully restored. He still reminded her of someone.

'Matthew's helping me set up a project,' said Mrs Knight.

'He might have done better helping you set up the easel,' said Lloyd.

She laughed.

'I locked the door,' said Matthew, handing her a key.

'Thank you,' she said. 'You've been a great help, Matthew.'

It was as he turned to leave that Judy finally nailed it. Michael. He reminded her of Michael. Articulate, easy with people, self-confident. And vulnerable. She remembered the bewildered, angular boy who had stared at the police activity, and thought of Michael, a little boy who had lost his mother in Woolworth's. Matthew and Michael, she thought. Hebrew names. Like Sam's, like her own. She knew a lot about names since trying to discover Lloyd's dark secret. She glanced at him, struck by a new thought. Was it *biblical*, this frightful name?

'We'll let you get on,' Lloyd said to Mrs Knight. He turned to go, then turned back. 'You wouldn't know where we'd be likely to find Sam Waters at this time of day, would you?'

She looked at her watch. 'Well,' she said, with a look that suggested a private joke, 'it's just possible that you'll find him in the car park.'

Half past two. Sam came to the conclusion that Caroline was not going to meet him.

He got out of the car just as another car pulled in, containing the chief inspector and his sidekick. Good legs, he noticed, as Sergeant Hill emerged from the car into the fine snow that had again begun to fall. In fact, she was all right, was Detective Sergeant Hill.

'Mr Waters,' said Lloyd. 'Just the man we want to see.' He walked up to him. 'Perhaps we could go inside?'

'Perhaps you couldn't,' said Sam. 'What do you want this time? Found tell-tale strands of navy blue velvet on the corpse?'

Lloyd blinked a little against the rain. 'Does Mrs Hamlyn's death touch you at all?' he asked.

Sam shook his head, then nodded to indicate a concession. 'As a facility, she will be sorely missed,' he said. 'By some.'

The sergeant held up a plastic bag. 'Have you ever seen this?' she asked.

He walked slowly up to her, and looked at the pen enclosed in the bag, his eyes widening in mock excitement. 'Is it a *clue*?' he asked breathlessly. 'Don't tell me – it's the murder weapon, isn't it?'

Lloyd came up to him again, his hands deep in the pockets of his coat. 'What do you suppose the murder weapon was, Mr Waters?' he asked.

'I know this bit,' said Sam. 'I say I didn't kill her by stabbing her with a poisoned fountain pen, and you say how do I know she was poisoned. Right?'

'No,' said the sergeant. 'I say how do you know it's a fountain pen?'

Sam's eyebrows rose, then he laughed. 'All right,' he said. 'For that, you can come in out of the cold.'

Sam let them into the flat, where the gas fire was belting out heat. He snapped it off and invited them to sit down, pleased that Sergeant Hill was there. He was going to have a little fun with the chief inspector's sense of fitness. And she was nice to look at. He wondered if Newby had even noticed her last night. She was his type: dark and slim, like Caroline. But Newby had been in a bad way, and none too comfortable, with the police there. Sam would be willing to bet that Newby couldn't even say what Sergeant Hill looked like.

'It's my pen,' he said. 'It went missing – but I don't suppose you're going to believe that.'

'When did it go missing?' the sergeant asked.

'Last night,' said Sam. 'I know I had it at dinner. I had to put some finishing touches to my speech. I thought I'd left it on the table.'

'Who was at your table?'

Sam grinned. 'Mr and Mrs Treadwell, Mr and Mrs Hamlyn, myself, some boring old fart of a governor and his good lady wife – I don't know their names, but I've no doubt Barry Treadwell does. Failing that, try Caroline Knight – she invited them.'

'When did you notice it had gone?'

'When I put my jacket on to leave the Hamlyns' flat,' he said. 'I had been visiting Caroline,' he added, by way of explanation. 'It wasn't there, so I looked outside for it, but it was too dark.'

'Where did you look for it?'

'I took a walk back across the playing-field,' said Sam.

'Are you sure you were still in the Hamlyns' flat when you noticed it had gone?' asked Lloyd.

'Yes,' said Sam.

'What made you notice?'

'I had had it in the inside pocket,' Sam explained, with great patience. 'The jacket was over a chair, with the inside pocket visible, and the pen wasn't there. Why in God's name do you want to know that?'

'It seems to me that it could have been when you were changing your clothes that you noticed the pen was gone,' said Lloyd. 'You know, transferring things from one set of clothes to the other.'

Sam frowned. 'Well, it wasn't,' he said. 'And so what, if it had been?'

'Then we could be examining the wrong clothes,' said Lloyd.

Christ. Sam went into the bedroom, picked up the jeans and sweater that still lay on the floor where he'd left them, and threw them down on to the sofa. 'I was wearing the dinner-jacket when I looked for the pen,' he said. 'It started to pour down while I was out – that's why it was still damp. I thought you were supposed to be a detective? But you're welcome to waste your time on these if you like.'

Lloyd was looking out of the window, his back to him. 'Thank you, Mr Waters,' he said. 'Of course, you are under no obligation. I appreciate your co-operation.'

Sam offered a suggestion as to what Lloyd could do with the clothes. 'Or get the sergeant here to do it for you,' he added. 'I'm sure she knows her way around.'

Lloyd turned from the window, his face dark and angry, as Sam stared at him defiantly. Sergeant Hill had taken it in her stride. Pity. He'd much rather ruffle her feathers – Lloyd was too easy.

'Well, Sergeant,' said Lloyd. 'The thefts are your province, I believe. Perhaps you could deal with that now?'

Sam felt the chill as she looked at Lloyd, and stood up. 'Yes, sir,' she said. 'If you'll excuse me, Mr Waters.'

'That's it,' said Sam. 'Put 'em in their place.'

She didn't exactly slam the door. She shut it very firmly. Sam grinned.

'Why didn't you tell us before that you went to see Caroline Knight?' Lloyd asked, in a sudden and disorientating change of subject.

Sam sighed. 'Where were *you* between ten and midnight last night?' he asked.

'Just answer the question,' Lloyd said wearily. 'You left the Hall at nine-thirty. What did you do then?'

'Before or after I raped and murdered Diana Hamlyn?' Sam asked earnestly.

'She was very probably raped and quite definitely murdered,' said Lloyd. 'It may be a joke to you, Mr Waters, but no one else finds it very funny.'

Sam smiled. 'I see it's turned into very probable rape,' he said.

'Very improbable would be a more suitable description – I'm aware of your interest in such things.'

'Mrs Knight has told us what happened between you and her last night, so you had better stop trying to be clever,' said Lloyd.

Sam felt as if he had been punched. 'The bitch,' he said, almost to himself, then looked at the chief inspector, waiting for him to say something. 'Nothing happened!' he shouted, when Lloyd remained silent. 'I misread the signals, that's all. I was more bothered about the bloody pen than I was about Mrs Knight, I can tell you that.'

'All right. You failed to find the pen. Then what did you do?'

'Came back here, changed my clothes, and went out.'

'Where did you go?'

'I went to a club in Stansfield.'

'What time did you leave here?' asked Lloyd.

'I don't know!'

'Just tell me,' Lloyd said wearily. 'A straight answer wouldn't go wrong, Mr Waters.'

'After eleven. Ten, quarter past. I don't know. I wasn't checking my watch.'

'Did anyone see you leave?'

Sam shrugged.

'Mrs Knight thinks someone was watching her last night. From the fire-escape – around eleven.'

'Oh – I'm a Peeping Tom now? The woman's paranoid, that's her trouble.'

'Did you see anyone hanging around?' Lloyd asked, raising his voice slightly.

'No.'

'I don't suppose this club has a name?'

Sam told him, and Lloyd wrote it down. He gathered up the clothes. 'You left Mrs Knight at ten past ten or so. Where exactly were you between then and eleven-fifteen?'

'Here, mostly.'

'Alone?' He walked over to the window, his back to Sam.

'Alone.'

'But you looked for the pen before you came back here.'

'Correct.'

'Did you see Mrs Hamlyn while you were out?'

'I didn't have to step over her corpse,' Sam said. 'If that's any help.'

'Did you see Mrs Hamlyn?' Lloyd repeated, getting angry.

'Yes, I saw her.'

'Why didn't you tell us that?'

Sam smiled. 'You didn't ask until now,' he said.

'When you saw Mrs Hamlyn,' Lloyd said, turning slowly to face him, 'did you speak to her?'

'No,' said Sam. 'She wasn't alone.'

'You saw her *with* someone, and didn't bother mentioning that to us?' he asked, his voice low. 'Who was she with?'

'I've no idea,' said Sam. 'I just saw his back view for a few seconds. They were going into the Barn. I can tell you what he was wearing,' he said. 'But it won't narrow the field much.'

Lloyd nodded. 'Dinner-jackets,' he said. 'Unfortunately, they weren't all as distinctive as yours.'

Sam looked at him for a moment. 'I didn't see a dinner-jacket,' he said.

Lloyd looked up sharply. 'What the hell did you see, then?' he shouted.

Sam smiled. 'I saw a school blazer,' he said.

They were in a burger bar in the Square – the centre of Stansfield's main shopping area. Outside, the afternoon light faded, and people walked, heads down against the incessant hard sleet which was turning inexorably back into snow; inside, they talked and laughed, and ate and drank, complained about the weather and their children's inability to keep still, or their unwillingness to eat what they had ordered.

'Would you like me to take that back?' Caroline asked, nodding at the box on the seat beside Philip.

'Sorry?' he said.

Pushing up the folds of her skirt ...

He replayed her question with difficulty. 'Oh, no,' he said. 'Thank you.' He glanced at the box. He didn't know what to do about it, really. Did they just accept that things might happen to hired clothes?

His fingers moving over nylon, finding bare skin . . .

She had seen him just as he was getting into the car to come here. He mustn't drive, she'd said. She would take him to the town. She was going anyway.

The muscles of her thigh growing taut to his touch; the brush of silk on his hand . . .

'It's just that it is a bit slippery out there,' she said. 'I could take it and meet you back here – unless you've something else to do.'

Touching her through the thin material . . .

'No,' he said. 'But it's all right – I'll take it myself.'

Pressing his hand between her thighs; her breath catching in her throat . . .

'If you're sure,' she said. 'We'll meet back at the car, shall we? In what – ten, fifteen minutes?'

'Better make it fifteen,' he said, reaching for his stick.

She buttoned up her coat as she got to the door, shivering as she stepped out, and they went their separate ways.

They just took the box; didn't even open it. Philip escaped from the men's outfitters, and walked cautiously over paving that seemed designed to catch him out. His back ached, his leg felt numb.

She had locked the car; sensible precaution. Things happened when you didn't. He stood for some time in the wind-driven snow that drenched the top deck of the car park.

'Philip, I'm sorry!' She came hurrying over to him. 'Did I lock you out?'

'It's all right,' he said. 'I've just arrived.'

It was getting worse; he could barely bend to get into the car.

'Philip – have you got a doctor in Stansfield?' she asked.

'Not yet,' he answered, as the pain made him close his eyes until it subsided.

'You should see someone,' she said, as he finally sat beside her.

'I'm fine.'

And he was; he had no stiffness, no aches, no gripping pain as he began all over again, starting with her coat. He never needed to undress; magically, his clothes disappeared. No slow, painful process of removing them. But he removed hers, item by item.

Slipping the blouse off; putting a hand to her hair, releasing it,

509

letting it fall over her bared shoulders. Unfastening her brassiere; drawing it away. Touching the small round breasts, his fingers moving delicately over the silk-soft skin; removing her skirt, her slip, revealing French knickers . . .

Not Marks & Spencer briefs.

'Would you like to come up for a drink?' she asked, as she pulled into the school car park.

Drawing her close, feeling firm buttocks under the soft, soft silk . . .

'That would be nice,' he said, wondering if he would manage the stairs.

She stopped the car, and he had to work out how to get out of it again. As he planted his stick on the ground, and heaved himself up from the seat, his eye met a faintly familiar figure. He looked up to see the police officers who had arrived with Sam the night before.

'Mr Newby?' the man said.

Chief Inspector Lloyd. Chief Inspector Lloyd. His mantra.

'Could we have a word, do you think?'

Philip turned to Caroline. 'Sorry,' he said.

'That's all right.' She smiled. 'Perhaps later?'

Later, he would be even more stiff. Later, he would be frightened of the stairs, and of her. 'Perhaps,' he said.

She ran up to her flat. If he could run; if he could run after her, chasing her, catching her. They would laugh, and hug . . .

He opened the door, and the flat was empty. Sam had turned the fire off. Damn the man – didn't he ever feel the cold? Of course he did. But it was macho not to care. Philip picked up the big box of matches he had purchased as a hint, and addressed himself to the task of getting down far enough to light the jets.

'I'll do it,' the girl said, smiling.

'I can do it!'

She looked a little startled. 'Sorry,' she said.

'No. I'm . . . You're right.' Philip handed her the box of matches. 'I can't do anything much,' he muttered through his teeth.

The fire's glow lit the darkening room. 'What do you want?' Philip asked.

'You were at the ball last night, Mr Newby.'

Philip nodded. Chief Inspector Lloyd, Chief Inspector Lloyd, he thought, as the pain gripped his back.

'Why did you leave?'

Chief Inspector Lloyd, Chief ... 'Sorry?' he said, too busy fighting the pain to hear what he had said. 'What did you ask me?'

'Can you tell us why you left early last night?'

'I was sick,' Philip said. 'I have to take pills. The doctor told me not to drink too much, but I did, and now I know why I shouldn't.'

The chief inspector nodded. The woman was taking out a note-book.

'What time did you leave the Hall?' she asked.

'I don't know. I was just about to throw up.'

'We've been told twenty past ten,' said Lloyd. 'Would you agree?'

Philip nodded.

'Mrs Hamlyn left at quarter past. Did you see her at all?'

'No,' said Philip, as his fists clenched. Carefully, deliberately, he relaxed his hands. 'Not in the gents'.'

'How long were you in there?'

'About half an hour,' Philip said, blinking with pain. He shifted his feet slightly, in the hope that that would ease the ache, but it didn't. 'It was busy, with the speeches having finished. I waited until everyone was gone before I came out. And I know what time that was. It was ten to eleven.'

'What did you do then?'

'I came here.'

Sam came in then, and acknowledged Lloyd and Sergeant Hill. 'Are you going to take a look at his dinner-jacket, or is that reserved for me?' he asked.

'I've taken it back to the shop.' Philip twisted round to look at Sam; it was a mistake. He held his breath for a moment, as his back seized.

'Highly suspicious, wouldn't you say, Mr Lloyd?'

'You left the Hall at ten to eleven, and came directly here?' Lloyd repeated, ignoring Sam.

'Yes,' said Philip. He felt the pain subside; he turned slowly to face them.

Sam walked into his line of vision, tutting, shaking his head, as though Philip had played a bad shot. He sat on the sofa, smiling slightly. Philip stared at him.

'Mr Waters says he was here alone until after eleven,' said the chief inspector.

Philip's head began to clear a little, and his heartbeat slowly returned to normal. Maybe he could sit down. He moved towards the sofa, and leaned heavily on the unfamiliar stick, lowering himself carefully down.

'I didn't come in,' he said. 'I didn't want company.'

'Where did you go?'

Philip thought for an instant before he answered. 'To the car park,' he said. 'I sat in the car.'

Sam tutted again.

Lloyd turned to him. 'You have something to say, Mr Waters?'

'His car was in the car park,' said Sam. 'He wasn't in it.'

'Mr Newby?'

'Sam must have just missed me,' said Philip, feeling flustered. 'I didn't stay in the car. I took a walk.'

'Weak,' said Sam. 'They don't like people who don't behave the way they think they should. They always do very definite things at very definite times and make a note of the witnesses present.'

'Wasn't it raining?' asked the sergeant.

'That's why you're so stiff,' said Sam archly. 'Walking about in the pouring rain like that.'

'Mr Newby,' said Lloyd. 'Did you see anyone in the car park?'

'Sam. I saw him leave. And – and maybe someone else.'

'Maybe?'

Philip couldn't be sure. He could have sworn, at the time, but, then, he had had a lot to drink. 'I was in the car with the window down,' he said. 'And I thought I heard someone on the fire-escape.' He looked up. 'There seemed to be a figure, but it might have been a shadow, or something. That's why I got out. That's why I was walking about in the rain,' he added, addressing himself to the sergeant. He found himself speaking almost at dictation pace as she noted everything down.

The chief inspector was interested. 'What did this person look like?' he asked.

'Oh – I don't know. It was too dark. It was just a movement – a figure. Maybe nothing at all.'

'Could it have been, say, Mr Waters?' the sergeant asked. 'Or me? Or the chief inspector?'

Philip frowned, then realised what she was doing. If he had seen someone at all, he must have got an impression, however fleeting a glimpse. But he couldn't be sure he'd really seen something. Maybe he was just giving himself an excuse. He looked at the assembled company. They were all different shapes and sizes. It couldn't have been Sam. Or the chief inspector.

'It could have been you,' he said to the sergeant. 'I thought it was one of the boys, larking about.'

'What did you do?'

'Nothing,' he said quickly. 'There was no one there when I got to the fire-escape. I thought I must have imagined it.'

They didn't comment; they thanked him for his time, and left.

Sam stood up when they had gone. 'Maybe we should do a runner before they stitch us both up,' he said.

Philip thought it was the mode of speech that probably irritated him most of all. Waters had been educated at a hideously expensive public school before getting a good degree at Oxford; he assumed a pseudo-cockney accent, unless he was rattled, when it would return to the received pronunciation which he more naturally employed.

'Maybe you should go and see your girlfriend,' Sam said, opening a can. 'If you can get up the stairs.'

Philip frowned slightly. 'Why?' he asked.

'She seemed a bit upset when I left.' Sam smiled. 'Must have been something I said.'

Slowly, Philip pulled himself up from the sofa. 'Like what?' he asked.

The smile remained. 'I may have forgotten my manners,' he said. 'What are you going to do, Newby? Hit me?'

Philip didn't speak.

'Now's your chance, son. She needs a shoulder to cry on. Nothing wrong with your shoulders, is there?'

Chapter Five

Caroline couldn't stop the tears. They'd started while Sam was still there, and that had made him worse.

She stared at the door when she heard the knock. Had he remembered some obscenities that he hadn't used? 'Who is it?' she asked, her voice betraying the tears.

'It's Philip.'

Philip. Come for his drink. Come to stare at her with his hungry eyes while he pretended to carry on a conversation. She didn't know why she had asked him up for a drink in the first place. She opened the door.

'What's he been doing?' Philip asked, limping badly as he came in.

She wiped away the tears, but they still kept coming. 'Didn't he tell you?' she asked, closing the door.

'He said he'd upset you,' said Philip. 'Why? What did he say to you?'

Caroline smiled, despite the tears. 'I really wouldn't like to repeat any of it,' she said.

Philip looked baffled. 'What's it all about?' he asked.

Caroline shook her head, and wiped the tears again. This time they stayed away.

'Tell me,' he said. 'You can delete the expletives.'

'That would leave a few pronouns and the odd conjunction,' she said.

There was, of course, a word for people like her. There were, as it turned out, several words. And they might not have shocked her, hurt her so much if he had been railing at her, shouting his graphic abuse; but he hadn't raised his voice once.

The gist was that she had caused the police to suspect him

owing to an overestimation of her desirability, that she had nothing that other women didn't have, and that what she did have was less than tantalising. He had not been reduced to a frenzy of sexual frustration because she had denied him her body, and she was deluding herself if she thought that she was capable of inspiring such a thing in anyone other than the sexual inadequate whose sick fantasies' – given vivid expression – fed her own.

'Let's forget it,' she said, as Philip, after much mental preparation for the effort, sat down at last. 'I promised you a drink.'

She poured two glasses from the bottle of wine she had bought in the town to give herself both a reason for being there and a drink to offer him.

'Won't you even tell me what it was about?' he asked, as she handed him his glass.

She sat beside him. 'Maybe he was just telling me some home truths,' she said.

Perhaps Sam wouldn't have upset her so much if she didn't feel so frightened, all the time. Someone had been watching her, perhaps whoever raped Diana. It hadn't been her imagination. And she had thought at the time that it was Sam. She shivered.

Concerned eyes looked into hers, and then he gave a little smile. 'Sam', he said, clinking his glass with hers, 'is a fake from head to toe. He wouldn't know a home truth from a home perm. If he happened to hit on one or two, then it was because he used machine-gun tactics, and he had to hit something.'

That was when she knew why what he had said about Philip had been the most hurtful part; that was what had made her cry. Because every now and then she could see the man that Philip was, behind the constant pain and the frustration about which Sam had been so crudely eloquent.

The Philip that Andrew had told her about; the Philip who lived his life and let other people live theirs, the Philip to whom people turned if they had a problem. Who always had some girl in love with him, who was always going to write a novel, and who had once described himself as living life in the bus lane. She smiled at the memory; Philip asked why she was smiling, and she told him.

He laughed. 'I've never understood yuppies,' he said. 'Screaming down a car phone in your Porsche and giving yourself ulcers doesn't sound like fun to me.'

'Why are you teaching at a school full of embryonic yuppies?' she asked. The wine was beginning to make her feel better. Philip was, too; for the first time, they were just talking.

'I liked the idea of being in the countryside,' he said. 'And of working with Andrew—' He broke off, his face slightly pink. 'Sorry,' he said.

'It's all right,' she said. 'I like talking about him.'

He nodded. 'And maybe I hoped I could get one or two of the boys to smell the roses.'

'Are you succeeding?'

'I have quite high hopes of Matthew Cawston,' said Philip. 'He likes reading – it's a start.'

'Andrew liked Matthew,' said Caroline. 'I'm never very sure that I do.'

'What's wrong with him?' Philip asked.

'I always feel as though he follows me about,' she said, and then wondered what Sam would have to say about that. 'He *does* follow me about,' she said defiantly, as though Sam were there.

'I don't blame him,' was all Philip said.

'And he's a bit too smooth,' she said. 'Too charming.'

Philip grinned. 'Well, there you are,' he said. 'That's one complaint you can't have about Sam.'

'There must be a happy medium,' she laughed.

'There is,' he said. 'Me.' He smiled at her for a moment without speaking. Then his face grew serious. 'Do the police really suspect Sam?' he asked.

'He's done his best to make himself seem suspicious,' Caroline said. 'It was only because they were asking about him that I ever told them about—' She broke off.

'About what?' he asked gently.

'Oh – I just . . .' She could feel herself begin to blush. At the memory, at Sam's subsequent thoughts on the matter. 'Sam made a pass at me last night,' she said. 'I encouraged him, I suppose. Well – not really. But I didn't discourage him. And then I . . .' She smiled, gave a little shrug. 'I would have said that I let him down, but he says it was no let-down at all, so I'm overestimating myself, as he pointed out.'

And it was true, she conceded, that the discovery that his pen was missing had made Sam even angrier than she had; she had put it down to sheer frustration, but Sam had assured her during his visit that it was because the pen meant more to him than anything she had to offer. Or a colourful phrase to that effect.

Philip put down his glass. 'This morning you said that you and he weren't involved.'

'We're not,' Caroline said quickly. 'I don't even *like* him!'

So why had she encouraged him at all? She waited, but Philip didn't ask the question.

'I know it makes no sense,' she said. 'But it's the truth.'

'I'd better be going,' Philip said suddenly, arranging the stick to take his weight.

'Philip – it's the truth. There's nothing between me and Sam.'

'None of my business if there is,' he said, grunting with the strain as he heaved himself to his feet.

'I want you to understand,' she said.

'Why?' But he sat down again, with a little grunt of pain. Caroline wished he would see a doctor; and maybe Sam was right, she thought. Maybe she was attracted to Philip because they were two of a kind.

They had both been damaged in an accident that was none of their making.

'I still haven't told you about my further enquiries into the thefts,' Judy said.

They had met up at Lloyd's car, the atmosphere between them frostier than the weather.

Lloyd grunted, uninterested, as they drove through the interminable snow to the main building. That was the second time she'd tried to give him chapter and verse on the thefts. All right, so she was going to make a federal case out of it. Let her. He hadn't wanted her to stay there, with Waters making remarks. It wasn't that he had one rule for Judy and another for other officers, he told himself. Her presence was hampering the interview, that was all. But he had wanted to annoy her. It was childish, but there it was.

'We've got a murder inquiry,' he said. 'I'm not interested in petty theft right now.' He pushed open the door at the top of the steps, standing to one side to let Judy through. Their footsteps on the wooden flooring echoed round the emptiness of the school building. But it wasn't like any other school Lloyd had ever come across.

'Is the entire teaching profession comprised of weirdos, or do they just come here to die?' he asked, as they climbed the stairs to Treadwell's office.

'Ssh,' said Judy. 'Someone might be in.'

'Would they care? Most of them seem quite proud of it.'

'Well,' said Judy, 'I did some checking when I had to come about the thefts in the first place.' The sentence was accompanied by a glare in his direction. 'And it costs less to send your child here, and it pays less to teach here, than at any other school of comparable size. So . . .' She shrugged. 'You get what you pay for, I suppose. Though it has as good if not better an academic record as the others.'

Lloyd toyed with the grammar lesson, but decided that it was too advanced, and too likely to get him a smack in the mouth. He wished he hadn't snapped at her. He wished he hadn't done a lot of things.

'So weirdos make good teachers?' he said.

'Looks like it,' she said. 'But, to be fair, Sam Waters is the only out-and-out weirdo, isn't he?'

'Is he?' said Lloyd, pushing Treadwell's open door. 'What about Hamlyn?'

A man rose as they came in. Not tall; thin, bespectacled, well into his fifties, possibly sixties. 'Mr Lloyd?' he said.

Lloyd, startled, nodded. 'I don't believe we've—'

'No,' he said, a little shyly. 'Robert Hamlyn.' He extended a hand.

Oh, God. Well, nothing to do about it now. Lloyd grasped the outstretched hand more warmly than he might otherwise have done. He had expected a much younger man. 'Mr Hamlyn,' he said, 'I am very sorry about your wife. We're doing all we can.'

He nodded, and looked down at the floor.

'This is Sergeant Hill,' said Lloyd. 'We didn't want to bother you with questions until you felt up to it.'

'I realise,' he said, lifting his eyes with difficulty, 'that you will have a great many questions. But – I would like to say something to you first, if I may.'

'Of course,' Lloyd said, sitting behind the desk. 'Would you have any objection to my sergeant taking notes?'

'None,' said Hamlyn, but he still stood.

Lloyd watched Judy become aware that Hamlyn wasn't going to sit down until she did. She took a chair from the wall, and she and Hamlyn sat down in unison.

'People here,' said Hamlyn, in his quiet, clear voice, 'find – found – my relationship with my wife difficult to understand.' He smiled a little. 'Perhaps I should say *even* people here,' he said. 'I couldn't help overhearing your conversation.'

Judy shifted a little in her chair. Lloyd nodded slightly. 'I'm sorry,' he said, there not being much more he could say.

'No need for apology,' said Hamlyn. 'Sam Waters calls us flotsam and jetsam – you call us weirdos. People have a need to label others.'

Lloyd took a breath, intending to defend himself, until he realised he really didn't have a defence.

Hamlyn continued. 'And it's true,' he said. 'In a way. The school has a – well, policy would be too definite a word – a tendency, let's say, to recruit from the ranks of non-career teachers, to put it politely. It's a matter of economy as far as the school is concerned, but it does have an odd side-effect. You see, sometimes those who aim for the top forget what they originally set out to do. By employing those who would be rejected by a more rigid system, the school gets – as your sergeant said – as good a result as schools charging several times the fee.'

Judy wasn't taking notes, but surely she should be, Lloyd thought. Wasn't this a lecture? Lloyd hoped that Hamlyn would get to the point in the end.

'And I am one such,' he said. 'I love what I teach. And I love being able to teach my way. Not teaching by numbers.'

There was a pause, but Lloyd knew that it was still not his turn to speak.

'I didn't become a teacher until I was almost forty. I was a bachelor, I was in industry, and one day I realised how much I hated it. They needed teachers, in those days, and I went back to college. I started out teaching in a private day-school, twenty years ago.'

The man spoke like a book. In neat paragraphs, with a space left between them. It was like listening to the radio.

'Diana was fourteen years old when I met her.'

Lloyd's eyes widened slightly, and he refrained from catching Judy's.

Hamlyn's hands were clasped in front of him. They twisted constantly and nervously, belying the calm delivery. 'It was wrong, obviously. I didn't even want it to be like that, but Diana ...' He hunched his shoulders slightly.

'Well, it was what she wanted, and I didn't want to lose her.'

Humbert Humbert lives, thought Lloyd. Lolita, on the other hand ...

'We married when she was eighteen,' he said. 'We ran away; at the age of forty-three, I eloped with an eighteen-year-old girl, Mr Lloyd. It doesn't do a lot for your career chances.'

Lloyd could see that it wouldn't.

'I think it had probably started by then. Her ... infidelity.' He looked up. 'I am assuming that someone – if not everyone – has told you about Diana,' he said. 'I was the first. But I was very far from being the last.'

'Someone did mention that she might have had a bit of a problem,' said Judy carefully, rescuing Lloyd.

Hamlyn nodded. 'I shudder to think how she would have lived if she hadn't married me,' he said, then looked away again. 'But, then, she might not have died.' He gave a long sigh. 'She couldn't help herself,' he said. 'She was perfectly ordinary in other respects.' He smiled sadly. 'She was sensible about everything,' he said. 'Except men.'

This time Lloyd couldn't resist sneaking a look at Judy. Baffled brown eyes looked back for an instant, before returning to her notebook.

'When I could no longer pretend that it wasn't happening, we had rows. We separated, even. But we weren't happy apart. You see' – the hands clasped and unclasped, the fingers twisting round one another – 'we were very fond of each other,' he said. 'But I was never very keen on ... the physical ...' His hands came together in a helpless little mime. 'In a way, I think that that's what Diana liked about me.'

Lloyd became aware that his mouth was slightly open.

'And I realised that I simply wasn't being logical. I was acting the aggrieved husband. I was doing what I thought other people would do. What other people expected me to do. But she needed me, and I needed her. So, we settled for a platonic relationship, which we both enjoyed very much. What Diana did was no concern of mine.'

Lloyd nodded, trying to look as if he came across this every day.

'It had begun to concern me – that is – I was concerned about Diana, with all the talk of disease, and so on. But other than that ...' He shook his head.

'Mr Hamlyn—' Lloyd began, but Hamlyn moved his hand just enough to indicate that he had not finished. Lloyd glanced at Judy again, but she was steadfastly writing in her notebook.

'I understand,' he said, 'that you have been questioning Sam Waters about my wife's death.'

Lloyd was taken by surprise at the sudden return to the matter in hand.

'I – we – are talking to everyone, Mr Hamlyn.'

'But you are paying very close attention to Sam.'

'I'm sorry – I can't ...'

'No,' said Hamlyn. 'Of course not. But I feel that I may inadvertently have caused you to suspect Sam rather more definitely than you should.' He paused. 'Last night, at dinner, I deliberately indicated that I believed Sam was with Diana.'

Lloyd scratched his forehead. 'But you didn't believe that?' he asked, tentative for the first time that he could remember since childhood.

'I had no reason at all to think that he was with Diana. She was involved with him – but that was all over eighteen months ago. Sam ended it.'

Lloyd saw the little frown that came and went on Judy's brow. 'You *know* it was Sam who ended it?' he said.

'Yes.'

'Did – er – did Mrs Hamlyn talk to you about her relationships with – er – other . . . ?' He tailed off, out of his depth.

'No,' Hamlyn said. 'But I'm afraid everyone knew about her new man, once they had been discovered together – and it isn't hard to tell when Sam is offended. Besides which, Diana simply wouldn't have ended it.'

'Mr Hamlyn,' Judy said, just as tentative as Lloyd had been. 'Forgive me. Would that have been the incident with the handyman?'

He nodded. 'All a bit Lady Chatterley, I'm afraid,' he said.

'Doesn't anyone do any work here?' Lloyd asked, unable to keep quiet any longer.

'The school wasn't open,' said Hamlyn, obviously feeling he had to defend what was left of the school's honour. 'It was during the summer break. And he wasn't a handyman, not really. He mended the odd broken window, but we have a caretaker for that. Treadwell got a two-year driving ban, and he needed a driver.' He gave a wry smile. 'I don't think he is ever entirely sober,' he said. 'That's *his* little drawback. We've all got one.'

Lloyd wasn't sure if he meant that it was a qualification for working at the school, or if he was being philosophical.

'Anyway, he called him a handyman on the books. The young man had a lot of time on his hands, and so did Diana.'

Lloyd lapsed into silence again.

'Treadwell discovered them – he was shocked, not unnaturally. Sacked the young man instantly. It was all round the school in no time, and Sam was far from pleased. I came in for some barely veiled comments about her availability, and just who was taking advantage of it – he presumably thought I didn't know what she was like. The truth was that Sam didn't know what she was like, and once he did it was all over, as far as he was concerned.'

Lloyd groped around for the question that would, he supposed, have a logical answer. But it was Alice-in-Wonderland logic.

'Then – Mr Hamlyn – why did you say that you thought she was with Sam?'

'I had my reasons. Childish revenge, I suppose. And I don't like Sam Waters. He was trying to make a fool of everyone, as usual, and I had no qualms about dropping him in it, as the boys would say. But I can't let you suspect him of murder because of what I said. I've no idea who she was with; I have no doubt that she was with someone. I suggest – purely from experience – that you look at the new man.'

'Mr Newby?' said Lloyd.

He nodded. 'That was the pattern,' he said. 'The handyman was new. Newby is the new man now, and Diana would doubtless be interested in him. He, of course, may not have reciprocated; it didn't follow that the new men were necessarily interested in her. But that was the sequence.'

Which number comes last in this sequence? Logic, thought Lloyd. It was all very logical. Judy would like it.

'Do you have any more questions you'd like to ask me?' Hamlyn said.

Yes, thought Lloyd. Why is a raven like a writing-desk, Mr Hamlyn?

'No,' was what he actually said. 'Thank you for being so frank with us.'

Hamlyn removed his glasses, putting them away in a pouch. 'I want you to find out who did that to Diana,' he said, standing up.

'We will,' said Lloyd quietly.

Hamlyn nodded, his eyes sad and trusting, like a basset hound's. 'I believe,' he said to Judy, 'that some men buy their wives flowers when they have erred in some way. That's how I felt. As though I had been bought flowers.'

Lloyd waited until the door had closed before he looked at Judy. He sighed. 'Well?' he said.

'Well.' She closed the notebook, her hand resting on it. 'And you think *our* relationship's irregular,' she said.

Lloyd put his hand on hers. 'Just not quite regular enough,' he said, and smiled. He didn't want to fight with her.

'He thinks we should lay off Sam,' Judy said, with her

disconcerting ability to switch instantly back to work. Lloyd had made the rule; only Judy ever kept it.

'Mm,' he said, reluctantly following suit. He told Judy Sam's latest revelation. 'But he says he saw her with one of the boys,' he concluded.

'One of the *boys*?' repeated Judy.

'I don't know why that should surprise you, in this place,' said Lloyd.

'Which one?'

Lloyd shrugged. He wasn't at all sure that he believed Waters anyway. He told Judy what Sam said he had seen, and she looked thoughtful.

'What?' he asked. He knew that look. 'What is it?'

'The boys were allocated ladies to dance with,' she said. 'Who did Diana Hamlyn get?'

For once, he had got there before her. 'I've checked that out,' he said. 'The boy has a dozen witnesses to prove that he went back to his table, and stayed there all evening. Good thought, though,' he said, smiling.

Treadwell walked into the office, preventing Judy from giving vent to her obvious irritation at his patronising approbation.

'Did Robert Hamlyn see you?' he asked. 'I told him he should wait in here.'

'Yes, thank you,' said Lloyd.

'How well did you know Mrs Hamlyn?' Judy asked, as Treadwell looked through papers in a drawer.

'Not particularly well,' he said. 'We didn't have a lot in common.' He found what he was looking for and straightened up.

'It's been suggested that she might have been seeing one of the boys,' said Judy.

Treadwell stared at her for a long moment before speaking. 'By whom?' he demanded, when he did speak. 'Who made the suggestion?' He made an impatient noise. 'As if I need to ask! There's only one person in this school whose mind works like that.'

'Then you don't think that there's any truth in it?' said Lloyd.

'Of course there's no truth in it! She would never have *dreamed* of having a relationship with one of the boys. It's just the sort of foul suggestion I'd expect from Waters!'

'But you've just said you didn't know her very well,' Judy pointed out, her voice quiet and reasonable.

'I didn't,' Treadwell repeated. 'But I did tell you this morning, Sergeant. Mrs Hamlyn was good with the boys.' He shot a look at Lloyd. 'And I don't want any ribald comments,' he said.

Lloyd's eyes widened. 'You weren't going to get any, Mr Treadwell,' he said angrily.

'No,' he said, slightly flustered. 'I do beg your pardon – I'm obviously too used to dealing with Mr Waters. Mrs Hamlyn understood the boys. Youngsters have problems with everything from acne to arson – she could deal with them, better than anyone else here. The deputy head has responsibility for pastoral care, and I had no doubt that it would be Mrs Hamlyn who provided it. Robert's too logical to understand what adolescents are going through, and Mrs Hamlyn would have been an asset. The suggestion is monstrous.' He closed the drawer. 'If you could let me know when you've finished with my office,' he said, by way of a full stop.

'Won't be long now,' said Lloyd.

Treadwell left, and Lloyd looked out of the window at the starlit night, and the frost which was already forming. So much for spring. A silence fell; idly he flicked through the little brochure which advised new parents of their responsibilities. His eyebrows rose as he read; according to Judy, it was cheaper to send your offspring here than to anywhere else, and he would need a loan just to get the clothes required. A policeman's lot.

'About the thefts,' Judy said.

God. He'd thought they'd reached a truce. 'We've got a *murder* inquiry, Judy,' he said. But really, he should have known her better than that. He knew it as soon as he had spoken.

'You never know, sir,' she said. 'It might help with your murder inquiry, sir. If it's all right for me to get involved in important things, sir.'

'How could it help?' he asked, trying to ignore her.

'I follow orders,' she said. 'I was told to work on the thefts, so that's what I did.'

Lloyd knew he was walking into something, and he didn't know what.

'I finally got Treadwell to do me a list. And one item hasn't been recovered. Something he described as . . .' She turned back the pages of her notebook. 'Here it is – a "niblick" – wasn't accounted for. I didn't know what that was, so I asked him.'

Lloyd closed his eyes. 'I know what it is,' he groaned.

'It's an old golf-club,' she went on. 'It was in the Barn one minute, and gone the next, apparently. It was stolen just before Christmas.'

'Why didn't you tell me?' he demanded.

'I tried to. Twice. You said you weren't interested.'

'What have you done about it?'

'I've got people looking for it – what do you think I've done about it? I'm checking who was here and who wasn't. I've given the lab details of the sort of club it was. I've—'

Lloyd held up a hand. She had, of course, done everything that he would have done. He looked at her, feeling ashamed of the streak of pettiness that had made him pull rank in front of Waters, of all people. 'Sorry,' he said. 'I expect I deserved that.'

'Yes,' she said firmly. 'You did.'

Sam opened the door, and smiled. 'Well, well,' he said. 'It's the fuzz.'

Chief Inspector Lloyd eyed him with distaste but, then, almost everyone did.

'What now?' Sam asked. 'Come to arrest me, have you?'

They walked in without being asked, and Sam stood extravagantly to one side, his arm extending an invitation to the empty doorway.

'Mr Newby,' said Lloyd unexpectedly. 'Is he in?'

'No,' said Sam, closing the door. 'He's upstairs, visiting. And that required considerable fortitude, let me tell you, because going anywhere at all is excruciatingly difficult for our Mr Newby at the moment, never mind tackling a flight of stairs.' He sat down. 'But, then, he lusts after our Mrs Knight.'

'Do you have another topic of conversation?' enquired the chief inspector.

Sam grinned. 'Now and then,' he said. 'But a sex murder on the premises does make you think a bit about the power of our sexual urges, doesn't it? I mean,' he went on, picking up a can of beer, 'it's an urge that gets Newby up a flight of stairs when he can hardly walk – even though he'd be too knackered when he got to the top to do anything anyway. If he *can* do anything, which I doubt.'

'Oh?' said Lloyd.

Another knock at the door; Sam raised his eyebrows. 'Popular chap I am, all of a sudden,' he said, opening the door to someone's chest. He looked up into the face of a young man who could have been nothing else on this earth but a policeman.

'Sir?' the young man said to Lloyd, failing even to acknowledge Sam, but at least refraining from entering without permission.

Lloyd went out, closing the door. Sam looked across at Sergeant Hill. 'Finally got around to wondering about our Mr Newby, have you? Caroline didn't tell you about him, did she? Oh, no. She enjoys it. As soon as someone takes a healthy interest in her, that's when she blows the whistle.'

'And Mr Newby's interest is unhealthy?'

'It all goes on in his head,' said Sam, tapping his own head as he spoke. 'And that's where she wants it to stay. Give her a touch of the real thing, and she has the vapours.'

'You mean because she rejected you she must be frigid?' enquired the sergeant.

'She's got the same problem as you, sweetheart,' he said. 'Nothing that a good seeing-to wouldn't cure.' She didn't react at all, not like the more volatile chief inspector.

'Sorted out your thefts, have you?' he asked, opening the beer.

'The inquiry is proceeding,' she said.

'When do I get my pen back?' he asked, twisting off the ring-pull. She smiled. 'Your pen will be returned in due course.'

'When?' he said. 'I want it back.'

'We wouldn't dream of depriving you of it,' she said. 'But the culprit hasn't been discovered yet.'

'You can't hang on to it! I don't give a shit who stole it.'

'I do. Your pen went missing on the night of the murder – it could be evidence.'

'Evidence my arse! You're doing this on purpose, you bitch. That pen's important to me, and I want it back.'

The door opened. 'Trouble, Sergeant?' asked Lloyd, coming in without even knocking this time.

'Nothing I can't handle,' said the sergeant.

'You should be a traffic warden, you know that?' said Sam. 'Hard-faced—'

'Mr Waters,' Lloyd said, timing the interruption to cut him off. 'Don't say it.' He sat down. 'Suppose you tell me again what you were doing on Friday night.'

'I was getting pills and potions, and goodness knows what all,' said Caroline. 'We hadn't been married long – I suppose that's why it hit me so hard.'

His mouth caressing her breasts, tongue tracing erect nipples . . .

'It must have been terrible,' he said. 'How long were you married?' He should know. Andrew must have told him.

Releasing the fastenings at the top of her stockings, sliding sheer nylon down long, long legs . . .

'Almost three years,' she said. 'It would have been our third anniversary that month.'

'Andrew and I had lost touch,' he said. 'I didn't even know he was married.'

His mouth claiming hers; their bodies coming together, only silk between them . . . her gasps at the thrusting pressure against the soft barrier . . .

'He'd lost your address,' she said. 'He was so pleased when you applied for this job.'

Hooking his fingers over the waistband, drawing the silk down; lips travelling back up the smooth legs, gently, expertly, stimulating her . . . her back arching, twisting her against him . . . her groan of pleasure as he entered her, repeated over and over with the rhythmic movements . . . her body writhing, shuddering under his; slowly bringing her to a climax, the soft moans under her quickened breath growing louder, louder, turning to cries of ecstasy—

'Why don't you let me join in?' she asked.

The rush of blood burned his face while everything else in the universe froze into solid ice. He could hear; he could hear the radio playing downstairs. He could hear the water gurgling through the old-fashioned radiator. He could hear the ever-present police call to one another. He could see; he could see the faded, threadbare rug beneath his feet. He could see scuff marks on his shoes. He could see the empty wine-glass on the floor. He could have seen Caroline, if he had looked up, but he couldn't look at her. Not ever again.

'I'm sure it would be better fun if I was doing it, too,' she said.

Say something, you fool. Say *something*. 'I was staring, wasn't I?' he muttered. 'I'm sorry – I . . .'

'You were doing a bit more than staring,' she said. 'You've been doing it ever since you arrived.'

'I . . .' He couldn't look at her at all. He tried to get up. 'I'm sorry, I'm sorry. I don't mean to do it. I don't know I'm doing it – I . . . well, I do, but . . .' He grasped the arm of the sofa, trying desperately to get to his feet. 'I'm sorry.'

'You don't have to go,' she said.

'Why don't you tell me to sod off?' It wasn't a question; it was a plea, mumbled, his eyes firmly fixed on his shoes. Why wasn't she angry? He could take anger.

'If you were anyone else, I would. But you're not. You're Andrew's friend, and I know you. Feel as if I know you.'

Oh, God, if only he could move. Then he could run away from this.

'Why, Philip?' she asked.

His skin was on fire again. 'I don't know,' he said. 'I don't know. I can't . . . can't . . .' His courage failed him.

'Can't what?' she said.

His shoes looked back at him, no help. 'I can't do anything else,' he said.

'Have you tried?'

He shook his head.

'Then how do you know you can't?'

'I know,' he muttered. Oh, God, let him get out of here.

She was pouring him another drink, handing it to him. He took it, looking at the glass, not at her.

'What does the doctor say?' she asked.

'He just keeps saying that it isn't physical.' That wasn't true; it was not all the doctor said. He said a lot of things that didn't help.

'That much was fairly obvious,' she said.

Oh, God. The humiliation burned on his face. Was that supposed to be some sort of comfort to him? It had all been in his mind; he hadn't had to wrestle with his clothes, to heave his body into doing what was required of it. Because it couldn't, he knew it couldn't. It could only make him want to die of embarrassment.

'Sorry,' she said. He could hear the smile in her voice, and he wanted to *die*. Please, please let me leave, he begged God, Caroline, anyone with the power to grant his wish. Please don't make me talk about it. Please let me die.

'Philip,' she said.

He stared at the rug. He wanted to crawl into its faded pattern, and fade with it. Disappear. Die.

'What sort of doctor?' she asked.

'Psychiatrist,' he muttered.

'Are you straight with him? Do you tell him everything?'

He had to look at her. She wasn't going to let him go.

She sat beside him, fully clothed. For the first time, he tried deliberately to have his fantasy, but he couldn't. He couldn't even have that, not now that she had faced him with it.

'I told him,' he said miserably. 'When it started. Total strangers – women in bus queues, girls behind the counter at the bank. I told him. I was frightened I'd molest someone. But he – he just says it's because I'm depressed.'

'He's probably right.'

Philip shook his head. 'That's *why* I'm depressed,' he said. 'Why can't the fool see that? I don't want pills and pep-talks. I'm frightened.'

'You're not going to molest anyone,' she said, smiling again.

'That's what he says.'

'What else does he say?'

'He says I'm avoiding physical contact, not looking for it. He says that's why I pick women I can't have.'

'What makes you think you can't have me?' she asked.

'You were Andrew's wife!'

'You were Andrew's best friend,' she said. 'I'm not going to let you turn into a dirty old man.' And she smiled again.

The knock at the door made him jump, jarring his back. It was impossible. Whatever she said, whatever the doctor said.

'Don't go away,' she said, going to the door.

'I believe Mr Newby's with you?'

It was, of course, Chief Inspector Lloyd. He always seemed to appear just when his discomfort was at its height. Philip reached for his stick, and even that was agony. He wanted his fantasy back, because there could be nothing else.

'I'm glad you're together,' said Lloyd breezily. 'Because you both reported seeing someone on the fire-escape outside the Hamlyns' bedroom window. I'd like to talk to you about that, if I may.'

Caroline was open-mouthed. 'You saw him?' she said. 'You saw him, too?'

Philip nodded, intensely grateful to Lloyd for the change of subject, even if it was to this one. 'Yes,' he said. 'Well – thought I did. Just a glimpse.'

'I didn't imagine it.' She shivered. 'I thought maybe it was just my reflection or something.'

Philip wanted to reassure her, but how could he?

'Well – perhaps we can get a reasonably precise time,' said Lloyd. 'Mr Newby – about when did you see this person?'

'I don't know for certain. It was just after I'd arrived in the car park. About five to eleven, or so.'

'I thought it was a few minutes after eleven,' said Caroline. 'I told your sergeant.'

'Still – we're agreed that it was about eleven o'clock,' Lloyd said. He looked at Philip. 'You didn't see whoever it was come down again?'

'No. It was just a figure – it was there, and it was gone. I thought I'd imagined it, too.'

'Did you put the bedroom light out when you left, Mrs Knight?'

'I don't honestly know,' she said.

'But you might have, automatically. In which case . . .' He turned back to Philip. 'He could have come down again without your seeing him. It's very dark out there.'

'Yes,' said Philip, his voice flat. 'But the light didn't go out,' he said.

'So where did he go?'

Philip shook his head. 'I don't know,' he said.

'No,' said Lloyd. 'Well – thank you both. I apologise for the intrusion.'

Lloyd went, and Philip got to his feet. He had the stick now, and he could leave at last. 'I'm sorry,' he said. 'I'm terribly sorry I upset you.'

'Don't go,' she said.

'I must.' He opened the door.

'Don't think you won't be welcome here,' she said. 'Please, Philip. Come back tomorrow. When you've had a chance to think.'

Matthew had watched as the daylight faded, and the playing-field emptied. They seemed to be checking every blade of grass. There had been a whole team of people in the Barn, looking for something. He had spoken to the pathologist; he had been pleased to be asked, and explained that the tiniest of objects could yield clues. Murderers rarely left anything obvious behind, not if they were intent on getting away with it. Most of them weren't, oddly enough, he told Matthew. Some of them gave themselves up, some even killed themselves. But most just waited for the reckoning, and didn't bother to deny it.

The interesting ones were the ones who thought they could beat the investigation teams. But if they only knew, he said, what they could discover from mud, from blood – from anything that was found in the area. It wasn't just in Sherlock Holmes that footprints – he called them footmarks – and cigarette ends gave the murderer away. They really did.

He had shown Matthew how they took casts of footmarks, explained how even the way the soles were worn down was sometimes how they proved someone's presence at the scene. But the ground in this case had still been frozen, despite the rain, and hadn't proved much help. But there were other things, he said. He had explained how the injuries themselves could point to someone in particular – someone left-handed, for instance. And how they could work out how many blows had been struck – that, he said, gave you an idea of the state of mind of the attacker.

Matthew had been fascinated.

'Do you think forensics might interest you?' he had asked.

'I'm sure it would,' Matthew had replied.

The pathologist had beamed; a sudden, wide smile that changed his whole face. 'Then, you should talk to your careers master,' he had said. 'Do you have one?'

Matthew had nodded.

'If he needs to know anything – tell him to contact me.' He had given Matthew a card. 'I'll show you round,' he said. 'When we're not so busy.'

Matthew had watched him drive away, and had raised his hand in salute, still holding the card. It was the first profession that had ever really caught his attention, the first time he had ever known what he wanted to do. His father had suggested the law, which had had some appeal. But this was much better. Piecing evidence together, like a jigsaw. Proving what must have happened, perhaps even proving who must have done it, from tiny fragments of information. A piece here, a piece there, the pathologist had said. He did his job, the police did theirs and, if they were lucky, it all came together to prove or disprove someone's story.

Of course, he had said, they didn't always win. But there was always excitement, always urgency, always something interesting to work on.

It was what he wanted to do, he realised, as he saw the chief inspector and the sergeant leave the staff block, and walk towards the car park. He had been waiting for them when he met the pathologist, but he couldn't tell them anything. Not now.

'Right,' Lloyd said to Judy, as they sat in his car in the school car park.

Everyone else had gone with the daylight; they would be back at dawn, looking for the murder weapon.

'What have we got?' he asked.

Judy smiled. 'Do you really want to know?' she asked, reaching into her bag for her notebook, turning on the interior light.

'No, but I expect we'd better make some sense of it all, if we can.'

'We've got Newby. Whose explanation about what he was

doing between ten twenty-five and ten fifty-five is uncorroborated.'

'Except Sam reckons he's impotent,' said Lloyd.

'Sam reckons he's an expert on everyone's sexuality,' said Judy. She smiled. 'Including mine. But would Newby have had the strength to kill her? He can hardly move, and you can *see* he's in real pain. All the time.'

'But only since last night,' said Lloyd. 'If we are to believe Sam. Again. And if that's true – what happened to him? Would throwing up be enough exertion to do that to him?'

Judy shrugged. 'He could certainly walk better than that when I saw him last month,' she said. Something still bothered her about that. She would have to think about it.

'And both Caroline Knight and Philip Newby say that someone was hanging round the junior dormitory,' said Lloyd. 'What do you make of that?'

Judy looked up at the bedroom window, and the easy access it gave to the fire-escape door on the balcony. The window should have a lock, she thought, with her crime prevention officer's hat on. 'It's quite possible,' she said. 'The lab might come up with something.'

Lloyd sighed. 'All right,' he said. 'So what was he doing? Trying to get in? Was Mrs Knight going to be his victim if Newby hadn't turned up?' He thought for a moment. 'Unless he thought the flat would be empty,' he said. 'He might have been trying to get into the building to hide somewhere, *after* he'd killed Mrs Hamlyn.'

'I've got them looking for this handyman person,' Judy said. 'His name is James Lacey. But the golf-club doesn't make sense. He was long gone when it went missing.'

Lloyd grunted. 'It's not just the golf-club that doesn't make sense,' he said. 'It could just be a coincidence, I suppose. But I doubt it. That's what Freddie thought it was straight away.' He sighed, a deep sigh of frustration. 'I don't *know* these people,' he said. 'And Sam Waters is right about one thing.'

'Really?' said Judy, unwilling to concede that the odious Mr Waters was right about anything.

'Flotsam and jetsam,' Lloyd said. 'They all work here and live here, but that's it. They're all loners, they're all failures. Putting Diana Hamlyn in amongst them was bound to end in disaster.'

Judy nodded a little sadly.

'They don't like one another,' Lloyd went on. 'They don't trust one another. They accuse one another – but I'd swear not one of them has told us the truth. Sam Waters did go to a club, like he said. Sandwell checked up – that's what he came to tell me. They know him in there – he was there from about half past midnight until about two, according to the owner. But he says he left here at about ten past eleven. It only takes half an hour to get into Stansfield.'

'But Newby confirms that he saw him leave,' said Judy. 'And Freddie says she was dead by then anyway. Does it matter?'

'But where did he go?' asked Lloyd. 'To dump the murder weapon? But I'll let Mr Waters stew for the moment. He's coming to the station to make a statement about what he saw. I'll have a few more questions for him when he does.'

'He could be making it up about seeing a boy with her,' Judy said. 'Treadwell certainly thinks he was.'

Lloyd sighed. 'He could,' he said. 'And we ought to check up on that film he was supposed to be taking Caroline Knight to – it could be some sort of alibi. You said Treadwell isn't convinced that there was a film. We should pay the club secretary a visit.'

'I rang,' said Judy. 'You had to book – and Mrs Knight booked two tickets in January.'

Lloyd looked a little disappointed.

'You just want to see if the club secretary can get a pirate video of that film that was supposed to be on,' Judy said.

'How do you know about that?' he asked.

'Because I tried to watch it.'

'Why? I thought it wasn't your kind of thing.'

She gave a little sigh. 'Because I knew you'd be watching it,' she said. 'We might as well go straight to the pub,' she added quickly, before he could say anything. 'We don't want to keep Freddie waiting.'

Lloyd smiled. 'All right,' he said, and waited until she had got the car started before leading the way out of the school, and into Stansfield, and the car park of the Derbyshire Hotel.

'Anyway, Sherlock,' he said, as they sat down with their drinks. 'You scored a bull's-eye with the pen. How did you know it was his?'

Judy smiled. 'You know the pattern down the side?'

'Yes,' said Lloyd warily.

'When I looked at it more closely, I realised it was "SW" linked over and over again.' She smiled. 'And I enjoyed taking the wind out of his sails for a moment,' she said.

Freddie was good company when it was possible to steer him away from pathology humour. He had come with bits and pieces of information; the bag and shoes were covered with too many prints to be of any use. But the squashed shoe had been run over by a car wheel.

Judy frowned. 'Are you sure?' she asked.

Freddie didn't deign to reply. 'So there must have been a car involved,' he said.

Which sounded as though it hardly needed to be said, except that Judy knew what he meant. A car furthered his theory, which he didn't have, because he didn't have theories. The back seat of a car seemed a quite likely place for consenting sex, even to Judy.

'But cars aren't allowed up at that end of the school,' Judy said.

Freddie spread out his hands. 'Allowed or not, there was a car in the Barn,' he said. 'And we haven't found her buttons in the Barn or the field,' he said. 'I presume Mrs Hamlyn wouldn't go to a dinner dance with buttons missing from the front of her dress, so it's a reasonable assumption that they came off in the car.'

'Oh, good,' said Lloyd, his voice heavily sarcastic. 'All we have to do is find out which car it was. There were only about two hundred people there. Have you any idea?'

'We're checking,' said Freddie. 'It all takes time, Lloyd.'

A niblick fitted the bill, he said, and pointed out to Lloyd that he hadn't been so far off when he suggested a sand iron. Sam Waters's suit had yielded nothing of interest. He was delighted because he had apparently made a convert while he was at the school.

Judy excused herself to make a phone call, and ordered another slimline tonic when Freddie got another round.

'Did you have to?' Lloyd muttered, as Freddie went to the bar. 'I just want to get out of this place.'

'You're the one who made the arrangement for you and Freddie and I to have a drink,' she said. 'So we're having a drink. All right?'

'You and Freddie and me,' he said, and smiled.

Freddie came back with the drinks. 'We've found a couple of strands of grey wool on Mrs Hamlyn's clothes,' he said, also, it would appear, a saver of the best till last.

'Grey wool?' said Lloyd. 'Like a school blazer?'

'Could be,' said Freddie. 'Get me one of the blazers, and I'll tell you.'

When they left the pub, and got into their separate cars, she didn't go home, but followed Lloyd to the flat. She pulled in beside him, and got out of the car.

It was dark in the garage area. She couldn't see his face.

'Judy,' he said, his voice tired. 'I'm getting too old for this. Setting alarms, looking at watches. It's not for me.'

'No alarms,' she said, and it seemed that her voice echoed quietly through the buildings.

There was a little silence. 'Does this mean you're not going to stay with him after all?'

'No,' she said. 'But it means I can spend the night with you.'

'And then go home to your husband?'

She was cold, shivering inside her coat, and it wasn't just the weather. 'No,' she said. 'And then go home. Michael just lives there, too, that's all.'

She still couldn't see his face. Just his shape, as he stood irresolutely beside his car.

'I can't stay here anyway,' she said. 'It would be silly moving to a flat, just to have to move again in a few months.'

'That's Michael talking. I can hear him.'

Having a relationship with a mind-reader wasn't easy. 'It's true, all the same,' she said.

He came up to her then, and she could just see his face in the strand of light from the street-lamp. He was angry. 'Was it Michael you phoned from the hotel?' he asked.

'Yes.'

He looked at her for a moment. 'Do you mean we have Michael's *permission*?'

'No, of course not! I just told him I wouldn't be home tonight.'

'Well, you were wrong. Unless you've somewhere else to go.'

Judy's heart was beating painfully hard. 'What?' she said. 'You don't mean that.' She was shivering.

'You have no intention of leaving him.'

'I *have*,' she said helplessly. 'But not until the transfer. I made him a promise.'

'You made me a promise.'

'I kept it! I told him – and I *am* leaving. I just didn't know it would hurt him like this!'

'It was going to hurt someone,' said Lloyd. 'Just as long as it wasn't you.'

'That isn't fair!'

'Fair?' he said. 'What's fair? Is what you're doing fair? Go back to Michael, Judy. I don't want this any more. Do you understand? No more. I don't care what you do – leave him, stay with him, do what the hell you like. But don't come back here. I've had enough.'

He turned, and walked away, into the flats.

Judy waited motionless by the car, until she could no longer hear his footsteps on the stairs. Numbly, she drove away, her hands and feet automatically manipulating the controls, her mind blankly refusing to face the situation. The road seemed to steer; she made signals and turned corners, but there was no will, no decision. The car stopped outside the house, and the path took her to the front door. They key opened it, her feet took her into the sitting-room.

'Change of plan?' asked Michael.

'I don't want to talk just now,' she heard her voice saying, as she turned back into the hallway to go upstairs. She stopped, frowning, at the suitcases.

'I do,' Michael said. 'I'll be making an early start. Since you're here, we might as well get things sorted out.'

Still frowning with the effort of regaining her thinking processes, she went back into the room. 'Have you got a business trip?' she asked.

'No,' he said. 'I'm moving into the penthouse.'

The penthouse was the flattering name given to the flat at the top of the office block where Michael worked.

'Ronnie and Lisa moved into their cottage today,' he went on. 'Shirley and I are moving into the penthouse tomorrow. I've got the removal people coming on Monday – it's furnished, so we won't need much. But I want the stuff from my study, and the hi-fi and records, and so on. Just my own things.'

Carefully, Judy searched for her wits, and gathered them gingerly together. 'You and Shirley?' she repeated, her voice small.

'Oh, you don't know her. She came to work for us about six months ago.'

Judy stared at him, sudden tears pricking the backs of her eyes. 'Then . . . what was all that stuff about Woolworth's?' she said.

'Well – you'd just gone back to work. Seen Mr Lloyd again. I had to do something.'

'Why?' Her voice was a whisper.

'I couldn't have you leaving first,' he said. 'It would have spoiled the surprise.'

She blinked painfully as he smiled at her.

'What was all that about, this morning?' she asked, bewildered.

'I wasn't going to let you upstage me,' he said. 'Why should I make it easy for you?'

She gave an uncomprehending shake of her head.

'If you'd ever bothered getting to know me, you would have known it was rubbish,' he said, and shook his head as he looked at her. 'You were good enough to tell me this morning why you married me. Do you want to know why I married you? A reason that won't have occurred to you.'

She could feel the tears hot on her face.

'I loved you,' he said. 'But I don't any more. And I sincerely hope that your unexpected return means that I have screwed things up between you and Mr Lloyd.'

She turned and ran blindly upstairs. She was opening drawers, delving in the wardrobe, taking out underwear and clothes and shoving them into a laundry-bag. She couldn't see what she was doing because of the tears; she had no idea what she was taking.

Her toothbrush. She ought to have her toothbrush. She went

into the bathroom, elbowing Michael aside as he arrived on the landing.

Toothbrush, comb, make-up. She swept them all up, taking a sponge-bag from the back of the door. Some of the things fell as she tried to undo the drawstring, and she kneeled down, picking them up, trying to wipe away the tears. She got everything into the bag, and pulled the string tight. A nightdress. She would need a nightdress.

She turned to the door, and stopped. My God, Lloyd had never seen her in a nightdress, she realised, as she went back into the bedroom, with Michael still on the landing.

She was trying to open the drawer that always jammed, tugging at it uselessly as Michael came into the bedroom. The surge of anger served to open the drawer. She looked at him through a mist. 'Loved me?' she said, and it hurt to speak. She consigned the nightdress to the bag, and picked it up.

'We should talk,' he said. 'About the house, and so on.'

She ignored him.

'Where are you going?' he asked.

'Lloyd's.'

'Are you so sure you'll be welcome?'

'No,' she said.

She threw the bag into the back of the car, and sat in it until the tears subsided. She drove off, back to Lloyd. No, she wasn't sure she would be welcome.

But he would let her in. And that, she told the absent Michael, *that* was love.

Treadwell read for a while after going to bed, but he couldn't get interested. He leaned over Marcia to turn off the light.

'No, Barry,' she said.

Nothing had been further from his thoughts; her response was automatic, produced at the first sign of anything that might be construed as an overture. It had made him smile once, long ago; it was a hangover from their chaste courting days, he had thought, given that in those early months of marriage it had not apparently been a serious rejection. As time wore on, however, the cajoling and persuasion had become wearisome, the objective hardly worth the time and trouble expended on its achievement.

Without discussion, an understanding had evolved that his requests – it would be overstating the urgency to call them demands – would be met, despite the token protest, at infrequent intervals. This was one such, and he availed himself of the opportunity on the grounds that it might be a while before the next time, and it might serve to make him feel better. Marcia took little notice of the proceedings; he expected no more than her occasional compliance.

He supposed he must have slept, or he couldn't, presumably, have woken up. He had no idea what time it was; it felt like morning, despite the darkness. He looked across at the smudged blur of light on the bedside table. Six forty-five; it was morning, despite the blackness beyond the window, despite the lack of noise. Schools were unbelievably noisy places, with hundreds of feet scurrying along uncarpeted floors, hundreds of voices raised at once in separate, animated conversations. The walls echoed with sound from dawn till dusk; only now was the place still and silent. But this morning the silence had a different quality.

Treadwell got out of bed, shivering a little in the chill air of the room. He reached for his dressing-gown, and was still struggling with it in the darkness as he crossed over to the window. Outside, the dim lighting revealed the outlines of the buildings. Beyond them, though he couldn't see it, lay the playing-field. The rain that had drenched that dreadful night had gone as though it had never been; even the sleety snow had gone, and the ground was dry and cold once more.

Perhaps it had all been a bad dream. Perhaps the rain hadn't happened. Perhaps – Treadwell sighed – perhaps none of it had happened. Perhaps Diana was still vibrantly alive. And it seemed almost possible that none of it had happened. He had had dreams that had remained real for minutes after waking. How did he know? He couldn't tell what was real and what wasn't, standing here in the dark with the school lying as frostily still below him as Marcia had. It didn't look like a place where a murder had happened.

Treadwell left the bedroom, went downstairs, and out into the cold, dark morning. Past the staff block, across to the junior dormitory, going to where he could see the playing-field, its frost-covered surface gleaming as dawn broke.

He had had to see for himself the proof that it had all happened. He hadn't really believed that it had just been a dream, but some sort of desperate hope had made him go and check. And there they were, two lines of ribbon across the field, as if it had been marked out for a cross-country run. Tomorrow, once again, police would inch their way across the grass, looking for something, anything, to lead them to Diana's killer.

Treadwell turned away, and became consciously aware of the muffled sound. He had been aware of it all along, he supposed. The peculiar quality of this morning's silence was that it *wasn't* silent; sounds of the rude world were intruding. A sound. An engine, running.

Puzzled, a little tentative, he walked round the side of the junior dormitory. The sound was marginally louder, but not loud enough to be coming from one of the dark shapes in the car park. He walked slowly, disbelievingly, towards the sound, towards the private garage that came with the junior dormitory. His hand reached out of its own accord, and he tried to push the door open. Something was jamming it; cloth, paper, something.

He pushed harder, almost falling as the door swung up, releasing the dense, choking fumes into the morning air.

Chapter Six

Wearing Lloyd's spare dressing-gown, Judy pulled the cord on the blind, which ran up the kitchen window with a loud snap as it reached the top. Daylight slanted into the kitchen as the sun reflected on the hard frost.

The flat was a kind of antidote to Lloyd himself; it was even more tranquil in the early morning. Hardy British birds called to one another through the cold air, and below the window the village street still slept. So did Lloyd; it remained to be seen what he was like first thing.

She surveyed the fridge. Bacon, eggs. Good. Frying-pan – where did he keep his frying-pan? On the rare occasions that she had eaten in the flat, Lloyd had done the cooking. It was ridiculous that she didn't know where he kept the frying-pan. Ah – up there. She took it down, glancing out of the window at the sleeping street.

Bread. She opened the bread-bin, but only a few crumbs remained. He had used the last of the bread to make sandwiches last night.

During the drive to the flat, the shock had turned to anger; she had announced as Lloyd opened the door that since everyone was agreed that she was a selfish pig who never thought of anyone but herself, perhaps they could take that as read and skip the part where she got told it all again. Then, tight-lipped, she had told Lloyd what a fool Michael had made of her, just so that he could watch her jump through hoops. Lloyd had listened, and then had asked what she had had to eat.

She had realised that she had eaten virtually nothing all day, and he had made sandwiches. You should not, he had said, make commitments on an empty stomach. It gave you cramp.

Now she was hungry again.

It was a gas cooker, and she wasn't used to one. It was Lloyd's opinion that she shouldn't be allowed near any sort of cooker, but she could at least make breakfast, if she knew how to make the thing work. It was supposed to be automatic, but the clicking noises that it made when she turned the tap seemed to have no intention of lighting the gas.

She had just given up when she heard the kitchen door open, felt Lloyd's arms come round her waist.

She twisted round to look at him. 'Oh, it's you,' she said, smiling at him.

'I was supposed to get up first,' he said. 'And bring you breakfast in bed.'

She kissed him. 'I don't like breakfast in bed,' she said.

'You amaze me,' he smiled. 'Oh, well, the rose on the breakfast-tray is out, I suppose.'

'I'll bring you breakfast in bed, if you like,' she said. 'If you tell me how to light the damn cooker.'

'I never eat breakfast.'

Judy couldn't conceive of anyone not eating breakfast as a deliberate policy. Especially on a Sunday.

She kissed him again, hugging him close to her.

'What was that for?' he asked.

'For being such a nice man,' she said.

'Wait a minute,' he said suspiciously. 'What have you done with Judy Hill? I know all about body-snatchers – I'm a film buff, you know.'

'Shut up.' She hit him.

'What have I done that's so nice?' he asked. 'I thought I was horrible to you.'

Judy took the bacon out of the fridge, and set about finding scissors for the rind.

'How come you're up so early?' he asked.

'A thought occurred to me.'

He smiled. 'I know I'm going to regret this,' he said. 'A thought about what?'

'Diana Hamlyn.'

Lloyd nodded slowly. 'The earth moved for me, too,' he said.

'Doesn't it always?' said Judy, and smiled. 'I did put her out of my mind for a while.'

'So what brought her back?'

'In a way,' said Judy slowly, 'that *was* what brought her back. She never had that.'

Lloyd raised his eyebrows. 'I rather thought the whole point was that she got too much of that,' he said.

'No, she didn't,' Judy argued. 'Hamlyn says he loved her, but he didn't want her. And the men who did want her didn't give a damn.' She shook her head. 'It was so joyless,' she said.

Lloyd frowned, puzzled. 'That's what kept you off your sleep?' he said, his voice disbelieving. 'You're not developing a soul at this late stage, are you? I don't know if I could cope with that.'

'Don't worry,' said Judy, shaking her head. 'It was just a passing thought. But it made me think about Sam Waters.'

'How very distressing,' said Lloyd.

'He said he saw her with a boy.' Judy cut off the rind, and nicked the bacon as she spoke. 'How do you light this thing?' she asked.

'Ah,' said Lloyd.

'Ah?'

'I had a thought, too,' he said. 'I don't think the grey thread means much. All the boys danced with the ladies – I expect we could have found grey threads on any of their clothes.'

'But he says he saw her with a boy, nevertheless,' said Judy.

'You don't think that's just Waters stirring it?'

'Not necessarily. Do you have any tomato, or anything?'

'Mushrooms?' he suggested. 'Salad drawer. I tend to agree with the headmaster,' he said. 'She doesn't sound as if she would be interested in one of the boys. She wasn't interested in them when she was an adolescent herself. It was Hamlyn she went after, remember.'

'I don't think she was interested in a boy,' said Judy. 'Not for that reason, at any rate. But Waters's pen went missing during the dinner. From the top table. Suppose Mrs Hamlyn saw who took the pen, and *that's* why Waters saw her with one of the boys?'

'She takes him outside rather than make a fuss with all these people there?' Lloyd said, nodding slowly. 'Could be. Do you have anyone in mind?' he asked.

'How do you light this cooker?' she demanded.

'You have to use matches,' Lloyd said, frowning distractedly as he spoke. 'The automatic thing doesn't work.' He took matches from the cupboard. 'I'm the one who is supposed to come up with theories,' he complained. 'Not you.'

She applied the match to the grill, half of which remained unlit then exploded into life. 'That's dangerous,' she said, as she left it to heat up.

'So are theories, as Freddie never tires of reminding me,' said Lloyd. '*Do* you have anyone in mind?'

'Well – it depends. The other ladies at the top table were the wife of the chairman of governors and Mrs Treadwell. First, I want to find out which boys danced with them. Because they'd have access to the pen.'

'And?' said Lloyd.

'And if one of them was Matthew Cawston, then I've got someone in mind,' she said. 'Treadwell said that Mrs Hamlyn almost knocked Cawston over on her way to talk to Newby. And, apart from Newby himself, she only had contact with the boy she danced with and Cawston. So, if she was with a boy at all, he seems the most likely. And he's in Palmerston House, which is where the stuff was found.'

Lloyd was still frowning slightly as he went to answer the phone, which was ringing unaccountably early for a Sunday. 'And to think', he said, 'I just fell asleep while all that was going on.'

She smiled. 'You obviously inspired me,' she called after him.

'Huh,' he called back, as he picked up the phone.

Two minutes later, Judy was reluctantly turning off the gas, putting the bacon back in the fridge, and getting ready to head out to the school again.

They arrived to yet another tangle of emergency vehicles, and drove into the car park, almost mowing down the headmaster.

'I don't believe it,' Treadwell kept saying, over and over again, as they got out of the car. 'I don't believe it.'

Freddie was already there; he called them over to the garage. As they walked across the quiet car park, a banshee's wail made

Judy freeze. She looked up to see nothing more alarming than WPC Alexander at the balcony door, which would have benefited from some oil on its hinges.

'Sergeant Hill,' she said. 'There's a note up here, addressed to the chief inspector.'

They went round to the front of the building, and up to the Hamlyns' living-quarters. Lloyd read the note, then stood aside to let Judy see it.

'*Dear Mr Lloyd,*' it read, '*I am writing this to you in order to make it clear that I died by my own hand. I can see that my death in the middle of your inquiry into my wife's murder could seem suspicious.*

'*I wasn't happy until I met Diana. I was unhappy during our brief separation. I don't believe I can possibly be happy without her, and I cannot live with the belief that I caused her death. Forgive me for causing you more work, as I know I will.*' It was signed, and dated.

'I'll get the handwriting checked out,' said Freddie. 'And check it for prints. Just in case.'

Judy looked out of the open door at the scene below. Poor Mr Hamlyn, she thought. Calmly, logically, arriving at the conclusion that life wouldn't be worth living. Her eye caught the fire-escape on which the scene-of-crime people had been working. They had found some threads of material, and what might be blood-stains at the foot of the steps; they were working on the evidence as fast as they could, but it all took time, and Hamlyn couldn't face having any more time.

They went back down. Lloyd went into the garage with Freddie, and Judy went in search of Treadwell. At least he was alive.

As she arrived at the house, a motorbike drew up beside her.

'Excuse me.'

She turned to see a dark young man, who was removing his helmet the better to converse with her.

'I'm looking for a Detective Sergeant Hill,' he said. 'Is he here, do you know?'

'You've found him,' Judy said, smiling.

'Oh – sorry. The message just said . . . so I assumed . . . sorry.'

'That's all right,' she said. 'Did you want me?'

'You want me,' he said. 'Jim Lacey. I kept being told a Sergeant Hill was looking for me, but no one said what about, or where you were.'

'I think we kept just missing you,' she said.

'I'm on the move all day,' he said. 'Anyway, I heard about . . . well – what happened, and put two and two together.' He shook his head, and blinked a little. 'I still can't believe it,' he said. 'What sort of a nutter does something like that?'

'I'll find somewhere we can talk,' she said. She rather liked Mr Lacey, and at least he seemed more forthcoming than anyone else she had spoken to.

'I don't think you'll have to,' he said. He unzipped a pocket in his leather jacket. 'That's where I was on Friday night,' he said. He handed her a hospital appointment card. 'I was in a bit of a punch-up,' he said. 'I had to go to casualty. You can check up,' he said.

'Thank you,' she said, smiling. Mr Lacey was probably no stranger to the police, and he was anxious to prove that he had had nothing to do with events at the school. She made a note of his address.

'Since you're here,' she said, 'can you tell me anything about Diana Hamlyn?'

'She was all right!' he said, almost angrily. 'I know what everyone thinks, but – well, she was all right.'

Matthew Cawston was standing a little way off, watching what was going on, looking rather like a model for the sharp clothes he was wearing. She wondered if she was right about him. She had better go entirely by the book in case she wasn't – Matthew would know all about his rights, she was sure.

'We have got the right story about you and her, have we?' Judy asked Lacey, but she had lost her audience, as an older man came past them, and caught his attention.

'Des – how are you doing?' Lacey raised his voice to speak to the other man.

Des put down his tool-kit. 'How do you think I'm doing?' he demanded loudly enough to make people turn their heads. 'Have you heard what's been going on here?'

'Yes,' said Lacey. 'That's why I'm here.'

'Well, if you've come to pay your respects to her husband, don't bother. He's gone, too. This place has gone mad. It was never normal, but this is ridiculous. And you didn't help.'

'What do you mean, he's gone, too?'

'He did himself in. This morning.'

Lacey looked at Judy. 'Hamlyn?' he said.

She nodded.

'Poor old sod,' he said.

'Who's this, then?' asked Des. 'Another of your conquests?'

Lacey smiled. 'No. This is Sergeant Hill, Des. I'm a suspect.'

'What?' He cupped his hand to his ear.

'A suspect! They think I might have done it.'

He was smiling as he spoke, but it seemed to Judy that the heartiness was just a little overdone; he didn't want Des to think that Mrs Hamlyn's death had touched him.

'Get on! You couldn't knock the skin off a rice pudding, for all your leather gear and your motorbike.' He wagged a finger at Lacey. 'Didn't I tell you not to get involved with her?'

'Yes, Des.'

'Well. Won't be told, will you? You and your good for a laugh. She isn't good for a laugh now, is she?'

Judy turned as she heard the sound of Philip Newby's stick on the pavement. He acknowledged her, and went into the flat.

'What happened to him?' asked Lacey.

Judy turned back. 'Do you know him?' she asked.

'Well – met him. He was here for an interview. I'm not likely to forget – it was the day I was sacked.'

'What's that?' said Des.

'I'm saying that bloke was here for an interview the day me and Mrs H got caught,' shouted Lacey. 'What happened to him?'

Des leaned forward, eyebrows knotted together, to indicate that he hadn't quite heard the question, despite its having been bellowed.

'He was in a car crash,' said Judy.

Lacey shook his head.

'What was that?' said Des.

'Will he always have to use a stick?' Lacey asked.

'I don't know,' said Judy.

'What?' said Des. 'Why do all you people *mumble*?' With that, he picked up his tool-bag, and went towards the junior dormitory.

'OK if I go now?' asked Lacey, swinging his leg over the bike and kicking it into life.

'Yes,' said Judy. 'Thank you for coming.'

She watched as he roared off down the drive. She had rather enjoyed meeting Jim Lacey. He was the first person she had met who actually seemed to care that Mrs Hamlyn was dead. She hoped she wouldn't have to talk to him again, and grabbed Sandwell as he passed, handing him the hospital card. 'Check that out, will you?' she said sweetly. Barton General was not noted for its swift response to enquiries.

She had to pass Matthew on her way into the Treadwells' house. He smiled politely, and gravely.

Treadwell came to his front door, a large whisky in his hand. 'A bit early,' he said, ushering her in. 'But I needed it.'

Judy asked him which of the boys had danced with the other ladies at the top table, and he shrugged. 'God knows,' he said. 'And Marcia, I expect.' He tilted his head back slightly. 'Marcia!' he shouted.

Marcia appeared. She didn't speak.

'Who danced with you and what's-her-name on Friday night?'

'Lots of people danced with *her*,' she said.

'No – the boys.'

'Oh, that.' She went slightly pink. 'Sorry,' she said. 'I thought you meant—'

'Just tell her who danced with you,' he said impatiently.

Judy looked apologetically at Marcia Treadwell, though why she felt she should apologise for the woman's own husband she wasn't sure.

'I can't remember who the other boy was,' she said, a little fearfully. 'But Matthew Cawston danced with me. Twice – the first dance, and then one later on.'

'Thank you, Mrs Treadwell.'

Marcia Treadwell took herself back to wherever she had come from.

DEATH OF A DANCER

'Mr Treadwell,' said Judy, 'the chief inspector and I would like to talk to Matthew. You should be present.'

'Why do you want to talk to Matthew?' he asked.

'It's about the thefts,' she said.

'Does it really matter about the thefts? Don't you think you've got more important things to do than that?'

'We'd like to speak to Matthew,' she repeated firmly, and went to the door. 'I'll find Chief Inspector Lloyd,' she said.

Outside, Sandwell was waiting with confirmation that an ambulance had picked up James Lacey outside a pub at 9.30 on Friday night, and that he had been attended to just after midnight.

'How did you get that so quickly?' she asked, in awe of anyone who could get an answer of any sort from medical sources.

Sandwell grinned. 'My sister was on night duty in casualty on Friday night,' he said. 'It's not what you know, Sergeant . . . .'

'Why the hell would he kill himself?' said Sam.

Philip looked across at him. 'Maybe he loved her,' he said.

Sam gave his opinion in two words, which was how he often communicated quite complex thoughts. Philip mused a little on the versatility of one small word, as he shifted slightly in his chair. He could move more easily again. He had spent a sleepless night, thinking about Caroline, but not the way he'd thought of her before. It wasn't a terrible, secret vice any more. It never had been. She'd known, all along.

And what had horrified him at the time seemed somehow to comfort him during the night. Despite the lack of sleep, he had been relaxed, for once, and the pain had relaxed with him.

'I take it you don't think he loved her,' said Philip, realising just how much he disliked Sam Waters.

'Who could love someone that everyone in the school was knocking off?' asked Sam, then grinned unpleasantly. 'Present company excepted, of course.'

'But she was loved,' said Philip. 'She was like a second mother to the juniors – you only have to look at them since it happened. You can't get a word out of the first-years. They loved her – why shouldn't Hamlyn have felt the same?'

'They haven't all topped themselves, have they? They've got more bloody sense.'

'Have you ever loved *anyone*, Sam?' Philip asked.

'Not a woman,' he said. 'Don't get me wrong, I'm not queer. Gay. Whatever they want to call it now. You just can't make a friend of a woman.'

'I'm not surprised, if you think of them the way you do.'

'That's rich, if I may say so. Can't go to jail for what you're thinking, eh, Newby?'

Philip felt himself grow pink. Did everyone know? Had it been that obvious? It seemed it had, as Sam went on.

'At least I can do something about it,' he said. 'And it's all they're good for.'

Philip sighed. 'Am I supposed to go digging round in your psyche to find out that someone let you down in your impressionable youth or something?'

'I don't want you digging round anywhere near my psyche,' said Sam. 'Save it for your girlfriend.'

She had said he should come back; and he should, if she wanted him to. He owed her that. And it might prove whether or not her shock cure had worked. He rose, wincing a little. But he had got up without having to think about it; it was a considerable improvement.

He was only slightly out of breath as he knocked on her door; not bad at all. He heard the bolt being drawn back; he must get a bolt for his room, he thought. Especially in view of the thief's activities. It wouldn't surprise him if it was his flatmate who was stealing, just to cause mischief.

Caroline was pale. Her hand shook as she bolted the door again.

'Are you frightened of something?' he asked. Not him, obviously. She'd locked herself in with him.

'I don't want anyone just ... walking in,' she said, going over to the window.

'Sam's not been here again, has he?'

She shook her head. 'And he's not going to be,' she said. She didn't speak for a long time. Just stood, looking out of the window at the increased police activity.

'Robert killed himself,' she said, at last.

Philip made a grunt of acknowledgement.

'I didn't. I didn't think I could go on living without Andrew, but I didn't try to stop living.'

'Killing yourself isn't a normal reaction,' Philip said, alarmed, going to her. He forgot, briefly, that he couldn't walk the way he used to, and had to hold his breath until the pain passed off. He stood beside her. 'You *can* live without him. Robert could have lived, too. He just . . . panicked, I imagine.'

She looked up at him. 'Maybe I should have killed myself,' she said.

'Caroline,' he said. 'Look – come away from the window. Sit down.' He manoeuvred her to the sofa, and sat her down. 'You've had too much death to cope with,' he said, carefully sitting beside her. 'Do you think that's what Diana would have wanted him to do?' he asked. 'You can't think it's what Andrew would have wanted. He was crazy about you. He told me you'd altered his whole life. He was really upset because I'd missed you—' He broke off, realising what he was saying.

'What's wrong?'

'I've just remembered that,' he said.

A lot of memories came flooding in on top of that. Too many. Not everything. It was disjointed and confusing, but such a relief that he sighed with satisfaction.

'What have you remembered?' she asked.

'He kept telling me he had a surprise for me. Then eventually he told me about you. He said I'd like you.' He smiled. 'He was right.'

'He said I'd like you,' she said, with an answering smile.

Philip reddened. 'I've made it a bit difficult for you,' he said. She shook her head.

' "*Everything's gone wrong*," ' Philip said, frowning, as another snatch of that day came back to him. Andrew had said that – just like Caroline had when she met him on the first day of term.

'What?' said Caroline.

'Oh – I was just remembering what Andrew said. I'd had the interview, and you were due back, but you had got held up.'

She nodded.

'And some crisis had happened here,' said Philip. 'I had to get back to London, but I'd missed my train.' He gave a bitter little smile. 'I can't even remember what was so bloody important now,' he said, looking at his stick. 'But he really wanted me to meet you.' He smiled. 'I'm glad I have.'

She smiled back. 'You're so like him,' she said. There were tears in her eyes.

Tentatively, Philip put a hand on her shoulder, patting her.

She drew back. 'You can't give me a cuddle if you're hanging on to that,' she said, taking away his stick.

He held her close as she literally cried on his shoulder. Nothing wrong with his shoulders, like the man said.

The heavy smell of exhaust fumes still lingered in the air around the junior dormitory, and once again the school was alive with uniforms; once again an ambulance stood by helplessly as another dead body was examined; once again Matthew watched the aftermath of sudden, unnatural death.

But this time the scene was sunlit and incongruous. Night seemed the right time for alarms and excursions; the professional, quiet urgency with which these people performed their duties suited a cloak of darkness, and it seemed out of place on a day when the bright winter sunshine flashed its reflection on the windows of the cars that came in a continuous stream up the drive.

Faces appeared at the windows as the news was whispered through the waking school, and boys came and stood in small groups, keeping a discreet distance from the Hamlyns' garage, where all the activity was centred. Matthew hated being one of the crowd, one of those who gathered to watch while other people got on with the job.

He had liked Hamlyn; he was sorry that he was dead. But he *was* dead, and there was nothing he could do about that. That being so, he rather wished he'd found him. Then he would have been in the arena, not in the stands. One day, he would be. One day, he'd be the one called to the scene, like the doctor, who came out of the garage, a girl running behind him, trying to keep up with his long strides. The sergeant and the chief inspector followed, and stopped to speak to Treadwell. What in the world had he been doing, wandering about the grounds at that time in the morning? Matthew wondered if the police had asked him that.

They seemed to be looking over at him, all three of them, talking about him. He thought he was imagining things until they began walking towards him. Being singled out was better than being one of the crowd, but he didn't understand this, and that worried him.

'Could we have a word, Matthew?' asked the sergeant, pleasantly enough.

Matthew had never known dread. He became acquainted with it as he followed them to the headmaster's house, and into the sitting-room, where Sergeant Hill formally introduced him to the chief inspector. Mrs Treadwell eventually realised that she was surplus to requirements, and went off into the kitchen. Nothing ever seemed to touch her, Matthew thought, as he sat down at Treadwell's command. Murder, suicide – she looked exactly the same. No one else did.

Treadwell looked pale and shocked, his hair uncombed, his clothes hastily assembled. Matthew had never seen him without a tie. Mrs Knight had looked like death when he had seen her earlier; even Waters had been too preoccupied to give anyone the benefit of his opinion. But Mrs Treadwell just fluttered about, as usual.

'The sergeant would like to ask you a few questions,' said Treadwell, sitting stiffly on an upright chair.

Matthew looked politely at Sergeant Hill.

'Friday night,' said Sergeant Hill crisply, and Matthew could only be thankful that he had been allowed to sit.

Helpful. Be helpful, anxious to please, until you know what she knows.

Matthew nodded slowly. 'The night of the ball?' he said.

'You danced with Mrs Treadwell, I believe?' she said.

'Yes,' said Matthew, a genuine puzzlement pulling his brows together. 'All the boys danced with the ladies.'

'Yes,' she said, and opened a notebook. 'You took Mrs Treadwell back to her table when the dance was over?'

'Yes,' he said. 'Of course.'

'What happened then?'

'Nothing,' he replied, to give himself time to think.

She sighed. 'What did you do, Matthew? When you got to the top table?'

This was all wrong. She wasn't going to be a pushover. He should have come forward of his own accord, when he'd meant to. Now he wasn't sure how to play it.

'What did you do when you got to the top table?' she asked again.

She knew. He didn't know how, but she knew already. He was supposed to be telling her of his own free will – shamefacedly confessing, reluctantly imparting the rest of his story. This wasn't right; it wasn't *fair*. But he still had information; he still had something to bargain with. Still, he wouldn't rush in, he told himself. He had to change his game-plan, but he had to be careful; he had to trump the right trick.

'Nothing,' he said again, dropping his head, still hoping that reluctant confession followed by his specific knowledge might swing things in his favour.

'Did you take a pen, Matthew?' asked the sergeant.

He lifted his head and looked straight at her. He didn't think muted heroism would go down very well with her after all; directness might be the answer. And she knew; there was no point in denying it.

'Yes,' he said. 'It was just lying on the table, so I took it.'

Sergeant Hill nodded; Treadwell's mouth fell open as his face grew dark.

Chief Inspector Lloyd turned from his contemplation of the view from Treadwell's sitting-room window, where he had been taking no apparent interest in the interview.

'Did you steal the other things that have gone missing over the last eighteen months?' he asked.

'Yes.' Matthew saw a slight frown appear and disappear on the sergeant's face.

'Why?' said Treadwell, sounding betrayed. 'Why, Matthew?'

'Fun,' said Matthew, looking at the chief inspector.

'What? Speak up, boy.'

Speak up, boy. Somewhere, Treadwell had a headmaster's

phrase-book, Matthew would swear. He turned his head this time. 'Fun,' he repeated.

'Fun?' echoed Treadwell. 'You stole for *fun*?'

'Yes,' said Matthew. 'Everyone thought that one of the teachers was stealing,' he said, turning back to the sergeant. 'It was fun.'

'What did you hope to gain by it?' Treadwell asked, his face baffled.

'Nothing. It wasn't really stealing,' Matthew said. 'I was going to give it all back. I was going to leave it somewhere it would all be found after I'd left. That's not really stealing. I kept it all.'

'We haven't found it all,' said the sergeant.

'It was all there,' said Matthew.

'Well,' said Lloyd, 'we'll come back to that. What happened after you took the pen?' He sat beside the sergeant on the sofa.

'I was on my way back to my table when Mrs Hamlyn stopped me. She said she wanted to see me outside, and just carried on walking, as if she hadn't spoken to me at all. So I went out and waited for her.'

'Go on,' said Lloyd.

'She came out and asked me for the pen. I said I hadn't taken it.'

Lloyd looked up. 'Where did this conversation take place?' he asked.

'Outside the Hall, to start with,' said Matthew. 'But it suddenly started raining, and she didn't want to go back into the Hall because there were too many people going in and out of the cloakrooms. So we went into the Barn. She said she'd seen me take the pen. She said she'd have to talk to Mr Treadwell, but then someone else came in, and . . . .' He shrugged. 'I ran away.'

'Who came in?' Lloyd asked.

'I don't know. I couldn't see.'

'How long were you with Mrs Hamlyn?'

'I don't know – just a couple of minutes.'

'What was the point of running away?' asked the sergeant.

'I just ran. I wanted to get rid of the pen, because if I didn't have it she couldn't prove anything. I went back to the house, and waited for about half an hour, to make sure she hadn't followed me, or told anyone. Then I put it with the other stuff. I was going to get rid of it all.'

'I thought you said it wasn't really stealing?' said the sergeant. 'That you intended giving it back?'

'I did,' said Matthew. 'But I didn't intend getting caught. I could say she was mistaken – if I got rid of the stuff, no one would be able to prove anything. But then I couldn't, with the police all over the place. I didn't think you'd find it.'

'You were unlucky, Matthew,' said Sergeant Hill. 'We were looking for a murder weapon. You look everywhere.'

'I didn't think anyone knew about the loft,' said Matthew. 'You can't really see the hatch.'

'A piece of the black bin-liner was sticking out,' she said. 'You panicked a little. You were careless,' she said.

Matthew almost smiled. The pathologist had said that that was how people got caught.

Treadwell frowned. 'Is this amusing you?' he asked.

'No, sir,' said Matthew.

'Did you deliberately cause Mrs—?' He stopped. 'A member of staff to come under suspicion?'

'Yes, sir. Well, I didn't mean it to happen – not at first. But people suspected her, and – well, then I did do it deliberately.' He looked from one disapproving face to another, to another. 'I didn't think!' he said. 'It was just a bit of fun.' He dropped his eyes. 'I'm sorry,' he said. 'I realised that it wasn't right, making people think that she was stealing. That's why I took the pen.'

'Who are we talking about?' asked Lloyd.

'Mrs Knight,' said Matthew. 'But she wasn't *at* the ball, so I thought that if I took the pen people would stop thinking it was her.'

Lloyd sat back. 'So it was really a laudable act, was it?' he asked.

'No, sir.' Matthew was having trouble gauging the chief inspector, and decided that trying to convince him of his concern for Mrs Knight was probably not the most sensible course. 'I thought it would be fun to confuse them, now that they were convinced it was Mrs Knight,' he said. 'I was going to tell you all this.'

'Oh?' The sergeant, disbelieving.

'I was, honestly! But then . . .' He aimed his remarks at the chief inspector. 'I spoke to the doctor who was here,' he said. 'About pathology. Forensic science. That's what I'd really like to do,' he said. 'And I thought if I told you I'd taken the stuff I might not be able to.'

Lloyd nodded. 'Well, that remains to be seen,' he said. 'But why?' he asked. 'Why were you going to tell us?'

'Because it must have been Mr Newby who came into the Barn,' Matthew said. 'His car was parked in there.'

'You could have told us about the car without admitting to the thefts,' said the sergeant, still suspicious.

'I know. But . . .' Matthew paused. 'I know something. I saw something when I was – well, another time. Another time that I took things.'

Chief Inspector Lloyd looked at him, his eyes slightly narrowed, as though he was trying to read print too small for his eyesight.

'Matthew,' he said, 'you have admitted stealing various items over the last eighteen months.'

'It wasn't really stealing,' Matthew said again.

'I am going to ask you to come to the police station to make a statement. As Mr Treadwell is *in loco parentis*, he will accompany you, and will be present during the interview. You can be legally represented if you wish.'

Matthew looked at Treadwell, who seemed as though he might be going to be sick.

'We will contact your parents as soon as possible,' Lloyd went on.

Matthew thought Treadwell was going to faint.

Sam left the art room, feeling hungry. He knew what he wanted; he knew if he gave himself over to it, it would come. But he had to give it time, let it come to him, and he needed something now, something to tide him over. Caroline had said she wasn't ready for that kind of commitment. Thank God for that. He wasn't looking for Caroline's commitment; he couldn't understand how something so trivial as the gratification of sexual appetite could ever assume such dimensions. It would be like having to commit yourself to a plate of chips before you ate it.

Sam would eventually be ready for his commitment; he would work at it, coaxing the colour and light out of his brushes and on to the canvas until it released him, if it ever did. It was wonderful, and dreadful, and no woman could ever produce the feeling of exhilaration he had when he worked, the triumph, the sheer joy that he would experience on its completion. Or the terrible anticlimax of its being over.

In the meantime, Caroline would suffice. Right now, however, food would have to fill the gap being created by the images that danced out of reach; he wandered over to the canteen, but lunch wasn't being served for another hour. He used one of the slot machines, and bought himself a bar of chocolate.

He walked back along the lane, where the images grew suddenly sharper, as he bit into the chocolate. He stopped by the art room, then carried on. He must let the thought germinate, let it come in its own time. He walked slowly, lost in thoughts which were interrupted by the sight of Lloyd and his sergeant getting into a car with Treadwell and young Matthew Cawston.

He watched it drive away, saw Mrs Treadwell look anxiously after it, and quickened his step to reach her before she went back into the house. Matthew, she said, had been stealing.

Stealing may have been their excuse to take him away, but that wasn't why Matthew had been bundled off to the police station. Good old British bobbies. They could always be relied upon to go off at half-cock, firing his bullets for him, and incidentally sharpening the image in his mind; he could see it, he could almost touch it.

It was agony, forcing himself to go back to the flat. Thank God Newby wasn't there. He paced the room, feeling his way cautiously into the image; this was just the start. He had to hold back, had to wait, had to let it take its own time. His only desire was to seize a pencil, sketch his thoughts, but he mustn't. He mustn't force the hard, clear image on to paper, or it would stay like that, like a photograph. When it was committed to paper, it would be pliant, yielding to his pen over and over, until every detail, every line, every curve was perfect. And when it exploded on to the canvas, if he did it right, people who could see past their prejudices would cry for his slot machine, and they wouldn't know why.

He swore when he heard the knock at the door, and didn't open it. But the knocking continued, and he strode over angrily, expecting another visit from the constabulary.

A large, handsome man in a flash suit stood at the door, by no stretch of the imagination a policeman.

'Yes?'

'Where the hell is the headmaster?' the man demanded to know. 'I've tried the school, and his house. The man's nowhere to be found.'

'He's with the police,' said Sam. 'At the police station, I presume.' He smiled. 'We've had some trouble here,' he said.

'Trouble?' The man snorted. 'I'll say you've had trouble! And you're going to have worse trouble, believe you me! Where's his deputy? I want to speak to him.'

Sam grinned. 'I doubt if that will be possible,' he said. 'Unless you've got an Indian guide.'

'What?'

'Suicide,' said Sam, never a man to waste words.

The man opened his mouth, then closed it.

'He was married to Friday night's corpse,' said Sam helpfully. 'He's today's.'

'Now, look!' Sam's visitor was going an interesting shade. 'I want an explanation of what's been going on at this school!'

They'd be coming by the coach load by tomorrow morning, thought Sam. 'You're a parent, are you?' he asked.

'My name is Cawston.'

'Matthew's father?' asked Sam.

'You know Matthew?'

'Matthew is our head boy,' said Sam. 'But, even if he wasn't, I would know him. We don't have that many boys here. And do you wonder?'

'I want to know what the hell's going on!' Cawston roared.

Sam opened the door wider. 'Come in,' he said. 'I'll tell you all about it.'

*

Treadwell stared at the boy, who sat at the table in the interview room, brazening it out. Opposite him sat Chief Superintendent Allison and Chief Inspector Lloyd; the ranks bothered Treadwell a little. Beside him sat the solicitor, hastily called, wearing a Sunday sweater over his shirt and tie, to indicate just how much he was going to cost. Treadwell hadn't been able to reach Cawston senior yet; he had taken the decision for him, knowing that whatever he did it would be wrong.

'Do you know why you're here, Matthew?' asked the chief superintendent.

'I stole some things,' said Matthew.

'What Matthew means is that he took some things without permission,' said the solicitor. 'There was no intention permanently to deprive the owners of these articles.'

Matthew Cawston was far and away the brightest boy Treadwell had ever had through his hands; a brilliant career in almost any field he cared to name was virtually a foregone conclusion, and Treadwell had announced that the thief would be expelled. Announcements at assembly weren't legally binding, of course, and he doubted if he really would have carried out his threat in any event, whoever the culprit. The items stolen were so ridiculous, so haphazard, that financial gain could never have been the motive. He had been prepared to have a heart-to-heart with whoever it was, find out what it was all about. Even get them help if it seemed warranted. But Matthew? It simply didn't seem possible.

Matthew was his flagship; when Treadwell would casually suggest that 'one of the boys' show the parents of prospective pupils round the school, it was Matthew whom he detailed to do the showing-round. Clever, but not a swot; strong and athletic, but not a show-off. A tasteful, well-designed, colour-supplement advertisement for the school. A thief.

Perhaps he stole because he was bored, because everything came too easily to him, and he needed the excitement. Perhaps because his overbearing father and his volatile mother had failed him in some way. Or perhaps because underneath all the effortless academic achievement he was just a bad lot.

But, whatever his reasons, if only he had owned up sooner, it might well have been possible to drop the whole thing. To give the boy some sleepless nights, and then tell him that he was being given a second chance. It might even have been possible to keep the alarming Mr Cawston senior out of it, to tell the police that the school did not wish to go any further in the matter of the thefts, and quietly set the whole thing to rest. Why he stole was a question for the psychologists, and didn't really concern Treadwell.

But the sergeant's obsession with the thefts had made any glossing-over impossible. Damn the woman. And the chief inspector, and the chief superintendent. Treadwell would have thought he would have had more sense than to worry about the thefts when two people had died. And it was just the thefts, wasn't it? He cleared his throat.

Matthew looked at him briefly, before his eyes flicked back to the police.

'Don't you want to know what I saw?' he asked.

'All in good time, Matthew,' said the chief inspector.

Sergeant Hill came in then, putting a sheet of paper down in front of Lloyd. Allison read it over Lloyd's shoulder, and left the room. Treadwell was beginning to feel panicky.

'Did you steal a golf-club, Matthew?' asked Lloyd.

'What's your interest in this particular item, Chief Inspector?' asked the solicitor.

The sergeant glanced at Lloyd, and then she answered the solicitor's question. 'Matthew has told us that he took all the items which have gone missing in the last eighteen months,' she said. 'One of them is still unaccounted for. An old golf-club – a niblick, it's called. We would like to know what Matthew did with it.'

Matthew shook his head. 'I didn't steal a golf-club.'

Lloyd took a slow breath. 'The thing is, Matthew,' he said, 'it looks rather as though that club was used to murder Mrs Hamlyn.'

Treadwell thought he was going to die. The statement hadn't taken him by surprise; it had taken no one by surprise. They all knew that they weren't there about some thefts which barely amounted to ten pounds' worth of stuff. But he'd said it now. He'd used the word.

'I didn't take a golf-club,' Matthew repeated, still shaking his head. 'I didn't. But I saw something – why won't you let me tell you what I saw? I saw Mr Newby with—'

'You don't have to say anything at this juncture,' warned his solicitor.

'But I want to! I was going to, anyway! I thought that's why I was here.'

'Tell us now, Matthew,' Lloyd said. 'I'm listening.' But there was no gentle encouragement about his tone this time. This time he meant business, and Matthew obviously knew that.

And he told them, with the odd glance over to where Treadwell sat, about a scene he'd witnessed in the Hamlyns' bedroom between Newby and Mrs Hamlyn. Treadwell listened, his head swimming, hardly daring to breathe.

Lloyd listened, but he didn't comment, didn't ask questions. 'Think about it, Matthew,' he said, and he and the sergeant left. After about five minutes, she came back.

'Right, Matthew,' she said brightly. 'Let's get this statement down on paper.'

The sergeant went through every single item, asking where he'd taken it from, what he'd done with it, checking his answers off on the list she had made of the items she had recovered; Treadwell sat watching, still half-hoping that it was all some sort of nightmare.

He would have sold his soul for a drink.

Caroline pulled a tissue from the box, wiped her eyes and nose, and tried to smile. 'I'm sorry,' she said.

'Don't be silly,' said Philip.

'You must think I do this all the time.'

He looked shamefaced. 'I can't have helped,' he said.

'It only bothered me to start with,' she said, then felt the pain herself as he went crimson. 'Oh, no,' she said, taking his hand. 'I didn't mean to upset you. Please, forget it. It doesn't matter.'

'It does,' he mumbled, like one of the boys being told off. 'Even Sam knew.'

She sighed. 'Yes,' she said. 'He said as much.' He'd said much more than that.

He looked up, appalled. 'He *spoke* to you about it?'

She felt out of her depth. 'Well – yes,' she said. 'You know what he's like! He was trying to put me off – he doesn't think you have any right to fancy me.'

'He's right.' His head dropped again in an agony of embarrassment.

'He *isn't*!' She held his hand tightly. 'It's just another injury, Philip. Like your leg and your back, except it isn't physical.'

He nodded miserably. 'I know,' he said. 'You're right.'

'I'm always right,' she said, smiling.

'You're wrong about one thing,' he said, with a shy duck of his head. 'I don't fancy you.'

'No?'

'Diana Hamlyn told me,' he said. 'The first day I got here. She said I was in love with you. She was right.'

She smiled again.

'But I'd be no good to you,' he said again. 'A physical and emotional wreck is something I don't imagine you need right now.'

'You're not a wreck!' she shouted. 'And I think for a start that you should find somewhere else to live. I know Sam – he'll encourage you to think like that.'

Philip looked up. 'I'm hardly a threat to Sam,' he said.

She shook her head. 'You haven't got Sam figured at all, have you?' she said. 'Has he told you he's not queer yet?'

Philip's eyes widened. 'Yes, as it happens,' he said. 'He told me this morning.' He looked disbelieving. 'You're not saying he is?'

She shook her head. 'No,' she said. 'He makes do with women. But he doesn't like them. And he doesn't want to lose you to the opposition.'

Philip shook his head.

'Oh – you believe macho Sam's stories, do you? Philip – you've got more sex appeal in your left earlobe than he's got in his whole body. I should think Diana Hamlyn's the only woman who ever looked at him twice!'

'You did.'

'No. I didn't – I . . .' She couldn't explain. And now she was scared again, scared that she would lose Philip.

'You said you didn't discourage him,' he persisted.

'No, because I thought he could . . .' She looked at him. How could he possibly think he was less attractive than Sam, who would have carried on regardless if she'd dropped dead? She shivered, as she always did when she thought of it, and stood up to try to mask the involuntary movement.

Philip was on his feet, too. 'Well, he *can*,' he said. 'Which is more than I can do, as he pointed out to me only today.'

Caroline closed her eyes. Philip would have shown more consideration for an inflatable doll than Sam had shown for her. 'Is it that important?' she asked.

He nodded. 'It is if you can't do it,' he said.

'I don't believe you can't do it,' she said. 'But even if you can't, you'd still be a better bargain than Sam.'

'I have to go.'

'No – Philip.' She caught his arm. 'Stay, please. I don't expect anything from you. Just stay with me. I'm scared.'

He looked at her. 'You think Sam raped Diana because of you, don't you?' he asked. 'And you think he was watching you. That's why you're scared. Isn't it?'

She dropped her eyes from his, and nodded.

He moved to the door, and Caroline looked up as he opened it. He turned back to her.

'Sam wasn't watching you,' he said. 'And he didn't rape Diana.'

With that, he left, and Caroline had to sit down, or she would have collapsed.

No, no, not Philip. Please God, not Philip.

'What the hell's going on here?'

The large man who brushed off Jack Woodford's restraining arm stood in the doorway, his face apoplectic.

Jack shrugged, and Lloyd stood up, wishing, not for the first time, that he was taller.

'Mr Cawston,' said Jack quietly. 'Matthew's father.'

'We've been trying to get in touch with you, Mr Cawston,' said Lloyd, coming out from behind his desk, and extending his hand, just as though he imagined Mr Cawston might shake it.

'I was already here!' he roared. 'I wasn't letting my son stay at a place where—' He spluttered. 'And when I get there I'm told that you clowns have arrested him!'

'Matthew hasn't been arrested, Mr Cawston,' said Lloyd, taking Judy's chair, and putting it down in front of his desk. 'He's making a statement.'

'It's the same thing!'

'No,' said Lloyd. 'Do have a seat, Mr Cawston.'

'Er . . . Mr Waters is here, too,' said Jack. 'He says he's been asked to make a statement.'

'Oh, yes,' said Lloyd. 'See to it, will you?'

'Yes, sir.'

'Are you in charge of this murder?' Cawston demanded as Jack left, and Judy came in.

'No,' said Lloyd. 'Chief Superintendent Allison is in charge of the murder inquiry.'

'Then get him! I'll speak to the ringmaster.'

Lloyd bit his lip, and nodded, leaving Judy with Mr Cawston while he rang the chief super, who groaned as Lloyd told him what he thought of Cawston so far. 'I'll be right down,' he said. 'Don't say anything, Lloyd. Let me handle it.'

It would probably have been easier for Lloyd to stop breathing, but he went back to his office, and manfully parried Cawston's questions with non-answers until the super arrived.

'Mr Cawston,' he said, after Lloyd had effected a kind of introduction. 'You'll want to talk to Matthew—'

'I want to talk to you! What sort of a circus are you running here?'

Fifteen love. Lloyd had to admire the man's ability to choose a metaphor and stick to it.

'Certainly you can talk to me.' Allison smiled, politely awaiting a question. 'What did you want to know?'

'Why has my son been arrested?' demanded Cawston.

'Your son hasn't been arrested,' said Allison. 'He has been interviewed about the theft from his school of several items over the last eighteen months.'

'What?' Cawston frowned, shaking his head. 'That's not what they're saying at the school. They're saying you think he was involved with this tramp that's got herself murdered!'

No coincidence, then, that Mr Waters had arrived at the same time as Cawston, Lloyd thought.

'I can't be responsible for what "they" are saying, Mr Cawston. We're not saying anything of the sort,' said Allison. 'He has admitted theft. Whether there is a prosecution depends largely on the school.'

Cawston stared at him. 'Matthew?' he said. That took a moment to sink in; then he rallied. 'What the hell did he steal, for God's sake? The crown jewels?'

'The thefts were very minor,' said Allison. 'Only one of the items was worth more than a few pence.'

'And just because of that you cart him off in a police car in front of the whole school?'

'Matthew was brought here in the chief inspector's own car,' Allison said.

'Why was he brought here at all?'

It was weak-wristed; it landed at Allison's feet.

'He was being questioned about his most recent theft by Mrs Hamlyn less than an hour before she was murdered.'

Cawston rushed the net to scoop up the dropshot. 'I knew it! You're accusing him of murder!'

'No, Mr Cawston, we are not. But another of the stolen items is believed to be the murder weapon. If your son stole this item, then we are bound to ask him what he did with it, where he hid it, who might have had access to it – whether he was stealing on his own, or in concert with others. Matthew also wanted to give us information which he felt might be relevant to the inquiry into the death of Mrs Hamlyn. He is here to make a statement. Nothing more.'

For a moment, Cawston blinked a little as the conversational lob went soaring over his head, out of reach. But then he raced it to the base-line, and it came screaming back over the net. '*Believed* to be the murder weapon?' he said. 'You don't even *know*?'

'It hasn't been found yet.'

Lloyd watched Cawston's face with interest as several different reactions chased over them. Anger, disbelief, relief, worry. 'Not been found?' he said, in the end. 'So you don't know that anything he took was used to murder the woman, do you?'

'No,' said Allison. 'But we have to find out. His headmaster was with him, of course. Mr Treadwell thought it advisable to engage the services of a solicitor, who was also present. Your son was interviewed by Detective Sergeant Hill, who is a very experienced officer, and who is dealing with the thefts at the school.' He indicated Judy's presence.

Cawston swung round to look at her. 'And this woman's murder? Is she dealing with that?' he asked.

Allison inclined his head slightly. 'She is involved in the murder inquiry, yes,' he said. 'As one of the last people to see Mrs Hamlyn alive, Matthew is a very important witness. If he were my son, I'd sooner he was here than anywhere else.'

Game, set and match.

Cawston's anger turned to sulky co-operation. 'Can I see him? Can I talk to him, alone?'

Allison smiled, as a constable brought Matthew into the office. 'Matthew is free to leave, Mr Cawston. You can do anything you like with him.'

Lloyd blew out his cheeks as they all trooped out of his office, and sat down again, looking up at Judy. 'Well?' he said. 'What do you make of his story about Newby?'

Judy shrugged. 'He didn't tell us his car was in the Barn,' she said. 'But he couldn't have stolen the golf-club.'

'Why the hell would anyone *want* to steal it?' Lloyd asked.

'To murder Mrs Hamlyn with?' said Judy. She thought about that for a moment. 'With which to murder Mrs Hamlyn?' she suggested, as an alternative.

'In order to murder Mrs Hamlyn,' Lloyd said, with a grin.

'It can't have been that, can it?' she said.

'Why not?' said Lloyd sourly. 'They had a nymphomaniac, a kleptomaniac and a dipsomaniac – maybe they needed a homicidal maniac to complete the set.'

Judy laughed.

'But no one planned this,' he said. 'Even Mrs Hamlyn didn't know she was going to leave the Hall when she did. She took

Matthew out to try to get the pen back with the minimum of fuss, and got herself murdered.'

'If Newby's telling the truth,' Judy said, 'then it couldn't have been him that interrupted Matthew and Mrs Hamlyn.'

'He who,' said Lloyd absently. 'No. No, it couldn't.' He tipped his chair back, swinging it gently to and fro on its back legs. 'Sam?' he suggested.

'He admitted being there,' said Judy. 'Would he do that if he had something to hide?'

'He would if he thought that young Matthew had seen him,' said Lloyd. 'Wouldn't he?' He let the chair fall forward.

'But we saw him. That night. He couldn't have cleaned himself up that well.'

'Maybe we just haven't seen the right clothes yet.'

'Lloyd.' She gave him a look.

'It's not so unlikely! He changes out of that music-hall dinner-jacket into something more suitable for taking Mrs Knight out. Realises his pen's gone – goes looking for it. Runs into Diana, and kills her, for whatever reason. Goes back, changes into the jeans and sweater and leaves the premises altogether. We know he didn't go straight to the club, remember. He could have been getting rid of the golf-club, like I said.'

'But he wasn't going out with Mrs Knight by that time.'

'She seemed to think he was. She was all dressed up.'

Judy shook her head. 'She says she was going to go alone. And you can't take any more of his clothes, Lloyd. The man won't have anything left to wear.'

Lloyd smiled. 'Anyway, it might not have been necessary for him to change. He might just have gone somewhere to dry out before he went on to the club – Freddie doesn't think the killer's clothes would necessarily get dirty.'

'He thinks you can rape and murder someone in a downpour and not get dirty?'

'If she *was* in Newby's car, he wouldn't have to get dirty, would he? And the field was frozen – no mud. Freddie says her injuries wouldn't have caused that much blood to splash – especially not if he was at the far end of a golf-club. He might just have got very wet.'

'And you think it was Sam. On no evidence.'

Lloyd knew he had no evidence. But he had Sam. In the interview room. And there was something wrong with Sam's story, if only he could sort out what it was.

'I take it you wrote down what Sam said about his pen?'

'Yes,' she said. She found the page.

Lloyd listened as she read, closing his eyes when she got to the bit that mattered. How could he have just let it pass at the time? Because he let Waters get to him, that's how. He stood up. 'Let's go and have a word with Mr Waters before he leaves,' he said. 'There is something he did that night that could bear a little explanation.' He smiled. 'Or, rather,' he said, 'something he didn't do.'

He deliberately left it at that, enjoying watching Judy's brow furrow as she resolutely refused to ask him what he meant.

They found Waters having his statement read over to him. Lloyd waited until the constable had finished, and Waters had been handed a pen with which to sign it.

'It's an offence,' he said.

Waters looked up. 'What is?' he asked.

'Making a statement knowing it to be false.'

Waters sighed. 'I've had enough of this, Lloyd,' he said. 'Your superior officer is going to hear from me.'

'That'll be nice for him.'

Judy sat down in the seat vacated by the constable, and produced the notebook. The constable stood by the door. Lloyd positioned himself behind Waters.

'Let's look at your statement, Mr Waters. You say you noticed your pen missing, and went to look for it. But that's not what you told us, is it?'

Waters twisted round. 'Of course it is!'

'No. My sergeant wrote down exactly what you said. And you said you thought you had left your pen on the table.'

Waters sighed extravagantly. 'Oh, I do beg your pardon. You are a stickler for detail, aren't you? Bordering on the pedantic, I'd say.'

'So why didn't you go and look on the table?'

Waters swore, screwing up the statement. 'You're going to regret this,' he said.

'I'll tell you why,' Lloyd went on. 'Because you knew where your pen was. Diana Hamlyn told you what had happened – when you were with her.'

'I wasn't with her. I saw her, that's all. With Cawston. Going into the Barn. They left the small door open, and I went to see what was going on. I heard her tell him she'd seen him take a pen, so I knew it had to be my—' He pursed his lips. 'My expletive deleted pen.'

'And you went in.'

The constable had hastily started taking notes. What with him and Judy, this was going to be the best-documented conversation on record.

'No. I left her to it. I went back to the flat. I did exactly what I told you. Exactly what was in that statement.'

'Why?'

'Because I was getting soaked to the skin. It seemed the best place to go.'

'Didn't you want to get your pen back? You seem anxious enough to get it back now.'

Waters tapped his fingers lightly on the table as he spoke. 'I knew Diana. I knew she would go through all the proper channels in dealing with young Cawston. He was denying it – she wasn't going to get anywhere like that. I preferred to deal with him my way.'

'Which was?'

'A clip round the ear. Or two. I'd have got the pen back, don't you worry.' Waters smiled. 'But Diana's demise presented me with an opportunity for much more poetic justice. I let you take him away. And I hope you scared the shit out of him.'

Lloyd sat down on the table. 'Oh,' he said slowly. 'You let us chase after Matthew because he stole your pen?'

'Yes.'

'Or because it stopped us dwelling on the logistics?'

'I don't know words with that many syllables.'

Lloyd bent his head close, and spoke confidentially to Waters. 'Someone interrupted Mrs Hamlyn's interview with Matthew,' he said. 'Someone who seems to have had sex with Mrs Hamlyn, possibly in a car. Newby's car was in there.'

Waters didn't move. Most people pulled away when you got too close. 'Then I suggest you talk to Newby,' he said.

'I'm talking to you.'

'You have no right to keep me here.' Waters sat back in his chair. 'I will be making a complaint to your superiors. This is harassment.'

'How long were you with Mrs Hamlyn?' asked Judy.

'I wasn't with her.'

'Sure?'

'Of course I'm sure. I wasn't with her, I didn't rape her, and I didn't murder her.' He drummed his fingers on the desk. 'When are you going to let me go? I've got work to do.'

'As you said, Mr Waters. We have no power to keep you here. And I don't think you raped her,' said Lloyd. 'I don't think she *was* raped. But, then, you knew that all along, didn't you? So I think that perhaps you went with her, and failed to tell us that.'

Waters grinned. 'Not me. I would have, given half a chance. Any port in a storm, and all that.' He looked back at Judy. 'Even you would have done,' he said. 'I'd have thawed you out, no danger.'

Lloyd contemplated sending her away on some pretext, but he wanted to go on living, and Judy's policy was to ignore Mr Waters. 'So what went wrong?' he asked. 'She was there, the car was there.'

'And Matthew was there,' said Waters. 'Even Diana drew the line at an audience.'

Lloyd sighed. He'd hoped to trick him into admitting that he had been alone with Diana. He had failed.

'And, besides, I didn't want her to know *I* was there. I've told you – I wanted to deal with Matthew my way, and that would have been less than official. And I was getting soaked. I went back to the flat, changed, and went out.'

'At eleven-fifteen, or thereabouts,' said Lloyd. 'But you didn't get to this club until twelve-thirty. What were you doing?'

'I've already told you what I was doing,' Waters said. 'I have co-operated fully with your inquiry, as I will tell your superiors.'

'You have consistently *refused* to tell us what you were doing!' Lloyd shouted.

Waters raised his eyebrows. 'I picked up a prostitute, Chief Inspector. A hooker, a whore, a lady of the evening. That's why I waited until after closing-time – they're thicker on the ground then. Do you want to do me for kerb-crawling?'

'I want to know when you think you told me that before,' said Lloyd.

'I told you at the very start,' said Waters. 'It wasn't an inapposite adjective, Mr Lloyd. Crude, but not inapposite.' He smiled. 'You're going to catch it from your boss,' he said, wagging his finger.

Lloyd got up. 'She had better have a name,' he said.

Waters's smile grew. 'I couldn't give you her name if I wanted to. I wasn't interested in her name. But I don't have to worry about that, because you have found nothing whatever to connect me to Diana Hamlyn's murder, and you know it.'

Lloyd shook his head as the constable made a move to stop Waters leaving, and shrugged. He and Judy walked back along to the office, neither of them speaking. They sat down, and looked at one another.

'He's right,' said Judy.

She had a remarkable talent for stating the obvious. Lloyd wondered if it was worth deploying manpower to try to find whoever Sam was with. The best they could do was find her, that would prove Sam's story. The worst they could do was not find her, and that hardly constituted proof that he was lying.

'Even if it's true,' he said, 'he could still have killed her. She was probably dead before he left the school.'

'How would he have got hold of the golf-club?'

'God knows,' said Lloyd. 'Unless he stole it in the first place.' But that didn't make sense.

'Why did you say that you didn't think that Mrs Hamlyn had been raped?' Judy asked, after a moment.

'Because I don't think she was,' he said tiredly.

Judy stiffened slightly. 'You've joined the chorus, have you?

Diana Hamlyn couldn't have been raped; she was the school bicycle?'

'She was in Newby's car with whoever it was.'

'You don't know that!'

'Not yet, but I imagine forensics will prove it.'

'So because she was in a car she can't have been raped?'

Lloyd sighed. 'A car that wasn't going anywhere, Judy. All the evidence suggests co-operation.'

'The evidence suggests a not inconsiderable degree of sexual violence, according to Freddie,' she said. 'You've read his report. He *hurt* her, Lloyd.'

'Maybe she got more than she bargained for,' said Lloyd. 'A professional foul, Freddie called it. Perhaps that's why she ran away. Or – maybe it wasn't that unusual, as far as she was concerned.'

'She *wanted* to be treated like that? Is that what you're saying?' asked Judy.

'Possibly. Or at any rate put up with it, in order to get what she needed. Whichever, I think Freddie's right. I think she consented to the sex, and I am inclined to believe that she was killed by someone else. Someone who discovered what was going on, and didn't like it.'

The office door opened. 'A Mr Coleman to see you, Chief Inspector,' Jack said.

His look was one that Lloyd knew well; Jack was the only person he knew who could wink without batting an eyelid. He ushered in a small, plump man with a neat, greying moustache. He carried a large cardboard box, which he held protectively, not without difficulty, under his arm.

'Coleman, Coleman's Outfitters. I thought I really ought to bring this to your attention in person, in view of the circumstances. I do hope I'm not making a fuss about nothing.'

So do I, thought Lloyd. 'Mr Coleman, we welcome any help we can get in a murder case. Well – all cases, really. Do have a seat,' he said as Judy got up.

Coleman sat, transferring the box to his lap. 'I wouldn't want to send you on a wild-goose chase,' he said.

Lloyd was always chasing wild geese. One more wouldn't hurt.

'So,' said Lloyd, smiling. 'I gather the box has some significance?'

'Well – I think so. It was brought back yesterday by a customer – it's one of our hire suits. Now, normally, they're checked over – you know – just to see that we have got the same suit back, but yesterday – well, we're short-handed at the moment, with the stand at the Civic Hall.' He raised his eyebrows. 'You know,' he said. 'The exhibition of non-central traders – to let people know where we are, and so on. A number of my assistants are manning the stand, and so yesterday, when this one was returned, no one checked it.'

Lloyd frowned. It was hardly relevant, but it bothered him. 'But isn't your shop . . . ?' He pointed vaguely out of the window in the direction of R. J. Coleman, Gentlemen's Outfitters, smack in the middle of the town centre.

'Yes. But we also have a shop in Queens Estate. Mary Tudor Square. It's quite different. Young, casual – sportswear. You know.'

'Do you?' said Lloyd, startled. What was the world coming to? The Queens Estate shops had had to be boarded up even during working hours in the old days. You knew where you were with it. You could go to the Good Queen Bess at chucking-out time and make your arrest-tally look good. A gentlemen's outfitters? Lloyd shook his head. Queens Estate had fallen to the Yuppies.

'See?' said Mr Coleman. 'That's why we've got the stand. Anyway, we had hired out a number of suits to people at the school where – well, the young woman was – you know. And that meant we had a lot of dry-cleaning to sort out, so I decided to pop in this morning to see what was what before tomorrow. And . . .' He stood up with difficulty. 'I mean, we expect the odd soup stain, perhaps even a slight tear, but . . .'

Lloyd sat forward.

'I thought you ought to see it.'

He placed the box on the desk, and grasped the lid, inching it up to reveal folded tissue paper. Lloyd glanced at Judy as she came over to witness the unveiling, and the tissue was drawn away.

The jacket was smeared with mud; dark stains had dried on the lapels, and others, more visible at the time, had been subject to an ineffectual attempt to remove them. One pocket had almost been torn off. Lloyd carefully lifted out the jacket, laying it down, and picked up the trousers. More of the dark stains, under the waistband, and at the tops of the legs, were clearly visible. No attempt had been made to clean them up. The knees were caked with the thin, dried mud.

The shocked silence into which Mr Coleman spoke was almost tangible, and his words wedged themselves into it, seeming not to break it at all.

'It was hired by a Mr P. Newby,' he said.

Lloyd looked at Judy, at troubled brown eyes that held no hint of triumph.

Freddie was wrong.

Chapter Seven

Judy stared out of the window at the darkening sky, as, armed with a search warrant, they drove back to the school. She hadn't formed much of an opinion of Newby, except to register that he was an attractive man. She tried to remember what he had been like the first time she had seen him, when Mrs Knight had brought him into Treadwell's office. What had her impression been then?

Different, she thought. He hadn't been in anything like as much pain, of course. He had been able to walk better; much more quickly, deftly. There had been something almost dashing about him. And that was when she remembered.

'How the hell would he get hold of the golf-club?' Lloyd was muttering.

Judy closed her eyes. 'He didn't have the golf-club,' she said. 'He used his stick.'

'No,' said Lloyd. 'I thought of that, but Freddie said it was something wooden – it splintered. His stick's metal. And it wouldn't be heavy enough – these NHS sticks are—'

'His other stick,' she said, waiting for the explosion.

There was a silence, which was worse.

'What other stick, Judy?' he said, at last.

'Oh, I'm sorry, Lloyd. I *knew* there was something about him, and I couldn't think what it was. I thought it was just . . . Anyway, he had another stick when I saw him first. A walking-cane. Black. With a heavy silver knob.'

This time the silence seemed to be going to last for the rest of her life. But no such luck.

'Cawston was giving Allison a hard time,' he said conversationally.

The tone didn't fool Judy.

'I wonder what he's going to say when he finds out that the thefts had nothing to do with the murder at all,' he continued. 'I suppose Allison might let me off with my entrails intact. I mean, all he did was go three rounds with Cawston because of some mythical murder weapon that I said junior might have stolen.'

'I'm sorry,' Judy said again, as he drew a breath. 'But I wasn't at the school to see Newby, was I? I was there about the thefts – the man had only arrived that morning. I wasn't taking any notice of him.'

'Some ancient golf-club that we couldn't even find,' Lloyd went on, as if she hadn't spoken. 'Which was stolen last December. Which was kept in a barn. A *barn*, no less, from which anyone could have taken it, and from which young Mr Cawston denied taking it. And, to cap it all, it doesn't matter if he did take it, because Mr Newby used his stick.'

Judy apologised again. If she hadn't been so keen to get her own back on Lloyd, she might have seen the golf-club in perspective. She might never have seen the damn thing at all. Perhaps it was just as well she was transferring.

'Still, all is not lost,' Lloyd said, pulling into the school driveway. 'I'm sure if you need a beat bobby in Malworth you'll put in a good word for me.'

Oh, God. She would be second-in-command at Malworth. Where she would make a habit of getting everyone running round looking for the wrong thing, while overlooking the one thing that only she knew.

The squad car waited outside the staff block, and she and Lloyd met up with its occupants before Lloyd knocked loudly and officially on the flat door.

Sam Waters opened it.

'Christ,' he said. 'You've come mob-handed.'

'Is Mr Newby here?' demanded Lloyd.

'I expect he's in his room,' said Waters, standing aside as they trooped in behind Lloyd.

Judy watched as Lloyd strode across the room to Newby's door. He knocked, and opened it. She could see Newby as he lay stretched out on top of the bed; he was struggling to get to his feet as she walked across to where Lloyd stood in the doorway.

Lloyd held up the warrant. 'Search warrant, Mr Newby,' he said. 'Right, Sergeant.'

Judy took a step into the room, followed by the uniformed constables.

'No – wait,' said Newby, looking baffled. 'What do you want? What are you looking for?'

Judy took a breath. 'A silver-topped walking-stick,' she said.

She could hear a soft chuckle from Sam Waters, and turned to look at him. He smiled, and left the flat.

'I . . . I lost it. I think it might have been stolen.'

Judy looked back at Newby. Lloyd said that her look made strong men tremble; it certainly saved a lot of time when discovery was inevitable, and Newby was not a strong man.

He blushed. 'Bottom of the wardrobe,' he mumbled.

Judy opened the wardrobe, and moved some bed linen. Underneath was the cane, broken almost in two. 'Chief Inspector,' she said.

Lloyd knelt down, and looked at it, then at her. 'He made a better job of cleaning that than the suit,' he muttered, looking a little puzzled. He stood up. 'Mr Newby, can you tell me how your stick came to be broken?'

'It snapped,' he said. 'The doctor said it might. He told me I shouldn't use it.'

'Why did you lie when the sergeant asked you about it?'

Newby's skin reddened again. 'I had nothing to do with the murder, if that's what you think.'

'Then you have some explaining to do,' Lloyd said. 'Can you tell us how the clothes you were wearing that evening got into the state they are in?' Lloyd waited, but Newby said nothing. 'Where were you between ten-fifteen and eleven-fifteen on Friday night?' he asked.

'I've told you.'

'And you have nothing to add to what you've told us?'

Newby shook his head.

'Do you have your car keys, Mr Newby? We will be taking your car for forensic examination.'

Newby produced the keys.

'And you had better get your coat,' said Lloyd. 'It's cold out.'

'What's happening?' Newby asked.

'I'll tell you what's happening,' said Lloyd. 'You are being arrested on suspicion of murder, Mr Newby. You are not obliged to say anything, but anything you do say will be taken down, and may be given in evidence.'

The constables led Newby to the squad car.

'Here,' Lloyd said, giving his own keys to Judy. 'You take my car back.' He called to one of the constables just preparing to leave the search, and together they went to Newby's car.

The squad car swept away, followed, after a few moments, by Newby's car. Lloyd lifted a hand in salute as they drove off, and Judy walked slowly back to the car. They were never what you expected, even if you had seen it all before. Somehow, you still thought you would know. But no one ever did. Not neighbours, or friends, or colleagues. No one. And especially not the victim.

Waters was standing beside Lloyd's car. He clapped his hands slowly together as she approached. 'I told you so,' he said.

Judy got in, slammed the door, and started the engine, but Waters tapped on the window.

After a moment's hesitation, she wound it down, and he bent down towards her.

'You don't have to rush off, do you?' he said. 'You've got him now – you can take some time off.'

'I have work to do, Mr Waters.'

Waters leaned his arms along the window. 'I just thought that now that I'm no longer a suspect you might come out for a drink with me.'

'Thank you, Mr Waters, but I'm still on duty.'

Waters glanced over to where the other police officers were assembling at the van, ready to go home.

'It doesn't have to be right now,' he said. 'When do you get off?'

'I don't think it would be a good idea, Mr Waters.'

'Oh, come on,' he said. 'No hard feelings.' He winked. 'On second thoughts, I can promise you some,' he said.

'I'm driving off, Mr Waters. If you are still leaning on the car, you might get hurt.'

'But that wouldn't be a nice thing to do,' he said. 'And I can get you and your boss into trouble as it is, without your adding injury to insult.' He smiled. 'So why don't you just come out for a drink with me, give me my pen back, and I'll forget the whole thing.'

One hand dangled into the car, his fingers brushing her knee. Judy switched off the ignition and removed the keys before he thought of it.

'That's better,' he said, giving her knee a squeeze. 'I'm sure you can be nice when you want to.'

Judy smiled, and looked round at the police van. 'Well,' she said quietly, 'I'll tell you what . . .' She beckoned him closer to her.

And no one but the predictably and profoundly shocked Waters heard what she said.

Sam watched as she accelerated away. He had never really held out any hope of the sergeant; he had just wanted to rattle her. Instead, she had rattled him. My God, to look at her you would think she wouldn't even know words like that, much less use them. He looked over at the crowd of policemen getting into the van, and went into the staff block, slamming the door. He didn't go into his own flat; he took the stairs two at a time, and knocked lightly on Caroline's door.

He heard the bolt being drawn back, watched her smile fade. She tried to push the door shut again; he wedged his foot in the crack.

'Go away,' she said.

'I've got some news for you.'

'I don't want to talk to you,' she said.

'I was angry,' said Sam. 'I called you names. You're not going to hold that against me, are you? I'd rather you held something else against me.'

'Oh, shut up, Sam. And go away.' She tried to shut the door, but Sam's foot was immovable. A bit painful, with being crushed in the door, but immovable.

He smiled. 'Guess who the police have just taken away,' he said.

The pushing stopped, the door opened. Caroline was pale.

'Who?' she asked.

'That's better. Can I come in?'

'No.'

'Then I won't tell you,' he said, sing-song fashion.

She left the door open, and went back into the room. Sam followed, closing it. 'They've taken Newby away,' he said.

'Why? What for?'

'For murdering Diana, that's what for,' he said.

'It's a mistake.' Instantly, without thought.

'It didn't sound like a mistake. Murdered her with his silver-topped cane – doesn't that sound wonderfully decadent to you?'

'You're a liar.'

Sam shook his head. 'They came with uniforms, search warrants, squad cars – the lot.' He smiled. 'See what a narrow squeak you had?' he said. 'Entertaining him up here on your own.' He put his arms round her. 'But never fear – Supersam's here.'

She shook him off. 'Get out.'

'Don't shoot the messenger,' he said. 'I told you so, didn't I? I told you it wasn't healthy. You could have gone the same way as Diana.'

He saw her shiver.

'Just thought I'd let you know you can sleep easy in your bed tonight,' he said, and left.

He heard the door close behind him, heard the bolt being sent home, heard Caroline crying.

He was going to get something to eat.

Philip looked up as they came in. For some moments, Lloyd didn't speak. He looked at Philip rather as though he was considering whether or not to buy him, then walked to the window, and looked out.

The sergeant sat down at the table, her notebook at the ready. She didn't look at him at all. She turned the pages back, making little ticks here and there, then found a fresh sheet, and sat, pen poised.

Lloyd seemed to come to some sort of a decision. He squared his shoulders, and turned from the window. 'Right,' he said. 'You are going to tell us what you did between leaving the Hall at ten-twenty on Friday the fourteenth of February, and talking to us at three a.m. on Saturday the fifteenth. You are going to tell us in detail, missing nothing. And,' he said, leaning over the table, his face close to Philip's, 'you are going to tell us now.'

Philip moved back a little. 'I didn't kill Diana Hamlyn,' he said.

'Diana Hamlyn spoke to you, then left the Hall,' said Lloyd. 'You left five minutes later. What did you do after you left?'

'I've told you. I left because I was going to be sick. I went to the toilet – what would you have done?'

'Then what?'

'Then I was sick. When I came out I went to my car, and drove down to the staff block. I've *told* you all this.'

'No, Mr Newby. You omitted to mention that your car was in the Barn. Was there some reason for that?'

'No,' said Philip. Yes. Yes, there was.

'Do you have some sort of explanation of how your clothes got into the state they were in when you took them back to the shop?' he asked.

Philip didn't speak. He should have known he could never be that lucky. But he couldn't tell them. He didn't have to. They had said so.

'Why was your car in the Barn? I thought cars weren't allowed up there?'

'I get a special dispensation,' he said. 'I can't walk very well on the cobbles in bad weather.'

'Whose idea was it?'

'Mine,' said Philip. 'Barry doesn't mind as long as I park in the Barn and make sure the doors are closed so that other people don't get the same idea.'

But Lloyd was off on another tack altogether by the time Philip had finished explaining.

'How did your clothes get into that mess? How did you break your stick?'

'I fell. The stick broke, and I fell.'

'It must have been some fall,' Lloyd said. 'Where did you fall?'

Philip leaned his head on his hands, his mouth covered, his eyes shut. He didn't want to think about that.

Lloyd got up, and went back over to the window.

'Why did you leave the ball early?' the sergeant asked.

'I was sick. How many more times?'

'You left the toilets, and went to your car. Did you see Diana Hamlyn?'

'I did what I've already told you a dozen times.'

'Which is?'

'I drove down to the staff block, but the light was on in the flat, and I didn't want Sam's company. I'm sure you've seen enough of him to know why.'

The sergeant smiled, suddenly and involuntarily. He hadn't seen her smile before. He would probably have liked her if he'd met her in a more conventional fashion. She reminded him a little of Caroline.

'And then?' she was asking.

And then. Philip felt the heat on his face. 'I needed fresh air,' he said, not looking at either of them. 'I ran down the window and, as I did, I thought I heard someone's feet on the fire-escape. I got out of the car, and walked over, but I couldn't see anyone, so I thought it must have been a shadow or something.'

Lloyd shook his head. 'Not much there to get your clothes covered in mud and blood, is there?' he said. 'When's this fall supposed to have happened?'

Philip's head went down.

'All right,' said Lloyd. 'Let's talk about Mrs Hamlyn. She made advances to you, didn't she? In the bedroom of the Hamlyns' flat on your very first night at the school. Isn't that right?'

'Yes,' he said, baffled.

'And you turned her down.'

'Yes. How do you know that?'

Lloyd smiled. 'There was someone else in the room, Mr Newby,' he said.

Philip shook his head. 'No,' he said.

'Yes.' Lloyd sat back. 'The thief, Mr Newby. The ever present thief.'

Oh, my God. 'Who?' asked Philip.

'Well, since everyone else in the school knows, why shouldn't you? Matthew Cawston.'

'Is that why you took him away?' he said. 'Sam Waters said you thought *he'd* killed Diana.'

'Mr Waters is something of a sensationalist, wouldn't you say?'

'He's something,' agreed Philip.

'But back to Mrs Hamlyn. Did she give up?'

Philip shook his head.

'Did you give in?'

'No.'

'What did she say to you at the ball?'

'She asked how my leg was.'

'That's more or less what she asked you in the Hamlyns' bed-room, isn't it?' Lloyd got up as be spoke, and walked round the table, in slow strides.

'Yes,' said Philip. 'Matthew seems to be a reliable reporter of the facts.'

'So – this time. Was she making another pass?'

'Perhaps,' he said.

'Perhaps.' Lloyd left a space between the two syllables. 'You went out to your car. Did you see Mrs Hamlyn?'

He shook his head. He didn't know what else to do.

'You're sure about that?' Lloyd waited.

Philip wouldn't look at him, wouldn't answer. He didn't have to tell them anything. But they'd got his suit, and the car. His rea-sons for staying silent didn't exist any more, except that he *had* stayed silent, and they had found out anyway. So his silence looked worse than ever.

'Did you see Mrs Hamlyn?' the sergeant asked.

'No.' His eyes were shut. No one spoke. He could hear Lloyd come closer, and sit down. 'I got to the Barn,' he said. 'And as I went in I could see the rear door of the car standing open.' He looked up. 'I thought someone must have been trying to steal from it,' he said. 'One of the Barn doors had been opened a couple of feet, and I'd left them shut.'

They waited for him to go on, neither of them speaking.

'I looked into the back, and . . .' He looked down. 'And her tights and . . . things were on the floor of the car. And her bag.'

'What did you do?' Lloyd's voice was light.

'I stuffed the things into her bag and threw it out,' Philip mut-tered. 'I was angry.'

'And yet you considerately put her underwear in her bag before throwing it out?'

'I didn't want any of the boys finding it,' he said.

'What about her shoes? What did you do with them?'

Philip shook his head. 'I didn't see her shoes,' he said.

'You drove over one of them.'

'I didn't *see* them! I drove off, and did what I've already told you umpteen times.'

'But you haven't told us this umpteen times, have you? You didn't tell us this at all. Why?'

Newby shook his head. 'I – when Sam said you thought she had been raped, I thought she was just making trouble for him for some reason. Then you said she was dead. And you'd been looking at Sam's clothes. I thought . . .' He dropped his head in his hands. 'I didn't want to get involved,' he said. 'I knew what it would look like, if you saw my clothes.'

Lloyd sat back, hands behind his head, smiling at him. 'That is what it looks like, Mr Newby,' he said. 'Your story explains away any evidence of Mrs Hamlyn's presence in your car, and any of your prints that we might find on her bag. Very good. But it doesn't explain one thing.'

'I've told you. I fell.'

'No, not that. We'll come to that later. No – what bothers me is *why* she was in your car.'

What was wrong with the man? He'd just told him why she was in his car. 'I would have thought it was obvious,' he said. 'I was a decoy. That's why she came and spoke to me. She had arranged to meet Sam. It's obvious!'

'Don't you lock your car, Mr Newby?'

'The back door doesn't lock.'

'Who knows that?' asked the sergeant.

'I don't know! It's not a secret.'

'So you think that she was in your car with Sam Waters,' said Lloyd.

'Yes.'

'But she thought that you would be in the Hall until the small hours. Sam would have had the flat to himself. Why the back of a car? Why the back of *your* car, Mr Newby?'

Philip shook his head. 'I don't know,' he said. 'I didn't think – I just . . .'

'I think I know why,' said Lloyd. 'I think it was you she was meeting. You expected to find her in your car, and you did. But Sam had left early, so your flat wasn't available, and Mrs Knight was in the Hamlyns' flat – the car had to do.'

'No,' said Philip.

'Doesn't that make more sense?'

'It isn't true!'

'Look,' said Lloyd, crouching down beside him. 'I don't think you set out to rape her. But after giving you every reason to believe that she was ready and willing, I think she changed her mind. I think perhaps she was more interested in a stolen pen than she was in you, and you didn't like that.'

The frown deepened. 'What?' said Philip.

'Matthew had run away. She wanted to go after him, maybe. I can imagine she might have felt torn between you and carrying out what seems to have been regarded as her job. Pastoral care, Mr Treadwell called it. So, she let it go too far before she changed her mind.'

'What?' said Philip.

'Well, of course, that's just my scenario. For whatever reason, she changed her mind.'

'What?'

Lloyd rose. 'You do see what I'm getting at? I mean – whichever – she was obviously co-operating at that stage. But then – to go back to my scenario – she says, "It's no good, I'll have to try to find Matthew," or "I'd better speak to the headmaster," or her husband, or whatever. It was something like that, wasn't it?'

Philip's head was just shaking, all the time. He had no idea what the man was talking about.

'Well, maybe she was just fickle,' said Lloyd. 'But she changed her mind, and you didn't like that. She ran away from you, but you caught her, and you raped her. She got away again, you chased her on to the field, and this time you killed her. Otherwise how did your suit get covered in mud and blood? How did your stick get broken? You went back to your car, and that's when you threw out her bag.'

'Me?' said Philip. 'I chased after her? Like this?'

'Ah, but that's another point,' said Lloyd. 'You weren't like that, were you? You could move pretty fast before, according to everyone I've spoken to.'

'Not that fast.'

'How fast was that? How fast was she running?'

Philip sighed.

'Well,' said Lloyd. 'I'm afraid you are going to have to accept our hospitality for the night, Mr Newby. The forensic and pathology tests which we are doing will produce all the evidence we need to charge you. I suggest you think again about legal help.'

Philip shook his head. He didn't need legal help. Roll on tomorrow.

'What in the name of God Almighty is going *on* here, Treadwell?'

Thus had the chairman of governors greeted Treadwell, who had been home from the pub for about half an hour; long enough to consume one more large Scotch, and pour a second. The man must have been lying in wait for him, watching for him coming back.

Marcia had been home, but it transpired that she had stayed in the back room, not answering the phone, not going to the door. Because of the newspapers, she had said, when Treadwell had taxed her with it.

'Theft, rape, murder – suicide?' He came in, uninvited, past Treadwell; a small, round ball of self-importance with a ginger moustache and a bald head over which he persuaded lacquered strands of hair from a parting above his left ear. 'A pupil arrested – a teacher arrested? Do you imagine for one moment that the school is going to survive this?'

Treadwell shook his head. 'Drink?' he asked, waving his own glass by way of encouragement.

'Why not?' he said, sinking into an armchair, where the light from the table-lamp glinted on his frameless spectacles.

'I'll resign, of course,' said Treadwell, handing him an equally large whisky.

'Too bloody true you'll resign!' He took a gulp of his drink. 'But what good's that going to do? How many of them have already taken their boys away?'

Treadwell shrugged. 'I've been out all day,' he said.

'Who was minding the shop?'

Treadwell smiled weakly. 'Well,' he said, 'in view of the depletion of our ranks, I think probably Caroline Knight would take over.'

'Then we'd better find out.'

'Marcia!' Treadwell sat down on the sofa as his wife came in from the kitchen. 'Go and ask Caroline if she'll be good enough to join us,' he said, and watched her scuttle off.

'It was touch and go as it was, Treadwell. This place has been trading on a reputation it hasn't had for years.'

'Well,' said Treadwell into his glass, 'it's got one now.'

'I seem to remember you went on the wagon after you got banned.'

'Yes.' Treadwell topped up both their drinks. 'Struck me as silly. If I couldn't drive, why the hell shouldn't I get drunk?'

'Because you're supposed to be in charge of this place!'

'Now wait a minute,' said Treadwell. 'I didn't employ these people – I didn't employ Hamlyn or his wife. I didn't employ that so-called artist—'

'What's Sam Waters got to do with anything? You employed the murderer!' He leaned forward. 'And the so-called artist has been telling me some very interesting stories,' he said.

'I'll bet he has.' The chairman seemed to be regarding Sam in a rather more favourable light now that he was comparing him to rapists and thieves.

'Like how you found Mrs Hamlyn in the Barn with some odd-job man or other.'

Treadwell had another swallow of the water of life.

'How come the governors didn't hear about that? How come you sacked this man and kept Hamlyn on?'

'I didn't find Hamlyn in the Barn with the odd-job man.'

'You knew what that woman was like, and you did nothing about it. You railroaded Hamlyn's promotion through. You employed Newby – you insisted that we keep his job open. If you had acted responsibly, neither of these people would have been here, and none of this would have happened.' He finished his drink. 'Have you any idea how difficult it is to keep this place going at all?' He shook his head. 'We won't survive this,' he said again.

Marcia ushered in Caroline Knight. Treadwell looked up. 'Ah, Caroline,' he said. 'Have a drink. We're celebrating the demise of St Rasputin's School for the Sons of Gentlefolk.'

'No, thank you, Mr Treadwell.'

'Am I right in assuming that you took charge of the exodus?'

'Mr Dearden did, really. I manned reception when we realised the scope of the enquiries, and Mr Dearden actually spoke to them.'

'People wanting to know if their sons were still alive and kicking?'

Caroline's eyebrows rose slightly. 'Basically, yes,' she said. 'Most of the young ones have actually gone. Their parents haven't withdrawn them,' she said to the chairman. 'Most of them just said they would rather they had them at home until this was all sorted out.'

The chairman looked at her bleakly. 'Do you think they'll be back?' he asked.

'I don't know.'

She looked tired, thought Treadwell.

'This chap Newby,' said the chairman. 'He was pestering you a bit, wasn't he?'

'No,' said Caroline.

'Oh,' he said. 'Waters said something. Perhaps I misunderstood.'

'Or perhaps Mr Waters misunderstood,' said Caroline.

Treadwell made the mistake of draining his glass; now he'd have to offer his guest another. On the other hand, perhaps he just wouldn't. He picked up the bottle. 'Well,' he said. 'They've got him now. So it is sorted out, isn't it?'

Both the others looked coldly at him.

'Why don't we just ring these people up and tell them it's all right?' he said. 'The police have got him, and their children will be safe and snug in the corridors of St Bluebeard's for another term.'

The chairman rose. 'Well – thank you, Mrs Knight,' he said, and turned to Treadwell. 'You'd do well to leave that alone,' he said. 'The papers have got on to this – they'll want interviews, I expect. It seems that Mrs Hamlyn's activities are already public knowledge.'

Treadwell raised his glass to him. 'You shall have my resignation in the morning,' he said, and smiled at Caroline. 'You could
do worse than make Mrs Knight the head teacher, you know.'

'Head teacher of what?'

The door banged, and Treadwell looked up at Caroline. 'I've
never actually closed a school before,' he said. 'I've had to resign
before, but up until now I haven't had to count the dead and
injured.'

She didn't speak.

'Oh – don't worry. You won't find me in a haze of carbon
monoxide. You see, I don't think it was my fault.'

'Don't you?'

He was a little surprised. 'Ah – you agree with the revered
chairman. I insisted on employing Newby – yes, I did. I thought
he'd had a raw deal. Still do. It was probably because of the accident that he . . .' The booze was making him less inhibited than
usual. 'Don't think he was quite . . . you know.' He searched his
pockets for a cigarette. 'Do you smoke, Caroline?'

'No.'

'Ah, no vices.' He tapped his glass. 'I have a vice. A couple of
vices. But – you shouldn't be here, you know. We only take flawed
human beings at St Judas Iscariot's. Seconds. Factory rejects.'

'I think I'll go now, if you don't mind, Mr Treadwell.'

'I blame . . . well, I blame the school – evil spirits. Who do you
blame, Caroline?'

She looked at him. 'Not Philip,' she said.

'No. We agree on that. Not Philip. Philip was a victim of circumstance.' He nodded. 'Good night, Caroline.'

He finished his drink, and got to his feet. A little unsteadily, he
walked round the room, switching off the umpteen table-lamps
that Marcia favoured, lighting-wise. She had gone to bed, of
course. She always did when he was drinking. Silly place to go,
since that was where the one thing she was hoping to avoid
always took place. No barns for Marcia. No back seats.

No, Barry. He could hear her already.

*

Monday morning, and Matthew's parents were rowing, as usual. Only this time they were rowing in public, in Chief Inspector Lloyd's office, with Lloyd and the sergeant as their audience.

His father had made him apologise. They had been rehearsing all morning in the hotel room, until someone came to see his father, and released Matthew for half an hour.

So he had apologised. Then they had all started chatting about him as if he wasn't there.

'We'll have to find another school,' his mother had said. 'But I'm sure he can manage without for a week or two – he's had a terrible shock, poor lamb.'

That had started it. The poor lamb sat back and closed his eyes while they argued. He'd have liked to smoke, but neither of his parents knew that he did, and there would be hell to pay if they found out, even from his mother.

'He's got exams,' said his father. 'In three months.'

'He'll pass anyway,' said his mother. 'If he could get all these O levels at that place, he can pass a couple of A levels standing on his head.'

'He can't pass them if he doesn't sit them!' roared his father.

'Well,' said Lloyd, obviously trying to bring the interview to an end, 'I'm sure you have—'

'He is *not* going back to that place!'

Matthew knew his mother was more than a match for any chief inspector.

'This isn't really any of our—' tried Lloyd, and gave up.

'Why not?' demanded his father. 'They've got him now – it's all over.' He turned to Lloyd. 'Isn't that right? You've got him?'

'A man has been arrested and is being questioned about the incident,' said Lloyd carefully.

'All over?' said his mother. 'They arrested Matthew! What does that prove?'

'They didn't arrest Matthew,' his father said, his voice quieter. 'He confessed to stealing. And the school is *asking* us to keep him there when they could have been expelling him.' He turned to Matthew. '*Stealing*!' he shouted, aiming a cuff at him.

Matthew didn't even try to move out of its way, because it was never intended to land.

'Well,' said Lloyd again, 'if you don't—'

'The school say they'll forget about the thefts,' said his father. 'The police have got the right man now – Matthew's got very important exams to sit. Disrupting his schooling now is—'

'Disrupting his schooling? What do you think all this has done to him?'

'Very little, from what I can see!'

'You'd send him back to a school that allowed that sort of woman amongst growing boys?' She looked at Sergeant Hill. 'What sort of man would do that?' she asked her.

His father turned to him again. 'Did she try anything on?' he demanded to know.

Matthew shook his head.

'See? She left the boys alone – and the school didn't know what she was like.'

'Of course they did! And Treadwell couldn't care less!'

'He has resigned,' said his father, as though he was talking to a small child. 'That's why he doesn't care. They're appointing someone else. They've got the guy that did it. It's all over now.'

'You've just taken him out of that place,' said his mother. 'You can't change your mind now.'

'I'll tell you what I've just done!' his father yelled. 'I've just paid for a whole year's schooling! I've just forked out for a whole new bloody uniform! I've just heard how much that solicitor's charging, and I've just lost the chance of a bloody good contract because I had to be here, that's what I've just done! And he's going back, understand?'

Matthew saw his mother's head tilt slightly as the truth dawned, and she really did understand.

'That man at the hotel this morning,' she said. 'The one with the moustache. He offered you some sort of deal, didn't he?'

His father didn't reply.

'He did! You're going to send your son back to that place sooner than have to pay another school! That's why he was there in the first place, because it was cheap – and now what? A rebate? Is that what it is? A free term? Money's all you can think about when your son's *life* is in danger?'

'His life isn't in danger, you stupid woman! It was an isolated incident. Matthew only got involved because he was breaking the law himself. He's damn lucky not to be charged with it!' He turned again to Matthew. 'What the hell were you playing at?'

'It was fun,' said Matthew.

'Was it?' said his father. 'And this pen – that was fun, was it, taking it from right under this woman's nose?'

'It was getting too easy the other way. And I wanted to confuse them.'

'What?' His father frowned. 'What do you mean, confuse them? You're confusing me, I can tell you that.'

'They all thought it was Mrs Knight,' Matthew explained patiently. 'She wasn't at the ball, so if I could take something from the top table it would make them all suspect one another. It would have been better that way. It was a joke,' he said, with a shrug.

'Who's Mrs Knight?' asked his father.

'The history teacher.'

'What made them think it must have been her in the first place?'

'Her husband was killed in a car accident – she went a bit strange for a while.'

'In that place?' said his mother. 'How could you tell?'

Matthew laughed.

'You think that's funny?' asked his father. 'You thought it was funny to let everyone think she was stealing? Because she'd lost her husband?'

Matthew shrugged again; this time the blow did land. Tears of surprise and pain sprang to Matthew's eyes as his father turned to Chief Inspector Lloyd, and shouted over his wife's shocked protests. 'We're going, don't worry.'

Matthew found himself being pulled to his feet and propelled from the office. The final humiliation was when his father, still holding his collar, turned back.

'It's the school that wants protecting from *him*!' he roared.

Almost four o'clock, and Caroline was trying to conduct a class. It wasn't easy. She placed the card on the easel. 'This, for instance, might be how the tabloids would have reported the sinking of the Spanish Armada,' she said.

The facsimile paper, which she had drawn with painstaking care, should have produced a laugh. The banner headline read 'MY NIGHTS OF LOVE WITH WILL – EXCLUSIVE: ANNE HATHAWAY TALKS TO THE SUN', and down in the left-hand corner, with a couple of column inches, was 'ADIOS, AMIGOS!'

A couple of the boys smiled politely.

'Well,' she said. 'That's the idea, anyway.' She left it there; some of them might stop and read some of the other news items that she had culled from the history books to amuse them.

'The idea is to write up brief newspaper accounts of anything that takes your fancy during Elizabeth's reign. Any style you like. But factual, please. If you want to do mock-up newspapers like I've done, I can let you—' She stopped speaking as she saw Sam through the small glass pane in the door.

'I've got card and felt pens, and so on. Just tell me what you need. And these old history books – you might find the style a bit odd, but they're full of little anecdotes and things that you might like. Historians today don't believe in telling you that Drake fin-ished his game of bowls before he sailed.' She had expected there to be some interest by this point. 'Kitty says that you can use the typewriter in the office when it's available.'

'When do you want them by, Mrs Knight?' asked a voice at the back.

She smiled. 'End of term,' she said. 'You don't have to do it at all, if you don't want to. But, if you do, I suggest you do it in groups of three or four.'

'We'll be lucky if there are three or four of us left by the end of the term,' said another.

'Then, whoever is still here, if they want to do it, can do it!' Caroline shouted.

They looked startled; she would have thought that they would be beyond that by now.

'Look,' she said. 'This is difficult for everyone. I think the best thing we can do is put it to the back of our minds, and carry on as normal.'

Someone laughed. Sam was still hanging about. She looked back at the class.

'Will you be taking us for English, Mrs Knight?'

Oh, God. Philip. 'I don't know,' she said.

'Did he really kill Mrs Hamlyn?'

'I don't want this topic discussed,' she said. 'As far as I am concerned, this is a history period, and that is what we should be doing.'

The bell rang, and the last few words were drowned in the chair-scraping exodus. When the doorway had cleared of grey blazers, Sam was still there.

Caroline started putting things away in her briefcase.

'Did you do this?' Sam asked, after a moment.

'Yes.' She closed her briefcase.

'It's good. I didn't know you were artistic.'

'I'm not.' She got up.

'You'd have made a good draughtsman.'

He turned, catching her arm as she passed.

'Let go,' she said.

'Now, Caroline,' he said. 'I'm not a murderer. That's your other friend.'

'What are you doing here? What do you want?'

'I've started a painting.'

'Have you?'

'Yep.' He turned back, and smiled at the mock-up. 'But I don't actually paint – not for a while. I mustn't. I mustn't paint, or it goes wrong.' He let go of her arm.

She was listening, interested despite her desire to run away, and she put down the briefcase.

'This is a kind of gestation period,' he said. 'It makes me hungry.'

He was moving all the time. His hands would be in his pockets, then out; he rocked slightly on the balls of his feet. He was fidgety, nervous. She had never seen him like that.

'Then maybe you should go and have something to eat,' she said.

'I will,' he said, his head turned away, looking at the mock-up. 'But it's more than that. It sharpens my senses. My reactions. My appetites.' He turned to her. 'And you and I have some unfinished business,' he said.

'It's going to stay unfinished.'

'No,' he said. 'No, it's not. I'll come to your flat, and we'll finish it. OK?'

'I don't want you in my flat.'

'Fine. You come to mine. I'll be alone. My flatmate's moved out.'

'Find someone else, Sam.'

'That's like telling me to read the end of another book,' he said.

'What does that matter?' she asked, picking up her briefcase again. 'If you don't know which book you were reading in the first place?'

'Look – maybe . . . well, maybe I was a little quick off the mark. I'll behave better this time if you will.'

'There isn't a this time. I thought perhaps I needed you. I was wrong. I did behave badly, and I'm sorry.'

She walked out, leaving him standing by the easel.

Boys flowed like a grey river through the building, on the stair-cases, in the corridors, swollen by tributaries from the open classroom doors. She stood on the landing, and watched the building empty, pouring its contents out on to the cobbles. The grey streams ran down the slope, seeping along the lane, dribbling into the houses.

She became aware, gradually, that Sam was standing beside her.

'Happiest days of your life?' he said.

She shook her head.

'They were of mine,' he said.

All things considered, Lloyd thought, as evening fell, it hadn't been a bad day. Cawston senior had made junior apologise to Allison before they left, and he in his turn had been almost pleas-ant to Lloyd.

Freddie had promised to give top priority to an examination of all the things they had discovered; soon, it would all be over.

They had found the missing buttons in Newby's car, and they would find something on the stick, however carefully he'd cleaned it. The silver top was engraved with an intricate pattern, and anyone who had ever stripped paint from carved wood knew just how difficult it was to remove all traces. Microscopes were won-derful inventions.

And the clothes spoke for themselves. They had found his shirt under the bed, and you didn't have to be a pathologist to recognise blood-stains when you saw them on a white shirt. The mud on the suit gave all the classic indications.

But he wanted to know *why*. Why he had done it, why he had made such a half-hearted job of covering his tracks, come to that. Why had he just taken the suit back to the shop, for instance? Judy had asked that last night, and it still bothered Lloyd.

He had told himself that if law-breakers had brains the crime detection rate would be even lower than it was. He had told himself that the man must be severely disturbed, and didn't even think about the consequences. He had told himself that it was deliberate; he was, after all, already receiving psychiatric help, and he had subconsciously wanted to get caught, knowing that he'd gone over the edge.

But Philip Newby came across as a sane, level-headed, intelligent man who was suffering permanent injury from the car crash, and who was being treated for the depression which had resulted. So why, having done it, did he not either give himself up, or work a little harder to conceal the evidence?

Maybe he would be going for diminished responsibility, and try to cite his lack of a cover-up as proof that he was a brick short of the load. Maybe he had prepared some sort of story that would have satisfied the shop, had they asked, and thought that the police would never know. But he knew it wouldn't satisfy Lloyd, so he simply wasn't even trying it on him.

Lloyd stopped at the machine, got one plastic cup full of lethally steaming liquid for Judy, and punched the buttons again. He got his own, and looked round for a plastic thing with holes in it, but there wasn't one, and he had to grit his teeth, a red-hot cup in each hand, all the way down the corridor. Once, people had made him coffee. Brought it in. Instant, but better than this stuff which seemed to have been designed purely as a weapon. He had had to give instructions that it must never be served to a prisoner until it had cooled.

He got into the office, gave Judy her coffee, and sat down still feeling disconsolate. He was about to be given all the evidence he needed for a conviction, and he had expected to feel something.

Maybe triumphant, if he had felt he was putting away someone who deliberately preyed on women. Maybe even sad, if he felt that the murderer was just as much a prey to his own impulses. But all he felt, when he thought about Newby, was puzzled. Why would he suddenly do a thing like that?

Some of them were called by God. Seek out wicked women, use them, destroy them. Newby seemed to have about as much truck with God as Lloyd himself, and it did seem, now he came to think of it, a little bit as though he himself had suddenly raped and murdered someone. He smiled. Maybe he could be a character witness. It must have been totally out of character, a complete bolt from the blue, because Newby didn't split infinitives.

The phone rang; Judy answered it. 'Freddie,' she said. 'For you.'

'Freddie,' he said, picking up his extension. 'You've surpassed yourself this time.'

'I've had everyone working on it,' said Freddie. 'Since the crack of dawn. But it's not as simple as it seems. Before I start, I agree that Newby's clothes show all the signs. I know that you found what appeared to be the murder weapon in his wardrobe.'

Lloyd closed his eyes. 'Appeared to be?' he repeated dully.

'Lloyd – if Newby raped and murdered someone, it certainly wasn't Mrs Hamlyn.'

Chapter Eight

Lloyd looked at Newby for a long time without speaking. Judy settled herself at the table with her notebook.

'Well, Mr Newby,' he said, when he had got Newby practically squirming in his chair. 'It seems your stick didn't kill Diana Hamlyn – it's made from a different kind of wood from the murder weapon, and bears no traces of having been used to assault anyone. It seems that the blood on your suit is probably your own, and it seems that you are not the man who had sexual relations with her.'

'I told you that,' said Newby. 'Does this mean I can go?'

'I don't think you really believe that,' said Lloyd. 'You are a witness. A reluctant one, at that.'

'I had nothing to do with Mrs Hamlyn.'

'No,' said Lloyd. 'It seems that whatever you were doing to get into that state, you weren't doing it with Mrs Hamlyn. Her clothes are not muddy at all. None the less, it is your duty, Mr Newby, to help the police in any way you can.'

'I don't *have* to, though, do I? I mean – duty is a very nebulous concept. I am under no obligation to speak to you.'

Lloyd gave a concessionary nod. 'But then again,' he said, 'you have no right of silence. You did have – when we were accusing you of something. But we're not any more. And, clearly, you wouldn't be indulging in philosophical musings about duty unless there was something you're not telling us.' He sat down.

'Oh – so because I *haven't* committed a crime ...' Newby's righteous indignation petered out, and he covered his face.

'However,' Lloyd said.

Newby took his hands away, slowly.

'Your blood *is* a match for the stains found at the foot of the fire-escape,' said Lloyd.

Newby's face coloured painfully, and Lloyd glanced at Judy.

'Don't you think you had better just tell us?' she asked gently. 'We want to know what happened to you. *Did* you see someone? Was it a fight, or something?'

'No.' The word was muffled as his hands went over his face again.

Newby waited for her to speak, but Judy could play that game better even than Lloyd, though he would never admit that to her. Very few people could stand silence in the middle of an interview. They almost always felt obliged to expand upon the last thing said.

Judy just sat, and waited for him. Newby had spoken, and she would wait for ever for him to continue, if she had to. At least, that was the impression she gave, even to Lloyd. He took a stroll round the room, stopping to read the notices. He had read over half of the advice to people in police custody before Newby spoke again.

'I drove down to the flat, and I waited in the car park for the light to go out,' Newby said. 'I didn't want to see Sam, not after what I'd found in the car. I felt . . .'

Lloyd groaned silently. Not the same story again, please. He strained to hear what Newby was saying.

'I felt as though I'd been used. I *had* been. My car had been. Other than that, I wasn't much use to anyone. I didn't want to see Sam.'

Lloyd sat down opposite Newby as he spoke.

'My head still felt a bit woozy, so I ran the window down for some air. And . . . and I heard feet on the steps. And I thought I *saw* someone.'

There was another long, long silence.

'I went up after whoever it was. I'd had too much to drink – it was crazy. It's metal, it was wet and slippery – anyway, I went up.'

Newby's head was on his hands, his fingers digging into his scalp. 'There was no one there,' he said, his voice clearer now. 'But – but there was a gap in the curtains, and I saw Caroline. She –

she was changing, and . . . and I . . .' His face was crimson. 'I watched her,' he whispered.

'You watched her undressing,' said Lloyd, getting up. So that's what it was all about, he thought tiredly.

'Yes.' He took his hands away, but his head was still bowed, his face still painfully red. 'And then she saw me, and I turned to get away. I put all my weight on the stick, and it snapped.' He looked up. 'It had a crack in it,' he said helplessly. 'I shouldn't have been using it.'

Lloyd sighed. Deeply, audibly, dramatically.

'I fell, but the jacket pocket got caught on the railing. Then it ripped, and I went headlong down the steps. I tried to get up, and I couldn't. Eventually, I managed to kneel, and I realised my nose was bleeding.'

Lloyd started walking round the room while Newby spoke. He listened to him with half an ear, because the evidence from the fire-escape already bore him out, more or less, and they had discovered a thumbprint on the handle of the rear door of the car which wasn't Newby's.

'When you went into the Barn,' he said, interrupting whatever Newby was saying, 'did you touch the rear door of your car?'

'I closed it,' said Newby.

'How?'

Newby frowned. 'I closed it,' he said. 'The usual way – what do you mean, how?'

'What's the usual way?'

Newby thought. 'I – I just pushed it, and it slammed.'

'Has anyone had occasion to open it since?'

'Not to my knowledge,' said Newby pointedly.

'Thank you.'

Lloyd had a theory to work on. One that he had abandoned on seeing Newby's suit; one that had come right back into the reckoning.

'I was frightened that Caroline might have called someone,' Newby went on, having left a suitable interval to be sure that Lloyd had finished his detour. 'I was frightened people would come looking. I crawled away until I could stand up. And when I did I saw Sam go to his car, so I went to the flat, and lay on the

A TRIO OF MURDERS

bed. I was trying to get my clothes off when you came in with Sam.'

Lloyd turned to look at him. 'So you were Caroline Knight's Peeping Tom all along,' he said.

Newby closed his eyes, and nodded.

'Well, that solves that little mystery, doesn't it?' Lloyd shook his head. 'Mrs Knight may wish to take the matter further, of course, but I have more important things to do than waste time on you. You can go.'

Lloyd wondered what Mrs Knight would do. She could, he supposed, lose him his job. Sam Waters had said that Newby had been making a nuisance of himself with Mrs Knight; perhaps they should have put two and two together. He felt sorry for the man, but then he wasn't the one on whom he had been spying. And Mrs Knight would have to be told. 'Mr Newby,' he said. 'You're free to go.'

Newby didn't move.

'Mr Newby,' said Judy. 'I'll see if I can arrange a lift back to the school for you.'

'I don't want to go back there.'

'You can't stay here.'

Newby looked up at Judy. 'I'm not like that,' he said. 'Truly, I'm not like that.'

Judy looked a little nonplussed. Clearly, something was required of her. She smiled a little. 'Try not to make a habit of it, then,' she said.

Newby stood up, stiffly and painfully. 'I would like a lift back,' he said. 'If it's possible.'

Judy went to find out; Lloyd looked at Newby, who stared down at his feet.

'I couldn't . . .' Newby shook his head. 'I couldn't tell you.'

'You had to tell me in the end,' said Lloyd.

He nodded. 'I'm sorry I wasted your time,' he said.

'Do you think your arrival in the Barn scared them off?'

Newby shrugged.

Something had, thought Lloyd. So who was with her? He still thought that Waters, fresh from his rejection by Caroline, might well have taken advantage of finding himself alone with Diana

Hamlyn. The kerb-crawling had only been mentioned in case they found some evidence of a sexual encounter on his clothing. Another word with Waters was indicated.

'If you could come with me,' Judy said, coming back, 'I'll show you where you can wait. It might be a little while, but there aren't any buses, and it's cheaper than a taxi.'

Lloyd went back to the office, and gave some more thought to his theory. Sam had been with her, and something, someone had scared them off. Not Newby – he would have seen them. Someone before Newby. Someone who became enraged at what he discovered. There was the usual objection. How could he have got hold of the golf-club? But as he doodled he realised something.

He looked up when Judy came back in. 'So,' he said, smiling. 'The hunt is back on for your golf-club, isn't it?'

Judy nodded. 'We've done the immediate area,' she said. 'And all the usual places – the bins, and so on. We can move on to the school building proper, if you think that's likely.'

Lloyd agreed that they should, as the phone rang and he was summoned to Chief Superintendent Allison's office. It didn't sound as though it was going to be too friendly an encounter.

Lloyd knocked, and went in. He was not invited to sit down, as Allison carried on writing something for some moments.

'I,' he said, still writing, not looking up, 'have just been on the receiving end of what was called "a word to the wise".'

Lloyd arranged a look of polite interest on his face, just in case Allison bothered to look at him.

'I don't know about you,' Allison went on, putting down his pen, 'but I feel apprehensive when conversations start with those words.' He clasped his hands, making a steeple with his forefingers, and looked at Lloyd for the first time.

Lloyd kept his face expressionless, and just had to hope that it didn't come out as mutinous. He was clearly not being invited to speak until he was asked a question. Which, if he had got Allison's measure, would be coming up any minute.

'Samuel Cody Waters,' he said. 'How many times has he been seen during this inquiry?'

Lloyd pursed his lips. 'Oh – twice, three times ... I'm not entirely certain, sir. But Sergeant Hill will—'

'Don't bother the sergeant,' said Allison. 'If you've lost count, I don't wonder that he's beginning to feel like a marked man.'

'He was very unco-operative,' said Lloyd.

'That's not against the law, Chief Inspector.'

Lloyd gave a brittle smile. 'You're the second person who's told me that today, sir,' he said. 'I am aware of that. But a lack of co-operation does tend to draw out our enquiries.'

'Lack of co-operation,' repeated Allison. 'That's not quite what I've been told. Is it true that Mr Waters offered us both the sets of clothes that he wore that night for forensic examination?'

'Yes,' said Lloyd wearily.

'Did he come to the station voluntarily to make a statement concerning his movements that night?'

'Yes, sir.'

'Then I fail to see where this lack of co-operation comes into it. What did you want him to do? Write a thank-you letter?' He tapped the tips of his forefingers together as he spoke.

'The statement that he made was—' Lloyd began.

'Was what? False?'

'Not exactly,' said Lloyd.

'Did it contain any false*hoods*?'

'No, but—'

'But what?'

Christ. If he'd let him finish a sentence, he might find out but what. 'But he was using us!' he said firmly. 'Sir.'

'Using us? Oh – you mean because Cawston had stolen his pen? Well, yes – that would never do. Involving the police in bringing a thief to book? Whatever next?'

'Sir, I'm sure you know what—'

'Have you at any time during this inquiry found any evidence – circumstantial or tangible – to link Mr Waters with this murder?'

'No, sir.'

'Have you found any evidence that he has committed any offence of any sort?'

'No,' said Lloyd.

'Then it's hardly surprising that he resents being treated like a criminal.'

'He has been treated with—'

'With discourtesy and disrespect. Those were his words, Chief Inspector. Are they accurate?'

'He has been treated with as much courtesy and respect as he has shown towards us,' said Lloyd.

'Look, Lloyd. The papers have got on to this. Apart from the obvious circulation value of Mrs Hamlyn's activities, it appears that Waters himself is something of a celebrity in the art world.'

'He used to be,' agreed Lloyd. 'I'd have thought he would have welcomed the publicity.'

'Well, he doesn't! And neither do I. I've got telephone calls stacked up from papers wanting to know if we suspect Waters. Do we?'

'No, sir.'

Allison's eyebrows shot up.

'But I do think that he was involved,' said Lloyd.

'Think?' repeated Allison. 'This isn't a cops-and-robbers television show, Chief Inspector. Leave your hunches at home. And unless and until you have some justifiable reason to *believe* that Mr Waters can cast any light on the incident at the school on Friday night neither you nor any other officer is to question him on the matter again. Is that understood?'

'Sir.'

'Now – Sergeant Hill. I want a word with her. And I want you present.'

Allison sent for Judy, and Lloyd waited for her knock, feeling more apprehensive for her than he had for himself.

'Come!' said Allison.

Judy came in, and stood, hands behind her back, while Allison busied himself once again with something on his desk. But at least he looked at her when he spoke to her.

'Sergeant Hill,' he said. 'You are in charge of the inquiry into the thefts at this school, I believe?'

'Yes, sir.'

'Are we still holding property belonging to Mr Waters?'

'Yes, sir,' Judy said. 'It was one of the stolen items recovered by PC—'

Allison raised a hand, stopping her going into the detail that she was clearly about to give him. 'Is it the case that all the other items have been returned to their owners?'

'Yes, sir.'

'Why hasn't Mr Waters's pen been returned?'

Lloyd stepped forward a little. 'I thought it might have some connection with the murder investigation, sir.' He didn't dare look at Judy. 'I asked the sergeant to hold on to it,' he lied.

Allison nodded, and turned back to Judy.

'But, acting on information given to you by Mr Waters, you apprehended the thief. At which point you knew that the pen could be of no further use in the investigation. Mr Waters, along with others, agreed not to prosecute. Why hasn't Mr Waters's pen been returned to him?'

So much for his gallantry. He had got himself into trouble for being a male chauvinist pig, and all for nothing.

'I'm afraid I haven't got round to it, sir.'

'You will get round to it now. Today.'

'Yes, sir.'

Rain was suddenly thrown against the window, as the evening grew dark and blustery.

'And a point for both of you,' he said. 'Mr Waters also alleges that an investigating officer used obscene language to him. I understand that he declined to name the officer concerned, but I have been asked to draw the matter to your attention. As far as I am concerned, I strongly disapprove of unofficial complaints, and I do not want to know who it was, even if you find out.'

He stood up. 'What I do want', he said, 'is for the future conduct of this inquiry to be free of any such petty nonsense as this business with the pen, or the least hint of personal scores being settled. And I want that damn golf-club found!'

They were excused; back in the office, Judy took out her notebook, and began writing in it.

Lloyd sat down, disgruntled. 'Who the hell does Waters know?' he asked.

'It's all in the handshake, or so I'm told,' said Judy, still writing.

'Waters is a Freemason?' said Lloyd incredulously.

'According to Bob Sandwell, who knows everything,' said Judy. 'And so – according to Bob – is the deputy chief constable.'

'Wouldn't you just know?' muttered Lloyd.

'I've got some better news,' she said. 'At least, I think it is.'

'Oh?'

'I asked Mary Alexander if I could share with her until the transfer.'

Mary lived in the block of flats behind Lloyd's block. He smiled. 'Well, you would be nice and handy,' he said. 'But if you're not going to Barton you can't be sure it'll be in June. She might not want a lodger indefinitely.'

Judy smiled. 'You are in an optimistic mood today,' she said. 'I haven't finished. She said yes of course I could, but how would anyone know which flat I actually lived in? I can use her address and, if anyone asks, she'll say I live there.' She smiled. 'I'm sure she won't mind a phantom lodger for as long as it takes.'

Lloyd sat back, his hands behind his head, and looked at her. 'So this is it?' he said. 'You've moved in? For keeps?'

'You try getting rid of me.'

Lloyd smiled.

'Well,' she said. 'You heard what the man said. I'd better get the sensitive flower's pen back to him.' She opened the door, and looked back at him. 'How polite do I have to be?' she asked.

'A bit more polite than you were the last time, by the sound of it,' Lloyd said, picking up his coat. 'I'm coming with you.'

Lloyd tried out his theory on the way to the school. 'Changing your clothes isn't all that easy when everyone's in formal dress,' he said. 'People would notice.'

He could feel the pull of the wind on the exposed country road, and slowed down, despite his instinctive desire to drive faster to get away from it.

'If it was someone who returned to the dance, he must have,' said Judy.

Here we go, thought Lloyd, as he launched his theory. 'Or been noticeably wet,' he said.

'Like Treadwell?' she suggested. 'He never did tell me why he didn't phone Mrs Knight back,' she said, raising her voice slightly as the rain battered the car.

Lloyd was relieved; his theory might not get the bad reception he had expected. 'I've been wondering about him,' he said.

'He went looking for her,' Judy said. 'And got soaked to the skin. And he was gone from the table for quarter of an hour.'

Lloyd nodded. He had been thinking about it for some time; it made sense of Hamlyn's statement, and his suicide note.

'But where did he come by the golf-club?' Judy asked, right on cue.

'Ah.' He let his foot press slightly on the accelerator. 'He's one of the few people who *could* have come by it,' he said. 'He found it in the first place.'

'Last December,' objected Judy, like his straight man. 'It doesn't make sense.'

'Who says it was last December?' asked Lloyd.

'That's when it was stolen,' she said.

'Who says?' he repeated.

There was a little silence. 'Treadwell,' she said.

The journey back had been worse even than being arrested in the first place. Back to face Caroline finding out what a pathetic mess he was. Back to face dismissal and *everyone* knowing what a pathetic mess he was. Including Sam.

He had been relieved that Sam wasn't there, and had gone into his room, shutting the door, wishing he had a lock. He had closed the curtains on the dark evening, on the school, on everything, and now he lay on the bed, wishing he could just die. Hamlyn had had the right idea.

He closed his eyes, trying to block out his thoughts, but he couldn't. He had been accused of murder because he couldn't bring himself to tell them that he had watched Caroline through a gap in the curtains. His stick had snapped because it had a crack, and it had a crack because he had smashed it down on the table the day he arrived. He had smashed it on the table because of what he had become; because all he could do was look up women's skirts and down their blouses. Because of what he had become, he had watched Caroline through a gap in the curtains. A wicked, vicious circle from which he could never, never escape.

He didn't open his eyes when he heard his door-handle turn. Sam, he presumed. Caroline must have told him; he would be here to give him the benefit of his opinion. But he couldn't say anything worse than Philip was already thinking.

'They told me.' Caroline's voice.

Oh, God. Caroline. He kept his eyes closed. Make her go away. Please, make her go away. But she didn't.

'Well?' she said. 'Aren't you going to say anything?'

'They thought I'd raped Diana,' he said. He opened his eyes. 'I suppose I should take it as a kind of compliment.'

'Oh, for God's sake, Philip! Stop feeling so *sorry* for yourself!' She closed the door, and came towards the bed. 'There's nothing wrong with you.'

'What?' he said.

'I was ill, too – but I did something about it, for God's sake!'

'You pulled yourself together? Well, bully for you, Caroline.'

'Yes! And so could you, if you weren't just lying there thinking what a terrible thing happened to *you*, as though nothing terrible ever happened to anyone else!'

'It doesn't hurt when I lie on my back,' he said, offended.

'And if you're going to watch me undress . . .'

Philip's eyes widened as, arms crossed, she seized her sweatshirt.

'. . . then watch me. Don't peep through windows to do it.' She angrily pulled the sweatshirt over her head.

It landed on the bed; Philip picked it up, absently folding it neatly.

'All right, you were badly hurt,' she said, kicking off her shoes, unzipping her jeans. 'Maybe you'll always be in pain – so what? You're alive, Philip – Andrew isn't.'

He laid the shirt down on the table beside the bed.

'You can walk – some people can't even move!' She stepped out of the jeans, kicking them away. 'Can't feed themselves – can't even talk. There's nothing wrong with you except what's going on in your head.' She peeled off her tights. 'If you want to spend the rest of your life the way you are, then don't do it round me – go and have fantasies about someone else.'

The Marks & Spencer bra and pants were discarded impatiently, and she looked at him. 'It hurts you to undress?' she said. 'Right. I'll do it.'

And she did; quickly, efficiently, irritably, like a nurse who was already late going off duty, except that she got on to the bed with him which, as far as he could recall, the nurses had refrained from doing.

She lay beside him, her head resting on her hand, not touching him, not speaking. Just looking at him. For the first time, he looked into her eyes; they were beautiful, and he had never seen them before. Then she bent her head, and her mouth was on his. She pressed close to him as they kissed, moving against him, awakening sensations that he had almost forgotten. She drew away, and he reached out to her, touching her face, her neck, her shoulders.

'And if you're not in pain when you lie like that,' she said, smiling down at him, 'then lie like that.'

She was real. His tongue had found an unsuspected gap where a tooth should have been; she had a vaccination scar on her arm. He caressed full, slightly heavy breasts, and his fingertips found the occasional blemish as they moved down the small of her back to a bottom no firmer than it should be. He could see a little broken vein at the top of her thigh.

She was real. Hands that worked, that washed dishes and Marks & Spencer underwear were arousing him, exciting an eager, almost instant response from the hunger that had fed too long on insubstantial fantasy.

She was real. Her legs had tiny bristles on them that rubbed against his skin when their imperfect bodies joined together. She didn't cry out in ecstasy; it was over too soon for that.

Matthew would never forgive his father for what he did at the police station. Making him look a child, a fool, in front of the chief inspector. Making him come back. But that hadn't been as bad as he had thought. He was no longer head boy but, far from being shunned, he had been inundated with questions; his status as murder suspect – never actual, but not denied – had eclipsed the fact of his having been the thief, and what might have been a sticky return to the school had turned into a positive triumph. Newby's arrest had been attributed to him; he had liked that. Newby had been perfect; nervous, obviously having physically overstretched himself somehow. Being led on by Mrs Hamlyn every chance she got. And his car had been parked in the Barn; it had all made sense.

But he and Mrs Hamlyn hadn't been interrupted by Newby; Newby had obviously convinced the police of that, or they wouldn't have released him.

So he had been trying to piece together what he knew, and what he had gathered. He wished that he could be shown round the forensic laboratory while the investigation was going on; then he would know what they knew. As it was, he had to rely on what he'd seen, and heard. And overheard.

He frowned when it occurred to him. No, he thought. That would be impossible.

Or was it? The more he thought about it, the more he thought about the little things, like the doctor had said – the little insignificant incidents, snatches of conversation, moments – the less impossible it became.

Matthew smiled to himself. The police might know things that he didn't, but the traffic wasn't all one way. He knew who else could have stolen the golf-club.

He nervously licked his lips as he knocked on the door, which was answered by Treadwell himself.

'What do you want, Cawston?' he said wearily. 'I've seen more than enough of you lately.'

'I'd like to ask your advice,' he said.

Treadwell seemed to think this funny; he let Matthew into the sitting-room.

'At your service,' he said, pouring himself a drink.

'Mr Treadwell?' Matthew said. 'Should I say I'm sorry to Mrs Knight?'

'No,' Treadwell replied. 'It's possible that she didn't realise that she was the subject of gossip. And if she did, it certainly wouldn't help to know that it was a deliberate act.'

'It's just that she was so nervy,' Matthew said. 'On Saturday. And I realised that she'd been that way since the accident really.' He dropped his eyes from Treadwell's.

'What's the accident got to do with it?' Treadwell asked.

'I must have made things worse for her. I'd really like to tell her I'm sorry.'

'That's too bad,' said Treadwell. 'I'm not giving you that luxury. And if I hear that you have said one word to Mrs Knight about the thefts I will kick you back out again, Cawston. I'm still the head for the moment, and don't think I wouldn't do it. Now, go away, and stay out of my sight.'

Matthew left, just as Sam Waters crossed the road to the lane; he followed a little way behind as he went to the canteen, waiting outside in the wet, windy darkness while Waters ate three courses, still watching as he strode away from the canteen.

He stepped back into the shadow of the doorway as Waters passed him, deep in thought, then followed him back into the lane, and saw him go into the art room.

He walked quickly along the lane, and knocked on the door. On getting no reply, he walked in.

'What the hell do you want?' Waters roared.

'Sorry, sir,' said Matthew. 'It was just that I saw the light going on, and I thought perhaps someone was messing about in here.'

'Well, they're not, so you can just piss off.'

'Sir,' said Matthew, determined to say what he had really come to say.

'Oh, for Christ's sake – what?'

'Sir – you know that I stole those things?'

'Yes, Cawston, I know that you stole those things. And I know that you stole my pen. And I knew that was why you were with Mrs Hamlyn, but I didn't tell the police that because I thought you deserved to be scared out of your wits. I trust you were.' Waters sat down at the table as he spoke, but he wasn't relaxed. His foot tapped quickly, as though he was listening to fast music.

Matthew realised what he had said. '*You* were there,' he said slowly. 'You were there when Mrs Hamlyn spoke to me.'

Waters's foot stopped tapping. 'You mean you didn't know?' he said.

Matthew shook his head. But he knew now. And the police had seen Waters over and over again, but they hadn't arrested him; it fitted. It all fitted.

Waters's foot began to tap again, slowly this time. 'What do you *want*?' he demanded.

'I'd like to ask a favour, sir,' said Matthew.

'From me?'

'Yes, sir,' he said. 'You see, everyone thought it was Mrs Knight who was stealing.'

'You made bloody sure everyone thought it was Mrs Knight.' He jumped up again, and paced the room.

Matthew nodded. 'I want to apologise to her,' he said. 'But Mr Treadwell won't let me talk to her about it.'

'Why not?'

'He thinks she'd rather not know that I was doing it on purpose,' Matthew said, then took a deep breath. 'But I'm sure she already knows,' he said. 'I mean – she'll have worked it out, won't she? It could hardly have been coincidence. Not all those times.'

Waters snapped his fingers, still hearing his music. 'What's that got to do with me?' he asked, sitting down again, hooking one leg over the other, his foot moving, moving.

'Will you tell her I'm sorry?' he asked.

Waters grunted.

'And – sir? Could you tell her that I didn't take the golf-club? I want her to know that.'

Waters frowned. 'What golf-club?' he asked.

'The one that went from the Barn just before Christmas,' said Matthew, watching him carefully.

Waters frowned. 'What about it?' he asked.

Matthew's eyes widened. 'Didn't you know?' he said. 'The police think that it's the murder weapon.'

Waters again stopped his constant movement just for a second. 'Do they now?' he said.

'Will you tell her, sir?'

'Why pick on me, for God's sake?'

'Well,' said Matthew. 'She's a friend of yours, isn't she, sir? I mean – I've seen you go out with her.'

'You know she's a friend of mine,' repeated Waters, in a low voice. 'You've seen me go out with her. You know too bloody much, Cawston. You know everything that goes on round here, because you never stop watching people, do you?'

Matthew had always watched people. People were usually very interesting.

'Will you speak to her for me, sir?'

'Yes! Stop calling me sodding sir and piss off!'

Matthew turned to go.

'And Cawston,' Waters called.

He turned. 'Yes, s—' He bit off the rest of the word.

'Don't play with fire,' he said.

Perhaps it *was* still all a nightmare. Treadwell poured himself a considerable pre-dinner whisky, and checked the drinks cabinet. He'd have to go to the off-licence for more soon. At least he could drink it in the open. He could get as drunk as he liked, because he was all washed up anyway.

Unless it was a dream, of course. In which case he could still get as drunk as he liked. And when he woke up Diana would still be alive, and he wouldn't even have a hangover. He watched Marcia lay the table for one. She wasn't speaking to him because he was drinking. It was no great loss; she was not one of the world's great conversationalists.

He wished Matthew Cawston hadn't mentioned the accident. How much did he know about what went on that day? Sometimes, he thought that Matthew knew everything about everyone. It was an uncomfortable thought.

Why, when God knew how many people were swooping on the school to take their sons away, did the Cawstons, of all people, have to bring theirs back? He had come in that morning with his father, who had said that after some discussion it had been agreed that Matthew should after all finish his education at the school. Matthew had looked a touch chastened; it was to be presumed that Mr Cawston had had enough of his smart-alec son. He had even been made to apologise.

'I'm very sorry for all the trouble I've caused you,' he had said. 'And thank you for being prepared to overlook what I did.'

It had been a bit like watching a hostage read a prepared statement. But the slightly mutinous look had gone with this latest visit, to be replaced by a Uriah Heep humility; it didn't suit him. And it hadn't given Treadwell the satisfaction he had hoped it might when he had dismissed Cawston from his presence. Why did he have to go and mention the accident?

The doorbell rang, interrupting his thoughts on Matthew. Marcia announced the arrival of Chief Inspector Lloyd and Sergeant Hill, and retired to the kitchen, presumably to eat her solitary meal. Treadwell didn't mind his being interrupted; he didn't really feel like eating.

They came in, bringing with them the cold, blustery night which he had managed to shut out with the help of his liquid refreshment.

'Mr Treadwell,' said Lloyd. 'We wondered if you could tell us a little about the golf-club.'

Treadwell frowned. What did they want to know about that for? 'Well,' he said, 'it's not bad. Not bad at all – not sure if you need to be a member. But' – he looked at his watch – 'you'd have to hurry. They stop serving quite early.'

From the looks on their faces, he didn't think that that could have been the information they were seeking.

'No, Mr Treadwell,' said the sergeant. 'The golf-club – the one that went missing.'

'Oh!' Treadwell frowned again. 'Someone said Newby used his stick,' he said. 'Are you still interested in the golf-club?'

'Mr Newby has been eliminated from our enquiries,' said Lloyd.

Suddenly, Treadwell felt very sober indeed. 'Not Newby?' he said.

'No.'

Treadwell sat down heavily.

'Does that bother you?' asked Lloyd.

'No,' he said. 'No. I'm glad. I like Newby.'

'May we sit down?'

'Oh, yes, yes.' Treadwell waved an expansive arm at the chairs. Not Newby. He'd have to tell Lloyd. But not with that damn woman here.

'About the golf-club,' said Lloyd. 'You know exactly when it went missing?'

'Yes. Saw it before lunch – rang the chap who might be interested, and arranged to have lunch with him. At the golf club, as it happens,' he said, with a weak attempt at a smile. 'Went back to pick it up, and it was gone.'

'When was this?'

'December the ... whatever it was. It's on the list.'

'You're sure about that?'

'Yes. When I asked Mrs Knight to organise a do for the sesqui-centennial, I said I'd like to include the older boys in some way. I thought that perhaps we could clear the Barn, and have a disco or something, but it wasn't possible, so we just let them come to the proper do. Anyway, it was when I was seeing if clearing it out was feasible that I found the niblick.'

'When my sergeant came about the thefts, you didn't mention the golf-club.'

'No, I'd made a note of them all, but I hadn't made a proper list. And it slipped my mind – I mean, it didn't even belong to anyone.'

'You said you'd let her have a list, but the first time she saw it was on Saturday.'

'I forgot all about it,' said Treadwell. 'There weren't any more thefts reported.'

Then the man seemed to change tack completely. 'When we spoke to Mr Hamlyn,' he said slowly, 'he said that he had suggested that his wife might be with Sam Waters as some sort of revenge.' He looked politely at Treadwell. 'What do you suppose he meant by that, Mr Treadwell?'

Treadwell shrugged slightly. 'Revenge for Sam having had an affair with his wife, I suppose,' he said.

'But that was an amicable arrangement, according to Hamlyn himself. He and his wife had arrived at an understanding.'

Treadwell frowned. 'I don't quite know what ...' he said.

'We think he may have been trying to upset someone else. Someone at the table. Someone who had an interest in his wife. Someone who wouldn't be too happy to think that Sam was with her.'

Treadwell thought. The chairman? No, he decided. Too interested in himself, if he was any judge.

'He felt as though he had been given some sort of gift,' Lloyd went on. 'To ease someone's conscience. Could that have been his promotion, Mr Treadwell?'

'But I'm the one who put him up for promotion,' Treadwell said. 'The chairman just went along with it – very reluctantly, I might add. He thought Hamlyn was too old.'

'The chairman didn't leave the table,' said Lloyd. 'And Hamlyn believed that his remarks actually caused his wife's death. I don't think he suspected the chairman.'

'Then who?' said Treadwell.

'You went looking for Mrs Hamlyn, Mr Treadwell.'

Treadwell was totally bewildered. 'Because Mrs Knight wanted to speak to her,' he said.

'Why didn't you ring Mrs Knight back?' asked the sergeant.

Oh, God. He'd have to tell them. He opened his mouth a couple of times, but he couldn't. 'Chief Inspector,' he said, 'would it be possible – I mean, could I speak to you alone, do you think?'

'Sergeant?' Lloyd said.

'Certainly,' she said, getting up. 'I have something else to do.'

Lloyd twisted round as she got to the door. 'Judy!' he called, and got up, speaking to her too quietly for Treadwell to hear what he was saying. He came back into the room as the outside door closed. 'Right, Mr Treadwell,' he said, sitting down again.

'I couldn't ... well, not with a young woman ...' Treadwell wasn't at all sure that he could anyway.

'You were about to tell me why you didn't ring back to say that you had been unable to find Mrs Hamlyn,' Lloyd said. 'Why, Mr Treadwell?'

'Because I did find her.'

Lloyd just nodded, as though he'd known that all along. 'Well – I saw her.'

'Where?'

'In the Barn.'

Lloyd looked stern as he spoke. 'Why didn't you tell us this before?' he demanded. 'Why didn't you tell the chief superintendent that night? Why didn't you tell anyone at all, Mr Treadwell?'

'Because ... I had got it all wrong, you see. I hadn't got the picture – it took a while to get it all sorted out.'

'Three days?'

'No, well—'

'Then let's sort it out now, shall we?'

'I went into the Barn, and—'

'Wait. Did you expect to find her there?'

The wind howled round the house; Treadwell poured himself another drink.

'No. When I was on the phone, the small door to the Barn was open, and I could see Newby's car. I thought he'd left some time before that, and I went to see if he was all right. With it being so wet and slippery underfoot.'

Lloyd nodded encouragingly.

'But then ...' Treadwell ran a finger round his shirt-collar, which was damp with perspiration. 'As I got to the door, I heard ... sounds,' he said, producing the final word as quickly as he could.

'Sounds?' Lloyd frowned. 'What sort of sounds?'

'Oh, you know the sort of sounds!'

'No,' he said, sitting back. 'Suppose you tell me?'

For a moment or two Treadwell's lips moved, but nothing much came out. His hands moved, too, as though their waving about would suffice. 'Sounds,' he said again. 'You know. Sort of ... well ... moaning, heavy breathing – you *know*!' He hated Lloyd for making him tell him, but at least he wasn't that woman.

'Did she call whoever she was with by name?'

Treadwell gulped his drink, and shook his head. 'Not unless his name was God,' he said, in a heroic attempt at a joke.

Lloyd didn't laugh. 'If they were in the car, how were you able to hear so clearly?' he asked.

Outside, the wind and the rain danced wildly together. Diana had danced wildly, Treadwell thought, beginning to feel pleasantly hazy. But you would never have thought it to look at her. She had been pretty, and vivacious, but she had always dressed sensibly, and she had *been* sensible. Bordering on wise, even. But she had danced wildly. He smiled a little.

'Mr Treadwell? How could you hear what was going on in the car?'

He sighed. 'The rear door was open,' he said. 'I could see that when I went in.'

'Why did you go in?' Lloyd's face was unfathomable. He just asked questions, and listened to the answers.

'Because I had to put a stop to it. Suppose one of the VIPs . . .' Even now, in the new-found freedom of his resignation, Treadwell couldn't bear to think of it. 'I called out. Asked what was going on,' he continued. 'There was silence, then a sort of scuffle, and then someone got out of the car and opened one of the big doors. That's when I could see that it was Diana Hamlyn, as if I hadn't already guessed. I followed her, and she was going in the direction of the playing-field when I got out. Then I heard the doors being pushed open properly, and Newby's car came out.' He shrugged a little. 'He was driving very fast. Too fast. I don't think he saw me.'

'What did you do then?'

Treadwell reached for the whisky, and poured two this time, handing Lloyd a glass whether he wanted one or not. He took it; no nonsense about not drinking on duty. 'I walked around,' he said.

'In a downpour?'

Treadwell nodded. 'I walked around, thinking what a god-awful night it had been, and how I didn't want to go back in to the chairman and his wife and Hamlyn being so . . .' He took a deep swallow. 'But I did.'

Lloyd sipped his drink, and didn't speak. The wind huffed and puffed, but it couldn't blow Treadwell's house down, because it was in ruins anyway.

'I didn't ring Caroline back because it still wasn't eleven, and Diana was on her way home,' he said.

'Or perhaps,' said Lloyd slowly, 'perhaps when you followed her to the door, you picked up the first thing that came to hand. The golf-club.'

Treadwell felt once again as though he had turned over two pages at once. 'The golf-club? But it wasn't there any more and, even if it *had* been, why—?'

'You say it wasn't there,' Lloyd said, interrupting him. 'But I don't know that. It might not have gone missing in December. We only have your word for that. As far as we know, it could have gone missing on Friday night, and been put on the list on Saturday. Perhaps you picked up the golf-club, caught up with her as she crossed the playing-field, and killed her.'

Treadwell almost choked on his drink. 'Why in the world would I do that?' he asked.

'Because you were having an affair with her.'

'An affair? Me?'

'That's what Mr Hamlyn seems to have thought,' said Lloyd.

Treadwell almost laughed. 'I feel flattered, in a way,' he said. 'If Hamlyn thought that I could ever have coped with Diana.'

Dancing wildly with Diana. It was a nice thought, but he couldn't even talk about Diana's wild dancing, never mind take part in it. He put down his drink. He really shouldn't drink this fast.

'He thought that was why he was promoted. He said he felt like a wife whose husband suddenly buys her flowers. He thought you had a guilty conscience, Mr Treadwell.'

'If he thought that, he was quite wrong. I pushed for his promotion because he had already been passed over twice, and it wasn't fair. And, as I've already told you, I thought that Diana would have been an asset in that particular situation.'

'He thought that that was why you sacked Lacey. And you went looking for her, Mr Treadwell. Where you'd found her last time.'

'I went into the Barn for the reason I have given you,' said Treadwell. 'Yes, I did find her again.' He finished his whisky, his two-minute-old promise forgotten. 'Only last time it was a summer's day,' he said. 'And I could see all too clearly what they were up to.'

He looked at Lloyd, the whisky deadening the embarrassment he still felt when he thought of it.

'She couldn't have cared less,' he said. 'She laughed. She actually laughed. Said something about having been caught in the act, and laughed, Mr Lloyd. And there was I, shocked, embarrassed, looking as if *I* had been caught in the act.' Chance, he thought, would have been a fine thing. 'And that's why I sacked Lacey. It was something I could do. To prove that I was in charge of the situation.' He smiled. 'But I wasn't,' he said. 'Diana was.'

Lloyd nodded slightly. 'Have you any idea who she was with this time?' he asked.

'I presumed it was Newby.'

Lloyd shook his head. 'We know it wasn't Mr Newby,' he said. 'Diana was in his car with someone *else*?'

'She must have been,' said Lloyd. 'Do you have any idea who it was, Mr Treadwell?'

'I suppose it must have been Sam,' said Treadwell. 'Hamlyn was right.'

'Did you touch the car when you were in the Barn?' he asked.

Treadwell shook his head.

'You won't mind letting us have your fingerprints? Just so that we can make sure?'

'If you think it's really necessary.'

Lloyd put down his glass. 'If I think it's *really* necessary,' he said, 'I will fingerprint everyone who was here on Friday night. At the moment, I think it would merely be helpful, Mr Treadwell. And I'm sure you want to be helpful.'

'I don't mind,' said Treadwell, resigned. 'I think, to be perfectly truthful, that I am past caring.'

'You didn't go back in,' said Lloyd. 'Didn't you feel the urge to sack anyone this time?'

Treadwell shook his head. 'Do you know the play *An Inspector Calls*?' he asked.

'Yes,' said Lloyd, a little puzzled.

'We don't know what the consequences of our actions will be,' Treadwell said. 'I sacked Lacey. Lacey was a driver. I needed a driver, because I had been banned.' He raised his glass in a salute to the constabulary, and realised it was empty. 'And he came in handy, running errands to the town, picking people up, that sort of thing. He picked Newby up from the station when he came for his interview.'

Lloyd picked up his drink again, and sipped it. 'And he should have taken him back?'

Treadwell sighed. 'But he didn't, because I dismissed him. Told him to get off the premises. Newby missed his train as a result, and Andrew drove him back to London.' He shook his head. 'If I hadn't sacked Lacey, the accident couldn't have happened.' He poured himself another. 'I've felt responsible ever since. For Knight's death, for Caroline's illness – because she *was* ill, Mr Lloyd, even if stealing wasn't, as it turns out, one of the symptoms. I feel responsible for Newby's disability – for everything.'

Lloyd covered his glass with his hand, as Treadwell advanced with the bottle.

'So I didn't want to go back into the Barn, and face anyone. Finding her in almost exactly the same circumstances had brought it all back, and I didn't want to do anything about it at all. And I thought, then, that everything with Caroline was going according to plan, despite that. So I didn't ring her back.'

'And when you found it hadn't?' Lloyd hadn't forgotten his original question. 'Why did you tell no one about this?'

Treadwell gave a deep sigh. 'Robert said he'd had enough at about ten to one or so,' he said. 'And then, the next thing I knew, he was back. He came up to me at the table, and he said, "Diana's dead", just like that. "Diana's dead. Someone's killed her." ' He stopped speaking, as he remembered the moment.

'Go on,' said Lloyd.

'But I thought he'd been *home*. I thought he had found her with Newby, and . . . well, flipped. After the way he had been behaving at dinner . . . Anyway, when I found out what had actually happened to her, it was such a shock that I wasn't thinking at all. It wasn't until Marcia asked me who was minding the juniors that I realised that Diana had never *got* home. I said I'd have to go and tell Caroline what had happened, but Simon Allison suggested I send someone else. Quite right. I'd had – I'd been . . . I was drunk,' he finished defiantly. 'And because I was drunk I wasn't capable of sorting it all out.'

'When were you capable?'

'When I woke up next morning, with a thick head. Simon had said that someone was coming to see me, so I was going to tell him. But it wasn't a him! I didn't expect a woman, for God's sake! I couldn't tell a woman what I'd heard, what had happened!'

'That was two days ago. Why didn't you tell me? Or Mr Allison?'

'I was going to. But then there was Hamlyn, and Matthew, and I didn't know whether I was coming or going. Then you arrested

Newby, and I thought it was all over. I thought that was who she had been with, and now you had got him.'

Lloyd sat back, nursing his drink, deep in thought. Then he spoke. 'Why should I believe any of that, Mr Treadwell?' he asked.

Treadwell shrugged a little.

'How do I know you didn't follow her on to the playing-field and kill her?' he asked.

Treadwell looked at him. 'If Mrs Hamlyn was killed with the golf-club,' he said, his voice quiet, 'then . . .' He paused. 'Then you should ask Caroline Knight. She was with me when we found it. She'll confirm that it was stolen that day.'

Lloyd listened; but Treadwell still couldn't tell what he was thinking.

Caroline watched as Philip's eyelids began to flicker, and smiled at him as he opened his eyes.

'Have you stopped being cross with me yet?' he asked.

Caroline buried her head in his shoulder. 'I was cross with us,' she said. 'For letting the accident hurt us more than it had to. I haven't pulled myself together any more than you have.'

He kissed her, and she smiled. 'I told you you could do it,' she said.

'Not very well,' he said.

She laughed. 'Oh, Philip! It'll get better. Yesterday you were practically suicidal because you thought you couldn't do it at all. Are you never satisfied?'

'I was,' he said. 'But I don't suppose you were.' His arm tightened round her.

'I just wanted to be with you,' she said. 'I wanted to prove to you that you weren't a wreck, and . . . I wanted to prove to myself that I wasn't Andrew's widow any more.'

'But you are Andrew's widow,' he pointed out, showing the same literal turn of mind as Andrew himself.

'I was ill,' she said. 'After Andrew died. Really ill.' She smiled. 'I was seeing a psychiatrist, too,' she said. 'You're not the only one.'

He nodded. 'I know,' he said.

'But it wasn't helping. And one day I realised that I had to stop being Andrew's widow,' she said. 'I had to live my own life again, and I had to do it without the help of medicine men.'

'Perhaps you should have moved away from here,' Philip said.

She nodded. 'I wasn't thinking logically. I just wanted to prove to myself that I was still me. I needed to put some sort of full stop to widowhood.'

She stiffened as she heard the front door to the building open, relaxing when someone knocked at the flat door.

'I thought it was Sam,' she said. She wasn't looking forward to seeing Sam. 'Shouldn't you see who it is?'

Philip smiled. 'I don't feel like entertaining visitors,' he said. 'I don't know about you.'

Another knock; louder, going on for a little longer.

'It could be important.'

'Then they'll come back.'

A third knock. She and Philip stopped speaking, and listened as the footsteps went, and the front door banged shut. A woman's footsteps. Whoever it was, she had gone.

'What were you going to do?' Philip asked.

'What?'

'About stopping being Andrew's widow.'

She lay on her back, no longer looking at Philip, but still close, still touching him. 'I was going to sleep with Sam,' she said.

'Wasn't that a bit drastic?'

She laughed. Drastic hardly covered it.

'Why Sam?' he asked. 'Of all people?'

'Because he was a sitting duck,' she said. 'Always so keen to prove how macho he is. I knew it wouldn't be difficult to interest him in the project.'

'I got the impression that was his project,' said Philip. 'He put the idea into your head in the first place.'

No, she thought. It was the other way round. Sam had embraced the idea that a night with him would cure everything, but it had been her idea. But sex wasn't important. It had seemed to be before, but it wasn't. It *had* been important to Philip; that was why she had come to him. Because she could do something for him that his psychiatrist couldn't; it was as simple as that.

She turned, and kissed him again. 'It was my idea,' she said. 'Sam just tried to convince me that I was right, and he almost succeeded. I went out with him a couple of times, but I couldn't make myself get involved with him. So, I planned it all. For weeks. Friday night,' she said. 'That's when I was officially going to stop being a widow. We were going to a film, we'd be back late, he'd ask if he could stay, and I would say yes.'

'Simple as that?'

'I thought so.' She sighed. 'But when it came to it I couldn't.' She sat up and looked at Philip. 'I really did treat him very badly,' she said.

'You still think you caused it all, don't you?' said Philip.

She didn't answer.

'You didn't, Caroline. Sam might have gone with her, but he didn't rape her. They were in my car, for God's sake! I don't know why the police thought it was rape.'

Caroline shivered slightly. 'I do,' she said. 'Sam isn't what you'd call gentle.'

'Is that why you didn't go through with it?'

She shook her head. 'I couldn't go through with it because I had already stopped being Andrew's widow,' she said. 'I'd met you.'

'Are you waiting for someone, miss?'

The loud voice startled Judy, who was having a cigarette in Lloyd's car, and had opened the window in the vain hope that he wouldn't know.

'Oh, it's you,' said Des. 'You're the policewoman, aren't you?'

'That's right.' She pitched her own voice at his level.

'It's cold out here,' he said. 'I'm just going to do the boiler – would you like a cup of tea and a warm?'

Waters wasn't in his flat, so she had been unable to put into practice Lloyd's last minute instruction to be polite at all costs. She couldn't go back to Treadwell's, and Judy, crossly waiting in the car for Lloyd like a child outside a pub, couldn't think of anything much nicer than a cup of tea and a warm. She walked with Des back to the school, and the wonderfully cosy boiler room. She sat at a little table while Des filled the kettle, then watched, transported, as he opened up the bottom of the boiler, and removed the hot ashes.

The smell made her six again. Six, in her grandmother's cottage which her father had tried, without success, to make his mother modernise. He would tell her of the joys of electricity, how clean the cooker would be, how easy it would be to heat the house, how she wouldn't have to rake out ashes and heave coal about. He would offer to pay for all the work to be done. And she would say that she had always done it, and always would. And she always did.

Des's boiler was much bigger, even more trouble, even hotter, and more awkward. But, like her grandmother, Des expertly shovelled up the ash and deposited it in a metal container. 'Bloody nuisance, these days,' he bellowed, as he carried it to the door, and put it outside.

'Plastic bins,' he explained, as he came back and spooned tea into the pot. 'You can't put the ashes straight in any more. Got to let them cool down first.'

Perhaps, she thought, Des was a reincarnation of her grandmother, as he sat beside her, leaving the tea to brew. No tea-bags for Des or Gran.

'How long have you worked here?' she asked.

'Thirty years near enough. Since it was a real school.'

She smiled. 'Isn't it a real school?'

'That lot? You ought to know by now – you've been asking enough questions.'

Judy decided that being non-committal was the wisest course when everything you said had to be shouted at the top of your voice.

Des handed her a mug of tea, and indicated the milk-bottle and the bag of sugar, which had a soup-spoon in it.

'Des,' she said. 'Was Mrs Hamlyn involved with anyone at the school?'

Des laughed.

'I mean recently,' said Judy.

'I don't know about that bloke with the stick,' said Des. 'She might have been, but I don't think so. She went about with that artist for a while. She wasn't too fussy.' He drank some tea.

'Mainly, it was people outside,' he said. 'I'd see her driving off in the evenings. I think since the business with Jim she didn't want to cause any more trouble here.'

Judy didn't think she had the strength to go checking up on Diana's outside contacts. She could feel the increased heat on her face before Des began to shovel coal in on top of the fiercely glowing embers, banking it up for the night.

'Hard work,' she observed.

'No,' he said scornfully. 'I'm used to it. Antiquated, though – you'd think they'd spend some money and get a new one, at least.'

'How often do you have to do it?' Judy knew that on a cold Monday morning she would hate it, but right now it seemed like a lovely job, full of warmth, and the sights and sounds and smells of her childhood.

'Night and morning,' he said. 'Every day but Saturday. Let it out Saturday, and clear it out proper on Sunday morning.'

Judy smiled. 'So why were you raking it out on Saturday at lunchtime?' she asked. 'Don't forget, you're talking to a detective here, Des.'

Des's face was blank.

She laughed. 'Just a joke,' she said.

'But I wasn't,' he said. 'I wasn't here on Saturday. It's my day off. Always has been. I'm at home with my feet up on a Saturday.'

'You don't live in?'

'Not me. Never take a tied house. If you lose your job, you lose your home.' He frowned. 'Your lot used to have to have police houses, didn't you?'

'Mm.' Judy wasn't really listening. 'Someone was in here on Saturday,' she said. 'Raking out the boiler. I heard them. Myself.'

'Well, I'd like to know who was messing about with my boiler,' said Des.

Judy nodded. 'So would I,' she said, putting down her mug. They had searched all the bins; it was the first thing they did after the playing-field. 'Des – that container that you put out the back door – how often do you empty it?'

'When it's full,' he said.

'Do you have something I could use to poke around in it?' she asked.

Des walked slowly over to the boiler. 'A poker works best,' he said.

Judy smiled, and held out her hand, but Des pulled the poker back. 'No,' he said. 'These ashes are red hot. I'll look for whatever it is.'

And he looked, and they found it. The metal head, which wasn't going to burn up, and the murderer knew it. The metal head which someone had had to come back for, to rake out of the ashes before Des found it. Which couldn't be put into a dustbin, because the police were emptying them all.

Sam couldn't concentrate; he walked back over to the staff block, frowning as he saw the light. He hadn't left the light on. He never left lights on.

Caroline and Newby sat on the sofa, with the fire going full blast.

'I thought they'd banged you up,' he said to Newby.

'I've been released,' he said.

'Well, well, well.' Sam turned the fire down, and picked up a beer. 'So we've still got a murderer at large,' he said.

'Could we drop that subject?' Caroline asked.

'A bit difficult,' said Sam. 'It isn't every day even this place has a dead body in the middle of the playing-field.'

The knock on the door was all too familiar. 'Fat chance of the subject being changed,' he said, opening the door to find the sergeant. 'Good evening, Sergeant Hill,' he said. 'Do come in.'

'No, thank you.' She handed him his pen, and he signed a receipt with it.

'Is that all?' he asked.

'You've got your pen back,' she said.

Sam smiled broadly. 'Had your knuckles rapped, have you?'

'I was told you had complained, and I was asked to give you your pen back.' She took a breath. 'But I suppose I—' She stopped speaking as Chief Inspector Lloyd arrived.

'Now what?' said Sam.

'Not you, Mr Waters,' Lloyd said, his foot on the stair. Sam wanted to let him go upstairs, but he felt he had done enough already. 'She's in here,' he said.

Lloyd and the sergeant came in. Asking about the golf-club.

'Perhaps you could confirm when it went missing from the Barn?' Lloyd was asking Caroline. 'Mr Treadwell wasn't certain.'

'December the fourteenth,' she said.

Lloyd smiled. 'Very precise.'

'It's in my diary,' she said. 'Barry wanted to see if we could clear the Barn.'

'What's a golf-club got to do with it?' asked Newby.

'They think it murdered Diana,' said Sam.

Lloyd looked at him. 'No,' he said. 'We think someone murdered Mrs Hamlyn with it.'

'Sorry,' said Sam. 'It's a pity you can't arrest me for murdering the language, isn't it?'

The sergeant took Lloyd to one side, and spoke quietly to him.

'It seems,' Lloyd said, looking up, 'that the golf-club was indeed the weapon used.' He was watching their faces as he spoke; everyone's, not just Sam's. 'And perhaps,' he said, 'since I have you all together, one of you might know who Mrs Hamlyn was likely to have been seeing recently?'

Sam laughed.

Lloyd raised an eyebrow. 'All I know is that you have all told me – in your various ways – that she couldn't keep her hands off men. Odd that, because every man I speak to was apparently as pure as the driven snow as far as she was concerned.'

'You give me a guest-list,' said Sam, 'and I'll show you half a dozen blokes that I know about, and another half-dozen that I suspect.'

'Right,' said Lloyd. 'I'll do that, Mr Waters. Any information would be most helpful.'

Sam frowned. 'I don't see how,' he said. 'Everyone would be coming and going – getting drinks, going off and talking to other people, going to the gents' – how can you sort out who nipped out for a quickie with Diana? It would be like looking for a needle in the proverbial.'

'When it comes to a murder inquiry,' Lloyd said, 'we look for needles in haystacks and anything else they might be in, however unpleasant. And we very often find them.' He opened the door.

'Good night,' he said to the assembled company. 'Thank you for your time.'

Newby and Caroline, said good night; Sam let Lloyd almost close the door.

'A word of advice, Chief Inspector,' he said, catching the door-handle.

'Yes, Mr Waters?' Lloyd reluctantly turned to look at him.

'Whoever murdered Mrs Hamlyn would have had a hell of a job doing it when she hadn't just been screwing someone.'

Lloyd paused for a tiny moment. 'Thank you,' he said.

Sam stood for a moment at the door, as Lloyd and the sergeant left.

She had been going to say something when Lloyd arrived, he thought. He wished he hadn't tried to needle her so much. She had more go about her than most women. He might almost have found her good company, if things had been different. Oh, damn it all. She shouldn't have tried hanging on to Walter's pen.

Walter Smith, a year ahead of him in school, one of the half-dozen or so black pupils whose parents had somehow managed to get rich enough to send their sons there. Smith had looked after him; he'd kept him out of trouble. He'd interested him in art. And when they had finished university, and Sam had gone to art college, he'd had the pen engraved, with the 'WS' linked along the side, for Walter's birthday. It was his first design. Walter Smith was the only other human being for whom Sam had ever had any time, and time was the one thing that had been denied to him. His wife had given Sam the pen back when Walter died from a heart-attack at the ludicrous age of thirty. It could just as well read 'SW', she had said. Sam already knew that.

Sam closed the door, and swore.

Newby sighed. 'Is that aimed at someone in particular, or just the world in general?' Sam swore at Newby.

'Well, so long as we know where we are,' said Newby amiably. 'Did I hear Sergeant Hill saying you had *complained* about her?'

'Storm in a teacup,' said Sam. He paused. 'What do you think of the good lady sergeant, Philip?'

'I don't know. I haven't seen any reason to complain about her.'

'No, I want to know. I'll bet you wouldn't kick her out of bed, would you? She's your type – like Caroline.'

Newby blushed, not looking at Caroline.

'I mean, you could mistake her for Caroline, at a distance, couldn't you? You must have noticed. Does she get you going, too?' Sam watched Newby's discomfort with totally unconcealed pleasure.

'All right,' said Newby, looking up. 'Yes, I've noticed a resemblance, and no, she doesn't get me going. So whatever it is you're trying to do, give up.'

'Just as well she doesn't,' said Sam. 'If you ask me, her boss is knocking her off.'

'You would think that, wouldn't you?' said Newby.

'I'll bet I'm right,' said Sam. 'And I'll bet that you and the lovely Mrs Knight here have become more than just good friends since I saw you last. Which surprises me, Newby. I didn't think you had it in you.'

'Come on, Philip,' said Caroline, standing up.

'Don't leave on my account,' said Sam. 'I've got work to do.'

Rather you than me, he thought, as he left Newby to Caroline's devices, and went back to the art room, ready at last to start work. He knew he was right about them, and about Lloyd and his lady. And he hadn't given Caroline the message from Cawston, because now he understood it, and understood that he had never been meant to pass it on.

And he knew he was right about that, too. His work was surrealist, if it had to be given a name, but Sam painted people; not everyone realised that. He knew what made people tick.

He just didn't like them very much.

Chapter Nine

They were alone in Philip's flat, having passed up the school breakfast in favour of toast and tea.

'When all this is sorted out,' Philip suddenly said, his voice firm, 'we're getting out of this place.'

Caroline looked up quickly, making the tea she was pouring spill on to the table.

'Oh,' said Philip, flustered. 'Unless – oh, hell, I'm taking too much for granted. Sorry.'

'No,' she said, mopping up the spilled tea with a tissue. 'You're not. I just didn't know that you felt the same.'

He smiled. 'I told you I did.'

She finished pouring the tea, and handed him his. 'So you did,' she said.

'And we'll leave here? As soon as we can?'

'It might be difficult,' she said.

'No,' said Philip. 'We just get into our cars and go. To hell with this place – it won't last the week anyway.'

'I mean finding somewhere that we can work together,' she said.

Philip looked a touch uncomfortable. 'Ah,' he said. 'I wasn't really thinking about our working together.' He cleared his throat unnecessarily. 'In fact,' he said, 'I'm not so sure that it's a good idea, on the whole.'

'Of course it is.' She drank some tea.

'But . . .' Philip thought for a moment before carrying on. 'But I think that that's one reason why it was so difficult for you when Andrew died,' he said.

'I loved him,' she said.

'I know, I know.' Philip put down his mug. 'But if you had

worked somewhere different – well, that part of your life would have carried on . . . I mean, it wouldn't have altered. Whereas you were so close, so . . . involved with him that . . .' He dropped his eyes from hers. 'Well, you lost your bearings.'

'I've found them again.'

'Yes, but you should have a life of your own. You said so yourself.'

'I've got you,' she said, then wondered if all this was his way of backtracking on what he had said. 'Or am I taking things for granted now?'

'You've got me,' he said. 'I'm not sure why you want me. But I still think that you should have your own job, and your own friends. I'm not so sure that living in one another's pockets is a good idea,' he said again.

'That's what Andrew said.' She smiled at him, at the kind, concerned eyes looking so earnestly into hers. 'His exact words. I don't think it is living in one another's pockets. I think it's perfectly possible to live and work together, and be a team. That's not living in one another's pockets.' She drank some tea as she watched Philip prepare his argument. 'Sam's probably right about the chief inspector and Sergeant Hill,' she said. 'They manage.'

Philip shook his head. 'You don't know that he's right,' he said. 'And even if he is, you don't know that they manage.' He smiled. 'And even if they do, they don't *live* at the police station,' he added.

'We don't have to live wherever it is,' she said.

'Is that what you told Andrew?'

She laughed. 'We didn't have much choice,' she said. 'I talked him round.'

Philip smiled, a little uncertainly. 'Well,' he said, getting up from the table. 'Time enough to discuss that. We'd better get to work – if we have any pupils left.'

'I've got a free period,' she said.

'It's all right for some.'

She went to the door with him, and discovered the thaw. The weather had finally made its mind up; water poured from the roof as the snow melted.

Philip smiled. 'Spring,' he said. 'Just right for new starts.'

Caroline frowned as she saw the crowd of boys in the lane. She glanced apprehensively at Philip. 'What's happened now?' she said, her heart sinking.

They walked quickly towards the lane; Caroline wanted to run, but she kept to Philip's pace.

'Mrs Knight!' someone called as they got closer. 'Mr Waters won't let us in!'

She left Philip behind, pushing through the crowd of boys to the building. Through the window, she could see Sam, working on his painting, oblivious to everything but what he was doing. She let out a sigh of relief.

'It's all right,' she called to Philip, as he came through the crowd to her. 'It's just Sam being even worse than usual.'

Philip banged on the window, on the door; if Sam could hear him, and he could hardly not hear him, he didn't indicate it by so much as a twitch.

'Bang goes my free period,' Caroline said. 'Right, boys. Single file. You'd better go to my form room.'

The boys pushed and jostled into a wavy grey crocodile, and set off.

Philip shook his head. 'Trust Sam,' he said.

'What are we going to do about him?' asked Caroline. 'He can't get away with this.'

Philip glanced in. 'Leave him,' he said. 'He's being bloody-minded as usual. He'll probably unlock the door as soon as we've gone.'

'You'd better go to your class,' she said. 'I'll find something for that lot to do.'

'Right. See you at lunchtime.'

'Mrs Knight!'

Caroline sighed. It was obviously going to be one of those days, and she might as well accept it. She turned. 'Yes?' she said.

'Mrs Knight, Mr Treadwell said to ask you to go to his house, because the chairman of the governors would like to speak to you.'

Caroline looked at Philip, at Sam, at the small crocodile on its way to the main building, and back at the youth who had given her the message. 'Right,' she said. 'Please tell Mr Treadwell that I'll be along in a moment.'

The boy ran off, and Caroline thought. 'Philip,' she said, 'which group have you got?'

'5C,' he said.

'So you'll have a prefect, won't you? Can you ask him to supervise the class while you go and keep an eye on the kids in my form room? I'll be there as soon as I can get away.'

'All this so as no one finds out what he's up to?' Philip asked, with a nod through the window at Sam.

Caroline nodded. 'I think it's the least I can do,' she said.

Philip didn't seem convinced of the necessity, but he sighed, and shrugged his shoulders. 'All right,' he said.

She watched him go, walking quite quickly even on the cobbles, some confidence back in his step. He waved as he went round the bend in the lane, and she waved back, her heart light for the first time in months.

He was so like Andrew.

Sam worked quickly, with a thin brush and bright oil paints. Harsh colours, harsh subject. But every stroke was applied with infinite patience, total concentration. He had been with it all night; it had started as a mark on the canvas. Just one line, the dominant line, the angle from which everything else would follow. Building it up, piece by piece. And he wouldn't stop until it was finished; he never did. By the time he first loaded the brush, the painting was there, in his head.

It never quite looked like it did in his head. But sometimes it got close, and one day – maybe today – it would come exactly right. Red. Red, and white.

He had heard the commotion outside the door, he had heard the banging on the window. But he had heard the birds start to sing before the sun rose; he had heard the school waking up. Heard cars arrive, and people walking along the lane outside. You could hear these things, but you didn't have to listen.

It had been so long since he had painted, so long since he had felt the release that it gave him. Sometimes, he wished he didn't use it all up at once like he did; he wished he could cover it up and come back to it again and again. But he couldn't let go, not once he'd got it. If he left it, it might not forgive him.

So he worked on, and he heard more people pass, another group of boys congregate and disperse, another knocking at the door. People calling his name. Then it went quiet again.

Sam could see that there was very little left to do; he didn't want to let it go, and yet he longed to. He wanted to stand back and look at the image in his head. The image that had come to him, stealing up on him, covering his eyes so that he couldn't see it. That was the worst time, when he couldn't sit still, and he was hungry all the time. And this was the best time; the moments before he looked at it.

He laid down his brush, not looking at the canvas. With his back to it, he cleaned up, put everything away. Washed his hands. Tidied up the room. Once he looked, it would be over.

He looked, and it was there. The image in his head. It was there, on the canvas.

He sat down, elated, exhausted, his head in his hands. Too soon, the moment was over. Already, he could see that the image hadn't translated exactly. He hadn't got enough power, enough energy into it. He had taken too much care. He should have slashed some of the colour on. He should have . . .

But no matter. Another image would come. Because he was painting again. In a year, if he could survive it, he would have enough for another exhibition. Sam painted fast and furious when he was really working. Meticulous, but fast. Like a machine. Like a computer, programmed with the brushstrokes, with the image inside its brain in coded messages. Sometimes he felt that he could start in one corner and build the picture up from there, so little did he seem to have to do with its execution.

And now he could look at it dispassionately. It was neither perfect nor disastrous. It was – what was it one of the papers had called him? – technically sound. He smiled. A put-down. But he was used to put-downs. Nobody *liked* what he did, but people like Newby appreciated it. Art critics didn't. He recalled some of his reviews, knowing he would read them again if this one ever saw the light of a gallery. '. . . depicting the sort of obvious, crude, colourful violence that is exploited on the cinema screens every night', according to one. 'The substitution of machinery for women as a focus for the brutality is as subtle as it gets.' He was right. Violence *was* obvious and crude. It wasn't subtle; why should he be?

Another knock. Not banging, like before. Just a knock. Slowly, like an old man, he got up, and unlocked the door.

'Hello,' she said.

'Sergeant Hill.' His voice was hoarse. 'Come to evict me?' She gave him a little smile. 'No. I've come to thank you,' she said.

'What for?'

'Not shopping me,' she said.

'Oh, that.' He sat down again, wearily. 'I deserved it,' he said.

'Yes,' she said. 'But you could have got me into trouble, all the same.' She looked at him. 'Have you been here all night?' she asked. 'Mr Newby said you were painting.'

He sighed, running a hand over his stubbled chin. 'I've finished,' he said, a little wistfully. He waved a hand at the canvas which stood facing the wall. 'You can be the first to see it, if you want.'

She looked a little dubious at the honour. 'I don't know anything about art,' she said. 'You want Lloyd for that.'

'No,' he said. 'I want you.' He nodded to it. 'Go on,' he said. 'See what you think.'

With a slight shrug, she crossed the room. He watched as she walked round the easel; he saw her look of polite expectation vanish, saw her eyes unwillingly move over it before she turned her head away.

'Does it disturb you?' he asked.

'Yes,' she said.

'I hope you're typical,' he said.

Her eyes moved back to it. 'Who buys a painting like that?' she asked.

Sam smiled. 'You wouldn't fancy it hanging in your sitting-room?' he asked.

'Would anyone?'

He shook his head. 'Probably not,' he said. 'A collector might buy it, or a gallery. If my reputation survives the critics.'

'Turner's did,' she said.

'I thought you knew nothing about art?'

'I'm being taught.' Another look at the painting. A slight frown. 'Poor Mrs Hamlyn,' she said, and left.

Sam looked at it. Just coloured marks on canvas. An optical illusion. He smiled. He had told himself people would cry for his slot machine; the sergeant hadn't cried, but it had touched her, all right. And one was all you needed.

Philip ate alone. Caroline had never returned to relieve him of Sam's art class, and her attempts to save Sam from himself fell apart when the next class was refused entry to the art room, and she hadn't been around to organise cover. It had been sorted out, eventually, with classes doubling up. Sam had emerged after Sergeant Hill had seen him, only to shut himself in his room. When Philip had left the flat for the canteen, Sam's snores had followed him to the front door.

Treadwell had abdicated responsibility for the whole affair, and Philip had no intention of involving himself, so the rest of the day would presumably be as chaotic as the morning. Though not as chaotic as it might have been; the normally packed canteen was quiet, with so many of the pupils taking an unscheduled break, and the doubled-up classes were not much larger than the normal ones.

Philip looked up as someone came in at the other end of the long room. He half-rose, trying to catch her attention, then realised that it was the sergeant. He had thought, for a moment, that it was Caroline. He sat down again, his heart pounding.

Sam had planted the idea last night. Deliberately, maliciously. He had been able to ignore it then, but now . . .

He watched as Chief Inspector Lloyd joined the sergeant at the counter, his eyes never leaving them as they chose their meals, and sat down in a corner. The chief inspector was doing all the talking; she just sat, and toyed with her food like Philip himself.

Then Caroline really did come in, not stopping to pick up food, but coming straight to where he was, sitting down, her eyes shining with excitement. 'You'll never guess,' she said.

'I won't try, then,' he said. Seeing her made him feel better, and he actually began to eat.

'I've been offered a joint headship,' she said. 'With Mr Dearden.

They think they should have a woman head teacher because of the girls coming next year.' She smiled. 'No interviews – nothing. A straight appointment.'

Philip stopped chewing.

'Isn't it great?'

Philip didn't know which aspect of it he found least entrancing. He looked round the huge canteen, with its odd groups of people eating. 'Are you sure anyone will be coming next year?' he asked.

'Oh, I'll get it going again,' she said confidently. 'The way it ought to be.'

Philip smiled. 'Well,' he said, 'if anyone can do it, you can.'

She put her hand on his. 'I know I can,' she said.

'I just don't think that this place is for me.'

'It won't *be* this place! They've all gone, Philip. Or they're going. The Hamlyns, Sam – Treadwell.'

'It's still the same school,' said Philip.

'But it's not *their* school any more,' she said. She sat back a little. 'But if you feel you have to leave, then I'm coming with you,' she said.

Andrew's voice. *'If you've got to leave now, I'll have to drive you.'* Andrew's voice, his face. Even his car. He could see it all now. A warm sunny summer day. An open-top car. *'Everything's gone wrong. Caroline can't get back, and it seems that Treadwell's sacked the bloody driver.'* Getting into the car, Andrew irritated because Philip wasn't going to meet Caroline after all. *'Found him in the potting-shed with the maths teacher's wife, would you believe?'* he had said, as they drove off. The potting-shed. He'd called it the potting-shed, in fun. That was what had made him think that there was a garden. *'I've told Caroline she's got Diana Hamlyn to thank if I get led astray by the bright lights.'*

And if he got killed? Philip's eyes rose slowly to Caroline's.

'Philip? We don't have to stay. I just thought it would be good, because we wouldn't have to find somewhere that we could both work. We could do it right – teach them to stop and smell the roses.' She squeezed his hand. 'But it really doesn't matter, Philip. We'll go. We'll find something else.'

He looked at her, then let his eyes move towards the sergeant.

Dark, slim. *It could have been you*, he'd said to her, when she had asked.

The figure that he had glimpsed on the fire-escape; the figure that hadn't been there any more when he got to the top. Caroline had been there.

The police had suspected Sam because he had changed his clothes. Caroline had been changing her clothes.

But he looked at her, and he knew he didn't care. He couldn't leave without her, and he couldn't take her away when she was so enthusiastic about the job. He smiled, and shook his head.

'We'll stay,' he said. And he would be with her, whatever happened. They were a team.

'Are you deep in thought or in a huff?' Lloyd asked.

Judy put down her knife and fork and stopped pretending to eat. 'Neither,' she said.

He smiled. 'Oh – I almost forgot. It seems that single-handedly you managed to flush Sam out of his bolt-hole. He came out just after you left, apparently, and you are fast becoming a folk-hero.'

Judy managed a smile, but she couldn't get that picture out of her mind.

'Did he say something?' Lloyd asked, his voice angry. 'Because if he did—'

'No,' she said. 'No, he was fine.' She looked at Lloyd. 'I think maybe he was even nice,' she said.

'*Waters*?' was Lloyd's only comment.

She hadn't told Lloyd about the painting. He would only make fun of her.

'If you're not going to eat that, could we take a walk round?'

Judy looked out at the weather. Long spits of rain streaked the windows down one side of the hall, as the afternoon grew greyer and wetter. 'A walk round,' she said.

'A walk round to the car, then, if you're frightened of a bit of weather.' He pushed his chair back. 'Come on,' he said.

Matthew Cawston, alone, as usual, came in as they were leaving, his blazer spotted with the quickening rain, running a hand over wind-tousled hair. Polite. Pleasant. Debonair, even in his school uniform, as he had been the first time she met him. Not the vulnerable boy she had seen on Friday night, that she had been conned into thinking she saw in Michael. She felt foolish every time she thought of that. Sometimes, she knew just how lucky she was to have Lloyd. She ought to tell him that some time. They walked through the lane to the car park, and they sat in the car as the wind grew wild.

'Both Newby and Treadwell think it has to have been that nice Mr Waters who was with Diana,' Lloyd said.

Judy groaned. 'Oh, Lloyd. Aren't we in enough trouble? Don't keep going after Sam. Why would he want to kill Diana Hamlyn?'

'I don't think he did,' said Lloyd.

The wind murmured round the car, ready to let rip again.

'You think Treadwell caught them together,' Judy said, a little wearily. 'But that doesn't make sense.'

They had been through his theory on Treadwell; why, Lloyd had wanted to know, had Diana run away from him this time? She hadn't before. She had laughed, made a joke of it. So why run this time, unless he was chasing her with murderous intent? Which would have been fine, except that Freddie had just half an hour ago quite unequivocally confirmed that the golf-club was indeed a niblick, and the murder weapon. End of theory. It hadn't so far produced any more clues as to who had wielded it. All Freddie could tell them was that it had been wrapped in some sort of plastic, probably a bag.

Lloyd tapped the steering-wheel thoughtfully. 'Logic,' he said. 'You're fond of that.'

'All right,' said Judy. 'Let's look at it logically.'

'Let's.'

'We now know that the golf-club is the murder weapon.'

'Check.'

The wind suddenly blustered, rattling the window. Judy shivered, and Lloyd switched on the engine, putting the heater on full.

'And it was stolen last December,' she said, caught in a blast of cold air from the heater. Why were car heaters cold to start with? Other heaters weren't. That never seemed entirely logical to her.

'Check,' said Lloyd again.

Judy was aware that she was being manipulated in some way; he was making her go through his theory for him, whatever it was, so that she couldn't dismiss it out of hand. It had to be a Lloyd special.

'So,' she said carefully, hanging on to the logic. 'Either it was somewhere that the murderer just happened to find it when he needed it, or . . .'

'Or it was stolen for the purpose?' Lloyd supplied the alternative, unable to wait for her.

'And that's simply not possible,' Judy said firmly. 'You said yourself it wasn't. No one knew that Mrs Hamlyn was going to see Matthew stealing that pen. No one knew that she was going to leave the Hall when she did.'

Rain started to fall steadily, blown almost horizontal by the wind, drenching the car, streaming down the windscreen, blotting everything out.

Judy took out her notebook, flicking through the pages. *Eighteen months*, she kept reading. Eighteen months, she thought. She had written it down so many times. She frowned. 'Eighteen months,' she said.

'What?'

'I keep hearing it.' She pointed to the places in the notebook as she spoke. 'The stealing started eighteen months ago,' she said. 'The odd-job man was sacked eighteen months ago. Newby's accident was eighteen months ago.'

'That isn't coincidence,' said Lloyd. 'His accident happened *because* the odd-job man was sacked. And Andrew Knight was killed in the accident,' he said.

Judy looked up from her notes.

'Everyone thought Mrs Knight was the thief,' said Lloyd. 'Because the thefts began at about the same time. And she was having some sort of breakdown.'

'Yes.'

'So everyone thought she had stolen the golf-club, presumably,' he said.

Judy confirmed that with a nod.

'But because she didn't take the *other* things, everyone's discounted her. Yet she was the only other person who knew it was there. If Treadwell didn't take it on the off-chance of finding

Diana with another man . . .' He sat back. 'Sometimes things are just the way they seem. Mrs Knight did take the golf-club.'

'Why?'

'To murder Mrs Hamlyn,' said Lloyd. 'Your friend Sam Waters gave me some advice last night. Remember?'

'*Whoever murdered Mrs Hamlyn would have had a hell of a job doing it when she hadn't just been screwing someone.*'

Judy remembered. She hadn't written it down.

'The sex had nothing to do with it,' said Lloyd. 'It doesn't matter who she was with in Newby's car. It doesn't matter who discovered her. She was going to be murdered. She was *always* going to be murdered.'

'By Caroline Knight?'

Lloyd nodded.

'But if the golf-club was stolen in order to murder her, then it *has* to have been planned,' said Judy doggedly. 'And it couldn't have been.'

'Oh, yes, it could. It was. The murder was planned. The whole evening was planned.'

Judy's eyes met his. 'By Caroline Knight,' she said slowly.

'She planned everything. She arranged the date of the ball, and then she arranged to babysit rather than attend. She arranged to go to this midnight movie thing with Sam, so that Diana would have to leave early, and walk across the playing-field just when she did.' He looked at Judy. 'She happened to be running away from Treadwell, but that doesn't alter the fact that she was crossing the playing-field exactly when she would have been anyway.'

Judy was looking through her notebook again.

'But Sam almost spoiled it,' Lloyd said. 'He wasn't supposed to come until eleven o'clock, and there she would have been, all ready to be escorted to her midnight movie. As it was, he came early, and she had to get rid of him so that she could wait for Diana crossing the field. She kills her, and then goes back up the fire-escape. Newby saw someone who just disappeared, remember. That's because she went in the door on the balcony. And he said it could have been you. Caroline Knight looks like you, Judy.'

So she had been told. Judy turned the pages.

He looked up in the general direction of the Hamlyns' bedroom window, though nothing could be seen through the windscreen but the blurred shape of the building.

'And Newby went up after her, and watched her changing. We said whoever it was had to have changed, and we *know* she did. We've known all along. And why was she changing? Sam wasn't taking her anywhere.'

'But why?' Judy asked. 'Why would she kill her?'

'*An Inspector Calls*,' said Lloyd.

Judy frowned.

'It's a play. By a man called J. B. Priestley. It shows you that everything you do has consequences, some you might regret. Treadwell mentioned it – now I know why. He said he felt responsible for Andrew Knight's death, Caroline's illness – and everything.'

It was hot and stuffy now; Lloyd switched off the heater, and sighed.

'Because Diana Hamlyn chose to seduce Treadwell's driver, Andrew Knight died. Because Andrew Knight died, Caroline had a nervous breakdown. And now Diana Hamlyn's dead. That's what "and everything" meant. It all goes back to the accident. Eighteen months ago.'

'But why would she steal the golf-club?'

'Why not? Someone was stealing anyway. Chances are if she used something of her own it would get traced back to her. But if she stole something in the middle of a spate of thefts – something she had no intention of using for two months . . .' He spread his hands. 'Any real investigation would prove she hadn't stolen the other things, and no one would connect her with the golf-club. And that's exactly what happened.'

That wasn't what Judy had meant; she let it pass, as she read her notes.

'And remember what she was like when we saw her that night?' asked Lloyd. 'She was surprised when we said we thought Diana Hamlyn had been raped. Surprised – and worried.'

Judy found what she was looking for.

'She disposed of the club in the boiler room,' Lloyd went on. 'And retrieved the head on Saturday.'

There were more efficient murder weapons than an old golf-club, thought Judy. And Caroline Knight had got rid of Sam because she didn't want his company any more. She had changed because she wanted to see the film, simple as that. And she had been surprised at the rape, just like everyone else, because Diana Hamlyn was anybody's. And she was worried about the rape, just like all the women living in the school were worried. But Judy didn't voice her opinion, because that was all it was.

'Well?' he said. 'Say something.'

He moved slightly, inadvertently touching the horn. The sudden noise made Judy start, and she remembered something. Something relevant, but not something she had written down. She had facts – one that she had just remembered, with the sudden noise of the horn.

'Caroline Knight didn't go in by that door,' she said, almost absently.

Her logic took her through the notebook, ticking things off. Facts. Things she had seen. Heard. Incidents, like Jim Lacey turning up. Little things that she had puzzled about. Because a lot of things had seemed odd, to her. Not any more. As usual, it took Lloyd on one of his flights of imagination to make her see it. Because Lloyd always picked up the things that mattered; he would throw them down in a corner for her to sort out, and now that's what she was doing. Why entertain her lover in the back of a car? Who would *want* to steal a golf-club? Difficult, to change your clothes when everyone's in formal dress: people would notice. Sometimes, things are just the way they seem. What about her shoes?

'There's the window,' Lloyd said impatiently. 'She would use it to open the door.'

Judy looked up. 'I am the crime prevention officer,' she said. 'I know about sophisticated tricks like that.'

'Then why couldn't she have done it?'

'She could have,' said Judy, delighted as she always was when she could pick Lloyd up on his use of the language. 'I simply said she didn't. Or Philip Newby wouldn't just have heard footsteps, would he? He would have heard the door opening. It, if you'll pardon the expression, would waken the dead.' Not quite; Hamlyn had slept on in his fume-filled garage, when Mary Alexander had opened the door on to the balcony to tell them she had found the suicide note.

Lloyd stared at her. 'Yes,' he said, with the puzzled frown that he always had when his theories bit the dust. 'Yes.' The frown went, to be replaced with a slight defiance. 'Newby's covering for her. Maybe he was in on it. He was hurt in the accident, wasn't he?'

Now, she gave him her look.

'Oh, all right,' he said.

She smiled. 'Now,' she said. 'I'll ask you a question. It's your own question.'

'Go ahead,' he said, with a sigh. 'You look like a gun-dog. Who am I to argue when you look like a gun-dog? You are invariably pointing in the right direction.'

'Why *did* Mrs Hamlyn run away from Treadwell?' she asked.

The chairman had left, thank God, and Treadwell closed the front door with a deeply grateful sigh. The man seemed to think that he should have done something about Sam Waters barricading himself into the art room. There really wasn't much he could have done, even if he had wanted to, but Sergeant Hill had winkled him out, somehow. He didn't know where Sam was now, and he didn't care. He was having nothing to do with it. He didn't hire him, and he wasn't going to fire him. He would gladly hand that pleasure over to Mr Dearden and Mrs Knight.

He went through to the kitchen where Marcia was putting away the crockery. 'Lovely lunch,' he said. 'You almost put the old sod in a good mood.'

'Don't swear,' she said.

'You should have joined us.'

'It was none of my business,' she said.

'Marcia, Marcia. My sudden retirement from academic life *is* your business.' He stretched. 'Early retirement,' he said. 'I can see us now, pottering about the garden, joining the Darby and Joan Club—'

'Where?' she said. 'Where will this garden be? Where will we go? What will we do?'

'Don't panic.' He sat down at the kitchen table. 'He says he can get Stansfield District Council to house us. A flat, probably.' He smiled. 'We'll have to potter about the window-box, I suppose.'

'You've been drinking,' she said, and turned away.

He watched as she put away plates and cups, and stood up. 'Yes,' he said. 'I've been drinking.' He slipped his arms round her waist. 'Dance with me,' he said.

She stiffened.

'I'm not drunk.' He smiled at her. 'Not yet. We used to go dancing,' he said. 'You wouldn't dance with me on Friday night. You danced with young Cawston, but you wouldn't dance with me.'

'He wasn't drunk.'

He held her tight. 'Dance with me now,' he said.

'Don't be ridiculous! Let me go!'

Dance, Marcia. Dance wildly. Once. Just once. But you couldn't force someone to dance, he discovered, as he tried vainly to push her round the room. You couldn't overpower a woman just to dance with her.

The doorbell brought the undignified grappling to an end. 'I'll get it,' he said.

Detective Chief Inspector Lloyd and Detective Sergeant Hill. Wonderful. Come to arrest him for attempted dancing.

'I'm afraid we're going to have to take up some more of your time, Mr Treadwell,' said Lloyd.

'Well, I've got plenty of that,' said Treadwell, showing them into the sitting-room. 'Can I interest either of you in a drink? I'm going to have several.'

They shook their heads in unison.

'What embarrassing questions do you have for me today?' he asked, pouring himself a Scotch of magnificent proportions.

'We would like to ask you some questions,' Lloyd confirmed. 'And I would like you to get Matthew Cawston here, if you would.'

Treadwell frowned. 'What do you want with him?' he asked.

'We think he may have information which is relevant to this inquiry,' said the sergeant.

Treadwell picked up the phone, and caused Matthew to be found.

'On Friday night,' Lloyd said, as they were waiting, 'you went into the Barn. Were the big doors open or closed?'

'Closed,' said Treadwell. 'I couldn't see Diana until she opened one of them.'

Lloyd nodded, and asked no more questions until Matthew arrived, and was invited to sit down.

Lloyd asked Matthew the same question about the doors, and Matthew gave the same answer.

'And, when you were interrupted, which way did whoever it was come in?'

A frown crossed Matthew's brow. 'From the Hall,' he said. 'He came in the small door.'

'He?'

'Well . . . whoever.'

'And which way did you run?' asked Lloyd.

'The other way.'

'You had to open one of the big doors?'

'Yes.'

Lloyd looked at Treadwell, then back at Matthew. 'You were running away,' he said. 'I presume you didn't close it again.'

'No,' said Matthew guardedly.

'So who did?' Lloyd asked Treadwell.

'It's surely quite obvious,' said Treadwell, forced into talking about this again, with not only a woman but also a boy present. 'They wanted privacy,' he said, in a stage whisper.

'They?'

'Diana and . . . whoever she was with,' said Treadwell. Lloyd considered that. 'Privacy,' he said. 'Yes. Yes, they would. So *they* closed the big door again.'

Treadwell grunted.

'So why did they leave both the car door and the small door open?' asked Lloyd. 'Not much privacy there. You could hear everything that was going on.'

Oh God. Not in front of Matthew, of all people.

Lloyd smiled. 'I don't expect an answer, Mr Treadwell,' he said. 'I just wanted to be certain that we understood about the doors.'

Matthew half-rose from his chair.

'Oh – the sergeant has a few more questions for you, Matthew,' Lloyd said. He turned to Treadwell. 'I'm afraid you will have to be present,' he added.

Treadwell shrugged. He was still the boy's headmaster, just.

'The thefts, Matthew,' said the sergeant.

My God, the woman never gave up, thought Treadwell. 'Oh, really,' he said crossly. 'The school has agreed not to prosecute. And you are certainly not going to take up any of my time, plentiful though it is, going over all that again.'

'Before I ask you anything, Matthew,' said Sergeant Hill, as though Treadwell hadn't spoken, 'I have to tell you that you are not obliged to say anything, but anything that you do say will be taken down, and may be given in evidence.'

It would be taken down all right, thought Treadwell, as the sergeant's thick notebook made its usual appearance.

'And you can have a solicitor present, if you wish.'

Matthew shook his head, puzzled, smiling.

'You were stealing for eighteen months,' she said.

Matthew nodded briefly.

'Eighteen months,' she repeated. 'That's a long time.'

Matthew said nothing. There wasn't much he could say, Treadwell supposed. Time was relative, after all. It was a long time compared to a day. It was a very short time compared to a millennium. Treadwell didn't even try to sip his drink.

'No one ever saw you,' she said. 'No one caught you. No one suspected you. They even suspected someone else altogether, because you wanted them to. That was clever, Matthew.'

Poor Matthew, thought Treadwell. How do you react to that? A self-deprecatory smile hardly fitted the bill. Modest denial was just as bad. He almost felt sorry for him.

'So why did you get caught on Friday night?' she asked.

'Bad luck,' Matthew said.

'No. You were good, Matthew. You never took anything that mattered to anyone. You would wait for weeks and weeks between thefts, so that you could pick just the right moment, and just the right item.' She leaned forward. 'But this time you took something expensive. Something that meant a great deal to someone. Because it didn't matter what you took, did it? This time, you wanted to get caught.'

Treadwell's glass stopped at his lips, as he looked at Matthew.

Matthew frowned. 'Why would I want to get caught?' he asked.

'So you could get Mrs Hamlyn alone,' she said.

Treadwell put down his glass.

'If she actually saw you steal, she would have to do something about it,' the sergeant went on. 'And she wouldn't take you to task in front of all those people. She would take you aside.'

Matthew shifted a little in his seat. 'I don't see why I would want her to do that,' he said.

'You knew what she was like,' said the sergeant. 'You'd seen her in action. Trying to seduce Mr Newby the very day he arrived at the school. It got you going, didn't it? You wanted her. That would be even better than stealing – that would really be cocking a snook at everyone. Having a teacher's wife. And easy. All you had to do was get her alone, and indicate your interest. She was anyone's, wasn't she?'

Treadwell picked up his glass again. He wasn't sure how much of this he could take. If Marcia had ever spoken like that, he would . . . but, then, perhaps the sergeant danced.

'And she did take you aside. It started raining, and you went into the Barn. Even better.'

Matthew was shaking his head, smiling a little.

'When we began this investigation, it looked like a straightforward rape and murder,' she said. 'Then all sorts of things came to light. We found out what Mrs Hamlyn had been like, and we found out that the sexual intercourse probably hadn't happened on the field at all. So it was possible that she hadn't been raped. We found out that it had actually happened in Mr Newby's car – Mr Newby found her underwear there, so he knew she hadn't been raped. Mr Treadwell actually heard her with someone. He knew she hadn't been raped.'

Treadwell looked at Lloyd, who seemed to be having nothing to do with any of this. It was nonsense, anyway. Whatever Diana Hamlyn may have been, she certainly didn't get involved with pupils, and this woman was suggesting that it was *Cawston* she was with when he heard ... He didn't finish the sentence, not even in his head.

'But sometimes, Matthew,' said the sergeant, 'things are just the way they seem.'

Matthew had lost the supercilious look.

'Right at the start, we were asked who the hell would need to rape Diana Hamlyn. And the answer is – a pupil would need to rape her, if he wanted her. Mrs Hamlyn would have nothing to do with you, would she, Matthew?'

Matthew's face had the closed expression that Treadwell had seen when he had apologised to him, as Sergeant Hill went on.

'It did happen in Mr Newby's car. But Mrs Hamlyn didn't get in voluntarily, did she? You opened the door, and you pushed her in. She tried to struggle – kick. Her shoes came off. Outside the car. She was pinned down in the back of a small car – she couldn't fight you off. And when you had had enough you ran. Your first thought was to get rid of the pen, deny everything. So you ran to where you kept the things you had taken. And you left by the small door.' She glanced at Treadwell. 'That's why you found it open,' she said, and turned back to Matthew.

'You had stolen everything that had gone missing here for the last eighteen months,' she said. 'And when you put the pen away you saw the golf-club. Because you had stolen it, of course. Who else would want to? Sometimes things are just the way they seem.'

Treadwell took a gulp of whisky.

'You realised what you had done. You had hurt her – you knew you were in deep trouble. She would tell. She would report it. You couldn't rely on lying your way out of violent rape. There she was, making all that fuss, and there it was, a ready-made weapon.'

Not a flicker of emotion showed on Matthew's composed, blank face as he spoke. 'You said that Mr Treadwell heard her with someone,' he said. 'According to you, I was at the other end of the school by then.' He looked at Lloyd. 'She can't have it both ways,' he said.

'Mr Treadwell went into the Barn,' said the sergeant. 'Diana Hamlyn got out of the car, and pushed open one of the big doors. Just moments later, Mr Newby drove his car out, having spent some time removing the articles he had found in the back. So if she had been in the car with someone, then Mr Newby would have found whoever it was still in his car, wouldn't he? But all he found were the tights and pants that she pulled away from her ankles in order to run away before anyone saw her. And what Mr Treadwell heard was someone shocked, hurt, in pain . . .' She paused. 'And alone,' she said, looking at Treadwell. 'Moaning. Trying to catch her breath. And asking God to help her.'

'*Not waving*, Mr Treadwell,' Lloyd said quietly, '*but drowning*.'

Treadwell looked away. He didn't need poetry quoted at him to know that he had jumped to the wrong conclusion. The sergeant was doing well enough in her own more prosaic way. But he had gone in. He would have helped her. 'She ran away!' he said, in his own defence.

'Yes,' said Sergeant Hill. 'She ran away. She ran towards the playing-field. Towards home.' She turned back to Matthew. 'You knew she wouldn't go back into the Hall, not in the state you had left her in. She would go home. You ran to the junior dormitory, and you went up the fire-escape. But you saw Mrs Knight and you realised not only that Mrs Hamlyn hadn't reached home, but also that when she did Mrs Knight would see her. Now you really panicked. You had to get to Mrs Hamlyn *before* she got home. So you ran back down. And that's when Mr Newby saw you. He saw you on your way down, not up. That's why there was no one around when he got there. But he had caught a glimpse of you; he said he thought it was a boy, and sometimes, Matthew, things are just the way they seem.'

Treadwell knew that he ought to be on the phone to the solicitor. But, if Matthew hadn't thought of it, why should he? Everyone knew he was a drunken incompetent.

'You ran across the field; you met Mrs Hamlyn, trying to get home. And you made certain that she never did.'

She sat back. 'You thought you'd got away with it. But we got on to the pen, and you had to think fast. You tried to make us think it was Mr Newby. You had your story about him, which was true. You had raped Mrs Hamlyn in his car; that had to help. But it didn't work, did it? You had to think of someone else. Someone plausible. Since no one believed it was rape any more, it didn't have to be a man. But it did have to be someone who could have stolen the golf-club. And who was the only other person ever suspected of stealing? She even had a motive – you discovered that when Jim Lacey came here. You were there, Matthew. You heard him – everyone heard him. He was talking to Des, and Des is deaf.'

Treadwell put down his glass. 'That's why you came here talking about the accident!' he said. 'Making sure I remembered she had a motive. Knowing that she was with me when we found that club, because you were there, too, weren't you? Following her about, waiting for your chance to steal something.'

There was a silence after Treadwell had spoken; everyone looked at Matthew, who never took his eyes off the sergeant.

'You've got no evidence,' he said at last. 'You've twisted things to fit. But you've got no evidence to back it up, because it isn't true.'

'I think I have evidence,' she said. 'Or, rather, a witness.'

Treadwell looked at Matthew, who seemed distinctly uncomfortable. He looked back at the sergeant, waiting to see what she did next, his drink forgotten. He would have paid good money for a ticket to this show.

'You see, Matthew, you must have got terribly wet. We know you didn't get any blood on your clothes, but the golf-club just wasn't heavy enough. You had to get down into the snow and the slush to finish the job. You must have been wet through.'

Matthew sat up a little in his chair.

'And you went back to the school, once you'd killed her. You disposed of the club in the boiler room, and went into the Hall from the inside door. You were there only minutes after you had murdered Diana Hamlyn, and your clothes must still have been wet.'

Matthew's eyebrows lifted a little. 'Has anyone told you that they were?' he asked.

'They might not have looked wet,' she said. 'But you wanted to establish that you were in the Hall. So you asked the headmaster's wife to dance with you.' She moved forward again. 'Shall I ask her?'

Matthew didn't react.

'Marcia!' Treadwell shouted, making everyone jump.

She appeared, looking even more flushed and flustered than ever beside the cool, collected Sergeant Hill.

'Mrs Treadwell,' said the sergeant, 'you told me that Matthew danced with you on Friday night. Once when all the boys danced with the ladies, and once later on. Do you know what time that was?'

Marcia looked at Treadwell.

'Tell the woman!'

'About twenty past eleven, or so,' she said. 'I know, because I—'

'I want you to think carefully, Mrs Treadwell,' said Sergeant Hill, gently interrupting her. 'Were Matthew's clothes wet?'

She frowned. 'I'm sorry. I don't know what you mean.'

'It's hardly an oblique question, Marcia,' groaned Treadwell. 'Were his clothes wet or weren't they?'

'Wet?' she repeated. There was a long silence while she puzzled over the question.

The sergeant gave her an encouraging smile. 'Perhaps not wet,' she said. 'But were they damp?'

'No,' said Marcia.

'Are you sure?' the sergeant persisted, but it was a lost cause, and she knew it.

'I'm quite sure,' said Marcia. 'His clothes were dry.'

Trust Marcia. Trust her to be decided for the first time in her life when everyone else wanted her to be undecided. Treadwell watched her as she walked back into the kitchen, then turned to look at the sergeant.

She looked at Matthew, and gave a little shrug. 'I was wrong,' she said. 'Your clothes were dry.'

Matthew inclined his head a little.

There wasn't a lot more she could say, Treadwell thought. Cawston senior would have a field day with this. Sergeant Hill would be lucky to be directing traffic come nightfall. No wonder her boss had stayed out of it.

But she did have more to say, her voice crisp and clear in the silence.

'Why were they dry, Matthew?' she asked.

Matthew felt the dread again. He didn't speak; he didn't look at her, as her voice went on.

'According to you, you went out to speak to Mrs Hamlyn, and it started to rain. You went into the Barn. You were interrupted by someone, and ran away. Through the rain. The rain that was so hard that Mr Waters's jacket was still damp hours later. But you didn't get wet.'

'I waited in the House. For a long time. I told you that. I got dry while I was waiting.'

'And then you went back to the Hall. It was still pouring – Mr Treadwell got soaked to the skin just walking round the Barn. But you went all the way from Palmerston House, which is at this end of the school, to the Hall, which is at the other end, without getting wet at all. Not even damp. You were dry, Matthew. Your clothes were dry. How did you manage that?'

'I had my coat on.'

She shook her head. 'You didn't have a coat,' she said. 'I saw you in the crowd. You weren't wearing a coat, and you weren't carrying one. And only Mrs Hamlyn's coat was in the cloakroom. Try again.'

Matthew hated her. She had been cleverer than him. He didn't like that. But that wasn't enough. It couldn't be.

She smiled. A cold, hard smile. 'I'll tell you how you did it,' she said. 'We knew whoever did it had to have changed his clothes. And who could change out of formal dress without people noticing? Someone in a school uniform, that's who. You murdered Mrs Hamlyn, you ran back to the House, and picked up your old uniform. The one you had outgrown. The one your father had to replace this term. I imagine you stuffed it into one plastic bag, and the broken golf-club into another. You ran through the rain to the school.'

Matthew was beginning to panic again. The panic that had engulfed him when Mrs Hamlyn wouldn't stop sobbing like that, and he had run away, the blood pounding in his ears, still sure he could hear her when he got to the House. The panic that had made him careless with the loft door. He mustn't be careless. He mustn't panic.

'You burned the club, and you changed your clothes. You hung the uniform you're wearing now up to dry. No one was going to go into the boiler room until Sunday.'

How did she know what he had done? He wasn't left in doubt for long.

'I told you that I saw you later that night, Matthew. In the crowd. I saw someone whose trousers and sleeves were about an inch too short; a boy, still growing. But that's not how you looked last month. And it isn't how you look today. I don't think you get taller and shorter, Matthew.'

It should have worked. He had spoken to everyone he could think of about the accident, and the golf-club incident. It *had* worked; the rumours had hit the classrooms by lunchtime. Mrs Knight might have killed her, they were saying. The police are here again. Not enough for them to charge her, but enough to suspect her. Enough to keep him out of it.

It had *worked*. So why was he here? How did she know, how did she work it out?

'I know someone like you, Matthew,' she said.

Perhaps she read minds, too.

'He had me fooled,' she said. 'But I don't get caught the same way twice.' She paused. 'The next day, you went to help Mrs Knight set up a project in the school building. You raked the metal head of the golf-club out of the ashes, and put it in the ashcan. You picked up your uniform, and put it in your briefcase.'

It was all circumstantial. His father would get lawyers who could make mincemeat of her case.

'You can't prove any of this,' he said.

'Oh, yes, we can. You're interested in forensics – you should know that. We have a thumbprint. We have threads from your blazer. We have samples from the victim, and now we even have a thing called DNA testing. Genetic fingerprinting. Do you know what that is, Matthew? It means that all sorts of things can be proved that could once only be suggested. Paternity, for instance. Right of inheritance. Rape. Murder.'

Panic took hold; Matthew leaped up, and ran from the room, from the house, smack into the arms of two police officers in the doorway.

The sergeant came out, followed by Lloyd; Treadwell brought up the rear.

'You should have let her live, Matthew,' she said.

Matthew stopped trying to struggle free. It wouldn't get him anywhere even if he could. He hated Sergeant Hill.

'She wasn't about to tell anyone. Her husband had just been made deputy head. Think about it – think about her history. Think about the headlines. She wasn't going to report it – she ran away from Mr Treadwell sooner than have to explain.'

Matthew's eyes widened. She was right. She was right. And his body sagged a little, his weight taken by the policemen who held him, one on either side.

'But maybe Mrs Knight would have made her tell the police,' she went on. 'And we would have charged you. But what would have happened? A sixteen-year-old schoolboy and a woman like her? A nice middle-class sixteen-year-old schoolboy and a woman with a reputation like Mrs Hamlyn's? She had to have led you on. She had to have been asking for it. And the violence was . . . well, within reason, shall we say? A professional foul – that's how I understand it was described. And that's how they would have seen it in court. A guilty plea, a show of remorse and, my God, Matthew, you would have got so many Brownie points they would have probably sent her to jail instead.'

Matthew swallowed.

'But you murdered her,' she said. 'And perhaps she didn't die in vain. Perhaps she saved a lot of other women going through what she went through in that car.' She stepped back a little, and looked at him for what seemed like for ever.

'Now you can take him away,' she said.

He hated her.

They had put on his film. After all the other programmes, where no one would notice it. But Judy had; she had gone to bed without the attendant nagging of his fantasy. He got up when it had finished, and took his mug into his suddenly tidy kitchen; he wasn't sure he could get used to that. He couldn't just leave it, like he would have done before. He washed it up, put out the light, and went back through to the living-room. Television off, video off, lamp – his eye caught Judy's ashtray. He would have to add that to the list, he thought, examining it carefully before putting its contents in the waste-basket, as though the cigarette that she had stubbed out two hours ago might suddenly leap into life-threatening flame.

He went round doing his usual check of windows and gas-taps. Putting the cat out, he called it in his head. Not that he had a cat. Not that he would put it out if he did. He liked cats. He wondered if Judy would like one, and realised that she might loathe them for all he knew. It had never been discussed, because all he and Judy had ever talked about was work and the triangular relationship in which they had always found themselves. Now at last they had the time to talk about other things.

He tiptoed into the bedroom, and undressed in the dark, easing himself into bed beside her. He liked going to a bed that had Judy already in it.

'Was the film good?' she asked.

'Sorry,' he said. 'I tried not to disturb you.'

'Some things disturb me,' she said. 'You're not one of them.' She switched on the light, and smiled.

He put his arm round her, not sure whether to broach the subject that had been bothering him.

'Judy,' he said slowly. 'Was there anything personal in what you said to Cawston? About what Diana Hamlyn had gone through?'

She shrugged a little.

'You haven't been . . .?' He was getting like Treadwell, he thought.

'Raped?' she supplied, shaking her head. 'No.'

'But something,' Lloyd said. 'Something of the sort.'

She looked faintly surprised, then gave an unamused laugh. 'Yes,' she said. 'Something of the sort has happened to me.'

'When?' he asked, alarmed.

'Years ago.' She sat back a little. 'Lloyd,' she said, shaking her head. 'Go out tomorrow, and ask ten women in the street. I guarantee you that something of the sort will have happened to seven of them.'

He frowned.

'Oh – they don't report it,' she said. 'They aren't raped. They manage to run away, or someone happens to come along at the right time. Or they talk their way out of it. But they know what could have happened if they'd failed.' She smiled a little sadly. 'Something of the sort will have happened to Mrs Knight, and Mrs Treadwell,' she said. 'Something of the sort has happened to almost every woman you have ever met.' There was a little silence before she spoke again. 'If Alsatian dogs were as unpredictably violent as men,' she said, 'the breed would long ago have died out.'

Lloyd thought about that. 'So what's to be done?' he asked.

'I don't know. All I know is that when I saw Diana Hamlyn I knew it could have been me. But I lost sight of that, until I saw Sam's painting.'

Lloyd had seen it, too, now. He didn't care for it.

An elegantly shod foot, thrusting in from the edge of the canvas, kicking to death a slot machine that had failed to produce one of the red-wrapped goodies which were spilling out in its death throes, staining the snow-covered ground, trampled, crushed, no longer wanted. Only destruction would satisfy.

'I saw it,' Judy said, 'and I knew I was letting her down. Because that was what it looked like when we saw her, and that was what it *was*, whatever Freddie said, whatever anyone said.'

Lloyd nodded.

'Sorry,' she said. 'I don't actually hold you personally responsible.' She kissed him on the cheek. 'Good night.'

She left the light on; he liked to read. He picked up his book. Perhaps one day she would complain about the light, about his late hours; the honeymoon wouldn't last for ever. But he was almost looking forward to that. He looked at her, at the dark head on the pillow beside him, and swallowed a little as he remembered her arrival on Saturday night. Angry, hurt, clutching a huge blue laundry-bag.

But give her someone like Sam Waters, and she could hold her own all right, he thought with a smile.

'Did Sam Waters make a pass at you?' he asked. 'Is that why you said whatever you did say?' He hadn't asked what she had said; he was sure he would rather not know.

'Yes. I told him exactly what I would do to him if he didn't take his hand off my knee. And I meant it.'

He smiled. 'Was I once in danger of whatever dire punishment you threatened?'

'You didn't make a pass,' she said. 'You said: "I'm a married man with two children, and I'm falling in love with you. Is this going to be a problem?" ' She smiled.

He remembered. 'And you said yes,' he replied. 'How right you were.'

But it wasn't a problem any more.

'I can take you out to dinner!' he said, suddenly aware of the new world opening up. 'We can go to the pictures – we can go for walks.' He abandoned his book. 'We can go on holiday,' he said, beaming.

'I'll hold you to all of this,' she said.

He put out the light, holding her close in the darkness.

'Lloyd?' she said, after a few minutes.

'Present.' He stroked her hair.

'Is your first name biblical?'

Bello:

hidden talent rediscovered

Bello is a digital only imprint of Pan Macmillan,
established to breathe new life into previously published,
classic books.

At Bello we believe in the timeless power of the imagination,
of good story, narrative and entertainment and we want to use
digital technology to ensure that many more readers
can enjoy these books into the future.

www.panmacmillan.co.uk/bello

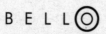

www.panmacmillan.com